Praise for the
LEGACY TRILOGY

"Ward has created a novel with such intention and craftsmanship that it brings back that feeling of excitement fantasy readers felt when discovering masters like J. R. R. Tolkien and C. S. Lewis."

—*Shelf Awareness*

"Expertly interspersing vivid action sequences with quiet, introspective stretches, Ward guides readers and characters alike through this winding, well-crafted saga. The result is an impressive series opener."

—*Publishers Weekly* (starred review)

"Packed with big battles, shadowy intrigue, and a large cast of characters, *Legacy of Ash* is an absorbing debut." —James Islington

"Epic fantasy as it should be: big, bold, and very addictive."

—*Starburst* magazine

"As intricate as a precision-engineered watch; as surprising as a precision-engineered watch with a concealed face-stabbing mechanism."

—Gareth Hanrahan

"An incredibly impressive piece of fantasy fiction." —*Fantasy Inn*

"This is the first epic fantasy book I've enjoyed getting immersed in for *ages*....A great fat romp in a brilliantly realised setting....I have lost sleep, forgotten food...and made this the thing I pick up every moment I can get." —*SFFWorld*

"A hugely entertaining debut." —John Gwynne

"A perfect blend of Martin's A Song of Ice and Fire and Bernard Cornwell's The Last Kingdom." —*FanFiAddict*

By Matthew Ward

THE LEGACY TRILOGY

Legacy of Ash
Legacy of Steel
Legacy of Light

LEGACY
OF LIGHT

Book Three of the Legacy Trilogy

MATTHEW
WARD

orbit

orbitbooks.net

Copyright © 2021 by Matthew Ward
Excerpt from *The Shadow of the Gods* copyright © 2021 by John Gwynne

Cover design by Charlotte Stroomer – LBBG
Cover illustration by Larry Rostant
Map by Viv Mullett, The Flying Fish Studios, based on an original
illustration by Matthew Ward
Author photograph by Photo Nottingham

Orbit
Hachette Book Group
1290 Avenue of the Americas
New York, NY 10104
orbitbooks.net

First Edition: August 2021
Simultaneously published in Great Britain by Orbit

Orbit is an imprint of Hachette Book Group.
The Orbit name and logo are trademarks of Little, Brown Book
Group Limited.

The publisher is not responsible for websites (or their content)
that are not owned by the publisher.

The Hachette Speakers Bureau provides a wide range of authors for speaking events. To find out more, go to www.hachettespeakersbureau.com or call (866) 376-6591.

Library of Congress Control Number: 2021933369

ISBNs: 978-0-316-45794-1 (trade paperback), 978-0-316-45795-8 (ebook)

Printed in the United States of America

LSC-C

Printing 1, 2021

For you, the reader, without whom no story
worth telling would ever be remembered.

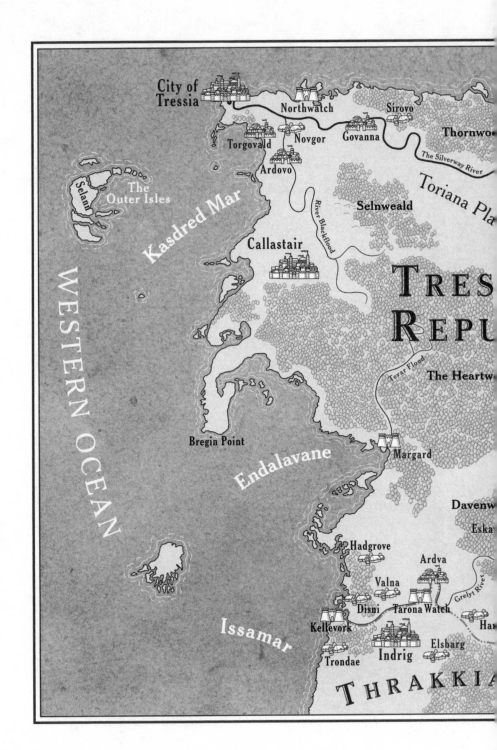

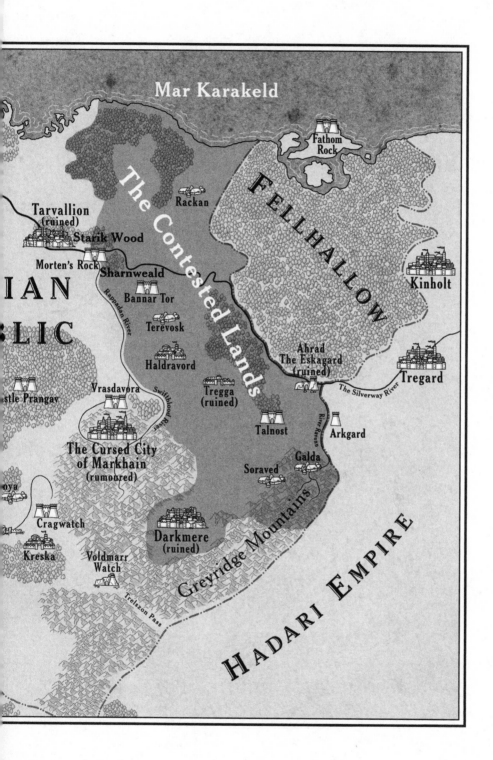

Mar Karakeld

FELLHALLOW

Fathom Rock

Rackan

Tarvallion
(ruined)

Starik Wood

Morten's Rock

Sharnweald

IAN

LIC

Bannar Tor

Terevosk

Ramadan River

Haldravord

Kinholt

Ahrad
The Eskagard
(ruined)

Tregard

The Silverway River

stle Prangav

Vrasdavora

Swithblood River

Tregga
(ruined)

Talnost

River Ferean

Arkgard

The Cursed City
of Markhain
(rumoured)

Soraved

Galda

oya

Cragwatch

Darkmere
(ruined)

Greyridge Mountains

Kreska

Voldmarr
Watch

HADARI EMPIRE

Trelazon Pass

Dramatis Personae

IN THE CITY OF TRESSIA

Viktor Droshna	Lord Protector of the Tressian Republic
Josiri Trelan	Head of the Constabulary
Altiris Czaron	Lieutenant of the Stonecrest Hearthguard; a Phoenix
Anastacia Psanneque	Definitely *not* Lady Trelan
Sidara Reveque	Adopted daughter of Josiri and Anastacia
Constans Droshna	Adopted son of Viktor Droshna, brother to Sidara Reveque
Stantin Izack	Lord Marshal of the Tressian Army
Vladama Kurkas	Steward to the Trelan household
Eldor Shalamoh	Scholar of Antiquity
Hawkin Darrow	Scoundrel
Elzar Ilnarov	Tressian High Proctor; Master of the foundry
Tzila	Viktor Droshna's seneschal and bodyguard
Konor Zarn	Peddler of wares and influence
Kasvin	A lost soul, awash on dark tides
Viara Boronav	Hearthguard at Stonecrest; a Phoenix
Adbert Brass	Hearthguard at Stonecrest; a Phoenix
Amella Jaridav	Hearthguard at Stonecrest; a Phoenix

IN THE CONTESTED LANDS

Sevaka Orova	Governor of the Marcher Lands
Roslava Orova	Repentant warrior
Zephan Tanor	Knight of Essamere
Silda Drenn	Pardoned Wolf's-head

IN THE HADARI EMPIRE

Melanna Saranal	Dotha Rhaled, Empress of the Hadari
Aeldran Andwar	Prince of Icansae, Regent of Rhaled
Kaila Saranal	Daughter to Melanna and Aeldran
Apara Rann	Repentant rogue
Cardivan Tirane	King of Silsaria
Thirava Tirane	Prince of Silsaria, Regent of Redsigor
Tavar Rasha	Jasaldar of the Rhalesh Royal Guard
Tesni Rhanaja	Immortal of the Rhalesh Royal Guard
Haldrane	Spymaster; Head of the Emperor's icularis
Elim Jorcari	Retired veteran, Master of Blackwind Lodge
Sera	Lunassera; a devoted servant of Ashana
Aelia Andwaral	Dotha Icansae, sister to Aeldran Andwar

ELSEWHERE

Arlanne Keldrov	Governor of the Southshires

DIVINITIES

Lumestra	Tressian Goddess of the Sun, known as Astarra in the Hadari Empire
Ashana	Hadari Goddess of the Moon, known as Lunastra in Tressia
The Raven	The God of the Dead, Keeper of Otherworld
Jack o' Fellhallow	God of the Living Lands
The Huntsman	Ashana's herald

GONE, BUT NOT FORGOTTEN

Malatriant	Tyrant Queen of Old, known as Sceadotha in the Hadari Empire
Kai Saran	Former Hadari Emperor, father of Melanna Saranal
Alfric Saran	Former Hadari Emperor, great-great-grandfather of Melanna Saranal
Hadon Akadra	Former Councillor, Viktor Droshna's father
Calenne Trelan	Sister to Josiri Trelan
Calenne Akadra	Imperfect mirror of Calenne Trelan, born of the Dark

One Year Ago

Jeradas, 24th Day of Witherhold

There are those who blame the gods for our failings, but pride was ever the cause.

from Eldor Shalamoh's "Historica"

The horsemen came at dusk, as they had the day before, and the day before that. Dark shapes hunched against Wintertide's cold night, spears held high. Flickering blue-white ghostfires set to ward against weeping, unhallowed things did little to cheat the mist. The world beyond felt distant. Unreachable.

And perhaps it was. Forbidden Places brushed the face of the divine, and none were more forbidden than this. Darkmere, ruined capital of Malatriant, the Tyrant Queen.

Though the gate was long gone to decay and sickly black ivy clung between the parapet's rotten teeth, the boundary wall was thick, and the gateway narrow. A dozen men could have held it. Rosa Orova had nearly as many Knights Essamere to hand, hawks glinting gold on hunter's green shields. And on the walls, the Drazina knights of Viktor Droshna's personal guard, black tabards drawn tight over banded leather and chamfered plate, the old Akadra swan repurposed. Named for the folk heroes of the old kingdom, they offered a rare glimpse of poetry in the Lord Protector's sombre soul. Just as his taking of the *Droshna* name – one born of Hadari fears, and now wielded as a weapon against them – spoke to old wounds gone unhealed.

A slow exhalation marked the end of Viktor's contemplation. He stood a head taller than Rosa, a brooding mountain, dark-haired and dark-eyed. The swirling sea-gold flames etched into his armour shifted as he folded his arms.

"How many today?"

"Maybe fifty. Why? Are you tempted to surrender?"

"To a mere fifty?" Viktor's mouth twitched, pulling at the old scar on his cheek. "Time was, you'd have settled that many alone."

Rosa suppressed a shiver. Five years, she'd tried to leave that day behind. The day she'd become something more than human, and also far less. That cursed woman belonged to history.

Five years ago, Viktor would have considered it poor taste to remind a friend of her failings. But neither of them were who they'd been. She was better. Not redeemed, exactly. You moved forward as best you could and hoped fresh deeds counted more than the stale. Rosa welcomed the moments of stiffness that presaged middle age. Ephemeral humanity wrested from eternity's clutch, though not without price. Ash-white hair was only part of it.

Yes, she was better. Viktor?

Viktor, Rosa worried about.

"They don't really want any part of this miserable place," she said. "But they can't look the other way with the mighty Lord Protector traipsing their territory. Pride paves strange roads."

He scowled away the title's formality. The air crackled with frost. It did that a lot around Viktor, lately. The shadow in his soul rising with his temper.

The northern reaches of the Greyridge Mountains weren't Hadari territory. Not by right. Like the rest of the Eastshires, they chafed beneath the white stag of Silsaria, one of the Empire's many kingdoms. Redsigor, the Hadari named it. Contested Lands whose conquest Viktor had sworn to undo. A rare failure in a life thick with success.

Pride paved strange roads.

Friendship paved stranger ones. Rosa had gladly followed Viktor to Darkmere, though Sevaka hadn't approved. She'd not said as much to Rosa. Not aloud. But five years of marriage eroded a wife's secrets as surely as the wind. Anything to escape the Essamere chapterhouse; the empty chairs and faded escutcheons where once song and mirth had hammered out. Roslava Orova, who'd so nearly been the Queen of the Dead, had instead become a mistress of ghosts in an ailing fortress.

There were others. Memorialia stones raised in every village stood stark reminder of empty houses, silent fields and borders desperate for defenders the Republic no longer possessed. Viktor had promised the expedition to Darkmere might change everything. Of the few truths Rosa yet clung to, one outweighed all: if Viktor promised a thing could be done, it *would* be done.

"We've come a long way to be here," she said. "Shame if it were all for nothing."

"My thoughts also," Viktor replied.

Three riders broke ranks in a muffled clatter of hooves. Steeds' snorting breaths fed the mists. Golden scale shone as they advanced beneath the city's wind-blasted walls and empty windows. Two Immortals trotted at the fore. One held a furled rust-coloured banner aloft. A naked blade, inverted in the tradition of parley, gleamed in the hand of the second.

The third rider was a slender man of Rosa's age, his armour dotted with glittering black gemstones. Where the Immortals wore close-fitting helms, he was bare-headed, his thin, olive-toned features twisted in distaste. Prince Thirava Tirane, Regent of Redsigor, seldom stirred beyond the comforts and walls of Haldravord. If he'd come so far south ...? Well, the estimate of fifty Hadari looked smaller and smaller all the time.

"They want to talk," said Viktor.

"Nice for them," Rosa replied.

"I could kill him." Once, the words would have been a joke, the unthinkable breach of honour framed by grim smile. But after years of tending the Republic's wounds, Viktor had little mirth to spare, and especially not for the Hadari. Nor, were she honest, did Rosa.

"You do that, could be we'll none of us get out of here alive."

"Then we'd better listen to what he has to say."

Viktor clapped Rosa on the back, hitched his claymore's scabbard higher on his shoulders and strode to meet the riders.

"You choose a strange place to partake the glory of Redsigor, Lord Droshna." Thirava spoke the Tressian low-tongue with an easterner's harsh accent, and measured politeness. The legend of Viktor Droshna had spread faster in the Empire than in the Republic. Tales of the dead raised, and impossible victory seized while gods warred. "Tell me, what fate would befall me, had I trespassed your land?"

Icy air prickled Rosa's lungs.

"That would depend on your reason," said Viktor.

Thirava narrowed his eyes. "And what is your reason, Lord Droshna?"

"My business is my own."

"In Redsigor, there is no business that is not also mine." Thirava's words hung heavy with the resentment of a man whose father clung to life and throne a little *too* resolutely. The captured Eastshires would never be the equal of the sprawling Silsarian heartlands. A prince in exile remained an exile, whatever titles he claimed and however many spears he commanded. "If you depart at once, you may live."

"And if we stay?" asked Rosa.

"Then you will find my hospitality equal to the task." Thirava's tone cooled to threat. "I lost kin at Govanna. I've not forgotten the dead."

Viktor's breath frosted the air. The ruins' shadows crept closer, black rivulets trickling over stone. The banner bearer flinched, then stared stoically ahead.

"Nor I," said Viktor.

Offering a tight nod, Thirava hauled his horse about and rode away, companions close behind, until the mist swallowed all.

"I doubt we'll live out the moonrise." Rosa shook her head. "I'm not sure why he bothered to talk at all."

Viktor grunted. "To show he's not afraid. I *do* have a reputation."

A small smile accompanied the words, an old friend glimpsed beneath the Lord Protector's dour mantle. The air lost its chill, the encroaching shadows receding as Viktor's mood improved. Then smile and friend were gone and the Lord Protector returned, like a helm's visor lowered for battle.

"Maybe you *should* have killed him," said Rosa.

"Maybe."

Rosa followed him back to the gateway, running the tally of blades. Thirava likely had hundreds. She'd thirty knights at the gate that protected the now-ruined inner city. Another twenty deeper in. Rosa knew herself equal to three or four. Viktor was worth at least a dozen – more, with his shadow loosed.

Not enough. But when was it ever?

Drazina knights stiffened to attention as they passed beneath the gateway.

"Captain Jard? Have everyone fall back to the temple." Viktor beckoned to his left. "Constans?"

The dark-haired boy emerged from a patch of shadow. "Father?"

Rosa stilled a twitch. Constans Reveque had a knack for moving unnoticed, a skill learnt while breaking parental curfew. Like Viktor – like all Drazina – he wore the black surcoat and silver swan of the vanished Akadra family, though he favoured frontiersman's dark leathers over steel plate.

Fifteen summers old and with Viktor as his patron, Constans would soon be granted a knight's plume. Or perhaps he wouldn't. For all that he was becoming the mirror of his long-dead blood father – not least in his precise movement and brooding eyes – Constans lacked Malachi Reveque's contemplative manner. Too often angry. Selective in authority acknowledged and respect shown.

He'd been quietly ejected from Chapterhouse Sartorov a year earlier – long before Grandmaster Rother had severed ties with the Republic and declared Fathom Rock an independent principality. That Viktor had taken on the boy as both squire and adoptive son – Constans' relationship with his previous adoptive father being only a hair less strained than his relationship with Rother – had struck Rosa as the wrong message. But as a man with few friends, Viktor remained unflaggingly protective of those he *did* possess. Malachi and Lilyana Reveque lay five years beyond his aid, but their son . . . ?

"Keep watch," said Viktor. "If the shadowthorns come, I look to you for warning."

Constans' eyes shone. A long dagger twirled about the fingers of his left hand and slid into a sheath on his belt. "At your order."

Ruined and overgrown streets fell away, the distant weeping louder as night thickened. A brazier hissed and crackled, then burst to blue-white flame as ghostfire caught anew in a waft of sweet-scented duskhazel.

The once-grandiose temple was more imagination than perception, buried by the collapse of its upper storeys and the windblown detritus of centuries. The entire western quarter was simply . . . gone, crushed by the collapse of clocktowers and galleries. The north fell away into a jagged precipice of broken tile and jutting sarcophagi. The centre, and its cracked altar, was clear only through recent labours. A great spiral stairway descended through the fitful glow of firestone lanterns. A handful of Drazina, stripped to shirtsleeves, formed a work chain on the outer spiral, toiling with baskets and broken stone cleared from below.

Rosa stared away from the leering, bird-headed grotesques that stirred so many old memories, her eyes lingering on burial niches, stale and silent. Some were cracked, others ajar. Yet more lay empty, their sarcophagi plundered by the same degenerate prizraks who wept and howled their hunger beyond the ghostfire perimeter.

The frontrunners of Jard's picket line set to work heaving sarcophagi to barricade the gateway. One cracked against the ground, spilling cloth-tangled bones across the nave.

Viktor peered into the spiral stair's lantern-lit gloom. "Master Shalamoh. What progress?"

No reply issued from the depths.

"Master Shalamoh?" Viktor rapped his knuckles against a lantern's metal crown, setting the light dancing. "A horde of shadowthorns gathers. You choose a poor time to test my patience."

A thin face appeared at the staircase's inner curve, accompanied by a voice too rich and deep for the speaker's cadaverous grey robes. "A horde? That's *most* unfortunate."

In the fortnight since departing Tressia, Rosa had witnessed nothing stir Eldor Shalamoh to excitement that had not been buried a century or more. He projected calm as readily as the very best of soldiers, his young man's vigour – despite his swept-back grey hair, Shalamoh was some years Rosa's junior – suppressed behind seemly facade.

"That's one way to put it," said Rosa.

He slid a pair of wire-framed eyeglasses from his nose and polished the lenses against a cuff. "Perhaps you should drive them off, Lady Orova? That's why you brought these brutes, isn't it?"

"If only we'd thought of that."

"Have you found the sanctum?" said Viktor.

Shalamoh's lip twisted. "I've found a door. *Fascinating* petroglyphs. But whether it's the sanctum or not, I can't say."

"Why not?"

"We can't get it open. Hammers, crowbars. Nothing works. Not even a crack."

Viktor started down the stairs. "Let me—"

"Father!" Constans burst through the temple gate, out of breath and cheeks flushed. He mantled the sarcophagus-barricade without slowing, boots skidding across stone. "They're coming."

War drums boomed beyond the walls. The fanfare of Thirava's courage found ... or more likely, of his reinforcements arrived.

Viktor froze. "How many?"

"At least three hundred spears," gasped Constans.

"Mount up!" shouted Rosa. "We'll fight our way clear."

The labour-chain broke apart, men and women running to their tents in search of armament. Others ran for the makeshift stables beneath the canted eastern roof.

"No." Viktor snatched a lantern from its hook. "We can't lose this chance."

Drums crashed to crescendo, and faded to nothing. Defenders froze, wrong-footed by sudden quiet and contradictory orders. Beyond the walls, a lone prizrak sobbed its hunger to the skies.

Rosa stepped closer and lowered her voice. "If we stay, we die."

Viktor turned on his heel. The air crackled with cold. A deep breath, and his features softened to something approaching friendliness. "Rosa, please. Trust me."

"That'd be easier if I knew why we were here."

He drew himself in, eyes imploring. "This is not pride, but necessity."

Grubbing around in forbidden Darkmere? Guided by an upstart scholar and the pages of an outlawed text? Five years before, it would have made for a special kind of madness. But Rosa scarcely recognised that world. So much of what she'd thought myth had been proven real.

But one truth remained. Whenever she'd doubted Viktor, others had paid the price.

"We'll buy you as much time as we can."

His hand found her shoulder. His eyes, hers. "I know."

Then he was gone beyond the curve of the stairs, Shalamoh in tow.

"You heard!" shouted Rosa. "We hold!"

Knights gathered to the barricades. Midnight black and hunter's green. Commander Tanor stood tall among the latter, a veteran of Govanna among untested Drazina.

Rosa drew closer. "Spread our lads and lasses out, Zephan. Let Essamere stiffen the line."

A ghost of a smile tugged at worn, Hallowsider's features. The Drazina were acclaimed as knights, but they weren't the equal of the old chapter-houses . . . and certainly not Essamere.

"I'll watch over the right, mistress. You the left?"

The left end of the barricade faced both the temple gateway and one of the navigable window arches. Where the fighting would be thickest, in other words. "You want the grandmaster's circlet that badly?"

The smile returned. "You'd rather you were bored?"

"The sisters shine for you, Zephan."

He straightened, pleased she'd invoked Lunastra alongside her radiant sibling. Hallowsiders didn't look to Lumestra alone to keep them safe. "Until Death, mistress." He strode away along the barricade of sarcophagi. "Gennery. Tolsav. Prasiv. You're with me."

The drums crashed back. Dust spilled from stonework. Rosa unslung her shield and took position with the Drazina at the gateway.

"The Lord Protector commands we hold, so we hold." She let her voice blossom beneath the approaching drums. Solidity. Certainty. Leadership was more than a bloodied sword. She'd been years learning that. Some never did. "Stand together. Do the dead proud, and—"

Ragged shrieks tore through the thunder of the drumbeats, and billowed madly into the night sky. Terror that shivered the soul without decency to first encounter one's ears.

To Rosa's left, Captain Jard paled beneath his helm. "Blessed Lumestra . . . What was that?"

"I doused the outer ghostfires." Constans' voice arrived at Rosa's shoulder, swimming in self-regard. "I thought it'd make things more interesting."

Shouts echoed beneath the screams. Bellowed orders. Rosa's mind's eye glimpsed the horror Constans had unleashed. Pallid, scarecrow-tatter prizraks falling upon the Hadari with tooth and claw, eyes burning like coals beneath thick red tears. Her stomach coiled in disgust.

"Reveque. You'll take position on the left, and your lead from Sergeant Danarov."

"I'd rather stay here."

She met the truculent stare head-on. "I didn't ask."

Eyes threatened refusal, but at the last he blinked. "At your command."

Screams faded, the prizraks slaughtered or driven back to the shadows. Drums regained dominance, their rumble louder with every heartbeat.

"*Tirane Brigantim!*"

A hundred voices washed over the ruins. Running feet thundered beneath.

"Here they come!" shouted Rosa. "Death and honour!"

"*Death and honour!*"

The gateway crowded with golden scale and rust-coloured silks. Swarthy faces roared challenge from beneath close-set helms. Ghostfires ripped and flickered.

An Immortal barged Jard's sword aside with his golden shield and vaulted onto the barricade. He died there, swept away by a slash that juddered Rosa's arm to the shoulder.

Others pressed behind, howling and screaming. Hammering at helm and shield. A young Drazina collapsed to Rosa's right, gasping for breath an opened throat couldn't claim. An Essamere shield took the woman's place, ramming her slayer back across the sarcophagus and into the press of bodies.

Spears stabbed across shield and stone. A thrust ripped Rosa's surcoat and skittered across her pauldron. Another scraped between the plates at her flank, rousing flesh to fire.

Details blurred, lost in red screams and ragged breaths. The judder of the parry. The bite of steel on flesh. The hot stink of death rising through the mist.

A war hammer struck Rosa's helm and set her world spinning. Reeling, she ducked the Immortal's second swing. His third strike crumpled the upper edge of her shield. She let it fall. Gauntleted fingers about the hammer-wielder's belt, she dragged him down behind the barricade. Her sword, now tight in both hands, crunched through armoured scales to split his spine.

"Until Death!"

Rosa screamed the words and reclaimed her place at the gore-slicked barricade. A fur-clad Silsarian clansman shied from her onset, and died before his sword touched hers.

Lumestra, but how she'd missed this! Even with her head ringing.

Even with skin hot and clammy with sweat and blood. Even with the fire of jarred bones and bruised flesh leaping through her veins. Battle brought bleak vigour.

She scraped a parry and sent another shadowthorn screaming into Otherworld. Her fist closed around a hank of filthy hair and slammed a helmless head against stone.

Why had she ever forsaken this? Allowed herself to become a tutor to recruits? To exchange the soldier's sword for the mistress' mantle? This was where she belonged. It was what she was *for*.

Then, as the fighting lulled and she sought an unbroken blade, she saw him.

He sat on a fallen keystone, hands folded behind his back and black goatee twisting quizzically below a mask of dark feathers. Tall, and yet with a suggestion that his true presence was vaster still; his coat rumpled and his tall hat scuffed.

Breath staled in Rosa's throat. The temple receded into grey, as did those who strove within, their clamour muffled beneath her stuttering pulse. The Raven. Had she drawn him there, by forgetting the lessons of times past and losing herself in slaughter?

"No ..."

She blinked and found no sight of him in a world restored to sound and colour. The patch of rubble on which he'd sat was empty.

The whistle of arrow and the scarlet hammer-blow in her shoulder came as one.

A crunch of knee on stone warned Rosa she'd fallen. The clang of steel that her sword had slipped from her grasp. A gasp sent fire raging through her lungs.

"Shields!" roared a voice.

A parapet of shields topped the makeshift barricade. The air clattered with cheated bodkins. The duller, wetter thump as others found flesh. Gaps showed in the shield wall. Fresh screams rang out.

Gold gleamed in the night.

Brow slicked with cold sweat, Rosa gripped the arrow tight, straining for leverage to snap the shaft. Her shoulder screamed and her hand fell. Shaking. Useless.

It wouldn't have been so, not so very long ago. She'd have ripped the arrow free without blinking. But that woman had been eternal, endless. Now she was ephemeral. Mortal.

Mortals died.

Black uniforms vanished beneath a rush of gold. A brother of Essamere slumped across the barricade, his helm crushed and a spear in his belly. Abandoning her useless battle against the arrow, Rosa closed her good hand about her sword.

An ear-splitting *crack* shook the temple. The ground heaved.

Stone plunged from the upper storeys, pulverising the dead and shattering flagstones. And the sensation . . . Not cold, not exactly. Cold was the mirror of heat. This was something else. Not the flipside of the coin, but another coin altogether. It felt old beyond words.

Drums fell silent. The Hadari bled away into the night, babbling their fear. Rosa stared towards the spiral stairway, giddy mirth spilling from her lips. "Took you long enough, Viktor."

But Viktor was nowhere to be seen.

Retreating footsteps faded. Survivors stirred to aid the fallen.

Hot blood rushing against cold skin, Rosa levered herself upright, her shoulder more heavy and numb than raw.

It *had* to be Viktor. He'd pulled similar tricks before; loosed his shadow to blind the foe and set them to flight. Granted brief life to the dead, if a boneless, puppeteered existence could be considered such. Always on the brink of disaster, as was ever a saviour's wont.

So where was he?

Leaving the barricade behind, she stumbled towards the spiral stair.

"Roslava." The familiar voice. Clipped and gravelly. Weary. Mocking.

She found herself face to face with the Raven.

"You promised to leave me alone!"

For the first time, Rosa saw the old temple in all its glory. The once-bare stone whorled with silver and gold; the roof restored and polished statues presiding over all, their arms outspread in welcome to supplicants shuffling about her like a rock in a stream.

Or so it might have seemed, but for the pervasive green hue and the inconstant, insubstantial nature of the crowd. Not living men and women, but drifting, empty-eyed ghosts, vaporous beneath the waist and indistinguishable from the ever-present mists.

Of the Hadari – of the knights – Rosa saw no sign. She heard nothing but the slowing, pulsing double-thump of her heart.

"I *have* left you alone," said the Raven.

"And yet here you are."

"No." He scowled. "Here *you* are. One foot in my world. One foot in Otherworld. Close enough to hear me."

He'd distracted her. Lined her up for the arrow, all so he could speak with her. She was dying, and the Raven had killed her. The revelation called for anger, but all was leaden – thought, emotion and being.

"Stop him," said the Raven. "You're the only one who'll listen to me."

"Stop who?"

"Your friend. The Lord Protector. He interferes with something he should not."

"He's doing what he must."

"No. He's doing what he *thinks* he must." Pain flared as he seized her shoulders, his tone darker, urgent. "I once told you that I'd been privileged with a glimpse of coming days. A future bleak beyond my taste. Though the details have faded like smoke, I know one thing: this is where it starts to go wrong. For us all. But for Tressia most of all. What is buried here must *remain* buried. Stop him."

Rosa pulled free, and nearly lost her footing. "Stop him yourself."

"I pledged to cease meddling. Breaking that promise won't prevent disaster – it will only alter its nature. But you . . . ?" He sighed. "Have I ever lied to you, Roslava?"

She yearned to say yes. But the Raven had never lied, though his truth was often poison. He'd even been kind, when she'd deserved nothing of the sort.

The double-thump of her heart ebbed. The space between the beats crawled to turgid agony.

When she doubted Viktor, others paid the price. But was that truth, or merely excuse for inaction? Viktor's triumphs always levied a price.

The Raven stepped closer. "Talk to him if you can. But stop him."

"How? I'm dying." It all seemed so distant. Unimportant.

Levity entered his voice for the first time. "One foot is not all the way. Let me give you a nudge."

Palms against her shoulders, he shoved her. She fell backward into the mists.

"Mistress?" Zephan crowded close. "Lady Orova?"

Mist thinned. Rosa found herself with legs splayed and a cracked pedestal at her back. The temple was again forlorn, the false splendour of Otherworld scrubbed away. Bodies lined the inner barricade. Some moving. Too many not. Those knights who remained bound one another's wounds and stared out into the darkness, waiting for doom to befall.

Good shoulder wedged against the pedestal, she edged upright. Her shoulder throbbed, the arrow's weight tugging at sinew. Oozing blood darkened her torn surcoat.

Zephan steadied her with a hand against her good arm. "Rosa?"

"Don't shout, Zephan. I'm not deaf."

"No, mistress." He winced. "It's better you don't move. The physician's coming."

For all the good that would do. Sevaka had begged her not to come to Darkmere. If only she'd listened. "I'm sorry, love," Rosa breathed. She refocused bleary eyes on Zephan. "The Hadari?"

"Gone. I've set Reveque to watch for them."

"Good." Every breath woke new fire, but pain was better than Otherworld's creeping numbness. "Snap the arrow."

He braced one hand against her punctured breastplate, the other about the shaft. A flash of pain and it was done. Through bleary eyes, Rosa stared at the splintered stump. Better.

She gripped Zephan's forearm. Should she tell him? No. He'd think her mad. Maybe she was. Maybe it was all born of lost blood and fleeting soul. "If shadowthorns return, hold them as long as you can."

"What about you?"

"I have to find Viktor."

"No. I can't—"

Rosa transferred her grip from forearm to shoulder. "You can. You will."

With an unhappy twist of the lip, Zephan stepped back. "Until Death, mistress."

Rosa limped towards the stairs, fighting to conceal a growing tremor. By the time she reached the first step, she abandoned all pretence, her good shoulder propped against the curved wall and the bad screaming as the arrowhead shifted in her flesh.

Down she went, knees buckling with every onerous step.

This is where it starts to go wrong.

She forged on. Clung to the Raven's words as mantra.

Halfway down, the drums sounded again. By the time she reached the piled dirt and broken stone at the pit of the stair, the sounds of battle raged anew. The Raven's words drove her on.

Mist shimmered in the lantern light of the half-excavated passageway. Alcoves yawned from the walls, the columbarium grander than in the temple above. Gold glinted, grave-hoard and offering. The not-cold sensation grew.

Great slabs of black stone emerged from the mist. One, split in two, lay flat upon the rubble. The other sat canted against the wall, its petroglyphs of piercing eyes and spread wings gleaming gold. The sanctum door, unbreachable by mortal toil, had yielded to Viktor's shadow. The force of its breaking had set the Hadari to flight.

Shalamoh scuttled to bar Rosa's path. He flinched at her bloodied aspect, then gathered himself to stillness, save for an outstretched, shaking hand. "Lady Orova—"

"Where's . . . Viktor?" The words ripped free, more gasp than speech.

"I caution against going further, lady."

This is where it starts to go wrong.

Rosa shoved him aside. Three more steps, and the mists swallowed scholar and shattered doors as if they'd never been.

"Viktor?"

There was no lantern beyond the doorway. The only illumination came from wisps of diffuse, whitish light that danced past her and vanished into the drifting shroud. Weary eyes glimpsed curved walls and a low, vaulted ceiling. Corvine faces leered from every pillar.

Stone skittered from Rosa's boot and into an abyss edged with broken tile and the remnant of a descending stair. No impact echoed up from the catacomb below.

"Viktor?"

She staggered across a gaping floor more collapsed than intact, past ancient tombs, the bas-reliefs familiar in style, and yet not. The stale scent of yesterdays grew stronger. White-green mist tinged with writhing black.

Viktor stood with his back towards her, shadow a shifting cloak about his shoulders. His hands rested on a glassy, black orb. Even looking at it *hurt*. As if it didn't belong in the living world. The orb, in turn, sat upon an ornate pedestal. Pale green cracks pulsed in time with the wisps dancing like glimmerbugs about his shoulders. Opposite, beyond the remnant of a frayed carpet, an empty archway loomed above unbroken stonework. A door leading nowhere.

What is buried here must remain *buried.*

Wisps bobbed past Rosa and joined the dance about the orb. Those that touched it vanished, swallowed by glimmering green. She shuddered, wracked by horrified recollection of her torment as the Queen of the Dead. Soul sparks, freed from those who fought and died above. The last gasps of the dying, drawn to the orb . . . and to what?

This is where it starts to go wrong.

"Viktor . . ." Speech was an excruciating effort now. "What are you doing? What . . . is all this?"

He didn't turn. Didn't move.

Two ragged breaths crept by, each accompanied by an unsteady step through coils of mist and shadow.

Three.

Four.

"I've found it," he said, his voice a rumbling, reverent whisper. "I *hear* them. I can *reach* them. This is where everything changes."

The last words, so similar to the Raven's, scattered Rosa's last doubts.

Galvanised to one final effort, Rosa shouldered Viktor aside and shoved the orb. It toppled free of the pedestal, struck the floor and shattered. A burst of viridian light left dark splotches on Rosa's vision. Glassy fragments spilled across the gaping floor and into the abyss.

"No!" Viktor spun about, eyes blazing. His shadow pulsed, hurling her against the empty arch. He bore down, face inches from hers. "Do you know what you've done?"

Ragged heartbeat slowed. Fire faded into numbness.

Viktor's brow softened, anger yielding to despair. For the first time since she'd entered the chamber, Rosa had the sense he recognised her. "Rosa?"

She tried to speak, but found neither words, nor the breath to give them licence.

Closing her eyes one last time, Rosa clung to the memory of Sevaka's face, and wondered if the Raven would be waiting for her in Otherworld.

Maladas, 26th Day of Wanetithe

I've lived my whole life in Tressia, and still the city
finds ways to surprise me. But in one thing it is
wholly dependable: the quieter the streets, the larger
the storm brewing somewhere out of sight.

from the diaries of Malachi Reveque

One

Soot spiralled through heavy snows, soaring over twisting alleyways and broad, cobbled streets, the rich woodsmoke from hearths mingling with sour blackstone from factory and forge. Priests proclaimed that blackstone tainted the air as surely as it did the soul. Altiris – who'd spent most of his twenty summers clinging to life in a slave's shack on Selann for his family's supposed transgressions – loved priests even less than the chill that had never quite left his bones, and rejoiced that the bitter scent banished both.

Tressia had lost much in recent years, but it seemed never to lack for priests.

At Altiris' side, Viara rubbed gloved hands together and stared gloomily along the nearly empty street. "I didn't realise we'd be walking halfway across the city."

"Exercise does you good." Altiris lengthened his stride, boots crunching on the thickening snows. A broad-brimmed rover's hat, woollen cloak and thick gambeson beneath phoenix tabard kept gooseflesh and shuddering joints at bay. "Gets the blood moving."

The cold had summoned a fair portion of Viara's blood to nose and cheeks, all of which conspired to shine brighter and ruddier in the lantern light than the scarlet ribbons woven through her blonde plaits. For all that she was Altiris' elder by three years, she looked younger – a soft-skinned highblood for whom service in the Stonecrest hearthguard was the first physical work she'd known.

She cast a longing look at the Brass Key's swinging sign – at shadows moving against windows hung with bright-painted wooden pendants with the silhouette of trees and angelic serathi. The tokens of the season. Muffled notes of ribald carols shuddered onto the street. "We've passed dozens of taverns already."

Altiris nodded at a pair of constables heading in the opposite direction. "Squalid dives, hardly fit for Stonecrest Phoenixes . . . much less for the Lady Boronav."

Lady Viara Boronav stifled a scowl at the reminder of the times to which her family had fallen. All the more reason to offer it. Life as an indentured slave was no more easily forgotten than the livid rose-brand on Altiris' wrist. The Boronav family had prospered from the oppression of the south. Even if Viara herself was too young to carry the blame, the sins of her kith hung close. There was joy to twisting the knife.

Especially as she so wanted to be liked.

"Yes, lieutenant," she replied glumly.

"'Altiris' is fine."

For all that Viara nodded, the correction fell flat. It was *supposed* to be largesse. A gesture of equality. Lord Trelan pulled it off all the time. Altiris never quite managed the right tone.

He longed for Lord Trelan's easy authority. The ability to make suggestions that were taken as orders. And if Josiri Trelan – separatist, outcast and apostate – could cheat monolithic tradition and become a hero of the people, then surely fate could be persuaded to allow the same for others.

To be acclaimed a hero in his own right. To have his opinion feted and his name celebrated. A decade ago, it would have been impossible, but with the decimation of ancient families by war and misfortune, the old conventions were coming apart.

Maybe there *was* opportunity, even for a lowblood southwealder. And wouldn't that be something? But for all that, Altiris was only a young man with a sword and something to prove, and there were plenty of those to go around. Other talents outshone the mundane.

He nodded to where the timeworn timbers and leaded window of the Ragged Wayfarer clung to the crossroad's eastern corner.

"Here we are."

"Thank Lumestra," Viara muttered. "My fingers are about to fall off."

They skirted the derelict townhouse on the crossroad's southern corner – its collection of huddled souls gathered around a guttering fire – and crossed the dunged roadway. As the last sparks of the year died, the lucky ones might find shelter in church or alms-house, some wealthy patron easing conscience by letting the downtrodden pass Midwintertide in fleeting comfort. But not tonight.

The city wall loomed, tarpaulins and scaffolds dark shapes against the billowing snow. One of a dozen new fortresses to bolster the city's defences. All of it behind a stout fence, and the silent, towering silhouette of a kraikon. Sunlight crackled softly across the giant construct's bronze skin and steel plate, the magic that powered its metal frame still vibrant, even in the snows. There'd be simarka too, somewhere close by. Kraikons were all very well for throwing a scare into trespassers, but the bronze lions were faster, and far more suited to running those self-same intruders down.

After the quiet chill of the streets, the warmth of the Wayfarer's hearth stole away Altiris' breath. The buzz of conversation and mournful refrain of an unseen piano were loud beyond words. Beneath the low, bare-joisted ceiling, the scent of woodsmoke and ale hung heavy with promise. Drifting eyes made incurious inquiry, then returned to the serious business of staring moodily into glass or tankard.

Not so the matronly woman behind the bar. "Lieutenant Czaron! Here to settle your tab?"

He met the glare with practised nonchalance. "Next week, Adela. On my word as a Phoenix."

"You said that last week."

"Did I?" The smile was for onlookers, not Adela, who was immune to such things. "If it helps, my companion's paying."

Adela snorted and turned her attention to another patron.

"Oh I am, am I?" murmured Viara.

"You wanted to talk. It's only fair. A lieutenant's wage doesn't go far."

She regarded him stonily. "I'm starting to believe what the others say about you."

"And what *do* they say about me?"

"That you're a rake who spends entirely too much time carousing with the likes of Konor Zarn, and not enough at minding your place."

"Folk invite me to parties. It'd be rude to say no."

"And miss the chance for a little social climbing? Absolutely."

"I'll take wine. There should be a little of the Valerun red left."

Taking her expression's descent from *stony* to *scowl* as his cue to depart, Altiris threaded his way through the crowd to an empty table beneath the window. Like so many of its era, the leaded upper frame trammelled a small, stained glass sun, though accretion of smoke had long obscured its radiance.

He peered at the crossroads, the fire in the derelict house just visible through the snow. Where he'd be, but for Lumestra's grace. Setting aside hat and gloves, he smoothed unkempt red hair to something resembling respectability and made silent note to spare a few coins on the return journey.

Viara slid a bottle and two glasses onto the table and sat on the bench opposite. "Adela says that if you don't clear your tab by the end of the month, she'll send her son to settle the debt."

"You're misreading the situation. She likes her little amusements."

She eyed the Wayfarer's clientele warily. "Yes, lieutenant."

Altiris frowned. "What's wrong?"

"People keep staring."

"You're a Phoenix." He filled both glasses with a flourish and set the bottle aside. "You'll get used to it."

Phoenixes transcended myth. The firebirds of legend who carried Lumestra's tidings through the stifling Dark that devoured all things. The hope that never died. Then again, it didn't hurt that even swaddled in a hearthguard's unflattering uniform, Viara was easily the most stareable thing in the Wayfarer. Enough to set hopeful hearts aflutter. All the more ironic – and not a little depressing – that Altiris felt no such stirring himself.

"If this isn't a squalid dive, I'm glad we passed up the others." Viara raised her glass, dark eyes on his for the first time. "Or is it that your debts are slighter here?"

Altiris took a sip of wine and made note not to underestimate her. "What was it you wanted to talk about, anyway?"

"It's complicated."

"I'm discreet."

Again that appraising, careful stare. "That I doubt." A sip of wine, and she sat back, lip twisted in irritation. "My father has . . . expectations."

"I see."

"He suggested working for Lord Trelan might restore lost opportunities."

Opportunities. A seat on the Grand Council that granted a generous stipend without asking much in return. Oversight of an office of state while others scurried around doing the actual work. Once a highblood's birthright, now callously ripped away by Lord Droshna's reforms. No Grand Council. No Privy Council. And no station to which Viara and her peers could aspire.

Time was, she'd never have lowered herself to join a hearthguard – even one so storied as the Phoenixes. Nobles went into the chapterhouses to earn a knight's plume. But with most of the chapterhouses gone or faded, and conscription making no exception for a family's wealth? Well, better to stand service in a noble's guard than trudge beneath a regimental banner or crawl around alleyways in a constable's tabard.

It explained her disgust that Altiris was welcome in what wealthy circles remained, even though she apparently was not. It remained a sour note with Altiris that his invitations from Konor Zarn in particular sprang not from personal regard, but because a phoenix tabard at Woldensend Manor's lavish balls implied rather more influence with Lord Trelan than facts supported. But it was better than nothing.

Motion beyond the window caught Altiris' eye. An officer in a Drazina's midnight black and silver swan drew into sight at the crossroads, his horse champing restlessly.

"And these opportunities haven't arrived?" he asked, eyes still on the street. "What do you expect? You've been at Stonecrest for what, a few weeks?"

"Two months. Lord Trelan hasn't even acknowledged my existence."

Beyond the window, the officer headed deeper into the city. A pair of cloaked Drazina knights followed in his wake. A low dray cart in theirs, its rider swathed against the cold. Four others brought up the rear. A heavy guard for something so unassuming.

"I'm surprised you didn't try for the Drazina," said Altiris. "Lord Droshna's ear is worth more."

"They wouldn't take me." She offered a self-deprecating smile tinged with bitterness. "I'm too short."

"Ah. I don't know what to say."

"Tell me how I can get Lord Trelan's attention. Lumestra, but I wasn't brought into the world to guard someone else's silverware!"

There it was. The entitlement. The sense that the world existed only in service to one's desires. It was disappointing, somehow, for a woman of Viara's obvious intelligence to be so blinded by her upbringing. But wasn't everyone?

"What makes you think I can help?" asked Altiris, his attention now on the inside of the Wayfarer more than on her. Something wasn't quite right, but the more he tried to determine *what*, the further he strayed.

"Can't you?" said Viara. "You live in the house, not the barracks. You dine with the family, and as for how you carry on with Lady Reveque—"

"That'll do." The last thing he wanted was to talk about Sidara.

Viara regarded him with a poisonous mix of uncertainty and embarrassment, afraid she'd overstepped. It'd be so easy to knock her down a peg or two. One more small act of recompense for old harms. But no. Childishness was all very well, until it crossed the line into malice.

Besides, Viara wasn't the only one who wanted to be liked.

Altiris took a deep breath. "Lord Trelan prefers deeds over words ... and bloodline. He's a man of action. Why else do you suppose he runs the constabulary?"

"Father maintains that action is vulgar."

"I'm sure he does. But it doesn't change the fact that if you want to ... "

That was it. The tavern was quieter, a small but significant number of faces having departed into the cold. Unheard of in the Wayfarer this side of midnight. And across the road. The fire blazed in the derelict, but its suplicants were gone.

Snatching hat and gloves from the table, Altiris started to his feet. "Come on."

Viara blinked. "What? I don't—"

"Do you want to catch Lord Trelan's eye, or don't you?"

The challenge did its wicked work. She emptied her glass and, with a last despairing glance at a bottle still half-full, followed into a snow-swathed world. A world Altiris swore was colder than before.

"What's going on, lieutenant?" she asked through chattering teeth.

Colder or no, the snow had definitely thickened, tracks and boot prints softened beneath soot-spattered white. Enough to follow, but not to show how many others had passed that way.

Altiris set off in brisk pursuit, exhilaration counteracting the chill. "A cart came through not long ago. Guarded by a half-dozen Drazina, no less. And just by chance, folk lose their taste for drink, and our friends by the fire forget the cold?"

"It's an ambush?"

"Half of one. The rest'll be up ahead somewhere. Probably before the Three Pillars checkpoint."

He quickened his pace. Viara's cry called him up short.

"Wait! If it is what you say, shouldn't we . . . you know?" She jerked her head towards the incomplete fortress, where the kraikon's magic sparked and crackled through the snow.

They should. They really should, but then there'd be no chance of taking credit for stopping whatever was going on. "We'll leave her out of this one." Seeing Viara wasn't convinced, he struck a winning smile. "But if you'd rather sit this one out, I'll understand."

Ambition won out, as he'd suspected it would, and she stalked on past. "Three Pillars isn't far."

They hurried on, following tracks that threatened to vanish at any moment. Bravado flickered as shuttered windows passed away overhead. For all that the city was home to thousands upon thousands, it was possible to be alone very quickly if you strayed down the wrong street. And in the frigid anonymity of the snows, every street could quickly become the wrong street. Especially in Wallmarch, where construction work had displaced so many and made potential lairs of most buildings.

A half-demolished warehouse passed away to Altiris' right, a church's lychfield to his left. The snows parted, strobing merrily in the light of a damaged lantern, half-hanging from its post.

The dray cart sat slewed across the road, crates jettisoned in its wake, horse staling into the snow as if nothing were amiss. Falling snow dusted motionless bodies, blood seeping scarlet through white.

"We're too late," murmured Viara.

Altiris crouched beside the nearest Drazina. The blood that had so alarmed ebbed from a bruise on the back of his head – his helmet lay a short distance away. "He's alive."

"This one too," Viara replied from nearer the warehouse. "But she won't stay that way without help."

Leaving the unconscious Drazina behind, Altiris clambered up onto the dray. The attack had been too precise, too efficient, to have been without deliberate goal. The kind of robbery the vanished Crowmarket had once conspired to so well.

"All right. We head back to the Wayfarer and raise the alarm."

Quicker to get the kraikon's attention than to reach the Three Pillars checkpoint. Besides, Drazina were more interested in inspecting identification papers than helping those in need – even their own.

The cart itself looked almost untouched, its crates and strongboxes still wedged in place. A sword, half-unwrapped from a bolt of velvet cloth, lay atop a burlap sack of the sort used to transport mail. A highblood's possession, if ever there was one, with golden wings as its hilt, and a large, many-faceted sapphire set in its pommel. Dulled through lack of care, and the blade's tang pitted with rust – but still, too fine a prize to leave behind.

Unless the robbers weren't yet done.

"Lieutenant? I think there are too many bodies."

They rose out of the snow as Altiris spun around, four dark-clad figures armed with knives and cudgels. Two, he recognised from the Wayfarer. The others were strangers. Unremarkable men and women you could cross paths with anywhere. A cudgel crashed down. Viara dropped without a sound.

"No!" Altiris drew his sword.

He went utterly still as a sheen of steel slipped beneath his chin.

"Put it down." The lilting voice was warm against his ear.

Gut seething sour, Altiris obeyed. The simplest of snares, and he'd rushed straight into it.

"That's better." The voice, maddeningly familiar, adopted a mocking tone. "I thought we were followed, but to find it was you? Been a long time, my bonny."

Stray memory flared. "Hawkin?"

"The very same. Haven't you grown into a fine young man?"

Hawkin Darrow. A southwealder like himself. Once trusted steward to the Reveque family, but in reality a vranakin of the Crowmarket. "I thought you were dead," spat Altiris.

"Thought, or hoped?"

"Longed for."

Bracing against the dray's floor, he slammed back into Hawkin. She yelped, and then they were falling over the cart's runners and into the snow. Altiris landed hard, his grab at her knife-wrist a hair too slow. But the wing-hilted sword, dragged from the cart during the fall, landed beside him.

He snatched it up. Hawkin shuddered to a halt, chestnut curls dancing and the tip of the pitted blade beneath her chin. Her eyes filled with poison, then bled into approval. "I always thought you showed promise."

She'd worn the intervening years well. Thinner, perhaps, the vivaciousness of youth – of the mask she'd worn while spying on those who'd thought her friend – eroded until only whip-thin essence remained.

So easy to ram the sword home and avenge old betrayals. But movement in Altiris' peripheral vision reminded him that Hawkin was not alone. Even if he fought his way clear after, her death would be Viara's too.

"Enough. Let her go." The speaker stood by the roadside, one elbow braced against the church's lychgate. A sharp-accented voice, a shock of ash-blonde hair and a black silk dress that was in no way practical for the weather. She drew closer, skirts dragging at the snows, and halted level with the motionless Hawkin. "No one has died. No one *need* die. Not for the Lord Protector's trinkets."

A rolling whisper billowed beneath her words, a breathy not-quite song that itched at the edge of hearing. One that flirted with melody but never fully embracing it, like waves rushing across an unseen shore. What showed of her skin above frilled black lace was pale in the manner of highblood fashion, but to a degree well beyond the limits of cosmetic powders and lacking their fashionable sheen. Her face was younger than Altiris' own. Ageless, blue-green eyes belied those slender years.

Altiris stuttered a laugh to hide his discomfort. "These belong to Lord Droshna?"

"They *used* to."

"Then you're a bigger fool than Hawkin."

"One of us surely is. Put down the sword."

The song's intensity swelled, its whispers no longer the burble of the shoreline, but the roar of a storm-wracked ocean. Altiris drowned beneath their rushing waves. He fell to his knees, heart hammering, lungs heaving for breath, his sword hand spasming and empty.

"No!" snapped the pale woman.

Altiris forced leaden eyelids open. The pale woman stood above him, sword point-down in her right hand. Her left gripped Hawkin's shoulder. The cart bucked and heaved as their companions completed the interrupted robbery.

Hawkin's knife glinted in the lantern light. "He knows I'm alive. He'll tell others."

The pale woman held her back without obvious effort. "And whose fault is that? You know the Merrow's rules."

Hawkin snarled and followed the strongbox-laden robbers into the darkened lychfields. The pale woman squatted beside Altiris, the sword at her shoulder and the ghostly whispers on the edge of hearing once again.

"I could have let her kill you," she breathed, her lips inches from his ear. "Think on that. Are you certain you're on the right side?"

Her lips brushed his cheek. Then she was gone, rusted sword and all, lost in the snow, whispers fading behind her.

"Viara?"

Clinging to the side of the ransacked cart, Altiris made it to his feet on the third attempt. Viara lay where she'd fallen, face down in the snow. Alive, as the pale woman had promised.

But the rest? Hawkin Darrow back in Tressia? The Lord Protector's possessions stolen? The Crowmarket resurgent? What more could the night throw at him?

A repeated, scraping thud sounded through the swirling snow. Metal feet falling on stone. Altiris' heart, already at a low ebb, sank further.

One last humiliation.

A gleam of golden eyes presaged the simarka's arrival. By the time the cast-bronze lion sat on its haunches before him and cocked its head in sardonic enquiry, Altiris had almost reconciled himself to what was to come.

"I need your help."

Tzadas, 27th Day of Wanetithe

Trust to the soldier who seeks no glory by the sword.

Tressian proverb

Two

Winter dawn crept in about the drapes, the memory of the pale woman's blue-green eyes lurking on nightmare's edge. All else was the sense of pursuit, of being quarry with nowhere to run, the reeve's hounds howling behind. Usual, for all they were unwelcome. Old memories that only showed their face at night, when Altiris' body slept and his mind wandered.

He banished Selann to the past, the sodden, weatherworn hovel of childhood yielding to his Stonecrest quarters. The attic room, while nothing to the expansive chambers enjoyed by the nobility, was larger than his family's entire shack. Thick carpet, rather than packed soil and cracked tiles. A broad hearth, and beneath the window a garden, not a muddy vale of crops to tend until arms ached and fingers bled.

Proof that the past was the past, and the future held only promise.

But those eyes. When Altiris closed his own they were with him still. Watching him as if he were prey. No. That wasn't quite right. As if she wasn't yet certain whether he *was* prey.

Are you certain you're on the right side?

The estate bell started him from reverie. Eight o'clock, and he still abed. Unacceptable, even if he'd been up long past midnight. Passing up a shave and all but the simplest ablutions in favour of haste, he dressed and took the stairs two at a time down to a hall resplendent with Midwintertide decorations. Not the wooden pendants of the impoverished Wallmarch, but glittering glass baubles and bright paper lanterns.

A nodded greeting to a maid – who bobbed a curtsey and hurriedly withdrew from his path – and Altiris quickened his pace toward the armoury.

"No call to be rushing around," a voice drawled from the drawing room doorway. "How many servants are you planning to trip over, anyway?"

Altiris halted to face his tormentor. "The hearthguard—"

"Are managing agreeably without you, lad. Brass and Jaridav have the gate. Beckon and Kelver the streets. Stalder the front door and Jarrock the patrol." Kurkas leaned against the door jamb and scratched beneath his eye patch. "What? Think I've lost the knack? Reckon my faculties are flaking?"

Not that. Never that. For all that Kurkas had traded a captain's uniform for the more respectable waistcoat and jacket of Stonecrest's steward – respectable, rather than *presentable*, because Kurkas could rumple good cloth with the merest brush of a finger – a lifetime behind the sword wasn't soon set aside.

Years that had struck black hair steel grey had slowed him little more than had leaving his left arm behind on the battlefield, twenty years before. Of Stonecrest's hearthguard, only Jaridav came close to besting him with any consistency. Altiris, for all that they sparred two or three times a week, counted victories on the fingers of one hand.

And they were good pairings. Jaridav's diligence would keep grizzled old Brass from slacking at his duties, and his poacher's eye would catch ill intent the younger woman might miss. And though Altiris hadn't considered it until that moment, Beckon and Stalder were barely on speaking terms – the result of a friendly card game turned less so with wagers laid. Keeping them apart was to everyone's benefit.

The realisation occasioned chagrin. He should have caught that. At least it had been Kurkas who'd covered his failing, rather than Anastacia, whose ratio of mockery to kindness was far steeper.

"And Viara?" Altiris asked, then remembered he'd used her personal name, rather than her family's, as was proper. "Boronav, I mean?"

"So we're on first name terms with all the nobility, are we? Or is it just the young and pretty ones?" Kurkas ignored Altiris' glare and forged on. "Light duties. She has one of the carriages, a satchel of correspondence and orders to take it easy playing at herald."

Altiris' shoulders unknotted a fraction. "No complications?"

"A lump on the noggin and a fearful headache, but that goes with the territory, doesn't it? You were both of you lucky last night."

Altiris scowled. Nothing travelled faster than failure. Then again, Kurkas seemed to know everything. "Going to chew me out for it?"

"Count my arms, lad. Tell me I've never made a mistake." He shrugged. "But I wouldn't mind hearing about it direct from you. In my day, vranakin didn't leave witnesses, and certainly not conscious ones."

Altiris grunted. "Maybe things have changed."

"Maybe. And as for being chewed out?" Kurkas levered himself upright. "It's not me you need worry about."

Tension returned to Altiris' shoulders. "She's here?"

"In the kitchen. Came home with the dawn in search of grub." He shrugged. "You'll have to speak sometime. Might as well be now."

He nodded farewell and strode across the hall, the limp unmistakeable. A reminder that formidable though Kurkas was, the steward had lived long years hard. Little by little, time was laying claim to a victory that vranakin and a legion of Hadari had failed to achieve.

"Vladama?" Use of the personal name still seemed wrong, but was sometimes necessary. If for no other reason than he and Kurkas occupied the same curious station in the Stonecrest household, being considered as close to family as commoners could. "Thank you."

The other halted, and offered a nod. "Just ... Keep it civil. Lady Boronav's not the only one with a throbbing head."

Sidara was, as Kurkas had promised, in the kitchen, one elbow propped against the tabletop and chin against her palm. Even staring moodily down into the remnants of a bowl of oatmeal – without giving any sign of *seeing* it – with shadows gathered beneath tired, blue eyes, and the frayed, once-meticulous plaits sporting a wispy golden halo of rebellious hairs, she lit up the room.

Many disdained as improper that a young woman who was both the heir to the Reveque bloodline, and by adoption a daughter of Trelan, should lower herself to association with a mere hearthguard – who was not only a southwealder, but once an indentured slave into the bargain. But sneers had only bound them closer. She'd been his confidante – and he hers – in joy, in heartbreak and in mourning.

Indeed, soon after Sidara had earned the Drazina's silver swan, she'd insisted Altiris accompany her to a ball at the Montesrin estate. One of the other guests – another newly elevated officer named Ivo Tarev – had loudly objected to Altiris' presence, insisting the [R] replace with: "upstart southwealder" be banished to the kitchens, or else prove his worth with a sword. Knowing Tarev to be far more skilled with a blade than he, Altiris had resigned himself to a humiliating retreat.

Only for Sidara to accept the challenge on his behalf.

By rights, the matter should have ended then and there. Bad enough that the Lord Protector disapproved of the once-common practice of honour duelling. Worse to fight such a duel against a woman the Lord Protector considered his niece. To do so in the full knowledge that Sidara wielded Lumestra's light in a way not seen outside of legend? Well, that took stupidity to soaring heights.

As matters transpired, Sidara hadn't resorted to magic. Blood streaming from a cut on her brow – the result of a sloppy parry and mistaken footing on the rain-sodden lawn – she'd extracted apology with her sword at Tarev's throat. Then, eyes shining and cheeks aglow, she'd taken Altiris' arm in hers and marched away. They'd spent the rest of the night on the edge of the Hayadra Grove, a bottle purloined from the Montesrin wine cellar emptied to the dregs, staring at the moon across the flooded streets of the western docks.

Then, in the light of the rising dawn, she'd kissed him. And the new day was suddenly very different to the old. The future he'd thought before him washed away and replaced by something wondrous and unexpected.

Not even two years ago, but it felt like a lifetime. Longer.

How the wall between them had arisen, Altiris still wasn't sure. Brick by brick, he supposed, in the manner that all such walls were fashioned. Hastened by Sidara's increasing responsibilities, mortared by words unspoken, and invisible until complete. He supposed it didn't matter. All that mattered was that the wall existed, and was not for climbing. Were he honest, he didn't even know when they'd grown apart, only that holding onto even friendship was a constant challenge. Anything deeper had long since been lost.

And for all that, Altiris still wanted to be near her. At least, until he was actually in her presence. Then all he wanted to do was leave before they fell to quarrelling. Living under the same roof would have been awkward beyond words, had either of them spent any more time at Stonecrest than necessity – or in Altiris' case, *duty* – demanded. At least Lord Trelan remained as ignorant of the widening gulf as he was of what had come before. Bad enough that Kurkas knew.

And Kurkas was right. They had to speak sometime.

"So you *do* still live here?" he said.

Sidara jerked upright, hand fumbling at a dislodged spoon before it skittered to the floor. The corners of her eyes and mouth rippled, then set rigid as surprise yielded to composure. "You're one to talk. Run dry of girls to impress with a Phoenix's uniform?" For all the words' barb, there was little in her tone. "Viktor insisted I sleep. He threatened to lock me out of the Panopticon and send me home under escort."

The Panopticon was the sole completed tower of the city's new defences. The uppermost floor was a triumph of engineering, more glazed than not, the multifaceted windows offering a view clear across the city. At night, firestone lanterns upon its pinnacle blazed bright against the firmament, birthing a more poetic name in those so inclined – the Tower of Stars.

Sidara set a hand to her mouth to stifle a yawn, undermining the righteousness of defiance.

"Maybe he's right." Altiris ventured past stove and pantry until he was level with the lopsided door that emptied onto the grounds. "You look awful."

Lips softened almost to a smile, but never committed. "And you're a fool."

He stifled a wince. Direct. Sidara was seldom anything but, and tiredness made her more so. "I called for help, remember?"

"You should have done it sooner. Viara wanted to, didn't she?"

"Who told you that?"

Old suspicions flared. Both simarka and kraikons were fuelled by the same magic running through Sidara's veins. A weaker, less versatile sort, but close enough kin that she could command them – at some distance, and without the aid of the lionhead amulets by which proctors had once achieved the same miracle. Few of those proctors now remained, and fewer amulets, hunted down and destroyed by the Crowmarket.

While the vanished amulet-bearers could only issue commands, Sidara glimpsed what the constructs saw, and caught snatches of what they heard. By anchoring herself in a particular one – blinding herself to others – its senses became fully her own.

Rumour persisted that the whole notion of anchoring was High Proctor Ilnarov's invention, and readily perpetuated by Sidara. That her view from the Panopticon encompassed a great deal more than stolen glances. Certainly the wealthy avoided discussing weighty matters in front of a construct as assiduously as the unabashedly criminal, and whether or not the eyes were aglow – the tell-tale that Sidara had anchored her presence within. Or at least wanted onlookers to believe so.

She sighed. "No one told me anything. But I know *you*, Altiris. Leaping into things with both feet, and never a thought for the consequences. From the very first day we met."

He bristled. Truth cut deep. Truth always did. She'd saved his life that day, giving of her light to drag him free of the Raven's clutches. A debt he could never repay. "I knew what I was doing."

"Clearly that isn't so, or Viara wouldn't have had her head split open."

"You're exaggerating."

"Really? What would you have done if Jaspyr hadn't happened by?"

Altiris had long since abandoned telling simarka apart. Dents and scratches aside, they sprang from a common mould. "I'd have carried her somewhere warm and sent for help."

She rose from the table, half a head taller than him, and as waiflike as at their first meeting. "And the others?"

The ambushed Drazina? As if *they* were his responsibility. "I—"

Sidara waved him to silence and went stock still, blue eyes drowning in gold.

Altiris glanced away, staring through the icicle-hung window to the mansion's gravel driveway and its crisp covering of snow. For all that Sidara's gift was a miracle, beholding it made him uncomfortable. Her magic diminished him in a way that bloodline or wealth could never achieve. She commanded Lumestra's sunlight. What was one upstart southwealder with a sword beside that?

A tremor crept up Sidara's arm. Lips thinning to a slash, she gripped a chair's upright beneath whitening knuckles.

Back in happier days, soon after the Lord Protector had entrusted her with the city's constructs, she'd confessed the difficulty of anchoring from down among the stone and shadow of the streets, rather than the Panopticon's lofty eyrie.

But whatever her failings, Sidara didn't give up on something merely because it was difficult.

After what seemed for ever, the glow faded from her eyes. She sagged. "Sorry. A housebreaker over on Middle Row. He put up quite a chase. I handled it."

Altiris winced. Time was, a housebreaker would have stood his sentence in jail, or as an indentured labourer on some distant farm, or quarry. Whoever Sidara had just handled would be lucky to escape with unbroken bones. One did not simply walk away from a simarka. "Is everyone all right?"

"Yes. As they should have been last night."

There it was. The tone that claimed authority despite parity in rank. That proclaimed she'd always be his better, however much Altiris knew she didn't believe it. Or hadn't used to.

"I had a duty."

"Really? Because unless Josiri tells you otherwise, your authority stops at Stonecrest's gate. In the streets, it's the constabulary, or it's me. If you see something, it's your *duty* to tell me, not play the hero because you feel you've got something to prove."

Altiris' cheeks burned. "*I've* got something to prove? This is the first time I've seen you outside the Panopticon in weeks."

Swaying, she waved a dismissive hand. "You're as bad as Viktor. Lumestra's light sustains me."

The old argument beckoned. The pointless, circular argument. But Altiris was too tired and frustrated to care. "Maybe it should sustain someone else. You hated that your mother wouldn't let you use the light to heal others. Now you can, and instead you're wearing yourself thin acting as an army of lawkeepers. You could be helping people! Or do you prefer to have them looking up to you? A Lady of Light enthroned in her Tower of Stars?"

Spots of colour touched pale cheeks. "I *am* helping people!" Aware she'd shouted, Sidara dropped her voice a notch, though lost none of her fire. "For the first time in my life, the streets are safe."

It wasn't an honest picture, for even Sidara's attention couldn't be everywhere. Some places were as desolate and deprived as Dregmeet had ever been, the streets trod hurriedly for fear of never leaving. "Then what happened to me last night? Did I imagine that?"

"You were only ever in danger because you chose to be," Sidara said icily. "I think that was my point."

And just like that, she'd won. It wasn't *her* fault that she acted as she did. Others made it necessary. *He* made it necessary. It wasn't true, of course – or not wholly so – but it was damn hard to argue against. So instead Altiris seized on something carefully unspoken during his report at the King's Gate watch house. He'd held it close even when Captain Tzila had arrived, hotfoot from the palace to hear a repeated account. No easy thing beneath the empty stare of her sallet helm, but he'd drawn strength from the memory of his identification papers being checked no less than three times. Even though it had long been decreed that all Tressians carry them, rather than just indentured southwealders, some northwealders still found ways to express their distaste.

"Sidara, Hawkin was there. She's back in the city."

Triumph faded to shock, then hardened to determination. "Then that's where I should be."

Sidara made it two steps to the door before exhaustion finally lost patience. She took an involuntary half-turn as her left leg folded beneath her, and flailed for purchase on a battered cabinet.

Fortunately, Altiris had read the signs, and caught her about the waist and shoulders. Somehow, he kept his balance – for all her slenderness, Sidara was not without weight – and stood bowed with her hands locked about his upper arm and neck, as if he were dipping the world's least coordinated dance partner – a title to which she was not without claim.

A glower born of embarrassment softened. "Thank you," she murmured.

Their eyes so close – closer than they'd been in some time – Altiris couldn't escape the small tell-tales of line and vein that spoke to more than weariness, but to long and sustained fatigue. For all Sidara's claims that her magic allowed her to function beyond the norms of sleep, she was a candle burning bright from both ends. Determined to safeguard others as she'd been unable to protect her parents, whatever the cost to herself.

Pride and pity fought for mastery.

"I'll always catch you," he replied softly. "Always."

For the second time that morning, Sidara softened almost to a smile. For the second time, it didn't quite get there. "You see? You can find appropriate words, when you try."

Altiris caught something in her expression not seen for months. A reminder that, though she'd never said the words, she regretted their estrangement as much as he. Just a glimpse, before composure returned.

With more dignity than grace, she pulled free and regained her footing. Unable to pass him to reach the door, she stood just beyond reach, arms folded and back to the kitchen table. "But from what I hear, your silver tongue's been getting a lot of practice. Does Viara know just how much?"

"It isn't like that. She wanted to ask my advice, that's all."

"Oh, I'm sure. And we both know you can never say no to a blonde, don't we?" Sidara stepped closer, tired eyes unblinking as they met his. "I'm returning to the Panopticon. I'm going to find Hawkin. And I don't need you trying to protect me."

Ironic, then, that the argument had begun – at least in part – because of her own overprotective instincts. But Altiris didn't rate his chances of finding another string of appropriate words to make her understand. So he said the only sensible thing, which was nothing.

The kitchen fell to silence, save for the dull *crump* and *scritch* of boots on the gravel beyond the window.

Still, Sidara didn't make any move for the door. Was she thinking, as Altiris was, what a terrible shame it was they knew each other so well, and yet so struggled to understand one another? Or was she hoping he'd attempt to stop her, and thus spare her the bruised pride of admitting she was too far gone to achieve anything?

The outer door creaked open. Constans slipped inside. He made play of stamping snow from his boots and stared at them in mock surprise.

"Oh, am I interrupting another quarrel? Alas."

The siblings had ever been stark opposites. Sidara, tall and fair; generous with herself and thinking only of others. Constans crept like a shadow into proceedings, and like a shadow one never knew precisely what he concealed.

Sidara scowled at him. "We're not quarrelling."

"Really?" The corner of Constans' lip curled into something Altiris suspected he thought appropriate to the moment's wit, but in truth merely looked sly. "Then something else must have set the birds to flight just now. A ghost, perhaps. Or maybe Kurkas was singing, and I missed it. Let me guess? You're angry that your southwealder bungled things last night?"

Altiris clenched a fist behind his back. His heritage was too often wielded as insult. Even in their fiercest arguments, Sidara never used it thus. Constans, on the other hand, delighted in doing so, though always denied it when challenged. Brave, for a boy not yet of age to thus needle a man several years his senior, but Constans had never lacked for a particular kind of courage.

"What do you want, Constans?" The icy tone Sidara had earlier wielded against Altiris had nothing to the one now mustered for her brother. Shades of the woman who'd once fought a duel for a south-wealder's honour. "You keep insisting this isn't your home. As a guest, it's proper you be escorted from the gate and received at the main door."

He spread a hand across his chest. "I did see the gate guard, as it happens. A tragedy that they didn't see me. And do I need reason to bask in my sister's radiance?" When no one took him up on the conversational gambit, he shrugged. "Father wishes to see Josiri."

Sidara's expression soured further, as it always did when Constans referred thus to the Lord Protector.

Altiris hurried to speak before she could. "I'll tell him. Where, and when?"

"The palace. Noon." A smile haunted the corner of Constans' mouth. "Do you think you can remember all that, or should I accompany you to make certain?"

"I said I'll tell him." Altiris met the irreverent gaze and held it long enough for Constans to glance away. Any victory that morning was welcome ... and maybe he could garner a second. "And where should I say you'll be, Sidara? If he asks, I mean."

A twitch of her cheek revealed that she'd caught the deeper meaning. "In my chambers. Sleeping. The rest of it ... " She sighed. "The rest will wait."

A glance at Constans. A shake of the head. An implicit warning to say nothing of Hawkin Darrow. A promise easily given, as Altiris had no intention of telling Constans more than he had to.

"I'll be sure to relay the message." He let his gaze linger on Constans a heartbeat longer. "You saw yourself in, so you can see yourself out, can't you?"

Three

The crowds had thinned by the time Josiri set out from Stonecrest, the snow trampled to mush by the morning's bustle, and bitter woodsmoke mingling with the sweet, rich scent of horse dung.

Even after nearly seven years at Stonecrest, Josiri still couldn't quite believe how *loud* the city contrived to be. It would be different tomorrow, when families flooded to church and priests recounted tales of how Second Dawn had rescued humankind from the cold clutches of the Dark. But today, the streets resounded with the rumble of wheel and the clatter of hoof. The ebb and swell of a thousand voices speaking at once, seeking to be heard: dockers, mill workers, processions of black-robed, holy serenes hurrying to dawnsong services and columns of marching soldiery. Stark contrast to a childhood lived in the now-vanished market town of Eskavord, followed by long years sealed in his ancestral home of Branghall at the orders of an equally extinct Council. There, Midwintertide's approach had ground everything to a halt. Here, the city barely paused to draw breath.

"I wish you'd agreed to a carriage," said Altiris.

Josiri sidestepped an oncoming cart and stifled a yawn born of too many late nights and early mornings attending to constabulary business. The young lieutenant had clung stubbornly to his side since leaving Stonecrest, vigilant for pocket-dippers, coshmen and the belligerent.

"You worry too much."

"Yes, lord," came the stiff reply.

The lad possessed a good, loyal heart. But he bore every error like a mortal wound. Pride kept a man rigid, but made him brittle, as Josiri had learned on the hardest of roads. With grey hairs creeping among the blond, he hoped never to repeat the lesson.

He spared a glance for Anastacia. In a street where every other soul was gloved and muffled against the cold, she glided atop trampled snows in a red silk dress – ankle-length, but leaving forearms and shoulders bare – and the unbound tresses of her white wig flowing behind. Heavy boots were her one concession to the elements, and those for grip, rather than warmth.

But then, a divine serathi surely felt little in the way of cold, and definitely not with her spirit trammelled by a body of unfeeling alabaster porcelain, jointed by dark leather where limbs flexed. The swirling gold patterns inlaid in her kiln-fired skin gleamed in the winter sun. Almost as bright as her obvious delight at the stares her immobile, beatific face drew from gaping passersby.

"My mother walked the city streets all the time when she was on the Council," said Josiri. "She always believed it better to be one of the people, than above them. How can I do less? And we both know it's last night that's really bothering you."

Altiris scowled. "I walked straight into a trap. The perpetrators escaped. Boronav could've been killed. It *should* bother me."

"I wonder what the head of the constabulary thinks? Oh, wait. That's me." Josiri sighed. "I read the reports. The attackers were organised. One of the survivors claimed the leader bewitched him."

The twitch of Altiris' lip lent credence to the suggestion. "It's probably true."

[[Bewitched?]] asked Anastacia, her smoky black eyes no longer lost in the curiosity of the crowd, but now intent on Altiris. Her singsong voice held, as ever, a trace of mockery. [[Who*ever* would possibly believe such a tale?]]

"There was something about her, Ana."

For all that no worldly power could convince Altiris to use Josiri's personal name, he displayed no such obstacle with her. That tradition offered no ready title helped. She wasn't Lady Trelan, for they weren't married. Mistress implied impermanence and a hint of scandal ... not that the latter would have troubled her any. Consort implied subservience wholly lacking. And her surname, Psanneque, wasn't really a name at all, but a grim joke played by old jailors, proclaiming her an exile. This, at least, was true.

[[What manner of something?]] The mockery was gone, replaced by sharp interest.

"A song. Whispers on the edge of hearing. Voices calling without words. I think ... " He hesitated, but forged on. "I think I blacked out for a heartbeat."

Josiri pulled him aside and into the lee of a boarded-up townhouse. The crowd flowed on past with nary a glance. "Blacked out? *That* wasn't in your report."

Altiris grimaced. "It didn't seem important."

Josiri considered. More likely, he'd been embarrassed. "You should have mentioned it. Details matter."

[[Was she very beautiful, this singer?]] The amusement returned to Anastacia's voice, but Josiri had known her too long not to recognise the seriousness beneath. [[Did she dazzle you?]]

"I don't remember. Truly I don't. Only her eyes."

With a thoughtful noise, Anastacia turned away, the matter apparently forgotten. Josiri had known her too long to be fooled by that, either. But he'd learned the hard way that she'd share her thoughts only when ready. And the conversation had already strayed beyond what was appropriate for a busy street.

"I'm sorry," Altiris murmured. "It won't happen again."

Instinct tempted Josiri to chastisement, but with passing years he'd come to distrust such urges. He'd lived too much of his life fearing his mother's disapproval. Even long after she'd embraced the Raven – out of pride, naturally. Fear of failure paralysed like no other.

"Yes it will. You made a mistake. Maybe several, but they were small, and are now corrected. There'll be more, because there always are." He paused, waiting until he was certain of the lad's attention. "Can I offer you some advice?"

"Always, lord."

"Atoning for errors past is honourable, even healthy. Until it becomes obsession."

Altiris snorted. "So you're also telling me I'm an idiot?"

No need to ask who'd beaten him to it. "Those aren't the words I used.

Nor do they hold the same sentiment." He glanced over his shoulder, but Anastacia was nowhere to be seen. "You want folk to look on you with respect – to see a hero – because that will make sense of everything. But it doesn't work like that. Actions in the light don't matter half as much as those taken in the darkness, where no one will ever know."

"Your mother's wisdom?"

"Viktor's. He was trying to push my head through a plate glass window at the time, but I'll spare you that."

Altiris blinked. "The Lord Protector did that? To you?"

"Some years ago I was in the throes of a terrible mistake. Wallowing in errors past. Viktor took it upon himself to enlighten me. Not my finest hour."

"I didn't know."

"Almost no one does. I'd rather that didn't change."

Altiris stood a little straighter, and for the first time truly met his gaze. "Of course, lord."

"Now, is there anything more you left out of the report?"

"No."

"Then we'll consider the matter closed." Josiri tapped the phoenix on Altiris' tabard. "As for Sidara? For all the sorrows she's borne, she'll never understand the burden we southwealders carry, will she?"

The phoenix, after all, was more than just a family emblem. It spoke to destiny, and to the delusion of prophecy. *A phoenix shall blaze from the darkness. A beacon to the shackled; a pyre to the keepers of their chains.* That delusion had killed Josiri's mother. It had claimed his sister. And in the end, it had been Viktor who'd freed the south – not from Tressia's Council, but from the Tyrant Queen Malatriant's lingering evil. For Altiris, who had not witnessed those events, the phoenix remained a symbol of hope, and of fate's kindness in dark times. But fate made landfall on strange shores once wind was in its sails. Josiri retained the emblem as his family crest to remind himself of that, and of what he owed to Viktor, good and bad.

"No, lord," said Altiris, the last shame falling from his expression.

"Good." Josiri glanced up towards the distant guildhall as scattered chimes rang out. Quarter to the hour. So much for arriving early. "Did you happen to see what has become of Anastacia?"

He peered past Josiri's shoulder, into the crowd. "Over there."

Josiri didn't see her at first, for he was looking at head height – itself an error, as his love's doll-like physique made her shorter than the common run of humanity. Instead, Anastacia knelt where the steep incline of Stanner Hill emptied onto the main thoroughfare, skirts puddled in the snow. Before her stood a wailing girl of no more than six or seven, her tatter betraying lean times, her tear-stained cheeks desperate sorrow.

The girl shied away as Anastacia reached out, and clutched her hands tight to her chest. To all evidence, no other paid them any heed, the passersby reflowing indifferently about them.

"Looks like she's made a friend," said Altiris.

Josiri threaded his way through the crowd, trying hard not to smile. For all that Anastacia delighted at playing the distant observer, the facade had worn thin with time.

He'd reached the middle of the street when a bellow of warning split the air.

"Look out! It's going!"

A dull rumble blossomed into rapid crescendo. The crowd's indifference dissipated, lost beneath the thunder of running feet as men and women ran for safety. A dark shape appeared further up Stanner Hill. An unhorsed wagon rushed backwards down the icy cobbles, bucking and lurching. Each jolt dislodged bottles into the street, the crash of breaking glass bright against the rolling boom of steel-shod wheels. The metal tip of its bridle-spar striking sparks behind, it demolished a lamp post and careened onwards to the hill's foot, headlong towards the girl.

"Ana!"

She looked up and shoved the girl clear. Then the wagon struck her trailing shoulder with a dull *crack*. Anastacia vanished beneath its wheels.

The wagon made it another dozen yards before the leading wheel struck a pothole. With a juddering groan, it slewed about, teetered and tipped sideways against a bollard, spilling what remained of its cargo into the road. Wine stained the churned slush red, its sweet smell sharper for the cold.

Josiri picked up his pace, boots skidding on the treacherous ground. "Ana? Are you all right?"

Wig dishevelled, her dress soaked through, but otherwise apparently none the worse for wear, Anastacia picked herself up from between the wagon's twin furrows. Waving aside Altiris' attempt to help, she made unsteady play of brushing herself down.

[[Of course I am.]] She staggered a pace, and stared forlornly at her torn and sodden dress. [[Such a waste. Wait! No! Don't even think about it.]]

Quick as a snake, she grabbed the retreating girl – who traded tears for an open-mouthed stare. The wailing began anew as Anastacia's fingers closed about her wrist. The emptied street refilled as opportunists sought plunder in the wagon's wine-soaked wake. No one gave Anastacia a second look.

"Ana . . ." Josiri began.

She crouched in front of the girl. [[I told you before. If you keep making that horrible noise, I shall eat you, and you'll never see your mother again.]]

The wailing ebbed. "You won't."

[[Oh, shan't I? And how do you know?]]

The girl's eyes narrowed. "Your mouth doesn't open."

[[Better. Maybe I shan't eat you after all.]]

She stood unsteadily, leaving the girl staring up at her with a mix of trepidation and curiosity.

"Oi! What have you done to my wagon?"

A florid-faced man half-ran, half-skidded down the hill, gloved finger jabbing accusingly.

Altiris strode to bar the newcomer's path, hand near enough to his sword to offer caution. Fingers still tight about the girl's arm, Anastacia whirled, the tangle of her disarrayed wig no longer hiding her otherworldly features.

[[It's more what your wagon did to *me*, and what *I'm* going to do to *you*, don't you think?]]

The man skidded to a halt, mouth half-open in a wary scowl. He shrank back from her black, witch's eyes. "Wasn't my fault. The chocks didn't hold."

[[And who set them?]]

He flinched as she took a step towards him.

Josiri cleared his throat. Anastacia could go from threat to action murderously fast. "Were I you, I'd concern myself with salvaging what's left of your wares."

Impossibly, the man's face fell further as he beheld the ruin with fresh eyes. Stood proud atop the wreckage, a cheering woman brandished an intact bottle. Glass shattered as eager hands made reckless search of what remained.

"Thieves!" Anastacia forgotten, the wagoner lurched along the trail of destruction, fist shaking. "Let it alone, dregrats!"

The girl laughed, then remembered she was supposed to be upset and fell silent.

"Ana, please tell me you're not stealing that child," said Josiri.

She cocked her head. [[I should leave her in the middle of the street, crying her eyes out and calling for her mother?]]

Survey of the street confirmed that if a distraught mother were close to hand, she kept a low profile. Beyond the growing scrum around the capsized wagon, there was no great concern on display elsewhere. Then again, stray children were hardly uncommon. The war had left far too many orphans. Not all had the good fortune of family.

With one last glance at the wagon – and electing not to get further involved unless bloodshed beckoned – Josiri offered the girl a smile. "What's your name, miss?"

She stared at him, weighing his integrity in that way only small children attempt. "Ella."

"And where do you live?"

"Near the church." She paused, then made proud proclamation. "Number 3."

Josiri knew of at least five churches within as many minutes' walk, and that was without counting the Lunastran chapel on Warren Gate, whose congregation claimed it a church even if the Lumestran majority did not. "Can you show me?"

A frown, a shake of the head. A wobble of lip and cheek promised fresh tears.

[[Don't do that. Or I'll do something appalling to you.]]

How the threat didn't set tears flowing again, Josiri couldn't conjure, but again the girl lapsed into silence. "Altiris, the Alder Street checkpoint is just around the corner. Would you mind?" He jerked his head towards the growing hubbub where the wagoner fought his losing battle against the tenets of finders, keepers. "And make mention of this mess, assuming word's not already travelled. You can catch us up."

The lad hesitated, concern written plain on furrowed brow.

"Lord, I—"

"I'm sure Ana will keep me safe."

Altiris nodded, squatted and held out his hand. "Why don't you come with me, Ella? Someone will find your mother."

Ella readily transferred her allegiance – and her grip – from Anastacia to Altiris. She stared back at her saviour until the crowd swallowed them up, eyes still red but no longer afraid. Delivered from a dark and fearful day by a serathi, though she wouldn't remember once terror faded. A good deed in the callous murk of an unthinking crowd.

Josiri set his back to Anastacia to hide his smile. In the distance, past the unhappy wagon and visible where the streets fell away towards the sea, a square-rigged merchantman furled sail on final approach to the docks.

[[Wipe that ridiculous expression off your face, or I'll eat *you*.]]

"I'm told you can't do that," he replied, deadpan. "When did you become a shepherd of lost children?"

[[I have been nothing else as long as I've known you. Some children are older and taller than others, that's all.]] Intrigued by the whimsy in her singsong voice, he was surprised to find her staring off to where Altiris had led the girl away. She swayed ever so slightly as she spoke. [[She was terrified, and everyone kept walking, even though all she really needed was someone who'd acknowledge her pain. I think I hate people.]]

"You couldn't have kept her."

[[The two you dragged into our lives are trouble enough.]]

Josiri forbore mention that adopting Sidara had been her idea. Constans too, though that had ended poorly. He'd many times considered formally adopting Altiris, but had always held back.

Sidara remained Sidara Reveque, out of respect for her wishes, and in memory of her father, whom Josiri had counted as a friend. But even before enslavement, the Czarons had not been of the first rank – nor the second, third or even the sixth. Adopting Altiris would make him a Trelan, and the name brought burdens to outweigh any benefits. Josiri had known one truth his whole life: Trelans were stubborn. But over the years, he'd reason to suspect another: Trelans also ended badly.

"Sometimes I wish we'd never left Branghall."

[[Part of me never did,]] she murmured. [[Things were certainly simpler.]]

"You should have heard them this morning. A blind man could see how they feel about one another, but something keeps getting in the way."

[[It's not for you to solve. They'll figure it out. We did.]]

He winced. He'd hated Anastacia when Emil Karkosa had first bound her to Branghall, resenting being forced to share confinement behind enchanted walls with a creature who delighted in playing the demon. All so long ago that Josiri barely recalled her old appearance, let alone what it had been like to embrace the woman of divine flesh she'd once been, rather than the clay she'd become. "And wasn't that fun?"

[[Eventually. As to what's getting in the way? Memories hang heavier than they'll admit.]]

"Not like us, eh?"

[[We *are* our memories, Josiri. A walking record of triumphs and failures.]] She sighed, a whistling, musical sound. [[What we've gained, and what we stand to lose.]]

Josiri drew closer, brow furrowed in concern. Melancholy was as rare to Anastacia's nature as kindness unleavened by sarcasm. "Is something troubling you?"

[[Nothing at all,]] she said sharply.

"You'll never win a starring role with delivery like that," he replied. "Needs more conviction."

Fingers *glinked* together as she clenched a fist. [[You'll think me foolish.]]

"I'd not dare." He took her arm, wishing that the pale mask of her face offered some expression – some clue to the thoughts beyond inky black eyes. "Tell me. Please?"

She glanced away. [[You're all going to die. All of you. And I'll still be here. Alone.]]

Her tone took him aback. She'd passed similar comment over the years, riven with anger. On this occasion, he heard only sorrow. "I've no plans to go anywhere."

[[But you will. Look at Vladama. He's faded so much these past years. Not that he's ever been anything more than passably domesticated.]] Asperity couldn't hide genuine affection. [[Some days, I'm almost afraid to blink, for fear he'll be gone. How many more blinks before it's you? Before it's Altiris . . . or Sidara?]]

The last was spoken with particular melancholy. A mother's dread for a daughter, undiminished by the lateness of their bond.

Josiri saw the shape of things now. After Calenne's passing, he'd assumed his family ended. Instead, it had grown, because family was more than blood alone. It was those one loved, and who would carry legacy and memory when life faded. For all the sorrow that brought, there was consolation alongside. But for Anastacia, who'd been immortal long before she'd been robbed of flesh? Family was regret waiting to happen. And she'd never been comfortable expressing weakness.

Holding her bunched hand, he slid his other atop the leather-joined fingers and squeezed, hoping as he ever did that some small measure of sensation would cheat the clay. "I don't think it sounds foolish at all."

[[And what does a fool know of foolishness?]]

"Everything and nothing. It's his gift, and his curse. But I understand. I do." Fury, he was used to. Disdain? Sardonicism? Glee? They were the cornerstones of Anastacia's being, all the more expansive for being loosed from divine spirit. But sorrow? He'd no map to chart a safe path, and no experience to serve as guide. "Maybe you're more human than you think."

[[What a horrible thing to say.]] She pulled away and stalked off across the crowded street. [[Come along. Viktor's waiting, and he's never been a patient soul.]]

Viktor. A man upon whom the past hung as heavy as the future apparently did Anastacia. Josiri stood still for a moment, staring down at the fine, white powder stark against his glove – aftermath of a porcelain fist clenched so tight as to wear the immutable away. Then he dusted his hands and set out anew, before she was lost to sight.

Four

"What bloody time do you call this?" The booming voice set the chandelier's crystals dancing. "Still, shouldn't expect military precision from a soft-bellied highblood, should I? I've a good mind to demand your resignation."

It wasn't exactly the tone with which one was normally greeted at the palace, not even when that greeting was delivered by black-tabarded Drazina, rather than a servant. Then again, Stantin Izack, Marshal of the Republic's armies – though he still wore a hunter's green sash proclaiming old loyalties to Essamere – was by no means ordinary. Despite the furrows in his tanned features and the remorseless recession of his sandy-blond hair, Izack remained a man to stand foursquare in a river's path and demand it choose another course.

"We were delayed," Josiri replied. "A mission of mercy. You wouldn't resent me that?"

Izack marched closer, footfalls hammering on the hallway's polished tile. Stern expression melted into a grin. "I'd only end up with your bloody job. I've enough on my hands with our illustrious 'army'. Sooner have a herd of sheep under arms."

[[Perhaps you should recruit some?]] said Anastacia.

"Don't think I'm not tempted, lady." He nodded greeting, then returned Altiris' clasped-fist salute. "All hands to the ramparts today, is it? Should be just like old times."

[[I'm sure the gallant lieutenant and I can take a turn in the gardens instead.]]

Izack shrugged. "I wouldn't worry. Like I said, old times. But I'd keep hold of your coats. He wants us on the balcony."

Odd, but hardly unheard of. The old council chamber held poor memories. "You *are* joining us at Stonecrest tomorrow?" asked Josiri.

Izack regarded him with veiled amusement. "That's the third time you've asked. Try to keep me away. That steward of yours has a nose for good brandy. Can't let him drink it all, can I?"

Josiri couldn't recall asking even once prior to that morning, but smiled anyway. "Vladama will survive the hardship, I'm sure."

Midwintertide was a time for friends, and for family. With so many of both dead or scattered, the ritual of a hearty meal in good company had become steadily more important to Josiri with passing years. Not that he'd ever convinced Viktor to attend.

There was no concession to Midwintertide within the palace. Neither bauble nor lantern decked the walls, no evergreen holly upon architrave or mantelpiece. The west wing, its offices and storerooms long since given over to the Drazina barracks, fell away behind. The iron gate barring passage to the east, and the suite of rooms comprising Viktor's living quarters, loomed ahead.

The clocktower belonged to the east, though no bell had chimed from the palace since the day Emperor Kai Saran had wrought murder within its bounds. Viktor had made the tower his private vantage, beholding the fragile city much as Sidara did from the Panopticon. A reassuring shadow glimpsed against the clockface lanterns when night fell, watching over his people as a protector should.

At least, that was what strangers perceived. Josiri knew Viktor too well. Whatever gaze he cast from the tower would be directed inwards. For all that he demanded much of those around him, Viktor ever saved his harshest judgement for himself.

The rest of the palace remained hidden behind locked doors and swathed in dustsheets, awaiting rising fortunes. Even Josiri, who'd seldom harboured love for the business of Council, experienced a pang to see the cold echo of empty corridors.

Ascending the grand stairway, they passed into the old Privy Council chamber. It stank of history; dust and thwarted ambitions brewed strong. It was impossible not to read disfavour in the stony frowns of councillors past, their likenesses rendered in granite and marble for posterity. The great gilded map showing Tressia's ancient domains still dominated the north wall, ever more a lie with the advancing years. Three counties remaining from a dominion that had once spanned a continent and challenged the territory of distant kings.

But not all was ancient and austere. A vast oil painting – as tall as Josiri, and twice as broad again – sat on a series of bowed easels. Curious, Josiri broke off to examine it.

For all he'd been present for the events depicted, it took effort of will to recognise them. The gold and green of Hadari warriors swarming through the plaza, held at bay by stalwarts in King's Blue. On the palace balcony – here gilded and glorious, rather than weather-stained and forlorn – two giants made contest. One was noble of brow and feature, his face contorted in righteous anger. The other, furtive and cruel – bloody sword dangling from his hand – was frozen in the act of being hurled from the balcony to his death. Tragedy and triumph, captured in oils.

"Who painted this?" For all that the name tormented the tip of Josiri's tongue, he couldn't place it.

"Mandalov. Been working on it for years, I gather." Izack drew up beside. "D'you like it?"

Every one of the hundreds of faces was unique, the emotions of the tumultuous day captured to perfection, the luminous trickery of pigment and varnish lending illusion of a scene one could step into, rather than merely observe. It took but a little effort to hear the clash of blades and the screams of the dying. But the rest? "A shame Mandalov doesn't have an eye for history."

Izack grunted. "Bugger's a charlatan."

The painting's prevailing medium was not oil, but artistic licence. There'd been no clash of armies, for Kai Saran had struck with but a handful of companions. As for other details? A dying Malachi Reveque was present, but depicted as a far older man. Constans and Sidara, whom he'd shielded from Saran's wrath, were depicted as little more than babes, when in truth Sidara had been on the verge of womanhood. Her expression, at least, was apt: filled with resolve, and bereft of fear.

Josiri shook his head. "Viktor commissioned this?"

"He's spoken of burning it. No one's had the heart to tell Mandalov. Reckon the daft bastard was hoping for patronage."

If that was so, then he'd misjudged his mark. For all that flattering portrayals were part and parcel of a noble's existence, Viktor had never encouraged them. If by chance the painting survived, it would do so as record of a past that had never quite existed. But then, that was par for the course. In Tressia's carefully curated histories, heroes were made villains, and villains erased or rehabilitated according to prevailing need.

"Am I on there?"

[[Here.]] Anastacia tapped the canvas. Midway between Viktor and Sidara, a bloodied figure confronted a dozen snarling Hadari. [[Aren't you small?]]

Leaving painting and Privy Council chamber behind, Josiri headed out onto the balcony – a space fashioned for dozens occupied by only a handful of cloaked and coated souls. Beyond the stone balustrade, the snow-clogged plaza stretched towards the treelined mouth of Sinner's Mile – the long, steep road up to the sacred Hayadra Grove. Where the streets had been busy, the plaza was near empty, and deep with drifted snow.

The cold noontide air banished the palace's warmth. Viktor's embrace did much to return it. He stepped away, the personal greeting reinforced by a rather more formal bow. As ever, he wore simple black garb, without cloak or armour, having learned long ago that his height and glower were intimidating enough – and often too much.

"Thank you for coming, brother." The basso voice that had offered threat to despot and Empress rumbled with affection. "I trust Sidara is resting? Her dedication should awe us all, but she should respect her limitations."

"Did we?"

Viktor offered a smile – they came easier to him in advancing years. He was now closer to fifty summers than forty, a tally betrayed by grey hairs amid the black. Josiri, who felt forever weary despite being a decade younger, envied his easy vigour.

"And Anastacia, too." Taking her hand, Viktor pressed porcelain fingers to his lips. "A pleasant surprise."

She cocked her head. [[Experience has taught me not to leave the two of you alone.]]

Her tone held reserve, as it always did in Viktor's presence. Though she often claimed to have forgiven the misjudgement by which he'd bound her to clay, absolution was an expensive commodity.

A smile tugged at the corner of Viktor's mouth, the old scar on his left cheek lending mockery where none was intended. "And who am I to question divine judgement? You're welcome, of course. Both of you."

This last, he addressed to Altiris, who lingered on the threshold.

"Thank you, Lord Protector." Altiris bowed, the tensing of his shoulders betraying courage gathered close. "I regret I wasn't able to prevent the theft of your possessions."

"That you failed does nothing to diminish my gratitude," Viktor replied solemnly. "But we can't afford to let this go unanswered. I assume you have the constabulary looking into the matter, Josiri?"

"It's underway." Now was not the time to remind Viktor that stolen goods vanished readily. For every fence weary constables locked up, another took their place, their wares as often scavenged from merchantmen lured onto the rocks by wreckers' lights as from common robbery. A booming trade in recent months, and one Josiri was determined to end. "Inventory of what was taken would help, of course."

"I confess I don't know. Most of it came from my great aunt's estate at Margard. She never cared much for order, far less making things easy on inheritors. One or two pieces, perhaps. A sword, in particular." He frowned in thought. "You won't mind if I instruct Constans to investigate on my behalf?"

Old discomfort stirred. "Constans? Is that wise?"

Viktor gripped his shoulder. "You mustn't take it so personally that he's faring better under my guardianship than yours, Josiri. The boy needed a firm hand, and has one. He's ready for broader responsibilities, and Tzila will keep him out of trouble. But if you'd rather he not become involved . . . ?"

Josiri sorely wanted to refuse. For all Viktor's claims of Constans' good character, his own experiences with the boy suggested otherwise.

Altiris gave a respectful cough. "Might I assist? I'd recognise the thieves. And the sword."

Viktor nodded. "An excellent idea. Josiri?"

"It's a lot of effort for a simple theft."

Viktor shook his head. "It's not the theft. It's not what they stole. It's *that* they stole. They knew precisely who they were stealing from. They made a point of it. That sort of audacity can't be permitted to spread."

Despite the blossoming scowl, Josiri couldn't escape Viktor's logic. Stealing from the Lord Protector was either supreme foolishness or open challenge. Better it was ended before others followed the example. With fortune, Altiris might serve as a brake on Constans' less suitable tendencies. And then there was the matter of the bewitching, half-remembered woman. Altiris, at least, knew to be wary of her should their paths cross.

He glanced at Anastacia, who shrugged, then splayed a palm against the wall to steady herself, seemingly having taken herself by surprise with the motion.

"Very well," said Josiri. "Altiris? Return to Stonecrest. Tell Vladama he'll be covering your duties for the immediate future. Then report back here."

A twitch of Altiris' eye betrayed worry that he'd overstepped, but he bowed and retraced his footsteps through the Privy Council chamber.

When he'd gone, Josiri at last turned his attention to the balcony's assembled company.

Izack had scarcely exaggerated when he'd spoken of old times. The gathering was the closest Tressia any longer had to a Privy Council. Men and women Viktor trusted to make sensible judgement and no abuse of authority. In many ways, it made for a better system. The Council's politics had tangled the Republic in chains of ambition. True, the current arrangement meant Tressia was a Republic in name only, but it had only ever been intended as a temporary state of affairs. And it wasn't as though others weren't consulted. Archimandrite Jezek. Eloess Nivar, Matriarch of Serenity for the church. Konor Zarn and his fractious guild council. Yon Trannar, Lord Admiral of the Navy. All had a voice ... it was simply that Viktor was under no obligation to listen to them *speak*.

Of those present, Josiri knew Elzar Ilnarov well, having shared – and inevitably *lost* – many a hand of jando to him on idle evenings in Viktor's chambers. Though stooped of figure and well into old age, Elzar remained a shrewd opponent, and one not entirely above bending the rules of the card game in his favour – though he inevitably denied such behaviour if caught.

In official record, he was Master of the foundry – second only in the Lumestran Church to Archimandrite Avriel Jezek. A stranger would never have guessed as much from his worker's leathers and dishevelled appearance. Elzar claimed such garb more practical than a proctor's golden robes – especially as he spent much of his life on the border overseeing repairs to the handful of battered kraikons who held the eastern watch.

The border itself fell under the responsibility of the woman with laughing grey eyes and unbraided blonde hair brushing the collar of her drab coat. She alone of the small gathering seemed to relish the cold. Propped against the balustrade when Josiri had entered the balcony, she now stood and flung her arms tight about him.

"Josiri. It's been too long."

He grinned and returned the embrace. Sevaka Orova, Governor of the Marcher Lands, was little given to concealing delight or sorrow, and nor were those in her orbit. "I didn't know you were in the city."

Sevaka stepped away, her voice growing nasal. "I arrived this morning. Summoned with nary a scrap of pomp. Most disgraceful. One is appalled." She arched an eyebrow. For a moment she was the twin of her departed and little-lamented mother, a cruel vision returned from an unmarked grave . . . save for a mischievous smile that Ebigail Kiradin would never have worn. Fingers splayed to ruffle blonde hair dispelled the illusion completely, though a tightness about her eyes remained. "Are you well?" she said, in her own voice once more.

"I am. Rosa?"

Expression cooling, Sevaka glanced at Viktor, now deep in conversation with Anastacia. "The same. She still won't talk about it, and believe me, I've tried." She shook her head. "I thought this was just another of their arguments. Her friendship with Viktor has always been . . . complicated, shall we say? But it's been a year. Would you speak to him?"

In point of fact, Josiri had several times discussed the Darkmere expedition with Viktor. However, he recalled no details beyond failure to recover Konor Belenzo's ancient texts. So much took him that way of late. In younger days as a rebellious wolf's-head, he'd dared write nothing down for fear of discovery or betrayal. Now, he dared not do otherwise. Which was unfortunate, as tired eyes increasingly found reading a strain. "Of course."

"Thank you."

Josiri turned his attention to the third and final member of Viktor's ersatz council. "Arlanne."

She offered a stiff bow, dark plaits bobbing behind a surcoat blazoned with the Prydonis drakon. Governor of the Southshires she might have been, but a military past seldom remained entirely so. "My lord."

Another one riddled with deference. Not quite as bad as Altiris, though it hailed much from the same source. A legacy of old days, when Arlanne Keldrov had been an officer tasked with suppressing the Southshires, and Josiri the imprisoned Duke of Eskavord. History had proved the wrongness of her duty, and for all that she'd since proven capable and fair, she'd never entirely rid herself of guilt.

"You're also a new arrival?" he asked.

"I've been here a few days." She offered a wintery smile. "Most of them waiting for the world to stop lurching. The passage across Kasdred Mar was not the kindest. Next time, I'll ride."

That left one other, though her vantage was as separate as her station. Captain Tzila stood perhaps a pace or two back from the double doors, unmoving and silent as greetings were exchanged, thoughts concealed behind the gleaming steel of a visored sallet helm. A scarf drawn tight across neck and lower jaw hid all expression. Below that, she wore close-fitting contoured plate of finer craft than that worn by other Drazina, softened only a little by the black silks of her cloak, tabard and bases long enough to have been a skirt.

Though her paired sabres were the only weapons on the balcony, she wore no blazon to proclaim allegiance. Tzila – she'd no other name Josiri knew – was Viktor's seneschal, separate from the Drazina hierarchy Grandmaster Sarisov oversaw, and free to act in the Lord Protector's stead. The Darkmere expedition had highlighted the necessity. Had Prince Thirava slain Viktor – or worse yet, taken him captive – the result would have been ruinous. Tzila, frankly, was expendable.

As ever, she offered no greeting save a slow nod. Tzila never spoke. Could not, in fact, were rumours true. Those same whispers suggested she'd once been a kernclaw – one of the Crowmarket's shadowy enforc-ers – and had helped Viktor scour vranakin sympathisers from the city after the Parliament of Crow's fall. Certainly, the gallowmen had plied a busy trade in the weeks after their toppling. Reason enough to conceal one's identity. Old grudges faded slowly.

Viktor crossed the balcony and leaned out over the plaza. "I apologise for calling you away from home and duty in so bleak a season, but what patience I have is a slender resource." He straightened, the shadows lengthening and the cold air turning ever more chill. "The shadowthorns have held the Eastshires too long. I do not have it in me to allow this state of affairs to continue."

Josiri winced in discomfort at Viktor's use of the name *shadowthorn* – one that suggested the Hadari were born as much of Fellhallow's tainted soil as Lumestra's divine light. Old propaganda, taken as fact by too many. Easier to kill an enemy perceived as less than human.

He found no surprise in the declaration itself. Viktor had ever been a protector. As a child, he'd lost his mother to vranakin footpads. Needless guilt had forged that boy into a soldier, and intervening decades had tempered the soldier into a champion. For all Viktor's strength, a piece of him remained anchored in the past, trapped in a failure for which no other held him accountable. It was the heart of his bond with Sidara, who blamed herself for her own parents' deaths, and for equally slender reasons. That the Eastshires remained oppressed vexed him terribly.

Izack looped his hands behind his back. "Noble goal. Can't fault it, but we're a long way from being ready."

"You claim your army unequal to the task, Lord Marshal?" Viktor replied without turning, his attention fixed on the gothic finery of Vordal Tower on the plaza's far edge.

Eyes narrowed. "We don't have an army. Not yet. We've unwilling recruits learning to march under banners they've not earned. It's a wonder the Hadari border isn't a damn sight closer to the sea."

"The Hadari border remains along the Ravonn." Still Viktor didn't turn. Nor did he raise his voice, though the darkening of his mood was as obvious as it was immediate. He'd never once acknowledged the existence of Redsigor. The Eastshires remained a stolen province – a temporary theft, albeit one that had stretched into years.

Izack's lip twisted. "There are veterans enough in the regiments who came late to the last war. But the rest? We've centuries of experience buried in the sod at Govanna, waiting for the light of Third Dawn. You don't replace that overnight."

"You've had five years," said Arlanne.

"And I need five more." Izack drew himself up, heels together. "You order me to do it, lord, I'll give it my best. That's my job. But I'm telling you, we're not ready. Now, if we had support from the foundry? That's different."

"You need five years?" said Elzar, his voice thick with frustration. "I need at least fifty . . . and the return of Konor Belenzo wouldn't hurt. I've ransacked every archive in the city, and I'm still no closer to learning how to return the smelters to operation."

"They're just machines, high proctor," Izack replied. "We've clever minds and canny hands enough within the walls, and more for hire out in Thrakkia. I say set them loose."

"And waving a sword about makes a soldier, does it?" Elzar offered apologetic smile for his sharpness. "There's a spiritual component to the process, Izack, and we've lost the secret. Oh, we kept everything running well enough, but when it stopped? I'm working by trial and error. Clever minds and canny hands will only get in the way, unless they're blessed with Lumestra's light, and the Goddess knows that there are few enough of those to be had."

The foundry's irreplaceable mechanisms had been destroyed during the vranakin uprising. A handful of the ancient machines had since been coaxed to life, but proctors themselves were not so easily replaced. The numbers of those born with magic had been waning for decades. The handful who remained were needed on the eastern border.

"What about Lady Reveque?" asked Keldrov. "I understand she's blessed in a way not seen for centuries."

She spoke carefully, unwilling to suggest that she harkened to rumour. Too many discounted the tales about Sidara as outlandish, or exaggerated. Until they saw for themselves. Then they believed.

"Alas, dear Sidara is untutored." Elzar shot a wary glance at Anastacia as she skirted Tzila and made her way to the balcony's northern extent. When she registered no offence, he pressed on. "What she does, she does by instinct – which is impressive, but unhelpful. She'd likely do more harm than good . . . not that I'm ungrateful for her service."

The balcony lapsed into silent contemplation of facts and figures that could not align. The army was inexperienced. Of the Republic's great chapterhouses, Sartorov had seceded. Prydonis had died on Govanna Field, and Essamere had never recovered. The nobility's hearthguards, once small armies in their own right, had been thinned by privation or else picked clean in Izack's search for competent officers. Where once the Stonecrest Phoenixes had been remarkable for their sparseness, Josiri's handful of men and women under arms was now considered grand to the point of luxury.

Sevaka stirred. "We needn't fight the entire Empire. There's little love lost between the Empress and Silsaria. Might be the Golden Court will stay out of things if we look strong enough."

Josiri considered. The Golden Court constituted a council of sorts, the kings and princes – and it was nearly *always* men, despite changing times across the border – of the Empire's myriad kingdoms playing twin roles of advisors and petitioners. Ambition lightly bound in exquisite silks and disguised by fine words. "What if they don't?"

"Our ships still command the seas of Mar Karakeld," Sevaka replied. "If the Empress sees enough sails on the northern horizon, she'll bristle the coastline with spears. She'll not sacrifice her own holdings to keep Thirava on a stolen throne."

Keldrov murmured agreement. Izack gave no sign of being convinced. Josiri, who knew the Empress Melanna Saranal better than anyone present, found no fault with him for that. He'd never had a taste for gambling with the lives of others. Nor, or so he'd thought, did Sevaka. Then again, she'd more reason than most to hate the Hadari.

"How is it in the Eastshires?" he asked, careful to avoid reference to what was very much the Tressian/Hadari border, however much Viktor wished otherwise.

Sevaka hesitated, a scowl distorting a face normally so ready with a smile. "Prince Thirava is not a man to forgive defiance. I understand most of the villages are little more than prison camps. The towns are under curfew. A few get out, but it's almost all meadowland and moor – simplicity itself to patrol. Those Thirava's outriders can't turn back, they shoot. Arrows do not respect borders. Master Tanor has Essamere on ceaseless watch, but they're few and the border long."

The lines about her mouth grew tight. "His knights are accustomed to digging graves."

Izack uttered a low, dangerous rumble. His left hand, level with his belt, clenched and unclenched about a sword that wasn't there. It had taken every argument at Viktor's disposal to have him leave Essamere behind and take responsibility for the army, but a knight he remained. Essamere's frustrations and failures remained his own.

Josiri closed his eyes, but there was no banishing the image conjured by Sevaka's words. He'd heard some of it through sources of his own, but had managed to stifle the horror of it with grim practicality. Whether or not the Golden Court marched to Thirava's aid, reclaiming the Eastshires would mean war renewed, and it was anyone's guess if the Republic would survive.

"And the Hadari claim to be honourable," murmured Keldrov.

"It would be a mistake to confuse Thirava's perception of honour with an entire people's," said Elzar. "It seems we need a miracle."

He addressed this last to Anastacia, who propped herself against the balcony and returned his raised eyebrow with a baleful stare. [[What you need, Master Proctor, is to refrain from foolish comment.]]

Elzar rubbed thoughtfully at his white-stubbled chin. "I merely meant—"

[[There is nothing I can do that you cannot.]]

"Enough." Turning, Viktor softened his command with a lopsided smile and spread his hands. "I didn't call you here to debate. The shadowthorns have held the Eastshires six years. Much longer, and what remains of our people will be so broken that it would be kinder to leave them be."

"The Southshires held out for fifteen years," said Elzar.

"The Southshires had hope. They had the dream of a phoenix who would burn away their chains. What do the Eastshires have? They are forgotten. We are blinded by our wounds. We allowed the Hadari to humiliate us in the very place we thought ourselves safest. They have made us timid where we should be awash with rage for what they've taken."

His voice shook with quiet passion, each word flowing from the next with the inevitability of a blacksmith striking steel. Too late, Josiri realised that there had been no coincidence in the meeting place, nor that each of them had marched past Mandalov's painting.

"Years ago, I risked everything to rescue our kin from bondage." Viktor shook his head. "I can't ignore what's happening in the east. How can you? You, most of all, Josiri? I understand that there are risks. Challenges. But we will find a way. Haven't we always done that, you and I?"

Josiri met his gaze, and was all but lost. That was Viktor's secret, one more dangerous than his shadow. He made you *believe*. No matter how dark the day, Viktor saw the future gleaming like sunlight. Only the roster of dead from the last war – from battles at Ahrad and Vrasdavora, at Tregga and Govanna, and a dozen more besides – kept Josiri from being swept along, and then just barely. Whole families obliterated at a stroke. Villages emptied, and farms fallen fallow for want of hands to tend their fields.

But the others? Sevaka and Keldrov nodded thoughtfully, if for different reasons. Sevaka, as kind a soul as any Josiri had ever met, was surely heart-lorn at the Eastshires' suffering. By contrast, Keldrov would consider the liberation of the east as another step towards atonement for the sins of youth – much as Viktor had once regarded the emancipation of the south. Izack would go wherever a soldier could stand between the defenceless and an enemy's spears. Tzila, as was her wont, gave no indication of her thoughts. And Elzar . . . ?

The aging proctor shook his head. "We're not ready, my boy."

"He's right, Viktor," said Josiri. "In lieu of troops, we need advantage. We don't have one."

Viktor glowered. "We will have every blade we require. Arlanne?"

Keldrov nodded. "I spoke with Thane Armund before I came north. He's prepared to broker for thrydaxes' services, if we can meet the price."

Izack fixed a grim smile. Elzar's brow creased in thought.

So Keldrov hadn't been part of the summons, but the reason for them – a herald bearing word of alliances struck with the thanedoms of the south. At last, Josiri understood why Viktor had allowed the meeting to play out as it had. All obstacles had been aired openly, and rendered moot by the promise of Thrakkian axes.

But he found little comfort. Thrakkian intervention altered the wager's odds, but a gamble it remained. Worse, a war of two nations would become one of three. Whatever betide, the dead of Govanna would not want for company.

"I agreed to serve as Lord Protector for five years," said Viktor. "They are elapsed, but I remained because each one of you, at one time or another, begged me to stay – to hold the Republic together, as I promised. It is in that spirit that I ask you to trust me now. Because though we might pretend otherwise, I've not yet fulfilled that pledge. Not until all our kin are free."

Elzar chewed his lip and nodded. "What do you propose?"

"That we begin moving regiments into the Marcher Lands – I defer to Izack's judgement as to which are most suited – along with whatever chapterhouses agree to join the campaign. Our soldiers will bear the burden of the reconquest, as is proper. The Thrakkians will merely discourage the Hadari from foolishness, and punish any that occurs."

"Then we'll be neck-deep in our own blood before we reach Tregga," said Izack.

"Not if we employ what constructs we have in the city alongside those already in the Marcher Lands."

"I haven't the proctors to command that many," said Elzar. "Not with any degree of skill."

Viktor shrugged. "Sidara has proved her worth within the city's bounds. It's time she did the same beyond."

[[No,]] said Anastacia, flatly. [[She is not a soldier.]]

"She wears a Drazina's uniform," Viktor replied. "That brings responsibilities. She owes this to the Republic. She's already agreed."

[[You had no right to ask.]]

"Sidara's no longer a child," said Elzar. "She can make her own choices."

[[Yes, and I imagine this choice suits *you* very well, doesn't it?]] Anastacia rose to her feet, her body quivering with anger as she bore down upon him. [[Her mother kept her from your foundry for a reason. You'd pluck the sun from the sky if you could, and set it in a lantern to dispel the very darkness you birthed.]]

"Be reasonable, lady," said Izack.

Anastacia took another trembling step, warning in her smoky eyes. [[This *is* me being reasonable. You'll know when that changes.]]

Tzila set her hand on a sabre. The threat of steel was all but worthless against Anastacia's porcelain flesh, but the motion marked an escalation no one needed. Josiri exchanged a worried glance with Sevaka and interposed himself between Anastacia and Viktor, arms outspread.

"Ana, please."

After an agonising moment, Anastacia stepped back.

Releasing a breath he hadn't realised he'd been holding, Josiri turned to Viktor and fought to quell a surge of annoyance at Viktor's presumption. Sidara was as safe in the Panopticon as she could be anywhere. The battlefield was another matter. Selfish to fear for the life of one young woman while her peers fought and died, but that was a father's privilege.

"When do you intend the campaign to begin?"

"As soon as the snows recede. A week. Perhaps two. Kraikons can clear the roads. Sunstaves can melt ice and grant firm ground."

Two weeks. How quickly the world turned. "I'll speak with Sidara. I want to be sure she comprehends what you're asking. You and I, Viktor, were shaped by decisions whose consequences we didn't understand. Whatever Sidara owes to the Republic, we owe this to her. And to ourselves."

He met the other's basilisk stare unblinking. Most crumpled beneath that gaze, but Trelans were stubborn, and Josiri's fear of Viktor was long dead.

"I agree with Josiri," said Sevaka, who owed more to Sidara than any other present. "We can set the rest in motion. There's no harm."

Viktor's gaze burned. "And if Sidara does, in fact, know her own mind?"

For all that he'd spoken in reply to Sevaka, Josiri had no doubt the question was for him. "If she can satisfy me of that, then I withdraw my objection."

[[Josiri?]]

He ignored Anastacia, his whole will bent on Viktor. "I will not be swayed on this, brother."

"Very well." Viktor gave curt nod, but his voice softened. "I would die myself before harm befell Sidara. You must understand that."

[[Josiri . . .]]

This time he turned, alarmed by the note of frailty in her voice.

That alarm redoubled as she staggered backwards, one hand pressed against her brow, and another grasping weakly at the balcony's balustrade. Her whole being, usually so forthright and seldom uncertain, seemed shrunken.

"Ana? What's wrong?"

[[I don't . . . I don't feel . . .]]

Another stumble. The small of her back struck stone. Balance shattered, she fell across the balustrade.

Josiri lunged. "Ana!"

His fingers closed on empty air. Viktor swore, his own desperate grab broken by Anastacia's not insubstantial weight. With a hollow cry, she plunged from sight.

As Josiri scrambled for the balcony's edge, the chime of stone striking stone cut through the crisp *whumph* of flattened snow. And beneath it another sound. One that stole the last of Josiri's breath and set worms writhing in his gut: the sharp, brittle report of shattering ceramic.

Voices rang out, though he didn't truly hear them. Just as he didn't truly see the dark figures forging to the balcony through the plaza's snows, or feel Viktor's hand on his shoulder. The world had shrunk almost to nothing, bounded wholly by Anastacia's motionless, spreadeagled body, and the golden light hissing from cracks in her once-flawless skin.

Five

Ignoring the ache in her shoulder, Rosa hefted the mallet and tapped the chisel. Friction between metal and seasoned wood flared as rich, smoky scent. Slivers of birch drifted to join the spoil at the half-carved statue's feet. She let the mallet drop and stepped back, examining her handiwork in the light of the basement's high-set windows and its single flickering lantern.

Still not right. The curve of statue's brow was too sharp, for one. Her left shoulder was definitely larger than the right. And the expression? Well, the less said about that, the better. But a noticeable improvement over the one that had come before, and leagues beyond than her first attempt.

Setting tools down on a hogshead, Rosa wiped her brow on a shirt-sleeve and swung her right arm back and forth, the heel of her left hand massaging the knot of scarred flesh at her shoulder. It didn't hurt as such, not any longer, but the stiffness persisted.

A polite knock sounded at the basement door. The newcomer's nose wrinkled at toil-laden air, though he forbore comment. Ravan Eckorov, Reeve of Tarvallion, fancied himself a man of refinement. He strove to comport himself thus, from pencil moustache and black hair oiled into place, to sombre raiment seldom in anything save perfect array.

"I hope I'm not interrupting?" As ever, his clipped pronunciation was impeccable.

Rosa shook her head. "I was just about finished."

"You know, I don't think I've ever been down here." Arms looped behind his back, he gazed into the eyes of the unfinished statue, taking in the snarl of lip, the murderous, imperfect scowl and hair that transcended imperfect chisel-work to offer the appearance of writhing snakes. "Repulsive fiend, isn't she? Anyone in particular?"

"Me."

"Ah." Eckorov cast a silk-gloved hand to the basement's rear, where shadows concealed other works standing watch among wine barrels and crates. Half a dozen more life-size pieces. Twice as many again reached no higher than knee or waist. "And these?"

"The same."

Venturing deeper into shadow, he peered at the nearest. The one it pleased Sevaka to call The Queen of Disappointment. "Please don't take this the wrong way, but have you considered getting a little more light down here? Or perhaps a better mirror? I'd be delighted to lend you one." Turning, he offered a polite smile. "Then again, that's not going to help with the horns, or the teeth, or the ... Blessed Lumestra, is that a tail?"

"It was Master Tanor's idea." Rosa propped herself against the hogshead. "There's a Lunastran ritual, practised by those who wrestle with the temptation of the Dark. They call it soul sculpting. You close yourself to all else and focus solely on the work. As the likeness takes shape, your flaw flows into the statue. Sealed away where it can't bother you or anyone else. The more statues, the freer you become. At least, that's the theory."

"And then you burn the statues, I suppose?"

"That would only free the flaw and leave me back where I started. You're supposed to work in clay, but it didn't *feel* right." She shrugged. "It's just as well Lumestra had more patience, or who knows *what* we'd have looked like?"

Of course, Lumestra hadn't imprisoned temptation in clay, but the souls of what had become humanity, temptation and all. Perhaps that made a difference.

"And you ... chose these delightful forms?"

"The flaw chooses its own shape." Rosa looked from one to the other, to the next. For all that they were monstrous, she always recognised her own face. But whether that was truly the flaw she chose to drive out – or her own subconscious sending unsubtle messages – she couldn't be certain. "You surrender yourself to the work, and what happens, happens."

"So that's why Lunastran chapels have such horrific statues," said Eckorov. "I did wonder. But I never saw you as a woman ruled by lust."

She caught the joke a fraction too late to prevent a scowl. "Anger."

"Surely not?" A courtier's politeness. He'd seen enough of her at her worst. "Is it having the desired effect?"

Rosa returned his easy smile with something tighter. "It's a work in progress."

"Aren't we all, Roslava? Aren't we all." He straightened, all business. "I came in search of a favour."

She'd known as much, of course. Eckorov was a busy man, and an infrequent guest at Brackenpike Manor. For all that little more than a quarter of Tarvallion had been reclaimed – the rest lay tumbled and ruined beneath the roots of Starik Wood – the population was large enough to fill the reeve's days with squabbles. Add to that the closeness of the uneasy border with the contested Eastshires, and Rosa wasn't wholly sure how he found time to sleep. With Sevaka called back to Tressia, his duties had redoubled. Though war had left Tarvallion – once the jewel of the Republic – in a sorry state, the villages of the Marcher Lands still looked to its reeve for leadership and redress.

Agreeing a favour, sight unseen, carried risk. But though Rosa no longer wore a uniform or bore a title, duty remained. "What do you need?"

"Those recent rumours have made the populace restless."

Rumours. Servants' whispers had furnished her with some details. Zephan Tanor had spoken of others at his last visit, the day before Viktor's summons. By no means a weak man – a grandmaster of Essamere could only ever be other – he'd shaken as he'd given account. Lost and weary souls, weeping for kin who'd not survived the journey from the Eastshires. Tales of houses burned, their tenants within. Of sons and daughters dragged away for slaves. And all of it behind a wall of Silsarian spears and the threat of war renewed.

Even thinking on it set the old fire smouldering in Rosa's gut – the desire to pick up a sword and march. She breathed deep and glanced at the unfinished statue. Still so far to go. The gap separating justice and vengeance was narrower than most thought, but still you could lose yourself between.

"Thirava's treating our people worse than animals," she said. "I'd say they've reason to be restless."

Eckorov scowled and tapped a knuckle against his lips. "No one's denying that. I've wearied Lumestra's ears with prayer. I've worn heralds ragged carrying reports to Lord Droshna, begging for more soldiers. To Grandmaster Rother, in the hope that Sartorov might consider standing with old friends." He scowled, but there was no taking back the criticism, even if there were few safer ears on which it could fall than Rosa's. "I understand that times are challenging all over. Already there's too much talk of taking up arms and marching east, whether or not the army chooses to follow."

Redsigor's spears against old swords and lumber axes? "It'd be suicide."

"You know that. I know that." Eckorov stared moodily up at the basement's windows. "But out there? There's a whole generation come of age who think things would have been different had they been old enough to fight. Too many remember only that we won the last war. They don't remember what it cost. I fear Tarvallion is dry as Sommertide kindling."

"Even kindling needs flame to catch."

"Does the name Silda Drenn mean anything to you?"

It did, though it took a moment for Rosa to chase the memory down. "A southwealder, isn't she? A wolf's-head who fought at Davenwood."

"This morning she arrived in Tarvallion, blown in on the Dawn Wind. She's preaching a tale of liberation and fury too many are ready to hear. Claims she can do for the east what the wolf's-heads once did for the south."

A seductive message, especially with folk looking for someone who'd take action. "She's a wolf's-head. Have her arrested."

"The trifling matter of the pardon aside, I'd like nothing more. But at least fifty swords arrived with her. More will take her side if I loose the constabulary. I've barely enough to keep order as it is. If there's a riot . . . ?" Eckorov shook his head. "No, I need someone to have a quiet word with Drenn. Persuade her, if possible. Warn her off if it isn't."

Rosa laughed bitterly. She'd expected a request for duelling tutelage funnelled from one of Tarvallion's wealthier families, or perhaps an undertaking to train the town's constabulary – who were certainly sorely in need of a soldier's lessons. But this?

"You want Josiri Trelan, not me. I didn't reach the Southshires until *after* Davenwood, and even then . . . "

She tailed off, memory bright with the flames that had reduced Eskavord to ash. Viktor's orders – and desperately necessary – but she'd carried them out. A woman with Drenn's reputation would remember that.

Eckorov set his back to the windows and fixed her with a level gaze. "I can't afford the time. A day for a herald to reach Tressia, at least? And I doubt Lord Trelan will drop everything to soothe my fears. You'll forgive me for saying so, but these days I receive more decrees from the city that I do tangible help, and more vagueness from Lord Trelan than action." He spread his hands. "Even if he agrees with my assessment and comes at once, that's another day, perhaps two. More than enough time for mischief, even if it's well intentioned."

That was the problem, wasn't it? For all Eckorov's obvious worry about riots, unspoken agreement with Drenn's goals lurked beneath his words. The reeve was too canny not to recognise that the situation with the Contested Lands would reach a head sooner rather than later. What made Silda Drenn dangerous in days of uneasy peace could make her priceless in the war of reclamation that had to be coming. She was a link to a romanticised past, proof that tyranny could not triumph for ever. That the tyranny she'd once fought had been willingly abetted by the folk of the Eastshires – as it had all Tressia north of Margard – was a detail perhaps better forgotten.

Rosa might have resented Eckorov his reluctance, had she not shared it. "I'm not exactly a diplomat."

"Drenn's far more likely to respect your past than she is mine – even if you no longer hold rank. And there's always going to be the tacit suggestion that you're acting with Governor Orova's authority." He shrugged and glanced meaningfully about the basement. "And if all goes poorly and the mob rouses? Well, they'll have no difficulty burning you in effigy, will they? Frankly, Roslava, you're the best option if lives are to be saved."

It really was that simple, wasn't it? "There's little less use than a broken sword," she murmured. "Save for a shield that shelters no more."

Eckorov frowned. "I didn't catch that."

"Doesn't matter." Decision made, the next words came easier. "Where can I find her?"

The sound of the crowd reached Rosa long before she arrived at the marketplace, borne by the same gusting Ash Wind that grabbed the tails of her jacket and tugged at her unbound hair. Quickening her pace through the snows, she steered north.

Even at that hour, the marketplace was crowded, the brightly coloured canopies of stall and barrow a reminder of what Tarvallion had once been. Far ahead, beyond the mismatched stone and tile of the houses, the ruined towers of Tremora Gardens pierced the skeletal winter canopy of Starik Wood's western extent. Bonfires blazed along the divide between the new city and the old, the reclaimed and the forsaken. On the forest's cusp, where firebreaks, iron fence posts and holy writ held forest demons and creeping vines at bay, folk slept poorly, each midnight *rat-tat-tat* on the windowpanes a reminder that not everyone who left Tarvallion did so willingly . . . or through ephemeral agency.

So easy to abandon the city entirely – certainly easier than constant vigil against the thornmaidens whose cruel, sweet song drifted through the reclaimed streets when the Ice Wind blew in from the north. But Tarvallion had long been the Republic's opaline heart, and Sevaka's first decree as governor was that it be reclaimed.

And so it had, after a fashion, but the new city was not the old. Its buildings had been raised over the course of months, rather than decades. Flagstoned streets had yielded to silted, muddy cobbles; firestone lantern-posts to braziers and oil-soaked torches. The Tarvallion of the present could have stirred no poet to consult his muse, nor minstrel to offer song. But it was *there*, and that counted for something. A rock upon the Toriana Plains, banners raised high at gate and tower to remind the Hadari of one, singular truth: we are still here, and here we mean to stay.

It took a special sort to meet the challenge of restoration. Hardy. Stubborn. And the trouble with stubbornness – as Rosa well knew – was that it respected boundaries little better than a thornmaiden's song. Defiance became a habit, and habits muffled good sense.

Case in point, the marketplace buzz was not that of greeting and barter, but an intemperate growl, conducted by a woman who stood atop a wagon's bench seat. Her left hand propped a strung bow against the seat. A quiver of red-fletched arrows hung at her thigh.

"Is the blood of the Marcher Lands so thin?" Drenn's voice pierced the hubbub with ease. Confident. Angry. Hard as stone. A trace of the guttural Thrakkian accent shared by so many in the south. "Less than an hour's ride from here our kin are suffering, penned in by spears!"

Rosa threaded closer, old instincts sifting purpose and intent. Most of the crowd were Tarvallion's citizens, or else merchants and travellers from nearby villages. The old and the very young, for much of what lay between had already been subject to conscription. A handful were riot-ously drunk, the day's takings already imbibed. Finer foods might have been scarce, but ale never ran dry. Blue-tabarded constables lurked on the periphery, watchful and with hands near swords they'd never have chance to draw if affairs turned ugly.

"In the south, we stood together," shouted Drenn. "We taught the Hadari the folly of hubris. We'll do it again in the east."

Halfway to the wagon, the crowd thickened, the transition from the curious to the truly interested marked by the press of bodies. Rosa resorted to shoulders and elbows to forge a path. She marked those who carried weapons – whose aspect was rougher and more weatherworn even than was normal for Tarvallion. Drenn's folk, seeded throughout the onlookers to prevent trouble, or perhaps provoke it.

"I don't need the reeve's permission, or the governor's blessing," Drenn continued. "The Eastshires cry out for aid. That's the only sanc-tion any of us require."

Now three-deep from Drenn's makeshift pulpit, Rosa was close enough to examine the woman herself. Wiry to the point of scrawny, and with a face so weathered by a life outdoors that she seemed a good decade older than Rosa herself. A misjudgement. Bounty posters ten years back had depicted a girl, not a woman. For all the romanticism proclaimed by playwright and poet, a brigand's life counted every year three times over. Her hair was cropped close, save for a single thin braid that snaked from beneath her hood to rest against a worn sunburst pendant.

As she opened her mouth to speak again, Rosa cut her off. "Tell them the rest, Silda. Tell them what it will cost."

A rumble rippled across the marketplace. Rosa's skin itched beneath unfriendly glares. Not just from Drenn's followers, but elsewhere in the crowd. Drenn's small gesture at waist height – easily missed, if Rosa hadn't been watching for it – stilled the former.

"You've an advantage over me, northwealder." Drenn levelled the last as a targeted insult – no easy feat amid a crowd of men and women no less northwealders than Rosa herself. Her eyes narrowed in examination no less thorough than Rosa's own, a ghost of a sneer rising as she took in the good cloth of shirt, waistcoat and jacket. "Won't you tell me your name?"

Was there a threat in the question? A reminder that a name made prey easier to find, especially in a denuded town like Tarvallion? If so, Drenn had severely misjudged.

"I'm Lady Roslava Orova, of Essamere and the 7th."

While neither shrunken Essamere nor the conscript-thick 7th any longer had claim on her, both had made her as she was. She'd forged her reputation under their colours. A reputation well known.

"That right?" Drenn's stare didn't waver above a thin smile. A woman well pleased with the sound of her own voice, and a rare moment of power over one who was her better. "And what does the Reaper of the Ravonn want with a poor daughter of Kreska?"

Rosa's lip twitched at the hated nickname. So Drenn *did* know her. "Only to talk."

"Your wife afraid to speak for herself?"

The jibe coaxed a chuckle from the crowd. Rosa kept her face impassive, and resigned herself to another morning's sculpture to banish reborn anger. "I'm here at my own behest. To greet a hero of Davenwood. I've always regretted that we never met. After all, we were so nearly allies."

She leaned into those final words, for the first time grateful that Viktor had so muddied the events surrounding Eskavord's burning that her own complicity was concealed even from rumour. She deplored the lie. Then, for his insistence of bearing the burden alone. The fires of Eskavord had been necessary. Every man, woman and child in the town had borne a fragment of Malatriant's spirit – had even one survived, the Tyrant Queen would have done so alongside, and the shadowthorns would be the least of anyone's worries. Now? Well, that was complicated, bound up in guilt and resentment. Rosa's feelings about Viktor had complicated further in the year since they'd been at Darkmere.

But even as Rosa wrestled with old memories, a cold fist clamped tight about her gut. Malatriant had influenced Eskavord across centuries, nudging the populace to revolt and rebellion until she was strong enough to consume them, body and soul. But what if a piece of her had survived the fires? What if Drenn's arrival in Tarvallion was more than it appeared? Her actions not entirely her own? Would she even know? So many of Malatriant's thralls had not until it was too late.

Drenn nodded, her eyes tracking across the crowd, a woman weighing possibilities of her own. The balance of the crowd's sympathies, perhaps. Then she offered a smile no less sharp than her tone, and jumped down from the wagon.

"Very well, Lady Orova. Let's talk."

Six

"Well," said Drenn. "This is cosy."

Cosy was one way to describe the back room of the Thief's Bounty. To Rosa's mind, *cramped* was more apt, the cracked plaster walls almost near enough to touch without rising from the table. A blazing hearth stacked high with wood and blackstone made the air closer still, and lent every breath the memory of battlefield pyres, blazing in the distance.

Drenn took another swig of her tankard and cast a pointed look at Rosa's own untouched drink on the windowsill. "I thought we were being friendly?"

Friendly – like *cosy* before it – flirted with the truth, more than committed to it. The shadows of Drenn's followers loomed large in the room beyond the door. As for the window? Twenty years ago, Rosa might have squeezed through into the gathering night and the marketplace's flickering braziers, but certainly no longer. Unwise to trap oneself thus, but she'd never been good at backing down from a challenge. Besides, what skills she possessed had merely rusted, not atrophied beyond reclamation, and she doubted Drenn was so foolish as to offer harm to the Reaper of the Ravonn.

Still, Rosa took a mouthful of ale. "You said you wanted to talk, but you've said little."

A slim, knowing smile. Drenn set her tankard down on the sill and leaned back in her creaking chair. "I've been thinking. We can do that, you know. Even in the south."

"And where have your thoughts led you?"

"To something I heard a couple of years back about your wife, Governor Orova." She leaned forward, dark eyes brimming with scandal. "That she died in the mountains, and that . . . thing . . . in your bed ain't nothing but a tame prizrak. Or maybe she's not so tame, eh? Maybe—"

The statues in Brackenpike Manor burning in her mind's eye, Rosa lunged from the chair. Hands closing about throat and wrist, she slammed Drenn against the wall, occasioning a spill of plaster dust from a ragged crack above.

Two burly shapes gathered in the doorway, hands slipping beneath their cloaks. Rosa ignored them. The first regret crept in as her pulse steadied. Not at what she'd done – or why – but at being so easily provoked. Not a diplomat? As severe an understatement as ever there was.

"So we're done being friendly, are we?" she murmured, her eyes on Drenn's.

The other gave an urgent wave at hip height. The shapes in the doorway withdrew. "I don't believe it, of course. Ain't the Raven's way, is it? Letting someone go. Dead's dead."

Rosa stepped away.

Released, Drenn coughed and rubbed at her throat. Then the smile was back – one more knowing than Rosa cared for. "So you *do* have a bit of fire yet. Go on, Lady Orova. Sit. I'll behave."

An impish flash of dark eyes threatened contradiction. Still, Rosa did as instructed. But her reasons for seeking Drenn hadn't changed. "Why are you here, Silda?"

Drenn reclaimed the tankard and shrugged. "I've not exactly kept it secret. The Eastshires need help."

"Your help?"

"Likely it's not the aid they're looking for, I'll grant you. But what else is there?"

Rosa caught no hint of the demagogic tone so readily wielded for the crowd. Instead, Drenn spoke low and earnestly, with no hint of mockery in voice or expression. "They've needed help for years. What's different now?"

"Little enough, and only for the worse." She met Rosa's gaze, lips scrunched in thought. "Months back, I ran into your friend. Lord Akadra. Well, Lord Droshna, as he styles himself now."

She paused, perhaps waiting for a response. Receiving none, she forged on.

"First time I'd been back to Eskavord since . . . Well, you know. Point of fact, I'd not long been back in the Republic. Thrakkians pay well for blades, and their men are drawn to scars like you wouldn't believe. But a girl gets bored even of that. It was like, I don't know . . . Like something was drawing me north."

Rosa stiffened, suspicions rekindled. Few of Malatriant's thralls had recognised how they'd been manipulated. A yearning. A desire. Drawing them close enough until all were one in the Dark.

"There I was, walking the ash fields. Nothing grows there any longer. Not for miles. You know where you are, soon as you cross the threshold. You can hear 'em on the wind. The dead." Drenn shook her head. "You reckon it's cold out there? Sommertide, this was. Barely a week after Ascension, and there was ice on Branghall's stones, and mist so thick you could barely see your feet."

The back room's warmth had become a distant memory, unable to contest the prickle of Rosa's skin. Was a piece of Malatriant lurking behind Drenn's eyes? If so, better to kill her now and risk the consequences, before Tarvallion inherited the chaos that had claimed the south.

Too late to regret coming to the marketplace unarmed. Not that she'd worn a sword since she'd woken on the hillside above Darkmere, her bandages sodden, Viktor a surly presence on the makeshift camp's perimeter and hope vacant from the eyes of her fellow survivors. Besides, Drenn had a knife strapped to her boot. Likely another concealed. And surprise was a weapon all its own. From there, easy enough to cripple or kill the brigand's minders . . .

She barely realised Drenn was still talking.

"I found Akadra not far from Branghall's ruins. Well, stumbled over him really. Damn mist. One of his Drazina nearly slit me. Then Akadra grabbed me, like you did just now. Reckoned he was going to do the job himself. He stared right through me." She shivered. "But I guess he didn't find anything, 'cos he let me go."

Rosa blinked, the choreography of murder unfinished. So Viktor had harboured similar suspicions about Drenn and set her free? Despite herself – despite shaken faith in her old friend – Rosa relaxed an inch or two. For all his failure of judgement at Darkmere, he'd surely take no chance with this? As for why he'd been at Branghall, on that day of all days? No need to speculate there. One failure hung heavier on Viktor than others. He'd made that Ascension pilgrimage for the last six years. A gesture granted to the dead of Eskavord and Davenwood. To one of their number, in particular.

She leaned forward, alert for trace of a lie. "He let you go?"

"*You've somewhere else to be.* That's what he said. He was right." The smile returned, if feebler than before. "Guilt brought me home. Tied and true."

"Guilt?" Rosa snorted. "You forget, I saw the bounty notices before the Council confirmed your pardon. You walked a bloody trail to Davenwood."

"Everyone I gave a ripper's grin wore an oppressor's uniform or took their coin. Their choices set 'em in the soil, not mine." She shook her head. "I'm a hypocrite, right enough. But not for that. For Davenwood."

"I don't understand. You fought at Davenwood. If you hadn't—"

The smile faded. "That's just it. I nearly didn't. A few of us, we'd a notion it might be better to let the Hadari win. No, not even that. That if we *helped* the Hadari win, we'd be better off under their boot than yours. Even if it meant fighting our own people. Thank Lumestra that Lord Trelan talked me 'round."

"I didn't know."

"I'm not surprised. Lord Trelan always remembers his friends, even when they're not exactly friendly. Keeps a secret well, he does."

Rosa knew so little about Josiri Trelan. For all that he and Sevaka had become fast friends, Rosa had never quite made the connection. It didn't help that she so often struggled with the personal, or that his meteoric rise from wolf's-head to Viktor's likely inheritor meant he transcended the structures of oath and authority by which she'd defined her life. But Drenn had offered a glimpse of a man careful not only with his own honour, but that of others. Another effort should be made, not just with Josiri, but with Drenn. Honour, like sunlight, could not reveal something not already there.

"So all this." Rosa cast a hand to the window. "Penance for throwing in with Kai Saran?"

Drenn narrowed her eyes. "For *almost* throwing in with Kai Saran." A twitch of the shoulder. "Maybe. Turns out all the pleasures of an easy life in Thrakkia can't keep conscience at bay. Figure it's time I did for others what Lord Trelan did for me . . . even if he seems to have forgotten the lesson himself. It's the city that does it. Spend too long there, and it changes you. Stops you seeing the world for what it is. It's only once you're outside the walls that you see things clear again."

That much, Rosa couldn't argue with. For all that humbled Tarvallion lacked the comforts of Tressia, it felt more grounded. Fashion. Intrigue. Politics. Things that had mattered so much in the city – for even resisting them was to play your own tedious part in the game – held less purchase here. But that didn't mean delusion was unique to the capital.

"You drag the people of this town along with you, you'll get them killed."

"That's war, Lady Orova. You of all people don't need a lecture on what it costs. Better a day lived free than endure a lifetime as a slave. Not that I'd expect a northwealder to know."

Northwealder. Now it stung. It was one thing to comprehend the horrors meted out on the Southshires by an unfeeling Council, another to truly understand what it was to live through them. "This isn't the same."

"Of course it's the same!" Drenn sprang to her feet, the fire of the marketplace in her eyes once more. "People are suffering, and the Lord Protector, like the Council before him, does nothing. Because they don't have the coin to be worth saving. Because they lack the right bloodline. Because it's easier to look the other way."

"If Lord Droshna is doing nothing, it's for a reason."

Rosa fell silent, surprised at her own words. Old habits died hard, even in the face of recent troubles. Worse, she felt empathy's first stirring. She'd come to defuse Drenn's recklessness, but now . . . ?

A memory clicked. The night the Council had formalised the Southshires' occupation. She'd only been a girl, years from squirehood. The first time she'd ever heard her uncles arguing. Gallan had abhorred the Council's actions, while Davor – who'd lost a sister in the brief civil war – had welcomed it. Three days, they'd spoken only to continue the argument. A frosty Ascension that had been, and warmth restored to the household only after Gallan put aside his principles to preserve his marriage. She'd no doubt the scene had repeated itself across Tressia. If others had spoken out – if they'd acted – the occupation might have ended years earlier. How many could have been saved? Was this the same mistake made over again?

She shook her head. It wasn't the same. The Eastshires suffered because, for all their vaunted talk of honour, the Hadari cherished it only when convenient. Provoking Thirava and the treacherous Empress who'd granted him the stolen lands would invite only disaster.

But still the pang of empathy remained. That, and treacherous desire for battle in a just and necessary cause. Because she'd lied to Eckorov as she lied to Sevaka. It wasn't anger alone that drove home the chisel. Stepping down as the Mistress of Essamere had been the hardest thing she'd done, for all that it had been necessary.

"Listen to me," she said, speaking to herself as well as to Drenn. "The Southshires were freed as much through the efforts of those in the north as in the south. Men and women who held back the worst of the occupation for years."

Drenn snorted and stared out of the window.

Rosa stood and seized her shoulder, forcing the other to meet her gaze. "If you provoke the Hadari, they will crush you."

"Only if they catch me. They haven't so far."

"And when they do?"

"Then I'll die, and when Lumestra raises me up into the Light of Third Dawn, I'll stand before her proud and unashamed."

A fanatic's answer. Or a soldier's. Maybe even a martyr's. The difference lay more in victory or defeat than unyielding fact. But Malatriant's influence wasn't the only thing absent from Silda Drenn. Save for her jibe about Sevaka – one that had only cut so deep because it was more true than it was not – she'd been courteous. She'd even used Rosa's title, which was *not* the behaviour expected from a wolf's-head bent on anarchy. In short, the woman in the Thief's Bounty was not the self-aggrandising demagogue of the marketplace.

It was just possible that Silda Drenn meant every word she said, but that only made her more dangerous, not less.

Rosa let her hand fall. "I've no doubt you'll convince folk to follow you. At the very least, you should be certain they're every inch as prepared to die as you."

Teeth flashed behind parted lips. "The good citizens of Tarvallion? I didn't come here for them, though I'll not turn aside any who understand what's at stake. I came here for you."

"Then you've wasted your time," Rosa replied coldly.

She stepped closer. "I've been watching you, just like you've been watching me. Your eyes don't lie, Lady Orova. You know something has to be done, but you're lost. For all you've pretended otherwise these past months, you're still a soldier. You need someone to *tell* you a war's worth fighting. Well, I've a war worth fighting, and it could use you. The people of the Eastshires need your help, in the way you never helped us of the south." She backed away, halting briefly in the doorway. "I'll be at Morten's Rock for two days. Tell the reeve if you like. Ring us in with constables and whatever you have that passes for soldiers. But if you've heard anything I've said, you'll come alone."

Then she was gone, her companions falling into step behind, leaving Rosa alone.

Seven

"Where is she? Where is my daughter?"

Tavar Rasha held his composure as an esteemed jasaldar of Immortals should, his weathered, olive-toned features respectful and every inch as enduring as the palace's vaulted oak ceilings. "Your daughter, *savim*? Is she not sleeping?"

Melanna bit back an unkind response. "Her bed is empty and her chambers quiet. Her night-maid was in the next room the whole time and heard nothing. Find her. Rouse the palace if you must."

Grizzled grey eyebrows furrowed. "She'll be found."

Rasha set off at a jog, golden-scaled armour rustling. Unthinkable for an Immortal to behave with such indignity – much less the captain of the guard whose authority was second only to that of the Imperial family's. But Rasha had two granddaughters of Kaila's age, and knew as well as Melanna that the heir to the Hadari throne wouldn't need to travel far to meet misfortune. A few paces might be enough, especially with a conclave of the Golden Court due that night.

Melanna told herself none would dare so obvious a blow against the House of Saran, but the words rang hollow. The throne was a prize grand enough to soothe any conscience.

She clenched her fists, aware of the losing battle against her fears but unable to sway its course. There'd been no guard set on Kaila's room. Tomorrow, yes. Additional precaution against cyraeths loosed from Otherworld by a dying year to settle unfinished business in the living world. Fleenroot and duskhazel were all very well, but stout hearts and steel served better. But such precautions shouldn't have been necessary at other times – not in the Imperial palace, which lay behind thick walls and a garrison of Immortals.

A thousand fates yammered for attention, each bleaker than the last. Where was the courage of the battlefield now? She'd thought herself tempered. Had she not walked divine realms and bartered with gods? But such deeds had been poor preparation for motherhood's fears. Those for a lost child, straying from safety. Not for the first time, Melanna understood a little of how her father had felt each time she'd picked up a sword. Though he'd gone to Ashana's care years ago, she felt closer to him than ever, and wished she could tell him so. That she could tell him anything. But for all that his gilded likeness now guarded the approach to Tregard's Triumphal Gate, Kai Saran was lost, blessed with Evermoon's tranquillity, or with a hunter's station in Eventide's court. And for all that the palace was seldom quiet, it always felt empty.

Voices echoed along the corridor, boots muffled by the rich weave of Itharoci rugs as Rasha marshalled the household to the search. An Immortal rounded the corner and drew to solemn halt.

"I am to stay with you, *savim*," she said. "Jasaldar Rasha wonders if you'd retire to the throne room, so you're easily found once there's word."

Melanna nodded, her eyes on the reflected lantern-light of a gilt-framed mirror hanging between the swirling linework frescos. She barely recognised herself. The woman who met her gaze had not a hair out of place beneath the filigree silver chains, no crease to her golden gown, nor a smudge to the powder that darkened her eyes to wells of shadow. The woman in the mirror yet resembled an Empress, despite fears brewing beneath. Melanna Saranal, Dotha Rhaled, Queen of the Silver Kingdom, and Empress of the Hadari.

Better to be that woman if she could.

That Empress would wait out the search in the throne room, as Rasha had not so subtly suggested – or perhaps in the solitude of her own chambers. A display of detachment and composure expected of one who was mother to a nation that spanned from the cold seas of Rhaled's northern coasts to the shifting deserts far to the south.

To worry over a single child – even of her own blood – would be proclaimed unseemly. A gift for those on the Golden Court who offered fealty to a woman only with reluctance. That might even be the point of the abduction – if abduction it was – to fuel whispers that it might perhaps be better for the Imperial consort to assume the throne. If it transpired that the disappearance was no disappearance at all, but merely the night-time wanderings of a sleepless child, the whispers would be more brazen still.

Melanna's father had never worried over such things, of course – nor his father, or his grandfather before that. Her earliest memories were of her sire breaking off from the business of state to comfort her tears, or scold girlhood's transgressions. Weakness was relative, and she was forced to prove herself twice over – once for her youthful twenty-five winters, and once again for committing the cardinal error of not being born a man.

Yes, the expected thing would be to retire, and let others conduct the search. But for all that motherhood's ambition had lain secondary to the birthright of rule, a mother Melanna remained.

Raven take them all, anyway.

She shifted her attention to the Immortal, still standing close by – but not *too* close. A little older than her. Old enough that she'd likely learned her trade masquerading as a man, identity concealed by a close helm, an uncinched belt and the loyalty of fellows who cared more for comradeship than tradition. Such was the reason Melanna discouraged helms within the palace grounds, where an Immortal's duties were largely ceremonial. Harder for staid elders to deny the warrior's path to a new generation of young women when others walked it plainly.

"What's your name?" she asked. Even an Empress could not know all who served her.

The Immortal hesitated, lip twitching in discomfort. "Tesni Rhanaja, *savim*. Daughter of Kael Rhanaja, who bore your father's banner at Coralta."

"My daughter is missing, Tesni. I intend to join the search. Jasaldar Rasha will find me easily enough."

She nodded unhappily. "As you will, *savim*."

Melanna retraced her steps to the east wing and Kaila's chambers, little caring that Rasha's Immortals had been there before her. Activity was as much the point of the exercise as discovery, an outlet for anxiety's strange energy. And besides, for all that Melanna trusted the royal guard with her life, the shepherding of children lay somewhat beyond their skills.

Barked command summoned maids with lanterns, and renewed search was made of bedchamber, washroom, nursery and neighbouring corridors. The adjoining chapel too, for though it had fallen out of use after Melanna's great-great-uncle's eastern campaigns had seen the House of Saran's family tree reduced to a single, sickly branch, it had been one of her favourite haunts as a young girl, and daughters were ever apt to imitate their mothers.

When the chapel's moon-shadows garnered nothing, Melanna returned to the bedchamber and had Tesni haul the wardrobe away from the wall. A few moments' brutal industry with a prybar and the door concealed within the oak panelling sprang open. But if Kaila had somehow found her way into the network of passageways woven through the palace walls – or had been forced to do so – it had been accomplished without disturbing the dust of decades.

Melanna left others to re-site the wardrobe, pulled aside the terrace drape and stared out into a night lit by stuttering blue-white ghostfires. Lanterns and the gleam of gold in the sculpted, snow-wreathed gardens told of Immortals carrying their search into the grounds.

Clouds parted and the snow of the terrace shone, the icicles of the fence beyond become glittering teardrops wept by a distant moon.

But it was another shape that caught Melanna's attention. A huddled bundle resting atop the snows. A wool-stuffed doll, one of two presented to Kaila on her fifth birthday but weeks before, the golden cloth of its armour dull in the moonlight. One of two, though that one had instantly been the favourite. After all, the other had worn a gown, and had not carried a sword.

Melanna fumbled at the door, mind and fingers numbly refusing to credit why the key wouldn't turn, nor the bolt unlatch. Only when she pushed at the door, a cry of frustration ripping free from the pit of her racing heart, did she realise the cause. The door had not been locked, merely pushed to.

She barely felt the night's chill embrace as she dropped to one knee and plucked the doll from the snow.

"*Savim?*" Moonlight yielded to Tesni's shadow, the sickly glow of the oil lantern drowning silver with gold. "You're not dressed for this, majesty. Please, come back inside."

Teeth chattering, Melanna clasped the doll between shaking fingers, and raised it for the other to see. Her hands shook so fiercely – though from cold or pent-up dread she could no longer say – that it seemed to jerk of its own accord.

"Three weeks, and this has never left her side. It was with her when she kissed me goodnight. The door was unlocked." She flung a hand towards the billowing drapes of the open door. "She might have reached the key, but never the bolt."

That made it abduction. Or worse.

No. She couldn't think that. Wouldn't think it. Corpses granted no leverage, only retribution. Willing back hot tears, Melanna gazed up at the moon, but found no more guidance there than she would have beneath her father's portrait.

Anger helped. It came easily enough, welling from appraisal of the night's failures. At her detractors, who held themselves to be men of honour, but who now struck through a helpless child.

Melanna snatched the lantern from Tesni's hand. Golden light revealed what silver had not: the shallow indentations of a child's footprints in the packed snow. They led away from the palace and out into the darkness.

She flinched as Tesni's hand fell upon her shoulder. "Go inside, majesty. I beg you. I'll fetch Jasaldar Rasha."

The low, practical words vied with Melanna's chattering teeth. But they'd no hope of besting the terrible, unsought imaginings of another huddled figure face down in the snow, or screaming into a gag as strangers bundled her away, wondering why no one came to help her.

Lantern trapped tight in trembling hands, she fled the terrace, following the sorry trail.

"*Savim!*"

Ignoring Tesni's cry, Melanna ran on into the night, Kaila's footsteps and the wan lantern her only guide. Her impractical courtier's shoes snagged as she crossed the stone garden's high wall. She left both behind in the sand and ran barefoot through the snows.

Shouts rang out as Immortals scattered through in the grounds hastened to pursuit. But Melanna had always been light on her feet, and heavy boots and armour were no friend to those who sought swift advance through snow.

That snow grew thicker as the formal gardens fell away into the wild, dark corner of the grounds – the old wood, where few ever trod. She stumbled on, feet numb to the relentless cold. Briars snatched at her dress. Golden silks tore. Blood welled hot on cheek and calf, and trickled away chill. Still she stumbled on, mind closed to all save the trail of footsteps that had become a muddled furrow in the drifted white.

The path widened to a glade, unseasonal roses black beneath snow. The gnarled oak with whom Melanna had shared many childhood adventures reached its wizened branches towards the stars. The ivy about its venerable waist rustled whenever thin breeze cheated the younger trees.

And there, between the oak's bulbous roots, her boots a poor match for her cotton nightrobes, and both of them thick with snow, Kaila Saranal stared back at her mother with a complete lack of concern.

"Madda? Have you come to play too?"

A sob of relief catching in her throat, Melanna gathered Kaila up and clutched her tight. There would be scolding to come, but not now. Let nothing intrude upon that one, perfect moment of relief, her daughter's arms tight about her neck and the illusion that she could ever protect her thus unbroken.

"You've earned such trouble this night, *essavim*," she breathed. "But it will come with the morning."

Tears restrained so long flowed freely even as she pressed Kaila's head to her own, the fears of kidnap and murder suddenly foolish. No intruder. No plot. No footprints in the snow beside Kaila's own. The door had been left unbolted through failing memory. The lapse couldn't be ignored, but it would wait. It would all wait.

Now the cold made its presence known. Holding Kaila tight, Melanna took her first faltering steps out of the glade. Beyond, the gardens were alive with lanterns and running feet.

Have you come to play too?

Melanna froze at the memory of her daughter's words, the chill at the pit of her stomach little to do with merciless Wintertide. "*Essavim*, why did you leave your room?"

Kaila pulled back, her eyes earnest, but confused. "The green-eyed king said we were to play a game. But when I reached the tree, he wasn't there."

The chill in Melanna's gut hardened to a lump of ice. She glanced at the oak, still and silent in the moonlight. Nothing about it was different, yet everything had changed.

Tearing free her gaze, she stumbled out of the glade to meet the approaching Immortals.

The cold lingered in Melanna's bones long after, despite the hall's roaring hearth and one of her father's old cloaks wrapped tight over the ruined dress. Even a generous glass of fiery tarakeet – the perfumed notes of violet and sage that same father had sworn a remedy for all ills of the soul – had done little to chase it out. Comfort had become fleeting commodity that night, its only bastion the knowledge that Kaila was again in bed, seemingly none the worse for her adventure. Four Immortals stood guard on the terrace.

The green-eyed king. Melanna told herself Kaila had lied to spare herself a scolding. She knew it wasn't so.

She knocked back the last of the tarakeet, and set her back to the fire. "First thing tomorrow, you'll send a messenger to Mooncourt Temple. The lunassera will take charge of my daughter's safety."

Rasha's cheek twitched. "The palace is the domain of the royal guard, *savim*. Your Immortals will protect your family, as we always have. It's—"

"Tradition?" He'd never have spoken thus in public. He understood loyalty. But in the privacy of her chambers, where few were permitted to tread? "Tradition would have been Kaila's death tonight."

"Might I remind you, majesty, that I argued the princessa's chambers be guarded long ago. You overruled me."

Melanna set aside a flash of anger. One aimed at herself, more than Rasha. "I know, and tonight I paid a thousand times for that hubris. I can afford no more risks."

"Then let your Immortals bear them, *savim*. We are glad to do so."

She shook her head, wondering how much she should tell him. "There are some perils steel cannot abate. I wish it were otherwise."

He tilted his head, brows beetling. "Is there something I should know, *savim*?"

Yes. No. She set her back to him once more and stared into the flames. Easier to find the words that way. "Kaila told me someone called to her. A green-eyed king within the trees."

He chuckled. "Is that all?"

"Is that *all*?" She rounded, fury at last warming what liquor and fire had failed to touch. "I see nothing amusing in any of this."

He held up a hand. "I meant no offence. It's simply that ... you used to play that game as a child."

"I most certainly did not."

Rasha clasped a hand to his chest. "On my life, *savim*. All the time before the Raven took your mother. You'd go to that same corner of the grounds and return from the old wood garlanded with black roses, all breathy with tales of a green-eyed king, who'd promised to make you his queen. I confess, your mother found it no more amusing then than you did just now."

Uncertainty wormed its way into Melanna's thoughts. "I ... I don't remember that. I mean, I recall playing among the trees. They were my fortress, and the old oak my keep. I played a hundred games of that sort, defending helpless bramble-fetches from Thrakkian pirates and Tressian knights. Singing with them. But the green-eyed king ...?"

Yet the more she thought, the realer the idea became. Like the aftermath of a dream long forgotten, all tangled emotion and fleeting image. A hand about hers. Her mother fussing over a cut from a rose's thorn. She'd died soon after that, broken beneath the hooves of a wayward horse. Long ago and yesterday all at once.

Rasha cleared his throat. Melanna blinked and looked up from a hearth whose dancing flames had sunk to unquiet smoulder, and wondered how long she'd stared at them without seeing.

"Forgive me, majesty, but if you've no recollection, why does it trouble you so?"

That she couldn't tell him. She'd done enough that night to make him believe her mad. "A messenger to Mooncourt at dawn, jasaldar. That is all."

She knew his expression even without seeing it. The frown of obedience fighting the slight levied against ability and honour. But unwelcome commands were an Empress' privilege.

"Yes, majesty."

The door creaked. Footsteps tracked away. Others drew closer, the unmistakeable tell-tale stutter of a man limping on a bindwork leg in place of the one with which he'd been born. Then hinges creaked, the warm currents of the hearth drawn into draught. Hands closed about Melanna's upper arms.

"I came as soon as I heard," murmured Aeldran, the warmth of his breath on her ear nothing to the concern in his voice. "Are you hurt?"

She nodded. "It looks worse than it is."

"You look as though you've lost a fight with a thorn bush."

An unfortunate comparison, but apt given her torn dress and scratched face. Decorum was a faded dream. She'd have to restore it before long. The Golden Court awaited.

"You'll address your Empress with respect," she said drily, "or not at all."

"Yes, majesty." For all the archness of the words, his tone was not without humour. Would that she could reply in kind.

"I needed you here tonight. Our daughter needed you."

The hands slipped away, and Aeldran with them. "I'm her father, not her nursemaid. I've duties of my own. Duties you gave me, Melanna."

Tradition laid no specific burden on the royal consort, and Melanna had availed herself of the opportunity to bestow as many upon Aeldran Andwar, Prince of Icansae and of Rhaled, as decency permitted. The Clan Council, the Veteran's Lodges, the Chancellery of Guilds. Anything to keep the Kingdom of Rhaled functioning as it should, leaving her free to shoulder the burdens of Empire – and in no few cases dismantle the web of preferment and nepotism those same organisations treasured so dearly. For the first time in Melanna's lifetime, worth was starting to be measured by more than the yardsticks of storied tradition and battlefield glories. A law of words, not swords, was taking root.

But Aeldran's evening' duties had been different. No one was more suited to welcoming Aelia Andwaral, Dotha Icansae, to Tregard's splendour than her regal brother.

And in truth, Aeldran was no more a poor father than she a mother. It was simply the way of things. Indeed, for the first half of Melanna's life, she'd seldom seen her own father for more than a few days at a time.

He'd been ever on campaign, carrying steel against Rhaled's enemies in places so many and so distant she'd struggled to learn them all, far less remember. Now she had to govern such places. To hear their concerns of famine and disorder, to meet with their worthies and make polite reply to false adulation.

For all that Melanna had spent more time in the palace in six years than her father had his whole life, her thoughts were too often afield, and Kaila in danger of growing up never knowing her mother. But there was still time to change that. At least, she hoped so. As Kaila's birthdays rushed past, Melanna dwelled more and more on the fact that her daughter's grandmother hadn't lived to see Melanna's seventh.

She turned from the fire to find Aeldran regarding her, his lean, rugged features without expression, but his eyes full of quiet compassion. He always read her thoughts better than she liked, and too often better than she deserved. A friend? Certainly. An ally? Without question. But nothing more, and most nights passed away in separate chambers and empty beds.

For all that it was to be expected of a dynastic marriage, Melanna had always resented that. The poor example set by her father, she supposed, who'd wed far below himself and thus jeopardised his own succession. A freedom she never could have indulged, even had a commoner snared her heart. But maybe that was fair, for had not her whole life been given over to following in her father's footsteps? Obsession was a jealous lover and tolerated no other.

All the more reason to reappraise her relationship with Kaila. What mistakes she'd made were hers alone, and should not be visited on a daughter. If the night was lesson of anything, it was that.

"Your sister is well?"

Aeldran's mouth twitched, acknowledging the change of topic. "She offers her greetings, and stands ready to, ah, rebuke Thirava for his part in tonight's excitement."

Melanna shook her head. Though Aelia's tongue was certainly sharp enough, swords were more often her method of expressing disfavour. "Thirava had no part in this."

"She knows. But the offer stands." For a moment, he looked as though he were about to say something else, but this time the thought was hidden so deep as to go undivined. "If there's to be nothing else, I'll leave you to prepare."

Offering a brief bow of the head, Aeldran left the room, pace unevened by the rigidity of the bindwork leg hidden beneath his robes.

Melanna stared at the closed door a moment, regretting that she so rarely returned his kind words with her own. Then she retired to her bedchamber and set about undoing the evening's damage. The torn golden gown she exchanged for one already laid out for her. Dirt, errant cosmetics and the aftermath of tears she scrubbed away. Eye shadow, she retouched – though this too could have been applied by other hands, she preferred to do it herself. There was nothing to be done about the scratches that would not draw greater attention, so those she resolved to bear without deceit.

With that done, the final part of the ritual beckoned. Pulling on her father's old cloak once more, Melanna drew back the drapes and crossed onto the balcony of living birch that overlooked the city. Her city.

Tregard remained beautiful as ever, the silver branchwork painted across wall and rooftop glorious even beneath an elusive moon. Ghostfires danced at every street corner, and from distant temple rooftops.

Save for a few hardy holdouts, cold had emptied the streets beyond the palace grounds, but a thousand lights at window and canopied porchway spoke to simple joys practised beyond the darkness. Those joys would burn brighter tomorrow. Midwintertide was a time for family, mourning the death of the old year and looking ahead to the bounty of the new. Her people. Her responsibility. The men and women without whom the Imperial throne was nothing, and whose service Melanna strove to re-earn each day.

She'd known it would be difficult. She'd never dreamed she'd be so isolated. For all that she was surrounded by courtiers and crowds wherever she went, there was no one she could really talk to. No one from whom counsel could be sought. As a princessa, she'd had her father, and the guidance of the goddess Ashana. Now fate had placed both beyond her reach, and she was alone.

Or almost so.

"I know you're there." Some folk, all the guards and walls in the world could not keep at bay. "You're growing predictable."

A shadow detached itself from the wall and drew back its hood. A streak of white shone against night-darkened auburn hair. Wry smile twisted beneath. "Both of us, or I'd not be here, would I?" Apara let the folds of her woollen cloak fall open, and joined Melanna beneath the frost-withered birch. She seldom felt the cold. Seldom felt anything in the years since Ashana had transformed her into a deathless eternal. "We all have our habits. You've become one of mine."

"Enough to make you abandon your others?"

"And leave so many beautiful things in the hands of an unappreciative few? I couldn't live with myself."

Melanna hung her head, marvelling once again at the peculiarities of friendship. Empress and Thief. Hadari and Tressian. High-born and low. They couldn't have been further apart but ... Perhaps that's why she felt safe with her secrets in Apara's care – a thief gave up nothing without cause. Or was it fate? Apara styled herself the Silver Owl, and the House of Saran had long ago embraced such a creature as its crest. Owls were sacred to Ashana, and the goddess had brought them together. Or perhaps it was simply that, alone of the world, Apara Rann expected nothing of her.

"Jack tried to take my daughter tonight." The words, spoken aloud for the first time, occasioned fresh chill. One did not speak the Lord of Fellhallow's name lightly. "He lured her into the woods. We were fortunate to find her before she froze, or ... "

She left the thought unfinished, not yet ready to dwell on other fates.

Apara's smile faded. "Why?"

"What else can it be?" She stared up at the moon. "Ashana has withdrawn from the world. She can protect me no longer. He wants to punish me for what I did."

"For what *we* did." Another would have questioned. Even Aeldran. But not Apara. She understood. She'd been a part of Jack's humiliation before the other gods. A bargain broken by a princessa and a thief in order to save a world. "Why now? It's been years."

"Divine habits run deep. I think he attempted the same with me when I was Kaila's age." There. She'd said it. The suspicion hung heavier than ever, especially in light of forgotten memories Rasha had roused.

"What can I do?"

"For now, nothing. The Golden Court meets tonight, and I can spare no thought for anything else. The lunassera will keep Kaila safe, but . . . " She paused, unhappy at making a request that might bring Apara to Jack's attention. " . . . but if you could spare an eye, now and then, you'd have my gratitude."

"Of course." Apara chewed her lip. "And the other matter?"

The other matter. With all that had happened, she'd quite forgotten. "We'll see how things go tonight. Sleeplessness shouldn't be shared without cause."

"I'm sure he'll appreciate it."

Melanna found Aeldran's chambers empty of all save servants, and none could say for certain what had become of him. The discovery provoked a flash of anger that seared away the fragile peace brought by Apara's visit, and Melanna's resolve to make amends for earlier curtness. While she hardly expected Aeldran to live like a hermit, for him to so swiftly depart the palace after all that had occurred . . . ? That he'd more likely sought out his sister's company anew than carousal did little to abate annoyance.

That ill temper fouled the long walk between Aeldran's chambers and Kaila's. The princessa, at least, was where she should have been, unruly hair spilled dark across the pillows.

But the room was otherwise not as expected. A large padded chair was set with its back against the drapes, its sleeping occupant all but invisible beneath swathed blankets. A serpent-hilted sword set across his knees rose and fell in time to gentle snores. A welling heart softened anger to chagrin.

Careful to wake neither occupant, Melanna kissed her daughter on the cheek and, after briefest hesitation, her husband on the brow. That first step back towards the door was the hardest of the night. So easy to linger in the dark, and leave the world to its own devices. But for all that the prince had chosen to be a father, the mother remained an Empress.

Setting the door closed, she went to be so.

Eight

The staff's strike echoed beneath the vaulted ceiling. The dull *thump* of brass on stone that called for quiet. An unseen usher uttered the expected words.

"In the name of the Goddess Ashana ... her Imperial Majesty, Melanna Saranal, Dotha Rhaled offers audience to the Gwyraya Hadar."

Trumpets blared, and a young messenger, not yet old enough to wear armour, but arrayed proudly in emerald silks and Rhaled's silver owl, drew on the rope. The golden curtain shimmered aside, and Melanna began the long descent into the throne room.

As a girl, Melanna had thought it a place apart from the rest of the palace – a foothold of the divine. Only when her father was away on campaign, and her grandfather in one of his more paternal moods, had she been permitted to wander beneath the high, vaulted ceiling – to peer up through the gilded hole in the roof and glimpse the burgeoning moon. She'd sat at the throne's foot while Emperor Ceredic Saran, ruler of a realm beset upon every border, had regaled her with stories of ancestors past and battles won. It was where she'd first heard how Ceredic's own grandfather Alfric had survived the razing of Baranagar and repaid the Tressians a thousandfold for its loss, seizing Tregard and setting his own fire-blackened and storm-smote throne atop the ruins as challenge.

Decades later, the gods beheld that very same throne – golden statues thrice the height of a man, bearing buttressed archways atop their shoulders. The Raven and the bellicose forge god Astor flanked the main door, the former with eyes of a watchful predator, the latter a brooding, bearded presence. Proud Astarra – whom the Tressians named

Lumestra – and sombre Endala made up the next pairing, one with a spill of sculpted fire for hair, the other with gentle locks cresting like flowing waves. Ashana stood behind the throne, the north star upon her brow, and a crescent moon in her outstretched hand. Hunched Jack faced her, his expression unknowable beneath a smooth mask. Of the seven divinities Melanna had been raised to acknowledge – though not necessarily revere – only cruel Tzal was absent, for no Hadari willingly bent knee to his forlorn and wicked majesty.

A trick of the artist's craft granted each the impression of paying homage, reaffirming Melanna's young belief in her grandfather's sagacity. Why else would the divine heed him so? How could ephemeral kings do other than accept his wisdom? These days, she knew better, her illusions about the unity of Empire shattered by a thousand petty quarrels. And having walked the glimmerless waters of the Celestial Clock she'd seen first-hand how little regard gods held for any save themselves.

She also knew why her grandfather had so often perched on the throne's extent – no number of cushions could make it anything less than bitterly uncomfortable. All things being equal, Melanna would much rather have stood.

She clung to the knowledge that tomorrow would be easier. With the chamber crowded for the Golden Court's Midwintertide banquet, she'd be permitted – nay, expected – to walk its bounds, offering welcome to monarchs, chieftains and petty worthies from two dozen realms. But tonight, with only the monarchs of the Gwyraya Hadar, the great kingdoms of Empire, gathered in a semicircle about the dais – if one ignored the heirs, advisors and shield-bearers who swelled intimate gathering to a small crowd – she had to endure not only the throne's discomforts, but also the ingenuine smiles of peers wary that the changes she'd brought to Rhaled would spread.

"Majesty."

Her cropped black hair glittering with silver-set rubies, Aelia Andwaral curtseyed. Where all others in the throne room were gaudy with ancestral colour and shimmering silks, she favoured a plain black gown decadent in its humility. Mourning for a nation crippled by war where others bore their grief proudly, or not at all. Aelia looked incomplete without a sword at her side, but the only blades permitted at conclave were those of the Rhalesh Immortals who ringed the dais. And, of course, the silvered blade whose scabbard hung from the throne's crooked armrest.

Melanna embraced her. "*Essavim.* It's been too long."

"You're walking into an ambush," breathed Aelia. "Tread with care."

Melanna withdrew, careful to give no sign of having heard.

"Majesty." King Cardivan of Silsaria offered a low bow.

She responded with a briefer nod. "Cardivan. You had safe journey?"

No need to ask where the threatened ambush lay. For all his snow-white hair, Cardivan Tirane was dangerous. Belated inheritance had left him with a taste for advancement and, though the bloodlines had long ago diverged, distant lineage from Hadar Saran granted a claim to the throne.

"I have never felt safer, majesty. I was comforted to feel your eyes upon me at every step."

"You overestimate the scope of my sight," she replied.

"Perhaps." Cardivan's smile lacked warmth. "I'm sure I'm never far from your thoughts."

"Nor I from yours."

She continued about the semicircle.

"Empress." Prince Thirava, Regent of Redsigor, was not the actor his father was, or perhaps he'd simply not yet learned to delight in deeds divergent from thought. His bow was stiff and resentful – offered to one he didn't consider his equal, let alone his superior. Nor did his thin, moustachioed features quite lose the ghost of a sneer. Then again, men of royal blood seldom lacked for arrogance, and arrogance – as Melanna's father had frequently reminded her – was more dangerous than a sword.

Like a sword, it was better met in kind than not at all.

"The Midwinter conclave is a place for the Gwyraya Hadar, not client realms, Prince Thirava," she said. "Your presence would be more appropriate tomorrow, before the full court."

His bleak stare met hers. "The traditions of our fathers are as dear to me as to you, majesty." The familiar insult was veiled just enough for denial. "I'm present as my father's heir."

Aelia gave a disdainful shake of the head. Melanna merely held Thirava's gaze, wondering idly if he'd the spine to brazen out the false claim. Herself included, the room held the monarchs of eight Great Kingdoms, but *nine* shields grounded at their bearers' feet – Thirava's personal blazon of a rearing stag distinct from his father's passant emblem. Three other heirs had come to conclave, and none with heraldry of their own.

"Then, as heir, I welcome you, and trust I shall not hear you speak further until tomorrow."

She continued on, greeting each monarch in turn. Prince Miradan – representing a father too frail to travel the long leagues from Britonis – gave a wry smile that might have been sympathy; King Haralda of Corvant a respectful bow. Agrana, Dotha Novona – the only other woman yet to cheat tradition and claim regal inheritance, and alas living proof that women could be as venal as men – offered neither.

Melanna took care to greet not only the kings of Kerna and Demestae, but also their heirs. She paid special heed to Princessa Nari of Kerna, who'd someday face a struggle as great as her own. Or perhaps not. That one as young as Nari's twelve winters had been permitted to join the Midwintertide conclave spoke to changing times.

The advisors she ignored entirely. Like her guards, trumpeters and servants, they were present only as extensions of their monarchs.

Formality attended to, and servants ushered to ply guests with wine and sweetmeats, the ancient throne could be put off no longer. Skirts whispering on stone, Melanna passed through the ring of Immortals, arranged herself as comfortably as its contours allowed, and raised a hand. "What business do you bring before the throne?"

As at the last conclave, the perennial issue of the eastern border and the febrile settlement with the Ithna'jîm dominated early discussions, with the usual accusations flying between Miradan and Haralda that the other marshalled insufficient spears to tame Itharoci phalanxes.

Dispute between Novona and Demestae followed, Queen Agrana venting displeasure at the taxes King Langdor levied upon her subjects' traders. For his part, Langdor retaliated with claims that a string of islands in Mar Karakeld – which a recent bequest had placed once again beneath the protection of Novona's trident, and not the Demestan bear – had been stolen through conspiracy.

Melanna spoke only in mediation. Aligning with one side would only alienate the other. Her father might have taken the risk, but he'd inherited a far stronger realm from Ceredic than she from him. Ravaged by the holy war of Kai Saran's Avitra Briganda, Rhaled's armies relied on the friendship of Icansae to safeguard the throne. Rhaled, and indeed the wider Empire – save perhaps the realms of Kerna and Novona who had taken no part in the Avitra Briganda – could scarcely afford another war.

Her peers showed no such restraint, offering glimpses of pacts broken and realigned to prevailing need. Corvant and Britonis might bicker about spears along the border, but they were united when it came to placing demands on the treasury for irrigation works and firm roads. For all that the Empire had begun hundreds of leagues south of where its capital now lay, wealth had ever lingered in the cities of the north.

Langdor remained an opportunist, picking and choosing his sides more on the principle of what would fill his coffers than what would benefit the folk of Demestae. Silsaria, Kerna and Novona were seldom in anything other than accord, with Cardivan often making generous concessions to Bodra and Agrana to keep things so. Redsigor, of course, offered no opinion, though Thirava's mind doubtless aligned with his father's. Aelia remained distant, but when she spoke, others listened. Icansae's voice carried weight, even though it was the least of the Gwyraya Hadar.

But for all the fire of discussion, compromise prevailed and hostilities were set aside. By the time the fires burned low and wine eased tongues, King Haralda took advantage of a lull in conversation.

"Majesty, I have a request on behalf of my people."

That was unexpected. Of the Gwyraya Hadar, distant Corvant was least apt to make trouble. But the word request covered a multitude of desires and ambitions. Perhaps Cardivan was not the architect of Aelia Andwaral's warned-of ambush.

"Proceed," said Melanna.

"We wish to raise a temple dedicated to your divine being," Haralda replied. "A goddess is loved more if her face is—"

"No." Melanna stifled a wince, the knowledge she'd spoken too hastily affirmed by thin smiles elsewhere. That the Corvanti espoused the divinity of Saran blood had ever been a source of contempt, not least because most deemed it a tool by which the ruling line controlled their populace.

"I can assure you, majesty, that only the finest artisans would be retained. Your divine image will stand as a protective colossus over Szadat. It will be so beautiful that all will have to avert their eyes, lest they be overcome."

Was he enjoying this? "I'm not a goddess, Haralda. You know this as well as I."

"You are too modest, majesty." His eyes drifted to the scabbard hanging from the throne. "Are you not Ashanal? A daughter of the perfect moon?"

He *was* enjoying this. Or perhaps he feared returning home rejected. Either way, refusing Haralda's request would be taken as affront. She'd trouble enough elsewhere without inviting more. Leagues counted for little when insult set armies to the march. However, for all that the Corvanti venerated the House of Saran, false claims of divinity would only sour relations elsewhere in the Golden Court.

But an answer had to be given.

Melanna let her fingers brush the sword's silvered hilt. The lunassera claimed metal held resonance of those who touched it in moments of great darkness, or great joy. Her father had wielded the blade at such times, but if a piece of his spirit lingered, it withheld counsel. But perhaps he held the answer, all the same.

"I'm humbled," she replied, "but my answer remains."

Cardivan offered a brief smile. Doubtless he'd encouraged Haralda's petition. Having his agents stir the Corvanti populace to the request would have been easy. Piety and priesthood were not always firm friends, and gold led wagging tongues astray.

Haralda shot a glance at his courtiers. "Majesty, I must ask you to reconsider. My people—"

"I cannot allow it." She paused, eking out the tension to add palatability to the following words. "Not until my father is given his due. Corvant endures through his sacrifices. Now he sits at Ashana's side on Evermoon, and wonders why he is so soon forgotten." She leaned forward. "Let the God Kai Saran stand as Szadat's guardian, and when I too walk the gardens of Evermoon, let your daughter petition mine, that I may stand beside him."

"An excellent suggestion," said Aelia.

Cardivan scowled, likely as much at the prospect of the throne passing to another woman as to another Saran. Agrana of Novona and Bodra of Kerna echoed his disfavour, though more guardedly. But the ambush was thwarted. None could argue that Kai Saran – the man who'd slaughtered the Tressian Council in their own stronghold – was undeserving of recognition.

Haralda nodded, colour returning to his cheeks. "It shall be done."

He withdrew to his shield. When no other showed inclination to take his place, Melanna allowed herself to relax. Perhaps she was getting better at this.

She rose. "Then if there are no other petitions, I call this conclave to a close."

Thirava stepped forward. "There is—"

"There is one further matter, majesty," Cardivan interrupted smoothly, throwing his son a warning look. "Redsigor's acknowledgement as a full kingdom."

Melanna reluctantly retook the throne. "At last conclave, we agreed Redsigor would remain a province until fully settled. The Empire does not need unwilling subjects."

"Your great-great-grandfather thought differently," said King Bodra. "As did his uncle before him. Neither my countrymen nor the Corvanti knelt willingly before the throne."

"And in each case, decades of strife followed," said Melanna.

"You'd compare the might of Corvant's armies to that of Tressian farmers?" said Haralda. Worship did not wholly eclipse pride. Rhalesh spears had run the Corvanti grasslands red before Haralda's ancestor had bent the knee. "What can they do?"

"Anarchy spreads like infection," said Aelia. "We'd be fools to invite it within our borders."

"Redsigor *is* settled," snapped Thirava, again forgetting he was not meant to speak before conclave or too angry to care. "The populace are recalcitrant, but they are learning. I have the matter in hand."

"I'm not deaf to what occurs between the Rappadan and the Ravonn." Melanna made a point of addressing her words to Cardivan, and not Thirava. "I'm troubled by much of what I hear. Curfews. Work camps. Executions. These are not our methods."

Cardivan twitched a shrug. "I'm sure what you hear is exaggerated. As for the rest? The Tressians make it necessary. They feed insurrection at every turn." He stroked his chin, the image of a man arriving at unexpected thought. "But perhaps Redsigor is not the issue."

"And what is?"

"That we have yet to finish what your father started," said Queen Agrana.

Bodra nodded, beard brushing against the shimmering blues of his robes. "The Tressians will never accept Redsigor as our territory. Sooner or later, they will send swords to reclaim it."

With those words, the true ambush lay revealed, confirmed by Agrana's nod of agreement.

"My father's war is done," snapped Melanna. "I will not reopen old wounds."

"It was no more your father's war than it is yours, or mine," said Cardivan. "It is simply how things have ever been. That is why Redsigor remains tumultuous, despite my son's ceaseless effort. Your caution does you credit, but courage has always served us better."

"There's fine separation between courage and foolishness," growled Aelia. "Accusing your Empress of cowardice crosses that line."

Cardivan frowned, his eyes still on Melanna. "I meant no such insult, majesty. We've all borne witness to your valour. You say Redsigor cannot be considered a full kingdom until it knows peace. Perhaps we should look upon this as opportunity to embrace the inevitable. And if you're too distracted to lead the campaign, well—"

Never more aware of the thorn scratches on her cheeks, Melanna rose and fixed him with an icy stare. "So now I am not only a coward, but I lack apt priorities?"

"Forgive me, majesty, but you were late to this conclave, and I understand there was some commotion earlier tonight." He radiated concern, all of it false. "I trust all is now well?"

Of course he knew something had gone awry, if not the full shape of it. Melanna trusted her Immortals and the servants who tended the royal quarters, but there could have been no concealing the hue and cry following Kaila's disappearance. "Yes."

"Ashana be praised. I know as well as any that the needs of a child alter a parent's perspective. On the blood we share, I swear I meant nothing more than that. I merely suggest that Thirava would be honoured to act as your champion in the campaign. He, after all, has the most to gain from success, and my son is ready for a throne."

Which meant Silsaria intended to lay claim to whatever Tressian lands were conquered, expanding the borders of its client kingdom of Redsigor. Doubtless, spoils had been agreed with Bodra and Agrana to ensure support. And that last line ... especially combined with the reminder of common ancestry? A warning that if Redsigor had no throne for Thirava to warm, Cardivan would look to set him upon hers. With Rhaled and Icansae weakened, and Kerna and Novona at his back, he might even manage it.

The simple thing to do would be to grant Redsigor the status Thirava demanded. Not all kingdoms were equal, and a client realm of Silsaria scarcely had more influence than a regent's province. But neither Thirava nor Cardivan would be content long. They'd scent blood in the compromise, and follow the spoor to its end.

"I gave my decision at last conclave." Again, Melanna addressed her reply to Cardivan, and not Thirava. "The peaceful settlement of Redsigor is not a sop to pride, or to conscience. It is the means by which those we invite into the Empire are proven worthy of a place within it ... and that he who would rule them has the proper balance of humours to be worthy of a throne. An Empire should be concerned with its people, not its land, Cardivan."

Aelia grinned. Haralda and Miradan nodded approval, as did one or two courtiers – though notably not those from Kerna, Novona or Silsaria. Nari of Kerna smiled, but shrank to stillness before her father could glimpse the small rebellion.

Cardivan's features went rigid. "Can I suggest you take counsel before making a final decision? With Prince Aeldran, perhaps."

"My consort and I are in one mind on this. And the decision is made."

"It's the wrong decision," snapped Thirava, stepping to join his father beyond the semicircle's arc. "Redsigor—"

Golden scales rustled as the Immortals beside the throne started forward. A needless precaution. Thirava wouldn't attack her any more than she him. Not that Melanna wasn't tempted. The goddess' silver sword would solve so many problems at a single stroke . . . but it would also create others. Her grandfather would have killed Thirava. Her father *might* have done so, though it would have been in the ritualised setting of a champion's duel. As for her great-great-grandfather? Well, Thirava would have been dead already. Power was a thief of patience, and Alfric Saran had never much of that particular virtue to begin with.

But Melanna had long ago sworn not to let the throne shape her. Cardivan was a lost cause, Thirava too. The others, however? There might yet be a chance to show them that wisdom was more than a drawn sword.

She held up a hand, bringing the Immortals to a halt. Cardivan, face now contorted with barely concealed fury, seized Thirava's arm and brought lips level with his ear. No words reached Melanna, but Thirava's poisonous expression told its own story. Tearing free, he retreated to his shield, leaving his father, composure returned, to offer a bow.

"If that is your decree, then we will respect it, of course," Cardivan said. "Saranal Aregnum. We serve the throne."

Saranal Aregnum. The old salute to an Emperor modified only slightly for an Empress. But Cardivan's second pledge held less weight, for it cared not who sat *upon* that throne.

"Then we are done," said Melanna. "In the name of the Goddess Ashana, I thank you for your attendance, and your service. Tomorrow is Midwintertide. A new year beckons. Let us welcome it in friendship, and as family."

One by one, the assembled monarchs bowed and departed the throne room, entourages streaming in their wake. When the last had departed, Melanna dismissed servants and Immortals with a wave of her hand. Then she sank back on the uncomfortable throne.

"Alas to see the bond between father and son worn away," murmured a voice. "I understand food tasters are in short supply in Silsaria of late."

Haldrane drew alongside the throne, robes swishing at the dais. His saturnine face was lost beneath hood's shadow, little more than a greying black beard, parted lips and perfect white teeth giving shape to thoughtful expression. Statues and drapes offered an embarrassment of hiding places, and the head of her icularis – her Eyes – had as much a knack for concealment as for secrets.

"I counselled against giving Cardivan the conquered lands," he said. "Now you see why."

"I'd little choice, as well you know."

"An Empress always has a choice," he replied. "It may simply not be the one she wishes."

Melanna sensed the deeper warning beneath the words. "Like that before me now?"

"War is coming. If not against Tressia, then to preserve your throne."

She'd once embraced war so readily. The chance to prove herself and thus claim her father's throne. Glory in victory, fortitude in defeat and honour always. But the Avitra Briganda had changed all that. So many thousands dead. Worse, the Avitra Briganda's consequences had nearly brought about the Reckoning of the Gods and the world's ending. Melanna shuddered to think about it even now. The recent past taught a harsh lesson: while kings and princes sought glory, those they ruled died in the mud.

"I won't do it," she said.

"You will." Haldrane spoke with weary inevitability. "Your forebears had to fight for the throne – to claim it, and to hold it. You will have to do the same. If blood is to be shed, better it be Tressian."

"And where will it end, Haldrane? On and on, and death the only respite. We should be better than this."

"Undoubtedly." A touch of amusement danced beneath the words. "But we are not. And you, my Empress, must deal with the world as it is, and not as you might wish it to be."

"And if I don't?"

"Then they will take from you everything that you value, and leave you with dust."

She snorted and shook her head. "You offer cold comfort."

"The year is dead. Cold comfort is all any of us have."

Nine

Having held off all day, the snows now determined to address the shortfall in glorious style. The street's firestone lanterns were lost behind a dancing, powdery white veil. Trampled paths, visible minutes before, succumbed anew. Not that Altiris minded a little snow – not so long as there was the prospect of a roaring fire and a stiff drink when the business was done.

Constans thrust his hands in the pockets of his coat and trudged unenthusiastically alongside. "This had better not be a waste of time."

Altiris doffed his hat and swept clear the brim. His work was undone almost as soon as he set it back in place. "Don't tell me you're afraid of getting a bit cold?"

"The cold doesn't bother me." The lad's tone shifted, churlishness yielding to mummer's exaggerated stage-inflection. "Let heavens rage and river crack, and still in wrath I'll stand."

The phrasing struck a chord. "Trastorov?"

Constans scowled, annoyed to be caught passing quotation off as sentiment. "Laniran. *The King of Fathoms*. Wouldn't expect a southwealder to know the difference."

"'My love lies buried, deep on deep. What heed have I for gods' command?'" Altiris finished, relishing Constans' surprise. "I know the words. I couldn't recall who wrote them, that's all."

Apt lines. Like the ill-fated King of Fathoms, the vranakin of Dregmeet had placed their faith in divine patronage, and they too had paid dearly in the end. The sunken streets were but a memory, flooded by the waters of Kasdred Mar.

Further north, the Silverway Docks had expanded into the new lagoon. But the kraikons responsible for clearing the wreckage of the drowned slums had been withdrawn before the works were done. In daylight, the ragged join stood plain – the unbowed timbers and bright stone of the new works yielding gradually to the sunken, decaying streets. Not so in the snows, which lent purity even to the undeserving.

Even Constans' edges seemed a little softer that night. The lack of Drazina uniform helped. But so did the lad's obvious affection for the playwright's words. Even the dread *southwealder* epithet had lacked customary sting. For the first time in years, Altiris conceded there might be someone worth knowing beneath the sneer.

"My father was a mummer," he said. "Knew all of Trastorov's works by heart, and a good number of others besides. After Exodus, he told them as bedtime stories to me, and to the children of the other slaves. They lose something when translated into the low-tongue, though. *Os lasdella darmanelna, dunmar—*"

"So you know a few fancy words?" And with that, Constans was back to normal. "Doesn't make you good enough for my sister."

"I didn't ask." Altiris scowled into the snows, the lad's matter-of-fact tone as offensive as the words. "And it's none of your business."

They trudged on in silence a few minutes before Constans found his tongue.

"I hope your tavernkeep hasn't sent us out chasing feylings."

"She hasn't." Adela had been speechless for a full minute after Altiris had set coins on the counter to settle his debt, and more than happy to talk thereafter. "I saw a couple of the brigands in the Ragged Wayfarer. Adela swore they were talking up a storm, promising work and a good meal for anyone who wanted it."

A promise uncomfortably close to those once offered by the Crowmarket. Allegiance exchanged for a full belly, and a tithe of all takings, be they from honest labour or criminal endeavour. Another pointer that the worst of old days might be returning.

Constans sniffed. "I don't want to be walking around in circles on some slattern's say-so. I've better things to do."

He hadn't, of course. What could be more important than retrieving the Lord Protector's possessions and bringing the thieves to justice? This was just more I'm-better-than-you preening. "Just remember, you're my responsibility and you'll follow my lead. Understand, *guardsman*?"

Constans held his gaze a heartbeat, then nodded.

Altiris pressed on, mindful of his footing on the steepening cobbles and alert for passersby who were a mite *too* interested. With tabards and armour shed and weapons concealed, he and Constans were about as nondescript as could be managed, but there was always risk.

Sparse streets emptied. Jettied eaves crowded murky skies, all sagging timbers and rotting windows. Pristine lamp posts gave way to wall-mounted lanterns with cracked glass. The blue-white flames of ghostfire braziers smouldered their sweet scent into the swirling snow. For all that the mists of Otherworld had drowned with Dregmeet, few were minded to take chances with vengeful spirits stirring beneath cold seas. Especially with Midwintertide so close.

Beyond, what had once been Birch Street veered north and south. The empty facades of its western edge projected from the lagoon's grey, snow-speckled waters, the retaining wall that had once stopped the street slipping away into Dregmeet proper now a weatherworn embankment holding seas at bay. Under clearer skies, Altiris had seen lights blazing beneath the waters. Sea fetches, some held them, luring the curious to a drownling's wedding. He was glad their light didn't carry through the snows.

Ahead, the spire of Seacaller's Church pierced the skies. A name once bestowed for a founder's determination to spread Lumestra's gospel across harbour slums now lent irony by rushing waters lapping against lychfield walls.

For the first time, the driving wind bore not only voices, but song – the curious atonality of carols brandished with more enthusiasm than skill. A common enough sound in the city's wealthier churches, but not in Sothvane. And certainly not so long after the dusktithe services were done. Try as he might, Altiris couldn't pick out the words.

He clung to the fleeting shelter of a crumbling brick wall, and wondered if he'd erred by not seeking assistance. He'd expected a furtive gathering, easily spied upon – or even overcome, were fortune with them – but not this. Even assuming most of the revellers were innocents, that didn't mean they'd take no side if it came to a fight.

Constans shook his head. "If they want to call Lumestra down from the heavens, they'd do better to learn the words. Hitting some of the right notes would help." He stomped his feet moodily. "Well, *lieutenant*? What now? I hear tell you're in charge."

What now indeed? How many waited inside? Temptation remained to return to Stonecrest, offer report and return with Brass and the others – maybe a few constables for good measure. Only that would risk appearing afraid – not least to Constans, whose dark eyes watched him with veiled amusement.

"We go in," Altiris said at last. "Ask a few careful questions – watch for familiar faces – and see from there."

"At your command." A sly smile undercut the acknowledgement's formality.

Altiris flinched as Constans' hand darted forward. Smile edging wider, Constans reached past his shoulder, plucked something from the wall and opened his hand. A bird's skull and a wreath of feathers. A crow charm, a vranakin warning to intruders. A tattered and miserable thing, but there was no telling how long it had hung there. Might have been years, months ... or hours.

Smile fading, Constans dropped the repulsive bundle into the snow and brought down his heel. "Better safe than sorry, don't you think?"

Altiris felt the watchmen's eyes on him as he passed beneath the lychfield's yew bower – and watchmen they clearly were, for all their lack of uniform or obvious weapons – but recognised neither from the night before. Seacaller's loomed ahead, light flickering through cracks in boarded-up windows. As he reached the door, the fitful carol died away. Muffled conversation rose in its place, footfall sounding on tile as folk moved about.

Judging the timing to be as good as any other, Altiris put his shoulder to the door. Warmth rushed to greet him, the brackish, earthy aroma of fish stew carried on its wings. And something else ... the frisson of a presence beyond ready contemplation. There was power in the dead, and in echoes of faith.

The congregation were not, as he'd feared, a huddle of vranakin. Or, at least, none were masked and garbed as such. Though that in itself was little comfort – nor had Hawkin and her accomplices been the night before.

But her brigands had all been strong, capable fellows. The church housed a worn, filthy rabble, spanning knee-high children to elders whose lined faces had borne witness to long decades. Altiris glimpsed a ragged uniform, a crutch to support a missing limb. Some huddled in groups about the candlelit nave, wooden bowls clutched tight. Others stood with backs to the walls, eyes suspicious. Indeed, the only folk with build and confidence to match the previous night's attackers – save another pair of obvious watchmen – laboured with pot and cauldron over a low fire set before the altar.

Not exactly the den of iniquity Adela had promised. But still, there was something off about the place. Not least that there was nothing of Lumestra to be found within sight. No sunbursts, no oak leaves – what serathi statues remained with their heads intact wore ragged blindfolds. No priest. No serenes. This wasn't a simple church offering charity. There was something familiar, though Altiris couldn't quite identify *what*.

One eye on Constans, he threaded a group of playing children and made a slow, incurious loop along the southern transept. As he passed a pillar, a heavy hand fell on his shoulder.

"What's your name, son?" growled a gruff voice. "What brings you here?"

Altiris froze. He turned about and stared up at a man of about Lord Trelan's age, heavyset with an unkempt beard. "I ... "

"We were told we'd be fed here." Constans' voice had lost its arch precision, nasal vowels replaced by something throatier – a better fit for the city's underbelly, and completely, utterly persuasive. More marked was the shift in posture, no longer the proud highblood, but something shrunken and cautious. "Please, we didn't mean to intrude, but my brother and me? We ain't eaten today."

"You're wearing good cloth," the man said with suspicion.

The sly smile returned. "Slipped over the wall and pinched 'em from Stonecrest, didn't we? For all the yammer about Phoenixes, the master of the guard's a lazy lump. Couldn't catch a limping cow. Would've had the silver, too, if we'd been quicker. But Devn here startled the mistress of the house."

Altiris stifled a scowl at the double insult. In Laniran's *The King of Fathoms*, Devn was the monarch's idiot servant.

The man grinned. "Well, you're here now. Come with me."

Altiris flashed Constans a glare – which the other ignored – and they followed to the altar's makeshift kitchen.

A woman pushed a bowl of stew into his hands. "The river provides," she murmured, without looking up.

Unsure of the proper response, Altiris muttered thanks and withdrew towards a pillar, careful to choose a vantage beyond earshot of others, but which offered clear views across the church. Constans joined him, the heavyset man on his heels.

"Eat," he said. "Sleep here tonight, if you've nowhere else. There'll be work come the dawn."

"What sort of work?" asked Altiris.

"The sort you don't ask questions about." A nod softened the reply. "Won't be nothing worse than you've already done. Name's Radzar. Ask for me, and I'll see you're taken care of."

A chorus of mismatched song erupted in a distant corner, soon joined by other voices. Constans waited for Radzar to pass beyond earshot, then hooked an eyebrow at Altiris, his voice quiet but back to normal. "Follow my lead, indeed."

Altiris took a mouthful of stew to avoid reply. It was surprisingly good, the salt of the fish – mudbream, or something similar – softened by thyme and hunks of potato.

"So what now?" pressed Constans. "We're not going to find anything worth stealing here, much less worth recovering."

Radzar was moving through the crowd, clasping hands and ushering folk to the altar. Altiris caught no indication that anyone else was paying them any attention. But for all that, a sour taste crept under his tongue. "It's like the stockade on Selann."

"Beg pardon?" asked Constans, his bowl already half-empty.

"There was an uprising. Lord Yordon's overseers dragged the survivors to the stockade, until they could work out who'd return to the fields without trouble, and who needed ... motivation."

"You think this is the same?" Constans replied, serious for once.

"It's not just walls and chains keep folk captive. The promise of food and warmth might do it. Or do you think anyone'd be here if they'd a choice?"

"Maybe. Folk are lazy, and free's free."

Spoken like a boy who'd never gone without. "Some, perhaps, but not all. Little tastes sweeter than food you've worked for – even if the work's nothing to be proud of."

Constans rolled his eyes. "Did *you* make trouble on Selann?"

Old pyre-flames flickered behind Altiris' eyes. "I knew better. They burned my father for witchcraft, and I knew they'd do the same to me if I offered excuse."

"There's magic in your family?"

Would that there was. "Not a scrap."

"Then why—"

"They caught him teaching children to read. Scratching letters into the mud with a stick. That was enough."

Constans pursed his lips and looked away. "That crack before – about you not being good enough for Sidara. I didn't mean it to be personal. Everyone's below her. My parents made that *very* clear. So does she, every time I ask her to join me as a Droshna. We're siblings. We should be together, but she can barely look at me."

Altiris grunted. He was unsure how to respond, for all that a reply was apparently expected. And Lumestra knew that an apology from Constans was a rare bird indeed. "It's forgotten."

"Viktor says I'm to think before I speak." He shrugged, not quite disguising the embarrassment of admission. "Sometimes my tongue gets in the way."

Surprise moved Altiris to his own confession. "Lord Trelan says I'm to think before I act. It might just be that we're not the right men for this job." A flash of white-blonde hair at the clocktower doorway caught his attention. "Then again . . . "

The pale young woman from the ambush. The one who'd stopped Hawkin from cutting his throat. Same blue-green eyes. Same black dress.

"There," murmured Altiris, twisting away so as not to be recognised in return. "That's her."

Constans followed his gaze. "She doesn't look like much."

Altiris closed his eyes, echoes of the woman's dizzying, drowning song rushing back over his thoughts, almost as tantalising as they were terrifying. Not someone to underestimate a second time. "She's bad enough."

"She's leaving."

Altiris opened his eyes in time to see the woman ghost through the main door and out into the night. A corner of his soul screamed at him not to follow. But the trail – never more than lukewarm – had gone cold. It was follow or admit failure. To the Lord Protector. To Lord Trelan. And to himself.

"Then so are we."

Between the black dress, the snows and the uncertain light from the Birch Street lanterns, they lost the young woman with the blue-green eyes twice in the first hundred yards. Footprints helped, but falling snow rapidly blurred hers to the point they were little different to other spent trails. Both times, Constans spotted her a heartbeat before Altiris, a nudge of elbow and pointed finger setting them back on course.

On she went, past the collapsed remnant of the portreeve's manor and Fennmoor orphanage. Altiris grew ever more uneasy, alert for a trap. But hurried glances behind revealed no pursuit, nor the suggestion of ambush lurking in the dark. What sounds there were came only from houses shut tight. As for the woman, she never once looked back, as unconcerned by the prospect of being followed as she was the deepening cold.

Then, just beyond the empty battlements of the abandoned Fellnore Vigil, she vanished beneath the shadow of a wood-framed warehouse clinging to the western side of Birch Street, picking a path across water-logged flagstones and vanishing into a doorway.

"Don't tell me we're blundering in behind her," hissed Constans.

"No. That's our way in." Altiris pointed to a second door a short way distant. The paintwork, like that of the wider warehouse, was flaked and peeling, but the padlock looked new, which it likely was. "Assuming you can open it."

A guess, but not much of one. Doors had never been much of an obstacle to Constans.

Constans snorted, and without a word picked his way across to the door. After a few seconds with an array of thieves' tools no upstanding citizen – much less a Drazina – should have possessed, he offered a sardonic bow and then eased the door open.

They entered into a corridor split from the warehouse's main bay by a wall of warped timber and smeared glass. In no place were the sloped and sagging floorboards less than three inches beneath the water. Thready black weed clung to the lower walls, filling every breath with a bitter, salt stench.

Beckoning for Constans to follow, Altiris edged towards the inner wall, careful to keep his head below the level of the glass and lamenting the inescapable fact that his boots were not so waterproof as he'd believed. Notwithstanding a small stack of crates and strongboxes, the warehouse floor was empty of everything save debris.

Three figures stood in the pool of light from a hanging lantern. The woman with the blue-green eyes, a much older man wrapped tight in thick wools and rich furs ... and Hawkin Darrow.

A hiss told Altiris that Constans had – unsurprisingly – recognised the woman who'd once held a blade to his throat. He set a hand on the lad's shoulder and a warning finger to lips. Thankfully, Constans offered a taut nod, his hand slipping from a dagger concealed beneath his cloak.

Satisfied, Altiris crept closer to the adjoining door and eased it open a fraction.

" ... told you not to come here." The young woman drew closer to the man. "It's dangerous."

"I had to see you. I had to—"

He broke off as pale fingers found his cheek. A scowl marred Hawkin's brow. The man had eyes only for the young woman.

"I told you not to come here," she repeated, voice hard. "I'm grateful for your support. But if you can't keep to our agreement, then there *is* no agreement ... and you will never see me again."

"I'm sorry." The man looked to be on the brink of tears. Heart-wrenching, perhaps, but for his obvious, desperate desire for a woman young enough to be his granddaughter. Such things were hardly uncommon, but his tone was a little too pleading, and oddly slurred. "Promise you'll come to me."

The woman smiled, the affection offered to a pet, not a lover. "If it pleases me."

Then Altiris noticed it. The familiar, whispering song echoing beneath her words, so soft to have gone unregarded beneath his quickened pulse. The blackout of the previous night took on fresh significance. More than ever, he wished he'd brought others to Sothvane.

The man clasped her hand tight. His face fell further when she drew it free.

"Go," she said. "Before I change my mind."

He stumbled away, but his gaze never left her until the outer door closed between them.

The young woman shuddered and shrank inwards. "You did right to send for me."

Hawkin made a disgusted noise. "He's pathetic."

"His coin's useful. Let him keep his dreams."

"I wish you wouldn't let them touch you."

"It means nothing." She kissed Hawkin on the cheek. "You needn't be so protective."

Again, the breathy song bloomed beneath her words, an insistent, scratching pressure against Altiris' thoughts. But Hawkin seemed not to notice, or at least so he thought at first. Then he noted the slight twitch of her eye, the expression of one who knows something to be amiss, but not *what*. The song grew insistent. The twitch faded, and Hawkin's expression smoothed. For all Hawkin's treacheries past, Altiris wasn't sure how he felt about that.

"What is it?" hissed Constans.

"You don't hear that?" murmured Altiris.

"Hear what?"

"Singing. Like whispers at the back of your thoughts?"

"No." He scowled. "Let's take them. I see one of Father's boxes in that pile, and Hawkin—"

Altiris tightened his grip on the lad's shoulder. "We wait."

Constans sneered. "You're scared of the other one?"

"Yes."

"She's barely older than me."

"I know."

Constans subsided, wariness in his eyes. Altiris withdrew his hand and turned his attention to the warehouse bay. The young woman picked through an opened crate, brushing appreciative fingers across a bolt of ruby silk. "Itharoci. This will fetch a good price."

Hawkin nodded. "I've a buyer lined up."

"It came from the *Moonchaser*?"

Hawkin nodded. "Brannin's wreckers wanted to keep it, but I persuaded them otherwise."

"Politely, I hope? The Merrow doesn't want to lose their services."

"They'll have the lanterns out tonight along Torda Crag, as promised. I offered first pick of the cargo."

The young woman smiled. "The river provides . . . or the sea."

Hawkin didn't quite return it. "As you say. You'll be away to see him now, I suppose?"

She nodded, already starting towards the door. "I'm already late."

Altiris' suspicions hardened to certainty. Definitely *not* the Crowmarket. Whatever Hawkin had embroiled herself in, it was something else. And if the other woman was reporting to her employer? Well, finding out the who and where of *that* was worth a little extra risk.

"Back outside," he murmured. "But carefully. We'll see where she goes next."

Constans offered no response, for he was no longer there.

The warehouse's outer door swung shut, the woman lost to the night.

Altiris swore bitterly under his breath and cast about. The boy had gone, and without so much as a whisper of sound. No mystery as to the why, not with Hawkin left alone and unawares. For all he silently cursed the lad, Altiris knew he'd only himself to blame for withholding her return. Constans would likely have done something rash regardless, but surprise made it a guarantee.

Where was he?

A moment later, he saw him. On the far side of the warehouse bay, advancing soundlessly on Hawkin with daggers drawn. To slip away was one thing, but to cover so much ground? Impossible, save that it plainly wasn't.

Hawkin turned in the same moment Constans lunged. A knife whispered from her belt and struck his dagger aside. He pitched forward with a yell as her boot thumped into his knee.

"You forget, boy, I always could play your games better."

Constans scrambled, the knife hissing over his head. Altiris ripped the door open and charged out into the warehouse, sword drawn. "Hawkin!"

Startled, she made a half-circle away from Constans, knife point darting back and forth and eyes wary. "So it's a reunion, is it?" she shouted. "Anyone else out there? Sidara? Apara Rann, perhaps? Why don't you all join us?"

Constans regained his feet, lips locked in a snarl. "We're enough."

"Hah! Always did have fine opinion of yourself." She let the knife fall and raised her hands. "So which of you's to do the deed?"

Shifting his grip on his dagger, Constans started forward.

"Neither," snapped Altiris, his gaze on the lad. "We give her to the constabulary. That's our duty. You want her life, petition the Lord Protector to play at hangman."

The warehouse trembled to running feet on the stairs and walkways above. Lantern lights spilled between slatted stairs. Altiris' heart sank as the first shiver of fear took hold. *Why don't you all join us?* A warning cry more than a jibe.

Hawkin shook her head. "Maybe you should have checked *I* was alone first, my bonnies?"

Three dark shapes upon the stairs became six. Steel gleamed.

"Go!" said Altiris. "We'll lose them in the streets."

The outer door burst inward with a rush of chill air. Another pair of heavies stood framed against the snow. Eight now – nine, including Hawkin. Far too many to fight and win. But what else was there?

"Constans?" Altiris spun on his heel in a failed attempt to keep their opponents in sight. "Back to back. It's our only chance."

The boy stumbled into the lantern's shadow, his expression wholly bereft of its usual sly swagger. "There are too many."

"Constans!"

"No. Sorry."

Altiris' angry glare fell on a calm, unrepentant face, pale in the darkness. Then the shadows surged, and Constans was gone, without footfall or motion to betray his passing.

"Where'd he go?" barked one of the heavies.

"Raven's Eyes," spat another. "A bloody witch."

Altiris threw down his sword, fear entangled by anger and confusion. Anger, for the lad's cowardice; confusion for the realisation that Constans Droshna, once Constans Reveque, had magic of his own.

Hawkin drew closer, her knife once again gleaming in a steady hand.

"Well then, my bonny," she said. "What shall we talk about?"

Josiri stared across the snow-stolen gardens without seeing them. Part of him knew the latticework gazebo made for poor shelter. That his gloved hands were as numb as his thoughts, and the rest of him soon to follow. Yet still he couldn't bring himself to rouse shivering bones. And so he sat upon the stone bench, watched the falling snow and damned himself for a coward.

"Josiri?" Sevaka's thin shadow darkened the gazebo's arch. "Kurkas said I'd find you here. I hope I'm not intruding?"

He shook his head, clearing numbed thoughts. "No. Of course not."

She drew closer, her cheeks flushed with cold and her grey eyes careful. "Is there any news?"

"I don't know. It isn't ... " Black clouds crowded in. "We put her to bed. It seemed best."

He'd forbidden the servants and all but a handful of others to enter the bedroom. Anastacia would hate to be seen as she was now. Her body split and shattered; limbs intact but golden light hissing from the cracks. Bad enough that all could hear her low, pained moans, but short of emptying the house there was nothing to be done.

The year was dying, and his love with it.

"I called a physician. He just stared until Kurkas dragged him away. I don't know what I expected him to achieve. She's always mended before. Elzar's tried. Sidara's tried. Kurkas suggested we send for a claysmith, and maybe we should." A sigh tore free, taking with it strength he couldn't spare. "Sidara's sitting with her now. I couldn't ... I ... She can't hear me. She can't see me. She can't feel my hand about hers. And every time she cries out, a piece of me dies. I'm sorry. I know how selfish that sounds."

Sevaka gathered the tails of her coat and sat beside him. An ungloved hand, sapphire ring glinting on a finger, snaked across his. "She'd understand."

"Are you sure?" He offered a wintery smile. "I keep thinking it's a dream. That I'll wake up, and she'll be stood there, scolding me for idleness. A collapsing mansion once buried her alive, for Lumestra's sake. What's a fall from a balcony compared to that?"

He paused, breathless, but the words wanted to come.

"I should have known something was wrong. She wasn't right at the palace. And before?" He stared at outspread fingers, remembering the clay dust of the morning. "Something was amiss even then. You know the worst part?"

Sevaka squeezed his hand.

Josiri let his eyes fall closed. "With everything she is – everything we've been through – I never expected it to be this way around. I thought she'd go on for ever. She even talked about it this morning. But this? I don't know what to do."

"Sometimes ..." Sevaka paused. "Sometimes it's enough just to be there."

"I know. I'll go back inside soon, but first I needed to ... Well, to stare. Recover a bit of that stony fortitude us nobles cultivate."

"I wouldn't know. I've never been much good at it."

He opened his eyes. "Me neither."

Sevaka withdrew her hand. "I was due in Tarvallion tomorrow, but I'll stay as long as you need."

"I won't hear of it."

"Josiri ..."

He shook his head. "This place is enough of a tangle at Midwintertide as it is, even without Ana. I don't need you under my feet." Knowing that she'd not believe that reason, he reached for another. "You've your own life, and if things on the border are as bad as you say, you shouldn't be away long. Which isn't to say I don't appreciate the offer."

"Why else have friends?" Rising, she stared out at the Ocranza statue standing untiring sentry amid the garden's skeletal trees. Anastacia hated it, claiming it too worn away to be decorous. Josiri only kept it in place to annoy her. "Tarvallion it is, though if you don't send a herald with news twice daily, I shall be back in a flash, and with Rosa in tow. You wouldn't like ... " The grin dissolved into a frown. "Queen's Ashes, I forgot about Shalamoh."

"Shalamoh?" The name was familiar, though Josiri couldn't place it.

"Some scribbler up in Highvale. Claims to be writing a history of the Republic. The *real* history."

"Then he'll be a man accustomed to disappointment, if he's not already."

Tressian history was a farrago of distortions and outright lies, as Sevaka knew better than most. For all that her blood family had once owned much of the city, they no longer existed, their pages torn from the annals.

Sevaka shook her head. "That may be, but he's pestering me about

Vrasdavora. Worse, he's gotten it into his head that I died there." Understandable, given that she had. "Endless questions. What was it like? Is the Raven real? Does Otherworld match the passages from Kendrial's *Vitsimar*? As if I've read the bloody thing. I keep hiding the letters – it won't go well for Master Shalamoh if Rosa sees them. But I can't very well go banging his door down at this hour."

Josiri rose, a small avalanche of snow cascading from his shoulders. A few minutes' conversation had rallied him more than an hour of staring. "Leave it with me."

"I can't ask you to do that, not as things are."

"Trust me, I might need the distraction." He forced a smile. "Or I can send Vladama. He has a way with words, and I think he could use the distraction as much as I."

"He looked to be on the brink of tears when I spoke to him."

"He and Ana are close, Lumestra knows why. But while we can't always choose our friends, we should always be grateful for them." Josiri embraced her. "Thank you."

"A herald by dusk tomorrow, Lord Trelan," she said, her cheek warm against his. "Or you'll see Rosa the next dawn."

Sevaka pulled away, halting at the gazebo's edge as if wanting to say more. Then she was gone into the night, and Josiri began the long walk back up to the house.

It was quieter than he remembered, the lanterns lowered and the servants withdrawn to their own chambers. That the hollow, mournful cries too had fallen silent added pace to Josiri's ascent of the stairs, tumultuous emotions again fighting for mastery. The last dozen paces to the bedroom he took almost at a run, but willed himself to calm before opening the door.

The room lay dark and silent, the hearth at a low smoulder and a single lantern lit in the bay window. Sidara rose from the adjoining chaise, her golden hair tied loosely back, her dress and shawl on the brink of disarray. Red-rimmed eyes spoke of a heart as ragged as his own.

"How is she?"

Sidara's cheeks twitched. "The cracks are spreading."

Josiri pulled a chair up to the bedside and took a cold, porcelain hand in his.

Anastacia offered neither word nor motion as response. No sign that she'd heard – or that she was even alive. With anyone else, the stillness would have meant the very worst, but Anastacia's clay body had ever lacked the small, unconscious motions of life. Josiri clung to that, and to the small shred of hope, for there was little else hopeful in her aspect.

What was visible of her porcelain flesh above the blankets was darker, somehow, than when he'd seen it last, its lustre faded alongside her spirit. The spiderweb cracks, limited to her back and shoulders in the aftermath of the fall, now crazed every inch of her once perfect alabaster skin. They too were cold and dark, the daylight fire characterising the magic Anastacia and Sidara shared barely a writhing flicker. Only the dark swirl of her eyes offered hope that some piece of her remained.

But for how long?

Josiri drew down a stuttering breath and raised Anastacia's hand to his lips. "Hello, Ana. I'm sorry I wasn't here."

Sidara drew closer. "Viktor visited not long ago. He spoke a lot, but he didn't *say* much. I think he feels responsible."

"He should." Josiri forced the useless anger down. For all that Viktor had sealed Anastacia's spirit in the porcelain body, it had been years ago. Nothing good came of dwelling on yesterday's mistakes. "Did he have any suggestions?"

"Only that he fears his shadow would make matters worse." She snatched a tear from her cheek. "He's probably right. Dark mixes poorly with the Light. But if it comes to it . . . "

Josiri nodded, his eyes on Anastacia's. "I'll give it until morning, then I'll speak to Viktor."

"What if he won't try?"

Seeing his knuckles whiten about Anastacia's, Josiri relaxed his grip. "He will. Get some rest. I'll sit with her awhile."

She shook her head, no effort now to abate her tears. "I'd rather stay."

Josiri held out his free hand. Sidara took it with both of hers and offered a watery smile.

"I keep thinking there should be something I can do. If it were you lying there, I could bind you with light. I did for Altiris. For Sevaka. But it doesn't work on Ana."

"You can't save everyone."

"Right now I don't want to save everyone. Just her."

"I know." Josiri didn't know what else to say. It was all too similar to the aftermath of his mother's death, wrestling with his own grief while trying to ease his sister's. Calenne. What would she think to see him now? She'd been barely older than Sidara when Malatriant had parted them for ever.

A polite knock on the door, and Kurkas slipped into the room. Sevaka had claimed him to be on the brink of tears, but there was none of that now. His eye touched on Josiri, on Sidara; on fixtures and furnishings – anything but the still, dark figure in the bed.

"Sorry, sah, but if you don't leave now, you'll be late for your meeting."

Josiri stared blearily up, wracking his brains for a glimmer of what Kurkas meant. He came up dry. "If it's constabulary business, Lieutenant Raldan can handle it."

"Not that kind of meeting, sir. Found this on the doorstep."

A gleam of silver arced towards the bed. Josiri let Anastacia's hand fall back onto the blankets and caught the pendant. A spread-winged owl, set in silver. His weary heart sank further. Beneath the gazebo, the last thing he'd wanted was to return to the bedside. Now all he wanted to do was stay. But maybe this was for the best.

"Josiri?" said Sidara. "What is it?"

"I have to go out again. I'm sorry." He leaned over the bed and kissed Anastacia's brow. "I'll be back soon. Make sure you're still here."

"She will be, sah," said Kurkas. "The Raven comes for her, he'll have a fight on his hands."

There it was. The sorrow Sevaka had spoken of, hidden in the crow's feet about his eye. The old soldier who resented leaving friends on the battlefield.

"I'm sure he will."

Rising, Josiri kissed Sidara on the cheek and went to seek a different battlefield altogether.

Ten

Josiri bit back a frisson of uncertainty as slipped through the aged, iron gate. Local rumour insisted that the house beyond the trees was haunted – or worse yet, cursed. Believers pointed to a previous owner who'd embraced the Raven in the bloodiest way possible; to an inheritor who'd vanished without trace. Other stories, most of them dating back to the day Dregmeet's mists had swallowed Silvane House, concerned depravity beyond words. These weren't true, but served to keep the curious away from a mansion long since boarded up. And yet still Josiri felt the clutch of old ghosts as he walked the overgrown path to a front door set ajar for his arrival.

The hallway was warm, the proof of a fire crackling away somewhere deeper. In fact, Silvane House looked more lived in than he'd seen it in years. Portraits stood sentry over the silent hallway, their dust sheets – like those of the furniture many decades older than Josiri himself – banished out of sight and mind. There was even a modest bronze statuette on the entrance hall table – the pouncing likeness of a beast as much flame as flesh, its hound's maw wide anticipating the kill.

Picking up the statuette, Josiri turned it over in his hands, admiring the craftsman's work and the intricate sapphires gleaming beneath the brow.

"It's a zaifîr," said Apara, arriving in the hallway without otherwise making a sound. "The Ithna'jîm use the real thing as guardians at their sacred sites."

The answer spurred flagging memory. He'd known that. Too tired, that was the trouble. "And this?"

"A burial token. It binds a zaifir to the dead, to protect them in Otherworld."

Josiri shivered and set the statue down. "So you're stealing from tombs now?"

Apara smiled. "Only from those who do. How are you, Josiri?"

"I've had better days. But I saw your sister."

Stiffness crept into her expression. "Sevaka? She's well?"

Josiri nodded. "Troubled, but aren't we all? You should see for yourself."

"I'm not ready. Maybe next year."

He sighed. The polite refusal had become ritual, and harder to bear that night than on past occasions. "There's going to come a time when there won't be a next year."

Her smile faded.

"I take it she's already here?" Josiri asked.

Apara aside, only one other was present in the drawing room. She stood at the hearth as one unable to feel its warmth, arrayed in green silks and her hair bereft of chain or jewel. Like Josiri, she bore the travails of a long and difficult day in the set of her shoulders, but offered a polite nod of greeting all the same.

"Josiri," said Melanna Saranal.

"Melanna."

As ever, he offered a shallow nod, though such was insufficient greeting for an Empress. She turned from the fire, dark eyes taking his measure. "You're troubled."

"Ana's dying."

The words, studiously avoided at Stonecrest, hung heavy between them, demanding challenge, pleading to be dismissed. But there could be only truth in that room. That, they'd agreed from their first meeting, seeking a way forward after the slaughter at Govanna. A meeting as secret from Viktor – and from the Golden Court – as those that had followed. Better to leave to imagination what would befall if Tressia's populace discovered she was within the city's bounds two or three nights out of every year.

"Is there nothing to be done?" Compassion blossomed beneath Melanna's accented words.

"One thing, perhaps," he replied, striving vainly for even tenor. "But it carries risk."

"Perhaps Apara should bring her to Tregard?" Melanna suggested. Over by the window, curtains drawn to hide the boards nailed to its outer face, Apara nodded. "It might be the lunassera can do for her what physicians cannot."

"Would Ashana approve?" Too late, he remembered that Melanna and her goddess no longer spoke, though the Empress had never explained why.

A glimmer of sorrow touched Melanna's eyes. "The Goddess' hatred for Lumestra's daughters is not as priests proclaim."

Josiri swallowed, touched by the offer for all he couldn't accept. It wasn't simply that to do so would place them both at risk – though it surely would – but because moving Anastacia from Silvane House to the Imperial Palace could be done only via Otherworld's shifting paths. For all that Apara had long since mastered the route between the two, reducing a journey of days down to a matter of minutes, Josiri dared not risk laying Anastacia's febrile soul before the Raven.

"She'd not survive the journey, not as she is," he said. "I can't be away long. If she ... Well, I should be there."

"I understand, and I wish I'd no need to add to your burdens."

"The Eastshires?" The walk from Stonecrest had winnowed the likely from the impossible and left only one.

"I need you to control your people."

"I might say the same to you," he snapped. "Thirava's drowning the Eastshires in misery."

"He says he is provoked," Melanna replied, her eyes darkening.

"And you believe him?"

She stared down at the fire, gripping the mantelpiece as if she wished it to crack asunder beneath her fingers. "I've no doubt there are trouble-makers, within and without, who provide excuse."

"A man like Thirava needs no excuse." Josiri's thoughts lingered on Viktor's decree that the Eastshires be reclaimed, no matter the cost. "If you cannot bring him to heel, it will be war."

"I know," she replied, voice rigid. "I've no wish to see another. But Thirava is ambitious and impatient—"

"And *you* are Empress."

Melanna looked sharply up from the flames, her voice bitter. "I am an Empress with sprawling borders, and not enough spears to defend them should the Golden Court tire of seeing me upon the throne. And even if I did? A woman who rules at spearpoint is a tyrant, not an Empress, and a tyrant's power is brittle, with only the appearance of strength." She sighed, anger fading. "I have not come seeking permission to do what I know to be best, Lord Trelan, but to warn you."

Josiri rubbed his temples. Telling Melanna of Viktor's resolve might force her to contain Thirava, but would more likely provoke pre-emptive war. Her people would come first, as would his own, were positions reversed. Though Josiri had not always loved the Republic, he remained Tressian, with a Tressian's duties. More than that, it would be a dangerous step over a line already muddied. One thing to negotiate the return of prisoners, or settle details of the uncertain border without risking the pride and pomp of official discussion. Quite another to betray the closest of counsel. Viktor might understand the former, but he'd never forgive the latter.

"I'll see what can be done," he said at last. "But I can make no promises."

"Nor would I trust those offered." Melanna's lips softened to a smile. "It would be improper to place my faith in a heathen. Go home, Lord Trelan. Be with your love. These woes will keep until the year is reborn. Maybe longer, if we deserve it."

"Maybe."

Stepping closer to the fire, he placed a small, velvet-lined box in Melanna's hand.

Her eyes crowded with suspicion. "What is this?"

"A gift. For your daughter. Most of my mother's jewellery burned with Eskavord, but a few pieces remained at Stonecrest." He shrugged. "The man who took possession of my family's estate auctioned off most of that, but this survived. It seems he couldn't bear to part with it."

Melanna tipped back the lid and drew out the silver chain, with its sole, perfect pendant of sun and moon entwined. The heavenly sisters in accord long-lost. "It's beautiful. But why?"

"Because Midwintertide used to be a time for gifts," he said. "And for all that our nations are different, they are both sticklers for tradition, so why not revive this one above all? A new year is upon us. Enemies make the finest friends. If that can be true for us, maybe it can for our peoples."

"You're a strange man, Josiri Trelan. Even for a Tressian." Melanna wound the chain back into its box, and set it shut. "But I thank you, all the same. May Ashana watch over you, and those you love."

Altiris stared at the grimy, uneven wall, and wondered why he wasn't dead. Not that he was ungrateful, though he remained mindful that bad things seldom happened to the dead, while being alive offered an infinite range of potential horrors. Location was another concern. Hawkin – no novice at skulduggery – had taken few chances. Between blindfold and hessian sack, since removed, he'd seen nothing as she'd marched him through the streets. Worse, she'd twisted him this way and that at every junction, foiling attempts to map the route by strides alone. He could have been anywhere.

The cell offered up few clues. The ever-present sea-tang narrowed things down little – the cool, damp air that spoke to being underground even less. Tressia existed as much below ground as above, and the Dusk Wind carried the scent of the waves far inland.

No. *Where* mattered little more than *why*. *Escape* rendered both moot – though Altiris was far from confident such a feat lay within his grasp. The timber door was solid, his hands were bound tight behind his back and an unknown number of enemies waited beyond. But what was the alternative? Sit quietly and wait for rescue?

Southwealders didn't do such things, and Phoenixes less so. And it wasn't as though there'd be help coming. Even if Constans deigned to fetch help – which seemed unlikely, given the lad's cowardice – how would anyone know where to find him?

Hunching into a sitting position on the rusting metal bench, Altiris turned attention to his bindings. Hawkin's experience showed here too, in wrists bound back-to-back and so tightly that even straining fingers barely brushed the rough strands. But perhaps the strands could be worn away . . . ?

Offering up the rope to the bench's upright meant adopting a contorted half-sitting, half-lying position on the floor, one shoulder braced against the wall and the other jammed beneath the seat.

Footsteps beyond the door sent Altiris scrambling back to his feet before he'd made even a dozen awkward passes.

A bolt clacked back. The door creaked open.

Blue-green eyes glinted amusement. "Should I ask what you were doing?"

Hawkin, though dangerous enough, was a known quantity. This woman was not. A head shorter than he and barely more than a girl, and she terrified him.

Altiris forced bravado into his voice. "On balance, I'd rather you didn't."

She shook her head in amusement and crooked a slender finger. "Come."

"Why should I?"

"The alternative's staying in here." The smile faded. "And I'll only make you otherwise. Dignity's *so* important, don't you think?"

"That trick with the singing?" He struck what he hoped was a convincing glare. "I'm ready this time. It won't work."

She drew closer. "You can hear it? Most can't."

Altiris fought the urge to back away. Her eyes met his. Vision blurred beneath the ghostly, babbling chorus. The confines of the cell fell away into vivid blue-green. He drowned alongside, thoughts treacly and lungs aching.

He pinched his eyes shut. There was daylight in the darkness, and he clung to it. The song faded beyond a whisper. Thought came easier. Salt-tinged air flooded starved lungs. When he opened his eyes, he found her watching him, lips pursed in thought.

"Perhaps you might resist, at that," she said. "But I can still have you hauled outside. Dignity?"

He hesitated, aware he'd won a victory – perhaps even a substantial one – but not how to use it. "All right. In the name of dignity."

He followed her beyond the cell and up a steep flight of stairs. Conversation stilled in the room beyond. From beneath a boarded-up window, eyes glanced suspiciously from behind hands of pentassa cards and the pitiful pile of coins set as stake. Further along, a woman in a tattered naval coat leaned against cracked paintwork and folded her arms, her appraisal ending in a sneer. All were of the same cast as the ruffians from the warehouse. Men and women not to be crossed without a sword in hand and superior numbers at your back.

Only when the room was left behind in favour of another flight of stairs – this one edged by a banister long since fallen on hard times – did the buzz of conversation resume.

"Friendly bunch, aren't they?" asked Altiris.

"Here." The young woman opened a door. "And keep a civil tongue. I can hide your body where it'll never be found."

Altiris stepped into what had once been a well-to-do study, at least before a leaking roof had tarnished metal fittings and set wallpaper peeling. Curling papers crowded a filthy, warped desk. A cracked mirror faced empty bookshelves. At the room's far end, a man stood silhouetted before a blazing lantern, his features hidden deep in shadow.

"This is him?" asked the man.

"It is." The young woman stepped inside the room and closed the door. "I know he doesn't look like much, but he's persistent. Hawkin thinks we should kill him."

"I fancy she does."

Robbed of visual clues, Altiris focused on the man's voice. Ageless, with a city-dweller's languid accent. Wry. Confident. Gruff, also, but with a fuzzing burr that suggested he was speaking outside his normal register. All told, as worthless as a face he couldn't see.

"Who are you?" Altiris started forward. "What—?"

"Kasvin?"

The young woman grabbed Altiris' arm and dragged him back without obvious effort. Kasvin was stronger than she appeared.

"Forgive my manners." The man spread his hands in apology. "You'll understand I must maintain a degree of privacy. As for who I am? You can call me the Merrow."

Altiris frowned, recalling the name from the previous night. "So you're in charge?" He threw a disdainful look about the room. "I don't think much of your lair. It's a new low, even for the Crowmarket."

The man chuckled. "The Crowmarket is dead, as you well know. Though I confess we share some of the same concerns. As for the house? It's nothing. A meeting place."

"Meeting who?"

"Tonight? You. Tomorrow. Who can say? I've learned to accept what washes ashore."

"The river provides?" said Altiris sourly.

"Precisely. Tonight, it provided you." He shrugged, the pattern of lantern light shifting. "You were at Seacaller's, weren't you?"

"I don't—"

An upraised hand cut him off. "Don't waste my time with denials. Some puzzles only ever have a single answer. You *were* at Seacaller's. What did you see?"

"Folk groomed for exploitation," said Altiris. "Food for favours yet to come."

"Cynical." The Merrow shook his head. "I suppose that's to be expected. This city sours everyone, and those who wear the rose-brand sooner than most. Is it really too much to believe that we feed the hungry simply because they *are* hungry?"

That the Merrow knew he was a southwealder meant nothing. It was one of the first things anyone learned about him, whether Altiris wished them to or not. "Yes."

"Who'd feed them if we didn't? For all its faults, the Crowmarket strove to help those that greed left behind. Your master and his friends were quick enough to drive them into the sea, but they've done little to fill the void. The poorhouses are overwhelmed, and charity grows thin. For those hale enough to carry a sword, the army offers respite, but for the rest? What are they to do?"

"Lord Trelan is doing everything he can," said Altiris.

"Is he? When was the last time he walked Sothvane's streets? Can he hear the cries of starving children from behind Stonecrest's walls? Do its windows afford clear view of those shivering because their homes were demolished to site new fortifications?" The Merrow paused, a deep breath bringing passion under control. "I have lived in this city all my life, and even under the Council's worst excesses, it functioned. Everyone had a place, a body to whom they had recourse. The Crowmarket for the poor, the Council for the wealthy—"

"And southwealders?" growled Altiris. "What did we have?"

"You're right, of course. Privilege blinded me for the longest time. I'm not free of it. But that doesn't alter the fact that this city – this

Republic – is changing, and not for the better. Or do you suppose you were the only child of Exodus at Seacaller's last night?"

The Merrow stepped closer, then checked himself.

"There is a darkness growing in this city. It spreads from the Lord Protector, leaving those closest to him blind. Conscription. The Eastshires abandoned. The streets patrolled by automata, answerable only to a priestess in her alabaster tower."

Uncertainty only fed Altiris' swell of anger. "Watch your mouth!"

He hissed in pain as Kasvin dug her fingers into his upper arm.

"Josiri Trelan is a good man, as Malachi Reveque was a good man," said the Merrow. "But good men are easily deceived."

"But not you?" Even Altiris recognised his response lacked weight. Too many truths in among the lies. Or what he *hoped* were lies.

The Merrow tilted his head. "No. Not on either count. When you wore shackles, is this the future you hoped for? Or did you want something better? There is wealth enough in the Republic, but none of it goes where it should." His voice quickened, passion returning. "*This* is what we seek to address. Join us. Help us do for others what was not done for you. I know you're loyal to Josiri Trelan. I'll ask nothing that would set you against him."

The grifter's promise. The first path along a slippery road. Altiris' wavering resolve hardened to crystal. For all the Merrow's protestations of righteous cause, he was exactly as bad as the Crowmarket. "And if I don't? You'll have Kasvin 'convince' me, as she did Hawkin?"

"Hawkin Darrow is earning redemption," snapped the Merrow. "As are we all."

A crash of breaking glass sounded downstairs. Shouts followed. Close behind, a scream split the air.

The Merrow's head jerked towards the door. "What—?"

The door burst open, a merrowkin with a naked blade and a bloody brow framed against the landing. "They've found us! Go!"

The Merrow nodded. "Kasvin?"

Shoving Altiris towards the merrowkin, she ripped open mouldered drapes. The balcony door swung open onto a pitch black, snow-strewn night. "The streets are clear."

The Merrow started for the balcony.

"No!" Altiris stamped on the newcomer's instep. The man howled and staggered away. Altiris lowered a shoulder and barged him back through the door. Hands still bound, he ran for the balcony and the fleeing Merrow.

Kasvin's forearm took him across the throat.

A chair shattering to spars beneath Altiris' back. Crushed hands throbbing, he fought to rise. Kasvin glared down, her vicious hiss more serpentine than human. Her hands hooked, black fingernails like claws.

"Leave him!" shouted the Merrow.

Black skirts swirled, and Kasvin was gone. By the time Altiris regained his footing, so had the Merrow. The first snows drifted through the drapes and melted into the ruined carpet.

A wet gurgle sounded from the doorway, a *thump* close behind.

Altiris spun about. Constans stood above the erstwhile captor's body, a bloody dagger in his hand, and his lips twisted in that familiar, self-satisfied smile. Altiris blinked in surprise.

"You might say 'thank you'." Stepping forward, Constans slit Altiris' bonds. "This *is* a rescue."

Steel chimed downstairs. A ragged bellow bled to a scream.

Altiris winced as renewed circulation made prickly displeasure known. "You fetched the constabulary?"

"Better."

Then who? If there was anyone less likely to call upon Sidara than Altiris himself it was her brother. And the Stonecrest Phoenixes wouldn't have followed the manor's outcast son on his word alone.

When Altiris reached the top of the stairs, he had his answer.

Bodies lay strewn across the hallway, some slumped and moaning, clutching at mangled limbs. Most were unmoving, with the vacant, skyward stare of folk fled to the Raven's welcome. Three remained standing. Two merrowkin – one bloody and both bearing the rictuses of doomed men – and Captain Tzila, her twin sabres in mirrored grasp, their points downward.

With a ragged cry, the merrowkin nearest the stairs flung himself forward, sword arcing down at Tzila's shoulder in a two-handed grip. The other lunged in the same moment, a dagger spearing at her spine.

Even as Altiris opened his mouth to offer warning, Tzila spun her bloody swords. The black silk of cloak and bases awhirl, she stepped aside – each footfall, each flex of limb graceful and possessed of unflagging purpose. Her left-hand sabre severed the swordsman's arm at the wrist, the thump of the falling hand lost beneath the merrowkin's agonised scream. The right struck the dagger aside and loosed a bloody riposte that left his comrade clutching a torn face. Tzila turned a graceful gyre, and steel flashed to silence both.

Then, her arms again at her sides and her sabres angled down, she turned towards the stairs, her posture that of a mummer awaiting applause.

Awestruck, Altiris descended the stairs. Four dead. Three moaning their pain. Not a mark on Tzila in exchange. The blood spattered on breastplate and vambrace was most assuredly not her own.

"Are any of these your work?" he asked Constans.

A shrug. "Just the one back there. I try to stay out of her way."

No wonder. Altiris turned his attention to the motionless Tzila. He'd never seen her fight – never heard of anyone who had. Few who did walked away, it seemed. "Thank you."

She tilted her head to one side and, stiff-armed, levelled a sabre at a door hanging off its hinges and the cold night beyond. Unspoken though it was, the order was clear.

Eleven

Josiri started awake, scattering blankets to the floor. Inconstant nightmare bled away as reluctant fingers loosed their grip on the chaise's backrest. Bleary eyes sought sense of the darkness, urgent with the growing fear of something amiss.

Fumbling behind, he opened the drapes a crack. Moonlight granted shape to furnishings and the huddled figure on the bed.

A dream. Just a dream.

But as sleep's veil peeled away and turgid thought gathered to something approaching function, Josiri looked again at the bed, whose shape seemed somehow amiss.

"Ana?"

He rose unsteadily. The huddled figure was not a huddled figure at all, but blankets cast hastily aside.

At once, he recalled what had startled him awake, the *thud* of falling body now impossible to forget. Heart in his mouth, Josiri hurried about the foot of the bed.

Crunch.

Something gave under his heel. Hard, but yielding. He stared down at a dusty white smear speckled with smooth, irregular flakes. A piece of fired porcelain, crushed to powder. Daylight seethed from the remains, and faded to nothing.

The floor between the bedside and the suite's bathroom was strewn with such fragments. Most were no larger than a shilling, but over by the bedside table, moonlight gleamed on what was unmistakeable as the thumb and forefinger of a right hand.

Overcome by dizziness and with a sick, sour ache at the pit of his stomach, Josiri grabbed at the footrest.

Only then did he hear it: a low, breathy sound somewhere between a gasp and a sob. It stuttered and faded, muffled by the intervening door and the shrill buzz of Josiri's tumultuous thoughts. Earlier, he'd have given anything to see Anastacia crook a finger or twitch a hand. That she was moving about would have occasioned joy, but for the proof that she'd left so much of herself behind.

A stumbling swallow did nothing to clear a parched mouth. "Ana?"

A heavy, scuffed scrape sounded beyond the door. The sob faded.

Josiri edged closer, careful of his footing. Trembling fingers found the handle. The latch turned.

An icy draught from the open window stole his breath. The bathroom's curtains snapped and tugged at their mountings as if fleeing the darkness. Seized of sudden, plunging dread that Anastacia had given herself to both the night and the Raven, he ran to the window. Three storeys below the sill, the pristine snow remained unbroken in the moonlight.

Stepping back, he calmed the curtains and set the window closed.

"Josiri?"

He froze, the husky, trembling voice unfamiliar. Eyes strained as they readjusted to gloom. At the bathroom's far end, a blanket-shrouded figure hunched over the sink, head level with the mirror. Porcelain fragments lay strewn across the tiles.

"I'm here." He drew closer, more careful than ever.

For all that it had been a woman's voice, it hadn't *sounded* like Anastacia. It lacked the singsong resonance that had become so familiar. And the blanket ... Anastacia had never been modest, treasuring clothes for what they enhanced, and not caring what they concealed.

"Ana ... What's happened to you?" He swallowed. "How can I help?"

A curved piece of porcelain slipped from beneath the blanket's folds and shattered on tiles. This time, enough remained whole that Josiri saw it was not solid chunk, but thin, concave.

Dusty hands drew back the blanket's folds, revealing a stranger's face. Or not quite. Beneath the chalky dust and smeared blood, there were signs of the Anastacia he'd known before Viktor had sealed her in clay.

The button nose and high cheekbones; thin lips that made every smile fleeting and every frown a curse. Thick, dark stubble bristled at her scalp. Tears glistened on cold-stung cheeks. And her eyes ... no longer the swirling black of a trammelled spirit, but the white sclera and green irises of an ephemeral woman, bright and uncertain.

She reached for him with trembling hand, the last porcelain cracking and slipping away from her fingers. The low, halting sob again fluttered from parted lips, though now Josiri realised she cried not with sorrow, but disbelief.

"What's happened?" she breathed. "Something wonderful."

Her knees buckled, and she clung to him for support.

Heart fit to burst, Josiri clasped Anastacia's head to his chest, and held her tight until dawn.

Lunandas, 28th Day of Wanetithe

Midwintertide

From the ashen threads of the old year,
Lumestra wove the new, binding it with such light
and splendour as to ensure that the Dark would
hide its jealous face until winter returned.
And ever after, Midwintertide was a time of hope,
not despair, for all knew that where the Goddess had
wrought one miracle, others could follow.

from the sermons of Konor Belenzo

Twelve

Altiris lingered before the mirror, as ever uncertain of a reflection belonging to someone else. He understood what the Phoenix uniform asked of him – even if he'd made a mixed job of complying of late. The softer, closer cloth of the well-to-do was different.

Knuckles rapped softly on wood. Without leaving opportunity for response, the door eased open. Sidara's black Drazina uniform was – for once – in abeyance in favour of a rich velvet gown the same sparkling blue as her eyes.

"Are you coming down?"

Altiris tugged at his cravat. "When this is sitting straight, yes."

She shook her head. "You look fine."

Easy for her to say. This was her world, not his. Take away the uniform, and Sidara was still the Lady Reveque. With the Phoenix gone, what was he? A southwealder in a costume.

On the other hand, Sidara didn't go in for spared feelings. Maybe it didn't matter if it was a costume, so long as he wore it well.

"I'm surprised you're not in the Panopticon."

"Josiri would never forgive me if I missed today." Blue eyes shimmered gold. "Besides, I see plenty from here. I understand *you* had another eventful night."

He tensed at the reminder of black and red in the tally of deeds. Black, for information gathered. The woman with the blue-green eyes had a name. Kasvin. Add to that a description of the Merrow – though this was so nondescript as to be almost worthless – and confirmation that the Crowmarket was not resurgent. Last of the positives was that a constabulary raid had recovered stolen possessions from the Sothvane warehouse, acknowledged by a solemn letter bearing Lord Droshna's seal, delivered to Stonecrest before dawn.

But still the red hung heavier. He'd been captured. Worse, he'd endangered Constans. And then there was the matter of Hawkin Darrow. There'd been no way of avoiding her mention this time, which would only lead to questions about why he'd said nothing before.

"If I agree to come downstairs, do I avoid the lecture?" he asked.

"Strictly one lecture a week." She glided into the room, perfect posture softening. Lady Reveque slipped from her shoulders until she was simply Sidara. "I might have been a little brusque. I'm not at my best when tired, you know that."

"I think that may have been my point."

Narrowing eyes to slits, she punched him lightly on the arm. "It's not kind to interrupt an apology. I don't know why I bother." But the smile broadened.

Altiris returned it with one of his own, the unfamiliar suit less of a burden. "Nor me."

"Then we agree on *some*thing," she replied, mock-archly. "But about last night—"

"You promised no lectures."

"Hush." Sidara set a finger to his lips. "I'm glad you're still in one piece, that's all."

"Am I? My pride's seen better days."

"An acceptable casualty. Not everyone in my brother's orbit escapes so lightly."

Constans. Who'd displayed magic of his own, of a sort darker than his sister's. Sidara surely didn't know, and should be told ... but perhaps not at that moment, where it would only sour things. Another lie of omission. "He rescued me."

She scowled. "I know. He won't shut up about it."

"He's here?"

"I'm as surprised as you are. In the kitchens, of course. Scavenging from plates meant for others. He gets taller, but he doesn't get older – not in any way that counts." She straightened, Lady Reveque once more. She crooked an elbow for him to take. "Are you coming down, or not? If only to save me from Josiri's guests?"

"Leave you alone with those ruffians? Never."

In the event, no ruffians were present amid the lanterns and decorations of Stonecrest's hallway. Nor were there any servants, who'd still be labouring in the kitchens – although they, like the hearthguard, would be well compensated for their efforts, and soon released to their own celebrations. Another of Lord Trelan's foibles. Stonecrest's worthies would be left to their own devices from the stroke of one until the next morning.

The chime of the brass doorbell drowned the murmur of conversation from the drawing room. Reluctantly disentangling himself from Sidara, Altiris slipped back into duties scarcely set aside, and slipped the bolt. Izack stood on the porch, a cloak cast rakishly back from the shoulders to reveal an immaculate hunter's green Essamere uniform beneath, rather than the blue of the regular army. He, at least, had chosen to be himself.

He stepped inside without invitation, and delivered a weighty clap to Altiris' back. "Well, well, well. If it isn't the hero of the hour. Eventful night?"

Altiris glanced over his shoulder for rescue, but Sidara had gone. "I've had quieter."

"Dregmeet may be drowned, but the dregs will always be with us. Only good thing about conscription is that we get to sift the mire." Izack shrugged off his cloak and set it on a crowded hat stand fashioned in the likeness of a gnarled tree. "Reckon I could manage a captaincy, were you interested."

Altiris blinked. Army captaincies went to the sons and daughters of the nobility – those schooled in war by the knightly chapterhouses. For all that he recognised Izack's offer as being born of the army's hard times at least as much as his own worthiness, he swelled with pride. Him, a southwealder. A proper soldier. A proper *officer*.

"Truly?"

"I don't waste time being a tease," Izack replied. "I won't pretend it won't mean some hard lessons, mind. Josiri's a good man, bless him, but he's no concept of soldierly discipline – you just have to see the way he dresses to see that. But I've confidence you'll learn."

"Th-thank you," Altiris stuttered.

Izack hooked a lopsided grin. "That a 'yes'?"

Altiris hesitated. Loyalty to Lord Trelan was part of it, but not the whole. Mistakes made in Tressia's backstreets were one thing; those committed on the battlefield were tallied in soldiers slain and battles lost.

He wasn't ready.

To his surprise, no shame accompanied the silent confession. Maybe, just maybe, he'd learned more the previous night than he'd first thought.

Aware that Izack was still waiting for an answer, Altiris stiffened himself to reply. "I—"

But Izack's attention was elsewhere.

Altiris followed his gaze across the hall to a petite woman in a clinging, bare-shouldered red dress, a white wig worn loose across her shoulders. Mischievous green eyes glinted in an ageless, beautiful face – one more expressive than it had any right to be, and flushed with colour lacking only a day prior. The Anastacia of before had been intriguing, even beguiling. Now, she was little short of stunning, and impossible to imagine any other way.

Izack's throat bobbed, voice lost in the gulf between sight and acceptance. A feeling Altiris understood only too well. Even forewarned by Kurkas, he'd stared too. The one solace of his fumbling about in Sothvane was that he'd not witnessed the decline presaging the miracle. He could only imagine what Lord Trelan had endured.

"Close your mouth, Lord Marshal." Anastacia sipped from her glass and fixed the luckless Izack with an impish stare. Strange to see the emotion in her voice mirrored in her expression. A tune once played on the edge of hearing now loud enough to shake the roof tiles. "It's not polite."

"I . . ." Izack blinked and rallied magnificently. "D'you mind excusing me? I need to throttle his lordship. Never fear, I'll be humane."

Altiris frowned, the pieces coming together. "He didn't tell you?"

"Bloody didn't. I knew you'd been ill, lady, and that you'd recovered. Even said a bloody prayer, didn't I? Me! Well, it was more a threat than a prayer, but what's the difference when no one's listening?" He shook his head. "Nothing about . . . this."

Anastacia grinned. "Drool if you must, so long as you do so discreetly."

"Generous of you, but I don't want to set a poor example for the lad."

"I'm sure his mind's on higher things. As would yours be, if you had one."

Lord Trelan appeared in the drawing room doorway and cleared his throat. "Ana, please don't provoke Izack."

Turning a pirouette of swirling skirts, she slid a hand about his waist and adopted sullen expression. "But he's so *very* provocative."

"I think you mean easily provoked."

"I know what I meant."

Rising on tiptoes, she kissed him on the lips and withdrew to the drawing room. Lord Trelan shook his head to disguise a blush of pleasure, and beckoned for Altiris and Izack to follow.

As with Midwintertides past, it was a modest gathering. Her glass refilled, Anastacia stood beside the mantlepiece, deep in conversation with Sidara and High Proctor Elzar Ilnarov – who was for once wearing his golden robes. Constans, perhaps banished from the kitchens, stood close to the battered old grandfather clock, and about as far from the other guests as could be managed. The ladies Orova had been guests the previous year, the thane of Indrigsval the year before that, but no others – within Tressia or without – rated invitation. Ironic, that so many who'd once disdained Lord Trelan would have paid dearly for a seat at his table.

No one expected to see the Lord Protector. Habits held long were hard broken.

"Lieutenant," said Elzar. "May Lumestra bring you wisdom in the coming year."

Altiris accepted a proffered glass with only a frisson of discomfort. For all his rank, Elzar's easy manner encouraged familiarity – partly because he looked no more at home in his robes of state than Altiris felt in cravat and waistcoat. "I'll take anything she offers."

Elzar grinned. "You see? It begins already."

The rich, bitter wine was a distant cousin to anything served in the Ragged Wayfarer – better even than the libations that flowed like rivers at Konor Zarn's infamous parties. Stonecrest's cellars ran deep.

"Josiri mentioned your foray into Sothvane," Elzar went on. "I'd no idea conditions were so bad. Poverty is tenacious, but there's always more that can be done."

Altiris mumbled noncommittal reply. Beneath the bright lights and decorations of Stonecrest, with the waft of fine food heavy on the air, it was impossible not to hear how Elzar had spoken of Sothvane as a world apart. Not quite the othering once inflicted on the Southshires, but near enough to make Altiris feel all the more a fraud.

Maybe for all the Merrow's criminal bent – for all his misplaced loathing of Sidara and the Lord Protector – he wasn't wrong about everything.

The whirr and click of the grandfather clock gave way to a peal of tinny chimes. Kurkas emerged from the dining room – his steward's array no less dishevelled than on any other day – and raised his voice.

"Ladies and gentlemen, dinner is served."

The dining room drapes were closed, the outer world banished beyond rich weave. The candlelit table creaked beneath the weight of serving dishes and platters. Cold meats and roasted, fowl and haunch. Potatoes piled high beside the crisp batter of Issamar flatcakes and sour chutneys, pickled fish and a small garden's worth of vegetables. There was even a tureen of spiced jakiri – a dish Izack had discovered a taste for while stationed at humbled Ahrad. Bottles of red wine clustered about the centre of the table; white cooled in the snow beyond the sash window. A regiment of cakes and sweet pastries waited in tight formation off to one side.

All told, enough food to feed two-score souls, let alone the mere eight gathered in the dining room. And there'd be more in the kitchens and the servants' quarters and the barracks. No one at Stonecrest went hungry at Midwintertide.

Lord Trelan reached the head of the table. His mouth creased sheepishly. "I may have overdone things."

He overdid things every year. He considered it important to do so – to thank the living for their service, even as they toasted the dead. But this year was more lavish than most, and had grown so at the last moment with cooks roused long before first light. Little doubt as to why, not with Anastacia standing at his side. Before her porcelain days, she'd earned quite the reputation for indulgence – a pleasure stripped away by the onset of clay. With sensation restored? Well, Altiris understood his master's overreaction.

Altiris took his place at the table. He, Sidara and Constans along one edge. Izack, Elzar and an empty chair along the other, and Anastacia facing Lord Trelan across the mountainous vista of food.

"If that's all, I'll be off," said Kurkas. "If you need me, I'll be in the kitchens."

Lord Trelan shook his head. "Sit, Vladama. You belong here."

"You shouldn't drink so much, sah." Kurkas scratched beneath his eyepatch. "Sours your judgement something rotten."

Slipping behind, Anastacia set gloved hands on his shoulders and her lips to his ear. "Sit, Vladama, or I'll break both your legs. Don't want to upset the guests, do we?"

Elzar shook his head in dismay. Constans grinned. Kurkas sank into the empty chair with palpable air of wounded dignity. "You win, plant pot."

She reclaimed her glass from the table, swayed gently, and took a sip. "Of course I do."

Lord Trelan cleared his throat. "Now that's attended to—"

The doorbell chimed.

"I'll go."

Relief creasing his worn face, Kurkas clambered to his feet, only to be halted halfway by Anastacia's hand on his shoulder. She seemed not to notice, intent instead on draining her glass to its dregs.

Lord Trelan set his own – barely touched – glass aside. "I can answer my own door, just this once."

Josiri checked the scabbarded sword was in its habitual hiding place in the hat stand before reaching for the door. Midwintertide or not, it didn't pay to be careless. Yet the creak of the door revealed neither a Hadari assassin, nor a tattered scoundrel, but a brooding shape in simple black cloth. The lack of escort was not unexpected. Reputation was a shield all its own.

"Viktor?"

A scowl tugged at a scarred cheek. An outward manifestation of inner awkwardness, and ever a herald to confession. "I find my thoughts snared in the living and the dead, and would prefer not to confront them alone. Does your invitation stand?"

Josiri stepped aside. There was ever a certain joy beholding Viktor in discomfort. His heart opened so rarely as to occasion creaking of the hinges. "There's enough to feed half the palace."

Viktor made no attempt to cross the threshold. "That's not what I meant."

Their argument over Sidara's fate? That wasn't yet settled, and it was typical of Viktor – and infuriating besides – to suggest regret without actual apology. But quarrels could come later. "You're always welcome."

The scowl blurred. At last, Viktor crossed into the house and thence to the dining room. His reserve wilted only a little in the face of Sidara's embrace.

"I'm glad you're here, Uncle." She paused. "Or should that be 'Lord Protector'?"

"I left the Lord Protector at the palace. He's a grim sort, and not to be trusted in polite company. 'Viktor' will suffice until I'm his prisoner once more."

Izack, who'd not only purloined a bottle of brandy in Josiri's brief absence, but also lowered its level by considerable degree, thumped the table in approval. "Too bloody right!"

Viktor made his way around the table, offering greeting with a clasp of hands and, in Kurkas' case, an embrace that left the other looking every bit as discomfited as Viktor himself had at the door.

"Are you well, old friend?"

"Can't complain, sah. It's been a while."

"The price of responsibility, as well you know."

"Not me, sah. Just a simple steward, tending my betters."

Viktor moved on to Anastacia, who held out a gloved hand for him to kiss. "When the herald brought word, I hardly dared believe. Flesh from clay, as beneath First Dawn. A midwinter miracle, when they are needed most."

The curl of her lip might have been precursor to sneer or smile. "Is Lord Droshna moved to poetry?"

"Lord Droshna is grateful that at least one of his past mistakes is unmade, even if he's bemused as to the means."

She withdrew her hand and tilted her head. "I've no answers for you, Viktor. My mother always delighted in mystery. She'd be pleased that to have birthed another, even in death."

Josiri heard fragility beneath the bravado. She'd offered him no deeper explanation. Awash in relief, he'd forsworn deeper enquiry. Truth was, it wasn't so simple as Anastacia having been restored to her old self. The spirit he'd first known had been as immune to physical harm as to liquor's embrace. Just as the fuzziness of her speech hinted at wits on the road to intoxication, her gloves and painstakingly applied makeup concealed scores of scabs and scratches earned in the sloughing of porcelain skin. A spirit would not have been afflicted thus, nor a divine serathi, who bled golden light, not mortal ichor. But she'd insisted she was well, and stridently dismissed trifles of infirmity.

Concerns remained, and Josiri was determined to see them aired. But they, like Viktor's designs for Sidara, would wait.

With a final solemn bow to Anastacia, Viktor took a place hurriedly set for him. Elzar rose with the stiffness of advancing years, cleared his throat and waited for Josiri to find his own chair.

"We come to the close of the seasons." The words, more strident than was Elzar's custom, echoed in the gloom beyond the candleflames and set hairs bristling on the back of Josiri's neck. "Lumestra commands us to greet the future unafraid, and unburdened by the past. To treasure those we hold dear, but not to forget those who came before. Speak their names, while the mists draw nigh and Otherworld comes close to this world bereft of sun. Let the dead live again in this brief Dark, that we may move forward when dawn rises."

Izack raised his glass in toast, levity for once absent. "Aharan Izack. Finest brother a man could want. Even if he couldn't tell one end of a sword from the other."

He glanced at Constans. The boy shook his head and stared down at the table.

Sidara frowned, though Constans was hardly alone in silence. Elzar sat apart from remembrance, as priests always did. And Anastacia invariably disdained the ritual as "ephemeral nonsense".

Sidara's expression cleared as she raised her own glass. "Malachi and Lilyana Reveque, who strove always for others and never for themselves."

"Ezhan Czaron." Altiris' glass joined the growing circle, tribute to a long-dead father.

Kurkas hesitated, as he did every year. Then he dribbled more brandy into his glass, and hoisted it high ... as he did every year. "Sedrin Costra, you reckless, charming bastard." He raised his voice and stared up at the ceiling, daring a response from beyond the mists. "And Revekah Halvor? You still owe me for a bloody eye."

Laughter rippled along the table. Josiri smiled, lost in bittersweet memories. Kurkas wasn't the only man to have crossed swords with Revekah and come away the worse. She'd fought all her long life, against Thrakkian raiders, Council occupation and Kai Saran's Immortals. And at the end, faced with a battle she couldn't win, she'd gone defiant into flame.

He caught Viktor staring at him, brow furrowed in unspoken question, and nodded assent.

Viktor added his glass to the toast. "Calenne Trelan."

"Katya Trelan." Josiri raised his glass. "Though I dread what she'd say to see me now."

Of the nine gathered at the table, three had fought *against* his mother during the Southshires' doomed secession; two more were heirs of a family whose vote had loosed the war. Altiris, at least, Katya would have approved of. Maybe even Elzar, for her quarrels with the Council had never encompassed the church. As for Anastacia? Who was to say?

"As the Old Year dies, and the New draws in ... " Elzar tailed off as Anastacia rose, trembling glass extended and voice wracked with rare uncertainty.

"To my mother. To my sisters. To Zorya." The words spilled as water through a millrace, gathering speed as confidence returned to a voice that seldom possessed anything else. "To brief, brilliant souls who strive for more in moments than those who squander eternity."

She scowled, and looked as though she were about to say more. Then she sat abruptly, and added her glass to the circle.

Elzar let silence reign a moment, then nodded. "As the Old Year dies, let us go forward into the New. In gladness and not in sorrow, safe in the promise that we will all walk together in the Light of Third Dawn."

"*In the Light of Third Dawn.*"

Glasses chimed, one against the other. Candles were blown out, lanterns roused and drapes drawn, the Dark of old banished from the room as Lumestra had once banished it from the world.

"And now that's done with, can we eat?" said Elzar. "I'm starving."

Anarchy descended. Settings were treated as mere suggestions, rather than shackles. Diners exchanged places as readily as plates. Jokes were broached, memories shared and stories told.

Izack, no mean trencherman, somehow found breath between forkfuls to extol Viktor's triumphs on the eastern border and then segued guilelessly into a far less flattering tale – one involving rich wine, a tender gut and a convalescence that stretched into the following night. Viktor brushed the first aside with habitual modesty, and glared sourly at the second, murmuring darkly – if ineffectually – about deliberate poisoning by a rival, and finally leavened discomfort with a self-effacing shrug.

As appetites failed before the table's impossible challenge, Anastacia, now noticeably slurred in speech and manner, spoke at length of golden streets, vibrant gardens and stained glass shining like gemstone. Goaded by Elzar, she even sang. Though Josiri understood none of the words, the lanterns seemed all the brighter while the notes lingered, and his heart lighter.

None listened more enraptured than Constans, who scribbled notes on a scrap of paper, and afterwards quizzed Anastacia on the form and meaning of the lyrics. But whatever power had moved her to sing had dispersed, and she sought to change the subject.

Unexpectedly, Viktor rescued her by launching into a recital of the *Heinrada's Lament*, which he claimed a Thrakkian deepwinter tradition. The guttural words held no more meaning for Josiri than had Anastacia's song, and were very certainly nowhere near as melodious. Viktor frequently claimed he'd no mind for music, and to hear him sing thus was a rare and unusual treat. His basso delivery sounded genuine enough, and Constans provided running translation – his proud expression for once bereft of slyness.

Unfortunately, by the time the bold Heinrada stood alone against the drakon who'd devoured his father, Kurkas chimed in with a translation of his own, one tending less towards epic poetry and the valour of heroes, and more towards a mummer's farce – complete with directions from the god Astor that Heinrada should demoralise the foe through a display of bared buttocks. Mirth redoubled when Viktor unexpectedly joined Kurkas in sabotaging his own performance, matching the steward's falsettoed parody so precisely – in meter, if not pitch – as to reveal that this wasn't the first time they'd played such a game.

Constans bristled at Kurkas' levity but, at Altiris' suggestion, the matter was settled by a duel, fought at arm's length across the table with chicken bones for swords, and eagerly cheered on in all quarters. When it was done – and Constans the winner – toasts were offered to victor and vanquished, to old friends and new, to the absent and the estranged. Having drunk to the valour of Essamere, it seemed only fair to do the same for Lancras, Fellnore and vanished Prydonis; to the dwindled bloodlines of Reveque, Trelan and Akadra.

Bottles ebbed, and wits drifted on seas of wine and brandy. The company retired to the drawing room, and conversation grew subdued, for all that it remained companionable. There, as at table, Sidara and Altiris were rarely apart, for all that they seldom came into actual contact. Still, the two remained a study in contrasts, Sidara effortlessly confident and Altiris wary.

Afternoon bled steadily towards evening, and a pentassa deck was fetched in preparation for games of jando. All were destined to lose to the cardsharp who styled himself high proctor. Even when Josiri marshalled six players against him – Altiris and Sidara chose instead to rabble-rouse from the comfort of a hearthside chaise – Elzar took every hand, and for all of Izack's accusations of skulduggery and false dealing, was never once caught in the act. It helped, of course, that Elzar – like Constans – had scarcely touched a drop all afternoon.

And then, too soon, the time of parting arrived, heralded by carriages on the gravel driveway, and reinforced by the arrival of a polite young officer of the 1st. As guests both unsteady and sober made farewells, Josiri sought words fit for the burden on his heart. Family was more than blood, and to have so much of it so close and complete – if only for a few hours – was a rare and wonderful gift. He found none and, when Viktor requested leave to speak, gladly assented.

Viktor nodded, steady and clear-eyed despite drink taken – which, now Josiri thought on it, had not been to any great quantity, though the lack had been artfully concealed.

"I should have done this long ago." He looked from one to the next, ending with Josiri. "I know what folk say of me. That I'm distant, even heartless. Some of you have said worse, and I've certainly deserved it. But though my words may be lacking, never doubt my affection. You are my friends, and more than my friends, and dearer to me than life itself. Whatever gods listen or care, I gladly thank for today, and those days that led us here. Have you anything to add, brother?"

There it was. Proof that despite the quarrels behind and yet to come, they were more alike than not. A peculiar friendship, but shouldn't the unusual be treasured all the more?

"Not a word." Josiri clasped Viktor's hand and embraced him. "Safe travels."

Thirteen

Tarvallion blazed with light, the bonfires at the forest's edge joined by lanterns welcoming the coming year and ghostfires warding off the vengeance of the past. And above them all, the full moon, soft silver amid the stars. From her vantage in Brackenpike's unruly terrace garden, Rosa fancied almost to see the city as it had once been, the towers of old reflected in the clash of lights – a promise of what might one day be again. History was ever a cycle. It walked old paths unless guided anew.

"So this is where you're hiding?" Sevaka let the outer door fall closed and joined her beneath the ivy bower. A heavy black shawl atop cream and silver gown was her one concession to the night's chill. "The ceremony at the grove dragged on longer than I expected."

"Did everyone behave?"

"More or less. With rumours flying, there's little appetite for religious quarrels. The cloudless night helped." Teeth glinted in the dark. "It's a brave soul who threatens a Lunastran with the moon looming large."

"It won't last."

"I know." Sevaka sighed. "When war comes, too many Lumestrans will forget hardships and triumphs shared. They'll see only a people who don't worship as they do – worse, who revere the same goddess as the shadowthorns. But today, at least, they stood together in celebration. Maybe they'll remember that."

"They'll remember it because you'll make them."

"That's me. Sevaka the Tyrant. Everyone trembles at my name."

Rosa grunted. It was precisely *because* no one feared Sevaka that she was so effective a governor. Fear was the vexed harvest of the unknown, and Sevaka left no uncertain ground in which such crops could take root. Those who came to her with grievance or need were assured of fair hearing; those who transgressed the law were equally certain to face justice. Empathy and retribution, wielded as shield and sword. For all that Sevaka had so often been derided as weak – not least by herself – there was steel in her soul. No one in Tarvallion doubted it.

"When were you going to tell me that you're leaving?" asked Sevaka.

"After supper. I didn't want to sour the day." The wind shifted, bringing with it bitter cold and the sweet, tantalising scent of Starik Wood. "How did you know?"

"Because you told me, just now. But you've been distant since I returned. I know the signs." She drew the shawl closer and sat down on the stone bench, back to the house and eyes on the moon. "It's the Eastshires, isn't it?"

"Do I have no secrets at all?"

A frown flitted across Sevaka's face. "That's not for me to say."

Her hurt was plain for all it went unspoken, and all the worse because Rosa had no words to ease it. "Our people are suffering, and I've been playing at sculptress. I can't be that woman any longer. Folk are gathering at Morten's Rock. They mean to fight Thirava."

"Soldiers?"

"Men and women who won't stand by any longer."

"Do you rate their chances?"

"Against the stag of Redsigor, and the owl of Rhaled flying close behind?" Bleak anger flared at the memory of Melanna Saranal, the woman who'd blighted Rosa's life for so long. The prospect, however unlikely, of catching her within sword's reach was never less than grim delight. "But they're our people too. I'm Essamere, or at least I was. A shield first and a sword second. If I can make a difference, I belong there."

Sevaka sat in silence for a time, lips pinched in thought. "Perhaps we both do."

"You don't mean that."

She sprang to her feet, cheeks taut with the first flash of anger. "Don't I?"

"You're needed here. You know that."

"And if I say you're needed here also, is that not enough?"

"By you. By no one else."

"Is. That. Not. Enough?" Sevaka turned away, the storm of her anger passing as swiftly as it had come. "I'm sorry. I know that's not fair."

Rosa's doubts, never far from the surface, urged her to recant. She'd never been at home on the battlefield of the heart, where victories were fleeting, and so often indistinguishable from defeat. She slid her arms about Sevaka's waist and held her close.

"It should be enough," she said. "I'm a fool that it isn't. I wish I could live a lifetime here with you, and let the world pass by. But I can't. I'd not be myself, and if I'm not myself, then what are we but a dream?"

"The last time I let you go off without me, you almost died," murmured Sevaka.

"I might say the same of you." Except there was no almost about it. Sevaka had been two days cold in the ground before the Raven had breathed her back to life.

"At least you know what became of me after Vrasdavora. A year, and still I know almost nothing of what happened at Darkmere."

Jumbled, incomplete memories swirled through Rosa's thoughts. Stifling. Infuriating. "There's nothing to tell. Nothing I *can* tell. There are flashes, faces. All else is swallowed by black fog, and the memory of something . . . " She pulled away, a hand rubbing unbidden at the long-healed scar beneath her shirt. "When I reach out, it pulls further away. It's all I can do not to scream."

She broke off, overcome by the sense of a precipice, hungry for the piece of her that had escaped. Skin prickling with cold sweat, she swallowed to soothe a parched mouth and urged her racing heart to slowness. Little by little, it ebbed, terror alongside. She opened her eyes to find Sevaka regarding her with worry.

"Why didn't you tell me before?"

"It's not your concern."

Sevaka snorted. "I won't even dignify that with a response." Warm fingers enfolded Rosa's and gripped them tight. "Zephan was there. Can't he fill in the gaps?"

She hesitated, but with the truth half in the open, what harm in speaking of the rest? "Not enough. That I was delirious with the arrow's strike, and stumbled away just as the Hadari launched their second attack."

"I see." Sevaka's lip twisted. "Is that why you won't speak to Viktor? Because you're worried you fled? That you failed him? Rosa . . . You can't make amends by pursuing a hopeless cause."

"I won't speak to Viktor because *he's* the reason I can't remember!" Rosa snapped, the words loose before good sense counselled against.

Sevaka stepped back, frown blossoming. "How can you know that?"

How to explain the lump in her heart? Blazing hot and cold as ice. "I *know*."

"What reason could he possibly have for doing such a thing to you?"

"How can I answer that when I can't remember?" She scowled, the poor argument already unravelling, contradicted by her own words. "Maybe he merely wanted me to forget. If so, he has everything he sought."

Sevaka's eyes widened, disbelief crowding out concern. "Why haven't you said anything?"

"If you could see your expression you wouldn't have to ask," Rosa said bitterly. "My own wife doesn't believe me. Why should anyone else? I don't know I believe it myself, some days."

That wasn't true, of course. It was simply that most days she tried to *convince* herself it wasn't true.

"I know what it sounds like," she went on, softly. "I owe Viktor my life and my sanity, so how can I think this of him? Maybe I *am* deluded. Maybe I'm even envious of what he's achieved. But for him, the Republic would all be Redsigor. But if I'm wrong, I can't make peace with it, not if I take a chisel to a thousand dreadful statues. If I'm right, I can't *prove* it, much less explain why it was done. But what's happening to the east? *That*, I can do something about, even if it's almost nothing."

"And if I forbid it?" asked Sevaka. "If I summon up constables and have you confined?"

"If you love me at all, you won't," said Rosa.

"That's a cheap card to play."

Rosa flinched. "Or the very dearest."

Sevaka threw up her hands. "You almost *died*, Rosa. I know the scars that leaves better than anyone."

A shadow passed over her eyes. For a full month after her Raven-sent resurrection, Sevaka had woken screaming in the middle of every night, shying from spirits only she could see, babbling about wounds she no longer bore. She'd been pale as ash the day of her investiture as governor. Those night terrors had been intermittent in the years since, but still there were occasions where Rosa woke from sleep to find Sevaka sitting in the darkness, eyes unseeing and the names of people she'd never met spilling from shuddering lips. Even when the Raven let you go, he left his mark.

Rosa dipped her head, haunted by the reflection of her own heartbreak in Sevaka's eyes. "I wish there was another way. But I have to do this. I've made so many mistakes. I can't shake this sense that I'm on the verge of making another."

Sevaka shook her head. "Then go."

Rosa frowned, as surprised at her tone as her shift in expression. "Pardon me?"

"I'm not blind, Rosa. You've tried setting aside the warrior to be a wife of leisure, but it's not you. It never could be." Lips danced a thin, sad smile. "If I hold you here, even to help you, I'll be no more myself than you for staying. Save one life. Save a thousand. Do whatever you must to fill the hole that's eating you inside out, and do it with my blessing. Just promise me you'll come home."

Sevaka's voice shook as she spoke those last words, but she didn't flinch from them.

Rosa took her hands and held them close. The temptation arose to gainsay every word she'd uttered, to wish it all away and stand for ever in that moment. "That's no easy promise to keep."

"You'll keep it all the same, or else I will don scabbard and plate as my mourning weeds, and visit such horror on the Hadari that the Raven will weep. If I am to no longer be myself, it is only fair I should choose what I become." Bright eyes met Rosa's. "But you should have told me about Viktor."

Even now, Rosa couldn't be certain Sevaka believed her. Perhaps it was better she did not. "I know. Forgive me?"

"Upon your return," Sevaka replied, speaking with a hint of humour for the first time. "Not before."

One last embrace beneath moonlight, clasped tight enough for its warmth to linger through lonely days to come, and Rosa pulled away.

"Until Death, Rosa." Sevaka offered the Essamere oath with wavering smile.

Rosa kissed her, hand cradled to her cheek. "Death failed to part us once before. It won't succeed now."

Then, before doubts returned renewed, she strode away, leaving behind a promise she doubted she could keep.

Fourteen

"Madda, this is *very* boring."

Kaila's claim was credible enough, for Melanna's patience chafed just as readily. The never-ending procession of kings, princes, viziers, sons and – Ashana be praised – occasional *daughters* had begun with the setting of the sun. It would continue at least an hour, until the throne room was full and the feast begun. A ceremony of greeting that made little account for weariness, much less a child's wandering attention. Such was the price of calling the Golden Court to conclave.

"Boredom is fine training for royal life, *essavim*." Aeldran – standing at Kaila's side a little behind Melanna, but a pace in front of the silver masked and white-robed lunassera handmaidens – laid a hand on the girl's shoulder. "Now stand up straight, and do honour to your mother."

Melanna gazed out across the throne room, at the impenetrable array of friends and foes gathered beneath the golden likenesses of the divine that towered over all. Highborn mingled with the low – a rainbow of gold-edged silks, shining in the firelight as old acquaintances and perfect strangers laughed, loved, quarrelled and danced. Haldrane's icularis would already be plying their trade in the smoke-wreathed hall, garbed as servants and bodyguards, sifting secrets from idle conversation, intent from arrogance. The never-ending game played to preserve the throne. One Melanna feared she was losing. Cardivan was plotting, and even the icularis could not hear everything.

At the foot of the dais, beyond the ring of Rhalesh Immortals, the usher's staff rapped against stone, dragging Melanna's faltering attention back to the business of the evening. "Prince Sailra Kerem of Abkarn."

"Empress." Sailra made a low bow, oiled black hair brushing against a starched collar. He pitched his voice with precision born of practice – quiet enough for seemliness, but loud enough that it carried over the swell of chatter and the musicians' soft flutes. "It pleases me to reaffirm the fealty of both the House of Kerem, and the great kingdom of Abkarn. My mother regrets not having made the journey, but the years weigh heavily upon her shoulders."

"My thanks, *savir*." Melanna offered a gracious nod. So many words to convey so little of worth. Far from being a great kingdom, Abkarn was a client realm of Demestae – half a dozen clans clinging to cold northern shores. Prince Sailra's fealty? Words proved nothing, only deeds. As for his ailing mother, her absence arose more from dislike than infirmity. Either that, or the Dotha Abkarn had the unenviable misfortune of having lingered on Otherworld's threshold for Melanna's entire reign. "Please, carry my greetings with you upon your return."

"Majesty."

Sailra withdrew, replaced almost at once by a prince of neighbouring Drusan. Melanna greeted the newcomer in turn – and the next, and the next – all the while acutely aware of her daughter's fidgeting.

At last, the line petered to nothing, the first of the evening's duties complete. Longer conversations were yet to come. Haldrane had forewarned that at least half those gathered beneath moonlight sought audience, whether to petition, to complain or simply out of hope that they might draw notice, and thus patronage.

Melanna rose from the uncomfortable throne and knelt before Kaila. "You have done well this evening, *essavim*. I'm proud." The girl straightened, her cheeks colouring with pleasure. "And for that, I offer you a choice. You may stay, and continue to earn my regard by enduring what will be a very dull evening for one so young, or you may retire and Sera will tell you more stories of Ashana."

Kaila glanced up at Aeldran, as she ever did when presented a choice by her mother. Then she nodded. "Stories."

"Stories it shall be." Melanna kissed her on the forehead and stood. "Sera?"

The handmaiden offered a slight bow, white robes whispering. "A pleasure, Ashanal."

Melanna stilled an involuntary twitch at the honorific. "She is not to enter the inner gardens. Is that understood?"

"Of course." Sera dipped her head, lips forming a solemn smile beneath the silvered half mask. Were Jack truly roused to malice, he'd think twice before challenging the lunassera. The Goddess might have withdrawn from the world, but her handmaidens remained. "Come, my princessa. We will speak of wolves and wisdom, and a love that was not. A fine story for Midwintertide."

Kaila trailed readily behind as Sera withdrew, the remainder of the lunassera walking at respectful and watchful distance.

Melanna watched them leave the room of false smiles and brilliant silks. Freedom she no longer had. Kaila seemed somehow older than the night before. Illusion, certainly, shaped by her changing place in the world. But altered perception only reminded how little time mother and daughter spent together.

Aeldran turned his back on the crowded hall. "At her age, my grandfather had me attend every meeting of his court. I had to stand still and silent, without relief or food, while his chieftains bickered and guzzled themselves insensible."

A not uncommon tale, for all that Maggad Andwar had been a most uncommon brute. "And you think I should inflict the same on our daughter?" said Melanna.

He shook his head. "I spoke in envy, not instruction. Let her be young for as long as she can. In any case, the throne will turn her grey long before her time."

"As it has me?" Melanna had untangled the first grey hair from her brush that very morning. She'd found the sight morbidly transfixing. Strange to hold mortality in the palm of one's hand.

"You are Empress, Dotha Rhaled. Your beauty will last as long as you live. It is practically law." Aeldran kept an infuriatingly straight face. "Why, I understand that in Kerna, King Bodra's grandmother is accounted the vibrant flower of womanhood, and she's been dead at least six decades."

"One lifetime is enough," murmured Melanna. "So long as my mistakes are buried with me."

His brow knotted, lending prominence to furrows not present at their first meeting. When he spoke, he did so in tones too soft to carry even to the ring of Immortals. "To live is to make mistakes, *essavim*. To fight is to correct them."

"Now *that* sounds like instruction, and not envy."

"I would never dare instruct an Empress," he replied. "But to my wife, I offer advice. Your beauty lies not in your form, but your fire. I rise to greet it every morn, but others have forgotten. They're breaking you, inch by inch. Have them see the fire again."

Bowing low, he descended into the whirl of merriment, a pair of Immortals breaking from the dais to serve as escort. Melanna watched as he mingled with the crowds, one faithful soul amid hundreds about whom she'd only doubts. Aeldran's advice was sound, for all that he perceived only half of her troubles. Suspicion of weakness so readily became truth, believed by all.

Perhaps a display of strength *was* required, if not the one Aeldran meant.

The old, overgrown wood sat untouched by the palace's radiance. The cold made mock of cloak and gloves as readily as the shadows did Melanna's lantern. Every step occasioned creak of branch and scuttle of an unseen *something* lost to briar-wreathed gloom. And yet the path was wider than it had been the night before, the frost-hung undergrowth parted in welcome.

A hundred childhood nightmares that might not have been nightmares at all clamoured for attention. Melanna pressed on along without backward glance. No fear displayed for Tavar Rasha, who'd pleaded against this course long past propriety's bounds. And none shown for he who waited at the wood's tangled heart.

And Jack *was* there. Melanna felt his attention upon her at every step. The heady, oppressive weight of anticipation. The last time she'd stood in such a presence, Ashana had watched over her as a mother should. Did she do so now? With the moon bright above, there was always that chance, for all the long silence between them. Melanna shook the thought away as she stepped into the clearing.

This time, she stood before Jack as a mother, not a daughter. Her strength would serve.

The ancient oak loomed black in the darkness. Inscrutable. Vast enough to crush her beneath a single branch, were it so inclined.

"Will you speak with me, Lord Jack? One monarch to another?"

A hunched, gangling shape detached from the oak's shadow. Robes the colour of decay brushed the snows. A wooden mask, plain barring a scar across one eye, peered from beneath a ragged hood. Branch and briar unfurled from the undergrowth and tugged at his robes, supplicants straining for a blessed touch.

{{Are we equals, Melanna Saranal?}} His voice was the drone of thousand insects, the rustle of leaves in the storm. Green fire blazed in the mask's eye sockets. {{Are we friends?}}

Melanna swallowed. She'd forgotten what it was to stand before the divine – to be dwarfed by the presence of something that wore ephemeral form merely because it chose to do so. And then there was the scent arisen with his coming: sweet putrescence and the musk of black roses. One breath, and lantern light shimmered a hundred colours. Senses fell mute even as they screamed longing.

"That isn't for me to say."

He raised an arm, spindly rag-wrapped fingers reaching to brush Melanna's cheek. {{I would have had it so, despite your disrespect.}}

She turned her head, skin crawling. Disgust banished fear. "Your actions speak otherwise. You swore to leave me be, and a bargain with the divine binds all parties. So why do I find you creeping about my gardens?"

{{I swore no claim on you so long as Ashana forsook her own.}} The leer returned to his buzzing voice. {{Concerning your daughter, no bargain was struck.}}

Fear returned, anger with it. "She's a child!"

{{As once were you. She will grow, and I am patient.}}

"Why? Why does the line of Saran matter so much?"

{{Because I will not be cheated twice in as many generations.}}

Twice? Her father had thought to trade his own life in exchange for support on the battlefield, but had been deceived into instead offering Melanna as a bride. What else had he pledged? What had he kept from her? "Tell me."

Jack creaked closer. {{Your mother desired a prince's love. When the moon was dark and Ashana blind, she buried a straw doll at Cairnroot. Ten years of wedded bliss, one for each drop of blood shed upon the doll.

Then she was to come willing to a graven throne at Glandotha. She agreed so easily, but her promise became a dream.}} His tone grew cold, bitter. {{When I offered reminder, she gave herself to the Raven out of spite.}}

Melanna grabbed at a branch to contest a world trembling beneath her feet. Her games beneath the oak. She'd been Jack's reminder of bargains unfulfilled, as Kaila was now hers. And her mother's fall from the horse – no accident, but a deliberate act.

She doubled over, fighting for breath. Had her father ever suspected his beloved's death had been no accident, but the only freedom she'd hope of seeking? Better Otherworld's peace and the hope of Evermoon than the mouldered, spiteful madness of Fellhallow's brides. Had her parents' love even been true, or a potion brewed of maiden's longing and Jack's enchantment? And the son Kai Saran had desired, but was ever denied . . . had that too been Jack's doing? Gifts given and taken in the same breath.

Starving lungs at last found breath. Fury burned away the cold, fed by Melanna's recollection that the Lord of Fellhallow's bargains ever ran crooked; that he was apt to offer in trade something his supplicant already possessed, but did not know. Jack was deceiver – a refuge for the desperate. Reading deeper meaning into his claims was to conspire in one's own deception. Aethal Avandal had been an Immortal's daughter, without rank or wealth. How impossible it must have seemed that the Imperial heir might have risked his own standing for her. How easily she might have been deceived into seeking divine aid.

As for the rest? The past was the past. The future had brought her to the oak.

The world steadied. Melanna stood tall, the last fear burned away. "I came to deliver a message. In friendship or otherwise, it remains the same. Whatever bargains were struck in the past, my daughter is no part of them. You have a forest, and I an Empire. Fire levels all."

Jack hissed and shrank back, broken and pitiful, some trick of manner granting expression from a mask otherwise bereft. She dared him to read the bluff in her words. Few among the Gwyraya Hadar would countenance war against a god, just as Fellhallow, whose roots burrowed across mist-bordered worlds, was more than a mere forest to be razed. But as with Jack's bargains, what was *believed* was more important than what was *true*.

{{What claws you have, when roused.}} Jack's buzzing tone offered no clue to thoughts lying behind. {{The time will come when you have to choose between your desires and the good of your subjects. Your father – your mother – clung to the former. What, I wonder, will you choose?}}

He melted into the oak's shadows, the air crisper for his passing. Melanna stood motionless, trapped beneath an outcome that offered scant victory, for all it felt nothing like defeat. Breath frosting, she retraced her steps to the wood's perimeter and the formal gardens beyond.

"Empress." Tavar Rasha broke from the knot of Immortals, concern crowding his battle-worn features. "You're pale. Are you harmed?"

Melanna gave a vigorous shake of the head. "No. I've all that I needed."

She felt his eyes on her, hoping to glean thoughts in her expression. She'd given no explanation for her descent into the wood, just as she'd offered none for leaving the throne room. How much did Rasha suspect? Perhaps, he merely thought her mad. That would be fair, as Melanna could no longer be certain of sanity. The sense that her life was not – had never been – wholly her own was unshakeable.

"The Golden Court awaits your pleasure." Rasha's tone conveyed disapproval absent from the words. Rumours concerning her absence would be spreading. Gossip made no account for rank.

"I know." She stared back at the wood, no longer a child's refuge against the world, but an intruder amid the lawns, twisted and malevolent. She'd faced down a god – moreover, without drawing on authority other than her own. That, at least, was a victory. The ephemeral confrontations yet to come held no dread. "I'm ready for them now."

He beckoned to the nearest Immortals. "You'll permit us to escort you inside?"

"No." She smiled. "But you may accompany me there, if that is your wish."

Rasha gave her an old-fashioned look, but let the matter drop. For her part, Melanna gazed again at the wood. The vantage from which Jack had spied upon her, and her family. The snare by which he'd thought to steal daughters from their mothers. *Show them your fire*, Aeldran had said. Metaphor was well enough in its way, but she could do better.

"Burn it, jasaldar. Every tree. Every briar. Tonight."

Fifteen

Viktor stared broodingly into subdued streets as the carriage made a jolting, shuddering crossing of the bridge, his expression no less a warning to unquiet spirits than the blue-white crackle of ghostfires. Elzar knew better than to take offence. Lumestra knew there was little in the city's broken skyline to offer encouragement for the year ahead.

There'd been a time, a few years back, when it seemed the Republic had been turning a corner – the corrupt bickering of the Council ended, the Hadari border quiet. Now Elzar's hopes of glorious rebirth had faded like the foundry's flames. Sunlight no longer graced the city as once it had, and with fall of night it seemed so different as to be alien. Maybe it was just imagining, wedded to an old man's failing sight. Or perhaps Lumestra truly *was* dead, as Anastacia readily proclaimed.

A whinny, a squeal of greased axles. The carriage eased to a halt at the palace's marble stairs. Viktor roused himself. "Hedvin will take you home if you wish, but I hoped to prevail upon you a while longer."

Elzar stifled a yawn, the prospect of warm hearth and soft bed never more appealing. Late nights were long behind him. But such offers were seldom made whimsically where Viktor was concerned. "Of course."

Viktor thumped a hand against the carriage roof. The door opened. Constans stood to attention beyond, the boy a reluctant shadow beneath the lanterns of the palace approach. Further up the steps, four Drazina and two simarka stood watch at the gate. Viktor dropped to the ground, grace as ever belying stature. Elzar gratefully took his proffered hand, and lowered his twinging bones into the snow.

"Will that be all, father?" asked Constans.

"It will," rumbled Viktor. "We'll speak in the morning."

Constans bowed and walked away, soon naught but a shadow in the greater dark beyond the ghostfires.

"He's very formal," said Elzar, following Viktor up the steps. "I hardly recognise the boy I once wrestled from the branches of a hayadra tree."

"He's learning his place in the world, and his responsibilities."

"Not as fast as he might, from what I hear. A little too fast with his hands, and faster to throw around his name … and yours. It could be he's a very different young man when your eyes aren't on him."

"That too is part of the lesson," said Viktor. "Better he learns it young than its lack ossifies with age. Had I been wilder in my youth, I might have made fewer mistakes since."

Little consolation for those who were Constans' unwilling tutors, who – if rumour held true – bore the cost of goods purloined without payment, but Elzar held his tongue as they passed into the palace.

For all that there were always Drazina in sight – Kai Saran's lesson, at least, had been well learned – the corridors felt empty. Elzar almost found himself wishing for the days of the twin councils, and the crowds of petitioners with their voices raised in quarrel. Few petitioned Viktor, and fewer still with raised voice.

Only Captain Tzila held post at the entrance to Viktor's chambers in the old clocktower. She offered a low bow as they approached, cloth whispering across sculpted steel armour.

"The high proctor and I are not to be disturbed," said Viktor.

Tzila inclined her head in acknowledgement, her helm's empty gaze lingering on Elzar perhaps a moment longer than necessary. But he'd lived too long to quail before theatrics, even of the bleak sort Tzila practised.

As ever, Viktor's chambers held a peculiar sense of abandonment. The sense that someone had lived there once, and might one day do so again – but not today. It wasn't for any lack of cleanliness, for in that regard every inch of shelf and carpet was pristine. More, everything was *too* orderly. Not a book out of place, or a scrap of paper discarded at a careless moment. Nor did the room terribly suit Viktor, if truth be told. The ornaments, the chandelier; the sumptuous cloth of chair and drape. Costume worn for others. The approximation of what a man in his position should aspire to, rather than what he wanted.

Elzar gratefully accepted a glass of sweet caldera wine, and sank into a fireside chair. "Thank you, my boy. May I say it was good to see you out and about today? I know it meant much to Josiri."

Viktor made no move to find a seat, just as he'd forgone pouring himself a drink. "I'm not always free to act as I wish." He shrugged. "A Lord Protector's burdens."

"Nonsense."

He glowered. "Is it? I think this is the first Midwintertide I've not been on the road. Every town and parish demands my presence. Conscription numbers are falling, and the fortifications lag behind schedule. Worse, every guild, merchant and banker expects me to solve their squalid quarrels."

Elzar chuckled into his glass. "This was always your problem. Thinking yourself alone, when in truth you've only yourself to blame for isolation."

"You think I don't rely enough on others? I handed the army to Izack, the constabulary to Josiri—"

"And promptly raised the Drazina to do the work of both," Elzar countered, "and in a manner answerable to you alone."

"The provinces have never been more independent."

"And yet both Sevaka and dear Arlanne – like Josiri and Izack – are scarcely free to make decisions without you snorting down their necks."

"They told you this?"

"No," Elzar lied. "But I've seen it for myself. Or did you *not* summon us to a meeting yesterday only to impose your own view? It's not the first time."

Viktor frowned. "I thought you agreed with me about the Eastshires?"

"That's not the point. You're too used to ordering soldiers about. Folk trust you. Trust them in return."

"Or I'll become a tyrant?"

Elzar shook his head. "You can't save the Republic from behind stone walls, my boy, even if those walls lie mostly in your own mind. You have to walk in it. Otherwise, how are you to know what you're saving?"

Viktor paced back and forth, footfalls heavy and rhythmic. "Saving the Republic? Is that what I'm doing? Not so long ago, I was torn between riding south and staying to thwart my father's ambitions. You told me

I'd look back on that moment five years hence, and curse my easy life. You were right." He came to an abrupt halt and spread his hands. "Five years and more are ash upon the wind. There's nothing I'd not do to have them back, and hope alongside."

"You *give* folk hope, Viktor. You always have. But I'd forgotten about your father." Hadon Akadra had been so like his son. Arrogant, assured, and forever terrified at the prospect of losing control. But unlike his son, Hadon had lacked empathy, or else had it worn away by privilege. "Whatever happened to him, I wonder?"

Viktor's brow furrowed in distaste. "We can only hope it was what he deserved."

"In the end, that's all any of us can hope for." Elzar set the glass aside, untouched. "Viktor, what is it you want of me? I've known you too long to mistake purpose for friendliness."

He received a wry smile in return – or as close to such as Viktor ever came. "I need your help."

"You have it. Always."

The glower returned. "You shouldn't say that until you know what I have in mind."

Elzar chuckled. "You always did have a flair for the dramatic."

"I'm deadly serious."

"You're never anything but, even when you're smiling." Ignoring the protest of joints unhappy at being roused, Elzar stood. "How long have we known each other?"

"All my life, or as near as matters. Most of what I am, I owe to you."

Elzar's cheeks warmed, though the claim was true enough. Even now, he caught glimpses of the terrified boy who'd sought shelter in the foundry after footpads had murdered his mother. "And in all that time, have I turned you down?"

"Not once."

"Then you have your answer."

Viktor nodded to himself. An acceptable impression of a man mulling things over, for all that he'd surely made his decision long before. For all his strengths, Viktor was apt to imitate the mannerisms of ordinary men more than have emotion drive him thus. "This way."

Following him through the inner door, and up rather more stairs than he'd have wished, Elzar at last entered a room that matched Viktor rather better. No trace of elegance lingered in moonlight cast from upper windows. Battered tables were barely visible beneath cracked and curling books, furled parchments and wax-crusted candelabra. The drapes of the lower windows were threadbare, so thick with dust as not to have been opened in some considerable time. Deeper into the room, past the spiral stair that curled towards the clocktower's summit, unused furniture languished beneath sheets.

Only one corner seemed cared for. There, Viktor's flame-etched armour sat on a wooden mannequin. Steel brackets secured two swords to the adjoining wall. One was a claymore too heavy for most men to wield. The other sword was shorter, slender, with gold detailing at pommel and hilt. Its blade was rusted where the claymore was hale. A blue ribbon, frayed and fading, hung like a tassel from its grips.

Elzar set an elbow against the wall and sought to quell heaving lungs. "Couldn't we . . . have discussed . . . this . . . downstairs?"

"My apologies." Viktor plucked a tinderbox from a table and set about waking the candles to life.

Elzar tapped a dull lantern. "Something wrong with this?"

"These days I find candlelight easier on my thoughts."

"I find being able to *see* easier on my toes." Yet the candles took the spark readily enough. Silvered moonlight retreated before murky orange.

Elzar squinted at the nearest table, and the book spread open atop. "Is that Kendrial's *Vitsimar*?" Illuminated letters shone as the pages curled beneath his fingers. They were cold to the touch, despite the tower's warmth. "I haven't seen a copy since the provosts seized Abitha Marest's library."

The provosts, at least, were an institution he didn't miss. Too swift with accusations of heresy, and too cruel in their investigation. They'd been fortunate only to be disbanded at Viktor's command, rather than dragged to the gallows.

The last candle lit, Viktor set tinderbox aside and leaned across the table. "A copy, and incomplete. Our forebears were too scrupulous in scouring the Republic of the heretical."

"They probably thought better of leaving temptation lying around." Elzar eased *Vitsimar* aside and peered below. The apocryphal

Tzalamourn. Three volumes with illegible, water-damaged spines. And at the bottom, a slender volume whose title was undamaged, and whose block script was nothing but gibberish to Elzar's eye. Viktor might have failed to recover Konor Belenzo's treatises from Darkmere, but he'd apparently uncovered a good deal else. "Hysteria's one thing, but we both know it wasn't wholly unfounded."

"There's nothing of concern in those pages," said Viktor. "Old men opining on topics beyond their experience."

"Nothing worse than opinionated old men." Elzar let an edge creep into his tone. "Apart from *impatient* old men."

"The Republic is fraying. We haven't the strength to defend what remains, let alone reclaim what was taken."

"We went over this yesterday. The foundry can't help. I wish it could. But even if you empty the city of constructs, set the Reveque girl to marshal them in battle ...?" He sucked at his teeth. "Now, if you'd found Belenzo's testament in Darkmere, maybe even his schemata? That would be different."

"There was never much hope of that," said Viktor. "From the very start, Shalamoh was convinced Konor Belenzo's testament burned years ago."

"Shalamoh?"

"A historian, of sorts."

"That's a frustrating profession hereabouts."

"He'd likely agree," said Viktor. "If a copy of Belenzo's testament survives, it would hardly be in Darkmere. He fled Malatriant with little more than the clothes on his back. She'd surely have destroyed any trace of him left within her reach."

"You lied about your reasons for going?" Elzar said uneasily. "What were you really looking for?"

"This."

Viktor set a small chest between them and hoisted back the lid. The air cooled. Candleflame lost vigour. Inside the box sat a curved hunk of black stone, or perhaps glass. The longer Elzar looked, the more translucent it seemed, the pale green lines sparking and cracking beneath the surface. He wanted to turn away, but the stone *called* to him, and not in a manner he cared for.

"What is this?" he breathed.

"A vranastone, or part of one. It's a bridge between our realm and Otherworld, for it belongs wholly to neither. Malatriant used it to pluck souls from the Raven's grasp. Shalamoh found passages referring to how she'd rip them apart and scry the future in their screams."

"Delightful." Elzar shuddered and looked away, dark spots dancing behind his eyes. "I thought you'd sworn off meddling with the dead. After Govanna—"

"This is different. At Govanna, I compelled corpses." Viktor tensed, his brow set. "You've no idea of the strain of fracturing yourself across thousands of unwilling vessels. Even then, they couldn't fight. The old tales are wrong. Malatriant never commanded the dead – she hollowed out the living. I haven't the stomach for that."

"I'm glad to hear it," Elzar said feelingly.

"You?" Viktor smiled without warmth. "You who always urged me to embrace my shadow's bounty, and never to fear?"

"To everything there are limits, my boy." They loomed closer that night.

"Are there? Or is it simply that the act should always be proportionate to the need?"

Elzar met his gaze, careful his eyes weren't drawn again to the stone. "And what act calls you, Viktor?"

"The kind for which I have ever striven. The necessary." He rested a hand on the stone. "Izack claims the experience of centuries is buried at Govanna. He's wrong. Only their bodies are there, and those are worthless. The Raven took everything of value. I mean to reclaim it."

"Viktor," Elzar began carefully, "the spirits of Otherworld are at peace. They walk the mists until Third Dawn."

"Can those taken before their time ever truly be at peace? And what if there *is* no Third Dawn? Lumestra is dead. Whatever hope we are to have, we must make for ourselves."

Elzar's cheeks stung at his bluntness. "Anastacia put this foolishness in your head?"

"No. But she's the key." Viktor lowered his voice, the words gaining fervency. "When I bound her to clay, she was but a spirit, shattered in the fall from Lumestra's realm. What was a prison for her can be salvation for others."

"Salvation? She *loathed* that body. I nearly wept with joy to see her today."

"And what if that gift can be shared with others?" said Viktor. "All this time, I thought I'd made her a prison, when it was a chrysalis! Seven years, and she's flesh and blood once more. What if that could be seven years of service in the army, thereafter free to live a life renewed? We demand *ten* of our conscripts, and I dread to think how few will live to see them out. Think of it. You know what Anastacia was capable of. As formidable as a kraikon. More! Imagine what we could achieve with an army like that."

Elzar scowled to hold temptation at bay. "The Lady Anastacia was a serathi. Divine. You've no surety what worked for her will do so for ephemeral souls."

"Lumestra crafted us all from clay, serathi *and* human. We are all after-images of her light."

"Scripture is no more a guide to the past than history. It's interpretation, not truth."

"Your whole career, you've sealed light into bronze and called it life." Viktor leaned closer. "Just as Lumestra did with clay at First Dawn. I'm proposing nothing different."

It made more sense than Elzar cared to admit. The foundry was in disarray precisely because no one understood its craft. Generation upon generation of proctors, following the form of what they were taught, and never truly comprehending. "Kraikons are little more than slaves. You'd have us inflict servitude on the souls of our dead?"

"Kraikons serve thus because they haven't the wit to do otherwise," Viktor replied. "They only mimic life. Tell me, has Anastacia ever struck you as one labouring under bondage?"

Elzar snorted. "Not lately."

What if the kraikons and simarka were witless not because they weren't souls, but because they were *fragments* of souls, stolen from Otherworld through imperfect means? Was that why proctors felt drawn to give them names? To read quirk of personality in a faceless construct? The more Elzar lingered on the thought, the more troubling it grew. Light and Dark were so often mirrors of one another. Were Malatriant and the foundry so different? Konor Belenzo had once been her closest disciple, the foundry his bequest.

"The Raven," he said slowly. "He will permit this?"

Darkness writhed at Viktor's shoulder. Or perhaps it was a trick of the light. "I don't intend to give him a choice."

Elzar rubbed his brow and sank against the wall, more drained than he'd felt in years. "And you want what from me? My approval?"

Viktor skirted the table and laid a hand on his shoulder. "This isn't something I can do alone." A faraway look came into his eyes. "I tried, once before. I patched the threadbare soul as best I could, but my gift is born of the Dark, not the Light. It proved ... It was not the balm I intended."

Elzar bowed his head. He'd heard rumours, of course. That Viktor had somehow drawn his beloved Calenne Trelan from Otherworld. Matters had ended poorly, but they'd never spoken of it. He'd never found the words to try. "I'm sorry."

Viktor shook his head. "Don't be. Today, I have hope, because today I beheld a woman of clay restored to flesh and blood."

"What you did to Anastacia, you did without light. That was your shadow alone."

"But it wasn't. The artist who smithed her body was once a proctor. He folded light into the clay as part of his art. A spark only, but it was enough."

Doubt slid away. But then, Viktor was always convincing when roused to passion. He could have talked the stars from the sky. "The dead are at peace. We haven't the right."

"Then why do cyraeths roam the mists where the world runs thin? Why do we mourn?"

"Oh, my boy," Elzar shook his head. "We mourn for our sake, not theirs. The dead are beyond such things."

"And if you're wrong?" Viktor paused, a man readying for another sortie. "If there are those in the Raven's keeping who'd seize the chance to return? Who'd readily shelter their countrymen and their kin? I'm not asking you to help me forge an army. Not yet. One willing soul. Help me prove that it can be done, or that it cannot."

It was all probability. The fruits of success set against the consequence of failure. And beneath it all, the cruel possibility that Viktor asked nothing Elzar hadn't already spent a lifetime pursuing. He could refuse, but what would that make him when armies marched and the bodies piled high? The young sacrificed on the stubbornness of an old man?

And just like that, Elzar realised he'd already made his decision. "When?"

"When else? The year is dead, and Otherworld draws nigh to claim it. We will never have a better opportunity."

Sixteen

"What *are* you doing?"

Altiris started, the cloth-wrapped roast chicken falling the last inch into the box. Turning his back on a dining table strewn with half-eaten platters and other makeshift containers, he found Sidara staring at him from the servants' corridor.

"I thought you'd gone to bed."

"Plainly."

"And everyone else?"

"Constans left with Viktor and Elzar. Izack a few minutes ago, bellowing a song whose lyrics I won't repeat." She stepped closer, more silhouette than substance with the lanterns lowered to conspiratorial flicker. "Josiri's helping Ana to bed."

"It's strange, seeing her drunk."

"I'm just glad she's still here," said Sidara, voice thick with pent-up emotion. "I cried myself to sleep last night, for fear she'd be gone when I woke. So let her be drunk. Let her be anything she wishes. I think it's a new experience for her."

"But not you."

"My blood's magic." She drew closer, defiant tone more convincing had she not stumbled and grabbed at the table for support. "I don't *get* drunk."

"Good grief, no. That table walked clean into *you*." That by itself was no proof. Sidara had never quite left the clumsiness of girlhood behind and could readily snag toe or heel on a completely unblemished surface.

"There's no need to crow. Just because *you've* barely touched a drop."

"I didn't want to make a fool of myself."

Despite everything, Altiris had enjoyed the afternoon more than he'd expected. It was impossible to stay intimidated by Izack for long, and even the Lord Protector – or *Viktor*, as he'd insisted on being named – was much less terrifying when unshielded by formality and armour.

Sidara closed the last distance, eyes on his and flecks of gold glinting amid the blue. "Looking foolish around me never seems to bother you."

"If you must know, it bothers me more."

Altiris silently cursed the admission, teased forth by a combination of perfume, proximity and old memories far headier than the sparing sips taken in toast.

"I wish it didn't," she said softly. "It shouldn't."

He blinked, taken aback as much by the sympathy in her expression as her voice. For the first time, he wondered how large a part his pride had played in their estrangement. That perhaps it wasn't just Sidara who'd changed with her responsibilities.

She drew closer still. Close enough for wine-laden breath to contest the perfume. "Altiris?"

"Yes?"

"Where are you taking the food?"

He deflated, half-formed fantasies dissipating. "Sothvane. So many folk there have nothing. I'd make a difference, if only for one night." He paused, gathering words to match uncertain feelings. "Some of what I saw yesterday ... I've forgotten where I came from."

Sidara pursed her lips. "Does Josiri know?"

Altiris suspected Lord Trelan would approve, but he hadn't actually *asked*. Lord Trelan had been so distracted of late, worn down by his duties to the point that Altiris feared he took in little of what he was told. And one way or another, Anastacia likely had his full attention now. "Most of this will spoil long before it's eaten, even if we divvy it up between everyone on the estate."

"So he *doesn't* know."

"Are you going to tell him?"

"I haven't decided yet." She shot him a sly smile. "What's it worth?"

"What did you have in mind?" he asked carefully, wary of ice creaking beneath his feet.

"You could kiss me."

Treacherous heart skipped a beat. He could, he really could, but for the suspicion that what began sweetly would sour by dawnbreak.

"I might," he managed, on second attempt. "If you ask me again in the morning."

The smile faded, though Sidara's tone remained more playful than offended. "You think this is the wine talking, don't you?"

"I hope it's not."

"There's only one way to know."

"Aren't you always chiding me for being reckless?"

The old year was dying. Maybe it was better to look to the future than the past. Encouraged by a faint gleam of teeth beneath perfect lips, Altiris leaned in.

"Cart's hooked up," said Kurkas. "We can go whenever you're . . . Not interrupting anything, am I?"

Altiris straightened. His gaze shifted from Sidara to Kurkas, the one suddenly a long stride further down the table and shoulder tilted away; the other propped against the doorway, wearing a thick outdoorsman's coat and a wholly unconvincing expression of innocence.

"Nothing at all," he said wearily.

Kurkas nodded to Sidara. "Evening, miss."

"So you're part of this, Vladama?"

"Quite sure I don't know what you're talking about, miss." The parade-ground stare was back, Kurkas' eye fixed on the wall somewhere behind her.

"She knows," said Altiris.

Sidara nodded. "She knows. She's coming."

What? More worrisome than the prospect of Josiri's disapproval was the uncertain reception to be had in Sothvane. Altiris had no assurances of safe passage, only hope. And if that hope was mislaid? Well, he was willing to take the risk. And he knew better than to try talking Kurkas out of joining him. But to gamble Sidara alongside . . . ? "It might not be safe."

"If it's safe enough for you, it's safe enough for me." Her defiant stare wavered. "Bad enough that Josiri and Viktor don't trust me to know my own mind. Prove you know me better than that."

Altiris frowned, certain now wasn't the time to ask what she meant by that. He glanced at Kurkas, and found no help in the steward's carefully immobile expression. Sidara watched him intently throughout, her pleading no less evident for going unspoken.

"All right," he said at last, "but on one condition. Viktor left the Lord Protector behind at the palace. I need you to leave the Lady of Light here. No magic. No simarka. No judgement of anything you see. Agreed?"

She nodded, and offered a grin Altiris hoped he'd not soon have cause to regret. "Agreed."

No danger waited on Sothvane's streets, at least. Cold, or perhaps fear of year's-end spirits, kept most folk inside. Those remaining offered the cart barely a glance as they shuffled along, a manner Altiris remembered well from his time on Selann, where curiosity too often earned an overseer's beating. It didn't do to show interest in things that didn't concern you.

Little by little, the tumbledown structures of the flooded shore replaced built-up streets. Seacaller's church stood proud amid the leaping ghostfires, boarded-up windows ablaze with light. Altiris dropped from the bench seat and eyed the lychfield gate. Half a dozen bulky figures, bundled tight against the cold, stood gathered around bonfire's fading light. What had seemed a fine idea in the warmth and safety of Stonecrest grew entirely other.

He glanced up at his companions. Sidara had exchanged lustrous blues for drab greys, unplaited her hair and scrubbed makeup away. Only the most suspicious soul would have recognised the Lady Reveque. Kurkas always looked like he'd crawled out of a gutter.

"Let me do the talking," Altiris murmured.

"Whatever you say, lad," Kurkas said airily. "I'm just along for the ride."

For all his nonchalance, Altiris noted that Kurkas' hand had fallen level with the bench seat's overhang, where three swords sat bundled in an old cloak. He nodded, and started towards the lychgate.

A hooded head rose from the flames. Others followed, the attention more curious than belligerent.

"Who goes?" bellowed one.

"A friend." Altiris tugged his glove free, baring the southwealder's rose-brand.

"You think that mark buys anything?" sneered another. "Plenty carry it on their skin but not their soul."

The wind bore notes of fiddle and flute from within the church's battered walls. Watchmen shuffled closer, line spread wide to forestall flight. Altiris gritted his teeth. Intimidation or actual threat, it wouldn't matter if they jarred Sidara into breaking her promise.

"Not me," he said. "I bring gifts."

"Only the river brings gifts down here," replied the first watchman.

Uncertainty shivered Altiris' spine. Should he claim to be merrowkin? That might open the way, but making such a claim without being able to back it up would only make things worse.

A third watchman pushed his way through. "Devn? I thought that was you." Radzar beamed through his unkempt beard. "Ain't no work tonight. Didn't anyone tell you? It's Midwintertide."

The poor joke elicited a rumble of laughter.

Altiris relaxed. "I did my share earlier. Why else would I have gifts to offer?"

Radzar squinted, wary now of a joke at his expense. "Show me."

Glad to be again on firmer ground, Altiris retraced his steps to the cart. Shooting suspicious glances at Kurkas and Sidara, Radzar followed. "Who are they?"

"Friends."

Radzar grunted and folded back canvas. "Bless me." He opened one box, then another, suspicion yielding to wonder. "Where's all this from?"

Altiris shrugged. "It won't be missed. Does the rest matter?"

"Not to me. Bring it through. Tie up outside the church. I'll find willing hands." He gave a low whistle. "Shouldn't be hard."

The watchmen parted. Kurkas guided the cart beneath the lychgate's ivy-wreathed arch and to rest alongside the church. Radzar's chain of willing hands was in place moments later, ushering the bounty inside with such eagerness that even with Sidara's help Altiris could barely unload swiftly enough.

"Who's Devn?" She tugged a box free of the cart's bed and pushed it into an old man's eager hands. Her cheek twitched at the grimy, tattered clothing, and again at the stoop of his gait as he bore the box into the church.

"Blame your brother," Altiris replied. "He thought he was being funny."

She rolled her eyes. "Why am I not surprised?"

Altiris reached into the cart, his hand settling not on a box, but a crate. A dozen ale bottles glinted. Frowning, Altiris saw others behind. "Vladama?"

The steward eased up from his slouch against the cartwheel. "Can't think how that lot got in there." He shrugged. "Still, they're here now. Like you said, won't be missed."

Sidara stifled a burst of laughter. "You're a rogue, Vladama."

He sniffed. "No manners, you young folk. Ain't a feast without a good drop or two, is it?"

Altiris winced. Leftovers – even on such grandiose scale – were one thing, but this? "And Lord Trelan?" he murmured.

"My problem, not yours." Kurkas glanced at Sidara. "That's right, ain't it, miss?"

She pursed her lips in thought, eyes on the ragged congregation. "If that's what you want."

Radzar ambled over as the last crate vanished inside. "Where'd you say this lot came from?"

"I didn't," Altiris replied. "The river provides."

The phrase wove its magic. Radzar grinned. "That it does."

"See it's shared out fairly, would you?"

Radzar jerked a thumb towards the door. "You mean you're not coming in? Don't be daft. Folk will want to thank you."

A tempting offer. Deeds done in the dark were all very well, but to be acknowledged in the light ...? Part of Altiris wanted – *needed* – that. But a higher profile meant risks. "Thanks, but—"

"Of course we are." Sidara slipped her arm through Altiris' and dragged him towards the door. "You'll see to the horse, Vladama?"

"I'm not sure that's a good idea ... " Altiris cast about for the first name that came to hand. Sidara was too rare a name to be risked. " ... Ceren."

She caught on fast, the smoothing of her brow chasing away brief furrows. "Don't be ridiculous, *Devn*. I could use the warmth."

With no help to be found in Kurkas' grin, Altiris reluctantly let her lead him inside.

The wall of heat and sound took his breath away. Fires burned in hollows dotted along either transept, the nave cleared of pew and rubble to create a space where couples danced to the whirl of flute, the thump of drum and heel. Not the formal dances Altiris had endured in Lord Trelan's service, but the abandon of jig and reel.

Distribution was well under way, but without sign of the disorderly scrum Altiris had feared. Folk queued before the altar as they had on his last visit, meats and morsels handed out to all who sought them. Bottles were broached, their contents decanted to mug and tankard.

Radzar, bottle in hand and never long without a grin, introduced them to all who crossed their path, a parade of names and faces Altiris forgot at once. Sidara flinched from the first clasp of hands, but mellowed inch by inch, overcome by gratitude and fellowship.

Still, she remained watchful, as did Altiris himself. The life of the Lady Reveque was worth more to the opportunistic than a Midwintertide meal. He relaxed only a fraction when the church door creaked open and Kurkas – cloak hitched high about his shoulders to conceal a sword worn at his back – took up position beneath the boarded-up east window.

At last, Radzar was called away. Altiris politely disengaged from the press of bodies. Skirting the makeshift dancefloor's crowd, he leaned against a pillar, careful to keep both Kurkas and exit in eyeline. Sidara settled beside him, her shoulder against his.

"Is this what you expected?" he asked.

"You've spent years in my world," she replied, eyes on the dancers. "I wanted to walk in yours awhile."

"This isn't my world," he snapped. "It shouldn't be anyone's."

Her face fell. "That's not what I meant."

But she wasn't wrong. The room was awash with echoes of those rare nights on Selann when the guards were at their ease, and the workers free to revel. The small adjustments to hem and collar, letting threadbare cloth ape something finer. For all the dance's abandon, there was formality to partners offered and accepted – the acknowledgement that there should be form to such things, even in poverty. The pride that led a man to keep a fiddle hale in a life where music was luxury.

It might not have been Altiris' world, but it was close enough.

"I know," he said. "I'm sorry. Old memories."

"You never really talk about your past."

"There's not much to tell. Days working the fields. Nights huddled around a fire, hoping never to catch an overseer's eye. And hungry, all the time." He shrugged, as if doing so robbed the recollections of their power. "I've lived more in six years at Stonecrest than in all those that came before. Wearing the phoenix means the world to me."

"Because it freed the Southshires?"

"Because it represents hope," he said. "My father always claimed the phoenix was a herald of better times to come, and he was right. I wished he'd seen it for himself, him and my mother both."

"*A phoenix shall blaze from the darkness,*" quoted Sidara. "I found a pamphlet in the streets when I was little. Mother called it treasonous doggerel and cast it in the kitchen fire, but I've always remembered the illustration of flaming wings stretching into the skies. There should always be light in the darkness."

"Your light?"

"Maybe. It's still such a mystery to me. Some days I don't know what to make of it." She shook her head and stared at the dancers. "Just as I'm sure 'Ceren' wouldn't know what to make of all this."

Belatedly, Altiris realised that in his scramble for a name, he'd plucked another from *The King of Fathoms*. The glint in Sidara's eye warned that she knew it too. "Probably not."

"Uh-uh. So you're a fool, and I'm an arrogant princess. Is that how you see us?"

That she sounded amused more than offended little eased sudden discomfort. "That's not exactly ... Look, it was the first name that came to mind."

"I see." Eyes narrowed, she stepped back and held out a hand. "Dance with me."

"Pardon?"

"Dance with me, *Devn*, or I'll make a scene."

Her eyes flickered gold, leaving no doubt as to the manner of the spectacle. Admitting defeat, Altiris allowed her to lead him to the nave. He returned her curtsey with a stiff bow, feeling eyes upon him more than ever.

Then the music whirled anew. The tension in his stomach smoothed away and his blood roused to flame.

The church, the smoke, the warmth of fires; fears of safety and uncertain menace. They drowned beneath wildling notes, smothered by the stomp of boot and clap of hand. Brief breaths offered a hand about Sidara's wrist, her hand, her waist. Each time she spun away, skirts hitched and cheeks aglow, only to return, the moment theirs alone, that strange intimacy found only in a crowd.

The Sidara who so readily made butchery of a formal dance was gone as if she'd never existed. Caught up in the moment, Altiris forgot to wonder who'd taught her to turn such a step. Surely not Sidara's sainted mother. He decided it didn't matter. Certainly not in that moment where, for the first time in months, he found himself at ease in Sidara's company. More than that, he felt *whole*. Even a glimpse of Kurkas grinning from his self-appointed vigil couldn't sour the moment.

Eventually, that moment passed as all moments must, occasioned by bursting lungs and jellied legs. Laughing, they withdrew to the quiet of the south transept and the support of an empty pew.

"Queen's Ashes, but I enjoyed that," gasped Sidara, smoothing bedraggled golden locks from her eyes. "I'll pay for it in the morning, but it was worth it."

Altiris, shirt heavy with sweat and his calves already moaning displeasure, stared back across the nave. Others had already stolen their place. "You seem . . . I don't know. You seem different."

"Maybe I am. Or maybe it's you."

Easy to deny, but for the fact he'd come to that very conclusion before leaving Stonecrest. "It's possible."

Sidara shook her head. "Ana's forever telling me I'm growing old too young. Last night, watching her slip away – what I *thought* was her slipping away – I finally understood what she meant." She looked up, unblinking. "I should dance whenever I can, and with whomever I want, because we're none of us here for ever."

Altiris reckoned he should have had a good response. The idiot smile was all he could muster. "Ana taught you to dance like that?"

"Of course. She, at least, thinks first of my desires." She shrugged. "Viktor wants me on the border, fighting the Hadari. Josiri wants to keep me safe in the city. Neither asked my opinion. They just repeat their own as if it *were* mine."

A chill crackled across Altiris' spine. Sidara, in the path of the shadowthorns? As a Drazina it had always been a possibility, but somehow remote. "And what *do* you want?"

"You ask that as if it's the easiest question in the world."

There was hurt beneath the words, deep and cloying and thick as tar. Unsure what to say, Altiris struck out in a different direction. "Izack offered me a captaincy in the 1st."

She stiffened, suddenly serious. "Did you accept?"

"I'm wondering if I should, if you're leaving for the border."

"You'd find someone else to quarrel with."

"Maybe I don't want to."

Sidara snorted. "You still shouldn't accept the commission."

"Because I'd be no good, I suppose," he replied bitterly.

"No. Because you're meant for something more."

"Me? I'm just a southwealder who's been lucky."

"You're not *just* anything, Altiris. Not to me."

"And how's that different to what Lor—" He broke off, thinking better of using the title in such uncertain company as Seacaller's, for all that no one seemed to be listening. "To what Josiri wants for *you*?"

"I've a nicer smile." She favoured him with one to prove the unarguable point. "I've lost too many of those I love. It's part of what's making me old. Help me stay young?"

He frowned. "You've lost me."

The smile turned sly. "It's nearly morning. Are you really going to make me ask again?"

I might, if you ask me again in the morning. Words spoken a few hours and a lifetime ago, out of fear Sidara hadn't meant her own.

Sidara drew closer, eyes shining with expectation. Altiris slid a hand behind her jaw, to the nape of her neck, and gently drew her closer still. She reached out, a small sigh fluttering between them, and closed her eyes.

In the moment before their lips met, blue-green eyes bored into Altiris' from across the nave, undimmed for the bodies between. Shaking her head in caution, Kasvin waved a black-gloved hand in beckoning.

Altiris dropped his chin to his chest, thoughts ablur with possibilities. None of them good.

Sidara's eyes snapped open. "Altiris?"

He swallowed, the camaraderie of Midwintertide fading. The ruined church was no longer thronged with the unfortunate in need of alms, but vengeful merrowkin with blades close to hand. He looked up. Kasvin had gone, but Kurkas was still on post beneath the east window.

"Go to Vladama," he murmured, barely loud enough to be heard over the music. "Now."

"What is it?"

A difficult question, not least because he didn't yet have the answer. "If I'm not back in five minutes, I'll look to the Lady of Light for salvation."

She didn't like that, not one bit, but she stood. "Five minutes. Then dawn arrives early."

A rumpled lip, words unspoken, and she made her way through the congregation. Allowing himself a last, lingering look, Altiris set off in the opposite direction.

He found Kasvin in an antechamber off the north transept, alone save for a statue of Lumestra who'd long ago parted company with her head. She sat perched on the sill of a boarded-up window, skirts a black stain across filthy stone.

"I'm here," he said. "I'll not fight. Just let the others go."

"So noble." Pale lips parted in a sneer, but Altiris heard nothing of the creeping, seductive whispers. Her manner stood in sharp contrast to how he'd seen her last. Calm, rather than feral. Honeyed words in venom's stead. "Relax. You're in no danger. Nor's your doxy. The Merrow was right about you. He'll be insufferable for days. More insufferable, I should say."

He frowned, clinging to confrontation even as it veered away. "You'll forgive me if I don't believe that."

"You still don't understand, do you?" Kasvin dropped from the sill. Her skirts barely rippled above soundless footsteps. "We're only your enemies if you choose."

"Even after the trail of bodies we left in your safehouse?"

"You didn't kill them, and they'll be avenged soon enough." The promise was grimmer for its lack of boastfulness. "It felt good to make a difference tonight, didn't it? If only for a little while."

"Lord Trelan's generosity made it possible, not mine." The lie flowed smoothly enough, for it held at least a grain of truth. Or would do so tomorrow, after forgiveness was sought.

Kasvin laughed, music in a minor key. "No it wasn't. He's too close to the Lord Protector. He's made his choice, even if he doesn't know it. You should make yours before the chance slips away."

Her fingertips brushed his cheek, then she passed through the doorway and lost herself in the crowd.

Seventeen

Viktor gripped the sheet, anticipation too heady for denial. In the workshop's candlelit gloom, aspiration seemed more dreamlike than ever, and it was in the nature of dreams to run awry. He caught the amused curl of Elzar's lip and forced hands to stillness. Everything that could be done *had* been done. The path ahead was strewn with obstacles, but he could walk it. The sheet slipped from the table's raised lips with the barest tug, billowing clay-dust glinting softly.

Elzar ran his fingertips across the mannequin's porcelain brow. "I didn't know you'd a sculptor's skill. I'm impressed."

Viktor grunted the compliment away. "There are many things I never believed myself to be. This is merely one more."

The words belied long and disheartening nights honing a skill. They concealed the catalogue of misshapen and misfired fragments boxed away at the chamber's rear.

Even now, the mannequin possessed little of the artisanry that had made Anastacia's vanished form such a wonder. The white expanse of samite porcelain was ungilded and bereft of decoration. The features plainer and lacking likeness – more kin to the impartial mask of a mummer performing as Judgement in a carnival play. But the womanly proportions were stylised, rather than grotesque, the stitching of the leather joints immaculate. Less a doll, and more a twin to a kraikon's stylised form. No, that wasn't quite right. It put Viktor more in mind of the Ocranza statues that stood silent guard over well-to-do estates, their original purpose – the warding off of evil spirits – forgotten to all save a few, and admired more for their craftsmanship than anything else.

It wasn't perfect, but nor would it be needed for ever.

Bundling the cloth aside, Viktor unhooked the gold-hilted sword from the wall. Setting it upon the doll's chest, he folded the lifeless arms atop – table and occupant become parody of an ancestral tomb. His fingers dwelled a moment on the sapphire ribbon.

"Always the soldier," said Elzar.

Viktor shook his head. "The Hadari believe that beloved metal retains a spark of soul. It's why recovering this sword was so important. I doubt we'd ever find her without it."

"Didn't you tell Josiri it belonged to your great aunt?" Despite his wry tone, Elzar's eyes remained serious. "I remember dear Abonia fondly, of course – such a wonderful singing voice – but I don't know I'd deem her a fit candidate for what you have in mind."

"I told him that *most* of what was stolen belonged to her." Seeing the explanation convinced little, Viktor reached for another, more truthful, response. "I didn't want to offer false hope. The sword was Calenne Trelan's. The one she lost at Davenwood."

Elzar rubbed wearily at stubbled jowls. "Are you certain this is a good idea? Calenne—"

"You're free to change your mind."

Elzar lapsed into silence, eyes downcast. Viktor wondered if he should have told the whole story from the first. Already, he asked Elzar to contravene scripture and tradition – some might even stir the dread word morality into the mix. To undermine that with the appearance of obsession would have been folly, and whatever else Viktor considered himself, he was not a fool. A shadow-draped witch, steeped in the Dark, certainly. Arrogant, perhaps. A man who aspired to much and always achieved less? Unfortunately. But not a fool.

"You've not walked Eskavord's charred fields," he murmured. "Malatriant's demise drew Otherworld close enough to touch. The locals hear the anguish of those she took. They feel it on their skin. They say it goes deep into the clay."

Elzar frowned. "Viktor ... it's not wise to look for meaning in the mists."

"Perhaps at this moment I am not wise. But I *am* driven." Urgency crept into Viktor's voice, as much at the prospect of disaster as success.

His shadow, ever apt to mischief when emotion ran awry, shifted in his soul. "Calenne Trelan proved herself a leader whose mettle we sorely need. For all that folk say I won victory at Davenwood, she made it possible. I could leverage all manner of claims, but the truth is simple. If I can save only one soul from the Raven's grasp, it must be she. A part of me has been lost these seven years. Calenne is its keeper. I would be whole again, and have her be whole with me."

He fell silent, overcome by the strain of speaking from the heart. Love was a peculiar spur to thus provoke courage and fear.

Elzar's expression cleared. "You've given so much of yourself to others, my boy. Refusing you now would be truly selfish, don't you think? I just . . . " He paused, brows beetling. "I only hope what you're looking for is what you find."

"It is."

"Then we should begin. The night's slipping away."

Viktor nodded, lacking words to thank a man who'd been guide and confidant his whole life. Crouching, he retrieved a ewer from beneath the table. Inky water sloshed within, offering no reflection.

"From the Black River at Coventaj." With reverent care, starting at the head of the table, Viktor emptied the vessel across the doll. Water pooled about its limbs, contained by the table's high rim, leaving the porcelain figure a lily in a bleak pool. "My mother spoke often of the goddess Endala's empathy for women taken by cruel means. Kendrial writes that the river is her blood. I see little harm in stacking the deck."

Elzar's eyelid twitched. "Coventaj is forbidden."

For a heartbeat, Viktor stood again in the cavern buried far beneath the city's deepest tombs, the cruel eyes of pale, lissom statues glittering malice as he pushed his thrashing father beneath the waters of the Black River for the final time. "Then I am nothing if not consistent. Everything we do tonight is forbidden, by one mandate or another."

"True enough." A chuckle faded, serious again. "And what is my role in this abomination?"

Candlelight dimmed as Viktor drew the vranastone fragment from its casket and laid his hands upon it. His vision swam, a piece of him already drawn across the veil between worlds.

"Call forth the light." His voice fell flat and muted. Vision paled alongside, the world's crispness smoothing away into mist. "Link me to the doll. Treat it as you would the grounding of magic into a new-made kraikon. Leave the rest to me."

"Gladly."

Elzar breathed deep. The air about his shoulders shimmered gold, enveloping both Viktor and the doll. Viktor's shadow hissed displeasure, recoiling from the splendour. Once, he'd have let it, powerless to curb the wilfulness of the Dark buried in his soul. But that helplessness belonged to a younger man – one afraid of his birthright. He brought the writhing shadow to heel with but a thought. Cloaking himself with it – with the Dark – he lifted one hand from the vranastone, and laid it atop the rusted sword.

The workshop peeled away to a misty street. Windows and rooftops reached crookedly into the skies. Listless etravia spirits, pallid in flesh and form, and vaporous below the waist, drifted along tangled thoroughfares without acknowledging Viktor's presence. Indeed, he wasn't truly there, just a piece of his soul, cloaked in shadow. Concentrating, he perceived the cracked plaster of the clocktower hidden behind, the candleflames guttering as if in draught. The golden spark of Elzar's magic.

None of which forestalled the rise of gooseflesh, or the strange certainty of being unmoored beneath a stark, viridian sky.

Nausea gathered, as it had the first time Viktor had walked the Raven's domain. The vranakin thief Apara Rann, unable to resist the shadow he'd rooted in her soul, had been his guide. She'd dragged him more than he'd walked, his senses overwhelmed and his shadow screaming. Not so this time. Calenne's sword throbbed beneath his hand, guiding him on.

He followed the spoor, the fragment of spirit within the sword calling to the whole. He threaded the ethereal crowd through town and field, along cobbled road and sunken tracks whose mud clung to his boots. Cawing shapes murmurated overhead, their cries deafening and vengeful.

He quickened his pace.

The path led on through a field of stone. Tombs jutted from the soil. Upturned swords grew like trees, their hilts spread as branches. The sounds of battle rose to clamour. The etravia, Viktor's companions upon the impossible road, passed beyond the cusp of mist, leaving him alone.

All save one.

She stood within a ring of swords, beneath a canopy of crooked, black trees. Unmistakeably Calenne for all that she was not. The slenderness of feature, the firm cheekbones and noble brow . . . even bereft of colour and bleeding vapour, they'd long ago seared themselves into Viktor's mind. But the expression? In their brief, blessed time together, Calenne had been by turns waspish, proud, solemn and gleeful. The empty-eyed soul had none of that, not even simple curiosity. A canvas without colour or form. The tyranny of Otherworld – the longer one walked its mists, the less of you did the walking.

Was he too late?

"Calenne?"

Viktor reached out. His fingers passed through hers. At once leaden and numb, they fell to his side. Chest heaving with icy spasm, he collapsed to one knee, thoughts awash with raven cries and the thrum of wings.

((Viktor?)) Golden light shimmered. Elzar stepped closer through the mists, voice and form no realer than anything else in that world. ((What can I do?))

"Stay . . . Stay back." Viktor forced the words through chattering teeth and stood, his good hand held up in warding. "Leave me be."

Elzar faded, lost to the mists. Viktor blotted out the raven-song and willed life into his frozen arm. A mistake to touch the ethereal with ephemeral flesh. He'd known, but in the moment had been unable to help himself. The stony heart of Viktor Droshna was a lie. Calenne had made it thus long ago.

Fingers prickling to life, Viktor let his shadow flow outward. He cloaked himself in Dark, a shield against Otherworld's malice. He reached out once more. This time, his fingers closed around the spirit's. Gentle. Mindful of his strength and her frailty.

"Calenne," he breathed. "It's time for you to come home."

At last, the etravia responded. Her brow softened, features gathering to panic.

"You shouldn't be here."

Her voice was barely an echo. A memory. But for all that, it set his soul alight. Unmistakeably Calenne. He clasped her other hand, holding both tight. "Nor should you."

Lips pinched tight. For the first time, Calenne truly resembled herself. "Poor Viktor. Always so certain you know what's best." She shook her head, strands of ghostly matter wisping away. "He's here."

Viktor turned, following her milky gaze. Clouds gathered like a bloodstain in the mists, the thunderheads of a storm, the white devoured by the black.

Before he could move, they smothered him.

He clung to Calenne's etravia and reached into his shadow, desperate for a means of defence.

The storm passed as swiftly as it had come. Clouds parted, and Viktor stood once more in the workshop's candlelit gloom. Failure thick in his throat, he stared down at empty hands. At the doll's lifeless body. Sword and vranastone sat motionless in the black water alongside.

Gloved fingertips brushed the blade. Smoke curled upward from the caress.

"No!" Viktor stared in horror as the sword crumbled to rust.

"Have you not learned your lesson?" Immaculate in coat, hat and feathered domino mask, the Raven looked up from the doll, and planted his walking cane between his legs. His goatee twitched a frown. "I told you before. I will not be stolen from."

Elzar gaped, the light about his shoulders fading to nothing. "Lumestra preserve us."

"Ha!" the Raven replied. "I doubt it."

Viktor glanced down, clenching and unclenching his fists, barely able to breathe for sorrow. So close. He'd held Calenne in his hands. Part of him still felt her now, for all that she was nowhere to be seen. "Can you steal from a thief?" Sorrow winnowed away until only anger remained. "She doesn't belong to you!"

The Raven shook his head. "What a man you are to see people as possessions. I am but a guardian ..." His expression lost what little friendliness it contained. His gravelly voice grew deeper still. "And one who is fast running out of patience."

"Calenne Trelan belongs to the living, not the dead."

The Raven sneered. "So like an ephemeral, laying eyes upon the moment and thinking it eternity. She belongs to *herself*."

Candles hissed and sputtered. Viktor took an involuntary half-step back, uncustomary fear thickening his gorge. The Raven wasn't merely in the room, he *was* the room. His being filled every nook and cranny.

"There is a balance to life and death," said the Raven. "It isn't yours to break. I'd hoped Roslava might reason with you. Alas that you didn't listen."

"You turned her against me!" Viktor snapped.

The candles dimmed another fraction. "I opened her eyes to a truth already known, nothing more. Why do you suppose she's always doubted you?" The Raven tilted his head. "Perhaps we should ask her. Oh, that's right. We can't. Not after what you did."

"What's he talking about?" croaked Elzar.

"At Darkmere. She shattered the vranastone." Viktor told himself he'd nothing to feel guilty over. Had his shadow not stolen Rosa's memories, too much of what she'd seen could have been misinterpreted. A mistake, perhaps, born of a desperate moment, his mind reeling from unexpected separation from Otherworld. But it lay in the past, and not for changing. And what had come after? The pursuit through the rain, Silsarian spears ever drawing closer. He'd atoned for his transgression in blood. "I'd no choice. I—"

"Viktor?" Elzar glanced at the Raven, and back to Viktor. "What did you do?"

"I erred," he replied. "A rash action taken when I was other than myself."

The doubt in Elzar's eyes was a blade in Viktor's heart. Words were ever deadlier than swords, and the Raven wielded them well. But why wield them at all? A god could call upon better, and yet he sought to cow and convince, or else break Elzar's faithfulness as he had Rosa's. Had the Raven been certain of snuffing out Viktor's life, he'd have done so already, without theatrics. And that left only one possibility.

The Raven was *afraid*.

At Darkmere, Viktor had sensed the Raven's presence and his hesitance both. He'd assumed the Keeper of the Dead had resorted to manipulation out of fear of the power rooted in the city's stones – power kin to Viktor's shadow. There was nothing to call on here save himself. Was that enough? Viktor had never considered the possibility before, but now recognised its logic. His shadow was of the Dark, and the Dark was older than the Raven – the Keeper of the Dead was a brittle umbra beneath it.

He could be fought. Be beaten. An impossible feat, save for one who had always thrived on challenge. Viktor ravelled in a shadow dissipated by his expulsion from Otherworld, gathering it to purpose.

Again, the Raven stepped closer.

Viktor stood eye to eye with the Keeper of the Dead in the fading candlelight. "Whatever I have done, I remain a protector of my people. A man forever limited by doubt. To embrace the former, I gladly move beyond the latter."

"Your people?" The Raven punctuated a gravelly laugh with a *rat-tat* of his cane on the floor. "It's about you. Everything always is, whatever you claim. Viktor Akadra . . . I'm sorry, Viktor *Droshna* . . . the man who cannot fail because he doesn't know how. Look what pride has made of you. You cannot outrun the Dark."

Viktor reached out for the last of his shadow, so goaded by the other's scorn that he almost missed the snare within the snare – the reason *why* his shadow was so diffuse. He hadn't lost his grip on Calenne – he'd never really held her. His shadow had done that, and a portion of his shadow remained in Otherworld, with her. They were still connected, one to the other and both to the doll by Elzar's tether of light. If he lashed out recklessly with his shadow, as he'd so nearly done, Calenne would slip away. With her sword destroyed, he might search a lifetime and never find her.

Viktor threw sidelong glance at Elzar. "I am not always the man I wish to be. I can only ask that you trust me."

For all that the old proctor was haggard and pale, he nodded. He *knew*.

The Raven's narrow gaze shifted to Elzar. "Don't listen to him. You can't—"

Viktor loosed his shadow. It ripped into the Raven. Not only his ephemeral form, but the vast, smothering presence beyond mortal sight. The god screamed in fury, cane abandoned and arms rigid.

The room filled with the shriek of bird voices, and the thunder of black wings. Candles toppled, or were extinguished in the backwash. Drapes danced and tore, bathing the room in moonlight. Books thumped to the floor, their pages shredded and scattered to a maelstrom of pale, forbidden leaves. Breaking glass chimed bright.

Viktor flung up a hand to shield his eyes. Talons raked bright rivulets of pain across scalp and shoulders; the wet rip of beak tugged at cloth and flesh. Choking on carrion stench, Viktor drew his shadow tighter about the Raven ... but through it all, held Calenne's soul tighter still.

Elzar screamed.

"Elzar!" Viktor turned. The old man was naught but a pale glow in the writhing, shrieking mass.

In that moment of distraction, the Raven tore free. Viktor's shadow howled and dispersed like smoke in the wind.

Breathless, Viktor fell to his knees. He strove to regather his shadow, but every flaring of pain, every ear-splitting shriek, drove it further from his grasp. The part of it – the part of *him* – anchored to Calenne lost ground with every racing heartbeat.

"Petulant child!" The squalling flock parted before the Raven. His form shimmered. The goateed gentleman in formal garb. An elderly, dark-featured woman in widow's weeds. One then the other. Both and neither. "I warned you of arrogance."

Viktor grunted through gritted teeth, panic rising as the last of his connection to Calenne began to slide. Bellowing, he struck at the Raven with what shadow remained.

For his troubles, he received only laughter, and the talons' bloody caress.

"Do one thing, and do it well," snapped the Raven. "Ephemerals weren't meant for more."

Viktor's frustration and despair spilled free as a wordless roar. The Raven had the right of it. He couldn't contest the Keeper of the Dead without relinquishing his grasp on Calenne.

He couldn't.

Better to let the Raven claim them both than be for ever apart. Except ... Except to embrace death was to abandon a Republic that looked to him for protection. He who forsook that charge was unworthy of peace – even the peace of death.

He had to let her go.

"Forgive me," he breathed, the words lost beneath the wingbeats.

Golden light flared. The swarm shrieked, boiling away to the workshop's corners. The Raven staggered, hands clasped to his face. Elzar slumped against the doll's table, a wan, tottering form in the moonlight, his golden robes bright with blood. The tether binding Viktor to the doll trembled.

"Bring her home," gasped Elzar.

The Raven screeched and his flock rallied. A moment bought. But a moment was enough. Shadow resurgent, Viktor lashed at the god's ephemeral form. It tore like paper, the left half of his being dissolved into black, starlit smoke.

The Keeper of the Dead screamed.

The flock squalled anew, a tornado of talons and wings spiralling around the ruined workshop. Then it too scattered into smoke, and the Raven was gone.

Viktor staggered upright into drifting feathers and the dancing fragments of torn manuscripts, unable to credit the evidence of his senses. A dozen frantic pacings of his heart stuttered before triumph yielded to tragedy. The tether was gone, his purchase on Calenne's soul with it. He'd bested a god – perhaps even dealt a mortal blow – but that achievement was nothing to the writhing, gnawing loss devouring him from within.

He swallowed, stoic facade crumbling beneath the weight of tears.

"She's gone," he breathed. "She's gone."

Elzar offered no reply. Viktor found him amid the workshop's wreckage, shoulder propped against the doll's table, eyes sightless and still. Careless of the blood, of his own screaming wounds, he knelt and embraced the man more responsible for his raising than any kin. Who'd taught him not to fear his shadow, and how to wield it; to trust to his instincts, however others maligned his actions.

The man he'd led into the clutches of death itself.

Clutching him tight, head cradled against his own, Viktor strove for words that might reach into Otherworld. That Elzar might hear before his soul slipped its last mooring in the living realm.

The ripple of water and the scrape of a porcelain hand clutching at the table's edge banished them unspoken.

[[Viktor?]]

Endas, 4th Day of Dawntithe

A warrior's duty is to protect those in need.
All else is sophistry.

from the Saga of Hadar Saran

Eighteen

Grey dawn gathered reluctantly beyond the eaves of Ganadra Wood, driving night's murk into the layland's long shadows. Fresh snow lent the illusion of peace. Impossible to see the rubble of village and homestead razed in the Avitra Briganda or the mournful crops of lychfield headstones. A blank canvas upon which swords could paint a new future, for good or ill. Artistry which suited Rosa better than the sculptry of recent months.

Edran spat into the brambles, his expression furled in habitual disappointment. "He's late."

A big man – he surrendered little in height to the distant Viktor Droshna – Edran epitomised Silda Drenn's followers. Unkempt, suspicious and lacking the discipline that was soldiering's foundation, his weapons were nonetheless oiled and free of rust.

"We wait." Drenn kept her eyes to the rolling eastern hills hiding the town of Yelska. Haldravord, and Prince Thirava's makeshift court, lay leagues beyond. Her bow was strung, her quiver muffled with wool-cloth to still the clatter of arrows. "Castir said he'd be here, so he will."

The soft-spoken words earned a flurry of scowls from the assembled wolf's-heads – with Drenn in command, it was impossible to think of them as anything else – but they subsided. Drenn had tighter control over her followers than most. She knew when to listen, and when to stand firm – a knack of leadership some went their whole lives without learning.

"I'd hate to think we made this early start for nothing." Rosa drew her cloak tighter, vapour dancing on her breath. "You're certain he'll show?"

"Nothing's certain." Drenn twitched a shrug. "Castir's close enough to Thirava's chieftains that he can come and go as he wishes."

Rosa scowled. The prospect of what Castir might have traded to earn even conditional trust sat sour in her gut. "You trust him?"

Drenn nodded. "Wouldn't give him coin for a horse, but in this ...?"

"A hundred things could go wrong," said Edran.

"True. Shadowthorns are paranoid, even around those they reckon they've tamed." Drenn's wolfish grin was echoed readily by others. "But they ain't paranoid enough. Not yet."

They numbered seven in all. Seven vagabonds crouched in the treeline's sparse cover. Enough to travel in safety without drawing attention. A mix of old comrades from Drenn's time in Thrakkia, and Heartwealders capable enough to not get themselves killed.

"Want me to take a look?" Jonas was one of those Rosa had chosen, a straw-haired farmhand. He'd joined up in Tarvallion's marketplace, eager to prove his worth.

"Sit down, boy." Edran shoved Jonas to his knees, provoking a ripple of laughter. "Have patience."

"I didn't pick this spot on a whim," said Drenn. "You'll have to trudge half a mile to see something we can't."

Jonas fiddled with the brass ring on his left hand and scowled away embarrassment.

Paces further north along the wood's ragged extent, Mirada hugged her shoulders close and offered a thin smile. "Don't be so keen. Adventure'll find you soon enough. Might wish it didn't. Right, Kalar?"

Kalar grunted in agreement. Rosa was certain the two were deserters. Mirada's swordplay was too honed to be self-taught, too efficient to have been tutored. The stiffness of Kalar's bearing betrayed him – not to mention the small, almost undetectable pause at the end of his every reply. The one otherwise home to *my lady* or *sir*.

Not long ago, Rosa would have distrusted both, but the difference between desertion and her own retreat from the army existed only in formality of language. She and they were more the same than different, and certainly had more in common than with Solveik, the Thrakkian who completed their small band. He wore the plain black claith of a thrydaxe – sellswording being an honourable trade in the south – but the entwined serpent-brands on his forehead spoke of one cast out from his thane's service. Rosa hadn't asked why. You didn't.

A year before, she'd been mistress of Essamere. What was she now?

"There," rumbled Solveik, his Tressian low-tongue accented and halting. "Northeast."

Rosa followed the jab of gauntleted finger to a distant hilltop and the slash of a drystone wall, half-hidden beneath snow. A dark shape swaddled in a woollen greatcoat clambered over the crest and stumbled up the gentle slope towards Ganadra Wood.

"At last." Edran stomped his feet. "Time to get moving."

"Wait," hissed Drenn. "Something ain't right."

A tingle at the base of Rosa's spine offered similar conclusion, though reason hadn't yet caught up with instinct.

"Of course something isn't right," said Mirada. "We're up at the crack of dawn, shivering parts and pieces off. Sooner we get him, sooner we get back to a fire and warm food."

Rosa stared northeast to the weaving trail of footprints and the figure hurrying at their head. Close enough now to read the urgency of his movements, to catch brief glances cast behind. "He's being pursued."

Edran snorted. "By cyraeths, I suppose? That being why we can't see them."

The hilltop behind the fugitive came alive with shadowthorns. A dozen men on foot. Three riders. Swords. Shields. Even a few spears. As far again behind the fleeing Castir as he himself was from the safety of the trees.

Drenn's fingers brushed her sunburst pendant. "We're done here."

Edran and Solveik nodded. Kalar stared stonily at the approaching pursuit. Mirada scowled.

"What?" Jonas' eyes widened. "We just abandon him?"

"We head back through the woods," said Drenn. "And we pray to Lumestra that we reach the horses before the shadowthorns tumble to us."

"And the folk captured at Bresanna?" asked Rosa. "Castir knows where they've been taken."

"*Maybe*," Drenn replied. "I said *maybe* he knows where they are."

Rosa met her frosty glare unblinking. Word of Bresanna had reached

Morten's Rock the morning after she'd arrived. The village razed and the populace taken – those who hadn't been slain. They'd already lost a day making contact with Castir. They couldn't afford another delay.

And as for Castir himself ... ?

"Either way, we need him," said Rosa. "And he needs us."

She stood. Drenn rushed to check her, hand outspread and features tight. "You're too new at this, *Lady* Orova." She hissed emphasis into the title. "You've not got damn Essamere at your back now. Surprise and numbers. We don't have those, so we slink away. That's how we live to fight another day."

Rosa rode out the scorn, her own anger rising to meet it. No small part of it was levelled at herself, for Drenn was right, for all that she was also dead wrong. "It's also how we *lose*."

"Say we go down there," snapped Drenn. "There's two shadowthorns for each of us. Even if we get Castir out, what will it cost?"

Rosa slapped her hand away. "I came to you to help save lives. That starts with one." She stabbed a finger down the slope. "That one. Or I've no business here at all."

"Then go." Drenn shook her head and stepped aside. "But you'll go alone."

No one else moved. Only Jonas looked at all torn, but of them all he was the most likely to get himself killed if he followed.

"I've been alone before."

Rosa strode free of the undergrowth, leaving trees and companions behind. She struck steady pace, swift of stride, boots crunching through virgin snows. Exertion crackled life into juddering muscles, driving out the chill. *Was* this rashness? Probably. You couldn't know until the moment was past, and by then it was too late.

The first warning sounded on the slope below.

The Hadari were strung out, a stuttered line trailing northeast. Good. She needed all the advantage she could get. Years ago, a dozen shadowthorns would have been nothing, but she'd been younger then. Younger, and eternal and thus proof from death. Now, Rosa felt every one of the intervening years twofold. The old wound pulled at her shoulder, stiffer than it should have been.

Castir – if Castir it was – fell headlong into the snows and rose shivering.

The leading Hadari quickened, swords drawn. At the end of the shadowthorn line, a horseman rowelled his steed, a spear held high to catch Ashana's sight.

Rosa's sole skidded on a hidden stone. Regaining balance, she stifled the mounting urge to break into a run, to have the uneven contest done with, one way or the other. Instead, she slowed. The cold was greedy. It would take all she offered, and leave her with nothing. The Hadari hadn't learnt that lesson, or were too caught up in dreams of glory to care.

Dreams of glory ended in the grave. No one knew that better than she.

Castir fell again as she reached him. Hand about his elbow, she dragged him upright and gazed into a face flushed red with exertion.

"Keep going. Make for the trees."

Garbling thanks, the eastwealder scrambled away.

Rosa swept her cloak open, hand on a sword not yet drawn.

The leading Hadari bellowed, his cry booming beneath brooding skies. He broke into a run, sword cleaving wildly at the air, as if vigour alone won battles. There was no caution in his dark eyes, only the gleam of youth burdened with duty unfulfilled and a name not yet made.

Rosa's sword sang as it left the scabbard. An old comrade, come again to the battlefield. Without altering pace, she stepped inside the clansman's swing. A thrust between his ribs left him dying in the snow, burdens gone and name forgotten.

She swept the bloody sword high, the old battle cry spilling free. "Until Death!"

Now she ran. To close the distance and fill the morning with blood.

The second shadowthorn died as swiftly as the first, without even chime of steel to mark his passing. The third was slower, cannier, but his parry came too late. Rosa's sword jarred on bone. He fell, clutching at a gushing sword-wrist. A backswing ended his cries, and she ran on.

Shadowthorn voices raised to fury. Gold gleamed along the footprint trail. A havildar in golden helm and heavy scale rose high in his stirrups, sword sweeping in Rosa's direction even as he bellowed orders.

A helmless brute with a milky eye blocked Rosa's path, a tall, steel-rimmed shield steady and a spear thrusting at her belly. A scraping parry and the spearhead flashed past her side. A kick to the shield-boss staggered its bearer.

Warned by a thunder of hooves, Rosa dived aside, the shieldsman untouched. The sharp, wrenching tug at her neck and the sound of tearing cloth came as one. The world spun in a dizzying spray of snow that ended with a jarred shoulder against frozen ground. As she blinked red-black splotches from her eyes, the horseman wheeled about, spear lowered for another pass.

Tearing free her cloak's remnant, Rosa stood. Breath a red wind, pulse a drumbeat that drowned all else, she hurled herself aside. The spear flashed past. Boots slewed in the snow, pitching Rosa sideways, and the milky-eyed shieldsman was on her again.

She chopped twice at the spear, strikes slowed by a tugging in her scarred shoulder. More shadowthorns closed the distance, snow spraying from their boots. Time and vigour – ever finite allies – were failing faster than she'd hoped. Beneath the hot rush of straining sinew, Rosa's bones were cold. With every gasping breath, icy tendrils clawed at her flesh.

"Ki vasta!"

The shadowthorn set his shoulder to the shield and barrelled uphill, seeking to barge her to the ground. Rosa loped to meet him. Falling to hip and heel, she slid to the shieldsman's left, shoulder level with his knee and sword slicing at his ankle. Blood spattered the snow. A howl of challenge became a pained shriek.

Rosa clambered upright. The shieldsman did not. Stalking a pace back uphill, she ended his cries in a red gurgle.

Again, the hoofbeats. Again the flashing spear. Tossing sword from right hand to left, Rosa seized the dead man's spear.

It wasn't an accurate throw. The spear was too awkward, too heavy. The speed the rider was closing, it didn't need to be. The horse screamed, legs tangled about the shaft. Man and rider went down in a whirl of armoured robes and flailing hooves.

Without waiting to see who rose from the carnage, Rosa planted a foot on the milky-eyed shadowthorn's chest and tugged free his shield. Taller than she was accustomed to, the balance off-centre, but with breath coming ever more ragged and three more shadowthorns closing about her, she needed every advantage.

Five shadowthorns down, and her cloak the only loss. Not bad, for a knight far out of practice. She was good for one more. And if she could manage one, why not two, or three, or four?

Maybe it had been recklessness. But sometimes, recklessness was all. Sevaka would understand.

An arrow hissed into the snow at her feet. Downhill, past the advancing swordsman, a rangy shadowthorn archer nocked another.

Rosa knew she had to move. To set herself side-on to the archer and the shield square in his path. Knew it, but was powerless to do so. She was back in Darkmere, arrow buried deep in a screaming shoulder, life slipping away.

The air whistled with the sound of an arrow in flight.

The Hadari archer spun about and pitched into the snows. Another scream sounded behind Rosa, the *whumph* of a falling body close on its heels.

"Vaega af vaega!"

A sword shattered beneath the strike of Solveik's colossal axe, the strike enough to split the wielder's torso nearly in two. Weary thoughts catching up with events, Rosa stared uphill. Jonas, his sword bloody, stood over a dying clansman. Edran plucked the spear from a second while Mirada ran him through. Kalar watched from a short distance away, arms folded, a bloody knife in each hand and a body at his feet.

As the last shadowthorn shield shattered beneath Solveik's axe, the havildar spurred downhill. He made it a dozen yards before Drenn's arrow took him in the neck. His horse stumbled to a confused halt.

"Edran! Get that bloody nag. We can use it." Drenn half-ran, half-stumbled down the churned slope to Rosa's side. "Next time, we leave you."

The words held rebuke, but her tone held something very different.

Rosa let her shield drop. "As you say."

Bannar Tor was the closest thing to a haven in the occupied Eastshires. What had once been a double ring of stone walls were now little more than grassy hummocks. The overgrown and subsided cellars served as shelter for Drenn's growing band, and the trees offered vantage for sentries.

Nevertheless, Rosa felt no safer than she had at Morten's Rock – itself little more than a fortified island at the merging of the Swiftblood and Rappadan Rivers. The soldier in her wanted battlements and towers. The fire, though? The fire she was grateful for. And the stew was scarcely worse than campaign rations, for all that its ingredients were scavenged or stolen. After the trials of the morning, she needed both.

Setting aside the empty bowl, she massaged her stiff shoulder. Cold and exertion had knotted it tight. "You're sure?"

Across the slab serving as their makeshift table, Castir threaded ink-stained fingers and scowled. Though much improved from their first meeting, the balding merchant still looked fit to bolt at first provocation. "That's what I heard. They've been gathering prisoners at Terevosk for the last week. From Bresanna and at least six other border villages. Might be three hundred, might be more. Word is the convoy's moving out for Haldravord at dawn. From there—"

"From there, it's back to the Empire," growled Drenn. "And a sale to the highest bidder."

Over by the doorway, Edran folded his arms. "Or sacrifice. Ashana never said no to a heart offered beneath moonlight, did she?"

"Pffff," Drenn waved a dismissive hand. "Unless you know different, Rosa?"

Rosa scowled. "Kai Saran was capable of any wickedness. His daughter is no different. We have to assume the worst."

"I don't know about that." Castir scratched his scalp, his eyes restless and empty, his voice thick with loss. "Only that they're going."

"Still not clear how a coin-rattler like you gets to hear about this," said Edran. "Been slaving your own kind?"

"No! I do a bit of trade where I can, of course, but nothing like that!" Castir bit his tongue. "My brother's . . . friendly with one of the chieftains. Things slip in quiet moments."

Edran growled. "If you're in so tight with the shadowthorns, why were they chasing you?"

"Wasn't supposed to be anyone in or out of Yelska, only I didn't know." Castir stared at the wall, cheeks taut. "Avin and Lukas held them long enough for me to get clear. They were good boys. They deserved . . . "

He broke off, bunched fingers to his mouth.

"How many guards on the convoy?"

The question came from Athaga Varalon, the greying, matronly woman who served as the third of Drenn's lieutenants, besides Edran and Rosa herself. Beneath belted chainmail, her serene's habit was patched and faded to the point of being unrecognisable. Her Lumestran vows were in rather worse order, the consequence of the late, unlamented Arzro Makrov ransacking Athaga's convent for sheltering wolf's-heads during the occupation of the south. She and Drenn had been together ever since.

"I don't know," said Castir.

"Won't be more than a hundred," said Drenn. "Maybe not even that, with the border how it is. Not like shackled folk can fight back, is it?"

Athaga nodded. "There's not much in the way of shelter at Terevosk. It's what? A stockade and a broken-down mining camp? I'll ask around. Odds are good one of our motley bunch knows it."

"So we're going?" asked Edran.

"With three hundred lives at stake?" Drenn shrugged. "We've better than a hundred of our own camped hereabouts. If I send lads across the border with tales of drudgery and blood sacrifice we'll double that before dusk."

"No," said Rosa.

Drenn laughed. "No, she says. The woman who ran headlong into a dozen shadowthorns."

"The *knight* who marched into battle, knowing what she faced," Rosa corrected. "You trawl the villages for every hothead with a sword, and we'll fill Otherworld with more of our own than the enemy. We do this with who we have to hand. We have the numbers. We have surprise. Someone told me that was the way we did things."

Drenn lapsed into silence, fingers toying with her sunburst pendant. "Athaga?"

Heavy shoulders shrugged. "We'll need a plan."

Rosa squinted up through the moss-choked hole in the roof. Noon was passing, and opportunity with it. "Then let's make one."

Nineteen

Melanna let the reports fall to the table. Despite the noonday sun streaming through the balcony door, the room seemed colder, the gilded splendour of her forebears muted.

"You're supposed to be my spymaster, Haldrane." She offered the rebuke softly, so that it wouldn't carry to the Immortals standing vigil beyond the chamber.

"And so I am privileged to remain." For all the smoothness in Haldrane's voice, his dark features were troubled. "But I cannot see everything."

"Human failing is one thing, but to miss armies on the march?"

"If you'd taken my advice and dealt with Cardivan as he deserves, it wouldn't matter."

"Have a care," rumbled Aeldran. Like Haldrane, he stood. Whatever the informality of private moments, he hewed to strictest protocol in the presence of others – regardless of the discomfort it awoke in his bindwork leg. Melanna had long since abandoned hopes of convincing him otherwise. "Even a spymaster should choose his words with discretion."

Haldrane gave a sharp nod of apology, setting silver threads shimmering in his midnight robes. "I lost many agents learning even this much. Nothing that leads back to Cardivan, of course. Disappearances on the road. Tavern brawls with curious timing. One by one, he is putting out my eyes."

Aeldran snorted. "These are the icularis that drove my grandfather to paranoia?"

"Maggad was paranoid from birth," Haldrane replied acidly. "As are so many Andwars."

Melanna stilled Aeldran with a glance. "We've enemies enough without quarrelling among ourselves. I'll have peace in my own chambers, if nowhere else."

He offered a stiff bow. "My apologies, *essavim*. And to you, Haldrane."

"I am but a humble servant. No apologies are required."

Melanna crossed to the balcony and stared out across the gardens. The charred remains of the old wood were a dark stain against snow. What she'd intended as a gesture of strength now felt more like portent.

Melanna caught the faintest scent of spices, borne from the noonday market held at the palace gates, dusky and tantalising. She'd have given anything to unchain her hair, exchange golden dress for simple robes and walk the stalls. *Almost* anything. And the part she couldn't give was the same as that which commanded her to stay.

Silsaria was gathering to war, with Novona and Kerna as its allies. Laxness hadn't shielded the mustering forces from Haldrane's sight. Marching armies sang out to be noticed. There *were* perhaps more warbands than was normal for the ailing winter, but not expressly so. Brigandage, repairs to crumbling fortifications, aid to beleaguered villages when snow-swollen rivers burst their banks ... even without war, there was much to occupy strong arms.

Haldrane's concern lay in warriors *concealed*. Pilgrims who weren't truly pilgrims. Trade convoys that bought little and sold less. Refugees fleeing landslides and floods whose extent had been sorely exaggerated, if they'd happened at all. Roamer caravans with folk ignorant of their own traditions. All travelling westward over long weeks to Silsaria's Rhalesh border. Singly, each was nothing to raise an eyebrow, but taken together ... ? Well, they boded ill, and not just for the Tressian Republic.

"What is he waiting for?" said Melanna.

Haldrane offered a minuscule shrug. "I understand Dotha Novona has no wish to antagonise you without cause. There's at least one ambitious nephew who'd overthrow her in a heartbeat if he could claim loyalty to the Empress as his rallying cry. It's why Agrana's fleets, as yet, remain in port."

Aeldran nodded. "But if the Tressians do anything provocative ... ?"

"Who'd blame Cardivan for supporting his poor, embattled son or others for supporting him? You'll forgive me for saying so, Empress, but family ever offers the finest excuse."

And the Tressians *would* offer provocation, sooner or later. Josiri had warned as much.

"Cardivan will still have to cross your lands, *essavim*," said Aeldran. "You can refuse permission."

Silsaria's western border was shared between Rhaled and Icansae. Even if Mergadir was bypassed, reaching Redsigor meant marching dozens of leagues across one or both neighbouring kingdoms.

"We haven't the spears to hold them." Melanna saw options no better now than at Midwintertide, when Cardivan's ambitions had lain revealed. "If I withhold consent, and they march anyway? Cardivan will proclaim my weakness from the mountaintops. It won't just be Kerna and Novona, but Britonis and Demestae too. And it won't be the Tressian Republic as the prize, but my throne."

"We could call up the Veteran's Lodges?" said Aeldran.

"The old and the broken?" Melanna shook her head. "After Govanna they'd be as likely to fight for Cardivan as against him."

Haldrane tugged at his goatee. "Then perhaps it might be best to wish Cardivan good fortune, and let him do as he wishes. Tragedy though it would be, the Tressians might even kill him."

Little hope of that. Neither Cardivan nor Thirava made habit of venturing near the front lines.

"And how many others will die alongside?" said Melanna.

"Does it even matter?" rumbled Aeldran.

She glared, temper's reins slipping from her grasp. "Silsaria is a province of Empire. They are all my subjects, and rely on me for wisdom when it is lacking in their own king. Or is it your judgement, husband, that I should concern myself with the well-being only of the Rhalesh?"

Aeldran Andwar, Rhalesh by marriage but Icansae by blood, bit his tongue.

Melanna rounded on Haldrane. "And what happens if Cardivan rouses the Republic to fury? Who will face their wrath when the last Silsarian stag flees the field? Or do you suppose Droshna will content himself with the border restored? He'll see only that the Hadari Empire again offered nothing but blood and steel, and will repay it in kind. I did not assume the throne to preside over needless death!"

Hypocrite.

Neither said it, but Melanna read the sentiment in their eyes. She'd seized the throne with blood-slicked hands – the altar of her ambition lay lost beneath the bodies of friend and foe. Those who'd followed her, and those who'd barred her way. The princessa who would be Empress, no matter the obstacle. For all that tradition had forced her to that path – for all that hers *was* the story of Empire, played out generation after generation – the burden of the dead grew with each passing year.

Haldrane shrugged. "Then I suggest we address the problem at its source. Cardivan winters at your great-uncle's villa. Well within the city's bounds and in easy reach. Such a terrible shame if he met with an accident."

"And why do you suppose he's still here?" said Aeldran. "If we remove him while he's under our hospitality – Ashana preserve us, if we *fail* – it will be civil war."

"No door can bar a Raven's herald, or so I understand."

Melanna scowled away the veiled suggestion. "If I resort to such methods, even once, I've already lost sight of what's important."

Haldrane crooked a lopsided smile, never more the tempter of wayward souls than at that moment. "I know. But I found the image of Cardivan's mottled body floating in a sewer rather soothing. It seemed cruel to withhold it." The smile faded. "I wish I could offer more, but there is death in the coming days. Even an Empress cannot prevent it. She can only choose where it falls."

Apara had always been a creature of the city. Rooftops and alleyways were her stalking ground. Ledges and gutters were handholds for a housebreaker with an eye for a bargain. Yet for all that – for all Tregard had been her home since she'd fled Tressia – the city didn't feel *right*.

It wasn't just that its walls held a fraction of Tressia's sprawl. Even beneath overcast skies it was brighter, more vibrant. Not just the streets themselves, with their brilliant canopies and painted shutters – the vines trailing from rooftop gardens that were never less than splendid come the spring – but the populace's mood. Folk held heads high in Tregard where her countrymen shuffled, downcast. Under winter sun, as it was at that moment, it bordered on the divine.

Or perhaps it just seemed so. The arched, covered roadway of Emperor's Walk had been designed to elevate royalty above the rabble as much as offer a private route to the mirrored temples of Ravencourt and Mooncourt. By rights, Apara should have felt out of place. A Tressian and a dregrat, trespassing on the territory of her betters. But wasn't that a thief's purview?

Besides, she was there by invitation, delivered to her house on the marketplace. Others in the small procession wished it otherwise. Not Melanna, of course, who'd issued the invitation and spoken at length of her quandary. Nor Kaila, who trailed behind with awed expression. But the lunassera?

Even with silver half-masks to guard their expressions, the handmaidens made it plain Apara was unwelcome, more likely for her sundered ties to the Raven than the country of her birth. Disapproving glances from the Immortals guarding the roadway felt more justified – even if there was little chance they knew the woman in expensive emerald silks was also liberator of so many fine things from so many unworthy owners.

But for the dreams, Apara might have been happy. They didn't come every night, but left her heart hammering and her skin slick with sweat. Last night had been the worst, details previously shrouded by formless horror stark upon waking. The past reawoken. Her mind and body not her own, urged to kill at Viktor Droshna's command. And then, as the blow fell, it was no longer Apara's mother beneath, but her sister Sevaka. A meld of old memories she'd hoped to forget.

"Haldrane thinks I should ask you to *persuade* Cardivan," said Melanna.

And just like that, Apara was back in Dregmeet. Another piece of her unhappy past. The ruined church, and the stream of petitioners seeking grim favours. She'd not taken a life since coming to Tregard. "*Are* you asking me?"

The ripper's life was behind her, and good riddance, but friendship was friendship.

"I don't want to. It'll only make it easier next time. Before long, it'll come so softly I won't even stop to think."

Apara's shoulders eased. "What will you do?"

"Something I don't want to. It seems that's what it means to be Empress."

"You could always *persuade* him yourself."

A wan smile. "That really would make things worse."

"What would it make worse, Madda?" Kaila piped up, proving once again that a child's hearing scaled proportionately to the awkwardness of what could be heard.

Apara crouched, mock-stern. "It's unbecoming of a princessa to eavesdrop on her elders' conversation, *essavim*."

Kaila narrowed her eyes and promptly ignored the rebuke. "You don't make any sound when you walk, do you know that?"

Melanna stifled a burst of laughter. Apara regarded Kaila with rather more wariness. Most folk didn't notice that. "I've learned to be very careful where I tread, little one."

"Will you teach me?"

"Whatever you like, as soon as your mother thinks you old enough."

Too late, Apara recognised the insult in offering to teach thief's skills to the Imperial heir, but Melanna merely smiled and continued on.

By turns, they arrived at Mooncourt Temple, the arches of Emperor's Walk bearing them far above the snow-crowded gardens. Folk of all ages roamed beneath the bare-limbed birch trees, or sat in silent contemplation at the edge of the fast-flowing stream. Ashana's voice was louder in the bounds of her temple, or so it was said, her blessings unwavering. That was why so many of its cloisters were given over not to worship, but healing for those who would recover, and respite for those who would not.

Another archway – another pair of Immortals at stiff attention – and they passed into the temple itself. Beyond a broad balcony, the birch trees of the sanctum mound reached for the open sky. There were no celebrants in sight, only the white-robed temple guards. Warned of the Empress' coming, the priests offered privacy by clearing the cloister.

"I'll go the rest of the way alone," said Melanna. "You'll watch Kaila?"

Apara nodded. There should have been no need of her presence, watchful or otherwise. Not with sanctum guards and lunassera close by, and Immortals within cry. But not all Melanna Saranal's memories of Mooncourt Temple were happy ones. "Of course."

The smile returned. "You might even teach her a little of your careful tread. But nothing of persuasion, if you please."

"Blessed Ashana, I beseech you. Guide your ephemeral daughter."

The old prayer came easily enough, for all that Melanna loathed to speak it. Bargains had been struck and promises made, and she knew so little of the rules governing either. Eyes clasped shut, she breathed deep of the root-woven temple mound's musty, bitter air. Listened for some sign that the goddess had heard, and half-hoped that she had not.

There was only the skitter of insects and the echo of her own breaths returned.

"Blessed Ashana, I beseech you. Guide your ephemeral daughter."

Jack had forsaken his claim upon her – a claim born of a father's folly – so long as Ashana did the same. Would *speaking* with the goddess also void that promise? That fear had held Melanna back ever since her coronation. Her heart quickened, the cool air of the chamber no longer soothing.

"Blessed Ashana, I beseech you. Guide your ephemeral daughter."

Were the roots already straining to claim her? To whisk her through the soil to the circle of Glandotha, and an eternity of madness as Jack's reluctant bride? Or would she not be reluctant at all when the curse claimed her? Would it be worse to revel in its clutches, as others did?

She pinched her eyes tight. "Blessed Ashana, I beseech you. Guide your ephemeral daughter."

"You shouldn't be here."

Melanna opened her eyes. A stranger in white priestess' robes stood before her, head cocked. A disapproving frown flickered in the alabaster light of root-set crystals. No. Not a stranger. It was more that the newcomer was somehow younger than at their last parting. Straw-blonde hair spilled past shoulders not yet filled out by passing years. A young woman yet slender with girlhood, rather than the heavenly mother she'd known. "Ash—"

"The Goddess Ashana lounges about on Evermoon in the company of her daughters while the valiant dead carouse – loudly – in Eventide. She can't be anywhere else." Even her voice was younger, its pitch a fraction higher and her speech less formal. "Don't say the name – don't even think it – and we can have a chat."

Melanna's heart eased. "What do I call you?"

"Madelyn. That's the name that goes with this." She spread her hands and gestured absent-mindedly at herself, as if surprised to see it. "Kind of. That other one goes with the ... rest."

Melanna thought she understood. The Goddess had spoken of a life before apotheosis. Had the woman remained young while the Goddess had aged? Had she set aside the piece of her that was divine, so as not to draw Jack's notice? Or was it all illusion?

The fear returned.

"Why did you call to me, Melanna?" Ashana ... *Madelyn* ... sat beside her on the stone bench, elbows propped on her knees and chin in her hands. "You know the risk."

Melanna swallowed. "Whichever turn I take, the road is knee-deep in blood. I've long since lost my taste for it."

"And you want the Goddess' help?"

Yes. "I know she can't, not without ... " Melanna's mouth fell ashen, her thoughts full of the bitter, broken creatures Jack had claimed as his wives. Not human any longer. Not even alive in any manner Melanna understood. Cursed testament to the Lord of Fellhallow's desire, bound for ever to the wooden circle at Glandotha. "My father once warned me of the scars battle leaves on the mind. I thought I understood. I didn't."

"You want to know things'll get easier?" Madelyn's hand found hers and held it tight. "They always do, sooner or later. But maybe not for you."

"An Empress' burden?"

"If she's wise." She shrugged. "It's way harder to be a good ruler than a bad one."

"And what would a good ruler do?"

"Do you need me to say? Or are you after my permission for a choice you've already made? Because I've nothing to tell you, in any case. This one's yours to bear."

Melanna scowled. This was her answer, after the risk she'd taken? Had it all been a waste of time and courage?

Anger faded to chagrin. Of course not. These moments, brief though they were, could only ever be a gift. Truth told, they were all she'd sought, though she'd not known until that moment. There had only ever been one way forward were she to remain herself.

"I just needed to see you." But there *was* a question, even so. "Why didn't you tell me that my mother offered herself to Jack?"

"Would that knowledge have changed anything?" asked Madelyn.

"It might have stopped my father trading me for advantage in battle," she replied sourly, even though the claim was unfair. Kai Saran hadn't known the consequence of his bargain with Jack . . . and if he had? He'd been desperate for victory, almost a stranger at their last parting. His final lesson, if one unintended.

They sat in silence for a time, its pleasure diminished by the knowledge that it couldn't last.

"I hear I've a granddaughter." Madelyn chuckled. "That word really doesn't go with this face, does it? Does she know about me? Not the scriptures, but the truth?"

"She will, when she's old enough to understand."

Wry expression turned serious. "Tell her now, Melanna. Not just about me, but about you. About your father. Everything you'd want her to know that no one else can teach. Because your time together's never as long as you think." She squeezed Melanna's fingers, tapped her hand thrice against her knee, and stood. "Call to me again, and Jack will hear. He's too sly to be fooled twice."

"But if I do call, will you come?"

"Goodbye, Melanna. Kiss Kaila for me."

Melanna lingered after the footsteps had faded, drinking in the sanctum's soft fragrance. A moment of peace, to be banished for ever once she stepped outside.

When she departed, she did so without backward glance, retracing her steps through the murky tunnels and into daylight. Apara and Kaila waited on the balcony where she'd left them. Stooping, Melanna kissed her daughter's brow, and ignored the suspicious glance offered in exchange.

"Did you find what you needed?" asked Apara.

"I think so." Melanna took a deep breath. "There's something I need you to do."

*

Cardivan arrived in the palace at sundown, dusk's purpled skies not yet faded to night. He came alone, his errant son having ridden home to Redsigor a day before. Ushered into the throne room by Tavar Rasha, he approached the dais with the stiff-necked composure of a man suffering indignity. That alone almost made it all worthwhile.

"My Empress." Cardivan's eyes darted left and right from Melanna, wary to see Haldrane present alongside Aeldran. Those who glimpsed the spymaster seldom kept their sight long enough to profit by the knowledge. Not once did he think to look up. Had he done so, he might have glimpsed Apara Rann, once again in thief's garb, crouched in the rafters midway between the godly statues of Ashana and the Raven, but higher than even their stern gazes. "You wished to speak with me?"

Melanna held her tongue, drawing out the moment as long as she dared. Was Cardivan wondering at the wisdom of leaving his substantial bodyguard at the villa? Not that Rasha would have allowed them into the throne room.

"I know what you intend, Cardivan," she said at last. "I will not permit it."

His surprised expression was masterful. "You have advantage over me, Empress. Perhaps—"

"The army gathering at Mergadir will not cross the border. Should it attempt to do so, I will meet it with spears. There will be war between the Kingdoms of Rhaled and Silsaria."

Cardivan snarled. "Your father led Rhaled to slaughter. Are the boys and old men left at your command worth three prime warriors apiece?"

Rasha started forward. Melanna checked him with a wave. "Perhaps not, but by midnight six thousand Icansae will stand with them."

Aeldran stepped closer. "Dotha Icansae recalls unkind words uttered at her coronation. My sister has never been one to repay insult in kind when steel might serve."

Blood drained from Cardivan's cheeks. He'd likely guessed that Aelia Andwaral would stand alongside Rhaled, but he could never have anticipated the speed of mobilisation. *That* had been possible only because Apara had carried the request through Otherworld's mists, reducing a journey of days to mere hours. She'd asked to be present in the throne room to see the fruits of her labours. Melanna hoped she had a good view.

"You've lost your senses," Cardivan bit out.

Melanna rose. "One of us has, certainly. So I am minded to present another option." She drew the Goddess' sword from its scabbard. Before Ashana had withdrawn from the world, its steel had burned with white flame. No longer. "Challenge my right to rule, here and now, and a sword will be found. No one will stand in your way."

Or perhaps not. Aeldran had agreed in words, but not expression. More fool him for his advice at Midwintertide. *Show them your fire.* Cardivan saw it plainly now.

Melanna descended the dais, blade pointed at the floor. "The throne is a sword's length away, my king. It'll never be closer. You need only fight for it ... and, of course, I am *only* a woman."

With obvious effort, Cardivan gathered himself to dignity. "This is not the end of the matter!"

Cloaked in brittle pride, he swept from the throne room, chased along by Haldrane's mocking laughter.

Melanna sheathed the sword and breathed deep until her toes tingled.

A victory well earned. Others would be needed.

Aeldran's hands found her shoulders. "You'll see he leaves Tregard tonight, jasaldar?"

Rasha bowed. "Gladly, my prince."

"What now, *essavim*?" Aeldran asked, once Rasha had gone.

"Now, I'll tell Kaila something of her grandfather," Melanna replied. "Beyond that? We shall see what the morning brings."

Twenty

The sentry's struggles eased as the dagger took his throat. Dying breath rushed warm against Rosa's palm. Hand clamped over his mouth, she dragged the twitching body into the headstocks' cabin. Drenn set the door to, and Rosa eased the body down beside the miner's winding cage. Kalar let his own burden drop with rather less care.

"See?" Drenn's smile was barely visible in the hooded lantern's backwash. "Nothing easier."

A dozen bedraggled men and women grinned agreement, but little could have been further from the truth. Reaching the air intake tunnel had required a tortuous moonlit climb, then a sweaty hour clearing a partial collapse. Then a stooped, shuffling procession through darkness – as often waist-deep in cold, stagnant water as not, and sometimes swimming beneath the surface – rock scraping shoulders and blackstone-damp's acrid taste thick on the tongue.

Rosa had taken every step short of breath and with pounding heart. Down in the depths of Terevosk's abandoned blackstone mine, soldiers' courage was nothing. All the worse that Fenner, a wiry fellow who'd escaped Terevosk's razing years before, moved through flooded tunnel and across stone spoil with blithe unconcern.

It had taken every inch of Rosa's self-control not to cry out in relief on reaching the lift shaft. Even the long climb up creaking ladders – the miner's cage had rusted long ago – had been welcome respite. And the heather-scented air at the top? Like rising from the depths of the Dark into the Light of Third Dawn.

As the tallest of their number, Edran had suffered the greatest

number of scrapes. The deserters Talar and Marad. Jonas, his youthful
face pinched in a combination of worry and excitement. Castir, torn
between heartache and rage had muttered darkly about ensuring his
sons' sacrifice not be in vain. Athaga Varalon, her serene's garb caked
in sodden grime.

The rest were southwealders who'd survived the purges after the
Battle of Davenwood. Solemn, quiet folk, exuding grim professionalism.
Like Drenn, they busied themselves unwinding oilcloth from quiver and
bowstring. Unlike her, they eschewed ash longbows for shorter weapons.
A little less than three feet long, they lacked the longbow's range and
sheer killing power, but in the confines of the mining camp, such was
unlikely to matter.

"Glad to be out of there," Edran murmured. "Priests are right, blackstone's evil."

Kalar snorted softly. "Superstition."

"Maybe." Drenn shrugged. "But it ain't just our priests, is it? Surprised
the Hadari didn't drown this place."

"Who says they didn't?" Edran rejoined. "More of it was underwater
than not."

Rosa prodded a corpse with her foot. Not even an Immortal. Just a
clansman mustered from some far-off valley. That the guards had been
posted *outside* the cabin spoke to a fear of escaping prisoners more than
incursion. She forgave the Hadari for not recognising the possibilities.
Without Fenner's memory and gloom-tempered eyes, she'd never have
found her way to Terevosk.

Beckoning for Castir to douse the lantern, she eased open the door.
Even beneath moonlight and crisp snow, the mining camp was less
than beautiful: a handful of squat, tightly packed brick buildings clustered within a stone and timber stockade. Storehouses and workers'
lodgings, lacking all artistry. Terevosk itself – a mile downhill along the
cobbled roadway – had once been picturesque, but Terevosk had burned
during the Avitra Briganda. The mine survived purely as a makeshift
fortress – walls intended to keep wolf's-heads from plunder now served
an invader's purpose.

To the north, directly before the pithead door, ghostfire torches crackled blue-white atop the gate, granting shape to a half-dozen sentries.

Others patrolled the wall-way. Yet more stood sentinel. All eyes were outward. Beside the gate, at ground level, a pair of blanket-draped horses stood tethered beneath a lean-to. The stall could have held at least two-score. A good sign.

She examined the buildings again, this time noting where footprints broke the snow. Westward, Silsarian flags – white stags almost silver in the moonlight – hung from high windows. Slush about the walls and smoke coiling from chimney stacks spoke to fires raging inside. The barracks. To the east, footprints ringed a windowless, two-level storehouse beside the canal's loading dock. The double doors, just visible through intervening buildings, had two guards. A third and fourth joined them briefly, exchanged a handful of words, and passed out of sight behind the storehouse.

Rosa ducked back. "Most of the horses are gone. Looks like Solveik drew them away."

Drenn looked up from stringing her bow. "How many left?"

"Two dozen in the open. There are fires burning in the worker's quarters off to the left. Could be another score. Could be a hundred. There's no way to know."

Edran scowled.

Drenn shrugged. "It'll be the former. Solveik knows how to make twenty men sound like an army. We take the gate and we'll have numbers on our side soon enough."

That was the plan. Three groups. One to create a commotion on the road and draw off the garrison. Another to wait in concealment in Elmgran Woods. And a third – Rosa's – to silence the sentries and open the gate for reinforcements to secure the camp and get the prisoners away. So many things could go wrong. But that was war. You did your best and sought success. The first stage was done. Now it was a race to complete the rest before the shadowthorns realised Solveik was leading them a merry dance across the moors.

"Let's get to it," rumbled Talar. "No sense pushing our luck."

Rosa nodded. "Silda? Jonas? I think they're holding the prisoners in the canal storehouse. Thick walls and sturdy doors that we won't have time to break down. We'll need a key." Jonas nodded, his fingers fidgeting where they gripped his sword. Rosa pressed on. "Athaga—"

"The gatehouse, then the barracks. I know my business, northwealder."

Rosa fought a flash of irritation. "Be about it quietly."

Athaga scowled, but nodded. Clasping her fingers briefly in the sign of the sun, she drew her sword and slipped out into the night. Edran, Castir, Fenner and the rest of the southwealders went with her.

"And us?" Mirada shared a glance with Kalar. "Don't trust us, your ladyship?"

"Go prowling for strays. One shout and this is all for nothing. But watch for the signal arrow."

A flaming arrow from Elmgran Woods meant it had gone wrong in the worst possible way, and absent shadowthorns were returning to camp. It grew likelier with every passing moment.

Mirada and Kalar departed in whisper of movement.

Rosa glanced at Jonas. "Ready for this?"

He nodded a trifle unconvincingly. "Yes, lady."

"Silda?"

Drenn set an arrow to her bowstring. "Until Death."

Rosa suppressed a wince. Not at the sneer beneath mimicry of Essamere's battle cry, but at the reminder it offered. A knight had no place playing at murderer in the darkness, and yet here she was, because no other means would serve.

"Stay low," she told Jonas. "Keep your eyes open."

The first shadowthorn died as Rosa loped for the shelter of a sagging shed. Arrow in his throat, he tipped from the western stockade without a sound. His companion-at-watch perished a heartbeat after, his fall deadened by gusting wind. Two of Athaga's southwealders hugged the stockade wall and crept towards the gate. Others picked their way around a snow-draped spoil heap and bore down on the stables.

"They're good," whispered Jonas.

Rosa dragged him behind the shed, careful nothing showed above the windowsill. "Worry about yourself."

He scowled, cheeks colouring.

Shoulders against timber, Drenn slunk towards the shed's eastern corner and risked a glance towards the storehouse. "Patrol's at the main door again. How do you want to do this?"

Rosa closed her eyes, picturing what she'd seen from the pithead.

"Jonas and I'll deal with the patrol. Can you drop the shadowthorn on the wall?"

Drenn patted her longbow. "Nothing easier."

Rosa turned her attention to Jonas, wondering if she should have kept Kalar or Mirada close. The lad's heart was in the right place, but cold-blooded killing – in silence, no less – was no work for amateurs. "You good for this?"

He nodded, eyes sharp with offence. "Yes, lady."

She pointed to a stack of mouldering pit props and then at a barge's cradle on the paved canal side. "Move when I move."

Rosa broke cover, reaching the pit props in five loping strides. The wallward sentry was still where she remembered, attention – if he had any – fixed on the hillside. The patrol was still out of sight, somewhere between storehouse and canal bank.

Glancing behind to confirm Jonas was still there, Rosa ran for the barge.

Four steps – halfway there – the wallward sentry turned. Bad luck, nothing more. With the wind in the east, he couldn't have heard her footfalls. He stepped back, hand cupped to his mouth, and crumpled as Drenn's arrow took him in the eye.

For a heartbeat, Rosa feared he'd pitch forward and plunge into the canal – alerting the others as surely as any warning cry. But Drenn had timed her shot to perfection. Dying momentum brought the sentry's knees against the stockade parapet. He vanished into the night.

Rosa reached the barge cradle a heartbeat later, nerves buzzing with near-discovery. As Jonas stumbled to stillness beside her, the patrol rounded the storehouse corner: two shadowthorns, muffled and cloaked against the cold, weapons scabbarded.

Rosa held up five fingers, tucking them down one by one as the patrol approached. When she reached one, she closed on the farthest shadowthorn.

He died with Rosa's hand across his mouth and her dagger slicing a ripper's grin. The second perished a heartbeat later, Jonas' takedown smoother than Rosa's own. Then again, he'd two working arms, where her shoulder was already throbbing protest against exertion and cold.

She eased the body to the ground. "Well done, farm boy."

Jonas scowled. "Even farm boys fight when brigands creep out of the dark. The army ain't—"

He broke off, eyes staring wide past Rosa's shoulder.

She spun about, face to face with a Hadari.

The shadowthorn's mistake was going for a weapon instead of raising the alarm. The sword was only halfway drawn when Rosa's lowered shoulder struck leather breastplate. The shadowthorn slammed into the storehouse wall. Rosa's punch scattered wits far afield, the guard's hood falling back as she fell.

"Well, well, well," said Drenn, arriving like a ghost at Rosa's side. "Must be bleeding the shadowthorns out if they're sending their daughters."

"I wouldn't count on it," Rosa growled, thoughts thick with memories of the treacherous Melanna Saranal. "Things are changing across the border."

Drenn drew her dagger. "No matter to me."

Rosa grabbed her wrist. "She's no danger now."

"She's a shadowthorn." Anger crackled beneath the hiss.

"And she's out of this fight."

"What about the next fight? Or the one after that?"

Rosa met Drenn's gaze dead on. Five years before – Raven's Eyes, even *one* year before – it wouldn't have mattered. She'd have slit the shadowthorn's throat herself. "We came here with a clear purpose. Don't lose sight of that."

Drenn narrowed her eyes. "Hands off."

Rosa left it a moment longer, then let her go.

Drenn stalked wordlessly around the storehouse corner.

"She's right," murmured Jonas.

Rosa shook her head angrily. "Chasing death only makes you a killer. A soldier has to be something more. The Republic needs soldiers, not killers."

He nodded. "Yes, lady."

The last of the sentries was dead by the time Rosa reached the storehouse door, a pattern repeated across the mining camp. Athaga's southwealders had made short work of the gate guard and the stockade rampart was clear. The gate itself hung wide open, Edran and Castir beckoning the first wave of wolf's-heads into the compound.

A dozen wolf's-heads became two dozen, became two score.

"I killed this one." Drenn kicked the corpse at her feet. "Hope that's all right?"

Rosa passed up the bait and stared at the door. A padlocked chain held a heavy wooden bar in place. No hope of the prisoners getting out under their own means, but with the camp filling with wolf's-heads, that wouldn't be an issue for long.

But for all that, something didn't sit right, though it took a moment to isolate the prickle of suspicion. Try as she might, Rosa heard no sounds from within.

Corpses didn't have the warmth to melt snow. The cold would hold off the smell.

"Silda, search the body. We need the key." Rosa jerked her head towards the storehouse's far end. "Jonas, check the others."

He set off. Drenn, longbow discarded and already squatting beside the dead guard, glanced up. "What's eating you, Orova?"

"There's no sound."

"Might be drugged. Your lot did that all the time in the south. Keeps 'em quiet. Biddable."

Your lot. The words stung. "And if not?"

Drenn froze, expression hard as flint. "Then I'll flay every scrap of skin off that one you left alive, and you'll do well to stay out of my way."

A crash of glass and a *whoosh*. Orange flame leapt into the night.

Even as Rosa turned, a blazing bundle shattered a second barracks window. Arms spread against the kindling fire, Athaga bellowed wolf's-heads into a line across the doorway.

A shadowthorn ran into the night, half-dressed and unarmed. He made it three paces before Edran hacked him down.

Missiles rained down, bottles stuffed with oil-sodden rags and alchemist's powder. A few struck the barracks' walls, liquid fire dribbling along brickwork. Others lodged in roof tiles and crackled merrily away. Most went in through the windows, feeding the dry, hungry roar of the flame.

The first screams sounded.

Rosa snatched Drenn to her feet and slammed her against the wall. "I didn't agree to this!"

"They're the enemy," gasped Drenn. "They deserve whatever we give 'em."

A trio of Hadari burst from the barracks door, swords drawn and smoke gouting on their heels. Bowstrings hummed, and they fell dying in the muddy snow.

Athaga tossed another fire bottle through the doorway. Shadowthorns stumbled out of a side door and died beneath the open sky. Still the screams raged inside, fires leaping against the dark sky.

"This is how we win," hissed Drenn. "By treating them *exactly* how they treat us."

Rosa stared, a sick feeling worming through her gut. Killing warriors was one thing. She'd led her share of ambushes. In war you took what advantage you could. But in an encampment this size there'd be servants, perhaps wives, children . . . none of whom would have ridden out to pursue Solveik. That was different to her, even if it wasn't to Drenn.

She took refuge in the mission. "You're not thinking! The shadowthorns will see the flames! They'll know!"

Drenn glowered, unrepentant. "No point to a message gone unseen. If Solveik's done his job, there isn't a shadowthorn closer than Yelska. We'll be long gone before anyone arrives to mourn the ash. We know all about mourning ash in the Southshires. You saw to that, Lady Orova." She held up a rusted key. "Now, you gonna let us get this done?"

Rosa growled and stepped back.

"Oi, Castir! Magram!" shouted Drenn. "Give me a hand, would you?"

Drenn set key to lock. Not trusting herself to speak, Rosa turned away. It didn't help, not with the barracks blazing into the sky and shadowthorn dead clustered about the doorways. All looked to be warriors, but that made no account of the poor souls screaming within.

Steeds slewed in the mud beneath the stockade gate. Carts rumbled in behind, the better to bear away any captives incapable of walking. Assuming any still lived.

Rosa scowled, riven by disquiet.

Chains rattled behind her. The bar hit mud. Swollen timber creaked on hinges.

"No!" gasped Castir. "This can't be . . . "

Rosa stared through the open storehouse door. Not at the

lifeless bodies she'd dreaded to see, but something that was, in its way, even worse.

Empty.

Drenn stalked across the threshold, hands spread to encompass broken crates and rotting machinery. "Where are they, Castir?"

"I don't understand," he moaned. "They were here. I was told they were here."

She sprang, dagger at his throat. "Where are they, you worm?"

Rosa started towards them. "Let him alone, this—"

A wolf's-head turned from the rampart, hand cupped to his mouth. "The signal! The signal!"

An arrow blazed against the northern sky, heralding a shift in the wind and a rumble of thunder.

No. Not thunder.

Drenn forgotten, Rosa ran for the rampart and took the ladder's sagging rungs two at a time. The woman at the summit ignored her, eyes wide as she stared at a hillside of horsemen riding at the gallop. Not wolf's-heads, but Hadari – lightly armoured outriders at the fore, and the golden scale of cataphracts gleaming in the moonlight. Easily three hundred. Probably more. Far more than accounted for by the absent garrison.

Instinct blamed the fire from the barracks, whose light would travel far on such a cold, clear night. Reason acknowledged that there'd been no time for reinforcements to muster, much less travel.

Thirava had baited a hook and they'd swallowed it.

"Close the gate!" Rosa shoved her way past a gawping wolf's-head. "Raven's Eyes! Close the bloody gate!"

With the gate shut, they might hold the camp long enough for some – perhaps *most* – to escape through the flooded mine. But if the Hadari breached the walls . . . ?

No one moved, paralysed by the prospect of galloping death. Others fled into the night, snow churning from their boots as they scrambled for illusory safety. Arrows whistled from the walls and vanished into the mass of riders. Others thudded into the palisade as outriders offered reply.

Screams split the night. A stray shot plucked at Rosa's sleeve. A woman collapsed at her feet, mouth full of blood.

At last, the west leaf of the gate was closing. Someone in the throng had kept their wits. The east hung ajar. Shinning down the gatehouse ladder, Rosa threw her good shoulder against the heavy timbers and heaved. Boots skidded in the mud. The gate barely moved. Snarling, Rosa planted her feet anew and heaved again. Timber shuddered beneath arrow strike. The ground shook to the rising tremor of hooves.

Another shoulder planted against the timber alongside hers. The gate inched inwards, picking up speed as the newcomer found firm footing.

"So much for this being a rescue," rumbled Edran.

"There was never anyone to save," said Rosa.

The big man grunted. "A trap, was it? I'll wring Castir's scrawny neck."

She thought back to Castir's pallid, horrified face. "He didn't know. He was used. Like these poor souls on the hill were used."

The most callous of traps – one that required a sacrifice of one's own kind to sell the illusion. One more reason to hate Thirava.

Almost closed. Barely space for two men to walk abreast.

Rosa glanced behind. "Stand ready with the crossbar!"

The gate bucked, hurling Rosa to her knees and Edran sprawling into the mud.

An Immortal crashed through the gap, tasselled sword flashing. "Tirane Brigantim!"

Blood streaming from his neck, Edran slewed into the gate approach and vanished beneath the hooves of newly come shadowthorns. As Rosa struggled to stand, the gate swung inward beneath a mass of men and steeds and flung her against the wall. Her head chimed against stone. The world upended into a mouthful of mud and snow.

Rosa's thoughts rushed red and black, drowned by the pulsing, throbbing clamour of hoofbeat and scream. Vision blurring and gut crowded with nausea, she grabbed at the wall. Trembling knees pitched her forward as she tried to stand. By the second attempt, the passion of battle stirred. It drove out the cold, the uncertainty – the ache of the old wound and the horror of unfolding events.

Strength returned to a body sorely in need.

Eyes regained focus, and gazed upon slaughter.

Bodies clogged the space between gate and barracks. Athaga Varalon's mismatched garb was recognisable in the leaping flames. Others too.

Men and women whose faces Rosa knew, even if she'd not yet learnt their names. Shadowthorn horsemen roamed the buildings, running wolf's-heads to ground with sword and spear. Screams choked the air, within the walls and beyond. She'd have been dead already, but for the shelter offered by backswung gate and stockade wall.

Movement in her peripheral vision set Rosa spinning about, sword ready. Her head throbbed.

Jonas. Pale. Harried. A lad barely clinging to his wits. "What do we do? They're killing everyone!"

Rosa clapped a hand over his mouth and dragged him deeper into the relative safety between gate and wall. Another band of cataphracts trotted into the camp.

An arrow whispered from the south. The leading cataphract pitched from his saddle. A second. A third. The survivors milled about, voices raised in alarm as they sought their assailant. A masterless horse cantered past Rosa's hiding place, spattering her and Jonas with mud.

She glimpsed a lone archer atop the canalside storehouse, silhouetted against moonlight, arms ablur as she nocked and shot. Outriders' bows sang in reply. The silhouette shuddered, the longbow falling to rest in the gutter. Transfixed by four arrows, Silda Drenn toppled from sight.

Rosa tightened her grip to stifle Jonas' gasp of dismay. Cataphracts spurred toward sporadic fighting beyond the pithead cabin.

Rosa counted to three, and relaxed her grip.

"What do we do?" she breathed. "We get out of here, if we can."

The words fell sour. Retreat was bad enough, but to abandon comrades? But the battle was over, even if it wasn't wholly done. It had been over from the moment the Hadari had breached the gate. Maybe before the signal arrow had been shot. More than ever, she was glad to have talked Drenn out of rousing the border villages.

"Have you seen Fenner?" she asked.

"He's dead. Talar too." Jonas shook, though with fear or anger, Rosa couldn't say. "They're all dead."

No sense trying for the mine. Not without a guide. If there was to be a choice between a spear in the back or drowning in the darkness, she'd choose the former.

"Stay close."

She crept to the edge of concealment and glanced about. Not safe – nowhere in the mining camp was safe any longer – but no obvious eyes either. She broke cover and ran for the cataphract's masterless horse.

The first guttural cry rang out as her hand closed around the trailing bridle. "Surrender!"

Swinging up into the saddle, Rosa pulled Jonas up behind and drew her sword. "Hold tight, farm boy."

She kicked back her heels. The stolen horse galloped for the gate. Cataphracts – newly come to the slaughter – rowelled their steeds to the charge.

Jonas tightened his grip about her waist. Old memories flashed. Riding into the teeth of a shadowthorn charge on the border, only then she'd a sturdy shield and chamfered plate armour. The Fall of Ahrad, where she'd crawled from the rubble and battled Ashana's antler-helmed demon. Only there, she'd been a bloodless eternal, strong and fast beyond ephemeral ken. But still, she'd a sword, and a steed. As complete as a knight of Essamere could wish.

"Death and honour!"

She swept the leading cataphract's spear aside and left him dying in the saddle. The rider behind him scraped a parry, and then Rosa was through the gate, howling vengeance as she reached the road.

Bodies littered the hillside, black against snow, the panicked wolf's-heads ridden down without mercy. Their slayers roamed the slope between Terevosk's fire-levelled ruin to the north and the dark eaves of Elmgran Wood further west. More curious was the knot of cataphracts a quarter mile along the road, their posture that of bodyguards, not pursuers. Had Thirava come to see his trap sprung?

"Rosa!"

The thump of galloping hooves accompanied Jonas' warning. An outrider rowelled his steed, sword levelled in challenge. Rosa tore her gaze from the distant entourage and goaded her horse towards the new threat. His sword buckled beneath Rosa's first strike. Her backswing took his spine.

Rosa circled her horse about, eye again on the distant cataphracts. It *was* Thirava, his opal-set armour black among the golden scales of his escort. A coward claiming glory for a one-sided slaughter without even drawing his sword.

The outrider's horse made to canter away. Rosa snatched up its reins. Wild voices and the drumbeat of hooves warned of approaching Hadari. "This one's yours."

Jonas clambered across to his new mount, eyes darting at the closing riders. "Where do we go? We can't fight them all."

"Ride west. Keep your head down, and don't look back. Do you hear me?"

His brow creased. "Me? What about you?"

"Go!"

She slapped the flat of her sword against his horse's haunch. The beast took off as if all the revenants of Otherworld were on its heels, Jonas clinging to the reins for dear life. Maybe he'd have a chance. Maybe he wouldn't, but where Rosa was bound, there was no chance at all.

Sword high, she sprang away along the road.

Now the cataphract escort broke formation, a rank of three spurring to intercept the upstart who sought their prince's head.

"Until Death!"

Rosa's cry dissolved into wild laughter. Gods, but there was glory in a lost cause! More in a good death. A good death for her, and a bad one for the self-styled monarch of Redsigor. The red of battle rose within her, and she let it bear her away.

She felt the first cataphract's death. The parry of the spear. The crunch of steel against golden scale. Blood hot across her sleeve. Not so the ones that followed. Those, she lost to the red, to the rhythm that cared not where the sword fell, only that it bit deep and slid free. Pain was a distant sensation, and one discounted so long as arm retained strength. There was only the road, and a shadowthorn tyrant who'd lived too long.

Arrows whistled through the night.

Rosa's horse screamed.

The strike of the roadway scattered the red of battle and drove breath from Rosa's lungs. Her sword skittered away across the icy road. Blood seeping from a dozen small wounds, she dived after it. A galloping horse barged her to the snow.

When she stood, it was into a ring of spearpoints, levelled from horse-back by golden-helmed Immortals. Failure coursed cold, bringing with it pain that refused to any longer be ignored.

"Lady Orova," said Thirava, safe beyond the thicket of spears. "It's been too long."

Maladas, 5th Day of Dawntithe

A man is naught but memory clad in rot;
History seldom more than ambition draped in lies.

from Eldor Shalamoh's "Historica"

Twenty-One

A week earlier, Paszar had been a thriving village tucked into the shoulder of the hillside, bright with Midwintertide decorations. Now, charred timbers and stone walls jutted from a black, ashen stain in the snow. Dawn's bloody light spilled across churned mud, conveying Lumestra's wrath at the slaughter.

Bile thick in his throat, Zephan Tanor slowed his steed as he reached the gate's remains. Haste helped no one now. He barely noticed the knights of his thin column do the same. They'd ridden hard from the Tarvallion vigil on unbarded horses – the 7th mustering in their wake – without time to don more than gambeson and breastplate. Few matched a knight's romantic ideal in such a state, much less Zephan himself. He knew all too well that below his shock of black hair his face was lined and weary.

"I want sentries to the east," he shouted. "If the shadowthorns return, they find us ready, do you understand me?"

Though if the Hadari returned they'd gobble up thirty knights no less easily than the half-dozen who'd fought and died alongside Paszar's militia at the ford.

The rear ranks peeled away. Zephan spurred on. Bodies lay where they'd fallen. Some were burned beyond recognition, charred, skeletal hands scrabbling at filthy cobbles or reaching skyward. Others bore only the spear thrusts that had stolen their lives. Once the one-sided battle had reached the gate, it had become slaughter.

Taradan trotted his horse alongside Zephan's, his expression grim. His left arm, bandaged about the wrist and hand, twitched in its makeshift sling; blood crusted his hair. Unlike the rest of the column, he wore full plate. A shieldbearer stationed at Paszar's tiny vigil, he'd carried warning to Tarvallion. His fellows had joined the defence and thence gone to the Raven's keeping.

"I should have stayed." Emotion absent from Taradan's face crackled in his voice. A knight had a family of steel as well as blood, and there was no family tighter than that of a vigil. Especially in these days of Essamere's waning.

"They'd have killed you too." Zephan clasped his shoulder, receiving a taut nod in return. "You did right."

Zephan was far from certain he'd have done the same. Sometimes it took more courage to run than to fight.

He wheeled his horse about and gazed back at the column Taradan's warning had rousted. Thirty men and women. Nearly half the knights left at his command, and most of them yet to see a twenty-fifth summer. All bore expressions similar to Taradan's, though few were as accomplished at concealing emotion. Sorrow, frustration ... and above all, rage. The same corrosive brew ate away at Zephan's labouring heart. The Essamere of old, of Orova, Izack – or Tassandra, under whom Zephan had learnt his bloody trade – would have stopped this. The Essamere of today – *his* Essamere – would be fortunate to avenge it. The grandmaster's circlet felt heavier than ever.

Perhaps it was time to set it aside, as Sarella's letters insisted. To leave the futility of the border to another's care, and return to their manor house on the Karakeld coast. Raise daughters he hardly knew and worry over quarrels of fisherfolk and winter storms. He was yet to reach middle age, but the last five years had ridden him hard. And grandmasters of Essamere seldom made old bones. Would it really be so wrong to think of family first?

But that was the problem. He'd two families, and the family of steel needed him more than the family of blood he almost never saw. What right had he to speak to his daughters of honour if he abandoned those in need?

The circlet grew more burdensome still as they reached the church's remains. The trampled mud of the lychfield bristled with makeshift gibbets fashioned from beams and lamp posts – a man-made forest, hung with bitter fruit of ravaged bodies. Fifty or more in mismatched and ill-maintained armour, and the stag banner of Redsigor flying at the very centre. Not villagers. Something else.

"Merciful Lumestra," breathed Taradan.

Back along the column, someone retched. Zephan urged his steed closer.

Taradan spurred to join him, face hard. "Who do you suppose they were?"

"Wolf's-heads," Zephan replied. "Trying to do what we couldn't."

Taradan leaned over in his saddle, examining the ground. "Wagon tracks in the mud. These were brought here so we'd find them. It's a message."

"Or a reprisal." Zephan halted, his gaze on a slender woman hanging in the centre of the grisly display. Snapped arrow shafts bristled from her torso. The spars of a shattered longbow hung from her shoulders, the bowstring wound tight about her neck. The face, he knew from bounty posters. "Silda Drenn."

Taradan gave a low whistle. "So the shadowthorns finally caught up with her?"

Pressing a forearm to mouth and nose to stem the graveyard stench, Zephan dropped from the saddle. His pace quickened as he threaded the forest of corpses, searching for a face he hoped not to find. A hulking fellow, his beard plaited in Thrakkian style. An older woman, her face crosshatched with old scars. A grey-haired man, clad in a grubby phoenix tabard older than Zephan. A parade of strangers, forlorn and pitiable.

No Rosa. Thank Lumestra and Lunastra both.

He glanced back at Taradan. "She's not here."

The other narrowed his eyes. "Who's not here?"

Belatedly, Zephan remembered that Rosa's departure to Morten's Rock was far from common knowledge. It wasn't his secret to share, or his rumour to feed. Even if it did add another grim duty to the day.

"It doesn't matter." Swallowing his worries, Zephan pulled himself into the saddle. "Take charge. I have to speak to Governor Orova."

"About this?" Taradan jerked his head back towards the column. "Send Resadov."

He could, of course. A herald would be easier than delivering tidings in person. And not just because Resadov was a swifter rider. Murdering refugees from the conquered Eastshires was one thing, but razing a village in the Marcher Lands marked a brutal escalation. And then there was Rosa, who Zephan's instincts screamed was caught up in this. Better Sevaka heard that from a friend, even if all he could offer was uncertainty.

Zephan shook his head. "Some things don't fit in a letter. I'll be back before noon. The 7th will be here before then."

Taradan clasped his good fist to his chest. "At your command. What would you have us do?"

Zephan took in those the shield of Essamere had failed to shelter.

"Take them down," he bit out. "Bury them with their faces toward the dawn. And keep your swords close."

Twenty-Two

The sun shone for Elzar Ilnarov's interment. The alabaster trees of the Hayadra Grove gleamed silver, promising that death would last only until the Light of Third Dawn. Altiris supposed that was how most would read the morning. But Altiris had lived too long in Anastacia's company. He knew the truth. Lumestra was dead, and nothing awaited Elzar save the worms and the Raven's uncertain kindness.

"He's drawn a crowd." Kurkas framed the words with rare respect. The high proctor had borne both rank and responsibility lightly, always ready to spare a kind word or a helping hand. "Terrible thing to pass and for no one to care."

The crowd beyond the ring of Drazina was vaster than any Altiris had seen in many a year. And it was uncharacteristically subdued. Few had actually met Elzar, and Altiris couldn't quite free himself of regret at being intimidated by a man who'd touched the lives of others so carelessly. Of course, the presence of so many Drazina *encouraged* respect. As did the handful of battered kraikons and simarka – the closest Elzar had to family, though who knew if the constructs recognised their loss? Certainly, the simarka looked somehow mournful, but their leonine faces invariably did.

Altiris glanced up at the nearest kraikon. Did Sidara see him? She'd insisted on watching the ceremony from the Panopticon, claiming the best way to honour Elzar was to ensure the constructs' vigil didn't waver. Altiris had forgone argument. Since Midwintertide, they'd spent every spare moment together. If things between them were to stay mended, compromise would be necessary.

None of which helped Altiris feel any less out of place *within* the ring of Drazina, swan banners flying above, even as a leader of hearthguard. The space beneath the Shaddra – the eldest of the hayadra trees, situated at the centre of an ancient, ruined temple whose yawning catacombs stretched deep beneath the city – was thick with the great and the good. Karovs, Marests, Tarkans, Slendrovs and two-score other highblood lines. The abolished Grand Council reunited in memory of one who'd repeatedly refused admission to their ranks. Then there were the aspirant few who'd risen as the old bloodlines had fallen – raised up by the Lord Protector's patronage, through military prowess or simple wealth.

Little separated the two, save the fact that the highbloods' garb was notably behind fashion as wealth withered alongside influence. The two groups seldom mingled, the former despairing the elevation of the latter, and the latter in turn resenting that the former clung to fading status.

Altiris and Kurkas formed a third lonely assemblage, cravated and coated – neither one wholly comfortable at being present. Captain Tzila might have felt the same. Certainly she stood apart as they stood apart. But Altiris, who felt a chill every time the blank gaze of her sallet helm fell upon him, was in no hurry to plumb her thoughts, even were she of the mind – or ability – to share.

There was a fourth group, of course – those close enough to Elzar to serve in his cortège and offer the kiss of hallowed farewell to his golden death mask. Lord Droshna, Lord Trelan, Anastacia and Izack. Others were churchmen, or old friends from the humbled foundry. Lady Sevaka Orova and Governor Keldrov had made the journey from their respective shires especially.

Commotion broke out at the Drazina cordon. Raised voices, and the low growl of warning used by lawkeepers as a prelude to trouble.

"Is that Boronav?" murmured Kurkas.

Altiris turned. It took a moment to recognise Viara in a sober gown of midnight silk and a silvered shawl, her blonde hair scraped back into severe plaits as befitted her family's status. Outraged expression, jabbing finger and a cluster of black-tabarded Drazina gave shape to the quarrel, if not the detail.

"Want me to have a word?" asked Kurkas.

Altiris hesitated. Viara wasn't representing Lord Trelan's Phoenixes, so technically wasn't his concern. And most Drazina guarded their responsibilities with vigour bordering on mania. Just a day before, a sergeant of the Karov hearthguard had spent a weary afternoon in the Oscastle cells for intervening in a clash between three Drazina and a street keelie. But Viara was a friend, and it wasn't so very long ago he'd had his own scuffle with a cordon in the Hayadra Grove.

"I'll go." With another glance up at the kraikon, he trudged off through the snow.

Viara broke off from her argument. "Altiris? Lieutenant! Will you talk some sense into this ... *individual*?" She gestured at the sergeant in command. "My carriage threw a wheel. Father expects me to represent the family."

Altiris turned his attention to the sergeant. "What's the problem? This is the Lady Boronav. Let her through."

The other man, possessed of both brow and jawline Altiris thought more suited to a darkened alley, gave an unapologetic shrug. "No papers."

"They're in the carriage."

Viara's expression held only worry. A fading family like the Boronavs couldn't afford to lose face, much less suffer direct humiliation at the hands of common soldiery.

"That's as maybe, lady." The sergeant's emphasis on *lady* was so slight as to escape notice ... at least, unless you were a southwealder, and accustomed to hearing scorn beneath a smile. "Move along, or we'll take you down to Oscastle and wait for the papers to show up together."

"This is absurd." Fighting a growl born of his own past and Viara's distress, Altiris dug into his inner pocket for his own tattered documentation. "I'm Lieutenant Altiris Czaron of Stonecrest. Lady Boronav is one of my hearthguards. I'll vouch for her."

"And are those her papers, sir?"

"No."

"Then I can't let her through."

It was the tone that did it. Like so many of the overseers on Selann. The casual, uncaring authority of a petty man granted power over others. Altiris took a half-step forward. "Now, listen to me—"

The sergeant stepped back, hand on the hilt of his sword. "We don't need trouble, southwealder."

A pair of Drazina loomed closer. Parallels with Selann grew more striking still. Altiris told himself no harm could befall him in broad daylight, in the Hayadra Grove – at a crowded funeral, no less – with Kurkas close by and Sidara seeing all from her Tower of Stars. But old fears weren't easily dispelled.

"This *is* exciting, isn't it?" Constans appeared at Altiris' shoulder. His Drazina uniform was immaculate, his voice breezy. But for once, Altiris wasn't wholly certain of his habitual mockery. The boy looked pleased with himself – no surprise there – but Altiris swore he caught the briefest of sidelong winks. "Whatever is the commotion, Sergeant Goroda?"

Goroda nodded at Viara and Altiris in turn. "One without papers, another making trouble."

"That's not—" Altiris started.

Constans waved him to silence. "You *are* a brute, sergeant. Maybe he thought it the only language you understood. Let her through."

Goroda's face flushed, his brow knotting. "Standing orders—"

"Are issued by my father." Constans cocked his head, innocent in voice and expression. "Which of us do you suppose knows his mind better?"

Goroda froze. On the one hand, he faced the immediate humiliation of submitting to orders issued by a boy twenty years his junior. On the other lay the sterner prospect of the Lord Protector's disfavour. Without another word, he rejoined the cordon, the other Drazina melting away alongside.

Constans offered a low bow, the familiar smirk in place one more. "Better?"

Viara beamed. "Very much, thank you."

Altiris nodded, uneasy. He'd no sympathy for Goroda, but Constans' solution sat ill. No objections to a bully put in his place, but were Constans' nebulous authority and motivations any better? "Why?"

The boy shrugged. "Last week, you relied on me and I wasn't there. Today I was. And I've not had my sister or Josiri bending my ear about *how* it was I came to not be there, so that means you've not told them, so I owe you for that too."

The words provoked a flush of guilt. Altiris had certainly *meant* to discuss Constans' magic with Sidara, but had not yet conjured means of doing so that wouldn't risk renewing old distance. Mumbled explanations about why he'd asked her to leave Seacaller's at Midwintertide had come close enough, but had, at the last, been forgiven in exchange for a kiss. Likewise he'd said nothing to Lord Trelan, whose focus had understandably been on Anastacia's recovery.

Still, Constans' words, spoken simply and with obvious artifice, went some way to allaying concerns. Good deeds and ill were defined by intent, and for the first time in recent memory, Constans' motivation had been sound. Perhaps that lad was learning, after all.

"Thank you."

Constans grinned and started uphill. "If you'll excuse me, I've duties. Innocents to save. That manner of thing."

Soon after, Viara was safely among her kind, and Altiris at Kurkas' side once more.

"That looked interesting," said Kurkas.

"Drazina throwing their weight around. It's handled."

Kurkas grunted.

"Altiris Czaron!" An aquiline man with long, oiled black hair wove his way through the press, the metal flask in his hand a match for stumbling gait. "The very gallant lieutenant I'd hoped to see."

Altiris glanced at Kurkas, who returned it stonily. "Lord Zarn."

"Konor." He offered the correction with a wobbly flourish. Lord Konor Zarn, once member of the Privy Council and one of the richest men in the city, had either started drinking early, hadn't yet finished from the previous night . . . or, as unkind rumour had it, hadn't stopped since the day Kai Saran had slaughtered the Privy Council, leaving Zarn the sole survivor. "Always Konor to my friends, and I do so like having friends."

Altiris stifled a scowl. Zarn's speech, louder than was proper for a funeral, had already drawn disapproving eyes.

"That's very kind," he replied, hoping the other would take the hint.

"Not at all. Not at all. Without your efforts, we'd never have recovered the *Moonchaser*'s cargo . . . even if someone promptly stole it from the stockyard all over again." He shook his head. "Can't trust anyone these days."

Altiris thought back to the flooded warehouse. To Kasvin and Hawkin's discussion of the wreckers' trade. "The *Moonchaser* was yours?"

"Alas, no more. She belongs to Endala's drowned garden." Zarn tapped him unsteadily on the cravat. "But that doesn't diminish my gratitude."

Altiris borrowed a page from Kurkas' book and stared at a point past Zarn's shoulder. "Just doing my duty, Konor."

"I hope you were commended. I've a feeling you're meant for better things."

Kurkas' stony expression adopted a hint of malice. Altiris stifled a sigh. First Izack, now Zarn. Hard to steer clear of recklessness when it brought such renown.

"A terrible shame about poor Elzar, of course," said Zarn. "Incorruptible, though I shan't hold that against him. His heart, I understand?"

"So I'm told," Altiris replied. "The Lord Protector was with him when he passed."

"I suppose that's something, though I'd prefer softer arms about me when my time comes." He tottered and patted the pocket of his brocade jacket. "I'm hosting a select gathering at Woldensend Manor tomorrow night. Might you put in an appearance?" He tapped the side of his nose. "Perhaps even persuade Lady Reveque to grace us with her presence?"

Altiris took care not to meet Kurkas' eye, uncertain what rankled more: the fact that his private life was apparently now the stuff of common rumour, or that Zarn's fine words had all been in pursuit of luring Sidara into his orbit. Closeness with the Reveque line, however implied, would only be to Zarn's benefit.

"Sadly, I'm on the duty roster," he replied. "Isn't that right, Vladama?"

Out of Zarn's sight, Kurkas grinned. "Must be, if you say so. You're the lieutenant, lieutenant. I'm merely a humble steward."

Zarn swigged from his flask. "A shame, but the invitation remains open." He scowled at the Shaddra as if seeing the tree for the first time. Eyes lingered on the black stain across her alabaster trunk, a blemish born from the blood of the Crowmarket's last pontiff. It had spread, year on year. Her branches no longer blossomed, and come spring there'd be black leaves among the gold. "Poor thing. Better to uproot her and have done."

Altiris winced. The Shaddra was holy, a gift from Lunastra to Lumestra. You didn't say such things, and certainly not at a high proctor's interment. "The sickness hasn't reached the other trees. The grove wardens believe it'll pass, in time."

Zarn's lip twisted. "But how deep go the roots? Rot's persistent. You never know how far it'll spread." He shrugged. "Until tomorrow, lieutenant."

"Wait, I didn't ... " But Zarn was already out of earshot.

Kurkas offered the ghost of a smile. "I think he likes you."

"He's more your type than mine."

"I prefer 'em sober." Kurkas gave a lopsided shrug. "Well, most of the time."

Altiris scowled. "Would you believe that's the first time we've spoken?"

"Hah! You've been at Woldensend at least a dozen times."

"The uniform was invited. I happened to be in it. Just like he's really inviting Sidara, not me."

"Cynicism's a terrible thing."

"But?"

"But you might be right. He'll want to watch himself around Lady Reveque."

"Afraid I'll challenge him to a duel?" Not that it'd be much of a contest, the state Zarn was so often in.

"You'd have to reach him before the plant pot." Kurkas shook his head. "Don't seem right, calling her that any longer. But it's good? You and her ladyship?"

Altiris fought a grin. "Better than good."

Kurkas clapped him on the back. "Make sure it stays that way. If the plant pot sees fit to chastise, you're on your own."

For once, the threat of Anastacia's ire held no fear. Were Altiris to find himself in need of chastisement, Sidara would likely not leave enough of him for her adoptive mother to menace. "Understood."

They stood without speaking as a distant hymnal echoed up from the subterranea, a sign that the private part of the ceremony was almost done. Altiris caught low, murmured snatches as Kurkas sang along, though the steward contrived to silence whenever Altiris looked at him.

As the hymn ended, the leading edge of the funerary procession emerged from the catacombs. Gold-frocked priests and black-robed serenes flanked the podium raised before the Shaddra. Archimandrite

Jezek, crimson robes almost invisible behind plumes of scented smoke, ascended the short stair to the summit. Altiris' small group swelled to five with the arrival of Lord Trelan, Lady Sevaka and Anastacia. Only Lord Droshna, arrayed again in simple black garb, stood apart. Though this too was swiftly rectified as Tzila strode to join her master.

"Elzar Ilnarov has returned to the Dark." The crisp, clear pronunciation of the city fought Jezek's rougher Treggan accent as he addressed the crowd, arms spread wide. "But do not mourn overmuch. One day, ephemeral corruption will leave us, and all shall walk together in the Light of Third Dawn. Such was Lumestra's promise. So shall it be. Lumestra wake us from darkness ... "

"*And lead us into the Light,*" the crowd answered with one breath.

Anastacia snorted and fell silent as Lord Trelan jabbed her in the ribs. Jezek withdrew from the podium, offering Lord Droshna a bow as they exchanged places.

The Lord Protector seemed in no hurry to speak. He simply stood at the podium's fore, head bowed, and hands tight about the rail. Lost in thought, or perhaps prayer. Murmurs of consternation broke out across the grove.

"Go on, you stubborn sod," breathed Kurkas. "Let it out."

Anastacia leaned close to Lord Trelan. "He wasn't made for this. You should rescue him."

Lord Trelan scowled, nodded and started toward the podium. He halted as Lord Droshna at last found his voice.

"In all the ways that count, Elzar Ilnarov was my father." Lord Droshna spoke slowly, picking his way through a thorn-choked path. "He taught me to trust myself. To stand for those in need where others thought only of what they might lose in the striving. Without his kindness, I'd be dead. Without his wisdom, the Hadari would have claimed the Southshires. Elzar understood, better than anyone, that a divided Republic is one doomed to fall. Some of you know the strain he placed on himself as he strove to restore the foundry. He died as he lived, putting others before himself. It is time we did the same."

He paused, the silence broken only by the moan and patter of wind-blown branches. Lord Droshna rose to his full intimidating height, support forsaken, and booming voice bereft of doubt.

"You will have heard, as I have heard, the horrors the shadowthorns heap on our kin. You will know also that we are not yet recovered from the last war. Any attempt to reclaim the Eastshires will cost us greatly. But as I stand here, in mourning for the man who made me, I find my thoughts with those we have abandoned. You've followed me for six years, and I have kept my promises as best I could. Now I make another: follow me one last time, and the Eastshires will be free! The Republic will be divided no more!"

"Death and honour!"

Altiris didn't see who voiced the oath, but gained volume and speed as new voices took up the cry. The hilltop, sombre moments before, embraced the challenge and roared with one voice.

"Death and honour! Death and honour! Death and honour!"

And through it all, Lord Trelan watched without words, lips pinched thin.

Twenty-Three

Maladas morn sparring was a Stonecrest tradition, and not to be set aside even for a wake. Even with brandy taken. In the preceding half hour, Josiri had watched the gambesoned Kurkas demolish Brass, Jaridav and Stalder. Now Altiris fought for the younger generation's honour in the snowy strip of lawn marked by four red pennants.

Cheers marked allegiance offered and wagers placed, the hearth-guard – all save Viara Boronav, who with family duties complete held the gate watch – split evenly between support of their present lieutenant and their old captain. Sidara, lately arrived from the Panopticon and a simarka watching mutely at her side, cheered for Altiris. Anastacia, arms folded and mourning garb exchanged for a red velvet gown, exhorted whoever seemed in greatest danger of losing. Sevaka, her threadbare naval greatcoat most unbecoming for a regional governor, beheld the contest with wry expression. At the opposite end of the sparring ground, deep within the formal path's statued colonnade, Tzila held immobile vigil.

"He's not bad, that steward of yours." Izack set his glass on the terrace's stone balustrade and offered hearty applause. "Can't imagine why Viktor let you steal him away."

Viktor's grunt did little to disguise an old friend's fondness. "He's not as good as he was."

"True. A dozen crowns says Altiris will carry the bout. Any takers?"

Altiris' riposte drew cheers from the lawn below. Sensing victory, he pursued the retreating Kurkas across the lawn.

"Gambling is best confined to battlefields," said Viktor.

"Suit yourself." Izack shrugged. "Josiri? Care to pledge allegiance with coin?"

Josiri dragged his eyes from the contest. "I'm sorry?"

"What's the matter? You've been off with the feylings ever since we got back."

He shook his head. "It'll keep."

"Hah! Bloody won't. Gloom is for funerals. Bad manners to drag it along to a wake." Izack emptied his glass and plucked the brandy bottle from the table. "Talk, or I'll hoist you by the ankles and dangle you from the terrace."

Josiri turned his attention back to the duel to hide a scowl. Not at Izack's threat, delivered without any real promise of follow-through, but the prospect of broaching a topic he'd hoped to air before Viktor alone.

He glanced at Viktor – at a face still marred from the tragedy of Midwintertide. Viktor had offered account of events with utmost reluctance, the shame of failure palpable. The clocktower window had shattered beneath Elzar's falling body, and Viktor had lunged through the shards to save him from the plunge. Wasted effort, if any selfless act could ever be truly wasted. At first appraisal, Viktor seemed collected, grief's claim broken by time and ritual. But his eyes were troubled. Loss, or because he saw the coming quarrel as plainly as Josiri himself?

"You set us on the path to war this morning, Viktor."

"About bloody time, too," muttered Izack.

Viktor set aside his glass. "I did only as the times demand."

Reasonable tone only made matters worse. Viktor was master of framing disagreement as consequence of another's misplaced sensibilities. For years, Josiri hadn't noticed. Lately, there was little more likely to rouse his temper.

"There's danger to enflaming the mob," Josiri replied. "And what if the Empress' spies heard your decree? We talked over moving regiments into the Marcher Lands, of securing Thrakkian aid, but that hasn't yet been done. Surprise was the highest card in our hand, and you've thrown it away."

Izack and Viktor shared a frown. Izack opened his mouth and closed it again at Viktor's gesture.

"Three regiments have reached Tarvallion this morning," said Viktor.

"Another two arrive before dusk. That gives us seven, including the 7th and 12th already on border watch. The thrydaxe host is camped in the eastern Heartweald, beyond reach of prying eyes. Two days, perhaps three, and we'll be prepared. Melanna Saranal cannot conjure spears out of the air."

"Or the grave?"

Viktor flinched at the reminder of the distasteful deed by which he'd won the Avitra Briganda. Josiri fell silent, the urge to apologise battling with the determination not to do so. So Izack had known about the gathering forces? Had Keldrov? Sevaka? Was he the only one in the dark?

He leaned on the balustrade and stared across the duelling ground. Kurkas was on the attack once again, Altiris' swordwork rushed and desperate. Kurkas went for the lunge ... only to halt, mouth agape and indignant, as a snowball cast from Sidara's hand broke across his temple. Anastacia's musical laughter washed over the terrace. Altiris rallied to a fresh assault.

"I wish we'd discussed this, that's all." Josiri hated how the words made prudence sound like ego. "I thought we'd no secrets."

Silence was his only answer, but consternation was palpable. A chill wriggled along Josiri's spine, instinct warning that his perception of events lay badly astray, though for the life of him he couldn't think why.

"We *did* discuss it," said Viktor. "Just yesterday."

Josiri blinked, surprised at the lie's smoothness. "I spent yesterday with Lieutenant Raldan, assessing constabulary reports and tightening patrols. He's convinced someone's settling old scores against the nobility. Lots of aging, wealthy men turning up dead – most of them with a reputation for less than chivalrous behaviour. You and I haven't spoken for days."

Again, the shared frown – this time tinged with concern.

"Begging your pardon, Josiri, but that's not so." Izack's tone mirrored his expression. A man who passed through life with all the delicacy of a cattle stampede now choosing his words with utmost care. "We met in the palace, the three of us, and thrashed it out. If this is an attempt to wind back the clock, it's not very bloody funny."

"I ..." The corners of Josiri's memory offered up nothing to match Izack's claim. "That didn't happen."

Viktor grimaced and laid a hand on his shoulder. "Perhaps . . . perhaps this was inevitable. Your responsibilities with the constabulary. The late nights and early mornings. Everything that's happened with Anastacia. The pressure—"

Josiri twisted free. "You think I'm coming apart, is that it?"

"I'm concerned," rumbled Viktor. "Examine the possibilities. Either Izack and I are both lying to you, you're lying to us, or . . . Perhaps you should leave the constabulary in Lieutenant Raldan's care for a few days. Spend some time with Ana."

"I don't need to."

Certainty wavered. Viktor, Josiri might have believed capable of the deception. But Izack? Falsehoods were alien to his nature.

"Please." Viktor drew closer, his voice thick with concern. "I buried a father today. Permit me concern for a brother. I need you whole. The Republic needs you whole. Whatever bedevils you, I'm certain a little rest will see it pass."

So like Viktor to wield loss as a weapon. But there *was* worry in his voice. Enough to offer a moment of pause. If Viktor and Izack were right . . . ?

Josiri swallowed a piece of his pride. "I make no promises."

Viktor sighed. "Of course not. But I suppose it will do." He chased away a shiver. "Perhaps we could continue this inside, where there's a fire?"

A chime of swords. A second. A third. Altiris retreated. Ignoring complaining muscles and burning lungs, Kurkas pursued, his attention split between his official opponent and one lurking beyond the boundary flags, a second snowball not-quite concealed between gloved fingers.

A repeated stumble confirmed the lad was tiring. Served him right for flamboyance. Age didn't so much bring wisdom as an appreciation for husbanding resources. A dashing blade flattered like nothing else, but terse, efficient swordplay *lasted* long after showiness was spent. Not that Altiris ever listened. Then again, nor had Kurkas. Losing arm and eye on the battlefield had been a lesson for the ages.

"Finish him!" Anastacia shouted, mercurial allegiance shifting once again.

Sidara made to shove her. Anastacia twisted away in a swirl of skirts and hooked an elegantly shod foot about Sidara's ankle, leaving her face-down in the snow and her improvised missile forgotten. Sidara's simarka escort tilted its head, curious at its mistress' misfortune. Kurkas tore his attention back to Altiris.

"D'you yield?"

Altiris brought his sword up to high guard, blade held two-handed and levelled like a spear. Showy. "A Phoenix never surrenders."

His challenge drew fresh adulation from the assembled hearthguards. All save Brass, who shook his head in despair.

"You ain't the first to say it," said Kurkas.

Kurkas feinted left and thrust. The blades barely kissed, making contact just long enough to tease Altiris' aside. A blur of steel, and it was over. Altiris froze with the point of Kurkas' sword resting an inch or two from his throat.

The cheers faded. Anastacia's slow, mocking applause echoed through their empty wake.

"Plenty of dead, defiant Phoenixes," said Kurkas. "Not so many still living."

Altiris' scowl faded to ruefulness. He dropped his sword into the snow and held out his hand. "I swear you cheat."

Sheathing his own blade, Kurkas clasped the lad's hand. "That's me. Bloody magic, I am." He shot Sidara – now on her feet once more, but her uniform still speckled with snow – an old-fashioned look of betrayal. "Even when it's two against one."

She smiled, pure innocence. "Just helping you stay sharp, Vladama." She ran her fingers over the simarka's sculpted mane. "Aren't we, Fredrik?"

Unable to resist, he returned her smile in kind as Altiris withdrew. Planting himself at the midpoint between the flags, Kurkas gazed about the duelling ground. "Any more takers? Maybe I'm tiring. Gives you a chance."

One by one, hearthguards shook their heads. Jaridav – a woman little older than Altiris, and far closer than he to learning economy of conflict – looked tempted to go a second round, but she too shook her head. Not that Kurkas minded.

"Want another go, Brass?"

He grunted. "If we make it a contest of arrows, sure."

Kurkas shook his head. Even with two good eyes and two arms to draw the bow, he'd never have outshot Brass, whose days as a poacher on the Akadra estate weren't as far behind as he liked to pretend.

"Lady Sevaka?" he called. "Care to show these dryfoots how it's done?"

She laughed. "Not seemly for a governor to be brawling with an old man, is it?"

"Afraid the old man will knock you on your arse?" The accusation came from Beckon, a lapse in decorum worsened by his own avoidance of the duelling ground.

Lady Sevaka straightened. The ragamuffin in the naval coat fell away, replaced by a woman of sharp-edged authority. "I'll gladly cross swords with *you*, young man. Do you accept?"

Beckon shook his head with enough force to set his cloak twitching, and scowled as his comrades guffawed at his expense. Lady Sevaka, her back again to Beckon and friendliness of aspect restored, offered Kurkas a wink. "What about Anastacia?"

The plant pot shot her an unfriendly look and plucked at her skirts. "I'm hardly dressed for it."

Kurkas shrugged, relieved and disappointed. True, Anastacia's scars were healing. She remained irrepressible and vital in manner. But she displayed marked reluctance to admit that her human body had limitations that ones of porcelain did not. Her revealing, bare-shouldered gown made no concession to the temperature; her shivering suggested she felt the cold keenly. On the other hand, he'd never won a bout against the old Anastacia. Could be they'd *both* learn a lot.

"Don't tell me you're scared, plant pot?"

She blew him a kiss. "Only for you, dear Vladama."

The response provoked another round of mirth from onlookers. It faded almost at once. Taking his cue from gazes directed past his shoulder, Kurkas turned about.

Tzila stood a half-dozen paces distant, within the duelling ground's boundary. Shrugging back her cloak, she drew her sabres and let the tips of the curved blades touch the snow in perfect symmetry.

Kurkas looked her up and down, drew his sword and nodded. Tzila was an infrequent presence at Stonecrest, but he'd heard enough – not least from Altiris' misadventures – to wonder how good she truly was.

"All right, captain. You're on. But one sword only, if you please. Go easy on these old bones."

After a moment's consideration, Tzila flourished her left-hand sabre back into the scabbard with a whisper of oiled steel. Kurkas rolled his stiffening shoulder and took position across from the midline. A low growl of anticipation rose into the bright morning.

The duel began slowly, as they so often did with unfamiliar opponents. Kurkas made little attempt to probe Tzila's defences, giving ground and contenting himself with brisk, efficient parries while attempting to read her style.

The parries came easily enough, though he recognised that she'd not yet begun her assault in earnest. But identifying her style? Another matter. Pieces were familiar. The textbook stances and guards drilled into any luckless sod who joined the army. A goodly bit of fencer's deportment too – more like dancer's steps than anything belonging to a battlefield. And on top of all that, he caught elements of the heavy, bombastic strokes favoured by Thrakkian thrydaxes. But none of it was quite *right*. Like his own swordwork, it reflected its origins, while separate from them. A technique personalised and honed to fluidity across decades.

Or ordinarily so. Tzila's grace and suppleness belied long years. The blank enigma of her helm concealed her eyes, and thus her intent. Each blow was swifter than the last, and her parries without flaw, always using the flat of her blade to check the edge.

By the time Kurkas had retreated halfway along the duelling ground, he was breathing hard, sweat prickling at his brow. Three paces more, and he abandoned all attempts to breach Tzila's guard, every scrap of vigour given over to cheat her blurring sabre.

"Come on, Vladama!" shouted Altiris. "Can't lose to a Drazina!"

Sidara elbowed him in the ribs.

Painfully aware he was running out of manoeuvring room, Kurkas bellowed and threw his weight behind the next clash of blades. His sword scraped along Tzila's until his plain crossguard locked with her sabre's ornate spiral hilt. Muscles screaming, he forced the trapped blades high and twisted beneath, using the turn's momentum to wrest Tzila's sword from her grasp.

Or rather, that's what *should* have happened.

Tzila's sword barely twitched. The flat of her empty hand struck Kurkas' back, tearing the sword from his grasp and sending him sprawling into the snow.

Spitting out a mouthful of mud and snow, Kurkas rolled over and found the point of Tzila's sabre at his throat. She stood immobile as applause and cheers rippled across the lawns, Kurkas' longsword at her shoulder.

"Not bad, lass," Kurkas breathed. "You win."

Tzila stood immobile, looking for all the world as if she'd not heard. Heartbeats thumped by, pace quickening as the moment of defeat shaded towards something disturbing.

Applause and cheers faltered.

Altiris' expression shifted from awe to concern. "He yielded. It's done."

Tzila swept the longsword off her shoulder. Kurkas dug his elbow into the ground as prelude to wriggling free. The sabre at his throat gave a warning twitch, and he froze.

With a shriek of injured cloth, the longsword sliced through the pinned, empty sleeve of his gambeson and drifted upward until the point drew level with his eyepatch.

She tilted her head, the blank stare of the sallet helm unreadable.

The first uncertainty trickled along Kurkas' spine. He resolved to chat with Lord Droshna about the good sense – or lack thereof – of employing what was almost certainly a kernclaw in his entourage. Sometimes it took a friend to make the obvious, obvious.

"You've made your point," he bit out, the words sour with humiliation. "Let me up."

The longsword tracked across the bridge of his nose to his good eye.

"Captain Tzila!" Altiris started forward.

A slender arm, sheathed in red velvet, held him back.

"Yes, we're all very impressed." For all that Anastacia's words were addressed to Tzila, her attention was on her fingernails, curled tight against her palm. Inspection complete, she looked up. "But if you're done picking on the elderly, perhaps you'd care to *test* yourself."

Tzila straightened. Kurkas exhaled relief as the swords twirled away to rest against her shoulders.

Sidara helped Kurkas to his feet. "Are you all right?"

"Never better." He glared at Tzila's retreating back, then across to where Anastacia shivered, the point of Altiris' borrowed sword planted in the snow at her feet. "You sure she's up to this? That captain is a killer."

"No." Sidara winced. "Five minutes ago she complained she couldn't feel her fingers."

Jaridav shrugged off her cloak and set it about Kurkas' shoulders. He offered a grateful nod. "So stop her."

"How?"

"Fair point." He glanced up at the empty terrace, and cursed the high-bloods for seeking warmer climes. "Jaridav? Find the Lord Protector, would you? Tell him things have gotten out of hand. We could use his brooding countenance out here."

"I'll go." Lady Sevaka departed for the terrace door at a jog.

Fighting shivers, Kurkas turned back to the duelling ground. Tzila and Anastacia stood a handful of paces apart. The former had discarded the longsword, again armed only with a single sabre.

"Don't talk much, do you?" said Anastacia, through chattering teeth.

Tzila twirled her sabre to rest in an approximation of low guard, and started forward.

"Wait!" Anastacia held out her free hand, fingers splayed. "I can't do this!"

Surprised by the concession, Tzila stumbled, off-balance for the first time that morning. Kurkas breathed a sigh of relief.

Anastacia frowned in thought, thrust her sword into the ground and seized the hem of her skirts in both hands. Stitches popped and fabric tore, slitting a dress easily worth six months of a hearthguard's salary to mid-thigh first on one side, and then the other. That done, she unbuckled the delicate, strapped shoes and kicked them away.

"*Now* I can do this." Anastacia tugged the sword free, and sprang.

Any pretensions Kurkas had to being a master swordsman evaporated in that first exchange of blows. He'd seen the plant pot fight before, but she'd done so with the blithe unconcern of one who'd known herself all but immune, and had thus favoured brute force over finesse.

This was wholly other, a blur of slashes and ripostes that Kurkas' eye struggled to follow. Not so Tzila, who somehow met every blow in kind, her twirling sabre on the move again even as the clash of metal faded. Yet there was an edge to the captain's motions absent before, the artistry of swordplay eroded by merciless necessity.

No one spoke. No one cheered. Looking about the duelling ground, Kurkas saw his own nervous awe reflected on the faces of hearthguards.

Tzila gave ground, her careful steps overcome by Anastacia's wild rhythm. Both resembled dancers more than duellists. But where the captain's motion belonged the formality of the stage, Anastacia's was the wilder pirouette of bonfires beneath starlight, her roamer's aspect accentuated by spiralling skirts and bare feet across the snow.

A shriek of pain. Blood spattered bright.

Anastacia reeled away, free hand clasped to a gashed shoulder, blood oozing between her fingers. Tzila bore down, a sabre now in each hand, the leftmost dripping red.

"No!" Sidara started forward, golden light gathering about her shoulders and the simarka on her heels.

Altiris, still weaponless, came a pace behind. Jaridav and Brass a pace behind *him*. Tzila halted, swords held at guard, but malice temporarily in abeyance.

A spreading bloodstain fouling her left sleeve, Anastacia staggered another pace and waved both away, her voice distant, pained, but also surprised. "It's nothing!" She set her gaze on Tzila. "I feel like I should know you. Why is that, do you suppose?"

Kurkas glanced towards the terrace. Where was Lord Droshna anyway? "It's past time this ended!"

"I agree." The plant pot turned shaking fingers this way and that, fascinated as the bloody trail trickled to fresh courses across pale skin. Her eyes drifted to Tzila's left-hand sabre. "But if we're cheating, we're *cheating.*"

A pair of translucent golden wings unfurled at Anastacia's shoulders, their light a match for that suddenly suffusing the blade of her sword. Eyes shining, she started forward.

A single step, and she screamed. She doubled over, daylight

wings evaporating. The sword slipped from her hand, metal turning cold and dark.

As Anastacia fell to her knees, Tzila sprang, sabres glinting in the morning sun.

Kurkas' borrowed cloak fell away as he flung himself forward, already knowing he – and everyone else – would be too late.

The morning's shadows lengthened.

"ENOUGH!"

Tzila froze at Lord Droshna's bellow. Her swords, inches from Anastacia's throat, whirled about and returned to their scabbards. Phoenixes rushed between the two, Altiris at the centre and blades bristling.

Sidara skidded to her knees at Anastacia's side. "Fredrik!"

Hackles high, the simarka loped to take up position between Anastacia and Tzila, its golden-eyed stare frozen on the latter.

"Captain Tzila!" Lord Droshna bore down, expression more thunderous than Kurkas had seen in many a year. "Return to the palace at once! We'll speak of this later."

She bowed and strode for the driveway. Lord Droshna reached Anastacia's side and with surprising gentleness helped her stand. She sank against Sidara, eyes red-rimmed and the left side of her dress bloody. Hearthguards looked on, appalled.

"What are you staring at?" demanded Altiris, his face pale. "You've duties. Be about them!"

One by one, the hearthguards withdrew towards the house, leaving Lord Droshna looming over those who remained.

"My apologies," he ground out. "This won't happen again."

"No," Anastacia rejoined hoarsely, teeth chattering and murder in her eyes. "It won't."

She didn't elaborate. Nor did she need to. Though given how swiftly her strength had failed, Kurkas doubted Anastacia could make good her threat. The indestructible plant pot of recent memory was gone, however much she pretended otherwise.

Lord Droshna grimaced. "Look after her, Sidara."

Lord Trelan appeared on the terrace, Izack at one shoulder and Lady Sevaka at the other. Suddenly haggard, he ran to help Sidara with Anastacia, but whatever words passed between them were lost to distance.

"What in Lumestra's name just happened?" asked Altiris.

"You're asking the wrong man," Kurkas replied, his eyes on the departing Tzila. "But you take my advice. If you find yourself on the other end of those swords for real, run away as fast as you can."

Twenty-Four

It wasn't Rosa's first time in a cell, bereft of all save stained and filthy clothes. Then, she'd been desperate, her life upended by events barely understood. Then, the hangman's noose had been welcoming prospect more than anything else. A release. An escape.

This was worse. Not because the dungeons of Haldravord Castle were fouler than those of the Tressian constabulary. They were much the same. Iron bars. Low ceilings. High, grilled windows to grant illusion of light. The acrid stench of a slops bucket inadequate to its mournful task. Creaking, slatted beds. Save for the muted roar of a crowd beyond the castle's thick, limestone walls, it was even peaceful, or near enough. Had Rosa been alone, she could have borne it, even with death a ready prospect.

But she wasn't alone.

They numbered thirty-one in all, now Solveik had passed during the night. The Thrakkian had gone to the feast halls of Skanandra without a sound. Rosa had rebound his wounds, clung to his hand as his eyes had filled with Skanandra's forge-light, but hers had never been a healer's gift.

Others would join him in death before the day was out. Too many listless eyes. Too many bodies gasping in restless agony. The living were twice the burden of the dying. Of the captured wolf's-heads, perhaps twenty were as uninjured as she. Indeed, most were haler still, for they'd not fallen from a galloping horse. Rosa's body was a sea of bruises and crusted cuts, sparse islands of unharmed flesh rare and treasured. Guilt was a sorer burden than pain, and grew heavier as spirits guttered and sank.

"You ask me, Solveik had it lucky." Jonas sat on the floor beside the heavy iron door, ankles crossed and elbows against his knees. Red-rimmed eyes stared at the Thrakkian's corpse. "If we're to die, better it be sooner."

No other accepted the bleak conversational gambit. Only Mirada, her narrow features just visible in the gloom, offered a twitch of lip to show she'd heard.

Rosa rolled off her creaking bed and to her feet. Vision blurred, reminding her of hours passed without food and water. "Soldiers don't wish for death."

"We're not soldiers." Jonas' voice shook as he spoke. "I should have stayed home."

Beneath the grime, his left eye was swollen almost shut. Riders had caught him just beyond Elmgran Wood. He'd not even landed a blow before they'd dragged him from his horse.

No other spoke, but expressions aplenty offered agreement.

"They'll come for us." Was it true? Once, Rosa would have wagered her life on Viktor's intervention. But now? She shook the thought away. Viktor was not the Republic. "If not the army, then Essamere. If it's at all possible, they will come. Our part is to make sure we're here when they do."

Mirada snorted. "Unless we can escape."

"Unless that, yes." Rosa stood before Jonas. "Get up."

He looked at her without truly seeing. "Why?"

His sorrow sought companionship with Rosa's own. Yes, he should have stayed home. But he hadn't. And he didn't need sympathy. He needed something to cling to. They all did. She let a little of the parade ground into her voice. "Get. Up."

Jonas rose, the confines leaving them almost nose to nose. More than close enough to read his eyes. Fear. Anger. And shame most of all.

"Bunch your fist to your chest." Rosa glanced through the dungeon's murk, making whatever eye contact she could. "Everyone who can. Do it!"

Mirada's lip twitched a small, wry smile. She at least recognised what was happening, but simply stood, rag-bound fingers clasped to her chest. Others joined her, shoulder to shoulder between the bars – even a few Rosa had assumed too feeble to obey.

"There's little less use than a broken sword," she said. "Repeat it."

"There's little less use than a broken sword." The reply was barely the sigh of a dying breeze.

"Save for a shield that shelters no more." She met Jonas' gaze, daring him to look away.

"Save for a shield that shelters no more."

"Come dawn or come dusk, I obey one command."

The lad's restless eyes steadied. His voice grew firm.

"Come dawn or come dusk. I obey one command."

"My vigil I'll keep. Until Death, I stand."

"My vigil I'll keep. Until Death, I stand."

"You're soldiers now. You're Essamere." A fleeting truth, for the full Vigil Oath was many stanzas longer, and written in the formal tongue. More than that, Rosa hardly had the authority to induct wolf's-heads into the order. But fleeting truths were sometimes enough. "Essamere stands together. They *will* come for us."

"And if they don't?" The bitter challenge came from Rosa's right.

"Then we face the Raven proud." Jonas faltered over the words. "And we wait for Third Dawn."

The challenger fell silent. Others, Mirada among them, even nodded. Oaths gave purpose, even in a cage.

Rosa only hoped it was enough.

Along the uneven corridor, the dungeon door creaked open. A tall, scarred man in golden scale stalked into sight, lips twisted in disgust. Men in Silsarian garb flooded in behind. Some carried shackles and lengths of coarse rope. Enough bore naked steel to forestall hope of escape.

The Immortal jabbed a gloved finger at Rosa. "This one."

Keys rattled in locks. Rough hands dragged Rosa into the passageway and slammed her face-first against the wall. Grit and lichen speckled her breath. Blood from fresh scratches warmed her cheek. She held anger close, knowing that to resist was death. Unseen assailants yanked her hands behind. Cold steel closed about her bruised wrists.

A shove spun her about to face the Immortal.

"Where are you taking her?" Jonas demanded.

A punch through the bars set him staggering. Clinging to failing scraps of temper as a Silsarian slipped a rope about her neck, Rosa held Jonas' gaze. "Until Death."

He raised a trembling fist to his chest. "Until Death."

The Silsarian tugged on the rope and hauled her towards the stairs.

Daylight offered Rosa her first true glimpse of Haldravord since the Hadari occupation. The town remained recognisable enough, thatch and tile above wattle and brick. But it *felt* alien. The statue of Lumestra that had long dominated the bridge between castle and town was gone, replaced by one of her sister Ashana, a crescent moon in one hand, and the full in the other. Deeper into the streets, austere timber frontages hid beneath bright canopies. And the last difference, so subtle Rosa didn't notice at first ... beneath the melting snow the streets were clean, the gutters unclogged where they so often overflowed.

Rosa stumbled on across cobbles, driven on by the twin masters of the rope about her neck and the swords at her back. A curiosity gawked at by robed men and women from stall and doorway, and less obviously from the paler Tressians who hurried past, heads bowed. Temper cared not for impotence and flared with every impatient jerk on the rope. By the time she'd been goaded through the marketplace – past the small scaffold about the remnant of a Lumestran shrine, and up the broad stairway to the reeve's manor – every tug of the leash demanded ironclad self-control.

The manor's interior was something from Itharoci myth, the tomb of some great king ushered into the mists by stores of undreamt wealth. Statues of bird-masked equerries lined every passageway, gemstones gleaming in their eyes. Golden tapestries hid the oak-panelled walls. Drapes were of patterned silk, rather than heavy velvet. High-necked vases and bronze figurines adorned shelf and table. Like Haldravord's streets, the Tressian supplanted by the Hadari.

Laughter and delicate song echoed all around.

And everywhere, robed servants and golden-scaled Immortals, liveried in the stag of Redsigor – the kingdom that yearned to be, but not yet *was*.

Rosa's captors escorted her through the double doors and into the manor's courtyard garden. A jerk on the rope brought her to a halt.

"Ah. Here she is." Standing by the pondside, Thirava extended a lack-adaisical hand. A boot in the back of her knee pitched her onto the path. "Lady Roslava Orova, late Council Champion and Reaper of the Ravonn. You recognise her, of course, Edgir?"

He addressed a dark-complexioned man at his side – one of two others gathered about the pond. Like Thirava, he wore flowing silk robes, though they were perhaps not so finely cut – midnight blue, and blazoned with the branches of a bare tree. A prince of distant Corvant? The other man wore the bear of Demestae, and a broad, ingenuine smile. Both clutched goblets, though neither brandished theirs so extravagantly as Thirava who, if not already in his cups, was well on the way.

Edgir grunted. "I do, majesty." Rosa was more or less fluent in the Imperial tongue, but his mournful accent made challenge of under-standing the words. "Six years is not enough to forget that harridan."

His face meant nothing to Rosa, but she recalled so few details of Govanna Field. Only the blood, and the screams, and the ineluctable, harrowing sense of her humanity in retreat.

Thirava quaffed from his goblet. "The wager is mine. Pay up!"

Edgir hesitated. Then, transfixed by a gaze gone unfriendly, he unlooped a purse from his belt. With obvious reluctance, he set it at the foot of a silver cat statue.

Rosa gritted her teeth and let herself sway. Feigning weakness was the only weapon she had. The knot of princes aside, the courtyard held only her leash holder and the two clansmen at her back – only the latter three were armed. Poor odds, but she was accustomed to those.

If only her hands had been free.

"Let this be a lesson to all that Thirava is a man of his word. A man who backs claim with deed." Thirava wheeled away, treading the narrow path towards Rosa. "Not so fearsome now, is she, my friends?"

She glared up at him. "Set me free, and I'll show you fear."

"I think not."

He upended his goblet. Wine trickled through Rosa's filthy hair and rushed away across back and shoulders. Self-restraint gone, she growled and flung himself at him. The leash dragged her to her knees.

Thirava laughed, his mirth echoed politely by the others. They didn't like him – that much was plain – though formality cloaked truth, just as it so often did among the Tressian elite.

He gestured to the Demestan prince. "You asked, Faethran, why I defy the Empress? Why my father does so?" Thirava wound his fingers through Rosa's hair and yanked up her head, baring her throat. Cold wine dribbled down her neck. "Take a good, long look. Do you suppose a creature like this would align herself with troublemakers and malcontents without her masters' blessing? Tressia never meant to respect the settlement of Govanna. They mean to wipe Redsigor off the map. *I* mean to defend it to my last breath. No *woman* has the right to order otherwise, Empress or no."

So Thirava's deeds went against the Empress' decree? Rosa's surprise yielded to contempt. It tracked all too well with what she knew of Melanna Saranal – like all Hadari, she spoke of honour and truth, but lacked strength of character. That the Eastshires' sorrows arose from her weakness, rather than her ambition, made her no less culpable.

Wrath gathered to Edgir's expression. "You blaspheme against the living goddess."

Thirava ripped his hand away, letting Rosa's head fall. "Do I? Your scripture proclaims the divinity of Emperors. Men, and the sons of men. It makes no accommodation for upstart daughters. I share the blood of Hadar Saran every bit as much as she. Am I too a god?"

Edgir's glower deepened. "She is divine. Chosen by Ashana herself."

"Is she?" Thirava spread his hands. "Then why does she permit the Tressians to slaughter my people? Why did she hold back after Govanna, and in all the years since? My sires have served the Imperial throne for generations. Silsaria's spears have defended that throne from those who would steal it. But she abandons us."

Edgir stepped closer, thought better of it, and returned to stillness, arms folded behind his back. "What is it you want, Thirava?"

Thirava crooked a sad smile – for show, Rosa had no doubt – and set the goblet down beside the wagered purse. "Only what we of the Gwyraya Hadar have always had: the support of friends in trying times. Tressia cannot be appeased. It cannot be cowed. Only annihilation will serve. When I ride to war, I do so not for myself, but for us all."

Faethran shook his head. "And the Imperial throne is, of course, no interest to you."

"The fate of my people. The honour of the Empire. These are the spurs at my flank. Anything else is a matter for the Gwyraya Hadar, and my cousin Melanna's shame – should she be capable of it."

Edgir straightened, a mask of formality again in place. "I will convey your message to my father."

"As will I," Faethran's eyes lingered on Rosa. "Of course, the message would travel smoother with proof in tow."

"She stays with me," said Thirava. "I trust your word will suffice?"

"Of course." Disappointment slithered beneath the words. "I wish you the joy of her."

Faethran bowed and left the courtyard. Edgir departed without word or gesture of respect. As soon as they were out of sight, drunken aspect slipped from Thirava's thin face, his expression turning thoughtful.

"You owe me a kindness, Lady Orova. Even leering Tzal would turn godly sight from what Faethran would make of you." He snorted. "There's a reason Langdor keeps him far from home. A king must have maidservants, must he not? And he can hardly do so when young women are terrified of entering the palace in case the prince is in one of his ... moods."

She glared at him. "Shadowthorns talk so readily of honour. But words are cheap."

Thirava twitched the fingers of an upraised hand. The rope went taut, hauling Rosa to her feet. He bore down, brief friendliness banished. "You'd talk to me of honour? The butcher of Govanna Field? The pale demon who swept out of the mist and cut down my brothers without a thought and licked their blood from her blade?" His eyes bored into hers. "And now I find you here, in my grasp. Demon no longer, but ephemeral flesh. The one will pay for the deeds of the other."

Bitterness crowded Rosa's throat. Not for the slaying of Thirava's kith, but for all that deed had wrought. "Terevosk ... You set that trap for *me*?"

Laughing, he shook his head. "Such pride you have. Can you hear yourself? No, Terevosk was simply politics. I needed a foray across the border – one large enough to spur my royal cousins to action. I was sorely disappointed that provocation had drawn so few ... but then fate delivered you into my keeping. How many swords were you worth at Govanna? A hundred? A thousand? You were worth ten times that just now. You were worth a kingdom."

Rosa stared past him. "You're a murderer."

He chuckled. "Murder is *personal*, and so little of current times is personal. My labours – my duty – is the elevation of Silsaria from a humiliated cur to the head of the hunt. If that calls for death, I shall not shirk the deed. Great men deal in death every day."

Rosa spat. "I've known great men. You're not even their shadow."

"I will be." He shrugged. "Melanna Saranal has had years to grow beyond mere novelty. She cringes from bloodshed and believes herself the better for it, but only bloodshed secures a throne."

The words were different, but the sentiment was all too familiar. Death justified by duty and ambition – and what was glory, save a melding of the two? The Reaper of the Ravonn, the Council Champion – even the Queen of the Dead – they'd revelled in death, made claim of necessity and always to serve their pleasure. In that moment, Rosa was almost grateful to Thirava – a near-perfect mirror of what she might have become, but somehow had not.

Thirava shook his head, a man dispelling pleasures deferred for present need. "As for you? Your passing *is* to be personal."

So there it was. "I'm not afraid of death."

"No, I imagine not. At least, not your own." Clicking upraised fingers, he strode away. "Bring her."

The marketplace, once empty, was now thick with crowds. Most were Hadari warriors in the gleaming scale of Immortals or the drab guard of tithed clansmen, but there were robed civilians too, and even a few dozen Tressian townsfolk – the latter regarded askance by their unwelcome masters.

A short, grubby line of shackled captives led to the scaffolded shrine, Jonas and Mirada at the fore. Two golden-armoured drummers stood atop the scaffold itself, one either side of a woman in silver half-mask and flowing white robes: a lunassera, a pale-witch. A shallow cart waited behind.

Rosa closed her eyes and sought solace in the knowledge that she'd die alongside comrades and they alongside her. But when the rope jerked again, it did so not towards the execution scaffold, nor to the line of wolf's-heads, but to the marketplace's upper terrace. An iron crow's cage rested on the cobbles, its pulley rope stretching away to a loading hook in the eaves high above.

"No!"

Rosa flung herself backwards at her leash-holder. Her shoulder struck his chest and both went down, her atop and he below. As he struggled to rise, she brought her head down. Cartilage crunched, earning blood and a scream of pain. She sprang away.

Something heavy slammed against the back of her head.

The world blurred drunkenly. Cobbles cracked against her knees.

"Gag her!" snapped Thirava.

Rosa's mouth filled with the bitter taste of cured leather. Hands hauled her backwards into the cage and drew ropes tight, binding her limbs to the iron bars, forcing her to stand. A leather strip across her brow forced her to stare straight ahead.

Golden armour retreated as vision regained its focus, replaced by Thirava's thin, expressionless features.

"You're a warrior," he said, "and I know the strength of a warrior's bond. You draw strength from those you fight beside, and they from you."

He slammed the cage door. Furious screams muffled by the leather gag, Rosa strained against her bonds. Anger gave way to panicked foreboding.

Thirava leaned close, nose inches from the cage. "I could tell you that this too is merely the great deed of a great man, but we both know it would be a lie. I could tell you that you're simply a lesson for your countrymen, but that too would be untrue. This *is* murder. My brothers cry out for vengeance. They shall have it. You will bear witness as your comrades get the knife. And then you will rot."

At his gesture, unseen hands busied themselves with the pulley. Creaking, the crow's cage lurched skyward. The marketplace reverberated to the thunder of drums. They rose in crescendo as swords goaded Jonas up the scaffold's steps.

"I'm sorry!" Her own fate forgotten and her heart raw, Rosa howled the words. The gag muffled them beyond recognition, and what remained was lost beneath the drumbeats.

Jonas halted before the lunassera. The drums faded, leaving uneasy silence behind. In that last moment, he stood tall, burdens gone from thin shoulders. He stared up at the crow's cage. No accusation in his streaming eyes, only pride. "Until Death!"

The lunassera's knife flashed. The drums began anew.

Twenty-Five

Josiri stared through his office's leaded window and out across the gardens. A mistake, as it offered a fine view of the duelling ground's flags and the dark stain of Anastacia's blood on snow. Too much had already gone badly that day. "You're certain there's no mistake?"

Arkadin Zaldov, master of Saint Selna's hospice, frowned. "The decree was very . . . direct. With the government ration withdrawn we'll struggle to feed our residents, let alone the countless others who rely on us for bread and a hot meal. Last year's harvest was poor. There are already shortages. Without access to the tithe-houses . . . ?"

He fell silent, his words eaten up by the hearth's soft crackle.

Josiri's mood sank further. The tithe-houses weren't meant to feed Thrakkian mercenaries. Their creation had been one of Viktor's first acts, though for more pragmatic reasons than mere charity. The Crowmarket had survived by winning the allegiance of the poor. Removing that leverage had finished the vranakin as surely as the trials and executions.

"Forgive me, but I'm still not certain why you've come to me, rather than speaking directly with Lord Droshna."

"Gaining audience with Lord Droshna is lately a challenge."

Ever a private soul, Viktor had been a recluse since Elzar's death, seldom seen beyond the palace walls. Grief did strange things even to the strongest men. "The Lord Protector sees the world in stark tones." Josiri forced a smile. "Sometimes he needs reminding of its subtleties. I'll discuss the matter with him."

Zaldov stood. "I'm in your debt, Lord Trelan."

A final bow and he departed, leaving Josiri alone with his thoughts.

Changing Viktor's course was never an easy task, and with war uppermost in his mind, it would likely prove more difficult even than usual. "Fortunately," he murmured, "Trelans are stubborn."

"They are certainly that."

Anastacia stood in the space lately occupied by Arkadin Zaldov, book in hand, a new gown in place and her bound shoulder hidden beneath a shawl. Sidara's magic had mended the worst of her wounds, but there was no hiding a worn face, paler than was healthy. Nor the stiffness with which she carried herself.

Skirting the desk's edge, he kissed her brow. Wonderful to feel warm skin beneath his lips, rather than clay. A reminder that not all Viktor's misjudgements abided eternally.

"You've no right to judge me," he said, "not when you promised to rest."

"I *am* resting." She ran her fingers across his cheek. "Or else I'd be drowning Tzila in the Silverway as we speak. I've not been hurt like that in a long time."

Humiliation vexed her more than hurt. Viktor's apologies – effusive though they'd been – couldn't soothe that away. Only time stood a fighting chance. "And now?"

She laid the book down on Josiri's desk, pages spread. He winced at the creak of an antique spine. "I'm angry."

"You're always angry."

"Tzila meant to kill me."

"Viktor claims things simply got out of hand." Josiri wasn't certain he believed that. Sparring so often stirred blood to foolishness. "He assured me she'll be disciplined."

"Viktor always has an explanation handy after the fact." Anastacia scowled. "You didn't see her fight. Cold and calculating the whole time. What she did to me was no more a flash of pique than her humiliation of Vladama. The cruelty was the point."

"Altiris told me you recognised her."

Anastacia shook her head, her voice thick with frustration. "I said I felt like I *should* recognise her, but who knows if that's even true? I'm only a piece of what I was, Josiri. The rest was lost. First, when my mother cast me upon this world. Again, when I tore free of Branghall's stones. And once more when I escaped the clay. I'm scattered far and wide." She

raised a hand level with her face. Golden light shuddered across fingertips and guttered out. "Is this what it is to be ephemeral? Seeing pieces
of yourself peel away as the days pass?"

She fell silent, small and vulnerable. Careful of her injured shoulder,
Josiri took her hands. "What can I do?"

"You can tell me what you and Viktor argued about."

He blinked. "I—"

"Don't deny it. I'd a fine view before you retreated from the terrace,
and you've been distant all afternoon. I can read you like a book." She
pursed her lips. "A short, moody book of uncertain wit."

"So we're not talking about you any longer?"

"No, we're not talking about *you*, apparently." She rolled her eyes,
vulnerability gone. "Don't make me beat it out of you. Someone told me
I'm supposed to be resting."

He stepped back, irritated to be so transparent. "I challenged Viktor's
decision to lead us into war. He swore we'd discussed it yesterday, and
that I'd agreed the course."

Anastacia's brow twitched. "And you hadn't?"

"I didn't *see* Viktor yesterday." Certainty had crystallised, the explanations of fatigue discarded alongside Izack's confirmation. The Lord
Marshal, after all, was a soldier and Viktor his commander. Military
bonds were hard-broken. "He lied to me, and now I find he's raiding the
tithe-houses to feed his soldiers."

"I see." She stepped halfway through the doorway, glanced left and
right along the passageway and re-entered the room, closing the door
behind. "Josiri ... you and I walked to the palace yesterday morning. I
went on to the Panopticon to see Sidara and you—"

He glared, sudden uncertainty gnawing at his stomach. "No. That's
not true."

Annoyance crowded her expression. "You spent most of the walk
complaining about that book you've been reading. It's not something
I'd forget."

He *did* recall something of the sort, but as Josiri paced the memory to
its extent found only shifting blackness akin to the tail end of a dream.
"I didn't see Viktor."

"What was your uncle's name?"

"I beg your pardon?"

"Your uncle. What was his name?"

"What does that have to do with anything?"

"Only that you won't tell me. Or that you can't."

"Ana, I'm in no mood for one of your jokes."

She glanced at the floor, lip twisting in discomfort. "Week before last, you got properly furious with yourself because you couldn't remember it. Ask Vladama. He was there."

"Ana . . ." growled Josiri.

She folded her arms. "Are you going to tell me? Or shall I ring for Vladama?"

Simplicity itself to end this nonsense, except . . . the name he sought lay behind the same shifting black as the day prior. Uncertainty rushed red, cold creeping behind.

Josiri's first thought was that Anastacia too was in on the game. Scowl deepening, he banished the unworthy suspicion. What malice Anastacia possessed, she wore without veil. How many friends was he prepared to believe engaged in deception? What if he *was* losing pieces of his past?

The red faded to nothing. A cold fist gripped his stomach.

"Taymor," said Anastacia softly. "Your uncle's name was Taymor."

Revelation brought no relief, only shame. "What else?"

She reached out. Frustrated, he twisted away.

"Little things," she said. "Unremarkable things. An appointment missed. A name forgotten. I thought nothing of it at first – ephemerals are such fragile creatures. But it's getting worse. It has been for a year or more."

Josiri closed his eyes. Ailing memory was hardly uncommon in the old, but he'd yet to see his fortieth summer. To be so beset so young made for a grim portent. And it wasn't as though he could look to his parents for comfort of lucidity. Both had died before their time, killed by the feud between north and south. Neither had lived beyond forty. Grandparents were dim memories. Calenne had always cursed the Trelan luck. What if she'd been righter than she'd known?

"A week ago . . . your little encounter with the cart. That wasn't about the loneliness of you living for ever, was it? That was about me, leaving you."

She nodded tersely. "I'm worried you're slipping away. I don't like it."

Her eyes dared him to mock the admission. Her voice simply sounded old, and sad. It convinced where words had not.

"I don't care for it myself." Better to hide behind levity. Better not to wonder how much of this moment would be lost in coming days. "Viktor told me I'm working too hard. Maybe he's right."

"That would be a first."

Holding her close, Josiri re-examined the previous morning. A walk beneath grey skies. The conversation – he preferred *critique* to *complaint* – about Ugo Genarin's meandering novel. Even a salute from a pair of Knights Fellnore at the mouth of Sinner's Mile. But nothing of the palace, or of Viktor.

The more he pushed, the more adjoining memories crumbled, as if those he'd lost sought to drag them into the void for company. There had been knights, hadn't there? At the foot of Sinner's Mile. Which chapterhouse?

His heart quickened.

Fellnore. They'd been Knights Fellnore.

Trembling with relief, Josiri drew back from the missing memories, lest he provoke total collapse. Too much like the sensation that took him when he ascended a tower, or stood on a cliff's edge. The fear of the precipice, and the macabre longing to hurl oneself off, despite that fear.

"I'll see a physician," he said. "Maybe there's something to be done."

"You know there isn't." Anastacia looped her arms around his waist. "Perhaps Sidara—"

"No." Josiri shook his head. "I don't want her to know."

"But if she can help you?"

"What if she can't? I won't have her bear that failure."

She sighed. "Then perhaps we should leave the city. Return to the Southshires. Live on the coast with the sea ahead and the hills behind. Maybe it *is* nothing more than fatigue." Her attempt at a suggestive smile fell flat, undermined by sorrowful eyes. "I could nurse you back to health."

Josiri shook his head. "Viktor needs me. The Republic needs me. Especially now."

"And what of your needs?" she demanded. "Or mine? Must they wait until I'm a stranger to you?"

"Nothing could make me forget you, Ana. Nothing."

"You'll never know it if you do. The loss will be mine alone." Sorrow quickened to anger. "This city? This Republic? They tried to take everything from you. You owe them *nothing*."

Josiri told himself she didn't mean to sound so selfish. There was, after all, simple pragmatism to her words. A man was his memories, and his were flaking away. He couldn't mourn what he didn't know he'd lost. Anastacia wasn't the only one becoming an echo of herself.

The study walls crowded closer, the woodsmoke-scented air suffocating.

"It's not about what I'm owed, Ana, but what I can *do* for others. I thought you understood that." Slowly, gently, he unpicked her embrace and held her hands tight. "Maybe this isn't as bad as it seems. Maybe it is, but I need to be myself as long as I'm able. Otherwise, the man who elopes with you isn't truly any longer the one you love."

She stepped away, lips pursed. "You're a fool, Josiri Trelan."

"Could be." Was there anything harder than arguing with a loved one who sought only to save you from yourself? "But I promise you, for once, I'll do nothing out of stubbornness. Let me think on it."

Twenty-Six

The solitude of a walk helped – if any excursion through the busy streets could be truly said to offer solitude. So long a prisoner behind Branghall's gates, Josiri had learned to treasure the freedom of setting forth from Stonecrest's door and wandering, hands deep in pockets and one foot in front of the other across cobble and flagstone, through alleyway and checkpoint, wherever whimsy bore him.

Yet there was no outpacing the black cloud in his thoughts. At best, the prospect of failing memory was set aside.

Perhaps he *should* speak to Sidara. He too often thought of her as a child to be guarded, rather than a woman growing into her own. He'd given reluctant blessing for her to join Viktor's campaign – distant though the prospect had seemed. Did he keep her distant out of concern for her well-being, or his own pride? He'd never been good at telling the two apart. His life with Calenne had been full of such false nobility, anchored by the certainty that amends could always be made. There was always tomorrow.

Until there wasn't.

Of course, Sidara wasn't the only member of his family who possessed talents beyond the mundane. Perhaps Viktor . . . ? But Viktor would take Anastacia's side, and insist on a temporary – or permanent – leave of absence. And then there'd be no one left Viktor considered a peer. No one to steer him away from the bleakness that so often overtook him.

And if I'm not a man any longer, but his after-image in the Dark?

Then I'll stop you. Whatever it costs me.

A promise made years before in a moment of hopelessness, but its power remained. With war looming, Viktor needed support more than ever. Better to let him believe it was overwork. Time for Lieutenant Raldan to receive overdue promotion. Let the constabulary tend to itself. Focus on being the Lord Protector's advisor . . . his conscience.

Josiri ambled to a halt, the crowd flowing on about him. Across the square, a pair of Drazina goaded a woman, face dark with fresh bruises, towards the watch house on Renner Square. A lone kraikon stood vigil beside the fountain, light crackling through a poorly patched rent in its left side.

Better to speak with Sidara soon, before war called her east. A brisk walk would bring him to the Panopticon soon enough.

As Josiri started away, his eyes lingered on the crooked street sign. Highvale. It took a moment to chase the name down. Shalamoh, who'd bedevilled Sevaka with questions, and thus courted disaster at Rosa's hands. A promise to warn him off had fallen by the wayside. Another victim of failing memory? Josiri didn't believe so, but supposed he'd better grow accustomed to asking that question.

That oversight, at least, he could put right.

Cutting across the traffic's flow – and almost ending up beneath the hooves of a dray horse for his trouble – Josiri struck out beneath Highvale's well-to-do townhouses. Asking around sent him to a doorstep flanked by a pair of Ocranza guardian statues. Hewn in the likeness of warriors from the Age of Kings, they were less fashionable – but in better repair – than the more refined examples of the craft that haunted the gardens of Shalamoh's neighbours, or those in Stonecrest's grounds, and Josiri wondered where he'd found them.

The door opened on the knocker's third strike. From Sevaka's account, Josiri had expected a fussy, awkward fellow – the invariable tendency of scholars and seekers. But the rake-thin man who offered Josiri a thoughtful look was something else. Aquiline brow and steely hair could never have belonged to one uncertain in word or deed. Only grey garb offered hint of the insubstantial – it was somehow less colour's absence than its opposite, as if both raiment and wearer touched the world lightly. His only obvious eccentricity lay in a pair of polished glass discs set in a metal armature resting upon nose and ears. Peculiar affectation for one otherwise bereft of jewellery.

"I'm well served for spiritual guidance." The voice was twin to appearance: seemly without warmth. "Ply your doggerel elsewhere."

Josiri narrowed his eyes, uncertain whether to be amused or affronted. "I've none to offer you, Master Shalamoh. I'm Lord Trelan."

Shalamoh blinked. The clipped voice grew friendlier. "Why, of course you are. Humblest apologies."

"I'd hoped to speak with you. I can come back if it's inconvenient?"

"I won't hear of it. Please, come inside."

The furniture of Shalamoh's drawing room was rather finer and better preserved than usually the case when cared for by an absent and solitary mind. Books, boxes and sheaves of scrollwork were immaculately shelved – a place for everything, and everything in its place. Even the low desk set beneath the rear window displayed mania for order. An old, leather-bound book was spread wide upon it, mouldered edges in line with the desk's edges and a small notebook to one side. Not for Shalamoh the practice of hurried jottings – every line was laid down in an elegant copperplate hand as perfect as any serene-copied illumination.

Refusing the offer of a drink, Josiri took up station beside a mantelpiece decked with golden figurines. Above, hung a map he tentatively identified as part of the vanished Kingdom of Tressia, though the borders and names meant little.

"I regret my confusion," said Shalamoh. "Certain of my neighbours have mistaken me for a sinner and task themselves to my salvation. They don't approve of my interests."

"You're a historian, I gather?"

"The Republic's official record reminds me of a garden, adroitly pruned." He offered a humourless smile. "Take your mother. For all the effort Ebigail Kiradin and her ilk bent to erasure, traces of Katya Trelan's works remain. She ended the Indrigsval border skirmishes, did you know? Hadon Akadra took the credit, of course. He was always canny when it came to opportunity."

"She never spoke of it."

Shalamoh nodded. "The archives are clear, if one reads the spaces around the words. What *isn't* spoken is often more powerful than what *is*. Facts can be erased, but the void echoes with the loss. A shame I never met your mother. I'm sure she could have given shape to many echoing voids."

"I'm sure," said Josiri, politely, though he'd little sense of Shalamoh's meaning.

"Perhaps you might spare me a little of *your* time? Preserve a morsel of your thoughts for posterity?"

Josiri bit back a growl. Shalamoh couldn't know his poor timing. "I doubt it'd be as illuminating as you think."

Shalamoh arched an eyebrow. "My thoughts, and my time, are my own. You need have no fear of disappointing." He strode to the desk and tapped the book. "There's little I find unenlightening. Take this, for example. What do you make of it?"

Josiri squinted at the yellowed pages, but the penmanship blurred and shifted whenever he bent his gaze upon it. "Very little. My eyes are tired."

"Are they indeed?" Shalamoh peered at him. "A passing weakness, or a persistent one?"

He hesitated, but saw no harm in the admission. "The latter."

Shalamoh tutted. "I thought so. I see it in how you hold your brow. Try these." He unhooked the metal and glass armature from his ears and held it out. "They don't bite."

After a couple of false starts, Josiri wrestled the eyeglasses into place across the bridge of his nose and the hooked arms over his ears. The room shifted. Shelf and cornice fuzzed at the edges, but the immaculate handwriting snapped into something approaching focus. "I don't believe it."

"Ithna'jîm work," said Shalamoh. "The curvature of the lens compensates for weakness in the eye. An artisan over on Delver Row said it was 'quite advanced for a heathen', though he's yet to replicate the technique. 'Heathen' is so often a word deployed by jealous minds, don't you find?"

Josiri regarded him with renewed respect. "You've travelled to Athreos?"

"Itharoc," Shalamoh corrected. "Athreos is merely the desert that lies in the way. So much easier to feel superior if foreigners scurry about in a wasteland rather than dwell in cities finer than this one. But yes, I lived there for a time ... but we're talking about this book."

He stared pointedly at the desk.

With a guilty start, Josiri remembered that they weren't supposed to be talking about the book at all – nor the Ithna'jîm – but Sevaka. Shalamoh's enthusiasm had swept him away. But maybe that was for the best. Shalamoh's eyeglasses still in place, he pored over the text. Tressian formal tongue, more or less, and familiar.

"The Saga of Hadar Saran?" he asked. "In Tressian?"

"A piece. I'm afraid the front half is quite illegible." Shalamoh offered a thin, pleased smile. "Remarkable, isn't it? You wouldn't know from that passage, but it's quite complimentary. Less so about Konor Belenzo. If the author's to be believed, our blessed saint escaped Darkmere by offering the First Emperor in his place. But then, it is a wicked world. That's why the populace cheered when Malatriant seized the throne. They didn't care that she was cruel. She was better than what had come before."

Josiri flicked through a handful of pages. "Where did you find this?"

"Where else? Darkmere."

The thought of someone like Shalamoh surviving the haunted ruins was quite impossible, unless ... "You were with the Lord Protector's expedition?"

Again the smile, though this time more distant. A man concerned he'd tripped over his own tongue. "I was."

"At his invitation?"

"You're free to draw your own conclusions, of course, but I'm afraid I couldn't possibly comment. Discretion is all."

Affirmation, or merely its appearance? Claiming to have Viktor's ear would open plenty of doors for a man like Shalamoh. "You were fortunate to make it home."

"Indeed," agreed Shalamoh. "But I've always led something of a charmed life."

"On that note ..." With a pang of reluctance, Josiri slid the eyeglasses from his nose and folded them shut. "You should cease pestering Governor Orova."

"Pestering?" Shalamoh's tone trembled with affront. "A few letters?"

"A few letters that might feed hurtful rumour."

"Ah. I see." Shalamoh steepled his hands and tapped his fingers together. "Can I assume that in declining your request I may not live a charmed life much longer?"

"I'm but the messenger. I said I'd discuss the matter with you, and I have."

"Ah. But another might be more . . . colourful in their disapproval?"

"You're free to draw your own conclusions, of course, but I'm afraid I couldn't possibly comment."

Shalamoh chuckled softly. "Very good, Lord Trelan. I do wish we'd met long ago. We might have learned much from each other. I might, for example, have taught you to offer incentives."

Josiri eyed him carefully. "Such as?"

"An hour with your good lady. Oh, nothing licentious, of course. But there are so many perplexing gaps in the Books of Astarria. I'm sure she could help me make sense of them. Over tea, perhaps?"

Anastacia had no shortage of opinions about how her mother's words had been captured by ephemerals. She might even welcome the opportunity. How much Shalamoh would enjoy the encounter remained an open question. If nothing else, he might have insights to offer regarding her recent transformation – if indeed it was as mysterious to Anastacia as she claimed. "I'll ask, but no promises."

"Naturally." The thin smile returned. "I'm indebted. Let me offer something in return. Four years ago, I found myself at Vrasdavora. Do you know it?"

Vrasdavora. Where Sevaka had died. "Only by reputation."

"It's not a happy fortress, little more than a graveyard nowadays. But graveyards – like old churches – so often hold traces of the divine. I spent a week there – sketching, copying down names from our headstones and the memorial the Hadari raised to their dead." He shrugged. "But one particular grave fascinated me. I simply *had* to glimpse inside."

Where was he going with this? "What did you find?"

"The grave was indeed occupied. The woman within not at her best, but recognisable enough." The corner of Shalamoh's lip twitched. "A man might be forgiven sending a few polite letters in light of that discovery."

The words provoked a new, unpleasant thought. Josiri had readily believed the tale the ladies Orova had spun of the Raven's mercy, for the word impossible had long since lost currency in his life, but Shalamoh's story offered a new explanation. "So you claim Governor Orova is an imposter?"

He'd worried about that himself at first – fears fed by nursery tales of markhaini spirits that stole the form of the deceased and feasted on the grieving. But such Cowled were said to betray their true form beneath moonlight, and he'd seen Sevaka many times thus since her death.

"I do hope not," Shalamoh replied. "That would be so very disappointing. The books of Astarria – at least the *early* copies – make no claim that a portion of the soul resides in the body after death, as we are told now. That came later. No doubt some priest had a sideline in selling shovels and tombstones. All that waiting around in the dark, waiting for Third Dawn. All a fiction. The entire soul is freed at the moment of death. All it needs is a new body . . . Governor Orova's apparently found one. Isn't that a wonder?"

"I'd be very careful about sharing your theory," Josiri said coldly, hearing blackmail in the story.

"You may depend upon it. The provosts may be disbanded, but any fool with a stout rope and a mob can arrange a hanging. Governor Orova has nothing to fear from me. Please tell her so." Shalamoh shrugged. "After all, she doesn't answer my letters."

Josiri nodded, still unsure what to make of Shalamoh. Plainly a clever man, but with no clear objective for that cleverness beyond its proclamation. A coveter of knowledge where others hoarded coin. But there seemed no malice in him.

And if blackmail was in the offing? Well, there was always Rosa.

He held out the borrowed eyeglasses. "Here. Very enlightening."

Shalamoh waved a dismissive hand. "Keep them."

"I can't possibly—"

"No, please. I insist. I've others. You're no use to anyone if you're not seeing things clearly." He chuckled. "Just don't forget your promise. Afternoon tea with a serathi. My father would never have believed it."

Twenty-Seven

Even with afternoon fading towards evening, Tregard's grand market remained alive with scent and sensation, the tantalising aromas of dry spices and cured meats mingling with the mellow bitterness of woodsmoke. Folk flowed beneath bright canopies, haggling, flirting or simply passing the time in conversation.

Melanna's father had once claimed that anything truly valuable could be found within Tregard's market – and always far cheaper than elsewhere – but so far as she knew he'd never stooped to shopping. For Kai Saran, such unwarriorlike tasks belonged to servants. Melanna had always found the market fascinating. The facets of a thousand lives on display, unguarded. And yet she'd seldom strayed among the stalls since ascending to the throne. The daughter who'd always yearned to become her father now resented the small ways in which her wish had come true.

All the more reason to walk the market now, and set Kaila a different example.

She gestured at a baker's wares. "Well, *essavim*? Which should we buy?"

Kaila stepped past Apara and rose up on tiptoes, brow furrowed and top lip fractionally overlapping the lower – a puzzled expression learned from her father. "The kitchen servants fetched bread this morning."

Which meant she'd been wandering the palace again. Not that there was danger so long as she was watched, and the lunassera had held unceasing vigil ever since Jack's attempted abduction. A handful of the sisterhood remained in sight even now, islands of white and silver as the crowd flowed respectfully around them.

Tavar Rasha and three of his guard stood closer still, visibly unhappy about even that small distance. But Melanna had insisted. Certainly, there were other Immortals in the crowd, bodyguards to distant cousins or other worthies, but there was no sense drawing attention. For those with malice of mind she'd a dagger at her belt and another concealed beneath her simple black skirts. And should the worst befall, Kaila had Apara to whisk her away. The thief's eyes saw more than Rasha's ever would.

"It's not good to depend on servants." Melanna crouched, bringing her eyes level with Kaila's. "Sometimes you will be alone. You must rely on your own eyes, your own ears and your own good sense. So I ask you again: which should we buy?"

Puzzlement yielded to earnest smile. Kaila's finger stabbed towards a slightly lopsided loaf at one end of the stall. "That one."

Melanna stood and addressed the stallholder. "How much?"

"Thirteen rialla."

Too much. Probably the woman expected to barter, but that in itself presented a problem. Melanna suspected most folk didn't recognise her without the jewels and gowns of state, but there was no guarantee. If she named a lower price and it was met only because she was the Empress, then that made a poor lesson for Kaila, and likely cheated the woman into the bargain. The realisation occasioned bitterness, a small pleasure stripped away. Perhaps that was why she'd avoided the market so long?

It didn't help that Apara watched her deliberations with obvious amusement.

Admitting defeat, Melanna counted out the coins and pressed them into Kaila's hand. "Pay the woman."

Kaila handed over the coins with stolid solemnity. Melanna scooped the loaf into her basket, and set the basket in Kaila's hands. "Guard it with your life, *essavim*."

The girl stood to something approaching attention. "Yes, my Empress."

The stallholder's lip twitched. So she *had* known.

Taking Kaila's hand, Melanna threaded her way through the crowd, stopping at one stall or another almost at random, buying goods merely for the pleasure of doing so. As she wandered, free of an Empress' burdens, the character of the stalls altered, the foodstuffs and garments of the day giving way to the coloured lanterns and complicated pleasures of the night market.

Eventually Rasha, no longer willing to wait on the periphery, wended through the crowds to join her. "I think it would be best if you returned to the ..." A weatherworn cheek twitched. "... returned home."

He was probably right. The night market operated on the fringes of acceptability, and was no place for an Empress to be seen, much less her child. For all that others of rank partook its intoxicating joys, seemliness was all. But it would be a while yet before the commerce of the day yielded to the hedonism of night, and Melanna – lost in the rare joy of untetherment from an Empress' duties, found herself in no hurry.

"I shall, in time." She gazed across the marketplace to where an elderly trader struggled to load his wares onto a low-sided dray. The man's arm was bindwork below the elbow, the artificial muscle fraying and poorly maintained. "Detail some of your Immortals to help that man."

"My Immortals are present for the Empress' protection," Rasha replied stiffly.

Melanna's eyes lingered on each visible Immortal in turn. "And I'm sure the Empress understands that if she can *see* four Immortals, there are as many again keeping vigil without armour to betray them." Rasha twitched a scowl, but said nothing. "And she surely trusts the lunassera to keep her safe."

"Very well."

Rasha offered a stiff-necked bow and withdrew. Apara's soft laughter chased him along. Soon after, the perplexed merchant found his burdens eased by a trio of Immortals.

A fourth appeared at Melanna's shoulder. "Jasaldar Rasha says I am to remain at your side, *savim*." A familiar voice, though her face lay hidden beneath the helm. Tesni Rhanaja.

"I'm sure he does." Melanna noted also that the lunassera now stood closer than before.

Kaila frowned. "Do you know that man, Madda?"

"I do not," replied Melanna.

"Then why do you want Shar Rasha to help him?"

Her use of the word *shar* – a corruption of the formal term for a respected citizen, used for kin that were not *quite* kin – provoked a smile. Another lesson beckoned. One Melanna herself had been too long in learning.

"He lost his arm fighting for the Empire, *essavim*. Defending all that we have and all that we are. It deserves honest service in return." She hesitated, recognising that the explanation belonged to a younger, more arrogant woman than the one she'd become. "And because I can. That's enough."

Kaila's expression knotted and unknotted as she wrestled with the concept. "Shar Apara says only a fool gives something away for free."

Face flat, Melanna stared over her daughter's head. "Oh, does she?"

"Not my words." Apara held up her hands. "I suggested it's wise to know what you're getting out of the deal, even if it's nothing at all."

Melanna looked from one to the other. Both wore curiously similar expressions, wary of being rebuked for a lie. "Apara is a rogue, *essavim*, and a rogue would make a poor Empress."

"Yes, Madda."

Would she remember any of this? Melanna's own recollections of childhood were so fleeting that she could hazard no guess. Maybe that was for the best, for there was truth even in Apara's cynical counsel.

"*Savim?*"

Tesni nodded sharply towards the sun-shadowed palace. A mounted messenger forced a path through the crowds, provoking curious gazes and angry voices. Any passersby who'd remained ignorant of the Empress in their midst would no longer do so.

Melanna's heart sank. A message, and an urgent one to provoke such commotion. The freedom of the marketplace faded as if it had never been, and the Empress went to receive it.

"So it has begun."

Aeldran stared from the terrace across the garden, past the ring of Immortals that guaranteed semblance of privacy from wandering servants, towards the blackened remains of the old wood. He'd been distant ever since they'd returned to the palace, at least to Apara's eye. Then again, she'd never had much of a knack for reading him. For all that she considered the Empress the closest of acquaintances, the royal consort remained a mystery that twin barriers of language and culture could not wholly explain.

Haldrane, a shadow in the dying sunlight, shrugged. "If Prince

Edgir's letter is to be believed, yes. He certainly spared no expense getting it here. There must be a trail of half-dead horses between here and Haldravord."

"You speculate when you should *know*," rumbled Aeldran. "Or should another assume your duties?"

Haldrane straightened. Ice crept into his tone. "The Empress may do as she believes best."

He, at least, Apara understood. A broker in secrets and whispers, Haldrane's anger was less at the accusation of dereliction and more at its truth. The icularis were failing too often of late. The sympathy didn't last. She didn't care for Haldrane, nor he for her. Each saw too much of their own duplicity in the other.

Melanna drew her cloak tighter. Her eyes too alighted on the fire-blasted trees, though Apara suspected for very different reasons. "The Empress believes that bickering solves nothing."

Apara suppressed a shiver. For all that Melanna looked no different than she had in the marketplace, she seemed many years older – a woman in her prime, in full command of self and situation. Even her voice was different, sharp and clear. Apara had witnessed similar transformations several times since their visit to Mooncourt Temple – not least when putting Cardivan in his place. Whatever she'd sought beneath the sanctum mound, she'd found ... at least in part.

Melanna's lip twisted. Imperial hauteur fell away. "The past is the past. We deal with events as they are."

Aeldran resumed contemplation of the gardens.

Haldrane sighed. "The attack on Terevosk itself is, of course, nothing. You'll forgive me, but a rabble counts for little in the grand scheme, no matter how storied their leader."

Their leader. Apara was trying hard not to think about that. Though they'd never spoken, she and Roslava Orova were sisters in law and tradition. She'd never had much family. Now it seemed she'd even less. She told herself what sorrow she experienced was for the idea of kin, not its truth. Sevaka's wife would never have thought kindly of her. And yet ... family was family, even if you didn't choose it.

"But the *symbolism*?" Haldrane went on. "Edgir may not be convinced, but he suggests Faethran was receptive enough. It makes for a powerful tale. Ancestral enemies strike against the Gwyraya Hadar and the Empress blockades those who seek to act? It'll play well with cynics and patriots alike."

"You sound as though you approve." Apara spoke more to drown uncertain feelings than to be heard. She wasn't even part of this council – merely a sympathetic ear. If council it was. It had more the feel of conspiracy than governance.

Haldrane hooked an eyebrow, his tone taking on the same note of disapproval it always did around her. "I find it best not to let pride interfere with judgement. It leads to underestimation, and if you'll forgive me, Empress, we are already guilty enough of underestimating the House of Tirane. I have warned you for many years that Silsaria was a boil to be lanced. Now it's too late."

"What would you have me do?" asked Melanna.

"Withdraw your blockade," said Haldrane. "Let it be known that you've been swayed by Tressian treachery, and will permit Cardivan – and those who follow him – to defend Redsigor and take whatever reprisals deemed due."

"You'd have the Empress be swayed by the actions of a rabble?" Apara wondered why she cared. After years away, she felt little kinship with her fellow Tressians, save one or two. "Your words, Haldrane."

He glared at her. "I didn't claim it a *good* option."

"Then why suggest it?"

"Because poor choices are all that remain," he snapped. "Almost *any* action now suggests weakness. Even peace with the Republic, if it could be arranged."

Unlikely, given Lord Droshna's unflinching manner. Apara preferred not to think of him if possible, nor how easily his shadow had once shackled her to his will. She'd sworn to die before letting that happen again.

Aeldran abandoned his vigil of the garden and folded his arms. "I know a part of what must be done. I should ride south, today, and take command of our forces at Mergadir."

Melanna shook her head. "I need you here. Kaila needs you here."

"One of us *has* to be with the army – especially if swords are drawn."

"Then I'll go. It's my banner, and my responsibility."

Aeldran exchanged a glance with Haldrane. Receiving the other's minuscule shrug, he limped across the terrace and laid his hands on Melanna's upper arms. "I've always admired your warrior's heart, but it leads you false in this. If you leave Tregard, you will be vulnerable. Rasha cannot protect you on the road as he can here, and I fear our forces at Mergadir will be swarming with Cardivan's agents. Ride south, and you invite death."

"That holds as true for you as for me."

He dipped his head, a wry smile playing about his lips. "Indeed. But I am not the Empress, merely her consort ... and consorts are expendable."

Melanna pursed her lips, swallowing vexed expression. "Not to me."

His hands fell away. "I'm glad that is so, but it changes little. The Empress must be above such petty concerns, especially now. She must preside with dignity while curs snap at her heels. But more than that, she must *live*." The smile faded. "I know inaction sits ill with you. But this is the way it must be."

Worry, hurt and frustration chased across Melanna's expression. One by one, they vanished. "Our daughter will expect your return. Do not disappoint her."

"Our daughter alone?"

The crease of Melanna's lips might have been a smile, though it vanished too soon for Apara to be certain. "As to the rest, if I am to be a caged Empress, I can still act to reaffirm the loyalty of wavering kingdoms. You will work with me on this, Haldrane?"

He bowed. "I live to serve, Empress."

For all his deference, there was something peculiar in his manner. But then, so much of Haldrane's manner was peculiar. Another oddity of culture, perhaps. For all that the Hadari were the same as Tressians, details of dissonance echoed strangely.

"Then leave us, both of you," said Melanna. "Farewells deserve privacy."

When Apara retreated from the terrace she found Haldrane waiting for her in the corridor.

"Might I steal a moment of your time?" He smiled, pleased with his small witticism.

Stranger and stranger. Apara could count on the fingers of one hand the occasions upon which Haldrane had initiated conversation. She drew back a step. An empty corridor invited the sharing of secrets, but the potential for so-called accidents around a man such as Haldrane was always to be respected. "Go on."

He offered a lopsided smile. He'd recognised her wariness. But then, she'd meant him to. "You've nothing to fear from me."

He'd never know how true that was. "You're right."

The smile soured. "We needn't quarrel. Indeed, I offer a gift – a detail not present in Edgir's letter, but confirmed through other means. Lady Orova lives, though I expect not for very long."

"I should care?" The response was rote, a defence against the actions caring might demand. "Why didn't you tell the Empress?"

"They share an … unfortunate history. Had I raised the matter, I've no doubt she'd have forbidden action."

"It's not for the Empress to forbid me anything."

Another of those damnable, Raven-may-care shrugs. "Then I misunderstood. Good day."

Apara watched him go, stomach sour with uncertainty.

The house was too small, too cramped, possessing only eleven rooms of modest size, and those filled to bursting by a moderately sized entourage. The furniture was worse. Not substandard, as such, but peasant's fare – workmanlike and barely comfortable. The gardens – too modest to be worthy of the name – were neither here nor there, for stepping outside invited dire consequences. Even in Tregard's Poor Quarter, far from the sight of city wardens and the Immortals of the palace guard, there were those who'd report that his regal majesty Cardivan Tirane had not been expelled from the city, as was commonly believed, but rather a decoy.

Cardivan consoled himself with the knowledge that it wouldn't be for ever, but still his temper slipped when his guest entered the drawing room. Haldrane had that effect on everyone. Temptation remained to cancel the meeting and offer the spymaster up to his champion's unhappy delights. Brackar's enthusiasm for pain was equalled only by his talent for inflicting it.

"Well?" he demanded.

Haldrane didn't answer at first, his gaze fixed on the cracked plaster above a soot-clogged hearth. "Aeldran Andwar rides south to take command at Mergadir. The Empress is to remain in Tregard, where she is . . . safe."

Cardivan leapt to his feet, the lumpen chaise rocking gently behind. "You promised an opening to exploit. Prince Aeldran's departure buys me nothing!"

"Be mindful of your tone, majesty," Haldrane replied icily. "I act as I do because the Empire can no longer afford indecision. If that means clearing your path to the throne, then so be it. But I'm not some lackey, bought and sold. Our goals align. Let that be enough. Or must I change my mind about our arrangement?"

Cardivan scowled. He reminded himself that Haldrane would surely have set contingencies against warranted aggression. "My apologies."

Haldrane nodded. "You underestimate how much she relies on her consort. Their bond may not be love, but it is partnership all the same."

"I need spears." With an effort, Cardivan kept frustration from his voice. "Aeldran's presence at Mergadir makes that harder. Aelia Andwaral might have been goaded to rashness. Her brother has the impatience of a stone."

"Forget the south. You've drawn away Rhaled's armies. Content yourself with that."

"How can I? Tregard is not without defenders, and I haven't enough men in the city to overcome them." In truth, Cardivan had rather more warriors in Tregard than Haldrane suspected. "I need an army."

Haldrane laughed under his breath. "You have one."

"With Mergadir blockaded, I have a hundred men." Cardivan cast an angry hand towards the unseen palace. "Not even enough to defend this squalid manse, let alone contest the royal guard."

Nor was that strictly true, but secrets had twice their value when kept from Haldrane.

Haldrane crossed to the cracked window. "Not so. An army is close enough, even if it is not the one you intended. You need only call for it. Redsigor was never the prize."

Lost in possibility, Cardivan forgot the spymaster's supercilious manner. "Thirava won't like it."

Haldrane snorted. "He doesn't have to like it, only obey."

Cardivan nodded absently, logistics now claiming his whole attention. It could be done, and swiftly. It carried risk, but all worthwhile endeavour carried risk. It was the mark of a great man that he forged on regardless, and bent history's flow to his will. "Redsigor was never the prize."

Twenty-Eight

Fingers brushed against the timbers of the boarded-up window. Not *her* fingers. How could they be when lacking any sensation save the sound? There was pressure, certainly. Instinctive acceptance of resistance against a piece of oneself, however distant.

Even sound, too, was lacking. Not just in the caress of fingertip against woodgrain or rough brick, but in what lay beyond. The bustle of streets steeped more in memory than present seeming. Dull, and yet not dull enough, just as the eyes beheld shape, but so little of colour. Here again, instinct inked detail, giving life to the drapes' rich black and shards of golden sunlight. Not seen, but known. A muted world, familiar and yet not. So close to nightmare.

Perhaps nightmare might be preferable. One awoke from nightmare. In nightmare, one didn't question the dearth of tell-tales that proved life's illusion. The flutter of breath. The imperceptible tremor of coursing blood. A hundred tiny sensations that told the mind that the body lived, and breathed, and *belonged*. All lost. Stolen in a whirlwind of raven feathers and cold clay.

Recent memory was jumbled. Frantic. A storm of frustrated emotion, soothed by embraces scarcely felt and rumbled solace that had comforted even with meaning lost to madness. Little by little, she'd come to understand her misfortune. She'd held witness as that same fate had befallen another. A lifetime ago, then and now bridged by . . . what?

She lacked words to frame the experience. There was only a lingering sensation of acceptance, swaddled in green-white mist. A feeling of stillness. A sense of more lost in transition than gained.

A low moan easing from clay lips that did not feel, Calenne Trelan rested head and hands not hers against the boarded window, and wished herself gone back into mist.

Turning about, she stared into a candleflame's soothing flicker and felt something stir deep within. A memory, or perhaps a dream dissipated in the moment of waking. She could almost see—

"I sought to prevent this."

Calenne spun, the motion unsteady with the weight of clay limbs both too heavy and too light. [[Who is that?]]

Her voice awoke fresh pang. Hollow, as her thoughts were hollow. Worse was the glimpse caught in the free-standing mirror. The silk dress was finer than any she'd owned in life, trimmed with lace and shaped by artful corsetry. The body beneath was pale as death, the polished clay face blank, expressionless – the mask of a mummer playing the role of Kismet. Fingers traced the scuff marks at the temple where, keening, she'd striven to drag it free. The wig, at least, was like enough to what her hair had once been – dark as moonless night, and braided close. Taken as a whole, it was all much less beautiful than the doll made for Anastacia. So much plainer and cruder.

An intruder's presence was nothing. An intruder at least meant company.

What more could he do to her than had already been done?

Shadow stirred beyond the candlelight, beyond the sofa, the tables and the stack of books provided for a glimpse of comfort in the bare brick room with barricaded windows and a locked door. An unsteady goateed presence in frock coat and battered hat bled away into a veiled, elderly woman in Hadari mourning silks. These two facets shared only the ruin where the right-hand side of their faces should have been. The darkness of a starry sky swirled beyond, a hole punched clean through the world. A glimpse of something vast, hidden behind a figment of flesh that shifted between vying aspects.

The memory of breath caught in Calenne's throat. [[Stay away from me!]]

Yet she felt a bond. A tether. Even a yearning. The echo of kindness offered and received in a mist-laden world.

To her surprise, the Raven halted. A hand rose to forestall panic, and might have done so had not the fingers bled wisps of vaporous starfield. "You need not fear me."

[[I'm *not* afraid of you.]]

The Raven shrugged. "I'm not your enemy in this." He chanced a step into the candlelight. "You know how you came to be as you are?"

Calenne hesitated. [[Viktor saved me.]]

"He *stole* you. Out of selfishness, I might add."

[[He loves me.]]

That much she believed, however contorted her feelings about his recent deeds. About tearing her from contentment into a world robbed of sensation. Ungrateful though she felt, Calenne couldn't say with certainty she was glad of it. Was a life lived unfeeling and *other* any kind of life at all? What of future and family? What of being shunned for a freak? Did Viktor's love grant him the right to act as he'd done?

The Raven's fluctuating image stabilised as the old woman, the deep, gravelly voice yielding to something drier. "Does he?" The woman shuddered away, and the man returned. "I think it's not Calenne Trelan he mourned all these years, but Viktor Droshna's pride."

[[Viktor *Akadra*.]]

The Raven's form shifted. She shook her head. "Not any longer. Did he not say? The Hadari named him for the Dark at his command, and he wears their curse proudly as mantle. They fought a war out of fear of what he might become, and in their terror midwifed that very fate." He scowled. "*Ephemerals.*"

[[He loves me. He does.]] She clung to that certainty in a life otherwise washed away.

"He styles himself a man who cannot lose," he replied, "and yet he lost you. That loss drives him far more than affection. And look at you. Do you suppose you any longer set his pulse aflame?"

Calenne fought the urge to glance at the mirror. Fought, and lost. The stranger with the doll's aspect stared back. Of course there was nothing of desire in the form. But then their brief, strange courtship – if it could even be called that – had been chaste, a bond born of shared souls more than desire. Or did she simply tell herself that to justify the void where her own desire should have lain?

[[Did Josiri still love his demon?]]

Josiri. Had he survived the aftermath of Davenwood? Had Anastacia? Calenne had the feeling she'd once known, and many other things besides. Snatches of ephemeral life, glimpsed through Otherworld's veil.

The Raven closed, skirts swishing about her feet. "You shouldn't resent a few missing memories. Worse than that gets left in the mists." She sighed. "Yes, your brother's love for my niece endures. But Josiri and Viktor are very different men."

[[Viktor is a *better* man.]]

The Raven shrugged. "I'm sure you know best."

[[I know better than to listen to the Raven.]]

He closed the distance in an eyeblink, palm against the spot where her breastbone should have been, the swirling starfield bleeding like smoke across her dress. Calenne felt no sensation, of course. Just pressure. An itch one couldn't scratch. She'd have wept, had she means to do so.

The Raven leaned close, her lips level with Calenne's cheek. "The feeling. Here. The one you can't describe. The loss you can't shape. You're pining for my realm. You belong to me. Your soul knows it, even if your mind rebels. Still, I suppose we should both be grateful. The last time he tried this, the poor soul was torn in twain. Half to my keeping, and half to his."

Calenne pulled away. The ache of loss ebbed, but did not abate. [[So you claim to love me more?]] She lent anger to the words. [[You're Keeper of the Dead. This is the concern of a landlord for his holdings, or the gamekeeper for a poacher's venison.]]

The Raven pursued, the remnant of his face contorted to fury. Candles scattered before him, spilling wax across the wooden floor. Calenne retreated until her back pressed up against the boarded window, his face an inch from hers.

"You are a mote among millions. A grain of sand upon the shores of a dozen worlds. I'm a keeper. A guardian. A caretaker. Even a curator. What love I have is the very driest form of affection. And even so, that love is greater than Viktor Droshna's. However he once beheld you, you're now nothing more than a mirror to his success and his failure."

The Raven winced beneath her veil and stepped back, shoulders hunched and head low.

[[You're wrong,]] Calenne's words quickened, confidence and defiance building. For the first time since waking to a world of unfeeling clay, she started to feel like herself. [[It's your own pride that's hurting. You say Viktor stole me? Perhaps he did. And I'm guessing you resent the theft of even a single "mote". Viktor *hurt* you. If I serve as a mirror to anyone's failure, it's yours!]]

The Raven straightened, humours again aligned to hauteur. "Perhaps there's some truth there. Certainly, I wish him harm for his deeds, and those he will yet attempt. But you should consider that Viktor Akadra is no longer the man you remember – if indeed he ever was."

[[Get out.]] Calenne hurled a book from the table. It fell far short of the Raven and skidded across the floor. Apparently Anastacia had her greatly bested in strength, as well as beauty. [[Leave me alone!]]

"As you wish." The Raven cocked his head, a sad smile twisting his goatee. "But you might ask your dear Viktor about his sudden fondness for candles, when firestone lanterns may yet be the only magic the Republic possesses."

She turned about and was gone, leaving Calenne feeling both more and less like herself.

Viktor turned the key and hesitated, his fingers at the door handle. What would he find within the sanctum? He'd departed the tower before dawn, drawn away by Elzar's funeral, leaving behind a woman whose welling black eyes – he hoped – held the first sign of sanity.

His heart had urged him to remain and ease Calenne's distress, as he had most waking hours in the days prior. But doing so would have betrayed Elzar's sacrifice. And it had been sacrifice. For all the clutter in his life, the high proctor had always perceived the world clearly, his certainty a rock to the last. His passing left a void impossible to fill. It could only be honoured. Observance held the sorrow at bay. Sorrow, and the speck of guilt that could not be dispelled, only ignored.

But hope more than sorrow gave Viktor pause. Hope that Calenne would at last recognise him. Accept him. That she was indeed what she seemed, and not some Dark-born demon. This last he feared more than any Hadari blade or lost cause.

Viktor gripped the handle. The door eased inwards into candlelight.

"Calenne?" He spoke softly, habit urging him to clandestine behaviour even though there was no other in the clocktower, Tzila aside, and his secrets were safe with her. "Calenne, can you hear me?"

[[Yes, Viktor. I'm here.]]

His heart leapt. Better than hearing Calenne speak in coherent, measured tones was the sight of her sitting on the high-backed sofa, legs tucked demurely beneath. The morning after her return, she'd scrabbled at the door, howling like a caged beast. Even yesterday, she'd huddled in the corner, head buried in her elbows. She was even *reading* – at least, she'd a book spread open across her knees. One of several volumes purchased based on imperfect memory of those she'd possessed at vanished Branghall.

"May I enter?"

She glanced up from the book. [[You're already here.]]

He still wasn't accustomed to the voice. She *sounded* like Calenne, but not completely. As if a piece were missing. Viktor told himself it was the clay that made it thus, and wasn't an indication of a greater lack – or one accidentally filled with the Dark. He'd made that mistake before, and chanced disaster. But even though a fraction amiss in character, her tone offered hope. Confidence. Certainty. Maybe even fondness.

He set the door to and edged into candlelight, searching the expressionless face for warning of relapse. "What are you reading?"

[[*The Turn of Winter.* I never finished it. I thought it might make me feel ... That I'd feel ...]] Voice crowding with emotion, she closed the book and stared at the cover. [[I'm sorry. After all you've done – after everything it's cost you – I know it's selfish to behave so. I have *not* been a decorous guest.]]

"You've suffered an ordeal." Heart brimming, Viktor knelt before the sofa and cradled her hands. "I'd have paid any price to have you returned. I've longed to hear you speak."

She shook her head. [[Even if my voice is no longer my own?]]

"Even then."

[[And what of affection? Of love?]]

"It is my hope it endures." He spoke slowly, choosing his words with utmost care. "I will do all I must to reforge it. But I place no expectation on you. My world is brighter for you walking in it, even if we must do so apart."

[[Prettily said. Has the Black Knight been reading poetry?]]

For all the mirth in Calenne's voice – for all the softening in posture – Viktor sensed his answer hadn't been the one sought. That he'd perhaps even misread the question. "Would that I had the time. Duty is a heavy burden."

[[Wasn't it always?]]

"It grows ever weightier." Viktor realised he was staring at the patch of floor where Elzar had breathed his last. He tore his attention back to Calenne. "When we spoke in Otherworld, you gave the impression you'd beheld something of the mortal world. What do you recall?"

Pulling her hands free, she set fingers against her temples as one massaging away a headache. Recognising the pointlessness of the motion, she let them fall to her lap.

[[I remember the wind in my hair at Davenwood. The glory of the charge and the joy of finally being someone I liked. Maybe even someone you could respect. Then a sword, white with flame. My horse bolted. I fell into Skazit Maze. And she ... she was waiting for me.]]

"Malatriant."

Porcelain hands clenched and unclenched, dark leather creaking at the joints. [[I tried to fight her ...]] She met his gaze, black eyes swirling. [[It would be better if you assume I know nothing thereafter.]]

He clasped her hands anew. How much to tell her? Seven long years had passed since Davenwood, filled with people Calenne had never met and deeds that would matter little. Start with the simple things. The folk she'd known and loved, Josiri most of all.

Viktor rose and pulled up a wooden chair. Sitting opposite, he launched into a fractured retelling – one he feared was less coherent even than it sounded. The aftermath of Davenwood and Malatriant's rise. The ascension of Kai Saran to the Imperial throne and the Avitra Briganda that had heralded his own elevation as Tressia's Lord Protector. He spoke of Josiri and Anastacia, of Revekah Halvor, Vladama Kurkas and Armund af Garna, and other comrades who'd marched beneath Davenwood's phoenix banner. Of the challenges ahead, and his determination to recover the lost Eastshires. Of his hopes that porcelain might in coming years soften to flesh.

But even amid the telling, he kept details shrouded. He said nothing

of his hope that Calenne might take up arms and fight for their countrymen. That commitment, Viktor judged, would come in its own time
and was not his to force. Likewise, he drew a veil over deeds to which
he'd pressed his shadow out of need, recognising them as mired in
complication – one or two acts, in particular, for which he still felt keen
regret ... necessary though they'd been.

Shafts of daylight from the boarded windows glowed red with
evening's fire, and surrendered to darkness. Hunger, thirst, and even the
brooding business of war grew distant, lost in the rising joy of shared
company sought so long.

And it *was* Calenne. As candles burned low and the chamber's shadows lengthened, he set his own free to test every facet of her being. It
was *her*. The true Calenne he'd sought in Otherworld, and not some
doppelganger conjured from the Dark. More than that, he found no trace
of the Dark about her. No weave of shadow and spite to patch a soul yet
part in the Raven's jealous grasp. The discovery, so long in arriving, left
him breathless to the brink of tears and quite unable to speak.

She mocked him for his silence, marvelling at the Black Knight's speech-
lessness. But it was not without kindliness. When she enquired what had
struck him so, Viktor found no words to serve justice by the tangled emotion, and instead spoke of Elzar's last moments. Grief walled away spilled
free. Despairing the weakness, he pinched shut his eyes to force it back. He
opened them at the pressure of a small porcelain hand upon his shoulder.

Silence reigned, no words exchanged and none sought. A long, cherished moment plucked from the world's travails, and one ended all too
soon when Calenne retook her place upon the sofa.

[[Josiri at the Republic's heart,]] she said at last. [[What would our
mother say, I wonder?]]

Our mother. That alone marked her different from the Calenne of yes-
teryear, who'd vehemently declaimed familial bond. Wisdom, it seemed,
was not the sole province of the living.

"He is my rock," said Viktor. "He has saved me from myself so
many times."

[[No doubt being insufferable all the while?]]

"At times, but no more than deserved. Where others would back
down, he stands firm. He's fearless. As all Trelans are fearless."

[[You mean *stubborn*.]]

"I do. But the Republic could use a little defiance in this hour."

[[Then war is inevitable?]] Calenne spoke flatly.

Standing, Viktor faced the corner where armour and sword hung. "I wish it wasn't. But the road ahead is choking in blood and darkness. I see a way through. At least, I pray I do. Folk have given me their trust, and already I'm straining it to the limit. I will deliver on my promises. I must. Otherwise everything I've done will be for nothing."

[[Simpler to be a monster with a sword?]]

"Would you believe I miss those days?" He shrugged, though felt little of that nonchalance. "I never sought peace, nor simplicity, but now they're all I crave. It's my dream that we might perhaps seek them together, but I know that's a conversation for the future. Whatever happens next, my world is brighter with you returned to it. I'm glad to have someone I can truly talk to."

[[You have Josiri.]] She rose in a swish of skirts. [[I'd like to see him.]]

The request he'd dreaded. "Not yet."

She tilted her head in suspicion. Under other circumstances, it would have cheered Viktor to see how swiftly she adopted mannerisms to compensate for an expressionless face. [[What aren't you telling me?]]

He grimaced, but acknowledged the moment no occasion for half-truths. "That dream I spoke of. Some years ago, I lived it for a time. A quiet life on the Thrakkian border with a woman I loved more dearly than life."

[[I see.]] Was that jealousy in her tone, or his hope of finding it? [[Who was she?]]

Viktor breathed deep. "After you . . . After Eskavord, something inside me broke. In my grief, I allowed the Dark to soothe my hurt. From it, I wove a woman I thought was you. Only when the malice of the Dark asserted itself was the lie revealed. I unravelled her once I learned what I'd done, but her memory lingers."

Calenne went utterly still. Viktor somehow managed to avoid babbling through the silence. Justification would only make matters worse.

[[And Josiri knows of this . . . creature?]] she asked at last.

"I fear that if he learns of someone calling herself 'Calenne Trelan' he'll react badly."

She shook her head. [[Oh, Viktor. I swear I don't know whether to thump you, or embrace you.]]

"Whatever you think is right. But I must ask you to remain in this room for the present."

[[I grew to womanhood in a cage, Viktor. I find the prospect no more appealing now.]]

"It won't be for ever. A week, perhaps two. Explanations will go easier once the Eastshires are settled. In the meantime, our people can't afford me to be distracted. Tzila will stand watch when I cannot. You'll have everything you need."

[[Except freedom.]]

"In time, I swear. Even if we must sail far from this city to find it."

She snorted. [[We? You're presuming a great deal, Viktor.]] The words cut cold, but her tone held wryness.

"Have you ever known me to be anything other than bold?" he asked. "In any case, I must take my leave. There's much needing my attention and I've already indulged myself longer than I should."

She beheld him, arms folded and thoughts unreadable. Then, step by hesitant step, she offered brief embrace. [[I'll withhold the thumping for another day. Take it as a sign that our dreams may not be so far apart. But if I might make one request?]]

"Name it."

[[Candles are more romantic than practical – especially for reading. Perhaps you could arrange for some firestone lanterns? I'm sure that's not beyond the mighty Lord Protector.]]

A simple request, and impossible to deny without explaining how painful he found their light of late. "For you, Lady Trelan, he will see what can be done. Though they, like so many things, are in short supply in this embattled Republic."

Calenne lost track of time after the key turned, her thoughts abuzz with revelations, recounted tales ... and evasions.

Evasions, above all. For all his talents, Viktor lacked a dissembler's tongue. Not that his artlessness did her any good, for she'd nowhere to start unravelling the suspected half-truths. The world she'd returned to was too different to the one she'd left. And Calenne allowed that there were many honourable reasons to keep things unspoken. Her own sanity for one.

Such as it was.

The room – her *prison* – grew smaller, the lengthening shadows closing about her like a fist.

A memory jarred loose. Words uttered in mist. *Poor Viktor. Always so certain you know what's best.* Her words. As true now as before. Much as she wanted to trust Viktor, she needed answers. She needed the open sky, and her feet free to walk as she wished. Decide for herself if new life was blessing or curse. Those things could not be hers if she obeyed Viktor's wishes.

Returning to the window, Calenne ran a hand across the lowermost board. Gravelly laughter echoing about her, she closed her fingers about its edge.

Twenty-Nine

Waning moon stared down on empty streets. Hawkin Darrow had lived through three city-wide curfews, and others targeted at specific districts. But for all that, this *felt* different. Resentment hung heavy on the smoke-bittered air. For all that the citizenry had cheered proclamation of war on a distant border, they'd little stomach for consequences nearer home. Food, already hard enough come by in certain neighbourhoods, would grow considerably scarcer.

Foremost of all, Hawkin had never seen well-to-do streets so quiet. Even during curfew, highbloods thought restrictions were for others, not them. Not tonight. The wealthy streets around Strazyn Abbey were deserted. The Drazina reputation at work. A curfew-breaker cornered by the constabulary might attempt a bribe. Getting snatched up by swan-tabards meant a beating. Worse, if you didn't have papers. The rules were changing.

Thus Hawkin clung to the shadows, flitting between lamp posts with ears pricked and eyes wary. The streets themselves she knew well enough – especially those bordering the Abbeyfields estate's overgrown ruins. *Not* where she wanted to be. Too many memories.

But choosing the course wasn't in the shadower's gift.

Three dozen paces along the narrow, lantern-lit street, the wisp of Kasvin's white-blonde hair halted. Her bare-shouldered and high-hemmed gown was a poor choice for the bitter night. Hawkin hunkered close to Abbeyfields' overgrown railings and clung to shadow.

Kasvin's blue-green eyes lingered on the patch of darkness. Hawkin breathed deep, cold air stinging her lungs, and beseeched the Raven to conceal her. If Kasvin called out, Hawkin knew she'd show herself and confess. Better to brave the gnawing, sorrowful hurt of the young woman's disappointment and come more swiftly to sweet forgiveness. Even now, part of her longed to do so. The small, mangled part of her that craved a word, a gesture, a kiss.

Hawkin would have cut it out long ago, were such a thing possible. But it ruled her whenever Kasvin was near, suffocated her in adoration. So much that she forgot her disdain for the younger woman's firebrand principles.

It had taken weeks to realise it was happening at all. She'd actually thought herself in *love*. Imagine that. Giddy at the knees for a slip of girl. She hated Kasvin for making her believe those scars had healed. But only when Kasvin was elsewhere.

The longing worsened, tugging at Hawkin's stomach. Clamping her eyes shut helped. If she revealed herself, she'd learned nothing.

When she opened her eyes, Kasvin was gone.

Heartsick ache faded to relief. Worry over an escaped quarry followed close behind.

Hawkin wasn't even certain why she'd ever come back to the city. But she couldn't leave now. Privation and war would make fertile recruitment ground for the Merrow, as it had the Crowmarket before. And what benefited the Merrow – assuming he existed, for she'd never met him – benefited those in his shadow, if they'd wit to seize the opportunity.

And there *had* to be opportunity. Didn't there? Not that she was against feeding the hungry or getting medicine to the sick, but she'd yet to see even a hint of profit in the enterprise. And there was *always* profit for someone. Might as well be her, if she could wrangle it.

Cursing under her breath, Hawkin left the shadow and advanced as swiftly as slush underfoot allowed.

"Let's see your papers!"

Hawkin froze, even though she knew the challenge wasn't meant for her. It had come from the streets ahead, past the memorial to the Weeper Plague – a dozen statues of men, women and children in funeral garb, hands clasped to their eyes.

A scream. The *thump* of a falling body. A whisper of song, half-heard on the night-time breeze. Achingly familiar, somehow.

Heart pacing with worry for Kasvin and her head wary of discovery, Hawkin concealed herself among the statues. Halfway between the corner and the tumbledown abbey gate, Kasvin stood atop a Drazina's crumpled body, bloody dagger in her hand and spreading stain at her feet. She had one arm wended about a second Drazina, hand cupped about the base of his neck and her lips against his.

The song faded. Hawkin's throat tightened with jealousy. Swallowing, she reminded herself it wasn't real. Or was it? Jealousy was of the heart. If it was felt, it *was* real.

More convincing was the passionless embrace. The Drazina's fading, ineffectual twitches. When he went entirely still, Kasvin let the body fall. He hit the cobbles, dark fluid rushing from his mouth and nose. Kasvin strode on towards the abbey as if nothing had happened.

Hawkin lingered, jealousy falling away into the empty, gaping pit beneath her stomach. Raven's Eyes, but what *was* Kasvin?

The easy thing to do – maybe the *smart* thing – was walk away. From Kasvin. From Tressia. From the Republic itself. Even now the thought offered a pang of dismay. Hawkin steeled herself. She'd been vranakin, hadn't she? On the cusp of earning a kernclaw's feathers. She'd beheld the rotting horror of the elder cousins and the malice of the Crowmarket's pontiffs. This was no worse.

Resolution bled away as she reached the corpses. Not so much because of the one Kasvin had stabbed. Hawkin had left too many with a ripper's grin to feel ought but mild approval for the cleanness of the blow. But the other? Bloated, mottled blue skin gave the appearance of a corpse dragged from the river. Fibrous black weed clung to lips and nostrils, twitching in the water puddled beneath his head. The smell, too, was of the deeps. Decay dredged from a silted canal.

Lips pursed, Hawkin stared again at the empty abbey gate. Kasvin's footprints marred crisp snows. Follow or flee?

Follow.

She advanced with uttermost care, walking only in her quarry's footsteps. They wended across the silent grounds, beneath the broken-rib arches of the long-vanished roof and through a gap in rusted railings raised to keep the curious at bay.

Not that the curious ever trespassed Strazyn Abbey.

Hawkin tried to forget the tales of how its lone, abandoned bell tolled without touch of human hand. That the deepest foundations had once belonged to one of Malatriant's Abdon Temples, where sacrifice and bloodletting had conjured demons from beyond the mists. By the time the snows gave way to the crypt's uneven stairs, she was trembling. Every sound – every wisp of shadow – promised some terrible fate. And none more so than the pitch black of the crypt.

Fearful she was on the cusp of some terrible mistake, Hawkin drew a hooded lantern from beneath her cloak, coaxed the crystal to life, and pressed on.

Bereft of guiding footprints, she trusted to instinct, to the tell-tales of scuffed stone that marked recent passage. The straight stair gave way to a long, bowing columbarium, burial alcoves crowded with cracked urns and tangled with tree roots. Insects scurried away as Hawkin twisted the lantern to and fro, picking a path across debris from a collapsing ceiling. Blank-eyed serathi statues watched her progress.

A door loomed to the left. Ajar, it was barely distinct from the columbarium alcoves. Indeed, its maker had clearly wanted it so, for it was less a door and more a pair of alcoves set on a deep hinge. Closed, she'd never have seen it. The cold, dry odour of the crypt gave way to something musty and older still.

A worn spiral stair lay beyond, walls unadorned save for patches of pale, lichenous glow. A dozen steps down the treacherous stones, the air shimmered. For a brief moment, Hawkin felt distant, unmoored – as if she and her body were no longer one and the same. Then the first ripples of song echoed up from below, and the sensation passed.

Product of a single voice, it wasn't the whispering, breathy song of the streets above, but a sweet, echoing refrain that resonated about her heart. The rush and ripple of running water deepening the melody. With fumbling hand, Hawkin doused the lantern, trusting to lichen-light to be her guide.

No door waited at the stairway's foot, merely an opening onto a vast, natural cavern whose crowded, girthsome stalactites and stalagmites evoked a shark's maw. A flagstoned path wended through the maze, flanked here and there by cold, white statues. Beautiful young women with hungry smiles. A far cry from the disinterested, serene serathi watching over the columbarium. Opals glistened in place of eyes, but no dream of avarice could have persuaded Hawkin to pry one free. At least one statue's pallid skin was smeared with what looked to be dried blood.

Song and rush of water blossomed in greeting as she edged along the path. Stalagmites yielded to glimmerless black water. Kasvin knelt on the rocky bank, hands outstretched. Even in the gloom, she shone. As if the lichen woke light for her alone.

Coventaj. The old name, half-suspected, emerged out of memory. You couldn't live in the city and not hear whispers. The Black River of myth that flowed from a land of giants and into worlds beyond without ever once touching the sea. A forgotten shrine to a vanished goddess. Endala, whose lover Tzal had drowned her in those same inky waters . . . or she'd drowned him. There were stories of both and neither, and a hundred justifications for the betrayal. Hawkin, who'd poisoned a wife dearly loved years before, understood that. Some things were true even when they were not, love foremost among them.

She'd wept as she pressed the seldora-laced rag to Vona's mouth, and begged her not to awaken. But at the last, soul-wrenching moment eyes had brimmed wide in accusation and pain. That moment had survived the years, experienced anew in midnight dreams. But it had been Vona or both of them, and so it could only ever have been Vona alone. The Parliament of Crows had ordered the murder as much as a lesson for Hawkin as retribution for Vona's killing of Crowfather Athariss. They'd sought to remind her of her true family.

Now both families were gone, and as Hawkin concealed herself among stalagmites, she recalled that the drowned goddess Endala was patron of betrayed lovers.

The cavern's cool air turned colder still.

Still Kasvin sang. A mournful lullaby offered to oneself.

A tendril of black weed broke the river's reflectionless surface and slithered about her outstretched arm. Others joined it, their caress tender. Owner and pet, or perhaps vice versa. Kasvin sang on, sweet and sad, as black water soaked the sleeves of her dress.

"Must you do that? It's revolting."

Hawkin flinched. The voice had hailed from behind, further up the path. Had he seen her?

The singing faded. The tendrils slipped back beneath the river's surface. Kasvin stood, water spattering from her sodden arms. "Am I now beholden to you? Is that how it works?"

The gloom shifted as he joined her at the water's edge, the lichen-light never strong enough to reveal much. Tall. Thin. Fragile in posture and confidence for all that he made measured stride. Was this the mysterious Merrow?

"Did we have to meet here?" The voice was cultured, highblood in tone and accent, but Hawkin would have wagered both had been learned in later life, much as her own speech had shifted while in service to the Reveques. Mimicry of one's betters was a hard habit to resist. "Is there something wrong with my home? You're ready enough to make free with it when it suits you."

"Does this place unsettle you?" Kasvin's thin smile belied innocence.

"You know it does. I wish I'd never found it."

"You'd do better to wish you'd never had the need," she snapped. "Or had found the courage to live with your deeds."

"You called. I came." A fussy, peevish note crept in. "What do you want of me?"

"You've heard the news, I take it?"

"About the ration being withdrawn?"

"Not just that. There's talk of broadening conscription." She laughed. "Not even a day, and already the city's heaving with discontent. There'll never be a better time."

"For what?"

Kasvin offered no reply save a wry curl of the lip.

"No." The Merrow shook his head. "Too many will die. I began this to save people."

"You began this because I own you."

Hawkin wondered at that. There was nothing in the Merrow's manner to indicate he shared her blind, unwilling adoration for Kasvin. She heard only fear, and something darker beneath.

"People are dying already." Kasvin's voice burned. "Droshna is squeezing the life from this city. The people won't take it. When their children sicken and starve, they'll rise up. But that takes time. How many more must die before that happens? This is inevitable. Better to get it out of the way while the odds are in our favour."

"You've already decided to do this, haven't you?"

"Yes."

"Why do you even need me at all?"

"Because my influence fades with distance. Folk will die for me, but only when I'm close enough to see them fight. But the Merrow's name? That reaches clear across the city. Plenty will remember how you fed them. If you call, they'll come."

The Merrow stared into the rushing waters. "And if I refuse?"

"You gave me to the river. The Nameless Lady sent me back. If you'd prefer my vengeance cast a smaller net, you need only say. You and I can dance together in the Black River."

A cold smile accompanied the words, what Hawkin saw of Kasvin's face suddenly older and crueller. For once, she'd no fear of the compulsion offered by those blue-green eyes. Their gleam spoke of merciless undertows and jagged rocks. The beguiling young woman was an aspect now washed completely away.

The Merrow shuddered. "What do you suggest?"

"Droshna cut the government ration to feed his Thrakkian allies, but it hasn't yet left the city. We blockade the storehouses and the docks."

"We tried two years ago. He was ready then. He'll be ready now. It'll be a slaughter!"

"No, it won't. Because we're going to keep Droshna off-balance. Angry men make mistakes, and we're going to make him *very* angry. Maybe even angry enough to rip Trelan and the rest from their stupor and make them see what he is!"

"And how, pray, are we to do that?"

"We give our cause a figurehead he can't ignore."

"Me?" The Merrow shook his head. "I don't think so."

"Nor I," Kasvin replied acidly. "Yours is not a face to inspire confidence."

"Then who? You won't find support among Droshna's circle. Izack thinks only of the war. Trelan and the others are suffocating in his presence." He broke off. "You're not suggesting the church?"

"I doubt the Archimandrite will accept my petition. In any case, with the foundry in the clutches of the Reveque girl and the provosts dispersed, Jezek has little authority."

"Then who?"

"The river provides."

Kasvin picked her way back through the stalagmites, her lilting song echoing around the cavern once more. The Merrow didn't move, the set of his shoulders betraying unhappiness. Hawkin beheld both in sordid fascination. Profit she'd sought, and certainly there was profit here. The secrets of Coventaj laid bare to the right scholar, or even to the archimandrite. A word in the Lord Protector's ear about the coming blockade? Both would command a grand fee.

Not that she could leave without being seen.

This time, Kasvin didn't stop at the water's edge, but stepped into the river's flow. Skirts petalled about her waist then sank, dragged down. She strode deeper until only her head and the tops of her shoulders could be seen.

When she walked back to shore, a man's body emerged from the waters with her, draped across extended forearms at shoulder and knee. A naked, grey-haired man, his withered limbs tangled in black weed. A weightier burden than should have been possible, but Kasvin gave no hint of strain, nor missed a beat of her fluid, mournful song.

Stepping onto the bank, she tipped the body from her arms. It landed with a thud, and gave a retching, hacking cough. A stream of black water slithered across stone, and the coughing began anew, each convulsion accompanied by a flood as heaving lungs emptied themselves.

Draped in weed, he made it to hands and knees. "Where ... Where am I?"

The Merrow turned away, disgusted.

Kasvin knelt before the old man, skirts puddling about her. Her aspect again demure, enticing. "You're home, Lord Akadra. Your city needs you."

Lord Hadon Akadra, who'd disappeared without trace years before. Who'd been thought dead so long. Or, Hawkin realised sourly, perhaps *thought* didn't cover it. A trick of the lichen-light, so worshipful in Kasvin's presence, revealed a face pale and grey, marred by thick black veins beneath the skin.

Except the veins were *moving*. Pulsing like river weed.

Stomach curdling, Hawkin bit down on her hand to stifle a cry.

Too late. An age too late.

Kasvin's head snapped about. "Show yourself."

Hawkin felt the pull at once. The desire to please Kasvin and thus earn pleasure herself. Revulsion held it at bay. She bolted for the stairs. The Merrow moved to stop her, a black shape in the darkness. A shoulder to his ribs flung him aside, leaving the way open.

"Hawkin?" The anger was gone from Kasvin's voice. "There's no need to run."

The words crawled beneath Hawkin's skin and burrowed deeper. She blinked and called forth the horrors of the night as a shield. The drowned Drazina in the streets. The writhing weed in the river. Hadon Akadra's greying, inhuman features. They gave her the strength to forge on, though legs faltered.

When she looked up again, Kasvin stood between her and the stairs. "Stay . . . Please?"

Hurt, cajoling tone was poor match for knowing smile. Not that it mattered. Not so close.

One glimpse of her eyes, and Hawkin Darrow floated away on a blue-green tide.

Tzadas, 6th Day of Dawntithe

She beckons you with winsome smile,
With slender hands as cold as frost.
Her icy kisses brush your cheek,
And when you meet her eyes, you're lost.
The River Bride, she knows your sins,
The broken vows, the wronged, the dead.
And drags you down among the weeds,
To share her drownling's marriage bed.

Sothvane nursery rhyme

Thirty

Nothing like a morning constitutional to air the cobwebs. Or so Kurkas had repeated to himself at least three times since leaving Stonecrest at dawn. The walk was part of his informal routine now that military life lay behind. Not that passersby would have guessed. Given the cold snap of the morning he'd set aside steward's informal cloth for battered uniform, its golden phoenix dulled by the passing years.

That morning, aching muscles could have done without routine. Counting by the years, he remained several summers shy of his sixtieth birthday. But not all years were equal. Too many lost on the battlefield. Stolen away, lost in Otherworld's mists. A couple of days, most thought. It had been longer. Much longer.

But even though the morning breeze cut sharper than it should, Kurkas held his course. All the time in the world to rest when they laid him in the sod. So long as there was a good drop or two to drink along the way, all was to the good. Cut right down to it and the only thing separating old soldiers and new were the years between. The calling was the calling.

Near-deserted streets roused unease. Even in that early hour – even with the curfew only just lapsed – the cobbles should have been thick with labourers and tradesmen. What should have been rivers of humanity had slowed to a trickle, the streets quiet and seldom more than a handful of souls in sight.

As Kurkas neared Silverway Dock, silence and sparseness retreated before the growl of the mob. Five hundred or so men and women in work clothes and wool cloth facing off against as many again at the harbour gate. Where the first group held pickaxe handles, shovels and boat hooks, the second was unarmed ... all save the two-score watchmen and the portly man in harbour master's shabby finery who stood at their fore. Beyond the gate, the tangle of warehouses and merchantmen sat still and unattended save by circling gulls.

"You're all in violation of guild contracts!" shouted the harbour master. "Back to work, and we'll say nothing more about it!"

"And if we don't?" someone bellowed from the crowd's anonymity.

"Then I'll have my men clear the gates!" The harbour master jerked a thumb over his shoulder. "And your fellows here get your wages as well as their own!"

Fifty swords and five hundred fists against an equal number with improvised weapons and malice in mind? Good luck with that. And that was already assuming that the workers at the harbour master's back fought with him, rather than just watched the brawl from a safe distance.

Worse, a *third* crowd was gathering on the street's outskirts. Maybe folk looking for a bit of early morning entertainment, but you never could tell. And if fighting started? Weren't no such thing as bystanders then. You picked a side, or had one chosen. The brawl would become a riot, and there'd be nothing for it but screams and cracked skulls.

And it had been such a nice, *quiet* morning.

A constable rounded the corner from Tarbridge Lane and retreated just as quickly, heading for the nearby guardhouse. That lass, at least, had good instincts.

Not so the harbour master, who remained unaware how precarious his situation had become, or was so lost to indignation he didn't care. "You have until the count of ten!"

The watchmen drew their swords.

"One!"

The growl about the gate grew louder and deeper.

"Two!"

Kurkas straightened from habitual slouch and pushed his way through the harbour master's crowd, heading towards the blockaded gate.

"Three!"

A watchman gave Kurkas a filthy stare, received a harsher one in return, and stepped aside at the sight of the battered phoenix.

"Fo—" The harbour master turned his scowl on Kurkas. "This isn't Stonecrest business."

"How long d'you reckon it'll stay that way once I report back to Lord Trelan?"

Fresh jeers broke out at the blockade.

The harbour master's scowl darkened. "What do you want?"

"Ain't what I want." Kurkas set his back to the blockade. "What do *they* want?"

"Does it matter?"

His opinion of the harbour master, already low, plummeted sharply. "You've not asked?"

"No I haven't, because it doesn't matter." The harbour master raised his voice, no longer talking to Kurkas, but through him. "I've supply barges to provision. They're contracted for the work. They'll come to heel, or I'll send back to the palace for the Drazina. There's a war on!"

Civilians. Not even a day since Lord Droshna's declaration, and already they were puffing out chests and strutting around like dunghill cocks. "You want another one right here, right now? Because that's what—"

"And is war reason to rip food from our children's mouths? To fill Thrakkian bellies while kin go hungry? That's not my Tressia!"

The interruption was bellowed from behind Kurkas, the crisp, authoritative voice maddeningly familiar until he turned from the harbour master's paling features to see for himself.

"Impossible . . ." he muttered.

Lord Hadon Akadra stood at the blockade's forefront, looking about as out of place in such company as it was possible to be. It wasn't just the powdered face and immaculate clothes amid the garb and grime of earthier classes – nor even that Kurkas, like much of Tressia, had long given him up for dead – but that he was slumming it on the dockside at all. Lord Akadra had never been one for the common touch. A flogger during his time in the army and as heartless a judge as any found warming a bench in the city's courts. Not exactly the clay from which men of the people were fashioned.

More than that, Hadon Akadra didn't look a day older than when Kurkas had last seen him, near eight years back. Apparently, vanishing from the face of the world agreed with him. Didn't seem fair, considering.

The harbour master swallowed, amazement yielding to obsequious-ness. "Lord Akadra . . . I've orders direct from your son."

Lord Akadra strode closer, rubbing absently at his neck. "And when did Viktor ever know what was best for this Republic? He never listened to good sense . . . never listened." His eyes snapped to Kurkas, his voice regaining its crispness. "I know you, don't I?"

"Vladama Kurkas, sah!" Habit brought Kurkas to the salute. He stared past Akadra's shoulder without meeting his eyes. "Had the good fortune to serve in your hearthguard, sah!"

"And now you wear Katya Trelan's phoenix?" His voice took on a sour, gravelly growl. "No loyalty any more."

Kurkas passed up the obvious retort that Katya Trelan had been ashes long before he'd exchanged the Akadra swan for the Trelan phoenix. Long years in Akadra's service had taught him to pick corrections with utmost care. But still . . .

"Begging your pardon, sah, but we thought you were dead. Old Brass? Drove him to the bottle for sorrow, you did." Never mind that Sergeant Brass had drunk himself stupid out of celebration at being free of Akadra's exacting commands, and second out of shame for having mislaid his master. Pride made little account for fondness, or lack thereof. "Does the Lord Protector know the good news? Be glad to see you, he will."

"I doubt that." Akadra tugged at his collar. "After all, Viktor sent me away. But I'm back, and I will see things put right."

Exile? No wonder the Lord Protector had always been cagey about his father's fate. He'd let the old goat off light for being in deep with Ebigail Kiradin. Others had ended on the gallows.

Kurkas opened his mouth to reply, but Akadra's attention had slipped elsewhere – not to the harbour master, but the crowd swelling behind the increasingly dwarfed knot of watchmen.

"We look to our own!" he roared. "Not one sack of grain nor scrap of meat for my son's war! Not while there are empty bellies! I give you my word as the last of the Council: I'll stand with you if you'll stand with me! We feed our own!"

"*Feed our own! Feed our own!*"

New voices took up the chant. The blockade thickened as men and women slipped past the knot of watchmen to join their fellows at the gate. The harbour master bellowed orders that no one heeded above the din.

Kurkas sighed, plans for the day washed away alongside the harbour master's tenuous authority. It hadn't been Stonecrest business, but it was now, sure as cider was apples. As he forged his way back to saner streets, a young woman on the blockade's fringe caught his eye. Not so much for a black dress more suited to low lights, sweet drinks and private company, but for the fact that she alone wasn't chanting, and that she alone was smiling.

Izack shook his head, a man beset by that contrary combination of surprise and the inevitable foreseen. "The city's gone bloody mad."

Even by its own austere standards, the old council chamber was steeped in gloom. To Josiri's eye, little of it was the fault of the room itself, but the news that the occupants had brought with them. Mandalov's ridiculous painting, now bearing the plaque *Lord Droshna's Triumph*, offered sardonic counterpoint to recent events.

At least Captain Tzila was elsewhere. After events a day prior, the further she was from him the better Josiri liked it. Not that the Drazina were wholly unrepresented. Grandmaster Sarisov was a calm, composed presence opposite Josiri, his uniform and greying moustache immaculate and his swarthy features furrowed in thought.

Josiri flicked through the reports and his own careful notes, the handwriting crisper for Shalamoh's gift of eyeglasses. Stoppages and protests had overtaken the city's western half, halting shipping and slowing manufacturing to a crawl. Perhaps two or three government granaries had been spared the revolt – slim comfort, as there was no operable wharf to load the supply barges.

"It's not madness," he said. "Folk are worried."

"They *should* worry," snapped Sevaka. "About the Hadari."

Her features, normally so ready with a smile, bore a decade's worth of lines they hadn't just a day before. Of the morning's tidings, hers were the worst. Three border villages razed. Rosa missing. No wonder she was wound tight. For all that Sevaka was present in body, her soul had ridden east.

Archimandrite Jezek stirred in his chair. "The Hadari are leagues away. Our citizens are afraid privation is just around the corner. This could have been handled better."

Viktor scowled. "You take issue with this city's governance, my lord archimandrite?"

Jezek flinched. Viktor's relationship with the Lumestran church was a complicated and unfriendly one. What latitude Elzar possessed he'd earned through a bond closer than blood. Jezek was out of his depth, and knew it.

"The past doesn't matter." Ironic to hear those words uttered by Arlanne Keldrov, upon whom the past was such a weighty burden. She'd been a league beyond the city gates, riding for the Southshires, when the herald had found her. "What matters is our response."

"I've emptied the watch houses," said Josiri. "I've thrown a cordon around Silverway Dock and had the bridges closed to cut the flow of bodies to the protest. I've smaller watches set at the Bretherhithe and Fullwell wharves."

It wouldn't stop the determined. Too many alleys, sewers and rooftops to cover, and not nearly enough constables to do the job.

"How many layabouts are we talking?" asked Izack.

"Too many," Josiri replied. "If trouble starts, this will go badly."

At last count, the city constabulary had two thousands on its roster. Fewer, since so many of the younger and abler recruits had accepted commission in the Drazina. The crowds at Silverway Dock alone outnumbered those who remained.

"There *will* be trouble," said Keldrov. "Begging your pardon, Lord Trelan, but I saw it often enough in the south back in the day. Doesn't matter how peaceful it starts, there's always a hothead itching to strike the tinderbox."

"Even if there isn't, we'll have trouble elsewhere," said Izack. "I'd Konor Zarn twisting my ear not an hour past dawn, badgering about surety for his merchantmen. They're trapped in the estuary now the layabouts have raised the harbour chains."

Keldrov rolled her eyes. "How drunk was he?"

"Almost sober," Izack replied, deadpan. "If that doesn't speak to magnitude, I don't know what will. Filled with rare clarity, he was, and with the backing of the trader's forum."

"Then we go in hard and fast," said Sarisov. "My Drazina can handle it ... if the constabulary aren't apt to the task."

Josiri let frost creep into his tone. "I'm well aware how your knights 'handle' things."

"Then use the army instead?" suggested Jezek, apparently unaware of Sarisov's poisonous glare.

"The only regiments I'd rely on for this work have marched east," said Izack. "We've only the 20th within the walls. Not sure I trust 'em to know whose side they're on if this gets nasty."

Josiri gritted his teeth. "The aim is to end this with minimal bloodletting. The people have concerns. They're not misplaced. We should at least *talk* to them."

"And offer what?" said Izack. "Look, Josiri, I've every sympathy, but there's a reason we cut the ration. Armies march on their stomachs. Full bellies in the city won't do any good if the Marcher Lands are burning and the shadowthorns are at the walls."

"There must be *some* compromise."

Sarisov snorted. "Any compromise invites further disobedience."

Josiri bit his tongue. There was no arguing with a man like Sarisov. To the Grandmaster, he'd always be an upstart southwealder, raised above his station, and too lax with lawbreakers.

"Are we not going to discuss the other matter?" asked Izack. "Their ringleader?"

"We *did* discuss it," rumbled Viktor. "Whoever that man is, he's not my father. My father died years ago, at the Crowmarket's hands. He belongs to the Raven."

Josiri had heard the rumour of a vranakin bounty years ago. He'd believed it at the time, but now ... ? "Kurkas believes otherwise."

Rising, Viktor brought a fist down on the table. The air in the council chamber grew colder, the shadows longer. "Kurkas is mistaken!" The scowl melted, and he reclaimed his seat. "Vladama is a good man, and a better friend, but he's not infallible. Sevaka. Izack. You *knew* my father. And you, Josiri, saw enough to recognise his nature. Did he ever strike you as a man to concern himself with the appetites of the lowborn?"

Sevaka shook her head.

"Not unless it made them pliant," said Izack. "Always did have an eye for the ladies. Especially the grateful ones."

Josiri scowled. Hadon Akadra could never have passed for an altruist. A firm believer in inherited worth, and a natural order that favoured those already fortunate. But leveraging those concerns in others for his own gain would have been entirely characterful. "If it suited his goals, I imagine he was capable of anything."

Viktor's brow darkened, but his temper held. "Someone is manipulating my father's name to legitimise treason."

Treason. Cold pricked the back of Josiri's neck at the sudden escalation. Family history alone warned how swiftly and enthusiastically that stain spread.

"What if it's the Hadari?" said Sevaka darkly. "The icularis are just as active under the Empress as her father. They're capable of anything."

Josiri hesitated, certain Melanna's desire for peace was as genuine as his own. This was beyond her, whatever was happening on the border. But his instincts had been wrong before. "If the Hadari are responsible, tearing ourselves apart serves their goals. Viktor—"

Viktor cut him off, voice flat and hard. "Grandmaster Sarisov. I want the Drazina mobilised by noon. You're to break the blockade at Silverway Dock. If you can do so peacefully, so much the better, but I want this ended."

"At your command, my lord."

Josiri sprang to his feet. "Viktor, don't do this. We'll find another way."

Viktor's gaze met his, eyes full of the cold, stark pragmatism Josiri had come to both envy and revile. "Tell me, brother, do you never tire of being the sole dissenting voice?" He smiled without humour. "Were you alone on an island you'd bicker yourself into the Raven's grasp. This is necessary, or it will cost us all."

Josiri glanced about, seeking a shred of support. He found none. Sevaka wouldn't even meet his gaze. Only Jezek shifted with discomfort. Josiri found himself missing Elzar more than ever. He'd have known what to say. Viktor would have listened.

Or maybe he wouldn't. Maybe Viktor was right, and he lacked perspective. That was the problem about arguing with Viktor. The weight of his certainty crumbled mountains to dust.

"If we're doing this," Izack put in. "We can't do it slipshod. We'll want all the bodies we can get. There are still a handful of Fellnore and Lancras within the walls. Can't hurt to drag a few proper knights into this. Even if it means waiting until dusk to drop the hammer. I'd join you myself, but Lady Orova and I are riding back east. We've Thrakkians due in Tarvallion tomorrow, and someone has to keep that boozy lot from starting the wrong bloody war."

He spoke guilelessly, but then he always did . . . even when up to mischief. And there *was* mischief behind the suggestion, or so Josiri hoped. If Viktor agreed, it bought a few hours in which to defuse the affair.

"I'll second them to the constabulary, if they're agreeable," he said. "We're more flexible in our approach than the Drazina. And we *will* be there."

"Of course," Sarisov replied smoothly. "I expected nothing less."

Viktor nodded, his brow unknotting. "Then it's agreed. We'll speak afterwards."

One by one, the others rose and filed out, leaving Josiri and Viktor alone.

"I hope you're right," said Josiri.

Viktor twitched a shrug. "You always do. Sometimes only strength will serve."

As he too departed, Josiri realised how pale and drawn Viktor's features had grown, the mask of certainty worn for wider consultation abandoned in privacy. It went a long way to easing his concerns about what was to come. If only Viktor hadn't invoked strength – the virtue Ebigail Kiradin had prized beyond all others, and the justification for so much harm wrought in years past.

Thirty-One

With an aggrieved groan, the board came free. The crack of daylight widened. Startled, Calenne stumbled under the weight, one end almost slipping free of her grasp. A brief flurry of hands, and she was its mistress once more.

Straining for a sign her struggle had drawn notice beyond the locked door, she paced out the moments to a heartbeat she no longer felt. After a ten-count, she set the notched timber against the wall and peered at the window, which she now saw was boarded both outside and in. Where the inner timbers sat snug, the outer were slovenly fixed – affording entry to glorious daylight.

With a last wary glance at the door, Calenne pressed against the inner boards and gazed out.

Had she breath to lose, the vista would have stolen it. Her whole existence – *life* no longer felt accurate – she'd known only Eskavord. As a child, that town had seemed impossibly vast, untold wonders concealed in crooked streets and alleyways. Far below the jagged glass of the shattered window stretched a townhouse-fronted square capable of swallowing a quarter of Eskavord whole. Beyond, the skyline crowded with slate and tile, arrow-straight roads, skeletal winter trees and snow-covered gardens.

Standing on tiptoes, she peered down at dark shapes heading to and fro atop the square's melting slush. Insects scurried underfoot, unaware they were observed.

Brilliant orange tongues clawed and raged at the heavens where blocky roofs surrendered to a harbour's waters. Calenne gazed, transfixed, and wondered how it was that she could smell the smoke, the soot. How she felt the backwash of the flame prickle her skin.

Felt?

Suddenly, she was in the darkness of Eskavord. Unable to move – unable even to think – as fires blazed all around. The echo of pain that was hers, and yet was not. And all the while, the pressure of Malatriant's will. Smothering. Suffocating. Screaming as her thralls blinked out, consumed.

Overcome by nausea, Calenne stumbled from the window, hiding the flames from sight. Clay fingers *glinked* against unfeeling lips. She struggled for breath to subdue rising panic, forgetting she no longer had lungs nor diaphragm to command. Eskavord had been home. Tressia was as alien as her body. Alien, and impossibly, unknowably vast. Even if she escaped the clocktower, the streets would swallow her up.

Everything she'd known – everything she'd been – was gone. All save Viktor. Perhaps it was better that she remain contented with candlelight and his fleeting company. Whatever her misgivings, he *did* love her. He remained her one certainty.

And yet, Calenne found her gaze drawn back to the unfamiliar world and wondered what it would be like to walk beneath sunlight. To hear the small sounds of life swirling about her, even though she stood forever apart.

That freedom could be hers. What she'd seen of the clocktower's outer face was rife with gaping mortar and rain-worn sculpture – handholds enough for clear-headed descent. Especially if one possessed a body free of ephemeral fatigue.

Footsteps beyond the door dashed her reverie to pieces. She hoisted the window-board back into position. Iron nails snagged, then glided home. By the time the key clicked, Calenne had deposited herself on the sofa, a book spread across her knees.

Tzila said nothing, just as she'd remained silent during each of her brief visits across the morning – interruptions that had slowed and discouraged Calenne's small attempts at freedom.

There was something oddly familiar about the other woman – a voiceless contempt conveyed by cast of shoulders and angle of head. More than that, there was a wisp of . . . something. It maddened like an unscratchable itch. Kinship? Or perhaps her own frustrations projected? After all, Viktor aside, Tzila was the only living soul she saw.

Viktor arrived on Tzila's heels, expression clouded by that brooding, oh-so-familiar scowl. Tzila withdrew, pulling the door closed. But still Viktor seemed in no hurry to speak. For all that Calenne felt his gaze upon her, she'd the impression he didn't see her at all.

Swallowing guilt over disobedience committed and intended – one advantage of the clay was she feared no tick of expression revealing her thoughts – she set the book aside.

[[This room already has a surfeit of statues, Viktor. It needs no other.]]

Shoulders sagged, the scar on his cheek twisting. "My apologies. It's barely noon, and already I wish it were tomorrow."

[[The war?]]

"Someone has stirred the dockworkers to mutiny, and the rot spreads by the hour. Half the city lies at a standstill and if the supply barges remain embargoed, the Hadari will learn of our coming before we mobilise. Surprise will be lost, and the liberation of the east over before it has begun." He rubbed his face. "I knew the storm was coming. I've done everything I could to encourage it to break before the Hadari forced my hand. But the scale . . . ?"

So that was the meaning of the fires? Calenne nearly asked about them, but remembered in time what that knowledge would reveal. [[You make it sound like you wanted this.]]

"No sane man would want this. But sometimes leadership means accepting the inevitable, or even accelerating it so the timing suits your goals, and not your enemy's. I knew there were tensions. Conscription and other measures made them inevitable. I'd hoped for a brief flaring. One I could end with a minimum of harm. Now?" He shook his head. "I don't know."

Calenne suppressed a shiver. Sometimes she forgot that Viktor and the Black Knight who'd haunted her nightmares were one and the same. Not so at that moment. But even for him, this was bleak. Oh, not in the abstract. It was only when she sought meaning between the words that she glimpsed bloodshed.

[[And who is your enemy, if not the Hadari?]]

"He has gone to great lengths impersonating my father."

[[But he isn't?]]

"My father died after Davenwood."

[[There's no chance you're mistaken?]]

"I choked the life out of him myself." Viktor turned about, his expression defiant, almost begging her for challenge. "I saw the light fade from his eyes. He is with the Raven."

[[So was I.]] Calenne offered response by rote, lost in dismay. [[Your own father? Viktor—]]

"No other course would serve!" he snapped. "Whatever was good in my father died long before I slew the rest. Left loose in the city he'd have dragged it into the mire. His death freed me to search for you."

But of course, he'd never found her. She'd already been dead in all ways that mattered, swallowed up by Malatriant's resurrection.

Calenne stood, anger burning away the dismay. [[So it's my fault?]]

Viktor twisted away. "Of course not. My deeds are my own, my mistakes alongside. I do not tally my father's death among the latter. And now someone rouses my people to revolt in his name." He snorted. "My father would never have possessed the nerve. Now I've no choice. I must break them all to pieces or more will suffer."

In those words, Calenne caught a glimpse of the Viktor she remembered – the man driven to unhappy deeds through refusal to shirk duty. Had he come for counsel, or to unburden himself?

[[Have you spoken to my brother? Has he nothing to suggest?]]

Viktor's voice grew wearier. "Josiri? He has a good heart, but he doesn't grasp the situation's urgency. Sometimes I fear he's lost his fire. Maybe even that I'm responsible for the change . . ." The corner of his lip twisted, and Calenne sensed the following words would not be the ones originally intended. "He'll understand afterwards. He always does."

She seized the glimmer of opportunity. [[Then let me go to him, or have him come to me. Surely nothing bad can come of that?]]

"Not yet. I need to keep you safe a little longer."

[[Safe from Josiri?]]

"I fear so. I need time to explain, and after this morning I suspect he's too angry to listen."

She stuck out her chin. [[It's my risk to take.]]

"Can you not think of something other than your own desires?"

That same sternness had once shocked Calenne to her senses, slough-ing off the calloused selfishness of girlhood to free the woman within. But transformation cut both ways. The woman was not so easily cowed as the girl, adrift in the world though she was.

[[*My* desires? My wits had barely returned and you pressed me with your vision of a shared future. And today ...? Why did you come here, Viktor?]]

One eye narrowed. "To see you, of course."

Calenne advanced, reinforcing her words by jabbing an angry finger in his direction. [[I think you came to unburden yourself to the one person who won't – who *can't* – reveal your secrets. You don't fear what Josiri will think of me, but what'll he think of *you*.]]

He stiffened. "That isn't so."

[[Isn't it? You haven't asked how I am, or what I might want. When I state desire, you forbid it. Is this solicitude? Is this love? Or is this obsession?]]

There. She'd said it. And felt selfish even before Viktor's expression crumbled. Unable to contest the anguish in his eyes, Calenne stared at the floor, and cursed the shortness of temper that had ever led her to ruin. But at her core, she found only the glow of truth spoken.

Was the Raven watching? Was he laughing?

She took Viktor's hand. [[I'm sorry to speak this way, Viktor. I am.]] At last, she met his gaze. [[I think perhaps we are both of us more changed than the other perceives. Whatever we were – whatever we are to be – will take time to discover. It requires our patience and under-standing. If mine have fallen short, I apologise.]]

He stood immobile save for the rise and fall of his chest. The hurt smoothed from his features, leaving an expression bereft of clues to thoughts entertained behind.

"No," he said at last. "You need never apologise for speaking your mind, even when your thoughts are not gentle. What business have I claiming myself the protector of the Republic if a scolding tongue cleaves me in two?"

Melancholic humour laced the words.

[[Then stay awhile,]] said Calenne. [[We can talk.]]

He gave a rumbling sigh. "If only I could, but I have duties. My desires, at least, must remain subordinate to the Republic's. It may be that I see you little in coming days, but I will *always* return to you." He stooped to kiss her brow, the sensation as dull as all others she was permitted. "Whatever betide, I will again be your champion as I was so long ago . . . at least, should that be your wish."

The words mollified, though perhaps not as much as they should – chiefly because Calenne couldn't be certain whether it was business of governance that drew him away, or his own soured pride. He'd always had such a lot of that. They both did.

[[I'll seek no other,]] she replied softly.

Letting go her hand, he left the room.

After his footsteps faded, Calenne returned to the window and began work on the second board.

Josiri tugged the cross-belt tight, winced, and let the hasp out a fraction. The constabulary uniform fitted well enough, for all it was seldom worn. By the strict order of things, he faced no compulsion to wear it today – societal status trumped trappings of authority. But his authority would face challenges enough come dusk. Better to face them with the tabard's crown-badged epaulettes in place.

He examined himself in the dressing-room mirror. It would do. Thicker around the waist than he'd have liked – a reminder of how soft life had become. But there was no helping that.

The door shuddered beneath a knock.

"You wanted to see us, sah?" asked Kurkas, his voice muffled.

"Yes. Come in."

The door admitted Kurkas and Altiris. The former already wore his parade-ground stare, the latter a measure of wariness.

"You've heard what's to happen?" asked Josiri.

The two shared a glance.

"It's going ahead then?" said Kurkas. "Won't end well."

"That's why I'm going down there in person. I'm taking the hearth-guard with me. The more level heads about, the better."

"But not me?" asked Altiris.

"I need you to do something else. Both of you."

"Right you are," said Kurkas, deadpan. "Death or glory, is it?"

"Hopefully neither." Josiri drew down a deep breath. "We know how this goes once the Drazina are off the leash. Someone needs to find Hadon Akadra. If we can turn this into a negotiation, there's a chance."

Altiris frowned. "Didn't the Lord Protector dismiss the notion of his father being at the heart of this?"

Josiri hesitated, and threw tact to the winds. "I'm not convinced Viktor's thinking straight. I'm happy to take Vladama at his word."

"Gratified to hear it," Kurkas replied morosely. "Problem is, I don't rightly remember the elder Lord Akadra being one for negotiating. Nor the younger, for that matter."

Josiri offered a smile he didn't feel. "We work with what we've got."

"We'll make a soldier of you yet, sah."

"Please don't. I hate uniforms." He followed the wan joke with a shrug. "I'll keep things calm as long as I can."

Altiris looked scarcely happier than Josiri felt. "My place is with you, lord. Especially if you're marching into trouble."

"I've the entire constabulary at my back, and a smattering of knights besides. You're more use helping Vladama." Josiri raised an eyebrow. "I understand you're not unfriendly with some of the Sothvaners. That can't hurt. There'll be plenty at Silverway Dock."

"Not as friendly as all—" Altiris stiffened and threw a sidelong glance at Kurkas. "Who told you?"

"Sidara doesn't keep many secrets from Ana. You did more than deliver food to Midwintertide at Seacaller's, I understand."

If anything, the lad looked more miserable, not less. Probably wondering just how few of his secrets Sidara had kept in recent years.

"But more than that," Josiri went on, "it's because I trust you. Will that suffice?"

Altiris nodded, chagrin yielding to pride. "Yes, lord."

"Good," said Josiri. "No death, no glory. Just get it done."

Thirty-Two

The key turned. The door to the windowless strong room opened. Blue-green eyes glinted in the gloom. And even after everything that had come to pass it was all Hawkin Darrow could do not to fall to her knees and beg for an embrace. The heart wanted what the heart wanted, even when it was deceived.

What self-control remained, she maintained by clamping eyes shut and focusing on other senses. Damp air against her skin. The rattle of wind about the timber eaves, and the muted roar of a crowd. The brackish scent of the dockside – salt, seaweed and fouled water. Adoration came hard when mired in such scents.

"It won't work." Hawkin hoped it was true. "Slit me the ripper's grin and have done."

She clung to false defiance born in the still, empty space between the piece of her that didn't want to die, and the sliver that longed for Kasvin's embrace.

"Oh, I wouldn't kill you." Kasvin's voice held the innocence of a child at play. "I'd give you the knife. You'd open your veins with a smile. I'm told it's the sweetest release."

"Then why don't you try it? Because you love me?" Hawkin hated the hope beneath the words.

"Love?" Floorboards creaked. Kasvin's voice grew louder. "I'm a daughter of the Black River. Upon its waters, I floated one way and love another. Shalamoh told me that's why I rouse such desire. A barren heart singing for solace."

The night before ... the Drazina at Strazyn Abbey. Twitching. Lost in embrace and the whisper of song.

"You see?" said Kasvin.

Hawkin heard it now, billowing beneath the words and yet somehow always beyond grasp. She clung to the name. Not one she'd heard before. "Shalamoh? You mean the Merrow?"

Kasvin laughed. "He and I sought answers only the other could give. We traded."

"Did he have a choice?" she spat.

Kasvin drew nearer. Close enough to touch. Resolve melted. "Shalamoh loves only knowledge. I told him what I'd seen of the Black River. He revealed my purpose, inked in books laid down in the Age of Kings."

"Let me guess: a harlot able to command any price?"

Cold breath brushed Hawkin's ear.

"I am the poison in a miser's soul," Kasvin whispered. "The blade at a child-beater's throat. The tide that drowns a faithless lover. I am vengeance. I am death."

Something cold and wet slithered over Hawkin's hand. She cried out as another brushed her shoulders. A third wended about her ankle and drew tight. She recalled the sinuous weed beneath Coventaj, dancing at Kasvin's touch. Before she could stop herself, she opened her eyes.

There was no weed, only a whisper of movement that might have been its retreat into the shadows, and the smothering blue-green of Kasvin's eyes.

Except... those eyes no longer enraptured. Nor did suffocating desire rise to meet them. Only the growing confusion in the pit of Hawkin's stomach and the smirk frozen on Kasvin's face.

"I don't understand."

The smirk widened. "Follow me."

Aware she'd little choice, Hawkin accompanied Kasvin from the strong room and up sagging stairs. The warehouse itself was familiar enough – one of the many along Silverway Dock. One of Lord Zarn's. She'd cased it by slipping in among the work gangs. The loading floor was silent, the gantries and catwalks empty. A fortune in wares crated and ready to go, unguarded.

Another door waited at the top of the stairs. The only light in the office beyond came from brooding, purpled skies filtered through leaded windows and flecked orange from a burning warehouse. Hawkin glimpsed cargo barges and pontoons tied up at loading piers, forming a network of bridges. Or rather one long, T-shaped bridge connecting the ends of the lopsided horseshoe-shaped harbour with the nadir of its curve. Dockworkers ran south across the bridge, weapons in hand, to join others spilling into the harbourside streets. Others milled about bonfires, waiting for the call to battle.

Shadows shifted by the manager's desk. Hawkin stumbled back. "Lord Akadra? I didn't see you there."

"No ... backbone," he slurred, the words dredged from somewhere distant. "Just ... like a ... vranakin."

He hunched over the desk and stared myopically at her. Powdery makeup on his cheeks had cracked and flaked, revealing fibrous tendrils shifting beneath his skin. For all the contempt in his words, Hawkin heard confusion in his voice ... pleading. And the smell. The stench of silted waters was stronger than ever.

"Don't disturb his lordship." Kasvin closed the door. "He's barely holding together, and I might need another speech out of him yet. Something fiery, but dignified. A repudiation of old sins, perhaps. Men so often seek redemption as death draws near, so all will believe it."

Hawkin backed away from both. "What have you done to him?"

Kasvin shrugged. "He was given to the Black River long ago. It gave him back."

"So he's like you?"

"Does he look it? The Black River has no sons, only daughters. What little of him remains belongs to me, doesn't it, Lord Akadra?"

Looking for all the world like a man on the brink of tears, he gave a shuddering nod.

"Do you feel sorry for him?" asked Kasvin. "You shouldn't."

"I don't feel sorry for anyone," Hawkin replied. And yet there was something pitiable about the broken old man. "Why do you need him?"

"Because his son is destroying the people of this city." Kasvin's voice, normally so carefree, turned hard as stone. "He's killing us, bleeding away hope and purpose and all the while insisting he serves our interest. You know how many die before their time in Sothvane and Narrowfen? Six years, Viktor Droshna has ruled like a king, promising deliverance from war and sorrow, and all the while he takes our children and our lives and leaves nothing but scraps!"

Chest heaving, she steadied herself against the desk.

"I act for the dead," she said softly. "For children who die starving. For those brutalised for the crime of misplacing their papers, or lingering after the wrong tick of the clock. For the mothers who mourn their daughters, and widowed lovers whose future lies entombed. I hear them all, Hawkin. They cry out for retribution, and I must obey."

Hawkin went still, wary of offering provocation. "Why?"

"Because someone should have done it for me after Konor strangled me!" For a moment, Kasvin looked years older, coiled up with rage and heartbreak. But only a moment. "That's why the Nameless Lady sent me back."

"Konor Zarn?" The connection was inevitable, given the building in which they stood – to say nothing of how Kasvin's wreckers targeted his ships. Hawkin couldn't imagine the sot having either wit or courage for the deed, but she supposed liquor would have supplied both. "Some vengeful spirit you are. He's still alive."

Kasvin's smile turned chill. "For now. My reward for settling Droshna."

"Is that you, Alika?" Lord Akadra swayed side-to-side as he murmured. "I'm so very cold."

"Then do so." Hawkin wondered why she cared. "Sing with your barren heart, and wrap Droshna around your finger as you did me."

Kasvin shook her head. "You presume a heart to ensnare. He's a scion of the Dark, and the Dark seeks only to be whole. It knows nothing of love. It already is all that it seeks to be. And even if I could, it wouldn't be enough." She flung a hand to the window, encompassing the dockside. "They have to win freedom. They have to *want* it. Bestowed as a gift, they'll only cast it aside. A piece of us longs to be dominated, to be spared the burden of choice. To be one, as all were once one in the Dark. So we embrace tyrant after tyrant and scream injustice when their nature stands revealed."

Hawkin grasped little of Kasvin's meaning. But she understood being used, especially of late. "As you did?"

Kasvin glared. "You can go now."

Lord Akadra stared up from the desk, and regarded Hawkin with broken grin.

She shivered. "As easy as that? With the tale I could tell?"

Kasvin shrugged. "And who'd believe you? Your past is full of broken trust."

That truth stung more than it should. "Then why tell me at all?"

"Because one voice in Otherworld's mists screams louder than any. Love betrayed. Poison pressed to her lips ... salt tears on her forehead." Kasvin snorted. "Your sobs woke her. What would have been a gentle death in sleep became agony in the waking."

Hawkin swallowed to moisten a dry mouth. Vona. She forced a glare. Better to brazen it out and defy the aching, solid lump her heart had become. "I'd no choice."

"Do you suppose that matters?"

She clenched her teeth to still a trembling jaw. "So I'm to make amends?" The hoped-for sardonic tone fell short. "Join your cause, maybe? Redeem myself?"

"There is no redemption. The Black River will take you, sooner or later. By my hand, or by someone else's. Ask yourself how you want to live before that happens."

Hawkin swallowed again. Raven's Eyes, but she was shaking. With sorrow. With guilt. With fear. She couldn't tell where one ended and another began. "As if you care."

"No," Kasvin replied. "But I almost did, once. Before I heard Vona cry out for justice, I actually thought you and I might be friends. This warning is a gift to the woman I thought you were."

"Well this *is* romantic."

Even shouted, Anastacia's words barely pierced the now-familiar chant of "*Feed our own!*" bellowed from behind the Harrowmoon Street barricade.

Unfortunately, the same effort that carried the words to Josiri also laid them plain before his hearthguard, and no few constables and knights in his cordon. Ignoring Sergeant Brass's lugubrious smile, he decided humour was the better part of valour.

"Yes, dear." He offered an empty smile. "You didn't have to come."

He'd argued against it, for Anastacia was still pale from misadventure the day before. For all that the healing touch of Sidara's magic had kept her walking around, her blood remained at low ebb. But like most arguments, he'd lost, and the Stonecrest hearthguard had gained another member – albeit a temporary one who'd wrung every last drop of glamour from one of Jaridav's spare uniforms. The golden Trelan phoenix had twice the glory with her perfect scowl above the tabard.

More than that, the double-faced constabulary line felt woefully fragile, even with fifty knights of chapterhouses Lancras and Fellnore stiffening the ranks with broadsword and shield. To the north, the dockworkers visible atop the tangled, rope-lashed mass of furniture, wagons and shipping crates. To the south, a triple line of black-uniformed Drazina with shields, swords and crossbows ready – infantry to break the barricade and cavalry to run rampant behind – blocked the confluence of Harrowmoon Street and Altranner Row.

A storm about to break. That it hadn't already, Josiri credited to the fact that while the Drazina would have gladly begun breaking dockworkers' heads, their enthusiasm stopped short of trampling the constabulary cordon in between.

Which was precisely why Josiri had placed it there – far enough from the barricade that the intermittent barrage of half-bricks and bottles fell well short, but close enough to signal intent. Every minute of delay was one in which Altiris and Kurkas could find Hadon Akadra.

It wasn't as though he'd the numbers to keep the peace by force. Two hundred constables, fifty knights and fewer than a dozen hearthguard, sandwiched between thousands.

Were Lieutenant Raldan's reports to be believed, the picture was the same all along Silverway Dock. Six wagoner's roads, three narrow residential streets and innumerable alleyways. All of them blocked. But Harrowmoon Street was the heart. The broad, arrow-straight road led south from the Silverway River, swung a sharp easterly turn through the city's marketplaces and storehouse districts, and ultimately passed through King's Gate. Tressia's chief artery, and for that reason had drawn greater numbers of protesters and Drazina than elsewhere.

"A crossbow's not a knight's weapon." Viara Boronav's cheeks were almost as bereft of colour as Anastacia's. A daughter of a highblood line did *not* expect to find herself in this position. But she'd joined the

cordon readily enough. "Those Drazina are just jumped-up commoners ... No offence."

The last was offered with a chagrined scowl, belated recognition that
both Stonecrest hearthguard and constabulary held more commoners
than highbloods.

Brass spat on the cobbles. "Don't matter, long as they get the job
done." He spoke with the gruff resentment of a man whose own failed
transgressions lay long behind. "Not right, is it? Bloody dockers. Always
think others have it better. We're at war."

His words found agreement nearby. Josiri exchanged a glance with
Anastacia and stifled a sigh. So easy to see your neighbours as something
other. A lesson learned hard in the Southshires.

"We're at war with the *Hadari*," he snapped. "If this turns to bloodshed, we've all failed."

Brass stared at a horseman spurring from the Drazina lines. "That's
the case, I reckon we're getting our fill of failure pretty damn soon."

A pace or two distant, the rider hauled on his reins. Open helm
offered clear view of Grandmaster Sarisov's swarthy, moustachioed face.

"Lord Trelan." Annoyance crackled beneath the greeting.
"Commander Hollov tells me you refuse to withdraw."

"I don't take orders from commanders," Josiri replied evenly. "Nor
grandmasters."

"Need I remind you the Lord Protector wanted this matter settled by dusk?"

As if this could ever end in mere hours. "Dusk isn't yet gone, and rash
actions help no one."

Sarisov scowled. Much as Josiri had refrained from open agreement,
Viara's assessment of the Drazina had struck a chord. Good at taking
Viktor's orders, not so much at understanding the reason behind. Not
like Essamere. In that regard, Sarisov – a younger son of a middling
family – was no better than the men and women he commanded. A
blunt instrument of simple desires. Back when Viktor had first founded
the Drazina, Josiri had seen sense in that. Tressia had been on its knees,
and loyalty was important. And Viktor's insistence that Josiri take
command of the constabulary had offered reassurance that rule of law
would continue.

Yet in the years since, the constabulary had shrunk, while the Drazina had multiplied to meet the demands of garrison and checkpoint. Somehow, Josiri had never quite seen that before.

"I insist you withdraw," growled Sarisov.

Was that a threat? Josiri, his own belligerence rising to meet the other's, couldn't be certain. Not that it mattered. Trelans were stubborn, and Josiri had seen worse than Sarisov.

He drew himself up. "The constabulary keeps order in this city, no matter how much your Drazina have usurped that duty. We wait."

Sarisov's scowl deepened. The grandmaster could invoke Viktor's name all he wanted, but he'd never quite grasp the bond shared between Lord Protector and southwealder upstart. Josiri knew better. Viktor would be furious ... but Viktor had been furious before.

"Raven's Eyes ..." breathed Viara.

Josiri tore his eyes from Sarisov and followed her gaze to the barricade.

The protesters' chant faded to a guttural cheer as two limp, bloodied Drazina were dragged to the summit and hoisted as trophies. Alive or dead, it was impossible to tell. A sergeant's dagged chevrons hung from a torn tabard.

Josiri's grasp on events, so certain a moment before, spiralled away. The cordon had failed. Had a constable elsewhere yielded to Drazina authority? Had the luckless sergeant found a route through alleyways or buildings otherwise missed? Irrelevant now. Because if there were two, there'd be more. And because ...

"Faithless swine!" With a snarl, Sarisov wheeled his horse southwards towards the massing Drazina. "Get your rabble out of my way, or I'll ride them down!"

He rode off in a clatter of hooves, outstretched hand raised in angry beckon. A triumphant cheer rose from the barricade at his back.

"That went well," said Anastacia, her expression blank as she stared towards a barricade thickening with swords, cudgels and axes. "What do we do?"

Frustration sour at the back of his throat, Josiri raised his voice. "We get out of his way, and we go in behind." Stepping clear of the line, he let his gaze travel, meeting the eyes of constable, hearthguard and knight.

"We get the wounded out, and get them help. No fear or favour, and no questions. Am I clear on this?"

A chorus of voices roused to agreement. Knights and constables offered clasped fists in salute. Brass gave a reluctant nod; Viara an altogether more determined one. What was it about this damn city anyway? The best and the worst of human nature, all jumbled up so no sane man might tell them apart.

The first buccinas sounded and the infantry came forward.

Thirty-Three

Altiris crept to the alleyway mouth and peered across to the Tribute Street barricade, thick with attentive men and women. A glance back along the street revealed a thin constabulary picket. So far to the west – practically on the coast – no one expected trouble. "I know some of those faces."

Kurkas grunted. "Don't mean they remember yours. Midwintertide's a lifetime ago."

Altiris shook his head. Everything Kurkas had said was true, and backed by peril besides. Kasvin knew who he was, and from the steward's account she was at the heart of the disturbance. "You're a cheery soul."

"You ain't the first to say." Kurkas eased his sword an inch back and forth in its scabbard. Weapons aside, both were in civilian garb once more. "You sure your head's right in all this?"

Altiris had asked himself the same several times since leaving Stonecrest. "Worried you can't trust me?"

"I ain't judging. Not so long back, I cosied up with a notorious Southshires wolf's-head. Turns out Halvor and me had more in common than I did with the Council. There's more than one kind of loyalty."

"Sometimes they're the same," Altiris said firmly. "Lord Trelan wants this stopped peaceably. Those in the docks need this stopped peaceably. We're all on the same side."

"Yeah?" Kurkas scratched beneath his eyepatch. "Let's hope it stays that way."

The wind gusted, driving screams and hoofbeats from the eastern streets and making mock of Altiris' assertion. He took a breath. "Let's get it done."

"Moment." Kurkas eased his sword from its scabbard and peered back down the shadowed alleyway. "I hear you creeping about! Might as well come out. Be sociable."

The alleyway offered up no answer, but felt too still, too silent. As if holding its breath. Altiris drew his sword. "You heard the man."

A dozen paces back, where crates mouldered beneath a leaking gutter, the shadows shifted. Not dispelled by light, but withdrawing of their own accord. Hand tucked to his stomach, Constans offered a florid bow.

"Hold thy steel, the Jackdaw cried. A harmless knave am I."

Kurkas' blade drooped. "Touched in the head, more like, providing your own narration."

Altiris sighed. "It's from a play within a play. *The Court of Four Winds*, by—"

Kurkas narrowed his eye. "And the trick with the shadows?"

"What trick?" Constans straightened from his bow. "Your tired old eye's seeing things, Vladama. Perhaps Josiri might lend you those eyeglasses he's acquired. I'm told they work wonders."

"Uh-uh." Kurkas nodded meaningfully at his tabard. "Shouldn't you be with the Drazina?"

"Shouldn't you be with the constabulary?" Constans grinned. "Storming barricades isn't really my thing. It's so ... crude. And then I saw you creeping around. I thought you'd like some help. Unless you're planning on joining the protesters."

He spoke the latter with a smile, *almost* smoothing away the insult.

"We're to find Lord Akadra," said Altiris. "Bring him to negotiations."

Constans pursed his lips. "Does Father know?"

Altiris hesitated. A lie would have been easy enough, except the slender trust that had grown between them in recent days was about the only leverage he possessed. "Only if it works."

"Sounds fun," said Constans. "I think I'll help."

Kurkas growled. "This isn't a game, lad."

"I know that."

To Altiris' surprise, the reply held no levity. Constans was changing. And an extra body wouldn't hurt. "Lose the tabard."

Constans grinned and offered a salute. "Yes, lieutenant."

Kurkas cleared his throat. "A word, sah?"

Taken aback by Kurkas' deference, Altiris allowed himself to be led deeper into the alley.

"You sure about this?" murmured Kurkas.

Not a challenge, but carefully voiced concern. Altiris had assumed Kurkas held command of their foray. It seemed Kurkas saw it differently.

Pride and concern quarrelled for prominence. Altiris swallowed both. "There's no guarantee he'd let us send him away. Better to have him where we can see him."

"I could thump him?" Kurkas murmured. "He'd stay put then. Wouldn't be a bother. Been a long time coming."

"It'll be all right, Vladama." Altiris laid his hand on the other's shoulder. "Trust me."

"Right you are, sah."

There it was again: respect offered up only to a few. Now all he had to do was live up to it.

Altiris turned back to Constans. Without the tabard to disguise his rake-thin figure and grubby shirt, the boy looked a dyspeptic match for the poet he so often claimed to be. "No killing."

Accepting the crisp nod at face value, Altiris straightened his sword belt, and strode towards the barricade, hands raised.

A stone cracked off the cobbles. A heavyset, red-haired woman shouted from the summit. "What d'you want?"

Altiris inched his hands higher. "To help!" He stifled a wince. It was true, wasn't it? Help took many forms. "Name's Devn. I was at Seacaller's for the dying of the year. Radzar will vouch for me."

The first sweat prickled Altiris' shoulder blades. Were there bows behind the barricade? He'd be an easy target if so. Kurkas and Constans slowing to a halt on either side did little to set his mind at risk. Their deaths would be on him. No wonder Kurkas had ceded authority.

"Radzar's gone to Harrowmoon Gate," shouted the woman. "You're out of luck."

Harrowmoon Gate. Right in the thick of things. No getting in that way.

"Now listen," said Altiris. "We—"

"I recognise him." An older man reached the barricade's crest. "Saw him talking to the Merrow's woman a few nights back. Let them through."

"You heard!" Altiris ignored a sidelong look from Kurkas and glanced back towards the constabulary cordon. "Come on! Before that dozy lot get interested."

The woman scowled. "Let 'em through!"

Altiris jogged to the barricade and began to climb. A hand found his, the southwealder's rose tattoo faded and scarred, and hauled him onto the uneven rampart of crate and roofbeam.

"Glad to have you," said the older man, a hint of Selanni burr roughing the edges of the words. "We can use you, if you're up for a fight."

"Wouldn't 'ave come all this way, else." Constans clambered to join them, aristocratic speech abandoned for the rougher manner he'd mantled at Seacaller's Church. For all his claim of not treating it like a game, he was enjoying the pretence. He reached down to aid Kurkas' ascent. "Wouldna miss this for the world."

A second, taller barricade blocked the street where warehouses yielded to dockside, fronted by ladders and its outer face bristling with wooden stakes, rusty blades and glass shards. Altiris suppressed a shudder. Once the ladders were removed, and climbing done by hand ...? At least fifty protesters were in sight upon the summit. Upraised voices spoke to many more mustered behind.

"That's fit to ruin someone's day," said Kurkas.

"If it comes to it." For all reserve in the protester's voice, pride shone through. "We'll not let the Merrow down."

"You mean Lord Akadra?" said Constans.

"Doesn't matter what he calls himself, long as he's speaking for us." The fellow jerked his thumb towards a quintet of dockers. "We've got this sewn up here. If you're serious about helping Radzar, Torin's heading to Harrowmoon Gate. Tag along with him."

Altiris nodded. It seemed unlikely Hadon Akadra would be anywhere near the fighting at Harrowmoon Gate, but hanging around Tribute Street wasn't achieving anything.

"We'll do that, thanks."

Blood oozed up over Josiri's fingers as he tied the makeshift bandage tight. The Drazina bucked and moaned on the cobbles, limbs thrashing. The wheeze and whistle of fading breath spoke ill of the lung.

"Easy, son." Josiri smoothed a hand across the fellow's brow. The sweat-sheened skin was cold to the touch. "Stretcher! I need a stretcher!"

He tore his eyes from the ailing Drazina and gazed into disaster.

The first of the Harrowmoon Street barricades had fallen easily enough, but there'd been another behind. Sarisov's Drazina, expecting open streets and a horseman's killing field, had ground to a halt against wooden stakes. Easy prey for the barrage of arrows, quarrels, rocks and refuse from the warehouse windows. The approach, already thick with bodies from the first assault, had filled with dead and dying Drazina.

Still the buccinas sounded, and black uniforms hurled themselves at the barricade with the growl of men and women lost to battle.

In the street behind, constables and hearthguards advanced beneath the interlocked shields of Lancras and Fellnore, dragging wounded to the hope of safety and the illusion of help. One of the impromptu drakonbacks shuddered, broken glass and flaming rags scattering wide beneath the sharp crackle of alchemist's powder. A knight's surcoat blazed as the fire caught hold.

"We'll take him, lord."

Kelver stumbled to a halt at Josiri's side, a constable close behind with a stretcher fashioned from a Drazina's cloak. What few physicians Sarisov had brought to Harrowmoon Street were stretched thin. Had runners not summoned serenes from nearby convents and hospices, they'd have been overwhelmed long before. Anastacia's idea.

Josiri wiped a clammy hand across his face, and grimaced at the realisation he'd smeared himself with blood. "Get him to the Saint Tremere Convent."

Kelver glanced up from manoeuvring the Drazina onto the stretcher. He looked every bit as exhausted as Josiri felt. "The Revered Sister says they've no more room."

"Take him anyway. Tell her I appreciate her efforts."

Kelver nodded, and the stretcher party withdrew. One down. Hundreds to go.

Buccinas sounded. Wounded and saviours scrambled clear as another column of Drazina charged the barricade. The rattle of crossbows vied with the hum of arrows. Fresh screams rang out.

"Sir! Lord Trelan!" A sergeant of constabulary hurried north from the splintered ruins of the first barricade.

Josiri knew the face, but his name? It vanished into the seething darkness that had claimed so many recent events. He gritted his teeth against the frustration. His failing memory was the least of current concerns. "What is it?"

"Trouble. The physicians' shelter."

Josiri urged weary bones to motion.

A final unsteady step, and Altiris left the pontoon bridge for the pier's solidity. For all that the ramshackle bridge offered a shortcut across the crowded harbour, its sections bucked alarmingly with every lurch of the choppy, white-flecked tide. He'd kept meaning to take swimmer's lessons, but somehow it hadn't happened.

Constans grinning at him with every almost-misplaced stride hadn't helped.

At least the pier offered the illusion of solid ground, even with its tied-up merchantmen bobbing sedately with the outgoing tide.

"Now where?" he asked.

Torin pointed dead ahead, past the pier's tarped crates and the three-storey redbrick warehouse dominating the immediate harbourside, to the towering harbour gate. "Where d'you think?"

Half the dockside was on the move, bonfires and blankets abandoned as they swarmed to the gate. And from the platform beside the warehouse's loading gantry, an old, grey man shook an angry fist towards the streets, his dry voice coming and going with the rise and fall of the wind.

"Hold the line!" he roared. "Let them taste your mettle! Your determination! Let them feel the fury of the streets! Tressia can never ..."

The wind bore the words away, but Altiris had heard enough – the man's identity confirmed first by Kurkas' slow nod, and second by the young woman at the demagogue's side. Even distant in the grey dusk, there was no mistaking Kasvin for anyone else.

Constans drifted towards the pier's edge, falling – by seeming chance – into perfect step behind one of the dockers. Kurkas peeled off left, his pace lengthening to cover the ground between him and two others.

"Well then. I guess that's it," said Altiris, and buried his fist in Torin's belly.

Torin doubled over and staggered against a crate, but his left forearm somehow blocked the punch that should have driven him to the pier. His other filled the dusk with hot, red stars and a copper tang.

Reeling, Altiris lowered his shoulder and drove Torin into the crate. Once. Twice. Three times. After the third, the docker dropped gasping to his knees. A kick to the temple drove his wits away.

As the stars faded and his vision cleared, Altiris found Kurkas and Constans staring at him, each having struck two opponents cold in the time it had taken him to almost lose to one.

Or maybe not. Constans' right hand was empty, but his left held a bloody dagger.

"I said … no killing," Altiris gasped.

The boy shrugged. "He'll live, if he gets help."

Offering a grimace a fit match to Altiris' mood, Kurkas dragged an unconscious docker into concealment among the crates.

"Poor technique," he said. "Next time, go for the chin, or the back of the jaw."

Altiris rubbed at his cheek. "I'll bear that in mind." He peered up at a gantry platform now emptied of life. "Let's find Lord Akadra."

In reality, the physicians' station was little more than a timber yard's forecourt, forced open by constabulary swords. The stench of blood and waste and fear was almost overwhelming. The sackcloth-draped bundles against the east wall evidence of the battle fought and lost within the walls.

Josiri found the promised trouble in the yard's corner. A broken-nosed Drazina captain, helmet gone and his arm bloodied and bound, had a dozen blades ringed about a group of huddled protesters, all worse for wear than their captors. Three constables stood between, swords out towards the Drazina.

"What's all this, captain?"

"Traitors, sir. The Grandmaster wants them hanged. Take the fight right out of their mates."

Where was Sarisov, anyway? Josiri hadn't seen him since the first assault.

"Take 'em out," the captain shouted. "We'll string 'em from the guild-hall roof. They'll be seen clear across the docks."

"Nobody move!" Josiri felt a surge of freedom as something snapped deep inside. His temper, never quiescent, lent the words fire. "They're prisoners. *Constabulary* prisoners. They get a trial."

Drazina expressions crowded with doubt. Not so the captain's. "These are the grandmaster's orders ... sir. No exceptions."

He stalked closer until they were eye to eye – or more correctly, eye to chin. For the first time, Josiri realised just how imposing the other was. Not as tall as Viktor, but broader, and with the belligerence of a man well used to winning what fights he couldn't annul through intimidation.

"Then Grandmaster Sarisov can tell me himself!" Josiri snapped. "In the meantime, Lumestra help anyone who offers harm – much less summary execution – to anyone within these walls, because I'll see their heels dancing alongside. Am I understood?"

He glared about the gathered Drazina. One by one they sheathed their swords and withdrew into the courtyard proper. All save the captain.

"Watch your back, *my lord*," he growled. "Streets are dangerous right now, and accidents—"

A dull, meaty *thump*. The captain's eyes glazed over, and he slid sideways into a heap.

Behind him, Anastacia cupped a hand towards the courtyard. "Stretcher for the captain!"

A serene hurried over, her dark robes wet with another's blood and her lined face creased in concern. "What happened?"

"He hit his head on something."

The serene's eyes dropped to the carpenter's mallet hanging loosely from Anastacia's other hand. Lip twitching, she beckoned for help.

Josiri shot Anastacia a weary look and drew her away. "I had that in hand."

"I saw. Very stirring." Her eyes went wide in mock horror. "Please don't hang me, Lord Trelan. I'll be good."

"I doubt that."

"Charmer."

He frowned at the flutter beneath her words. The brightness of her eyes. "Have you been drinking?"

"Only medicinally." She let the mallet fall and gestured to erstwhile captives once more in the custody of constables. "What do we do about them?"

Josiri scowled. Today or in the future, the hangman's noose would claim them all. That was the law. He turned to the constable who'd first fetched him to the lumber yard. "Sergeant . . . ?"

The other frowned. Confused, maybe even offended. "Kressick, my lord."

Of course. Like so many figments claimed by clouded memory, it was obvious once reminder was offered. Josiri swallowed his frustration. "Escort them to the crossroads and cut them loose. The same for anyone else who can walk. Those who can't go to the King's Gate watch house. Lock them up, but give them whatever help they need. Then find Lieutenant Raldan and relay these orders to him. Understood?"

Kressick nodded. "At once, my lord."

Josiri turned his attention to the prisoners. "Go home. Stay there until this is done."

Disbelief turning to grateful nods, erstwhile captives shuffled away, Kressick and his constables in loose escort about them, leaving Josiri alone with Anastacia.

"I meant what I said." She offered a small, genuine smile. "You *were* very stirring."

Mounting annoyance swallowed up the rare compliment. "It's all so bloody pointless!" he snarled. "A few days of this and we won't need the Hadari. We'll tear ourselves apart!"

His third battle in Tressia's streets. The first time, he'd fought alongside Viktor to thwart Ebigail Kiradin's coup. In the second, he'd led the city against the Crowmarket. He regretted neither. But this? There was no purpose to any of it.

Anastacia kissed him on the cheek. "Sometimes all we can do is all we can do."

"Then where's Viktor while this city slides into chaos? Why isn't he here?"

Her focus shifted past his shoulder. "Be careful what you wish for."

Josiri turned. Beyond the serenes and physicians and wailing wounded of the timber yard, a new formation of Drazina drew up beside the gate, Viktor a brooding shadow at their head and Sidara at his side in full Drazina uniform.

For the first time in long hours, Josiri felt a surge of hope. Anastacia following in his wake, he hurried to the street.

"Sidara? Thank goodness you've come," he gasped, breathless. "We've wounded that could use your help."

She pursed her lips, regret flickering across her golden eyes. "I can't."

Hope faded, leaving sourness behind. "I don't understand."

A piece of him did, even before the ground shook. Before Viktor offered a weary glance and shrug of the shoulder. "That's not why I brought her."

The first kraikon rounded the crossroads, golden light sparking from rusted armour. Another followed. A third. They strode past Viktor's escort and formed up, shoulder to shoulder, across Harrowmoon Street. A flood of simarka loped to join them. If anything was worse than the slaughter at the barricades, it was this. An echo of days past when the people of Eskavord had risen up against northwealder oppressors and the Council's proctors had cleared streets.

Josiri glanced from Viktor to Sidara. "You can't ask this of her."

Sidara's expression tightened. "I want to do this."

"Viktor—"

"Don't treat me like a child!" snapped Sidara. "People need my help."

"It's her choice." Viktor moved to stand between them, the growl in his voice speaking to patience at its last ebb. "But if you wish, I will make it yours. This cannot spread. Sarisov has failed, so I must look to other means. If you forbid Sidara to act, I will honour your decision . . . then I will be forced to do so in her stead. You know what that will mean."

Objection rooted in fear for Sidara's safety – perhaps even for her innocence – shrivelled before a new, horrific prospect. Viktor's shadow, whose chill grasp blinded or drove men mad. Most folk knew it from rumour if they knew it at all. If it were loosed in the city . . . *against* the city? The citizenry would no longer look to their Lord Protector with trust, only fear. The consequences were incalculable.

"It'll only be a fight if they force it," said Sidara, her voice level. "You know what kraikons can do. So do they. If a reminder will serve, then it shall, but my sword-siblings are dying. What would you do, Josiri?"

"It's your decision, brother," said Viktor.

"You know it isn't." Josiri met Anastacia's gaze, received a small shake of the head, then focused on Sidara. "Do what you must."

She nodded tersely, a daylight halo spreading across her shoulders.

With a groan of strained metal and a crackle of light, the kraikons started forward.

Thirty-Four

The warehouse's emptiness did little to settle Altiris' jangling nerves. The roar of battle was too close. Near enough to separate individual screams from the cacophony, each one a mark of a life ended. They drove him on through the darkened, empty loading bays and storerooms, each step swifter than the last. Kurkas and Constans ran to keep pace, the steward brisk and professional as he checked each doorway, the boy moving always with a flourish to an audience only he could see.

"Nothing doing down here," said Kurkas, as they came to the stairs. "We going up?"

Altiris took the steps two at time, the timber creaking under his weight. The musky scent of silted water – never absent from the harbour – grew stronger.

Constans scowled. "Zarn's a cheapskate. Roof's rotten through."

They reached the mezzanine landing, the web of pulleys and walkways stretching into the shadows of evening. To the right, the door to the outside gantry-walk. To the left, the manager's office. A trail of smeared, slime-laden water stretched between, broken tendrils of black weed twitching and writhing in the uncertain light of a lone lantern.

Altiris crossed to the office door. "It's not the roof."

Constans paled. "Queen's Ashes . . . What is that?"

"That woman we saw with Lord Akadra? We cross her path, don't look into her eyes."

Kurkas scowled. "A fine time to mention that."

Altiris grimaced. "We're not here to fight."

"Might not be our choice." Kurkas drew his sword. "Still, we're here now."

The door handle turned smoothly. A last, deep breath to reinforce faltering nerve, and Altiris stepped into the office.

No lanterns burned within. The dull, angry glow of the setting sun cast long and brooding shadows. A desk sat between door and window, the huddled silhouette of a man slumped in the chair. A pool of weed-strewn water glimmered beneath.

"Alika?" The wheezing, bubbling voice was barely recognisable as belonging to the man from the gantry. His head bobbed up and down. "Is that you? I can't see anything any longer."

"Who's Alika?" murmured Altiris.

"His wife. Dead for decades." Rounding the desk, Kurkas opened his mouth to address Lord Akadra. Whatever words he'd meant to speak faded away, his jaw suddenly slack and his eye bulging.

Instinct screaming at him to do otherwise, Altiris made the mistake of looking down at what was left of Lord Akadra.

Beneath the smeared and cracked face powder, Lord Akadra's skin was mottled and swollen. Glassy, milky eyes twitched in red-rimmed sockets. Raw, peeling lips cracked an imbecile smile. Everywhere the skin pulsed and shifted as black, fibrous tendrils writhed beneath. Others showed through lesions above the water-stained cravat, and beneath the sodden cuffs of his jackets.

Altiris pressed a hand to his mouth to block the stench. Constans retched and doubled over.

"Alika?" moaned Lord Akadra, the smile fading. "Where are you?"

"I guess he didn't look like this before?" asked Altiris.

Kurkas grimaced. "Lord Akadra? It's Captain Kurkas."

"Kurkas?" A burbling cough drooled water across the desk. "Still filling Viktor's head with fool notions, I suppose?"

"Yeah. Hangs on my every word, he does."

The mottled brow creased. "You were always so ... " Fists clenched, he rocked gently back and forth. "Always so ... "

Before, Altiris had entertained the possibility that Lord Akadra was the mysterious Merrow. But even discounting the decaying state of the *thing* wheezing at the desk, it shared nothing with the urbane, upright stranger who'd sought his help. "Don't reckon we can negotiate with that."

"It *is* a shame," said Kasvin. "There's never much holding them together when the river gives them back. Memories. Regrets. Bound together by slivers of Dark."

Altiris spun around, sword out. Constans took a long step into shadow.

"Your work?" Kurkas' eye didn't leave Lord Akadra. "He weren't a good man. Not even close, but he didn't deserve this."

"Lord Trelan wants peace," said Altiris, careful not to meet her eyes. "Help him stop the fighting before it's too late."

"But I want *this*," said Kasvin. "The people are awake. They've forsaken fear! It's made them strong enough to claim their freedom and avenge those they've lost to privation and cruelty. What care I for the desires of those who remain sleeping?"

Whispers of song danced louder, insistent. Blue-green eyes swirled. Altiris heard his sword strike the floor before he realised he'd let it fall. Constans stumbled, a rapturous smile plastered across normally cynical features. Kurkas sank to his knees.

Altiris pinched his eyes shut as his own legs buckled, and sought the flash of daylight that had saved him a week before. It rose in answer to need, golden rays unfurling first into a phoenix, then to a likeness of Sidara, her hand outstretched. Fighting to breathe – even to think – Altiris reached out and found something cold beneath his palm. Opening his eyes a crack, he glimpsed his fingers curled about his sword.

The song grew insistent, Kasvin's frustration felt more than heard.

"She can't protect you," she hissed. She glided nearer and planted a naked foot on the sword's blade. The vision of Sidara faded, smothered by blue-green. "She's just an echo."

The last spark of daylight flickered out. Cold fingers brushed Altiris' cheek.

"Open your eyes." Kasvin breathed. "Adore me. Dance with me in the Black River."

"That ain't fair," said Kurkas. "Everyone knows he can't swim."

A wet ripping sound vanished beneath a shrill scream. The whispering song vanished. Altiris opened his eyes as Kasvin toppled backwards,

Kurkas' sword buried between her ribs and black blood welling up over the blade.

"Lassie, were you ever barking up the wrong tree," said Kurkas.

"What . . . ?" Blinking away blue-green after-images, Altiris stumbled upright. "How did . . . ?"

"Adoration, she said." Kurkas shrugged. "Fire needs fuel. Thought it'd be better to play along."

Women and desire were poles apart in Kurkas' world. At least, unless they were offering free brandy or the favours of the shield wall. Kasvin could have scratched at him all day, and her claws would never have found purchase.

Altiris glanced at Constans, now propped groggily on one knee. "You all right?"

The boy stared at the motionless Kasvin. "I'm . . . not sure."

Outside, the sounds of battle shifted, the screech of abused timber contesting scream and cheer. Running to the window, Altiris saw crowds streaming in retreat from the Harrowmoon Street gate. Bronze glinted in the setting sun.

"They've brought up kraikons." Long shadows promised more to come. "What do we do?"

Kurkas swore softly. "We take this sorry pair down there. Show both sides what they're fighting for, and hope it shakes sense loose."

Altiris glanced at Lord Akadra, still rocking back and forth in his chair. "That'll work?"

"You got a better idea?"

"I do." Lurching to her feet, Kasvin locked both hands about the sword, slid it free and cast it aside. Black blood gushed across the floor. Where it fell, feathery tendrils sprouted, swaying like windblown corn. Her dress rippled and writhed.

Skirts unravelled into a mass of thick black weed. It framed rippling, pallid flesh and blue-green eyes gone the colour of midnight – Kasvin bounded by an ever-shifting cage of lashing, serpentine fronds that was both an extension of herself and something wholly other.

Kurkas roared and vanished beneath the writhing mass. Tendrils ripped the sword from Altiris' grasp, then wended about his arms and legs. At Kasvin's gesture, they hurled him against the window. Glass cracked beneath his cheek. The stench of the river clogged his throat.

"Hey!" Constans started towards Kasvin. Moving with deceptive sluggishness, Lord Akadra rose from his chair and snared the boy in a sodden, twitching bear hug.

Kasvin surged towards the window. Eyes rimmed with black blood bored into Altiris', beguiling no longer, but murderous. Merciless.

"The river will carry you all away," she hissed.

Fronds coiled about his throat.

The barricade that had defied the Drazina shattered to matchwood beneath the kraikon charge. Men and women screamed, crushed beneath falling timbers or the remorseless advance of animated bronze. A handful of protesters held their ground, only to be bowled over by pouncing simarka.

Most fled.

Hawkin watched from the tannery rooftop west of the Harrowmoon Street gate. No saving the revolt now. Less a retreat, and more a rout, driven toward the pontoon bridge by the constructs' onset and vengeful Drazina massing behind. How many were merrowkin? How many were bystanders, roused to revolt by demagogue's decree? How many would die?

Not her problem.

She started thinking otherwise, she'd end up like Apara Rann, who could've been an elder cousin of the Crowmarket ... maybe a crowmother. She'd thrown it all away, and for what? For conscience? For the approval of those who'd ground them all into the filth? Kasvin had been right. You couldn't make amends to the dead.

Turning her back on the Merrow's dying dreams, Hawkin ghosted across the tiles to the tannery's southwest corner. Finding handhold at drainpipe and rough mortar was second nature. Soon she stood in the alleyway. Free of Kasvin's nonsense, if not her shadow.

From there, slipped latch and a flurry of skeleton keys gained entrance to a draper's storehouse. She kept below the level of the windows, warned to keep a low profile by boots and shouts in the adjoining street – the glimpse of Drazina uniforms beyond the glass. A game played many times at the Crowmarket's behest.

Another thwarted lock, another alley. A hundred yards and she'd be at a sewer access – as good as home free as could be managed. One eye on the alleyway's streetward end, she slipped the other way.

The dull *thud* of a punch – a pained grunt – sent Hawkin scrambling for the cover of an unevenly bricked-up archway. A dozen paces ahead, blocking the turning that led to salvation, a Drazina threw another punch. Her victim sprawled across the alley, ending in the unsympathetic arms of another knight, who held him fast.

Drazina. Called themselves lawkeepers, but they weren't really. Not like . . .

Not like Vona.

"Think you can run?" crowed the first Drazina, fist bunched. "After all your lot have done today?"

Her gauntleted fist snapped the young man's head about.

Hawkin recognised him. Rass Maridov. Ioan Maridov's boy. Little more than a child, for all his gangling frame. He'd been at her wedding a lifetime ago. The elder Maridov had been one of Vona's constables, and one of her closest friends. He'd died during the Crowmarket's rising and the streets had claimed Rass, as they had so many. Only there'd no longer been a Crowmarket to feed him, had there? Only the Merrow. Hawkin had seen him around, at Seacaller's and other meeting places, always taking care not to be seen in return.

She glanced away as another punch landed. A broken tooth skittered into the gutter.

Not her problem.

Even if Rass had given her a flower as she'd walked to the aisle, smiling with that mix of earnestness and embarrassment boys so often did at the prospect of a touching deed. Even if how the Drazina were fixing, he'd end in the soil, not a cell.

He'd made his choices, and there were other ways into the sewers.

Hawkin retraced her steps. She closed her ears to another lingering moan. She didn't owe Rass anything. Didn't owe anyone anything. Raven's Eyes, but even Vona wanted her dead, if Kasvin spoke true.

Vona would have hated the Drazina. Would have hated *this*.

Not her problem.

It was therefore very much to Hawkin's surprise when she reversed course a second time. Boots skidded on treacherous cobbles as she picked up speed.

Lost in her cruel business, the first Drazina didn't look up until she was within two paces. A cry of surprise gurgled away as the dagger's kiss opened her throat.

Hawkin reeled as the body fell, breath ragged and the second Drazina's cry of alarm ringing in her ears. Released, Rass collapsed to the filthy cobbles. Hawkin sprang over him, one hand slamming the Drazina's sword-arm against brick. The other cut his throat as cleanly as it had the first's.

Inexplicable tears welled up as she let the body fall.

"I'm not doing this again," Hawkin muttered. "I'm not. I'm *not*."

"Hawkin?" Rass stared at her from beneath a swollen brow. "'s that you?"

She twisted away. "Get out of here."

Without backward glance and shaking at every step, she made for the sewers.

Gasping for breath, Altiris tore at his bindings. Fingers found no purchase on the fleshy, musculous weed. Murky splotches danced before his eyes.

Far below the creaking window, the leading edge of the rout reached the T-shaped pontoon bridge. Hastily lashed sections bucked and shuddered, the wind-chased harbour waters rushing across swollen timbers. A woman slipped and plunged beneath the waves, lost from sight. Other folk surged along the spine of the T in hopes of bypassing Drazina clustered at the docks' southern reaches and coming safe to the eastern and western quaysides.

And behind, remorseless in their advance, came the kraikons – a dozen now in sight, forging straight for a bridge crowded with hundreds of struggling souls.

A bridge that couldn't possibly take their weight.

A chill gripped Altiris' heart. One separate from heaving lungs and blood roaring in his ears. "They're all going to die," he gasped. "The first kraikon that reaches the bridge will drag them all into the harbour."

Fronds convulsed, smearing him across the window. Altered

perspective revealed the shattered remnant of the Harrowmoon Street gate. The golden daylight halo as Sidara advanced amid a knot of Drazina.

Kasvin stared blankly down at the harbour. "Good."

"Good?" Constans thrashed in Lord Akadra's grip. "What happened to freedom, you crazy—"

Akadra clamped a rotting hand over the lad's mouth.

"Look at it!" snapped Kasvin. "They won't forget this! The city will see – the Republic will see – and the next uprising will be larger still."

"Maybe," gasped Altiris. "But those who followed you here will be dead. You don't ... want that."

Kasvin snarled. Fronds slammed Altiris to the floorboards. "Don't presume to know my desires!"

He tried not to look at the undulating mass of tendrils where he'd last seen Kurkas. "You wanted ... to help people." The words came harder now, the breath behind rare and painful. "You asked ... if I were on the right side. Maybe I ... wasn't. Are you?"

The first slackness crept into the weeds.

Altiris tore his hand free, fingers closing on something half-glimpsed with failing eyes. Strength returned at the feel of the sword beneath his hand. Fronds severed beneath steel with a wet, squealing hiss. Kasvin shied, weed thrashing protectively.

"You think that toy can kill me?" she shrieked.

Not after Kurkas had run her through to so little effect. Silver might have done it, or fleenroot or one of the other traditional remedies for demons and divine. But not steel.

Altiris dragged a strand of severed weed from his throat, weary beyond words. "Sidara doesn't realise what's happening. But she'll listen to me." He forced himself to meet Kasvin's stare. "You want to prove you're better than Lord Droshna? That you give one single damn about these people? Now's your chance."

Kasvin surged forward on a carpet of weed, fingers hooked to claws. Halfway, she shuddered to a halt. Shrinking inward, she fell to her knees, fronds winding in until the dress was again just a dress – albeit one gaping and torn. Released, a spluttering Kurkas clambered to an elbow. Only Constans remained a prisoner, trapped in Lord Akadra's grasp.

"Go," breathed Kasvin.

Altiris hesitated, wary at her sudden change of heart.

"Get out of here!" gasped Kurkas. "Move your bloody feet!"

Altiris fled the office and took the stairs two at a time, footing guessed at more than found. His missed it entirely at the first landing, his shoulder slamming painfully into the wall. Riding the momentum, he scrambled on.

On the dockside, the tumult of voices was deafening. To the west, kraikons loomed above the labyrinth of crates. Across the harbour, the pontoon bridges swarmed with struggling men and women, the slow trampled by the swift. Already, Altiris saw bodies floating with the wave tops and bobbing against merchantmen's keels. And still the kraikons marched on.

Straining for breath, a stitch stabbing at his side, Altiris ran on towards daylight.

A meaty hand closed about his collar. Another twisted the sword from his grip.

"Where d'you think you're going?" growled the Drazina. Altiris' ribs creaked as the other flung him against a crate. "I've got a runner!"

"I'm Lieutenant Czaron of the Stonecrest hearthguard," Altiris gasped. "I have to get to Lady Reveque!"

"You have to shut up," snarled the Drazina. "Or do I make you?"

Altiris told himself that it'd have been different had he been in uniform. He didn't believe it. "Listen to me, I—"

A gut punch left him on his knees, sucking for breath.

A man with a knight-captain's star approached. "Do we have a problem?"

"No problem," the Drazina replied. "Just a dregrat, selling a line."

Altiris fought the howling, hollow feeling in the pit of his stomach and made to stand.

"Lady Reveque . . . I must—"

A kick rattled his jaw and drove him to his knees. To the west, the kraikons marched on, the pier's timbers sagging beneath their weight.

"No!" Altiris cast a desperate glance across the harbourside. He could *see* her, only a matter of moments and a score of Drazina away. "Sidara! Sidara!"

The shout earned another kick.

"Take him to the wagons. Drag him if you have—" The knight-captain broke off, a shadow falling across his face. "Blessed Lumestra!"

Then he was gone, snatched away by a storm of black tendrils.

The remaining Drazina scrambled back, Altiris forgotten.

"To me!" he shouted, his voice cracking with fear. "Crossbows! I need crossbows!"

Then he too was gone.

Staggering upright, Altiris glanced behind.

Kasvin towered over the quayside's edge, riding on a carpet of black weed like a mummer on stilts. Fronds danced about her, the two bellowing Drazina dangling helpless from ankle and arm. A splash and one was gone, lost to the harbour waters. The first crossbows rattled. She staggered, black flights buried at belly and shoulder, the crest of weed undulating and dipping as pain sapped concentration.

"Demon!" a woman screamed.

A crossbow clattered to the dockside, its wielder dragged into Kasvin's embrace. Her eyes met Altiris'. Intent needed no words to grant it shape.

He ran headlong, ignored now by Drazina with more urgent woes. "Sidara!"

Crossbows clacking all around, he closed the distance. A Drazina barred his way, sword drawn.

"Stand aside!" shouted Sidara. "Let him through!"

Gasping, Altiris drew to a halt before her. "You ... you have to ..." He broke off, lungs heaving.

Golden eyes gazed into his, a gauntleted hand going to the wounds on his face. "What happened to you?" A scream sounded behind as another Drazina fell foul of Kasvin. "Blessed Lumestra! What's *that*?"

"Doesn't matter," gasped Altiris. "Stop the kraikons!"

"What? No! Do you know how many have died? How much has been destroyed? The dissidents must face justice, or it'll happen again."

"The bridge won't hold. You'll take them all to the bottom of the harbour."

She scowled. "I know what I'm doing."

"Sidara, please—"

"Why are you here, anyway?" Eyes narrowed in suspicion. "Queen's

Ashes . . . That night at Seacaller's when you sent me away. You're one of them, aren't you?"

"No! Lord Trelan—"

A high-pitched shriek drowned Altiris' desperate reply. Kasvin, body bristling with quarrels and weed flailing furiously about her, struck the quayside with a sickening thud. She lay unmoving in a slick of black blood.

The first kraikon reached the pier's end.

Altiris grabbed Sidara's shoulders. "Listen! Think what you will of me. That I'm one of them. That I'm not. It doesn't matter, but you have to stop the kraikons. Now!"

She wasn't listening. He saw it in her eyes. Too afraid of failing in her duty. Of disappointing Lord Droshna. Or maybe she simply didn't believe him. A minute, maybe less, and he could win her around. But the people on the bridge didn't *have* a minute. They had moments, and the only way to buy them more was to throw everything else away. Burn one bridge to save another.

"I'm sorry," he breathed.

Sidara frowned. "About what?"

Resolve faltered, riven between need and desire. Then Altiris swung as clean a punch as he'd ever thrown. Knuckles connected with the back of Sidara's jaw.

He caught her as she fell, golden light fading from her eyes. Abused muscles screamed beneath the weight of woman and armour. He turned frantically back towards the kraikons.

All now was gamble. If Sidara had been in direct control, they'd stop and await new instruction. But if she'd set them loose and merely nudged them from moment to moment, then it was all for nothing. Kasvin's sacrifice. His own. Future's dreams dashed on the grey harbourside stone.

Golden light crackling about their eyes, the kraikons shuddered to a halt.

Brief elation bleeding away, Altiris kissed Sidara's brow one last time as the Drazina closed in.

Thirty-Five

Brooding clouds filled the grey evening, though Rosa couldn't be certain whether they belonged to the heavens or her wandering mind. Thought throbbed, diffuse, a complement to parched mouth, aching joints and a stuttering, muffled drumbeat behind her eyes. After a day spent shivering in the crow's cage – nearly two without food or water – dream eroded reality's shore. So many times, she'd glimpsed Sevaka through the gloom. So many times, she'd faded into memory.

A stab of pain and warmth across her cheek brought her awake. Eyes opened into a storm of black feathers as the bird scrambled away from its erstwhile feast.

Rosa coughed and bit down, the leather gag bitter beneath cracked lips. Had it been a crow, or a raven? Was the Keeper of the Dead watching?

Perhaps it would be better to close leaden eyes and leave them thus. Defiance was all very well, but who any longer was she being defiant *for*? Those for whom she'd striven to set example were dead, throats cut by the pale-witch in the marketplace below. Dead eyes and accusing stares glimpsed in dream. Jonas, Mirada . . . even Drenn, though she'd at least died on her feet at Terevosk, not slaughtered like cattle.

Wind set the cage listing. Commotion in the marketplace drowned the sigh of rope and rusting iron. Carts rumbled from the reeve's manor, gold bright beneath rope-lashed tarpaulins. Soldiers marched alongside, swords drawn and shields raised. A near-endless procession, driven by trumpet and drum, and then gone.

The streets fell silent and the rain came again, drenching Rosa's sodden clothes anew, the sweet scent of it maddening for being so close. But the gag refused parched respite as readily as speech. The corners of her mouth were red raw from it.

Little by little, the soft patter bore her into dreams of mist and sable wings.

When a blare of trumpets brought her back, stars blazed in a cloudless sky, the waning moon reigning in the heavens. The marketplace was again full. A sullen Tressian crowd waited beyond a line of rust-coloured shields, white stags shining in moonlight. Immortal gold gleamed on the scaffold, the silver of a hooded pale-witch close by.

A new blare of trumpets, and a dazzling procession descended the manor house approach. More Immortals, the foremost bearing a gilded stag-banner, and all in rich, fur-edged cloaks. Thirava strode at their heart, silk robes iridescent beneath torchlight; the gemstones of his silver crown glittering fit to challenge the stars. The monarch of Redsigor in all his glory.

The cage jerked and plunged. It crashed back as iron struck cobbles, jarring Rosa's aching knees and spine yet further. The cage door shrieked open. Rough hands dragged her into the open.

Abused flesh refused even to stand when bonds were cut. Feet dangled uselessly as two Immortals, faces hidden behind close-fitting helms, dragged her to the scaffold.

Still, defiance remained. It burned at Rosa's core. But it was walled in by the same leaden ice that kept limbs shivering and fingers twitching.

"Behold, people of Redsigor!" Arms outspread, Thirava approached the scaffold's edge. Even his voice hailed from someplace afar. Or maybe Rosa was far away, falling into mist. She could almost smell it – that peculiar scent of yesterdays and lorn memories. "*This* is the price of insurrection and the fate of all false saviours."

The crowd offered no reply, or so Rosa believed. The fall of the cage had set her head raging anew; every faltering glimpse shaded red, every sound rushed with the waves of an invisible sea.

She barely felt it when the Immortals hoisted her high by arm and hip – the better for the crowd to see. Even keeping her head up was beyond her. She hated her weakness. The eternal she'd once been would have found the strength to fight. The Queen of the Dead would already have been free, and reaped every soul in the marketplace in retribution. To be those women again, if only for a moment.

Long enough to glimpse the fading horror in Thirava's eyes as she took his life.

"Tonight the moon smiles upon us." Thirava's dry accent thickened beneath the Tressian words. "Ashana will have Lady Orova's heart. The hands she raised against my rule will go to the fire!"

The old ritual, the stuff of Hallowside tales and nightmares. Barbarism the shadowthorns claimed behind them. The heart carved from living flesh and offered as feast to the wolves of Eventide. The hands incinerated so that even in the Light of Third Dawn she could hold no weapon. Better to receive the ripper's grin given to Jonas and the others.

"Henceforth, this is the price of transgression!" shouted Thirava. "This is my land, and you my subjects. In coming days, when I return in triumph, I will reward faithlessness and loyalty with equal generosity!"

In a swirl of robes, he set his back to the silent crowd. Rosa's world lurched as the Immortals lowered her to the scaffold. Not one pair of eyes met hers. She forgave them. She wouldn't go to the mists resenting others' fear. Essamere, Viktor – even Drenn's wolf's-heads – all had owed the eastwealders protection. All had failed.

The Immortals dragged Rosa past the pale-witch to stand before Thirava and stripped away the gag. Lungs heaved, drawing down the first unstoppered breaths in forever. The rich, rose-petal scent of perfumed robes parched her throat anew.

From some heretofore unknown reserve, Rosa found strength to raise her head and meet his preening, self-satisfied gaze. "Thought ... I was to ... rot."

He leaned closer, nose almost touching hers. Thin lips cracked a malign smile. "Opportunity beckons, and plans change." A gloved hand brushed her cheek, his thumb smearing the bloody gouge from the crow's beak. "I'm sure this will prove just as memorable."

"I'll come back for you." For a wonder, she managed the words without gasping.

A backhanded slap rocked back her head.

"Brave words," Thirava sneered.

Rosa managed a dry, bitter chuckle. He might have witnessed her deeds at Govanna Field, but he'd not truly understood what the Raven might grant her, if she asked. "No."

Uncertainty broke the arrogant sneer. Glorious. Better would have been to hear the Essamere battle cry, and see a host of knights in the street, Sevaka at their head. But some things weren't to be.

"Show the Goddess her heart!"

Thirava descended the scaffold and withdrew to his bodyguard. The righteous ruler, standing proud beneath his heraldry. The crowd stirred to a low growl. More the moan of a tortured beast than anything uttered by human folk. The wall of clansmen turned about, shields and blades levelled at the onlookers.

The growl receded, but did not entirely fade.

Rosa was soon in motion again, held upright before the pale-witch by Immortals' gauntleted hands.

Again, Rosa cursed sundered strength. Two Immortals and a single lunassera should have been nothing to her, not with her hands free. Yes, escape would have been impossible, but she might have ended Thirava's sneer. Raven's Eyes, but wiping the calm, appraising stare off the pale-witch's face would have been enough.

The lunassera's dagger came up, raised high above her head with ritual decorum. Behind the silver half-mask, grey eyes remained cold, expressionless. But below the mask's curlicued lower arc, cheeks twisted to a knowing smile. Cheeks that were somehow wrong. Not quite the olive skin so common among the Hadari. More the weathered tan earned from a life outdoors.

"Until Death," murmured the lunassera.

Rosa blinked at a decidedly Tressian accent. And not only Tressian, but the drawl of the city's worst slums.

The dagger blurred. The Immortal to Rosa's left collapsed, bloody hands flailing at a ragged throat. A second blur, and the other pitched backwards off the scaffold.

Unsupported, Rosa hit water-stained timbers. Fresh pain blurred to old harms.

Bloodstained robes pooling about her, the lunassera dropped to Rosa's side. "Can you fight?"

Rosa crawled half-upright on trembling arms. Her right buckled, the throb of her scarred shoulder darkly vibrant. "No."

The first cry tore free from stunned onlookers. Thirava bellowed a slew of urgent, guttural Hadari. The lunassera hung her head. "Don't go anywhere."

The dagger left her hand as she rose, a pained scream and heavy thud speaking of a victim found. Stooping briefly to snare an Immortal's sword, she ran for the scaffold's stairs.

The crowd's growl deepened.

Cheeks hot with worthlessness, Rosa again tried to stand. The effort used every scrap of breath in her lungs, but her arm held.

At the top of the stairs, the lunassera's kick sent a clansman tumbling into the marketplace. Steel scraped as she turned an Immortal's blade. Gasping, daring her ailing body to betray her, Rosa gathered one knee beneath her, then the other.

The crowd's fury found bitter crescendo, the rolling, rumbling sound of surging floodwaters, or an avalanche gathering pace. Harsh shadowthorn voices rose in contest.

Silsarian shields buckled as men and women came forward with fist, stone and boot. The outer marketplace descended into anarchy, Haldravord's abused populace finding their fire in a moment of doomed courage. Some hurled themselves at Thirava's retreating escort and died for their bravery.

"Send to the castle!" howled Thirava. "We need cataphracts!"

A stone caromed off the side of his head and he vanished behind his men's shields.

A clansman died on the scaffold stairs, a knee bent beneath him by the stomp of the lunassera's foot. Another went to the Raven with his mouth agape and a sword in his throat. An Immortal, chancing the opening, barrelled into the gap, taking the steps two at a time and his sword hacking down. The lunassera brought her sword about to parry. Steel chimed, and the sword ripped from her hand.

"Get up," Rosa hissed to herself. "You're not dead yet."

The Immortal's blade hacked down. The lunassera's mask split in two. The sword crunched through bone. She dropped to the top step, a hollow cry tearing free.

The sound of a woman dying in her stead drove Rosa to her feet, no weapon but momentum and the will to act.

She struck the Immortal, the motion half shoulder charge, half outright collapse. He clubbed at her with an armoured sleeve. The world bucked, precarious balance lost. It took all Rosa had left not to fall. The Immortal's sword came about.

"No!"

Impossibly, the lunassera lunged between them. Her empty hand formed a fist. Steel gleamed beneath moonlight, metal talons hissing free from the robes' voluminous sleeve and punching through the shadowthorn's scales. He sagged, and was gone.

The lunassera staggered. An empty hand tore the ruin of mask and hood free. No horror of mangled flesh and bone lay beneath, just a pale, ragged scar drawing steadily closed, and a wisp of black blood steaming silver in the moonlight. Rosa had seen such wounds before. She'd *borne* such wounds. The lunassera was an eternal – delivered from death by divine patronage, and bound to the living world by obsession.

More surprising was the face revealed. A likeness impossibly similar to one Rosa dearly loved. Auburn hair where Sevaka's was blonde. The cast of features older. Harder. Uncertain.

Trumpets shook the night sky. Fresh screams rang out as hooves clattered on cobbles. The darkness of the street shone with cataphract scales. Spears dipped as they goaded horses to the charge. The marketplace became a tide of surging, desperate bodies, running for safety that didn't exist.

"Who are you?" gasped Rosa.

"I'm family."

Rosa glared at the bloody talons bound to her would-be saviour's wrist. "You're a kernclaw."

"Once." The eternal's expression shifted, adopting earnest cast of brow. A perfect match for whenever Sevaka believed Rosa was being difficult. Which was often. Her voice grew in confidence. "I came to get you away from here."

Rosa backed away from her grasping hand. The dizziness returned, worse than ever. The pounding in her head tinged everything black. Even the moon seemed darker. "No, the others . . . we have to help."

A street could be held, maybe horses stolen. Some could escape. Some would live. But even as sluggish thoughts formed, she knew Thirava wouldn't forgive this. He'd fill Haldravord with blood.

Again the eternal reached for her. "It's already over. They had their moment. It's more than most get."

The words were rational, for all the woman's urgency. But Rosa had never done well with reason. "I'm staying," she rasped. "If you want to help me, you'll stay too."

She bent, fingers straining for a fallen sword. Fatigue and injury finally lost their patience. The scent of Otherworld stronger than ever, the world rushed black. Her last memory was of arms beneath hers and the eternal's weary voice.

"Why are the selfless always so stubborn?"

Thirty-Six

Jaridav saluted as Josiri stepped onto the upper landing. She looked no happier than he felt.

"Lord Trelan."

"Amella," he replied. "You can stay out here."

She sank gratefully into the wooden chair at the landing's curve.

Stooping slightly where the ceiling sloped, Josiri picked his way past lantern sconces and the faded rendition in oils of Bregin lighthouse. Reaching the door, he rapped twice.

"Yes?" Even muffled by the door, Altiris' voice was thick with trepidation.

Stifling the temptation to walk away, Josiri entered the room.

Altiris stumbled from the armchair. "Lord Trelan?"

Eyes adjusting to the gloom – the lone firestone lantern was barely at half-light, and shadows clung to the sparse furnishings – Josiri waved him down. "Sit. Please."

The lad obeyed, a brow marred by the bruises and scrapes of the afternoon furrowing in concern. Josiri didn't blame him for that. He wore no phoenix tabard – only shirt and trousers – but formality remained. Strange to see him out of uniform so long. Midwintertide aside, Josiri couldn't think when it had last happened. Or more accurately, the last occasion he *remembered*. Frustration flickered at the silent admission. He tamped it down. Whatever Altiris had wrought this past day, he wasn't responsible for the curse of failing memory.

Words grew elusive, so he fell back on convention. "How are you?"

Altiris offered a mirthless smile and winced as the motion tugged at a bruised cheek. The Drazina had been less than gentle. "You tell me."

"Commander Hollov is calling for the highest penalty." Serenes had found Grandmaster Sarisov's body beneath the ruin of the second barricade. Some acclaimed him a hero. Josiri's own thoughts were less charitable. "Viktor's furious."

Altiris pursed his lips, no longer staring at Josiri, but beyond him. "And Sidara?"

"She'll be fine."

"That's not what I meant."

Josiri sighed. "Perhaps you should talk to her. It's house arrest. You'd still be in the house."

"I'm the last person she wants to see right now."

Josiri hadn't spoken to Sidara himself – dealing with the riot's aftermath had swallowed the rest of his day, and would likely occupy those to come – but the brew of betrayal and frustration Anastacia had recounted was one Josiri found all too credible, and familiar besides. Worse than the fact that Altiris had laid hands upon Sidara were the events he'd brought about. Sidara's first real action away from the Panopticon, and she'd failed. Viktor had been the first at her side once she'd recovered. Josiri hadn't heard what words had passed between them, but knew all too well that Viktor's disappointment was a difficult burden.

"If I've learned anything, it's that wounds only fester in silence."

Altiris grimaced. "I wouldn't know what to say."

"Lead with 'sorry'." Josiri perched on the end of the bed. "The army marches tomorrow, and Sidara with it. Don't leave things bitter between you. Don't repeat my mistakes."

The lad's eyes snapped into focus. "I don't follow."

Josiri hesitated, overcome too late by strange regret at sharing even that much. "My sister Calenne. Our last conversation – our last *real* conversation – was a quarrel. I said many things I shouldn't, and never had the chance to take them back. Nor did I have opportunity to apologise for years of lies. In the end, my lies killed her. I'd give anything to tell her I'm sorry."

Altiris set his shoulders. "That's just it … I'm not sure I *am* sorry. I wish there'd been another way, of course I do. But she'd have drowned all those people. I can't apologise for stopping that." He stared down at the floor. "Even it if costs me everything."

He spoke with unassuming determination Josiri wished he'd possessed at so tender an age. The early years of his own adulthood had been paralysed by resentment and fear. In a just world, Altiris would have been lauded for his actions. But for all Josiri had laboured to make it otherwise, Tressian justice was far from perfect. Or life too complicated.

That didn't mean he wasn't proud. "I know."

A wan smile chased across Altiris' face, smothered by brooding contemplation. "What about Kasvin?"

"Priests bound her with silver. The Drazina took her away." And she wasn't alone. Cells and barracks across the city were rammed with rioters awaiting judgement. A problem for the morning. "She'll answer for what she did."

"*What* is she?"

"Archimandrite Jezek insists she's a rusalka: a demon birthed from the Black River to corrupt wayward souls. Ana says much the same thing, only with more approval. I think they're cousins, after a fashion."

More childhood tales, woken from myth to reality. How strange life had become.

"You've spoken to her?"

"Ana says I probably shouldn't." Josiri frowned. "Why?"

"I don't think she's evil. She truly wanted to help people."

Josiri scowled. "Then she chose a poor way to go about it. Hundreds are dead. More will die of their wounds before the week's out. And the rest? Hollov's calling for a new wave of curfews, and greater leeway in enforcement. Kasvin's only made things worse."

He tailed off, lost in echoes of the past. Kasvin had provoked the city to unrest on a far grander scale than he'd managed in the Southshires, but if the intent was the same, could he truly judge her?

"It would have been thousands dead had she not let me go," said Altiris, his eyes on Josiri once more. "You only captured her because she helped me when the Drazina wouldn't listen."

You only captured her. Not *we*. "I see."

"Why didn't they take me too?" Altiris asked. "I'm surprised."

"I couldn't let them. Improper arrest warrant, you see. As head of the constabulary, I could hardly allow that."

Altiris frowned. "Improper?"

"Indeed. The warrant bearing Viktor's signature was made out for one Altiris Czaron. It had no claim on Altiris Trelan, you see."

The penny dropped, presaged by Altiris' disbelieving expression. "You lied?"

Josiri shrugged. "Not exactly. Pre-empted, perhaps."

Disbelief turned to suspicion. "In what way?"

"Only in that I led Commander Hollov to believe I'd already adopted you into the family, whereas technically I hadn't until just now."

"I..." Altiris shook his head and blinked furiously. "Say that again?"

Josiri grinned, glad to have reason. "I hope it doesn't offend."

"No ... No, of course not. Even if it is just a ruse."

Josiri stood and looped his hands behind. "It isn't. You're a Trelan now, if you wish it."

Altiris shook his head as if dispelling a dream. "But why? I don't understand."

As if that had a sole, simple answer. "Because when I look back on these last few years, I find that they've flown past, leaving little trace of the things I've said or the deeds I intended. I've put this off for so long, not wanting to burden you. I want to make it right, before another five, ten, fifty years fly past, and the chance is lost for ever."

"I ... I've not earned this honour."

Josiri shook his head. "Calenne always said the Trelan name was cursed. I've thought it often enough myself, but it's not true. The 'curse' is the consequence of striving to do what's right, regardless of the cost to ourselves. You saved hundreds from the river tonight." He cocked his head. "Tell me again how you've not earned this."

Altiris frowned. "They'll reissue the warrant. All that's different is that whatever happens to me tarnishes the Trelan name."

"It will survive a little tarnish." Crossing to the armchair, Josiri laid a hand on his shoulder. "Years ago, I did something eerily similar to what you did today, though you'll find no record in the official history – Malachi scrubbed it away. Melanna Saranal and her father didn't flee the field at Davenwood. They were captured ... I freed them."

"Truly?"

Josiri nodded. "Viktor made me an Akadra to protect me from the consequences. I'm hoping he recognises the irony. Reissuing the warrant will take time. Time in which Viktor's temper will cool."

Little by little, Altiris' expression regained a measure of steadiness. "You think he'll listen?"

This was no time for lies, however well intentioned. "I hope so."

Altiris rose and withdrew to the empty hearth. "You'll forgive me, Lord Trelan—"

"Josiri." He offered the correction politely, but firmly.

"Lord Trelan . . . I'm not so sure the Lord Protector who exists in your head is a match to the one running the Republic."

Josiri bristled at the words, but supposed them fair enough. Viktor was seldom lovable from a distance. Even up close, he made it challenging. Altiris had seen too little of him at either span. "It might be he'll surprise you."

"Maybe. But Kasvin insisted Lord Droshna was at the heart of everything wrong in the Republic. Every time, I rejected her claims. But today Lord Droshna won Kasvin's argument for her."

"You're wrong."

"Look around." Anger quickened beneath Altiris' words. "Is this the Republic you thought you were building? The Drazina? Checkpoints? The identification papers that were a blight on a southwealder's life now borne by everyone? We ate like kings of old at Midwintertide, and a dozen streets away folk had nothing!"

"It's not that simple!" snapped Josiri, temper rising at the ingratitude.

Altiris flinched, but held his ground. "I think it might be. Or as close as makes no mind."

Josiri gritted his teeth. "So now I'm wicked, or a fool? Is this how you speak to me, after everything I've just told you?"

To his surprise, Altiris showed no sign of backing down, but met his stare head on. "I'm honoured to be your son. You've been a father to me almost from the day we met. But if I can't speak to you honestly – especially now – then what's the point?"

Josiri bunched fists at his sides and breathed deep. Even now, he couldn't think *why* he'd taken offence. Altiris had said nothing untrue. Worse, Josiri had wondered at the greater part of it himself – why else parley with Melanna Saranal behind Viktor's back? Was this the price of passing years? To become so trapped by position and status that rejection became reflex?

Anger faded, leaving behind the hollow sense of foolishness anger so often does. "You see? Already you're speaking like a Trelan." He smoothed a hand across his brow. "But you need to stay at Stonecrest until we get this all worked out."

Altiris nodded, expression stiff. "Yes, lord."

Josiri let the formal address slide. Change took time. "Shall I tell Sidara you'd like to see her?"

He grimaced. "I'll think on the matter."

Again Josiri admitted defeat, though less readily. He resolved to speak to Sidara himself, for all the good that would do. The lass was stubborn. Another Trelan in the making. "Do so. Now is not for ever. It will pass, if we let it."

Altiris opened his mouth as if to say something, and closed it without a word.

Taking it as the closest he'd get to winning the argument, Josiri departed.

Viktor didn't relish setting foot in the Vaults. Too many memories. None of them good. Though the provosts were long gone, the scars they'd inflicted remained – not least in his flesh.

The presence of silver, too, was a trial. His shadow hissed and spat with every step. Artisans had worked the blessed metal into architrave and sill, fashioning flowing patterns that danced whenever light touched them. Beautiful, certainly, but they made every thought a chore, and every threshold a test of courage.

After Govanna Field, where the Raven's revenants had battled Fellhallow's forest demons, Viktor had suspected he'd need a jail capable of caging the divine. That was worth a little discomfort. And it wasn't as though the cells went otherwise to waste. Though it pained him greatly, Tressia remained as lawless in nature, if not degree, as before his ascension to the Lord Protector's duties. The cells were seldom empty. With the riots at Silverway Dock done with, the upper levels were full to bursting.

But one chamber remained isolated from the rest. The same, deep oubliette into which he'd once been cast, where the crash of waves and the shriek of gulls carried through the bars. The door had been replaced since Viktor's time, for the old had been torn from its hinges by one of Elzar's kraikons. Another debt owed to the old man. Another reason to ensure his sacrifice wasn't wasted.

Two Drazina guarded the door. Each wore a silver sunburst necklace against the skin. Archimandrite Jezek had insisted the shape of the metal was as important in thwarting a rusalka's wiles as the metal itself. Unable to ward himself with silver, Viktor had no choice but to trust in his shadow.

Ignoring the Drazina's salutes, he slid back the door's narrow inspection hatch. The prisoner remained a crumpled heap of torn skirts, chin against her chest. Silver shackles shone bright in the puddled moonlight.

He snapped the hatch back into place. "Leave us."

"My lord."

The Drazina withdrew. When they were lost to sight, Viktor unbolted the door and stepped inside. So close, there was no mistaking the otherness of her. It wasn't simply a matter of sight or scent: the pallid flesh, puckered and smeared with black blood where quarrels had struck home; the bitter, musty smell of clogged waterways. When his shadow examined her, he saw almost nothing at all, just a black, glimmerless tangle of river weed, wearing humanity as skin. Predatory, even in pain.

"I know you're awake," he rumbled.

Kasvin raised her head. Filth-fouled blonde hair snaked across her shoulders. Blue-green eyes, dim beneath the influence of silver, glared.

"So the high and mighty Lord Droshna faces me at last?"

Her voice was barely a whisper, and feeble. The wounds she'd taken on the dockside should have killed her thrice over. Viktor knew better than to trust appearances.

"I've greater concerns than the justifications of an insurrectionist."

"And yet you're here."

"Perhaps I was curious about the kind of creature who'd lead honest folk to a worthless death."

Kasvin laughed under her breath. "So much like your father."

The barb shouldn't have hurt. Wouldn't have, had Viktor's patience not already been stretched by his shadow's discomfort.

"You know nothing of my father!" The bellow echoed about the chamber. "My men found the remains in the warehouse. A poppet woven of river weed, entwined with glamour. A deception."

"No. It was him. Enough of him, at least. His pride. His arrogance. Even some of his memories. Everything I could salvage from the river." She let her head rest against the wall, a thin hiss passing her lips as silver manacles shifted. "He was proud of you at the end. After all, when the city raised its voice in defiance, you acted *exactly* as he would have, didn't you?"

"You know even less about me than you do my father," he replied coldly.

She leered, youthful guise replaced by something cold and cruel. "You and I, we're cousins in damnation. The tainted waters of the Black River pulse through my veins as the Dark does yours. Our very existence twists the world. Only *I* fight for those who have no one else."

"All my life, I have done only that." Stepping closer, he let a little of his shadow free – allowed it to enfold her. "I'm here to offer common cause. I've no choice but to lead the Republic into war. If you truly care for its people, you'll aid me."

He let his shadow coil tighter, closer, nudging Kasvin's thoughts in the direction that would serve best. He felt no guilt, not after all she'd done. If redemption required coercion, then so be it.

Her eyelids drooped, then closed.

Split lips twisted into a mocking smile.

"Do you really think that would work?" she said. "But thank you."

Growling, Viktor withdrew his shadow. It crept into his soul with faltering step, abasing itself for the failure. "For what?"

"For proving your nature beyond doubt." She jabbed a cracked nail at the ceiling. "Up there, they don't see you, not like I can. One day soon, you're going to break apart and the mask will slip. What you hope to be smothered by what you *are*."

"I'm a man."

"Are you?" There was no triumph in Kasvin's voice. Only weariness. "Do you believe that, or just think you *should*? I hear the voices of your victims. Those you've already slain, and those yet to come. Kill me. Send me back to the river. Another will come for you."

Regret bitter in his heart, Viktor stepped away. Perhaps employing his shadow had been a mistake. Perhaps, had he more time, he could have coaxed her onto a righteous path. Kasvin could have saved more lives than she'd waylaid. But he'd no such luxury. War called him away. Leaving her at his back – shackled or otherwise – smacked of folly. Given chance, she'd twist Josiri inside out.

With heavy heart, Viktor closed his eyes and looked on her only through his shadow. The deed was easier with the innocence of youth stripped away. Easier to kill the monster beneath those beautiful blue-green eyes. "Let them try."

Kasvin didn't struggle as shadow embraced her. Didn't cry out. Indeed, Viktor could have sworn she smiled in that last moment before her blood turned to ice.

Voices faded from the passageway. The sound of boots on the stairs soon after confirming that Jaridav's watch had ended, and Brass' had begun. Altiris let another hour while away, and wits to wander. Pulling coat and bundled haversack from beneath the bed, he opened the drapes.

The ailing moon watched over empty gardens three storeys below. Slowly, nerves jangling at the slightest *creak*, he eased open the window.

Warm air rushed into the cold night. Skin rose to gooseflesh. Between drainpipes and ivy, the climb would be simple enough. And he'd have to make the climb. For all of Lord Trelan's cleverness – Altiris couldn't yet imagine calling him Josiri, even in the privacy of his own head – there was no guarantee of escaping jail, or even the noose. Mutiny seldom invited leniency. Lord Trelan would fight for him, of course. But was there really any hope?

Especially if Kasvin were correct about Lord Droshna.

It was the simplest arithmetic. If Kasvin were wrong, then fleeing into the night would have few lasting repercussions. Were she right, then obeying Lord Trelan's wishes would, at best, cause all manner of distractions in a household that could little afford them. At worst, it would subject Lord Trelan to accusations of shielding a traitor.

And yet something held Altiris back. Urged him to close the window and wait to see what came with the morning. Stonecrest was *home*. Indeed, it was the only real home he'd known. Leave it now, and he might never return. Czaron or Trelan, he'd be a fugitive.

No. It was Sidara that held him back. The longing to see her, to explain . . . and to apologise most of all. What if she never returned from the east, or did so to find him hanged? Maybe Lord Trelan was right. Words left unsaid were the hardest burden.

Set against that was the fear that earning Sidara's forgiveness was now impossible. That even if she consented to see him, words exchanged would only worsen matters. If they fell to quarrelling, he'd have nothing but the bitterest of memories to sustain him. This way, at least, there was a chance at reconciliation. Better to have hope.

Before he could change his mind, he clambered out of the window.

Lunandas, 7th Day of Dawntithe

Family is more than blood, though blood brings
family together like little else.

Thrakkian proverb

Thirty-Seven

Viktor hesitated, furled knuckles an inch from Calenne's door. The morning had come too soon, as mornings often do, and the black mood of the night before had little abated. Anger provoked by argument with Josiri had formed unfair compact with self-doubt – often Viktor's worst trait, and one he could scarcely afford.

And so he hesitated, the desire to speak with Calenne held in the balance by the fear that he'd find only judgement beyond the door. She'd already proven her ability to wheedle out truths he'd prefer to keep hidden. He was proud neither of the bloodletting at the docks, nor the rusalka's death, but accepted them as necessary. Calenne, he felt increasingly certain, would not, and he'd no time to sway her mind. Her disapproval would become his doubt, and a man riding into war could afford doubt less even than mercy. Better to face her with triumph under his belt, and a free Eastshires to justify his deeds.

Strange how Calenne could be his greatest weakness, and his greatest strength.

He let his hand fall and turned his attention across the hall to where Tzila stood motionless as a statue.

"I'll return as soon as I'm able."

Tzila offered a slow, careful nod.

She, at least, understood. Or so Viktor assumed. Did she resent how he'd plucked her from her prior existence? It might explain the flashes of anger from a woman who was otherwise never less than carefully composed.

Viktor wished he believed resentment was truly the cause, but a lie practised on oneself was twice the falsehood. A tragedy, but Tzila remained an asset. Not the success he'd hoped for, but far from a failure.

"Keep her safe," he said. "Trust no one but Constans."

He turned on his heel and strode away. Calenne would wait.

Even in cruel times, everything was ceremony. That uncharitable thought was uppermost in Josiri's mind as he beheld the King's Gate approach.

The road was thick with assembled soldiery. The rich blue of the regular army, the last of the regiments bound for the Eastshires: halberdiers, shieldsmen and the humpback silhouettes of pavissionaires. The deeper tones of Drazina, though plenty would remain within the city walls. Perhaps fifty men and women in the grey cloaks of borderers, dispossessed by the Empire's spread. A smattering of knights in bright raiment – a couple of whom wore Prydonis scarlet. Then there were the kraikons, tall enough that they'd have to stoop in order to pass the gate and their bronze hides polished to a mirror sheen. And, of course, the pride of simarka, their leonine expressions inscrutable as they awaited instruction from Sidara to send them forth. It made for a glorious sight beneath the fiery dawn. Even through his misgivings, Josiri felt a stirring.

It helped that the morning's lively Dusk Wind swept Archimandrite Jezek's sermon out over the walls with nary a word of it troubling the ears of those inside. But for his gesticulations from the inner rampart of one of the new fortress towers, the casual observer might have been forgiven for remaining ignorant that he was speaking at all.

And there were observers aplenty. Families, come to catch last glimpse of their kin before departure. The inevitable slew of traders and opportunists. Pickpockets too, for a certainty, though Josiri hoped his constables – themselves weary from the previous day – would hold them in check.

His own possessions, at least, were safe enough. Kurkas had deployed the hearthguard to one of the wallward alleyways – a thin line of Phoenixes granting privacy for reluctant farewell.

"Doesn't he cut a fine, majestic figure?" said Anastacia of the distant Jezek. "Priests carry more authority when you can't actually hear what they're saying."

Sidara frowned away an inappropriate smile and ran fingers through her horse's mane. A knight's destrier, bred for battle. Tall though she was, when she stood beside it her head barely reached its shoulder. Josiri could see over it only by standing on tiptoes. At least she looked the part of a knight, arrayed in a Drazina's armour, golden hair hidden beneath her helm.

"He means well, Ana," she said. "If he offers solace, then where's the harm?"

Josiri marked unease behind her eyes. That peculiar mixture of excitement and trepidation that infected soldiers old and new.

He glanced down the alley. Kurkas had pulled the hearthguard back to guard against eavesdroppers. The quiet thoughtfulness Josiri had long taken for granted.

Mentally girding himself, he turned back to Sidara, whose gaze was again on the soldiery. "You know I don't want you to go. But someone recently told me – and at some volume – that it wasn't for me to make your choices."

She embraced him. It would have been sweeter but for the bruising press of armour. "Was I very rude?"

"'Strident' sounds more polite." Josiri held her head against his and fought the temptation to keep her there, safe, while the army marched. He felt foolish for caring so for a child not his own, and yet the ache was impossible to deny. "You're forgiven for both."

Sidara pulled back. Her eyes dipped to the cobbles, then touched on his. "Has there been news of Altiris?"

He shook his head, frustration swamping any words he might have offered. Easy to see that the lad thought he was protecting others, but understanding wasn't agreement. Was a father doomed to be ignored by his children, be they blood kin or no?

"He'll be found," said Anastacia. "And then he and I will have a friendly talk."

Friendliness was not uppermost in her tone. Altiris would no doubt find the conversation bruising, but he'd probably survive.

Sidara's face fell. "I honestly thought we'd got it right this time."

"You're young," said Josiri. "You've years ahead to figure it out."

"Perhaps." She drew up to her full, impressive height, a little of her mother Lilyana's fire returning. "Tell him something for me, if you see him?"

"Of course."

"Tell him . . . I'm sorry. His actions were his own, but I forced them. I should have listened."

Josiri blinked in surprise. "You did as you thought best."

She shook her head. "That's just it. I don't know that I was thinking at all. I saw only the dead. I heard only the cries of the wounded. I was determined to bring the fighting to an end, and it blinded me." Her throat bobbed. "When I came to, the harbour was choked with bodies. But for Altiris, it would have been worse. He probably hates me."

"He definitely doesn't," said Anastacia, drily.

"But hold that lesson close. It'll serve you well." Josiri scowled, fearing his words sounded like a sermon. What did she *need* to hear? "You've a good heart, Sidara, and you have it in you to help so many. But you can't help everyone, and your choices won't always be easy, especially—"

He stifled a yelp of pain as Anastacia drove an elbow into his ribs.

"What Josiri means to say," she said sweetly, "is that you should stay safe and remember that whatever happens, you're loved, and we're proud. As your mother and father would be proud."

Sidara's eyes danced from Anastacia to Josiri and back again, storm clouds parting from her expression. "Mother always said I was meant for more than being a knight."

Anastacia sniffed. "On this, at least, she and I agree. But today you *are* a knight. You can be something else tomorrow. Live to see it."

Smiling at last, Sidara embraced Anastacia. Then she nodded, bereft of words, and led her horse to join the muster. Anastacia slipped her arm about Josiri's waist, and watched her every step of the way.

Josiri gazed down at Anastacia. "That *hurt*."

"'Your choices won't always be easy'," she muttered. "I don't know what you were thinking."

"He thought to offer useful advice," rumbled a voice. "Weighty decisions carry a cost."

Josiri turned to find Viktor looming behind, arrayed in full, flame-etched armour for the first time in recent memory and a claymore strapped to his back. A black velvet cloak drank in the alleyway's shadows, making him twice the brooding presence. Something cold twitched at the base of Josiri's spine. For the first time in years, Viktor again looked as he had at the Battle of Zanya – the day he'd harried Josiri's mother into the grave. Older and greyer, certainly, but he was again the Black Knight of Calenne's nightmares.

Anastacia regarded him stonily. "Has the Lord Protector taken to eavesdropping?"

A wry smile tugged at Viktor's scarred cheek. "The Lord Protector came to apologise. Difficult times lie ahead, and I've quarrels enough without weathering those of my friends." He spread his hands. "I will allow nothing to happen to her."

"See that you don't," said Anastacia. "It would only bring to mind everything I owe you."

Viktor's account lay heavily in the red, but that detail seemed to trouble him little. "That you feel so strongly does you credit, but she's glimpsed a wider world. It's not for us to hold her back."

As with all Viktor's apologies, the conversation held little in the way of actual contrition. Josiri had long since abandoned expecting anything different. Though Viktor's temper cooled readily enough, admission of wrongdoing was seldom confessed.

"And Altiris?" asked Josiri.

"I've given orders no harm is to be offered. If he's found, he'll be held for trial."

Anastacia started towards him. "That's not good enough."

She subsided as Josiri laid a hand on her shoulder. The scars of her transformation shifted under his fingers, little concealed by the dress' thin fabric. "She's right, Viktor."

Viktor spread his hands. "Without a trial there can be no exoneration. The law must bind our friends as well as our enemies, must it not? A family name cannot be a shield." He sighed. "If he hadn't fled, it would be easier. But I promise you, it will all be gone into on my return."

Josiri held his gaze. "Maybe all of this should wait. After what happened yesterday—"

"The city is quiet."

"It's quiet because we've doubled patrols. Because we've checkpoints on every major street. The city's holding its breath, waiting to see what comes next. If there's another revolt—"

"There won't be," Viktor replied. "That's why I drew all this out, so it could be dealt with at an hour of our choosing."

The words, delivered so matter-of-factly, sent a chill down Josiri's spine. "Is there something you want to tell me?"

"I'm not blind, Josiri. I know what's been building. Folk are resentful. Sometimes with reason – often without – though it matters little when the end result's the same. The Eastshires call me, but I could hardly answer if I left an uprising at my back. That's why I cut the ration. Why I authorised wider powers for the Drazina." He shrugged. "It's strategy, nothing more."

Josiri glared, appalled. Though the admission wasn't quite kin to Altiris' accusations, it was far too close for comfort. "It's monstrous."

"The necessary often is. But now the city's humours have been bled. The architect of unrest has died of her wounds. I'm free to act. The Eastshires will be saved."

"I can't believe you did this," snapped Josiri.

"Someone had to," Viktor replied, unrepentant. "If you feel you can do better, brother, you'll have no better time to prove it. The city – the Republic – is yours, until my return."

"Me?"

"Of course." Viktor frowned. "Who else could I trust? Folk tempted to look on me as a monster will find relief in the fact that a gentler soul guides their fate. I've already given orders for the ration to be restored – in your name, mark you. As to the rest, you may do as you think proper. Commander Hollov is instructed to follow your orders … short of burning down the city or opening the gates to the Hadari. Though I advise against stripping back the checkpoints too far. Gratitude can be fleeting."

"So I'm yet again to tidy up after your mess?"

"I prefer to see it as you rebuilding what was broken. Such deeds have always suited your talents more than mine." He offered a grim smile. "I am called upon to break things elsewhere."

Josiri nodded, uneasy at Viktor's callousness. But his own advice to Sidara echoed through the empty spaces between his thoughts. Few choices were easy, and a Lord Protector's hardest of all. The city was a puzzle, and Viktor's solution a tidy one, for all its amorality. More than that – and unthinkable though it was – Sidara wasn't the only member of his strange family riding into the Empire's maw. Though Viktor was no more Josiri's blood than she, still they were brothers, and what led them to quarrel bound them all the tighter.

"We'll continue this discussion on your return." He held out his hand. "Be sure you live to endure it."

Viktor's smile broadened. Seizing Josiri's hand, he dragged him into a bear hug. "I fear death may seem too tempting when faced with the prospect . . . but I will try. Stay safe, brother. Rebuild our city. I shall do the same for the Republic."

Setting Josiri free, he bowed to Anastacia, who consented to Viktor raising her hand to his lips. Then he too strode from the alley, greeted by uproarious cheer as the citizenry marked his presence. Whatever malice Viktor had borne elsewhere, that morning he was again a saviour.

Anastacia watched him go, a pensive expression tugging at her cheek.

"Was he right?" asked Josiri. "Was this necessary?"

"I don't know. But if he disposes of his city thus, what hopes for the army he leads?" She shrugged, the moment forgotten. "I need a drink."

Buccinas blared and the army began its long, slow departure. First, a morning's march to Govanna, and from there upriver aboard transport hulks to Tarvallion. Cloaked and hooded at the rear of the crowd, Altiris caught brief glimpse of Sidara among the Drazina. Then she was gone, and he more alone than ever. It wasn't much of a farewell, but to stay away had been unthinkable.

The crowd dispersed, chivvied along by constables. Altiris went with them, careful not to draw attention. The constabulary might have let him be, but there were plenty of Drazina, many of them wounded from the day before. Better a wide berth – especially with his wits numbed by a sleepless night.

Too used to the luxuries of a warm bed, he'd managed only a few brief, shivering hours beneath the arches of Vrazdagate Bridge, and they'd been full of nightmare. He'd need something better, and soon. But what? He might find shelter at a hospice, or perhaps at Seacaller's. Both carried risks. Serenes wouldn't protect him from Drazina, and he could hardly count on a warm welcome from the merrowkin.

Lost in thought, he'd no warning at all when hands closed about his mouth and waist, dragging him into an alley. He spun around as the arms retreated, fist raised to strike . . .

"Constans?"

The boy held up his hands in mock surrender. "Stay thy wrath, a friend am I." He topped the overwrought greeting with a modest bow.

Altiris let his fist drop. "Shouldn't you be with the army?"

He gave a lopsided shrug. "Father wants me in the city. I'm to track down a dangerous fugitive."

No guesses as to who he meant. Altiris sank against the wall, more disappointed than he could easily credit. Constans wasn't so foolish as to try to take him without help. There'd be others nearby. The price of carelessness. "Do what you have to."

Constans frowned, perplexed and affronted. "Don't look so glum. I was joking."

"It's hard to tell with you."

He grinned and clasped both hands to his tabard. "Good. I've always wanted to be a mystery." Artlessly insouciant, he leaned against the opposite wall. "Do you need money? I'd offer you lodgings at the palace, but that might be counterproductive. Then again, it's probably the last place they'll look . . . "

Altiris brushed a strand of red hair back from his eyes and stared at Constans as if truly seeing him for the first time. He just about believed Constans was prepared to forget having crossed his path, but such generosity of spirit left him speechless. Estranged from one Reveque, he'd somehow grown closer to the other. An inequitable trade, but only a fool shunned fortune.

"I'm good for now, thanks."

That wasn't entirely honest. *Good* required a plan, but Altiris knew he was a hot meal and at least five hours' sleep from even having the beginnings of one.

Constans nodded earnestly. "If that changes, tell me."

"Why?"

"Because I'll give you some coin." He spoke slowly, carefully, as one burdened with an idiot. "You can then take that 'coin' to a place we call the 'market' – or perhaps a 'tavern' – and buy 'food'."

"I meant, why are you helping me?"

"You thumped my sister." The grin returned. "I've not been able to do that for years."

Altiris winced, sour memories rushing back. "That's not funny."

"Of course not. I'm not a jester." Shoulders still propped against the wall. "But I am your friend. Or I *think* so. I confess, I'm not very good at it. I've not had a lot of practice."

Breathing easier than he had in hours, Altiris offered Constans a smile. "You're doing fine."

"Just stay low, all right?" For the first time, Constans struck a serious tone. "Hollov has a bounty on your head."

"And your father?"

"He was angry last night. This morning? Who knows? He burns bright and brief sometimes."

That much tallied with Josiri's expectations. Maybe he needn't be a fugitive for ever, after all. "So I've heard."

Constans nodded. "Just keep your head down. If you need me, I'll be taking a stroll around the Hayadra Grove at dusk and dawn for the foreseeable future. Try not to be conspicuous."

"I'll do that." Altiris tried to express his gratitude, and came up dry of anything save the simplest words. "Thank you, Constans."

Constans pushed away from the wall and offered a florid bow, seemingly forgetting he didn't have a hat to doff. "What else are friends for?"

It was with no small relief that Hawkin reached the cover of the estate's trees. Sothvane had been alive with Drazina into the early hours, with shackles aplenty and little concern whose wrists they were snapped around. Even if no one recognised her, she'd no papers to present. When she'd gone to Old Eiran for shelter, he'd tried to turn her in.

It was getting so an honest rogue wasn't safe in Tressia.

She needed to get out. Back into the provinces where she could breathe. But that meant help. She daren't go to the Merrow – or rather Shalamoh, as Kasvin had inferred. No telling where she stood after that night in Coventaj. She'd no reason to trust him, and no leverage to make up the shortfall. So instead, she'd come to Woldensend. The Merrow's identity wasn't the only secret Kasvin had let slip.

Though the gardens were strewn with the wreckage of the previous evening's festivities – at Woldensend, every night was party night – there were no conscious revellers in sight. Plenty had passed out under the stars and slumbered through the dawn beside waning bonfires, reeking of wine, swathed in blankets, propped up against the garden's statues and surrounded by broken tableware – the dishevelled and the lamentably underdressed alike. Hawkin could have been three days dead and still threaded that insensate mass without disturbance. Indeed, her lithe fingers turned a tidy profit from purse and pocket long before she reached the garden's inner wall.

From there, a window offered ingress to the house. No guests to be found, and what few servants roamed the halls were no match for a woman who'd learned from the Crowmarket's finest. Nary a one so much as glanced in her direction as she searched the rooms. Servants' passages and connecting doors offered a wealth of evasions. Hawkin employed them all.

Before long, she found herself perched on the edge of a luxurious four-poster bed. Drapes twitched in the breeze from an open window hidden behind. Konor Zarn lay sprawled at her side, fully clothed, entangled in bedclothes and his dark hair spread across a makeup-smeared pillow. Less like a man who'd sought slumber than one who'd fallen into bed and passed out.

Revolting.

Hawkin slid a dagger from her belt. "Lord Zarn?"

An eye fluttered and peered drunkenly into the gloom. "Not now, Nadia. 'm trying to sleep."

A waft of stale wine accompanied the words. Whatever had become of the mysterious Nadia, she was almost certainly better off where she was.

Hawkin pressed the dagger's edge to his throat. "I'm afraid I must insist."

Eyes shot wide. Hawkin muffled a cry of alarm with her other hand. The dagger's twitch sent him back to stillness.

"I don't want to hurt you," whispered Hawkin. "In fact, we're going to be the very best of friends. You'll get me passage out of the city. In return

I'll not tell any of your rich, influential friends how you strangled one of your bedmates. You *do* remember Kasvin?"

Eyes widened further, the handsome face struck with horror. He nodded.

Hawkin counted to three and removed her hand. She left the dagger where it was.

Zarn's throat bobbed. "I . . . I need a drink." He moaned. "This is too much. All too much."

Hawkin's disgust deepened a rung or two. The last thing he needed was a drink. Likely he was still out of his skull from the night before. She slid away from the bed, careful to keep between his sozzled lordship and the chamber door.

"Call for help and you'll die."

Reaching his feet on the third try, Zarn tottered to a dresser and set his hand upon a decanter. Swaying, he wagged a finger back and forth. "I know you, don't I?" he slurred. "Hawkin . . . Hawkin Darrow. That's right. Never did get you into bed, did I?"

Ugh. "My name doesn't matter."

He splashed a measure of brandy into a filthy glass. Rather more across the dresser. "Kasvin . . . Such a pretty lass." He knocked back the contents of the glass and belched. "Such a pretty . . . I'm going to be sick!"

The dagger's threat forgotten, he stumbled towards the drapes.

"No! Wait!"

Cursing under her breath, Hawkin ran after him, free hand clawing for his shoulder. She reached him just as his desperate hand closed around the velvet folds.

Too intent on preventing his escape, Hawkin barely saw Zarn change direction. She certainly had no time to avoid the punch to her gut.

As spasming lungs fought for air, Zarn twisted the dagger from her grip and slammed her against the wall, hand clamped about her throat.

Eyes bereft of both drunkenness and worry bored into hers. "Let's start again, shall we?"

Thirty-Eight

Rosa woke with medicine's bitter aftertaste on a cotton tongue, and the cloying scent of balm thick in her nostrils. Winter sunlight crept about thin drapes. And yet there was shape enough to the bedchamber to warn of the unfamiliar. A low ceiling. Walls decorated with flowing patterns, dark against pale plaster. Furniture full of flowing shapes, where she'd grown up surrounded by stark practicality. And everywhere, the glint of gold. A delicacy of leaf and gilding that perfectly complemented oaken curve, rather than smothered it.

Stomach tight, Rosa reached for the bedcovers. Pain jolted from wrist to shoulder. A dozen other harms screamed for attention from beneath silk bindings. She pinched her eyes shut to hold them at bay.

"You'd do better not to move. The lunassera are skilled, but they're not miracle workers."

That voice. She knew it, but for a frustrating moment couldn't place it.

Haldravord. The eternal from the marketplace. Her saviour.

Rosa forced her eyes open and tracked the voice to its source. There. Between wardrobe and door. Jaw-length auburn hair, marred by a perfect badger stripe above the brow, her shadowed likeness almost twin to Sevaka's, but her gaze cold, clinical. A formal gown of blue silk, though Rosa noted its skirts were slit to the thigh so as not to constrict movement. In Tressia, the dress would have been thought provocative, even unseemly. But it seemed likely she wasn't in the Republic any longer.

Surrendering to the dull ache in her neck, she let her head fall. "Oh. It's you."

"Charming. I *did* save your life."

As Rosa's eyes adapted to the gloom, she decided the other's resemblance to Sevaka was little more than skin deep. There was no laughter in her eyes, and little kindness. "I didn't ask you to."

"Doubly charming." The eternal folded her arms. "My name's Apara Rann."

"Not Kiradin?"

"My mother gave me up to save me being an embarrassment."

All too easy to credit. "But you *are* Sevaka's sister?"

A thin, bittersweet smile. "She bears that burden, yes."

"And you're a kernclaw."

The smile faded. "No more than you're a soul-hungry apparition. The past is the past."

Anger growled. Rosa had trapped herself in the Raven's service through error. No vranakin wore a kernclaw's feathered cloak unwillingly.

"Why save me?"

"Because we're family."

Rosa gave a tired snort. "Family? You almost killed Sevaka."

"And I killed our mother. I took commission for our brother's death, though I didn't know him at the time." Apara folded her arms. "I did all these things, but was responsible for none."

Rosa sneered. "A likely tale."

"Choice is the privilege of wealth, and freedom. Now I have both, I'm trying to do better. Last night marked the first blood I've spilled in many years." Eyes narrowed. "Scorn is apparently my only reward."

Prettily spoken, for a vranakin. But fine words made poor shroud for foul heart. There was an angle to this. Where the crow-born were concerned, there was an angle to everything. "Where am I?"

"Tregard. The Imperial palace."

Rosa fought to hide dismay. No longer a ritual sacrifice, but a hostage against fortune. Thirava's pleasures exchanged for an Empress' cold calculation. She couldn't know how little collateral Rosa was worth. Viktor had proved that at Darkmere. Sevaka might attempt to sway him, but when had Viktor ever yielded to another's will? The brief vigour of waking bled away.

"So you serve the Empress now? I never thought a vranakin could fall further."

"Out of friendship. She's a good woman."

"She's an honourless despot." Old memories gave the accusation bite. War without declaration. Poison offered beneath a friendly smile. The Eastshires stolen. "Sarans were ever thus."

Apara drew closer, the first flicker of anger in her tone. "The Hadari Empire was falling into ruin, bled dry by decades of war. Now even the poor have food and shelter. Commoners are treated as something more than hands apt to hold a spear. When I first arrived, the only law was royal decree. Now magistrates enforce justice for pauper and privileged alike." She halted, composure returning. "If this is tyranny, I wish it had come to Tressia long ago."

Rosa scowled, reminded of what the Republic claimed to be, and seldom was. "It doesn't change her past."

"She's made mistakes," Apara said. "She's trying to move beyond them. That's all any of us can do."

It wasn't so much the words that struck a chord with Rosa, as the tone. They mirrored the mood in which she'd recently driven many a chisel into undeserving timber. She resented both. "So I'm to be your redemption? A path to divine reward?"

"I've seen gods up close. I want no redemption they can offer. You're alive. Don't overthink it."

Truth, or a sop to defuse argument? Sifting Apara's claims for verity was an effort fast sliding beyond reach. All Rosa wanted to do was sleep. "Am I a prisoner?"

Apara hesitated. "In truth, I'm not sure. Bringing you here has strained the Empress' friendliness." She twitched a shrug. "She's not fond of you. Something about broken truces and the slaughter of routed warriors. I didn't care to ask. I've no right to judge another's past. More than that, I've committed no few transgressions along the way. I'm to be called to account once I leave you. It may be I'm no longer welcome in the palace, or even the city."

Rosa found no lie behind the words, only melancholy. "Then why bring me here at all?"

"Because you needed help, and I didn't know where else you might find it in time. You've already slept for most of a day. The lunassera gave you an even chance of never waking up. You're tougher than you look."

Rosa's suspicions ebbed. Tiredness was part of it – sleep called her with every passing moment. But it wasn't the whole. She felt moved to offer something in return.

"She speaks of you . . . Sevaka, I mean. Not often, and never for long, but you're in her thoughts. You should see her."

Apara turned away. "I haven't the right. Not after what I did."

Rosa snorted. For the first time, they'd something in common. "For a woman who wants me to leave the past *in* the past, you're very attached to your own."

"So Josiri tells me."

"Josiri Trelan? How do you know him?"

Apara flinched. "We speak, from time to time."

Her reaction betrayed a loose thread, but where did it lead? "Another *friend*?"

"No. He's too close to Droshna for that."

A face that had thus far only flirted with anger now tightened with hatred. Of a sort Rosa had seen gazing back at her from a dozen clumsy sculptures. "Why do you hate Viktor?"

Apara reached for the door. "There are four guards in the hallway, and others beyond the window. If you offer any trouble, they'll kill you."

"That's probably wise, as I'll surely kill the Empress if I see her." Rosa forced the snarl from her voice. "Tell me about Viktor. Please."

Apara paused, hand on the doorframe. "Because he smothered me in shadow and made me his puppet. He broke me into pieces I was a year putting back together. Because even now I wake from nightmares, terrified my thoughts are not my own, but his." Turning, she shot Rosa a defiant glare. "I don't expect you to believe me."

The gaping hole Viktor had opened in Rosa's memory loomed larger than ever. No matter what she'd done since Darkmere – no matter how many sculptures she struck, how far she ran or the causes she threw herself into, there was no closing it. "I believe you," she said softly.

Apara held her gaze a moment longer, then left the room without a word.

"What were you thinking? Bringing that woman here?"

Melanna seldom employed that particular tone. It withered wayward courtiers and broke the stubbornest of warriors. Servants described it as being fit to rust gold, though never in her presence. She felt diminished whenever she used it, as if it were a concession to failures past – failures she should have recognised, and avoided. But sometimes, it was the only tone that would serve.

She needn't have bothered, for Apara stood her ground with the calm, polite certainty of a woman who found no fault with recent actions. "Should I have let her die?"

Yes. A woman who broke a flag of truce, as Orova had done at Vrasdavora, deserved to die. She who'd torn a fleeing army to ruin at Govanna Field deserved to suffer. How swiftly years of tolerance fell away. How quickly aspirations became lies. The anger – that howling, hot pressure about Melanna's heart – belonged to a vanished princessa, not the Empress. Aware that she fought a losing battle with composure, Melanna stared down at the thin desk and its bundle of interrupted paperwork.

"And the rest? Impersonating a lunassera?" Her voice surely carried beyond the chamber's thin walls to Immortals beyond. In the throne room it would have echoed like thunder. She lowered her voice. "Killing Silsarian warriors? My subjects?"

"Thirava doesn't hold them so. Just as he doesn't hold your laws to be his."

Apara's reply maddened precisely because of its truth. "I suppose you expect me to treat Orova as hospitality demands?"

"That's your decision, my Empress." Still, Apara offered nothing but calm. "She need only recover enough to manage the passage of Otherworld, and I can return her to Tressia. Keep her in shackles until then, if that is your will."

"I should have her executed, and you cast from the city."

"Then perhaps you and Thirava have more in common than any of us believed."

A smile softened the words, Apara plainly believing herself out of danger. Temptation flared to prove her wrong – punishment for thinking to know an Empress' mind. Melanna's father had done similar with his closest friends on many occasions. But she was trying so hard not to be her father, save in ways Kaila might respect.

"You presume a great deal on our friendship."

"I know. And I'm sorry."

"But you'd do it again?"

Apara hesitated. "Yes. You've set me a very clear example, *savim*."

The unabashed flattery dispersed anger's dregs. "Apparently that example extends to forgiving those who seek my death."

The smile broadened. "Can there be more decisive way to prove yourself her better?"

"You're speaking like a courtier."

"I've been practising."

"It *wasn't* a compliment." Melanna sighed and sank into a chair. "Why didn't you ask me first?"

"I was worried you'd forbid me," said Apara. "I imagine that's why Haldrane didn't tell you she was still alive."

"Haldrane?" Melanna threw her a sharp glance. "The river of my days is muddied enough without those I trust keeping secrets."

Distaste chased the smile from Apara's lips. "Do you suppose Haldrane has ever told you everything? I'd cousins like him. Full of preening cleverness that little reflected their ability."

Melanna shook her head, reminded again how little love was lost between thief and spymaster. "His ability is sound and, though I regret the necessity, there are many things I'm better off not knowing. An Empress' hands must be clean, even when they're slippery with blood." And there was already so much blood on her hands. "But it wasn't Haldrane I meant."

Apara nodded contritely.

Melanna sighed. "So long as the Lady Orova remains confined, I will visit no harm upon her. If she sets foot beyond her quarters without leave, she dies. Am I understood?"

Apara dipped a curtsey. "Of course, my Empress."

She retreated from the chamber, leaving Melanna alone with the morning's unfinished business. She sat in silence, thoughts not on the stack of reports and missives, but on Apara's deeds. Leniency was a fine, if dangerous, trait in an Empress. Had she relented because Orova was deserving? Out of Apara's friendship? Or simply to prove herself a better woman than once she'd been? Would it have changed her reckoning had Apara acted thus against someone other than Thirava? If she'd shed Icansae blood, and not Silsarian? Melanna found the lack of ready answer more unsettling than the inciting deed. The infuriating dichotomy of rule: that an Empress must be certain in all things, save her own mind.

A knock came at the door.

Melanna glanced up. "Yes?"

Tesni entered, a sheaf of papers in her hand. "Delivered a few minutes ago, *savim*. I apologise for keeping you waiting, but it seemed a conversation better left undisturbed."

Melanna sighed a smile and took the papers. "You'll flourish here."

Tesni bowed, her armour rustling. "Thank you, my Empress."

"Wait, please. They need only a signature." Returning to the desk, she armed herself with quill and blotter. Most days, a poor substitute for sword and shield, but not today. "Magister Savra seeks profit by the law. Now he'll see it from the other side."

A scritch of the pen, and it was done. Disappointing that a man she'd personally appointed had misused his office, but he was one among dozens. And now, a magistrate no more.

Tesni frowned. "Forgiveness, Empress, but is this so important?"

"You think I'm wasting my time?"

"No, Empress."

Melanna shook her head at the unconvincing reply. "I know this is a small thing. But even in unhappy times, small things count. They make the world better, even if only by an inch." She stared off across the room. "It's a notion alien to my royal cousins. They see only how the Empire may serve them. Do you think me mad?"

"No, Empress."

Tesni's second reply convinced no more than the first. Melanna silently forgave her and busied herself with sealing wax. For generations, Immortals had enjoyed the privilege of reflected authority, elevated by royal service. That too was fading as the nature of Imperial power grew more diffuse. Tesni, denied the right to an Immortal's scales for so long by the misfortune of being born a woman, perhaps felt as one might when arriving at a banquet only to discover the choicest offerings already devoured.

A press of the signet ring – her father's owl, it would always be his, even though it was now hers – and the task was done. "See that this is delivered to Vindicator Javeri before noon."

Tesni took the letter and withdrew, and Melanna was again left alone with her papers. Score upon score of small things to be attended, and the course of Empire improved, inch by inch. Better for her sanity that it was so, for larger events were spiralling into civil war. Worse, she was alone. Ashana forbidden to her. Aeldran gone. Haldrane and Apara had both deceived her, if by differing degrees, and would likely do so again. Oh, servants and courtiers and Immortals all remained and would serve until their dying breath, but it wasn't the same.

Despite the hour, she found herself nodding, the black squiggles of ink dancing in and out of focus. Too many nights broken by worry. Too many days drowning beneath it.

Melanna touched her eyes closed. Just for a moment, but that moment stretched out into indulgence. So much simpler in the darkness. So much quieter.

As she dozed in and out, a new scent graced her nostrils. The sweet, musky fragrance of springtime and fresh blooms, undercut by a heady, indescribable yearning. Bright blossoms in the dark.

The scent of Fellhallow.

She started awake into a room overrun with briar and black roses. The door was lost beneath a curtain of vines; the garden window at full hinge, the drapes rippling in the breeze. Melanna sprang to her feet, scattering papers onto a floor drowning in autumn leaves.

"Guards!"

What she'd meant as shout emerged as wheeze, her lungs overcome by Fellhallow's heady perfume. The same perfume that saw young gallants lured beneath the forest's treacherous eaves by Jack's beguiling, thorn-wreathed daughters.

{{Hush.}} Jack's voice crackled at her shoulder. Air turned damp and musky with his presence. His angular, jagged shadow bled across the floor, raising gooseflesh where it touched her skin. A gnarled, woody finger brushed her cheek. {{Beset on all sides. Abandoned by your allies. No one else loves you. Only I.}}

Heart racing, Melanna spun around. "How are you here? I burned the wood!"

Jack's rustling laughter filled every corner of the room. {{The forest always returns.}}

He reached to embrace her, green eyes blazing in the scarred mask, ragged cloak outspread.

Melanna's trembling fingers snatched a poker from the fire. "Guards!"

Darkness swallowed her up.

She struck the floor with enough force to jar every bone in her body, a gasping cry spilling free. Disoriented and sore, Melanna dragged herself to a sitting position, eyes darting. No vines. No briars. The papers she'd thought disturbed sitting in a stack upon the desk. The windows closed.

A dream. It had all been a dream.

The door burst inward. The room filled with golden scales.

"Empress!" Tavar Rasha stooped, his grey beard scarcely concealing a frown. "Are you hurt?"

"My pride alone," she replied, thick with chagrin. How foolish she must have seemed.

And yet . . .

The scent lingered, or something like to it. Soft. Tantalising. Intoxicating.

With Rasha's help, she stood. Something crunched beneath her foot. A dry, golden leaf, long out of season.

Ignoring the jasaldar's restraining hand, she strode to the window and stared out across the gardens. In the middle distance, beyond topiarised hedges and lawns bereft of snow, the soot-blackened timbers of the old wood were thick with green shoots.

Astridas, 9th Day of Dawntithe

The covetous embrace treachery for a handful
of coins, the generous for the greater good,
the righteous out of principle, and the wicked
because they know no other way.

Suspect everyone, and you will not be disappointed.

attributed to Rashat Tirane,
prior to his brother's untimely death

Thirty-Nine

Akamha stared out in the grey noon, resentful at a fate that had assigned him to Triumphal Gate on the coldest day of the newborn year. The snow had melted but hissing rain bestowed its chill through oft-patched furs and faded silks. The barbican guard house lay close enough to scent tantalising woodsmoke. But duty was duty, especially on Triumphal Gate.

Beneath the rampart, the flagstones of the Golden Way rippled south, broad and arrow-straight through the sodden fields beyond Tregard's dizzying walls. The road upon which Alfric Saran had first entered the city and claimed it for Empire.

Little of the original wall still stood, replaced stone by stone by a man determined to erase the city's Tressian heritage. Triumphal Gate was the road by which emperors returned in victory or defeat. Those same emperors and many more watched over it in death, from gilded statues thrice Akamha's own height. Attire reflected the afterlife to which they were held to have departed: jewelled robes for the quietude of Evermoon, bird-helmed equerries' hunting garb for sombre Eventide. To stand sentinel atop the parapet was to stand with the emperors of old. A rare and honourable duty when the sun shone and the whorling silver let into sandstone gleamed like a thing alive.

Not so much in the rain.

He halted beside the unlit ghostfire brazier and envied its sloping roof, far more effective at fending off the rain than his own sodden cloak. It and the many thousands of others scattered through Tregard's streets looked out of place, dark and functional where so much else in the city was pale and beautiful. But Akamha understood. He'd been in the Emperor's vanguard at the Rappadan, when revenants had come wailing out of the mists. If ugliness held back the Raven's servants and the dead when dusk fell, he welcomed it.

"A quiet day." Cadaman, havildar of the watch, nodded greeting as he reached Akamha's side. "Nothing good comes of quiet days."

Akamha stared down at the sparsely occupied roadway. A handful of wagons. Two dozen riders. A single shuffling column of villagers, wrapped tight and heads lowered against the rain. The distance, stolen by murk, offered little beyond the broad-shouldered statue of Kai Saran – the latest and loneliest of the road's guardians, for he'd no mirror on the western side to keep him company.

It had been worse at dawn and would be again at dusk, the broad archway queued solid for a half-mile. But with market well underway, it was hardly unusual for things to be so lifeless.

He shook his head. "The Goddess owes us some quiet."

"Ashana owes us nothing." Disapproval shone through Cadaman's careful speech. A gloved palm pressed against his leather breastplate, and the moon pendant worn beneath. "We *earned* this."

No mistaking the rebuke. There was status to guarding Triumphal Gate, if not as much as wearing an Immortal's scales. Marked them out as more than tithed men, whose spears paid a chieftain's debt of service.

Akamha set his back to the parapet and stared across the smoke-wreathed, jumbled streets to the golden smudge of the Imperial Palace. "How did the Empress earn that? She's lost every war she's ever fought."

Cadaman scowled. "Hush. Never know when an icularis might be listening."

Akamha swallowed. The glance left and right along the parapet came as hurried instinct. No one in sight but his fellow sentinels, for all *that* proved. "All I mean is it'd do her good to stand a watch in the rain."

The older man shook his head. "She did."

"Very amusing."

"Then it's Jasaldar Tarbarit's joke. Says she held watch right where you're standing, two winters back – all the way through the close of the year. All very secret. Tarbarit found out by accident." Cadaman grinned. "Took a liking to her smile and, on the last day of her stint, followed her halfway across the city, looking for the courage to make something of it. The sight of her falling into the company of Immortals near carried him off to the Raven. Spent days fretting about everything he'd said and done in her presence."

Akamha grunted, unable to picture her staid Imperial majesty offering a smile, and adopted a gruff imitation of the jasaldar's voice. "Wasn't a spear-maid rejected me, but the Empress herself." He spoke normally once more. "Makes a good story."

"I believe it. My Arina says she saw her in the marketplace just yesterday. No finery, few guards, and the princessa trailing along behind." He shrugged. "Others have claimed similar."

"Why would the Empress do such a thing?"

"I don't know," he conceded. "Her father never did, nor *his* father."

"Perhaps she's mad. Perhaps—"

A warning cry rang out further along the wall. Grey shapes gathered in the distance where sparse light yielded to rain's shroud. A rank of horsemen, advancing knee to knee along the Golden Way. The rank became a column. A hundred. Two hundred. Thousands, with spears close behind.

Now the cold came from within, not without. "Prince Aeldran's army?"

"They'd ride with banners unfurled, even in this," Cadaman bit out.

And there'd have been warning. Consort or no, tradition had to be obeyed, and no army set foot in Tregard without the throne's blessing. But even if the riders came with malice there'd have been warning from the sentinel posts along the road. That there hadn't been . . .

Trumpets blared. The leading riders quickened to a gallop. Those caught before them on the road broke apart and scrambled clear. The first shields came close enough for recognition. The Redsigor stag on its rust-covered field. One man, too slow, vanished beneath hooves.

Along the wall, another sentinel hauled on a watch-bell's cord. Chimes tolled warning high above the barbican. The rampart shuddered with the first rumbling groan of the gate mechanism; running feet on treacherous stairs as archers exchanged the warmth of the barracks for the outer air.

"This is madness," breathed Akamha.

Cadaman stared at the approaching horsemen. "Better theirs than ours. The gate will be sealed long before they get here. Foolish way to die." He jerked a thumb back towards the barbican. "Find the jasaldar. You know how he is about surprises."

"Yes, *savir.*"

Akamha ran for the barbican.

The clock, as dilapidated as everything in the squalid house, chimed noon. Cardivan raised his glass to the south in silent toast and took a mouthful of tarakeet. Early in the day to indulge one's vices, but bravery should always be recognised. And there'd be courage at Triumphal Gate soon enough ... even if not all of it was harnessed to a fit and proper cause.

Brackar entered without knocking, a habit forgiven for faithful service. Arrayed in a champion's golden finery for the first time since they'd arrived in Tregard weeks before, he offered a low bow. "Haldrane just passed the front gate. He's not alone. Should we hold him?"

Most men would have hesitated to suggest violence against the spymaster, much less offer to initiate it. But then, Brackar wasn't most men. A benefit of recruiting from places others did not. In Brackar's case, the jails of Tamrakash, and with the oft-broken nose to prove it. What he lacked in refinement he compensated for with unflagging loyalty. And, of course, a talent for focused violence. Naturally, Thirava disliked him. Considered him a brute unfit for a monarch's favour.

But Thirava had lessons to learn in the coming days – his proper place, among them.

Cardivan shook his head. "Let him come. Let them all come. Enjoy the moment."

Innate caution overwhelmed a frisson of delight as Brackar withdrew. No matter how carefully laid, plans could still go awry.

But where to receive his guest? From the chair in the raised bay window? Yes. That would do nicely. It would force all to look up, and render Cardivan himself in pleasing silhouette. For all that Ashana had her uses, what happened in the shadows was ever more powerful than the light.

But even as Cardivan took his place before the lace curtains, doubt assailed his heart. Even though all that could have been done had been done, there was always the possibility he'd fallen prey to arrogance. That the pieces he'd set into motion across the board would move in a manner other than the one he'd decreed. That was always the danger. Especially when opposed by a man like Haldrane, in whom ignorance – or the mere appearance of the same – shared uncanny likeness.

He took another gulp of tarakeet. The hot, sweet rush of liquor settled his nerves.

Too late for doubts. Enjoy the moment.

Haldrane burst into the room, a half-dozen city wardens and two robed and hooded icularis at his back. All were armed. Brackar hadn't mentioned that, but it wasn't unexpected. Brackar's own presence was inevitable – as was him taking up position, at his master's side – but no other of Cardivan's men entered the room. That spoke of more wardens outside and prisoners taken. Haldrane was little given to half measures.

"Cardivan Tirane." There was no friendliness in Haldrane's voice, but even now the words held a hint of sour glee. He, too, was enjoying the moment. One of them was deceived. But which? "In the name of the Empress, you'll accompany me to the palace for what I'm sure will be a brief imprisonment and overdue execution."

"On what grounds?"

"Your son leads an army against the city," said Haldrane. "Your doing, I believe."

Even now he distanced himself from conspiracy. After so many years a deceiver, did the man even know whose cause he served?

"I'm sure what I claim will be of no account." Bitterness came easily. Cardivan had supped of it long enough to savour the taste. "Do I take it that you've reneged on your promise to ensure Triumphal Gate stands open in greeting?"

Haldrane drew back his hood and offered a sly smile. "I recall no such promise. The men you sent to open the gate met with unfortunate accidents before dawn. And here you stand, trapped within the city while your son lays siege? Unfortunate."

Cardivan hung his head, hiding the emotion of the moment. "Why, Haldrane? You and I could have made this Empire great once more. The Empress is weak."

Haldrane stepped closer, palm resting on the sword at his waist. "The

Empress wearies of bloodshed. It's the only reason you're still alive. You had to be tempted to audacity. Arrogance is more dangerous than a sword, my king. But it kills far slower. I'll see to it."

"Arrogance. Where would we be without it? Nothing else drives men so readily to ruin and rule."

Haldrane spread his hands. "The Gwyraya Hadar will tolerate much from their own, but to move openly against the throne, without issuing challenge? None will stand with you now."

Cardivan sighed. "You're a clever man, Haldrane. Perhaps the cleverest." Raising his head, he met the other's dark gaze, and at last set free the grin that had been building since the first chime of bells. "But I don't think you're clever enough."

The gate mechanism, loud even over the clamour of bells and shouts, went silent in the same moment Akamha wrenched open the barbican trapdoor, the distinctive rumble of pulleys and gears fading away.

He shinned down the ladder, landing awkwardly in the outer guard post.

Empty. No sign of life between the simple hearth and the rows of bunks. Not even Melindri, who could always be relied upon to answer any summons behind everyone else.

"Jasaldar?"

Strike of hooves challenged chiming bells. Akamha glanced through an arrowslit. The riders were almost at the walls. Arrows whistled and holes appeared in the column, motes among a dust storm come to sweep into the city. But the gate would hold them.

As Akamha turned, a dark trail caught his eye. He sifted a scent from the air he should have noticed from the first. Blood. Leading towards the winding room door. The manner of trail heels might make when a body was dragged.

As he crossed to the winding room door, the gate's silence took on new meaning. A full half-minute for the mechanism to do its work. How long since he'd left the parapet?

Akamha drew his sword and wrenched open the door.

The winding room occupied the remainder of that floor, a broad high-ceiling space easily four times the size of Akamha's tiny house in

Tregard's Old Quarter. The gate's mechanisms filled much of that scaffolded space, a web of pulleys, counterweights and gears that came and went through floor and ceiling like the threads of some vast, intricate loom. What little space remained was full of the living and the dead.

The dead, with the pallor of fresh corpses. Melindri. Kovir. Others. All with gaping red ruin at the throat. The living, an even dozen in a mix of sentinel's garb and travellers' cloth, with naked blades in hand and hooded, unfriendly eyes. A slash of a sword, and a counterweight plunged into the darkness below. An unnecessary flourish to gears jammed tight with spar and steel.

"Akamha." Jasaldar Tarbarit, silks stained with blood not his own, turned about. "You should have stayed on the wall."

At last, Akamha found his voice. "What is this, jasaldar?"

"The start of something overdue."

It wasn't much of an answer, but then Akamha hadn't needed one. The winding room offered an embarrassment of explanation. The creak of foot on floorboard behind warned of what would follow. And yet he knew only anger. Close enough to courage in a man's final moments.

"Saranal Aregnum!"

The words more howl than speech, Akamha hurled himself at Tarbarit.

Forty

Surrounded as it was by taller buildings, the narrow balcony of Apara's house offered no view of the commotion. Instinct cautioned her to head back inside, pour something sublime from the carefully stocked liquor cabinet and leave events be. The timbre was too familiar, for all that she'd never heard its like in Tregard.

But that wasn't how it worked, was it? Tregard was her home. Either everything was her business, or nothing was.

With a last mournful glance at her lace-edged gown – bought with proceeds from a recent commission and first worn today – she sought higher vantage.

Drainpipe, rain-sodden trellis and a semi-dignified, dress-tearing scramble across contoured tiles brought her atop a neighbour's roof. Four storeys, where her own modest dwelling was two, and a view clear into the heart of Tregard's Old Quarter.

"No ... This isn't happening."

The streets were crowded with bodies. Most fleeing, some dead. Those advancing carried the rust shields of Silsaria. No ... Redsigor, though the difference mattered little. Apara watched, shivering with an echo of cold her eternal constitution no longer truly suffered, as a coordinated charge of riders and shieldsmen overran a knot of warriors in Rhalesh green. Further south, smoke gathered above the warriors' lodgings. And scarcely visible through the rain, the looming bulwark of Triumphal Gate, a vast Redsigoran banner streaming from the inner rampart.

Screams rose skyward. Bells fell silent, replaced by the screech of steel and the cries of battle.

With them came realisation. Cold hadn't set her shivering. Nor fear. "How dare you!" she screamed to an uncaring sky. "I was happy here!"

Go inside. Better yet, leave. Be happy somewhere else.

That was the old Apara talking. The one in thrall to the Crowmarket. Who'd stolen and killed for the pettiest scores. Who'd found strength almost too late. It wasn't the woman who'd saved a sister-in-law she didn't know. It wasn't the woman who counted an Empress as a friend.

Four storeys below, a Rhalesh warrior died beneath a Silsarian sword. The woman and child he'd sheltered fled deeper into the alley, unaware of the dead end.

No one to save them.

Only ... that wasn't true, was it? There was still a choice.

"Oh, this is going to hurt."

Apara stepped off the roof. The fall gave just enough time for regret to blossom into terror.

Bereft of warning or an eternal's constitution, the Silsarian crumpled beneath her with a dull *huff* and a crackle of breaking bone.

Impact drove the breath from Apara's lungs, leaving her no means to howl the pain of dislocated knee and snapped ankle. Her head chimed against flagstone, adding nausea and blurred vision to the dizziness of the fall. The woman dragged her daughter close, a hand across her eyes.

Already reknitting, Apara's ankle held as she struggled upright. Not so the knee, which folded, tearing muscle and ligament anew. She bit into her hand to muffle the scream, then jack-knifed onto her side. Gripping her lower thigh with both hands, she braced her thumbs against the offending kneecap. A scraping, wrenching shudder, another scream. It snapped back into place.

Not as bad as the aftermath of her teenaged fall from Vordal Tower – she'd barely clung to consciousness as Erad had relocated the bone – but bad enough.

The next time she tried to stand, both legs held. "Not my finest idea."

The woman backed away, the girl shoved behind her. "I pray you, serathi, spare my daughter."

The woman thought her a serathi? Apara stifled a gasp of unintended mirth. But then she was paler of feature than most in Tregard, and she *had* plunged from the sky. Speaking Tressian hadn't helped. Perhaps the woman could be forgiven for overlooking the lack of wings.

Stepping over the Silsarian's corpse, Apara stumbled to the alley's end. The fighting had moved on. "Get to the palace, *savim*," she replied, this time careful to speak in the Rhalesh tongue. "You'll be safe there."

The woman nodded, but made no move.

"Now!" shouted Apara.

The other flinched and fled the alley, girl in tow. Apara sank against the wall, memory of pain now more pressing than its present. Something else buzzed beneath it. Welcome and unfamiliar. Pride. The same pride she'd felt during Rosa's rescue. Seemed heroics were intoxicating. Worth a little pain. Worth a ruined dress.

"I just know I'll regret this."

She picked up the Silsarian's sword anyway.

The icularis cut down the two city wardens immediately to their front before the victims realised their loyalty lay elsewhere. Others perished in the same moment Haldrane spun around, his own sword whispering free too late and his habitual smugness given way to a mask of terror.

True to Cardivan's expectation, the spymaster didn't hesitate. An icularis collapsed, hand at a bloody throat. The second managed three whole parries against his former master's onslaught until he lay dead, run through as cleanly as a pig on a spit.

But Haldrane had made the mistake of setting his back to Brackar. Closing meaty hands about the spymaster's wrist and neck, the champion slammed him into the wall. Haldrane grunted as he dislodged plaster, leaving pale trails across his dark robes. Twice more, and the sword dropped from his grasp.

"Enough, Brackar," said Cardivan.

After a fourth collision – Brackar never being one to leave a task half done – he spun Haldrane about. Murderous eyes glowered from beneath a mottled, swollen brow.

Cardivan stepped closer. "We were discussing arrogance, I think. An organisation is only as strong as the men in its service. I've taken the trouble to discover which of yours value coin over loyalty." He glanced at the dead icularis. "I hope you weren't close."

"Your death will come an inch at a time," gasped Haldrane, the words whistling from the loss of a tooth.

Cardivan shook his head. "My fate – anyone's fate – is no longer yours to command. You can expect no rescue from your men outside. By now, they're already dead."

A glare was his only reply.

Cardivan drew a dagger from concealment in his sleeve. "You've expended so much effort encouraging me to indiscretion that you never questioned whether or not I could do it without you. Do you know how many swords I have in the city? The palace? You've been blind, Haldrane. And you chose it for yourself."

The spymaster went rigid as the dagger punched low in his belly, then jerked as Cardivan twisted the blade clear. But for Brackar's grip, he'd have fallen. The lack of a scream was somehow disappointing, and Cardivan considered indulging a second thrust in hopes of coaxing one free.

Deciding against, he stepped back. The gut wound was a slow, painful demise. Not quite the death of inches Haldrane had promised, but enough to serve as down-payment on decades of indignities. A second would only speed matters along.

Besides, the hollow look in Haldrane's eyes was worth a dozen screams.

"The Empress is as bad," said Cardivan. "So busy tearing down traditions, she's not thought about those she destroys alongside. I'm not saying it was easy. Not everyone will take my coin, and few of those who do hold any love for me. But they hate her more."

Haldrane said nothing. A breathless, sagging bundle in Brackar's grasp. Beaten. Pathetic. Cardivan grimaced. *This* was the man he'd been afraid of all these years?

Stooping, he wiped his dagger and hand clean on the robes of a slain icularis. The murmur of the city gave way to new sounds. The tolling of bells. Hoofbeats on flagstones. Raised voices. Screams. At last.

"You hear that?" he said. "My son is already in the city. Though you won't live to see my coronation, you might last long enough to see your precious Empress' head on a spike."

"No," gasped Haldrane.

"Come now, this will be over by nightfall." He withdrew to the window and drew aside the veil. Between the garden's unkemptness and the rain, he saw nothing of the streets. "I'm sure you can hang on that long."

"Not . . . what I . . . meant." Haldrane's voice hardened, the threadiness of recent moments banished. "You will never . . . wear the crown."

Brackar bellowed in pain. Cardivan spun around in time to see Haldrane lurching towards him, one hand pressed to his wound. The spymaster's gaze was no longer hollow, but determined.

Mouth dry, Cardivan stumbled, hands upraised to ward off the inevitable blow. He quite forgot the dagger in his trembling hand, and that Haldrane was dying.

"Guards!" he screamed. "Guards!"

Voices sounded on the landing. Haldrane shot him a look of pure contempt and veered towards the window. At the last moment, he toppled. A pane of glass shattered beneath him, and then he was gone into the grey afternoon.

Still shaking with fear and humiliation, Cardivan reached his feet as the first guard entered the room. Brackar was on hands and knees, gasping for breath but unharmed.

"Well?" howled Cardivan. "Get after him!"

Thief's instinct kept Apara to the shadows. Eternal or no, she wasn't a creature of the battlefield. She'd be a burden on a shield wall, and it on her. And besides, what few defences she saw of any kind seldom outlasted the sight. Tregard had relied too much on its walls and the promise of warning. Its garrison, thinned first by Govanna's aftermath and again by the blockade at Mergadir, had little chance of rising to the day's bloody challenge.

What Rhalesh warriors remained fought to the last. Street corners and alley mouths were thick with waterlogged dead. That emerald green tallied equal with Silsarian rust spoke of oaths fulfilled to the last breath, and heroes forgotten in the rain.

But Thirava had more men. And numbers mattered.

By the time Apara made it halfway to the palace, fractious battlefronts had disintegrated further, and Tregard's winding streets were full of triumphant men seeking plunder. Bodies of traders and travellers, householders and servants joined those of the warriors who'd perished in their defence. Children cried out for slain parents. The wounded crawled for the shelter of doorways.

Tregard, the heart of the Silver Kingdom – a city where Apara Rann had finally found a measure of peace – was drowning in spite and blood. Her heart broke to see it thus.

And here, in narrow roads similar to those in which Apara had learnt a vranakin's trade and yet so different, she found her hunting ground. In her wake, she left a trail of dead Silsarians who'd seen no danger in the bedraggled woman with tangled hair and a torn, filthy dress.

Those she saved from the sacking, Apara hurried to safer streets, or else hammered on nearby doors until frightened souls within offered sanctuary. Those moments were the only shafts of light in a miserable, soul-wrenching day. She found no joy in the killing, deserved though it was, but nor did she shrink from it.

As she reached the Great East Road, she spied Silsarians moving with purpose through the maze of broken traders' barrows. Four in all, and with a lumbering brute in a champion's finery at their head. Apara knew his sort, though they'd never met. An enforcer, moving with a bully's confidence. She read it in the sidelong glances of those who advanced in his shadow, as wary of their ally as whatever waited elsewhere. They crossed the line of dead, the brute casting glances up and down the street, then ran on into the opposite alleyway.

Apara halted in the shadow of a minaret and peeled matted hair from her eyes. Four trained warriors? Her stolen blade had long since lost its edge, and the day had offered plentiful reminder that the sword wasn't *really* her weapon. For all that they healed fast, the wounds still hurt. But the brute ... He'd the look of a man on the hunt. A man who dealt only in spoils that screamed.

Hefting her blunted sword, Apara ran across the flooded street.

A high-pitched howl from deeper in the alley set her running, the torn sole of her left shoe slapping at her heel. Unable to stop as she rounded the corner, she all but collided with the rearmost Silsarian. She twisted mid-stride and thrust. Steel grated against golden scale, and he fell. The blade, trapped between his ribs, ripped free of her grasp.

Warned by his dying scream, the others turned from the robed figure lying in the gutter, waters swirling pink as they trickled away from the unmoving form.

The brute spat into the rain. Lips twisted to a grin beneath his lumpen, disjointed nose. "And what are you meant to be?"

Apara recognised him now. Part of Cardivan's entourage. His champion, Brackar.

The others laughed, and stepped as far apart as the alleyway allowed. They the flanks, the brute to the centre.

Apara stared up into the rain. Grey clouds stared back. She wasn't sure what she expected to see. Maybe the goddess who'd made her eternal, witnessing what she did with the gift.

"I'm still working that out."

Planting her foot on the Silsarian's corpse, she ripped the sword free.

The rightmost Silsarian screamed a challenge and flung himself forward. Apara met his sword with her own and punched him full in the face. The close-set metal helm buckled under splitting knuckles. Cartilage crunched and he dropped, blood slicking his armour. The leftmost slipped on the treacherous flagstones and died with Apara's sword in his throat.

A shadow blotted out grey skies.

Apara barely felt Brackar's sword punch through her chest. It was when the point burst from her back, the hilt flush against her ruined dress, that pain found her. A lung spasming and sucking, she collapsed. Her sword fell from numbed fingers. Every breath tasted of iron. Every motion was exquisite agony. Worse than the dislocated knee. Worse even than when Hawkin Darrow had knifed her, years before.

"You'll never be anything now," growled Brackar.

Letting go his sword, he turned back towards his erstwhile victim, who in the confusion had crawled a pace deeper into the alley.

Apara closed her eyes and forgot the pain. Fingers splayed against the wall, she regained her feet, inch by painful inch.

"I don't . . . know," she gasped. "I think I'm . . . just getting started."

Brackar paled and stumbled away. It had been long enough now that he had to have realised she wasn't bleeding. For a bully, even one a good head taller than her, that would always be enough.

Slack-jawed and eyes wide with horror, Brackar turned tail. Hurtling past his victim, he vanished deeper into the alley.

Somehow, there was more triumph in his flight than in his confederates' death.

Apara's flesh only reluctantly gave up its grip on the sword, but she somehow got it free without screaming fit to alert every Silsarian for three streets. Black blood hissing silver along the blade, she cast it to the ground.

"Ow! Ow! Ow!" she swallowed hard, urging the pain to fade. It did so with uttermost reluctance. "Damn it!"

Brackar's victim reached up a trembling hand and drew back his hood. Mangled features stared out into the alley's sodden gloom. "Rann?"

"Haldrane?" She staggered closer, stride complicated as the ailing shoe at last gave up its sole. "You look terrible."

Bright blood trickling from his lips, he gave a wheezing, pained laugh. "I'll ... hold the Raven back long enough for you to get me ... to the palace."

She knelt beside him, at last noting the belly wound beneath his hand. Black robes had hidden the blood from a distance, but there was no disguising it now, nor the pallor to his face, or the sickly copper smell.

"You need a lunassera's care," she replied. "I'll call the mists, get you to Mooncourt."

"No time. Empress ... in danger."

"In the palace? It's the safest place she could be."

He laughed again, bleaker this time. "Enough that I've erred today. Don't ... follow my example."

Something in his tone set a chill racing along Apara's spine. "What did you do?"

Haldrane's chin sunk to his chest. "It's only treason ... if Cardivan loses. If he wins, he's Emperor. One house falls ... another rises. Tirane Aregnum."

She glowered at the evasion. "What did you do?"

But Haldrane's wits had flown, a stuttering, febrile chest betraying that the rest of him was soon to follow. Apara stared down, frustration and sorrow battling for mastery. Both yielded to rising fear. The House of Saran was more than Melanna.

Kaila. Was Cardivan so determined to rule that he'd harm a child?

Of course he'd do it. Brides of Brief Moonlight. Women and girls wed long enough for the husband to steal their dowry, and then the knife. A man like Cardivan wouldn't even blink at the prospect, not with the Imperial throne as the prize.

Her last weariness falling away into a bit of black, bitter wrath. Apara hauled the dying Haldrane onto her shoulder.

Forty-One

"Empress."

Elim Jorcari bore himself with a warrior's pride. The stiffness of back and shoulders that age could not entirely unmake. The eyes that promised defiance or respect according to status. A man, in other words, unimpressed by the throne room's splendour, or the stern visages of the golden godly statues staring down from on high. That he wore civilian silks and not armour – well cut, though the cloth was not the finest – struck a jarring note. But not so jarring as the rigidity of his tone, a man offering politeness but sparing no attempt to hide distaste. A warrior with attitudes as mired in the past as his battles.

Melanna elected to respect one, and ignore the other. She rose from the throne as he approached. Weaponless, of course. Her Immortals would have made thorough search. "Jasaldar Jorcari."

Grey brows beetled, his composure thrown. "*Ashar* Jorcari now, my Empress. My service is long done. I'm merely a citizen."

"My father spoke well of you, and I'm glad to receive you. I apologise that it must be you alone. My Immortals grow nervous with the throne room filled with old soldiers."

An exaggeration, for Jorcari had arrived with only a score of petitioners, cast in much the same mould as himself, and now waiting in modest comfort elsewhere. Melanna had long ago found the business of rule more easily settled in more intimate gatherings. Save for herself and Jorcari, there were only the four Immortals standing watch at the foot of her throne, and a maidservant waiting close enough for ready summons, but far enough away to grant the illusion of privacy.

Her eyes on Jorcari's, Melanna sat. "Especially those who come with grievances." The frown returned. Surprised by her directness, or appalled by it? Melanna had seen plenty of both, and the one turned swiftly to the other. "Can I offer refreshment?"

Impossibly, Jorcari went even more rigid. "No, *savim*. I came to deliver a message for Blackwind Lodge, nothing more. I will intrude no longer than I must."

Hard not to hear the double meaning. Outwardly polite, but beneath that the distaste for being in her presence. Six years of an Empress' rule couldn't erase generations of patriarchal attitudes. For a man like Jorcari, a woman could master the finest arts, toil in a field or construction site, even command an army of merchant caravans ... so long as she lacked the temerity to think herself a warrior. The Veteran's Lodges were full of such men. Men who'd have laid down their lives for an Emperor without a whimper, but regarded an Empress as affront.

"And what can I do for Blackwind Lodge?"

She knew some of it. The lodges had been founded as networks for warriors no longer fit to serve in battle, whether through advancing age, or infirmity of body or mind. A generous stipend from the Imperial purse kept them afloat, complemented by tithings of income from those members still able to find employment as bodyguards, watchmen or servants. But her father's disastrous Avitra Briganda had seen the lodges burgeon. Too many of the newcomers bore burdensome wounds, and thus became burdens themselves.

Jorcari stepped closer. Too close, by tradition. Immortals started forward, swords half-drawn.

Melanna waved them back. "Well?"

Jorcari's lip twisted, reluctance returning. Reason so often unmanned unreasonable men. Halting at the foot of the stairs, he stared not so much at Melanna, but *through* her. "We need land."

"Land?"

"Yes, my Empress. Good, tillable land. Used to be, we were few enough – and old enough – to survive on generosity while we awaited Ashana's call. But now too many of us are young, and there's not enough work to keep them from idleness." At last, he met her gaze. "But if they've fields to tend, they can feed themselves, their kin."

Melanna blinked. She'd expected a demand for a larger pension – one she'd have been hard-pressed to meet without howls of protest from the Chancellery of Guilds. But this? A far finer solution that balanced a man's pride with his need to be useful. Rhaled's treasury was no longer as capacious as it had once been, but the kingdom remained rich in farmland – if she could prise any of it from the grasp of its grain factors.

But maybe she didn't have to. Her father's old estate at Kinholt sat mostly empty, its expansive acres little more than overgrown muster fields for the town's wardens and havens for squatters. Aunt Aella would quibble, perhaps – the estate's custodianship had fallen to her – but even stripping back the wider grounds would leave generous gardens, and Aella would doubtless find consolation in being marooned upon a sea of toiling menfolk. Widowhood had, after all, done little to calm her passions, much to her sister's disgust.

"It's no small thing you ask," she replied, "but nor is to lay down—"

Melanna broke off, distracted by distant trumpets. And something else beneath. A low rumble, louder all the time. The sound of battle, drawing closer.

A cold hand closing about her stomach, she sprang to her feet and beckoned to the nearest Immortal. "Candrat! Find out what's happening!"

Tesni burst through the door, four Immortals at her back, weapons drawn. "Empress! The city is invaded! You need to come with us."

The hand about Melanna's stomach squeezed tight. "Invaded? The Tressians?"

There'd be cruel irony to that, given her father's final act in the ephemeral world.

"Thirava." Tesni slowed as she approached the throne. "Please, *savim*, you must come with us. You're not safe."

Thirava? Melanna felt no surprise, just sick inevitability and the first flicker of fear. She drew down a deep breath and sought stillness of thought. "Where's my daughter?"

"The jasaldar's gone for her," said Tesni. "She's safe, Empress. Think of yourself. We'll take you to Penitent's Tower. It's easier to defend."

Melanna glanced around. Penitent's Tower was formidable enough, though for the unhappiest of reasons – an aunt, distant in bloodline and passing generations – caught in the twin transgressions of treason and infidelity and walled up alive in her chambers. That kind of horror sank into the stones.

True, the throne room was by no means a fortress. But that hardly mattered. The entire palace *was* a fortress, and guarded by Immortals. There was time yet. But was anything truly certain now? Errors had led her to this place, and more would surely follow. One thing remained true: she was Empress and Dotha Rhaled. She'd duties beyond survival. She swallowed. Yes, even beyond her daughter's.

"I want to see the city."

Tesni frowned. "Please, Empress, that isn't wise. You must—"

"Must?" Ice crept into her tone. "There is very little I *must* do."

Tesni shared a glance with another of the new-come Immortals. "The balcony in Prince Aeldran's chambers would be best."

"Agreed." Melanna set brisk pace for the door.

Halfway there, she realised no one had followed. The maid screamed. Wet rasp of blade on flesh hurried close behind. The strike of steel and the grunt of dying men.

Melanna spun about. Tesni seized her by the throat. Blood trickled warm down her neck as the killing edge of the Immortal's sword kissed her windpipe.

Behind Tesni, Candrat shuddered and fell, a sword buried in his scales. One of Tesni's companions – another *traitor* – kicked the body clear and rounded on the maid, who fled screaming into the corridor. Jorcari backed away from another, hands held high and the warrior's pride gone from his shrunken posture. A third traitor lay dead beside the corpses of his victims. A fourth clutched an arm whose emerald silks were bloody to the elbow.

"After the girl!" snarled Tesni.

The injured Immortal left the chamber at a run.

Melanna forgot the sword at her throat, the tumult in the city and held Tesni's gaze as if it were the only thing in the world. Bad enough to be betrayed by one's Immortals – an act unheard of in generations of Empire – but by a woman who'd never have held that position but for Melanna's actions?

And Kaila. What of her? Tesni's every word and deed was now suspect.

A question that should have awoken terror instead lit a roaring flame.

"Where is my daughter?" growled Melanna.

"You will go to Penitent's Tower and await King Cardivan's pleasure," said Tesni. "Or I'll cut your throat here and now."

Melanna bunched her fists. A twitch of Tesni's sword forced a gasp of pain. It too fed the rising fire. "You had my trust. Where is your honour?"

"You can't eat honour, *savim*. And Cardivan pays well." Tesni's voice hardened, all trace of deference gone. "Now. Which is it to be?"

Rosa knew the sounds of strife well enough and, for all that it was unlikely, entertained hope that rescue lay at hand. She'd prepared herself for the possibility as best she could, rising and dressing in the shadowthorn robes left for her. With her whole body a bruise, she couldn't contest her guards – much less unarmed. But if another did so on her behalf, she stood ready.

Bellowed cries and a clash of swords drew her to the window. A fight had broken out in the garden below. Immortal versus Immortal – a dozen on one side, and perhaps a shade fewer on the other – though the distinction between the two parties was otherwise indistinguishable. Already one lay motionless, his blood seeping into the sand garden. Another reeled away, then limped back for more.

Perhaps there *was* opportunity. Apara had promised guards beneath the window. Likely they were already part of the brawl. When it was done . . .

Running feet in the corridor drew Rosa's attention to the door. They slowed, replaced by muffled voices.

"Open it up," said one. "Cardivan wants her dead."

"Thirava wants her to suffer."

"And who is to be Emperor?"

Rosa cursed under her breath. No tears for Melanna Saranal if her allies had turned against her – she'd earned that and more. But typical of her own fortune to be caught up in events.

But that didn't mean she had to roll over and die.

The lock clicked. The door crashed back. An armoured Immortal strode in, vast in the room's confines. Ignoring the complaints of muscles barely healed, Rosa snatched the heavy drawer – carefully worked free from the wardrobe not half an hour before – from the bed, and swung.

Eyes widened an instant before the timbers shattered across the golden helm. The Immortal staggered, and then Rosa was inside the arc of his sword, reaching for the dagger buckled at his belt. Fingers closing around leather grips, she snatched the weapon free and rammed its point up under his chin. He dropped with a wet gurgle, and then Rosa had a sword. The weight of it scattered the last of her soreness, cobwebs before the wind.

A second, helmless Immortal entered the room, her eyes cold and sword steady.

Rosa raised her stolen sword in salute. A little bravado couldn't hurt. "Until Death!"

Tavar Rasha was halfway to the throne room when the first sounds of battle reached his ears. Even in the silent contemplation of prayer, something had set instinct sparking. An Immortal was more than a warrior. He was a protector. A soldier. And a soldier knew when something was amiss.

Decorum be damned, he broke into a flat run and sifted grim possibilities. Disobedience – even riots – were not unheard of in Tregard. He'd himself drawn steel to put them down. But to hear one so close to the palace walls? And to say nothing of the timing . . . As jasaldar of the Imperial guard, he should have received some report, some warning.

He reached the princessa's chambers, noting with approval that here, at least, his Immortals knew their duty. Two stood on station, one to either side of the door. Except . . .

Rasha slowed, unable to pin discomfort on anything save nebulous unease. "Have you heard what's happening in the city?"

The two shared a glance. Garita and Devarni. Young men of promise, proven at Govanna.

"We've had no word," said Garita. "You've orders for us, *savir*?"

"Stay with the princessa. She's not to leave her chambers until I say otherwise. Am I understood?"

Both bowed. Rasha walked away, his mind calmer for knowing at least *part* of his world was as it should be. But as he took the first step, pieces of a puzzle clicked together. Its shadow revulsed him, but once witnessed could not be unseen.

"One more thing." He turned. "The lunassera set to guard the princessa. Where are they?"

"The Empress called them away," said Devarni.

Rasha's heart sank further. A good answer, even a credible one. But the hesitation behind it told all. He set a hand to his sword. The minuscule twitch of Garita's left eye confirmed suspicion. "Stand aside."

"I don't understand, *savir*," said Devarni.

"You don't need to understand, only obey. Move!"

A child's shriek sounded, muffled by intervening doors but unmistakeable in character.

Devarni's and Garita's swords were only halfway from their scabbards when Rasha's swept free. Folded steel shaped by the master craftsman Terrigan, a gift from Emperor Ceredic for preserving the Imperial bloodline at the Ravonn, there was no better in the palace – save the Empress' own – and no swifter hand.

The thrust that sent Garita scrambling blurred into a back-cut barely checked by Devarni's desperate parry. A boot against knee sent Devarni staggering, then Rasha turned his wrath upon Garita once more.

Swords screeched. The blades locked. Knowing Garita was younger, stronger, Rasha didn't seek contest but twisted a full circle anticlockwise, sword rolling about his wrist into an underhand grip as he reached his knees. Garita, still off-balance and facing the wrong direction, screamed as the sword pierced the unarmoured back of his knee. Rasha rose as his opponent fell. His whirling blow cheated the now-wavering sword. Garita's golden scales rushed red.

Rasha heard the strike of Devarni's blade before he felt it. The crunch of scales at his midriff and the sharp, melodious sound of silk and flesh slicing as one. The ice-hot agony of the wound. The warm spill of blood. Those came as he hurled himself at the traitor, shoulder driving the younger man against the wall.

Impact sent a fresh jolt through Rasha's side. A statue, struck by a flailing hand, shattered on the floor. Devarni grunted as ribs cracked. Rasha drove his sword up beneath golden scales. The grunt became a moan. Became nothing at all.

Flank sticky with his own blood, Rasha stepped away. Devarni's twitching body dropped beside Garita's. The sight cut deeper than pain, deeper than disappointment. His men. Recruited on his advice. What was one's blood when set against such error?

A second cry from beyond the door renewed clarity.

Anger burning away the pain, Rasha passed through the princessa's outer chambers. He spared no more than a glance for the crumpled lunassera barely concealed beyond the entrance, driven on by the crash of furniture and a child's sobs.

The Immortal framed in the bedroom door never saw him coming, and Rasha chanced no hesitation. His sword took her spine, and then only one remained. He, at least, was a stranger to Rasha. An imposter garbed in armour he'd not earned. He had the sobbing princessa by the hair, but still she fought, heels dug into the carpet and tiny fists pummelling uselessly at an armoured thigh.

Her mother's daughter.

The imposter paled as he caught sight of Rasha. Many did. Making no attempt to reach for his sword, he raised his hands. The princessa scrambled away behind the bed.

"She's unhurt." The imposter's Silsarian accent was unmistakeable. "You—"

The words vanished in a wet gurgle, his throat taken. Breathing harder than he'd like, the wobble in his right leg warning that Devarni's blow had gone deeper that he'd feared, Rasha sank to the floor beside the bed.

"Shar Rasha! Shar Rasha!" The princessa flung her arms about him, a bundle of dark-eyed disarray. "What's happening?"

"Nothing that cannot be put right, *essavim*. I promise."

He put a bloodied arm about her, holding her head close and hoped the words were truth.

Boots sounded in the passageway. A shout of alarm and drawn steel. Rasha sighed. Unfair to be caught in a lie so soon.

Kissing the princessa on the brow, he pushed her away. "Beneath the bed, *essavim*. Whatever comes next, you should not see."

For a moment, he feared she'd disobey, but she scrambled readily away. Rasha's own rising proved more of a challenge. Those parts of him that didn't ache had already stiffened. But it was bad enough to die in a girl's bedchamber. He'd not do so on his knees.

The anteroom filled as he reached the doorway. A dozen eyes. None of them friendly. All Immortals. All of them young. None of them with a sliver of the honour he'd sought to instil.

"I taught you all!" he bellowed. "This is how you repay me?"

"Stand aside, *savir*," said one. "Don't make us do this the hard way."

No. They didn't understand. His failure, as much as theirs. Rasha gripped his sword tighter.

"Do what you must. As will I."

Forty-Two

Palms slapped against the wall's ragged parapet. Altiris pivoted as fingers tightened around brick, legs sweeping up and over in one smooth motion. The landing was barely half as gracious, crunching through rotting crates unseen until too late. Cold air stinging his lungs, he staggered across the dray yard with a jarred ankle and drunkard's gait.

"After him!"

A watch bell's toll accompanied the Drazina's bellow. A scuff of boot on brickwork as the fellow attempted pursuit. Gauntlets showed at the wall's crest.

Altiris stumbled through the maze of tarpaulined bundles as new bells chimed, cursing carelessness and ill fortune. He'd not welcomed a fugitive's existence, but he'd been confident he'd survive it long enough to get his head together. But he and the city had changed since he'd last lived on the streets – the one softer, the other harder, crueller. Checkpoints and patrols, already commonplace, grew denser when you were on the run.

Breathing hard, he flung himself behind a crate and peered out. A Drazina jumped down from the wall. Another joined him. A flurry of gesticulations and they picked separate paths across the yard, swords drawn.

"Show yourself, Czaron! You're bound by law!"

Gritting his teeth, Altiris pressed his head back against the tarpaulin. Should've gone south. Should've left the city that first night, but it'd felt too much like running away. What he hoped to achieve by staying ...? Well, he'd not gotten that far.

He'd not done *everything* wrong. He'd steered clear of the south-wealder enclaves at Gelder Lane and Bannock Hill – places the Drazina would have been watching. But he'd been too trusting. Should've caught the glint in the tavernkeep's eye when he'd asked for lodging. He'd barely scrambled out of the window in time.

Footsteps tracked away left and right, towards the sunken-roofed warehouse, and away towards the wrought-iron street-gate. Safe. It wouldn't last.

A rumbling stomach reminding that his last meal lay long in the past, Altiris sifted poor options.

No hope of fighting the Drazina, not unarmed. That left evasion, but he'd singularly failed at that so far. And if he got clear, where could he go? He needed food, and sleep. Constans would have helped, but dawn lay long in the past. By now, the boy would've left the Hayadra Grove and returned to the palace. That left returning to Stonecrest – something he'd sworn not to do – or handing himself in at one of the constabulary watch houses. Safer than letting the Drazina take him, but it would involve Lord Trelan as surely as showing up at Stonecrest's gate.

"I see him!"

Altiris tensed. Dregrat's instincts, earned on Selann and honed in the city's back alleys, warned of the Drazina's ruse just before it drove him from cover. Still, the leftmost footsteps were coming closer.

Time to go, while he still could. *Where* would wait.

Footsteps to his left, towards the street. Right, it was. Get to the warehouse. Jump to the next roof. Shoulders pressed against tarpaulin, Altiris crept away.

"Got you!"

No ruse this time. Not with a Drazina blocking the steep valley between the crates. Altiris flung himself aside, shoulder scraping against covered timbers. A hand tugged at his coat tails. Straight line became a tightening arc, slamming him against the opposite crates.

Vision crowding with dark spots, Altiris gulped down a breath full of rain-sodden canvas. A knee cracked on cobblestones as the Drazina kicked his leg away. A cuff to the head sent red spots rushing to join the black.

"Get his hands bound," growled a voice. "I want those fifty crowns Hollov promised."

They forced Altiris' hands behind his back. Struggle earned him a second, heavier cuff. Constans had been right, he thought groggily. Hollov *was* taking things personally to levy a bounty of a year's wages.

Should've gone south.

Altiris' captor leaned closer. "Settle down, sonny. Dead pays less, but I'm not a greedy ... " A wheezy grunt sounded. The captor's grip slackened. "What the—?"

A scream. The soft, wet rasp of a blade on skin. A warm, wet spray splashed Altiris' neck.

The grip on his arms fell away. Crying out in revulsion, he reeled about. Both Drazina lay dead. Above their bloodied gorgets, ripper's grins beamed at the moonlit sky.

Hawkin stepped over the corpses. Raising a sardonic eyebrow, she pressed the flat of a fouled dagger to her lips. "Hush, my bonny. You're safe with me."

Altiris wiped a hand across the back of his neck. It came away red. The warm, copper stench set his stomach lurching. "I bet."

Bells chimed in the streets. Shouts and running feet. Too many to count.

Hawkin smiled sweetly. "Or you could stay here."

She ran for the warehouse. After a moment's futile hesitation, Altiris did the same.

The Privy Council chamber door opened a crack. Raldan leaned into the room, his face frozen in an expression of permanent disappointment – one many cited as proof that he'd not so much earned a career in the constabulary as been destined for it. "You wanted to see me, my lord?"

"Indeed." Sliding eyeglasses from his nose, Josiri rose. So peculiar to sit at the head of the table. To hold sway over a chamber where the Republic's worthies had conspired to destroy his family and subjugate his people. But for Anastacia's sly smile – she was not so much seated in the chair opposite Josiri as draped across it, her barely skirted legs hanging over one arm – he might have thought it a dream. "Join us, captain."

"Captain?"

Eyes crowding with suspicion, Raldan took a seat beside Jezek, weather-stained constabulary tabard tawdry beside the archimandrite's scarlet robes. On the other side of the table, Commander Hollov – an unsmiling woman of middle years now commanding those Drazina left in the city – drummed impatient fingers against the tabletop. Konor Zarn, representing the trader's forum, had at least made an effort to sober up, although his half-lidded eyes wandered readily.

By contrast, Anastacia's bright eyes and flushed cheeks betrayed an early start on Stonecrest's wine cellar – and not for the first time in recent days. Josiri suspected Jezek might have lectured her, were he not studiously averting his eyes from a dress whose neck- and hemlines didn't so much flirt with respectability as elope with it and thereafter leave it penniless in the gutter. For her part, Anastacia revelled in Jezek's veiled disgust as readily she did Hollov's jealousy and Zarn's open admiration. Not all pleasures of the flesh were pleasures of the flesh alone, and she'd missed them badly.

"The Lord Protector left the city in my charge," said Josiri. "I leave the constabulary in yours. You've more than earned it. And as head of the constabulary, you've a right to hear this first-hand."

"Which is what?" Hollov scowled. "I've business enough rounding up the perpetrators of yesterday's riot without mystery and intrigue . . . my lord."

"Actually. You don't." Josiri slid an envelope along the table, its blue wax seal agleam in the lantern light. "I'm declaring amnesty for everyone who took part in that disaster."

Hollov broke the seal, read in silence, then glared at him. "Amnesty?"

Anastacia grinned. "It means he's pardoning them."

"There'll be misery enough in coming days," said Josiri. "I won't borrow from tragedies past. We have become a nation of closed minds and empty hearts. Perhaps we always were. Perhaps I've played my part in that. We need to be better. Starting today, we will be."

Colour touched Hollov's cheeks. "Drazina lost their lives at the docks. What of their justice?"

"Or their victims'?" Josiri retorted. "I know I'm gaining a reputation for wandering wits, but I'm not blind. I've seen your knights' labours up close, and looked away more than I should. When I say the amnesty's for everyone, I mean *everyone*. Be satisfied with that."

Zarn's gaze snapped into focus, a wry smile forming beneath. It vanished just as swiftly. Hollov's scowl did not, though it *did* alter form, outrage adopting worried tinge. In that moment, Josiri knew without doubt that the Drazina had secrets he'd as soon as not uncover.

Jezek nodded sagaciously. The timidity Josiri had thought an unswerving part of his character had vanished as soon as Viktor left the city. The Lord Protector had that effect on churchmen. "Forgiveness is the highest virtue, commander."

"Is it more important than security?" she snapped. "How am I to keep order if we set the rioters loose?"

Josiri *almost* felt sorry for her. Might have done, but for how recent events had opened his eyes. "You won't." A second sealed envelope joined the first. "I'm rescinding the Drazinas' authority to enforce the law. That includes checkpoints, patrols, custodianship of the Vaults. Everything. You will return to barracks and await further orders."

Raldan cleared his throat. "My lord, if things turn ugly again ... No Drazina, no Lady Reveque ... ? The constabulary haven't the numbers to keep the streets quiet."

"Then we'll use other means." Josiri shuffled his notes, careful as ever in recent days that his blighted memory didn't lead him to over-look something important. "I'm also ordering the government ration restored. The trader's forum have agreed to handle distribution, and provide security. They want everything back to normal just as much as we do."

Zarn offered a boozy grin and thumped a fist on the table. "Indeed!"

Hollov glared. Anastacia rolled her eyes. Raldan offered a slow nod. "It might work."

"You're a fool." All pretence of respect had fled Hollov's eyes. "The streets will eat us alive."

Josiri held her gaze. Should he repeat Viktor's confession of provok-ing the uprising? Would anyone believe? "There were grievances. I'm settling them. Had anyone done similar twenty years ago, my mother would be here instead of me, and we'd all be spared the burden of this conversation."

"And if I refuse the order?"

A shiver chased along Josiri's spine. An excellent question, without ready answer. If the Drazina refused his order to stand down, he lacked the swords to compel them, and that would be the end of his slender authority. But such odds had seldom bothered Viktor. He wouldn't let them bother him.

"We are a Republic of laws, not revenge. I'm closing the door on this miserable chapter, and I expect you to do the same." He paused, lending aspect of afterthought to what was in fact cold calculation. Wandering memory or not, he'd no need of notes for *this*. "Lord Droshna gave me this authority knowing what I'd do with it. He can only be halfway to Tarvallion. By all means, send a herald to confirm my instructions. That is . . . if you think you know his mind better."

With an impotent – but entirely audible – snarl, Hollov looked away. "I hope you know what you're doing."

She strode from the room, leaving behind a chamber less oppressive than before. One by one, the others followed – all save Anastacia.

Josiri intercepted Raldan before he reached the door. "Keep a close eye for trouble, Erik. From whatever quarter it hails."

"Yes, my lord."

"And spread the word about Lieutenant Trelan, if you would. I want him found and brought back to Stonecrest."

Raldan clasped a fist to his chest and departed.

Josiri sagged against the table, worn away by the need to project confidence.

Anastacia unfolded herself from the chair. "Didn't Viktor warn you against favouritism towards kith and kin?"

"Viktor isn't here." He shrugged. "And how can it be favouritism if all sins are forgiven?"

"I can't *wait* to see you try that one on Viktor."

"The least of my concerns. There's nothing to say he won't reverse everything when—"

"If."

"*When* he returns."

Anastacia kissed him on the cheek. "Maybe you shouldn't let him. You handled that well enough."

"High praise indeed." Josiri hesitated. "You might have worn something suitable."

She crooked an innocent eyebrow. "The dress? It *is* suitable. I look stunning." Offering a rather less innocent smile, she slid her hands about his waist. "I can always take it off. It's not like there's anyone here any longer."

So hard to tell if she was joking. Especially as Josiri wasn't sure if he wanted her to be. "I think I'd like to get through at least one day in charge of the Republic without a hint of scandal, if it's all the same to you."

"Who's talking about hints?" The smile broadened. "If a thing's worth doing, it's worth doing with *abandon*."

Anastacia leaned in for a kiss, the sweet, sour tang of wine heavy on her breath. Hands gentle but firm about her wrists, Josiri disentangled himself. "*Not* the time to test the theory."

"Spoilsport." Affronted moue dissolved into a grin.

Josiri returned it willingly. For all his tiredness, he felt better than he had in months. As if a black cloud had come unmoored from his thoughts. Yes, there was every chance Viktor would be furious, but that was a problem for the future.

And he'd survived Viktor's wrath before.

At every moment expecting the door to burst open and admit a furious Tzila, Calenne eased the fourth window-board to the floor and stepped back to admire her handiwork. Or its lack. While the gap in the inner boards provided all the space she'd ever need to make her escape, the outer boards – replaced that morning – stared back in silent mockery.

"You really should have made more progress by now," breathed a voice at her ear.

The memory of her pulse racing, Calenne spun about. The Raven, unswervingly in his male aspect, stared at her from no more than a handspan away.

[[Leave me alone!]] hissed Calenne.

The Raven twitched a shrug and made no move to comply. To her surprise, Calenne found she was glad. With Viktor ridden to war, she'd no visitors at all save Tzila, who was no use for conversation *or* consolation. And though the Raven's expression wasn't entirely friendly, he seemed more *solid* than before, more mortal man than caged starscape.

He shrugged and stared past her shoulder. "My point stands."

Calenne growled, frustration getting the better of good sense.

[[There's no way to prop the outer boards in place once I get them free. I had to push them all the way loose last night.]]

"And yet you're still here."

[[They fell into the square. I thought the noise would draw someone.]] She glared, daring him to suggest that she'd bottled out at the last minute, terrified of the vast, empty city below. [[This morning, men came with ladders and set them back in place. I have to start over.]]

"Then do so." For all his easy manner, anger growled beneath the words. Anger, and what sounded like pain. "Or perhaps you prefer pining for your gallant Viktor?"

Viktor. Part of her longed for him to return, but the rest . . . ? [[If you're not here to help, go away.]]

His eyes flashed. "Are you *asking* for my aid?"

Calenne went still. She'd led a sheltered life, certainly. But not *that* sheltered. One did not ask favours of the Raven and end well. Whatever she and Viktor had become, she wasn't about to be a pawn in his quarrel with the Raven. At least, not under any terms other than her own. [[No.]]

He tutted. "Please yourself. But you might want to put things back. I fear your jailor is coming to check on you."

He stepped past her, and was gone. Calenne stared at the empty space left behind, then frantically busied herself with the boards. She had the last in place just as the door creaked open.

[[Yes?]]

Tzila offered no reply, not even her customary bow, and strode into the room. Her hidden gaze took in sofa, books, Calenne . . . and finally the window.

Phantom heartbeat tripping faster, Calenne stepped closer. [[I heard the workmen this morning. You needn't worry – I hid. I don't want people to see me like this.]]

Four statements. Three truths, one lie. For she hadn't hidden. In fact, she'd been struck by perverse temptation to remove the inner boards and lay herself bare. Might have followed through, but for fear that the shock might have sent the poor man plunging from his ladder.

The sallet helm's empty stare remained fixed on the window, for all that Calenne stood between. Fighting mounting panic, Calenne fished for a change of topic – anything to break her jailor's fixation.

[[Won't you stay? I could use someone to talk to. At least when I was at Branghall, I had my brother. There's no one here.]]

At last, Tzila's gaze left the window. Calenne flinched as her right hand came up, then stood frozen as fingers curled to stroke her porcelain cheek. Gentle. Soothing perhaps, had she been able to feel it. The gesture stirred half-forgotten memory. Not just the touch, but the tilt of Tzila's head – the slight easing of her rigid poise. Calenne could almost see the reassuring smile, hear words gently spoken. So familiar it was maddening.

[[Who are you, Tzila?]]

Tzila froze, a soft, hollow moan swelling to fill the space between them – the only sound Calenne had heard pass her lips.

[[You can tell me,]] said Calenne. [[It can be our secret. Viktor need not know.]]

The moan deepened to an animal growl, more wolf than woman. Tzila snatched her hand away and spun on her heel. The door slammed, Calenne's secrets intact, but in possession of more questions than ever.

"Is the sack really necessary?" asked Altiris.

"Not my secrets to give away, are they, my bonny?"

Hawkin's tone offered no leeway, so he lapsed into silence and pieced together what clues he had. They'd travelled a long way north through the city before Hawkin had insisted on tying the sack over his head, and a considerable way further after that. Not that distance alone meant anything. She could have led him in circles for all he knew. But the chair was soft and well upholstered, the room warm and smoky with a recent fire. The sounds of the city – such as they were at that hour – were distant. Come morning, bells and ships' horns might offer some clue, but now? He could be anywhere. At least she'd left his hands free. That alone offered hope that some extravagant murder wasn't on the cards.

Then again, given recent luck . . .

A door creaked somewhere off to Altiris' right. Carpet deadened the footsteps.

"Can I at least get something to drink?" he asked. "It's been a trying day."

The door clicked shut. Glass *chinked* on glass, followed by a glug of liquid. A glass pressed against Altiris' knuckles. "Here."

A man's voice, and familiar, though it took a moment to place. The Merrow. Shoulders prickling, Altiris took the glass.

Shadows shifted beyond the sack's rough weave. "Hawkin, my dear . . . is there a reason you present my guest thus?"

"It amused me," the reply came from somewhere off to Altiris' right.

The Merrow sighed and set about unwinding the belt from about Altiris' neck. Soon after, the sack was gone, and Altiris found himself staring up at a face that had been awash in drunkenness at Elzar Ilnarov's funeral.

"Konor?"

Zarn smiled. "Ah, so we *are* friends, after all. That should make this conversation easier."

"I don't . . . I don't understand. You're the Merrow? But you're a—"

"Respected member of society? Rake? Drunkard?" He shrugged and settled in a chair on the other side of the hearth. "I must beg 'no longer' to all of the above. But the trappings are sometimes *very* useful. Make yourself contemptible and no one heeds your actions."

"So it's all an act?" Altiris took a swallow and glanced about the room as the brandy did its warming, calming work. One of Woldensend Manor's drawing rooms. "But you've lost as much as anyone to the wreckers."

"Anything else might have attracted attention." He shrugged. "And so long as the goods go where they are needed, what does it matter?"

"What do you want, Konor?"

"All I've ever wanted: to help, and be helped in return. Those of us who see what's happened to this Republic have a duty to one another." He leaned forward, voice and expression earnest. "You *do* see now that I was right about Lord Droshna?"

"After the docks? Yes."

Zarn shook his head. "It's what Kasvin wanted, you know. To goad him into something that would dispel all doubt. I knew what it might cost, but she wouldn't listen."

"You're lucky she stopped at arguments," said Hawkin icily from her post by the drapes.

Altiris twisted in his chair and saw her staring balefully at Zarn. "What does she mean?"

"My relationship with Kasvin was . . . complicated."

"Was?"

"She's dead."

"She lived when the Drazina dragged her away," Altiris objected. "They subdued her with silver."

"And now she isn't," growled Zarn. He took a deep breath and spoke softly. "I'm not mistaken about this. We were bound, she and I."

"Murderer and victim," snapped Hawkin.

Altiris glanced from one to the other. If anyone had murdered Kasvin, it had been the Drazina on the dockside, but why then did Hawkin hold Zarn accountable? "You're not making any sense."

Zarn sat back in his chair, eyes swimming with old ghosts. "Once, I was to be married to the brightest, most charming creature in the city. Lumestra knows what she saw in me. I was arrogant and brash, three sheets to the wind more hours than I was not, and seldom given to kindness. A week before our wedding day, deep in liquor's embrace and hot with jealousy, I lost what little kindness I possessed."

"He rang her neck like a chicken's, is what he means," said Hawkin.

Altiris stared at Zarn, disgust mingling with puzzlement. "How long ago?"

"Twenty years."

"Twenty?" Though impossible, the words rang true. Kasvin had looked no more than sixteen summers, but her manner had belonged to someone older, more confident.

Zarn pressed on, the steady, confident voice turned halting and dull. "My father's bribes preserved me from accusations, but couldn't save me from myself. I crawled even deeper into the bottle, and there I stayed for ten long years, gnawed by self-loathing and my heart an open wound. Then I heard whispers of a river flowing through the Coventaj caves – of unhappy dead returned to new life and purpose. One moonless night, I broke open Kasvin's tomb and carried her worm-eaten body into the darkness. I set her adrift on the Black River, and begged Endala to send her back. The next morning, I awoke to find her standing at the foot of my bed, eyes shining. I have been her slave ever since."

Easy to see the form that slavery had taken. Altiris had felt its pull often enough. Longing that transcended desire. Zarn had lived that way for ten years, a puppet dancing in the glow of irresistible blue-green eyes. And yet Altiris could conjure no shred of pity.

"When the Crowmarket fell, Kasvin saw a chance to fill the void. The Merrow was never my idea, but hers. A name folk could rally around. It pleased her to make me play the hero – a fit reflection, she said, of a wasted, wretched life. She never missed an opportunity to remind me I was not that man, and that when I was no longer of use she'd drown me in the same waters that gave her life." Cheeks streaked with tears, Zarn offered a wan smile. "Now she's gone, all I have in me is to finish what she started."

"Why?" Altiris fought to keep a sneer from his voice. "To absolve yourself?"

Zarn snorted. "There's no redemption for me. When they put me in the ground there'll be teeth in the darkness, and I'll deserve every bite. My rotten soul was the token that bought Kasvin new life, and the Maid of the River always collects. I've known good men – six years ago, Malachi Reveque could have left me to die in the council chamber, but he broke a chair across Kai Saran's shoulders and dragged me clear – but I've no place among them. Kasvin is gone. Her purpose remains." He tapped at his temple. "She branded me with it, and I'm powerless to do aught else."

Altiris heard no triumph, no determination, no yearning for glory. Only the fatigue of a man tired of the dance and unable to leave the floor. For all his smooth words, Konor Zarn was a husk, hollowed out and filled with another's purpose. He might have pitied the man, but for the deed that had doomed him thus. "And what *does* she want?"

"To save this city from Droshna, before it drowns in the Dark." Zarn breathed deeply, composure returning to his face and manner. "Everything I told you before is true. You've witnessed some of it yourself. It's only going to get worse. Josiri is a good man. I've seen the proof of it this very day, but it won't last. Droshna has him broken and he doesn't even know it."

Altiris stared into his brandy. He wanted to contest Zarn's claim, but the words too closely mirrored his last conversation with Lord Trelan. "What do you want from me?"

"Proof. Something so damning that the city will *have* to take notice."

"And where do we find that?"

"Drazina, constable or hearthguard – there's always one ready to trade honour for coin," said Zarn. "I can open any room in the city, and take my pick of its contents. Any room, save one."

Hawkin drifted away from the window. "There's a chamber above the Lord Protector's quarters in the palace clocktower. I can't find anyone who's ever set foot in there. Except for that seneschal of his, and I know better than to waste my time trying to turn her head."

Tzila. Altiris nodded. "So the Lord Protector values his privacy. Highbloods do."

Zarn snorted. "What if I told you this is the room where the high proctor died?"

"They were close." The first doubt wormed its way into Altiris' certainty. "It's no surprise that he'd have wider access than most."

"And if I said that it wasn't Ilnarov's heart that killed him, but something else?"

Altiris narrowed his eyes. "How can you possibly know that?"

"Kasvin had a very . . . amicable relationship with death. Souls spoke to her." Zarn leaned forward, eyes burning. "Think it's worth having a poke around, while the Lord Protector's away?"

Unthinkable that the Lord Protector had killed Elzar, but that he harboured ruinous secrets? That the near tragedy of Silverway Dock was just the first of many? It was all too plausible. Or at least plausible *enough*. "Why me? The Merrow has an army to call upon."

"I don't need an army. Armies are *loud*. You and Hawkin will suffice."

Altiris looked up at Hawkin, her features unreadable. "And what's your stake in this?"

"Payment. What else?"

The challenge in her tone couldn't quite conceal the lie, but Altiris let it be. He drained the brandy dry and knew at once he'd need another before the night was done.

"All right. How do we do this?"

Forty-Three

As the cataphract column wound through drizzled, sullen streets, Cardivan almost heard the bells chiming for his ascension. Anticipation rippled through his veins, the ambition of a lifetime at last coming to a head. Worth the chafing of sodden armour, and more besides.

Battle still sounded to the east. No cause for worry. Inevitable consequence of his warriors reaching the Ravencourt barracks too late and finding it mobilised. Elsewhere, all was silent, Tregard's denuded garrison overwhelmed by sheer numbers and surprise. And the populace, as predicted, cowered in their homes. Come coronation, they'd cheer him. Kings came and went. Fiefs changed hands, and life went on.

A second, smaller column cantered out of the west and joined those gathered between the stag-banner. Uncomfortable as ever in the saddle, Thirava assumed an heir's proper place on his father's right just as the bruised and humiliated Brackar rode on his left. Not a speck of blood adorned Thirava's armour. As the father, so the son. A man did not need to wield the sword to claim victory by it.

"My king." Thirava's tone was a study in false deference. As ever. "Their ranks are broken, the palace surrounded. But I do wonder at the cost."

Cardivan regarded his son with weary distaste. So certain of his place in the world. So much to learn. "It's a sacrifice. An Emperor must not only be strong, but be *seen* to have strength."

"I might believe that were it your own men dying, and not mine."

"The throne will be yours soon enough, will it not? Sooner than I expect, I'm sure." He offered Thirava a sidelong glance. "Or do you think I don't know of your agents among my household?"

His son flinched. "I'd never—"

Cardivan waved him to silence. "It's a family tradition. Should you get the better of me, I'll deserve it. Dare I hope for competence elsewhere?"

Thirava scowled. "The Empress will be yours by dusk."

Cardivan let another street pass away beneath his horse's hooves before answering. "And our agents in the palace?"

"Loyalists hold the walls, their eyes outward. What occurs within is a mystery. I've given orders for the assault."

Cardivan nodded. Even if Melanna and her daughter had escaped his suborned Immortals, the distraction was enough. Action was all, and reaction death. Perhaps, had the Empress been free to rally her warriors, things might have transpired differently – whatever contempt Cardivan held for her person, he respected her ability – but now those warriors were dead or captive. She had no one.

Well, almost no one. A few hundred Immortals within the palace walls. The odd fugitive … Brackar's cowardice in the face of Apara Rann still rankled – and that it had been the Empress' pet Tressian who'd humbled his champion, Cardivan didn't doubt. One last bastion remained, and as the white boundary wall and iron gate of Mooncourt Temple came into view at the street's end, Cardivan rode to unmake it.

It wasn't much. A flicker of Tesni's gaze. Barely a heartbeat of broken attention. But to Melanna, wound tight with outrage and fearing for an absent daughter, a heartbeat was a lifetime.

Bracing a foot against Tesni's thigh, Melanna ripped free of the hand about her neck and the sword at her throat. The deed set her stumbling, the tangled skirts of her gown and impractical formal shoes offering little stability and less grip.

Melanna circled, trying to keep not only her attacker but the rest of the throne room in sight. Tesni's sword darted, sending her back the other way, the cowering Jorcari, the throne and the two other treacherous Immortals again lost somewhere behind.

Tesni hacked down. Melanna flung herself aside, losing only the trailing edge of a sleeve to the blade. A grunt sounded behind. A scream. Then

Tesni's sword stabbed forward once again, leaving Melanna no attention for anything else. Tesni bore down with short, stabbing blows. Melanna retreated, her every attempt to break left or right thwarted by steel.

"It isn't too late," she gasped. "Give me your sword."

Tesni offered no words, but Melanna read answer in her eyes. She knew that look. She'd seen it in so many faces. She'd recognised it in herself. The knowledge that bridges behind were in flames, and the only way forward was through the darkness.

Those same eyes warned Melanna of Tesni's next swing before it arrived. Ducking beneath the blade, she broke right, angling towards the throne. The throne, and the Goddess' moonsilver sword hanging from the armrest.

"No!" shouted Tesni.

Fifteen paces. A thunder of Tesni's footfalls sounded behind.

Ten paces. Melanna cursed ever having laid eyes on the formal gown.

Five paces.

An Immortal veered in from Melanna's right.

She twisted. The sword meant for her heart found empty air. Survival robbed her of balance. She fell, head, shoulder and hip cracking against tile. As she struggled to rise, the Immortal's helm blotted out the towering statues of the gods, and the throne room's distant roof. Slowly, deliberately, he spun his sword point downwards and grasped it in both hands.

"Tirane Aregnum."

The Immortal collapsed, cut down from behind. A withered hand found hers.

"Empress."

Jorcari helped Melanna rise, his manner again that of an unbending warrior. Behind him, the remaining traitor lay sprawled across the tiles, sightless eyes skyward. The old man bore not a scratch.

Planting a hand in Jorcari's chest, Melanna shoved him aside. Tesni's blade hissed between them. Melanna dipped and stood tall with a dead Immortal's sword in her hand.

Tesni struck again. Melanna met the blow with steel of her own, and welcomed the shiver of impact. For all that an Empress' duties had atrophied her bladework, her arm knew what was needed.

Swords scraped once, twice, three times. Tesni went back, the first fear in her eyes. A fourth exchange, and her sword skidded across the floor, chased along by the cry of pain from severed fingers. Her boot slipped on a smear of blood. She landed heavily, the ruin of her sword hand further slicking the tiles, the other outstretched to fend off the inevitable.

"Please . . ."

Melanna pursued, outrage cold as ice. "I offered you mercy. You chose this."

One sweep of the sword struck Tesni's warding hand away. A thrust silenced her for good.

Sick at heart, Melanna left the sword buried in the corpse. The sounds of distant battle swelled around her, much of it close enough to be elsewhere in the palace. A moment. She'd bought only a moment. How many of her household had Cardivan suborned? If he'd broken the legend of the Immortals, all were suspect. All who'd chosen to be at her side. How could she defend herself and Kaila, much less the Empire? She had a nation, and yet she was alone.

"Jasaldar Jorcari?" For all that she spoke softly, the words carried. "I owe you a debt I cannot repay, and now I must impose another. I've no notion of how matters lie beyond this room. It may well be that the palace offers nothing but corpses. But if your lodgemates live, would you find them, and bring them here? I need men about me I can trust."

"There is no debt, my Empress. If they live, you shall have them." He tilted his head, shrewdness gleaming in his eye. "But I must have your promise that you'll still be here upon our return."

For a moment, Jorcari was gone, and Melanna's father stood in his place, so clearly had he read her intent.

"I will not abandon my daughter," she replied. "I will know that she is safe even if I have to tear this palace apart with my bare hands."

He nodded. "Of course. But a dead mother is no gift to her child. Even for an Empress, patience is all."

Melanna scowled, but truth cared little for her worries. "Go."

Rosa saw not a living soul, warrior or otherwise, though this in no small part was due to her determination to go unseen. A Tressian loose in the Imperial palace was a Tressian of uncertain future – especially with the thrill of freedom running dry, and aching muscles a reminder of how close she'd come to death in recent days.

Of the dead, Rosa saw plenty, though which faction held ascendance was a mystery to her. Nor, in truth, did she care. Loyalist or traitor, they were all shadowthorns, and undeserving of mercy. Little would change if Melanna Saranal was dragged from the throne, save the lingering resentment that another had ended the woman who'd so soured Rosa's life.

Reaching the next corner, Rosa checked her pace. An open door, bodies sprawled about it, and a room beyond. The ragged, uneven breath of the dying. Sword gripped tight, she edged out into the corridor.

A helmless, grey-bearded Immortal staggered through the doorway, one hand pressed to torn scales on his right side. He looked more a slaughterhouseman than a warrior, for scarcely a scrap bore no blood. His sword came up, levelled in line with an eye crusted shut.

"Are you part of this, Lady Orova?" The voice was weary, but unyielding. "I should tell you I've orders to kill you, should I find you loose in these halls."

Rosa halted, her own sword at middle guard. High would have been better, but middle was easier on tired arms. "I've killed no one who did not first try to kill me." She tilted her head, trying to make sense of the shadows behind him. "Don't join them."

He cracked a smile. "The arrogance of Essamere. I expect nothing less." The sword point dipped, then righted. He swallowed hard. "Is your honour equal to your arrogance? Can I—"

He sagged against the architrave, leaving a scarlet trail as he slid to the floor. His sword chimed on tile, released from a twitching hand. A small girl in a soiled dress darted from the room beyond. Careless of the blood, she flung her arms about him.

"You mustn't die, Shar Rasha," she wailed. "You promised to find my mother."

Rosa drew closer, unsure why she did so. The child's racket would only draw attention.

Rasha put his sword-arm about the girl. "The selfishness of children. This is not how a princessa behaves, is it, *essavim*?" She gave no answer save tears, and he turned his good eye on Rosa. "I saw you fight, years ago. You broke the wall at Zaragon to save a wounded comrade. You were remarkable. And I marked you again years later, at Govanna, where you were death without mercy. Which are you now?"

Rosa shook her head, thrown by the question. She'd forgotten about Zaragon. A squalid brawl in the borderlands, as all such skirmishes were. A shadowthorn mace had shattered her shield arm. She'd been weeks recovering.

"I don't know. Maybe neither."

Dry laughter caught in his throat. "You at least do not seem a woman who would kill a child, and I . . ." Alertness faded from his expression. A wince brought it rushing back. "I am out of options. Bring Kaila to her mother, and we will both have our answers."

Rosa shook her head. "Why should I care what happens to the Empress' brat?" The question set the girl wailing anew. "The sins of the kith care nothing for age. She inherits her mother's crimes."

"Perhaps because she stopped the last war," breathed Rasha. "Because she gambled everything she holds dear on the hope of preventing the next. Or perhaps because a warrior's worth is not in who she kills, but who she is prepared to die for, and why."

Rosa glared, furious at his presumption. He comprehended nothing of the debt the House of Saran owed the Republic. Malachi Reveque slaughtered at an Emperor's hand. The Eastshires, conquered. The dead of Govanna, Haldravord and Terevosk. Prydonis obliterated and Essamere driven to the brink. Ten thousand unmarked graves along the Ravonn, and the proud fortresses of Ahrad and Vrasdavora cast down.

But Rasha's words echoed hints Josiri had dropped in the years since Govanna. Turns of phrase that suggested personal knowledge of an Empress who should have been no more than a loathed stranger. And Josiri was no fool.

Were Rasha's claims true?

Voices sounded in the corridor, back the way Rosa had come.

"Choose quickly," breathed Rasha. "While choice remains."

Ever since Govanna, Rosa had striven to be better, and had stumbled more than she'd succeeded – her failure to confront Viktor with what he'd done to her was only part of it. Did she share that with Melanna Saranal? And even if she didn't, what manner of monster abandoned a child to her death?

She took Kaila's hand. To her surprise, the girl made no attempt to pull away.

Voices grew closer. The wet, rippling sound of a cut-throat silenced a pained cry.

Rasha nodded. "The corridors are not safe. But there are passageways hidden behind. She knows them all." He brushed Kaila's cheek. "Beneath the tears, she's an imp of soot and secrets. But first, one last favour. Help me stand."

After brief hesitation, Rosa laid aside her sword and seized his wrist. Between that and the wall, Rasha reached something approaching upright, hand still pressed to the scarlet ruin at his waist. Seeing wordless question in his eyes, Rosa returned to him his sword.

A deep, stuttering breath, and Rasha twisted to face the pursuit. "I will trouble them one last time. How does it go? Death and honour?"

Rosa nodded. "Death and honour."

Death for Rasha and honour for her, and both of them his gift. For the first time in her life, Rosa found herself looking upon a shadowthorn – a *Hadari* – and wondered what fortune might have brought them had they met as friends. Her world grew suddenly more complicated, and her place in it far simpler. A shield, not a sword, and a girl's life beneath her aegis.

Offering Rasha one last nod, she gathered Kaila in her arms.

Halfway down the next corridor, the air behind shook to a battle cry in an unfamiliar tongue. Screams followed, the last more defiant bellow than cry of pain. Then a wooden panel swung outward beneath Kaila's probing fingers. In the darkness beyond there was no sound at all.

Four ranks of stag-shields and serried spears rippled apart. Brackar and Thirava at his side, Cardivan spurred forward to greet the woman who stood before the barred gate, figure-hugging white robes plastered to her skin by the rain. There would be others close by, no doubt. Concealed among the trees of the temple gardens, perhaps. Theatricality was the least of the lunassera's skills.

"You've no business here, Cardivan Tirane." Sera spoke evenly, no expression showing beneath the gentle curve of her silver half-mask. "Withdraw your spears, and the Goddess may yet forgive you."

Cardivan leaned low over his horse's neck, more amused than affronted. "You dare address your Emperor with insolence?"

"You do not rule here."

"But I will. The House of Saran is done. Come midnight, you will acclaim me beneath the moon." He stared up at the skies. A mistake, for no moon could have penetrated those clouds. Other men might have taken that as ill omen. "You are lunassera. Your service is to the throne."

Sera's head snapped up. "Our service is to the Goddess, and to those she claims as kin." She raised her hand, and a spear of silvered light and jagged, planar edges coalesced in her hand. "Withdraw your spears."

Cardivan couldn't quite suppress a shiver. He saw fear reflected in the faces of his warriors, in the reflexive tightening of Thirava's hand about the reins. The lunassera had a reputation that transcended healers' gifts. But in duty, there was weakness.

Quelling his fear, Cardivan sat high in his saddle, and raised his voice to proclamation. "If the Goddess claims Melanna as her own, let her do so. Let her Huntsman summon the mists and ride out with the Court of Eventide at his back." He stared past her to the temple, its white stone still bright, even through rain. "But if the lunassera leave this place, the wounded in your care will be left unprotected. The temple will be unprotected. I will raze it to the ground, and have the land given over to something useful. A pig farm, perhaps."

Murmurs rippled through the assembled ranks. Whispered expectation that the Goddess Ashana would not let such words pass unchallenged. But these faded when no bolt of searing flame leapt from the heavens, when no otherworldly hunting horn shook the sky. Absence brought reminder that Ashana had been distant since the close of the Avitra Briganda.

The shard-spear faded from Sera's hand.

Cardivan nodded, careful to keep his relief hidden. "This will all be over soon."

"Yes," she replied icily. "It will."

Somehow the simple, unprepossessing words shook Cardivan more than any that had come before. More theatricality? The lunassera rejoiced in playing at prophets, but prophecy was not truth.

"To the palace!" he shouted. "A new era begins!"

As he wheeled his horse about, the wind brought new clamour from the west. Sounds that had dominated recent hours roused again to wakefulness. The growl of battle and the strike of swords. Cardivan's confidence, battered on the rocks of Sera's certainty, began to fray.

"What now?" he snarled.

When Jorcari returned to the throne room, he did so not just in the company of two dozen lodgemates – all time-worn, and many with bindwork limbs as proof of valiant service – but also with Ori Chakdra, a havildar of the palace gate. As trustworthy a soul as any Melanna had known ... but then, trust was a coin greatly devalued that day. Blackwinders busied themselves barricading the doors with benches and tables. Jorcari escorted Chakdra forward.

The havildar dropped to his knees, head bowed. "My Empress, we failed you." His voice shook, wrath and humiliation in the balance. "Those I trust are hunting the faithless as we speak."

"How can I believe anything you say?" Melanna replied sourly. "For the first time, I'm glad my father is gone. To see this would have broken him."

Chakdra slid his sword from its scabbard. Grasping it by the blade, he offered her the hilt. "If you doubt me, strike my head from my shoulders. I offer it gladly."

Melanna took the sword, every passing moment of Kaila's absence weightier than the one before. Her father would have accepted the sacrifice. Haldrane would have urged it. Certainty demanded it. But if there was to be any hope in coming days, there had to be trust. Blind suspicion crippled as surely as any wound.

She reversed the sword and held it out. "Rise, havildar. There's failure enough this day. If I take your head, I must offer my own alongside. How many remain—"

Cries of alarm rang out. Blackwinders rushed towards the towering statue of Jack with scavenged weapons drawn. As Melanna joined them, she spied a half-height panel in the sculpted robes, so cleverly concealed she'd no suspicion of its existence. That she saw it now was only because it hung slightly ajar, frozen in the act of opening.

"Announce yourself!" she shouted.

A pause. Blackwinders edged closer, weapons levelled.

"Madda?"

For a moment, Melanna thought a longing heart deceived her ears. Then the panel creaked fully open. Kaila, her hair matted and filthy, her face streaked with dried blood, clambered into the room as if there were nothing unusual in the deed.

"Kaila?"

Melanna held her daughter tight. She'd no notion how long she knelt there, only that it wasn't long enough – could never be long enough. A piece of her world returned, and she the stronger for it.

She pulled back. Fingers probed for harms, and found nothing but grazes. "Are you hurt, *essavim*?"

Kaila shook her head, welling tears a match for Melanna's own. "Shar Rasha kept me safe. And her. She killed so many ... "

Fresh growls of challenge dragged Melanna's gaze back to the panel. Face unflinching, her rent and torn clothing covered in blood, Lady Orova cast a sword to the tiles. The Blackwinders closed in.

"Stop!" Melanna stood, once again little crediting the evidence of her eyes. Orova the truce-breaker, the widowmaker of Govanna Field ... her daughter's saviour? "Is it true?"

Orova staggered, a faltering hand leaving a crimson smear against the statue's flank. "If you don't believe your daughter," she said in halting, accented Rhalesh, "what surety can I offer?"

"And Jasaldar Rasha?"

"He died for her."

There was no parsing that swirl of emotion. Relief that Rasha had been true to the last. Sorrow for what it had cost him. Gratitude to the woman who'd slain more of Rhaled's loyal warriors than any save the Droshna himself. As Melanna floundered amid their confluence, the air grew chill, a scent of stale yesterdays rising to challenge the scents of woodsmoke and stale blood.

Green-white vapour spilled from a doorway no longer bounded by stone and timber, but swirling mist. A lifeless body draped across outstretched arms, a ragged Apara Rann stumbled into the throne room and eased her burden down.

"Haldrane?" Melanna pushed Kaila to Apara's keeping and crouched beside him.

The mists dissipating behind, Apara gave a sharp shake of the head. "I found him in the streets. He was all but gone then. I didn't want to bring him through Otherworld – it's stolen most of what was left – but he insisted. Cardivan's warriors are everywhere."

Haldrane uttered a great, wracking sigh and clutched and grabbed Melanna's shoulder. Red-rimmed eyes burned in a greying face. "It seems ... my warning has come too late."

She laid a hand on his. "That doesn't matter now. You need to live."

"I have erred ... this is my payment. I encouraged Cardivan, you see. Better to draw out his poison ... not fester in the shadows. Force you ... to deal with him in kind. But I was complacent."

The confession should have provoked anger, but Melanna found she'd none to offer. "You old fool. You should have listened to me."

"I should." A laugh gurgled in Haldrane's throat. Still prone, he craned his neck, bloodshot eyes taking in the chamber's occupants. "I would have had you ... force enemies and rivals to be resentful servants. Bound them with lies and protocol. The way of your sires. Instead, you've made them into allies. Your way ... will serve you better than mine."

"And what if it's too late for that?"

Haldrane gave no reply. He'd never again offer one that side of the mists.

Laying the lifeless hand across his chest, Melanna closed his eyes and stumbled to her feet. The loss hurt more than it should. She'd never liked Haldrane overmuch, nor he her. But for all his contrition, he'd also confirmed the horrific scale of what was underway. It wasn't just the palace. It was the city. Perhaps even the Empire. Was Aeldran already dead upon the road? Mergadir overrun? The twin thoughts squeezed every scrap of breath from her lungs.

"What are your orders, Empress?" asked Chakdra.

They were all looking to her for guidance. Not just Chakdra. Not just Jorcari and his lodgemates, but Apara ... and even Orova. Kaila seemed more confused than anything else, a blessing among dire times. What did she tell them? An Empress was nothing without warriors, and hers were dead, or gone. The business of Empire would continue readily without her. Few cared who ruled, so long as someone *did*.

It was over. The House of Saran had fallen. Not through Haldrane's hubris, but her own.

Jack had been right. She was alone.

"Do you hear that?" asked Jorcari.

And there *was* a new clamour in the streets outside. Battle renewed, and voices raised in unity, though the words were distorted.

Apara skirted Haldrane's corpse and stood eye to eye with Melanna, her voice too quiet for any other to hear. "The streets were empty when I found Haldrane, but as I entered the mists they were filling again." She glanced at Jorcari. "The spears of your garrisons are dead. But old warriors do not forget their loyalties. The populace has not forgotten all you've done since taking the throne. They're finding their courage, and learning that it burns hot enough to kill."

Melanna at last sifted words from the cacophony beyond the walls. *Saranal Brigantim*. Victory for the daughter of Saran.

Despair yielded to shame. Her Immortals were riven. Her garrison was gone – perhaps her husband and her armies too. But her people remained. And they fought for her.

She stared about the room, Haldrane's final words taking on fresh meaning. *You've made them into allies.* Apara. Orova. Jorcari. The absent Aeldran, if he lived. His sister Aelia. Even Haldrane. Her father would have made enemies of them all. For their allegiance, for their deeds – for demanding something of the throne it was not prepared to give. Some had been her enemies also, but not at that moment. How had Josiri Trelan put it, less than a fortnight and a lifetime ago? *Enemies make the finest friends.* The kindness he'd twice shown had echoed through her own deeds, and now brought hope out of despair.

Because Jack had been *wrong*. She wasn't alone.

"My place is with my people." Melanna's voice was once again something she recognised. "Those who would join me there do me the greatest honour."

Jorcari and his lodgemates knelt, hands clasped to their chests in salute. Chakdra bowed. Apara nodded, a smile banished as soon as seen.

Orova set her back against the statue, her face pale, but her eyes steady.

"I won't fight to preserve your throne, Empress, but I *will* guard your daughter's life with what remains of my own."

Melanna nodded, the response far more than she'd hoped. Strange to trust an old foe so completely and without doubt, but that was the tenor of the day. "So be it."

She stalked towards the throne. No fire blazed as she drew the Goddess' sword free of its sheath. No matter. She'd plenty of her own.

Forty-Four

They came without orders through the rain, without fanfare of trumpets and without shields. For every sword, there was a woodsman's axe, a mallet, a mattock, a scythe or a cudgel. What leaders they had were marked not by rank or golden armour, but by bellowed command. Veterans of the Empire's wars, leading not spearbands or cohorts, but friends and neighbours roused to purpose. No blazons of banners, no heraldry to mark allegiance. Just a rallying cry that hammered out beneath the bitter smoke from Triumphal Gate's burning barracks. It echoed along the stark black walls of Ravencourt Temple and into the streets.

"*Saranal Brigantim!*"

Safe among the two hundred cataphracts of his bodyguard, Cardivan stared down into the temple plaza with contempt beyond words. A mob remained a mob, no matter its allegiance. This last spasm of defiance would end when the gutters ran red.

Silsarian shields buckled, but held. The leading edge of the mob rippled. Screams contested the misguided battle cry, survivors of the Avitra Briganda and foolhardy citizens alike borne to the Raven's embrace on wings of their own impertinence.

"A shame this couldn't be avoided." Cardivan patted his horse's neck. "But they've only themselves to blame."

Brackar grunted, envious eyes never leaving the plaza. "They must be brought to heel."

"Indeed. I can be merciful tomorrow."

Jasaldar Amitra, his armour and the tails of his rust-coloured cloak

flecked scarlet from the day's labours, walked his horse along the formation's front. An old warrior, with the scars to prove it, he regarded the
one-sided battle with stony expression.

"There's no end to them, *savir*. Should I send a rider to Prince Thirava?"

Cardivan snorted. "We can manage this without my son's unique
brand of valour. Let him stay at Mooncourt, caging the holy drabs."
In the plaza, the shield wall stuttered and shifted as warriors fought to
contain a crowd thrice their number. One end curled back about the
fountain and the forest of cast-iron ghostfire braziers above. "But des-
patch a rider to Triumphal Gate to summon Ganandra's spears. And
send in your outriders. I want this city at heel before moonrise."

Amitra spurred away, upraised sword and bellow of command
forming waiting outriders into a wedge of spears. In the narrow streets
around the plaza, the mob might have fared better, but in the broad, open
ground before Ravencourt Temple, riders would tear them to pieces.

A shame to mar so great a day with slaughter, but the throne was all.
Not the city, and most certainly not the people.

With a blare of trumpets, the cataphracts spurred away.

Melanna beheld the palace's outer gate, the old, familiar frisson of a
battle yet to come buzzing beneath her thoughts. Fear. Anticipation.
The excitement she'd thought passing years had placed behind her. And
the impatience most of all. She was Empress. If she called for the gate
to open, its keepers would obey. The waiting would end. But premature
deeds were more dangerous than no deeds at all. The coming hour
turned on symbols more than haste.

Hardest of all was to wait in the saddle with the sounds of battle
washing over the walls. Her people, dying with her name on their lips.

She gripped the reins tighter and stared across the courtyard towards
the palace. Where was Apara? How long could so simple a task take?
Aware that scores of eyes looked to her for example, Melanna bit her lip
and resumed contemplation of an outer gate whose every knot and rivet
she'd come to know intimately in preceding minutes.

"Cardivan will not take your throne, *savim*." Jorcari spoke without
turning, his back spear-straight in the saddle and his eyes on the gate.
Clad in a mismatch of armour salvaged from the royal vaults, he looked

part Emperor and part brigand. As did the Blackwinders waiting in silence behind – all save those who had barricaded themselves within Penitent's Tower with Kaila and a Lady Orova who looked on the point of collapse. Emeralds glistened at helm and hilt, the heirlooms of Empire summoned again to the battlefield. Chakdra and his Immortals waited further back, the courtyard thick with wounded pride. Tarnished by the treachery of their peers, they'd not guard their Empress this day. "The people won't let him."

Melanna grimaced. "It's the people I fear for."

"That's *why* they won't let him." The wrinkled face dipped. The voice become a murmur. "To my shame, I might have taken Cardivan's coin five years ago."

The confession was little surprise. The Veteran's Lodges were bastions of the traditions Melanna had flouted. "What's changed?"

"My kin stopped living in the shadow of wars yet to come. They glimpsed a future beyond trumpets and shield walls. A gift generations of Emperors promised, but only you sought to deliver."

She stared at the gate, cruel imagination inking faces behind every scream. "And yet still they have to fight."

"Because they *choose* to, *savim*. Not because they complete a chieftain's tithe, or because their Empress seeks glory. This is not battle demanded by fealty, but offered in service. Do not reject the gift."

"I don't mean to." Melanna, her heart brimming with humility's contradictory pride, let her voice blossom for all to hear. "Whatever lies beyond that gate, the House of Saran owes you all a debt. I will see it repaid."

As if on cue, Apara – ruined gown exchanged for the same mismatched splendour of the Blackwinders – at last hurried across the courtyard, a rigid bundle in her hands. She set its brass-bound foot in the shaped stirrup alongside Melanna's knee and pivoted the rest for her to take. As it came upright, the swell of emerald silks streamed behind, setting free a spread-winged silver owl upon its glittering field.

Not her father's banner, which had been lost on Govanna Field, nor even her grandfather's, but that of her great-great-grandfather Alfric, who'd torn Tregard from a complacent Republic. That owl had once proclaimed the city the property of the House of Saran. Though its silks were tattered and moth-eaten, it did so again.

"Be careful with that," said Apara. "It's worth a fortune to the right collector."

Jorcari frowned. Melanna smiled. "You can do what I ask?"

"All this death has brought Otherworld close. The mists will take me wherever I've need. I'd rather be with you."

"I trust no one else to see that Triumphal Gate is sealed."

"But why? There's no one left to keep out. All of Cardivan's forces are already in the city. If this goes badly, you'll be trapped."

"Not me. Cardivan wanted this city. Let him choke on it."

Apara nodded and withdrew. Trumpets sounded on the outer wall. The gate rumbled open.

Melanna hoisted the banner high and spurred away. "Saranal Brigantim!"

With one voice, the city replied.

They kept coming. Inspiring to see, were one a connoisseur of doomed gallantry. Cardivan, who cared little for gallantry of any kind, merely found it remarkable that so many folk could be so deluded.

What matter that Amitra's charge had stalled? His horsemen had driven deep into the mob, splitting a single, unstoppable tide in twain, one half caught between the obsidian walls of Ravencourt and the outriders' spears, and the other being ground to offal between those spears and the advancing stag-shields. The dead of both sides lay trampled beneath, but discipline and superior weaponry would carry the day, as they always did.

One last effort, one last glorious charge of spears would turn the tide. But there were no spears to be had. The sloping street remained empty. No sign of Ganandra's warband, nor the others sent for since. Just the two hundreds of Cardivan's own bodyguard, and a trail of wounded being dragged to physicians' care.

That the clamour from the neighbouring streets seemed louder did little to ease Cardivan's mood. Seldom had he heard the hated name Saranal bellowed so often in so fleeting a span.

"Where's Ganandra?" he growled.

Brackar tore his gaze from the fighting. "I can find out."

"Yes. No. I need you with me. You!" Cardivan stabbed a finger at a nearby cataphract. "Triumphal Gate. Find Ganandra! I'll have his spears or his head! Leave the choice to him!"

The cataphract galloped away, cloak spread wide in the rain.

A great cheer went up from the plaza as the stag-shields reclaimed the fountain, driving the mob back towards the Old Quarter. A grey-haired veteran stood his ground amid his fellows' retreat, a great notched axe whirling bloody circles. A shieldsman collapsed beneath the heavy blade, leather helm and skull split open. The veteran sent another sprawling back, right arm parted from his body. Then the axe lodged deep in a shield, and vengeful spears came forward.

The axeman died with a mouth full of blood. Gaps opened up as the mob at last lost heart, old men and young scrambling away, abandoned by the Empress for whom their neighbours had fought and died. Drawing purpose for the uncertainty of their foes, the shields of Silsaria and Redsigor ground forward.

Cardivan nodded, indulging satisfaction. The moment he'd sought. The chance to join in a victory well won, for his men to see that he shared their travails.

He raised his sword high. "Tirane Areg—"

Trumpets blared from the west, drowning out the battle cry. A thunder of hooves swallowed all. The plaza's western streets – streets that had been empty moments before – filled with emerald green and beneath a silver owl, wings spread wide.

The Silsarian line, steeped in victory moments before, now died almost before they knew their danger, their shields locked tight against a beaten foe and their backs to bejewelled spears and gleaming swords, to merciless riders garbed in the armour of Emperors long gone into mist.

And at the head of the charge, a woman who should have been dead or captured or anywhere but there. The city had called, and the Empress had come.

Lost to a sudden, seething rage, Cardivan rounded on the nearest cataphract. "Find my worthless son! Tell him his future is dying beneath the walls of Ravencourt!"

Without waiting for reply, Cardivan thrust back his spurs.

Triumphal Gate's occupiers had expected trouble, but with the ramparts cleared their attention had been focused, along murder-hole lined passageways and iron doors closed to hold even the most determined of attackers at bay. A Tressian regiment could have ground itself to ruin on those stairs, outmatched by a garrison of a few score. But it had been a long time since Apara had troubled herself with front doors.

Its site chosen with care made possible by Otherworld's closeness to the ephemeral world, the mist gate cast her small company of Immortals into the heart of Triumphal Gate's barbican. The Silsarians – their eyes to the city rather than the chambers at their back – stood no chance at all.

Wiping her sword clean on a corpse's robes, she tallied the survivors of her assault. Three had died retaking the barbican. Two more had suffered injuries that would see them return to the mists before nightfall. Of the survivors, several were pale beneath their helms. Three more sat slumped against the wall, heads in hands. Not a result of wounds taken during the attack, but the malice of Otherworld's mists. What should have been a straightforward passage had been oppressive, suffocating – the mists themselves more grey than greenish-white. Apara had felt it during her foray to Haldravord, but had dismissed it as a projection of her own doubts about Rosa's rescue. Now she knew better. Otherworld and the Raven were bound, their moods linked. She wondered what had riled him so, and hoped never to find out.

"The doors are barricaded, *savim*."

The havildar even offered a small bow. To her. A Tressian and a thief. What should have called for amusement offered only solemn pride. "And the winding room?"

"This way."

Apara hesitated, her gaze stolen by a glimpse of Silsarian warriors through the narrow window. No more than a dozen, and all of them running for the gate as if the Raven himself were on their heels. And that might have been true enough. Though Tregard were still in uproar, the tone was different. Anger remained, but the fear was gone.

The winding room was a jumble of broken bodies and mangled mechanisms. Even had they been whole, Apara doubted she'd have understood their function.

"Close the gate, she said." Apara threw up her arms to encompass the baffling array of ropes, gears and pulleys. "I'd better go down and push."

A thunder of hooves far below drew her back to a wallward window. A column of Silsarian riders, Thirava's thin features readily identifiable even through the rain, galloped out of the tangled streets and vanished beneath the gate house. Moments later, she heard their hooves on the Golden Way's flagstones. Good riddance.

"Here!" The havildar stood in one corner of the room, his hand about a thick, grease-smeared rope stretched between a pulley and a jammed windlass. "This one."

Careful not to snag a foot on the dead, Apara moved to join him. "You're certain?"

"I held the watch here for five years." He shrugged. "Half these counterweights are for driving home the locking bolts, or raising the gate once it's closed. Not this. We split this, and the city stays sealed until we get lifting teams in place."

Apara plucked an axe from a nearby Rhalesh corpse. "Then we'd better get to it."

After years trapped on the throne she'd yearned for all her life, Melanna found freedom in that charge. The sword didn't care about politics, or the balance of power. It had no ego to soothe, nor temper to placate. It cared only that the hand wielding it was strong, and filled with purpose. On that day Melanna Saranal, Empress and Dotha Rhaled, knew purpose unflinching.

It didn't matter that her armour no longer fitted as well as once it had, or that the sword was heavier than she remembered. There was only the wind in her hair, the enemy ahead and the banner snapping behind. Raven take Jack, take Cardivan, take Thirava – take all those who'd worked so hard to fill her with doubt and shatter what she'd built. To the Raven with them all, and if it was she who sent them to his keeping, so much the better.

A Silsarian shieldsman screamed and reeled away, blood gushing from his shoulder. Another levelled a spear to pluck her from the saddle. Melanna struck the weapon aside and hacked down.

To her left, where the banner's burden left her vulnerable, Jorcari roared with every thrust of his spear. Blackwinders glutted Otherworld's mists with dead as only old warriors could. Behind them swept

Immortals desperate to restore tarnished honour, and an army of vengeful citizenry.

The shieldsmen broke, fleeing back across the plaza in one and twos, and then by the score. Outriders were dragged from their horses, or swept from saddles by Blackwinders' spears. Melanna parried a chieftain's vicious swing and struck him screaming from his saddle. Then there was only the fountain, a tideline of dead, a blur of gold as Cardivan's cataphracts galloped to the charge, and no time to do anything but meet it in kind.

Banner streaming behind, Melanna thrust back her spurs and gave herself to the madness.

"Saranal Brigantim!" roared Jorcari.

The rumble of hooves gave way to an almighty crash of spears and shields. Melanna's ears rang to the screams of men and horses. Her sword chimed as it met a cataphract's, the impact twisting her about in the saddle. Battle lines blurred, Silsarian gold bleeding away between the Blackwinders' emerald glory as the clash of armies yielded to intimate duels.

Catching sight of Cardivan, Melanna spurred on. A brute in champion's finery slewed to block her path. She knew him by reputation, and only for deeds of which no champion should be proud. A murderer hiding behind notions of honour he'd never understand. A braggart. A thug. Precisely the sort of man she'd expect Cardivan to choose as champion. He bore no shield, only a long-bladed headtaker sword that few had the strength to wield well.

Melanna met the first swing with a parry that shivered her arm, all but ripping the sword from her grasp. The second scattered golden scales from her shoulder, leaving a livid graze beneath. As the third hacked down, Melanna dug her knees into her horse's flank. She twisted as it sprang aside, and the blow meant to split her skull hissed harmlessly through the rain. A second nudge and her mare cantered clear through the anarchic melee.

"You don't match your reputation, *essavim*," Brackar leered as she wheeled about.

Melanna's skin crawled at the misused term of endearment. Worse, she felt the ache of muscles fallen fallow – the ironclad princessa of the past softened by an Empress' comforts. Brackar was stronger. The head-taker sword gave him a reach she couldn't match.

But she'd spent a life uncaring of her limits. She'd not change now.

A rolling *boom* swept the plaza, warning Melanna that Apara had done as she'd asked. Triumphal Gate was sealed. Cardivan would find no escape. And tangled in its echoes, something sweeter and sadder. A song of old memories and old times, borne aloft on a chorus of women's voices. Melanna had sung it herself, when the Goddess had moved her to do so, though she never recalled the words afterwards.

Far beyond Brackar, beyond where Cardivan sheltered behind the shields of his cataphracts, the roadway's crest filled with the white robes and glittering, ethereal spears of the lunassera.

Melanna's flagging limbs found new vigour. "I'm more than my reputation."

With a wolfish grin, Brackar rowelled his steed to the charge.

Melanna thrust back her spurs, sword levelled as a spear. No fear. No fury. Only a calm she'd never known. Peace amid the battle's rage.

Brackar let go his reins to take the sword in both hands. The killing blade swung to take her head. The rain ceased and the first sunlight split the clouds. And in that heartbeat, it seemed to Melanna that the Goddess' sword again found its flame for the briefest of moments. Or perhaps it was simply the sun's glory reflected from the steel, Lumestra offering aid where her sister could not.

In the end, there was almost nothing. A soft tug that travelled through Melanna's body and passed like rain on the meadow. Already masterless, the headtaker sword hissed over her head. Brackar's horse cantered on, his corpse still in the saddle, throat torn wide.

Melanna's eyes met Cardivan's.

Turning his horse, he fled.

What remained of the Silsarians joined him in flight, but of escape, they found none. To the north, there was only the citizen army. To the west, the plaza was thick with Immortals and Blackwinders. To the south, the lunassera. And to the east, the foreboding gates of Ravencourt Temple remained shut. A low, murderous growl rose in crescendo as the men and women of Tregard recognised the plaza for the cage it had become. Shieldsmen and outriders threw down their blades and cried for mercy. Cataphracts fought and died between the hammer of Jorcari's Blackwinders and the anvil of Chakdra's penitent Immortals.

Even as Melanna rode to join them, Cardivan's horse reared before a mace-blow. The would-be Emperor landed heavily, his helm rolling away across the flagstones. With a howl, those he'd sought to rule closed in.

"Enough!" cried Melanna. "Anyone who lays a hand on him answers to me!"

The onrush stuttered, halted, cooler heads prevailing over the rash. Cardivan gazed warily up at her from hands and knees, but said nothing.

Beckoning to a nearby Blackwinder, Melanna yielded the venerable banner and swung from the saddle. Weary muscles and chafed skin howled a symphony in tune with her injured shoulder. Making no attempt to hide discomfort, she bore down on Cardivan. Warriors of both sides, captives and victors, drew back from her – from the sword still slick with Brackar's blood – until Empress and presumptuous king were alone in a circle of blades.

"It's ended, my king," said Melanna. "The city is sealed. Your men will be hunted through the streets, and you will find escape only through my mercy or the Raven's gift."

There was no pleasure in this moment. None. In the victory, yes, but that victory had cost too much. Tavar Rasha. Haldrane. So many men and women whose names Melanna would never know, who'd fought for her when sworn protectors had cast aside all honour.

No pleasure. But perhaps a measure of justice.

Ignoring the stab of pain from a wounded shoulder, she spread her arms. "You venerate tradition above all, isn't that right, Cardivan? Tradition demands that we of royal blood settle our differences with swords." When he offered no answer but a dead-eyed stare, she pressed on. "Not long ago, I offered to duel you for the throne. I offer again. Face me in the ring of blades and, live or die, your warriors will go free. Or you can kneel without a fight. I'll spare your life, but they – every last one – will feed the pyres at Ravencourt."

The plaza went deathly silent. There were hundreds of prisoners in the plaza alone. Across the city, they surely numbered thousands. Kings and princes doomed that many all the time through arrogance and war.

But to do so now? When all Cardivan need do otherwise was to duel a *woman* he'd ever proclaimed his inferior?

Faced with the same choice, Melanna wouldn't have hesitated. But slowly, wretchedly – and without once even meeting her gaze – Cardivan cast his sword to the ground and sank first to one knee, and then the other. Proclaiming with bright clarion the esteem in which he held his warriors' lives.

And Melanna Saranal, who'd never had the slightest intent of sending anyone to the pyre, closed her eyes and revelled in the warmth of the sun.

Forty-Five

Her smoke-blackened features worn smooth by repeated rains, the serathi sculpted into the cornice looked as though she intended to continue her staring match with Vordal Tower for centuries to come.

A chunk of her right wing crumbled away under Altiris' hand. Stomach lurching and scabbard tapping at his leg, he scrabbled for fresh grip. A gloved hand grabbed his, arresting his descent. His other at last found purchase. Heart pounding, Altiris glanced up. Hawkin lay flat upon the broad ledge he'd sought to reach, arm at full stretch and teeth gleaming white in the moonlight.

"Thought you'd be better at this, my bonny."

Flushed with chagrin, Altiris planted his booted toe in an alcove and hauled his way up. Seemingly unencumbered by prybar, covered lantern and scabbarded daggers, Hawkin pivoted to give him space on the ledge, and let her legs dangle out over the six-storey drop.

Altiris sank beside her, every inch of his body within the ledge's outline, and his back flush against stonework. He glanced up, taking in the boarded window and the dark, motionless hands of the ancient clockface. He closed his eyes as the world reeled.

Twenty years lived, and nary a flicker of vertigo. Until tonight.

"I prefer staying close to the streets," he replied evenly.

She snorted. "Slip past a palace bursting with Drazina? Least the fall'll be quick."

Altiris scowled, the logic unassailable. Still, he was glad of the windless night, and the maze of scaffolding still in place from the window repairs. Better not to think about the alternatives.

"You good to keep going?" asked Hawkin.

He nodded, taken aback, his companion more like the woman who'd played at steward for the Reveques than the one who stole and murdered for the Merrow.

"After you," he said.

For reasons Altiris couldn't quite determine, the scaffolding's platforms ceased a full storey below the window they'd been erected to repair, even though the poles continued to the full extent. Nonetheless, Hawkin scrambled effortlessly up the last section of wall, ponytailed chestnut curls bobbing against the darkness and fingers moving instinctively from handhold to handhold until she stood on the ledge beside the boarded window. This time, Altiris joined her without unwanted excitement. Not that his pacing heart *quite* agreed with that appraisal.

Still, there was a beauty to seeing the city thus. The firefly rivers of its street lanterns, and the smoke spiralling away towards the moon. "I see why the Lord Protector chose quarters up here."

"His sort always like to look down on people. Even while they're raising them up." Hawkin stared north across the city, her tone reluctant, hesitant. "Do you think it's possible to atone for the past?"

"Zarn doesn't seem to care. Not really."

"I'm talking about me."

There was an odd vulnerability to her now – sharp contrast to the ice-edged woman who'd re-entered his life with the dying year. "You're asking the wrong person."

"Vona's spirit wants vengeance. Kasvin told me that sooner or later, someone's going to see she gets it."

Was Hawkin looking for the house they'd shared? That would have been near the palace. Nascent sympathy bled away. He'd not known Captain Darrow well, but she'd saved his life. "You blame her for wanting that?"

"I'd no choice."

"Plenty don't. They choose different anyway. *I* chose different."

She sneered. "Yes, you're a proper little hallowed sunbeam, aren't you?"

Sympathy now well and truly at its dregs, Altiris bared his wrist and the slave's rose-brand they shared. "I started out with nothing you didn't. You know that."

She turned away, lips tight and bloodless. "I just want to wipe the slate clean. Start again."

He sighed. Hawkin didn't want to make amends, but to escape consequence. Understandable, and somehow disappointing. "Maybe Zarn's right. Maybe you can't make up for the past. You can only do better in the future."

"It's not fair."

"Sometimes it isn't about what's fair. It's about what's right." Altiris fell silent, no longer certain if he was talking about Hawkin or himself. Lord Trelan. Sidara. He'd broken their trust, though in different ways, but couldn't for the life of him see how he could have done otherwise. "Perhaps none of this will change things for you, but it can't hurt."

She glared, again all hard edges and certainty. "You don't need to talk me around, my bonny. I said I'd do it, and I will. My word still means something."

Turning her back on the city, she unslung the prybar.

Calenne looked up from her book at the first scrape of metal on wood. At the fourth, she closed the pages carefully and set it aside. Torn between curiosity and concern, she rose, passing from the glow of candlelight to the gloom beyond.

A muffled grunt. A screech of unhappy timber. Muffled voices beyond the window. Housebreakers? Here? What should she do? What *could* she do? The fear of discovery, of being seen – the same fear that had held Calenne back from escaping the previous day – returned with a vengeance. More than that, there was no telling how the intruders would react.

If only Viktor had left her a weapon, but there were only the books, the broken mannequins and the paraphernalia of his mystical studies. Nothing with which to defend herself. Barely anywhere to hide among the sparse furnishings.

Something heavy struck the lowermost of the inner boards. Nails loosened by Calenne's own efforts slipped free at once, provoking a cascade of timber as those supported above fell away with a rumbling crash.

Echoes rushing around her, Calenne froze, awash in bitterness. Tzila *had* to have heard that. Her escape plan was as tattered as the window . . .

assuming she lived through what was to come. She'd no idea how durable her porcelain body truly was, and harboured no desire to find out.

A head poked beneath the boards. A sharp-eyed woman, only a few years older than Calenne had been at her death, in worn, vagabond's garb.

"There's no one here," she hissed into the night. "Just a dressmaker's mannequin."

Had she been able, Calenne might have smiled. There was a third path between confrontation and flight. With the intruder's attention still on her conspirator beyond the window, she let her hands drop a fraction further, becoming even more the image of the woman's mistaken glance.

Ducking beneath the remaining boards, the woman clambered over the windowsill. A younger, red-haired man followed her inside.

Altiris narrowed his eyes, willing them to adapt to the gloom. There was no light save from a lone candle burning on what had once been an expensive, veneered side table. The chamber had the feel of one untrodden for some time. The air had an attic's dry, stale odour, lacking the small smells and tastes of something occupied, or frequented.

"So much for the stealth of vranakin," he muttered.

"They were already loose, all right?" Gruff tone didn't conceal Hawkin's embarrassment. "How was I to know?"

Altiris crossed to the table. Picking up each of the small, leatherbound books in turn, he held their spine up to the light. Nothing useful. A series of romances held accorded classics by a certain kind of matriarch. Just racy enough, but not unseemly. "Make this quick. Someone may have heard."

"Don't tell me how to do my job, my bonny."

Hawkin unfurled her lantern's shield and roused it to life. The dull orange of firestone gave shape to several more wax-crusted candelabra and tables – one broken and canted over – and a pile of large, weighty books stacked beside a small chest. Fresh shadows gathered around the dressmaker's mannequin and above the cold, dust-laden chandelier. Altiris shuddered away a prickle between his shoulder blades.

"I don't like this."

Hawkin snorted. "Where's that Trelan courage now?"

Regretting ever having told her of Josiri's decision, he threw her a sour look and drew closer to the mannequin, which felt every bit as much out of place as the burning candle. Pristine, in a room thick with dust. The cream, panelled gown – chased with embroidered blue flowers and golden silk – was as perfect as the ribbon-laced wig and long-sleeved gloves. All were of more expensive make than Sidara ever wore. Only Anastacia favoured such garb, a habit that had survived transposition from clay to flesh. Had the mannequin's features been finer, there might have been a kinship between them. As it was, Altiris saw nothing but old regrets gone screaming past the threshold of fondness and into something pitiable.

"We'll not find anything." He sighed, unable to meet the mannequin's black, empty gaze any longer. "All this room hides is a broken heart."

Hawkin looked up, her lantern set aside and her fingers dancing yellowed pages. "Say again?"

"I think this is supposed to be Lord Trelan's sister, Calenne. She and Viktor . . . " He paused. How quickly sorrow humanised a man. "She and Lord Droshna were betrothed. The Dark took her, and he'd no choice but to kill her."

"Northwealders and their perversions. You're wrong, though, my bonny." She tapped the book and nodded at those that remained. "*The Undawning Deep. Testament of Ways. Vitsimar?* One of these'd set me up for life, with the right buyer. Be a bold man who left them on show, mind, even with the provosts gone."

Altiris nodded, uncertain whether to be glad or dismayed at finding the proof they'd sought. The false Calenne made it easier to recall the charismatic, companionable Viktor Droshna of Midwintertide rather than the brooding Lord Protector.

Hawkin knelt before the chest. "And what do we have here?" Hands dipping to her belt, she set lockpicks to work. "Might as well look. We've come all this way."

Altiris nodded, his eye drawn to a pale gleam just beyond the reach of Hawkin's lantern. Claiming the candlestick from the lacquered table, he edged further into darkness. The gleam became a porcelain hand, smooth and perfect. In the battered box beneath, he glimpsed other pieces: fragments of scalp and brow, the gentle curve of an arm, a section of torso made jagged by a break.

A torso? A dressmaker's doll needed only a padded cage. Face and hands were understandable enough, for they gave the seemliness of fashionable pallor, but to craft the whole thing from clay as these components had been . . . ?

He spun about, eyes on the maybe-Calenne once more and his thoughts mired in one other detail about Anastacia he'd forgotten until that moment. That the Lord Protector had been the one to seal her in clay in the first place. "Hawkin . . . ?"

Double doors crashed back on their hinges. Tzila stood framed against the lights of the stairway, the long silk bases and cloak lending her the silhouette of a drowned bride. Death in a doorway.

Altiris' stomach plunged seven storeys to street level. Drazina were one thing – the woman who'd demolished Kurkas and almost killed Anastacia was something else.

He stepped closer, a hand twitching at waist level, urging Hawkin towards the window. "Tzila . . . I'll come quietly. This doesn't have to be a fight."

She slid her swords free of their sheaths, turned them a double circle about her wrists and ran into the room.

If you find yourself on the other end of those swords for real, run away as fast as you can.

Kurkas' words ringing in his ears, Altiris drew his sword and ran to meet her.

His first parry was a thing of wild desperation, but it checked Tzila's right-hand sword a hand's breadth from his brow. Fear-heightened senses glimpsed a sliver of lantern-lit steel as her left stabbed forward. He twisted, the rip of cloth warning how close to death he'd come, and barely checked a second, vicious slash from her right.

Altiris stumbled back. His left hand closed about a freestanding candelabra. A convulsive jerk sent it toppling into Tzila's path. Bases whirling, she turned on her heel and it clattered past, crusted wax shattering across the floor. The spin became a lunge, and again Altiris stumbled away. A kick set him crashing into the boxes of broken mannequins.

With a cry, Hawkin landed on Tzila's back, ankles hooked about her hips, a forearm about her shoulder and a stiletto dagger in hand. Even as the Drazina bucked, attempting to throw her clear, Hawkin stabbed down through the gap between sallet helm and gorget.

Steel scraped against a second, hidden layer of armour. Hawkin's cry of dismay rose to a shrill of pain as Tzila dropped her left-hand sword and dragged her clear by the hair. Candles scattered as Hawkin thudded across a table and crashed into a wall. Her stiletto skittered away, bent point gleaming in the lantern light. Altiris forgotten, Tzila bore down. Her remaining sword whirled to a reversed hold, both hands about the grips.

Lungs stinging with clay dust, Altiris stumbled upright. No way he could beat Tzila. Join blades with her again, and he'd be dead in seconds. Even the thought turned his knees to jelly. Might even be that Tzila was destined to be the agent of vengeance come to settle Vona Darrow's score. Destiny ran strange paths. But fight or flee, it was still his choice – just like it always was – and that made it no choice at all.

"For the Phoenix!"

He roared the battle cry, drawing strength from the motto that had been his father's before it had been his own. A promise of life. A promise of hope. It scattered fear to the shadows until only purpose remained, and Tzila . . .

Tzila, her sword halfway to Hawkin's prone body, froze.

As Altiris hacked down, she turned, blank-eyed sallet gazing straight at him. Darting inside the sword's arc, Tzila grabbed him by the throat. Slowing not a step, she strode on.

Altiris' spine struck brick. The sword jarred from his hand. Gasping for breath that wouldn't come, he cuffed uselessly at Tzila's wrist. The strike of a boot numbed his knee as he made to stamp on her foot. Her own sword falling to her side, Tzila tilted her head and gazed incuriously back.

Black splotches gathering behind his eyes, Altiris stared past her shoulder.

The mannequin was gone.

Calenne reached the threshold of her prison, the brightly lit stairs beckoning her to freedom. It wouldn't be that easy – she was starting to realise that nothing in her new life could ever be so – but it was better than chancing the window, better than remaining to await Viktor's return.

As she made to cross into the light, a choked splutter brought her to a halt.

She glanced back across her shoulder to where Tzila had the lad pinned against the wall, his struggles fading. The lad the other intruder had called a Trelan. Who'd called upon the Phoenix. She'd been the Phoenix, if only for a day. For all she'd claimed the mantle reluctantly, it had been her choice. Because *not* doing so would have proved her the selfish, callow child so many others had thought her.

She'd been freer that day than all those that had come before.

But the lad was an intruder and the woman with him plainly a thief. What punishment Tzila doled out was deserved – in principle, if not degree.

Raised voices sounded below. A moment's hesitation and her escape would be cut. Might already be cut. She wasn't the Phoenix any longer. That woman was dead.

Who was she now?

Tzila's head jerked back, grappled from behind by a pair of gloved forearms. Altiris fell to his knees, the hand gone from his throat. Bleary eyes caught a flurry of limbs, some garbed in armour and midnight blue, others in cream and blue silk.

The mannequin, dress torn and wig askew, had Tzila in a headlock, one elbow crooked about her throat. [[Go! Get out of here!]]

The singsong voice settled it. She was like Anastacia had been, or almost so.

Shadow and light swimming about him, Altiris staggered upright. Tzila twisted free of the mannequin's grip. Dislodged, the sallet helm clanged across the floor.

A blank face of smooth porcelain stood revealed, one that lacked even the small refinements present in the mannequin's features. Dark vapour blazed from empty eyes beneath the brow. Mismatched twins – triplets, if you threw Anastacia's old self into the mix.

With a soul-wrenching, hollow howl, Tzila lashed out. The mannequin shied away, arm upraised in defence. Slivers of silk rained down, the tearing sound lost beneath the scrape of steel on polished clay. The mannequin's back struck the windowsill, and then she was gone.

[[Calenne!]] At once, a change swept over Tzila, confidence habitually worn vanishing from form and posture. She ran to the window, sword abandoned and hand reaching through the ruined frame. [[No!]]

Even beneath its beautiful, horrific singsong, Altiris heard the throaty accent of the south.

A window board shattered across Tzila's unfinished head, hurling her sideways.

"No, yourself," gasped Hawkin, dropping the board's remains. Breathing hard, she turned to Altiris, her eye black and her swollen right wrist cradled against her chest. "Time to leave, my bonny."

Chased along by the sound of footsteps on the stairs, Altiris stumbled to the window and leaned out into the night. No sign of the mannequin – of *Calenne* – on the scaffold. If she'd plunged to the square . . .

"Move!" snapped Hawkin.

He glanced back into the room. To the heretical texts that would have provided all the proof they'd ever have needed. To the chest, and whatever it held. All of it beyond Tzila. She'd have been on them already had she not stopped to restore her helm and the illusion of humanity. To stay was to die, and they had learned *something*, even if they couldn't prove it, and didn't understand what it meant.

Urged on by Hawkin's shove, Altiris crawled out into the night.

Jeradas, 10th Day of Dawntithe

You may always trust to pride to steer you ill.

from the Saga of Hadar Saran

Forty-Six

Cardivan Tirane didn't resemble a man who could have been Emperor. Few would have looked the part sealed up in the deepest of the palace's dungeons, flickering torchlight lengthening the shadows on craggy, unshaven features. The previous night's meal, untouched, spoke to lacking appetite or dearth of trust. A man like Cardivan would always suspect poison, for he'd no compunction about using it himself.

He barely reacted when the Immortal snapped shackles about his wrists, ensuring he remained close companion to the wall. Only when the Immortal withdrew, and Melanna ducked beneath the swollen lintel, did his eyes twitch. A brief probing, and they resumed a blank stare towards the barred window and its pre-dawn glow.

Waving her escort from the cell, Melanna sat on the slatted bench opposite and eased her skirts into place. The window's gentle breeze – the first sounds of the waking city borne upon its wings – softened the cell's rank stench and prickled the skin on the back of her arms.

Her city. It called for retribution.

"It's over." She spoke softly, resentful at how little satisfaction she found in the words. "Your warriors are slain, captured or routed. I've decreed occupation of the Tressian Eastshires be ended. Your son flees for the Silsarian border as fast as his horse will bear him, but he'll be taken."

At last, Cardivan shifted his gaze from the window. "Then it will be war. Kerna and Novona will not sit by and watch you destroy my kingdom."

"You might be surprised," Melanna replied. "You bought your allies with cleverness. How clever do you suppose you seem at this moment? As masterplans go, this lacks . . . gravitas."

"They will come," he snapped. "They fear that their crowns will be next. So they will strike first, and the Empire will tear itself apart. Your doing, Melanna."

Was he really so deluded? Or was he simply wielding the only weapon left – the only weapon Cardivan had ever cared for? The tongue left deep welts that seldom healed. Maybe it would have worked a year before. A month. Even a week. But for the first time in a long while, Melanna had no fear of words. Whatever secrets Kerna and Novona held, Cardivan's were out in the open.

"They might," she replied, her eyes ever on his. "Had I meant to unmake Silsaria, or even its royal line. I intend neither."

His eyes crowded with suspicion. "Then you're twice the fool."

For the first time, Melanna glimpsed mania at work behind. However motionless Cardivan held his body, his mind was racing. She leaned closer. Close enough to use the dagger concealed beneath her skirts, had that been her wish. Temptation remained to do so. The walls resounded with the howls of forefathers demanding that course.

"I merely make distinction between your actions and those of your people. You've never done aught save that which would favour you, Cardivan. Did you really think I'd punish others for that?"

Melanna saw truth written in the shift of his brow and the curl of his lip. He'd believed she would, for he'd have done the same. For all that he loathed the differences between them, he didn't truly perceive their scope. The realisation offered all the satisfaction that victory lacked.

"I'll levy no further punishment against those who followed you to war, save those who owed loyalty to me," she went on. "Those, I've ordered put to death, as their oaths demand. As for your throne, I've sent an envoy to Presarai. To your grand-niece Incalia, as it happens. With you a self-professed regicide and Thirava implicated in your conspiracy, she holds the succession. I have offered peace, a throne, and the friend- ship of Rhaled. Does she love you more than these?"

According to Haldrane's detailed files, Incalia loved her great- uncle not at all. She knew little more freedom than a cask of tarakeet, hoarded against the possibility of attracting a wealthy buyer once blossomed to full vintage – and for much the same reason. Haldrane's notes had also suggested that she was not the noblest of souls, but perhaps a crown would change her. Crowns had a way of doing that, if worn well.

"Women do not rule," growled Cardivan.

"You made that argument yesterday, and lost it in bold fashion." Melanna sat upright. "I've neither the desire nor the need to destroy Silsaria, much less the House of Tirane. But you, Cardivan? You who would have made my daughter a Bride of Brief Moonlight? I have the most ignoble urge to hurt you very badly indeed, and find I cannot resent myself for it."

Anger retreated from his expression. "Then I am to die?"

Typical that he found solace in that. A good death forgave all, and for all that Cardivan had failed in his ambition, there'd be those in his court who for long years after would speak about how he'd died defiant; free, despite the chains. The martyred King of Silsaria, immortal and triumphant, even in death and defeat.

Melanna shook her head. "You will remain my guest. Indeed, I'm having a room made up for you as we speak. One that affords a grand view of the city. You will see me walk the Emperor's Walk and watch as I ride out in full panoply on feast days. Should you live but a few more years, you will see my daughter's procession to sanctum to be acclaimed my heir. Who knows? Perhaps you will even outlive me, and be privileged to witness her coronation." *Now* she permitted herself a smile. "I condemn you not to death, Cardivan, but life."

Composure dissolved beneath an animal growl. Hands hooked to claws, Cardivan sprang. The chains went taut, his face inches from Melanna's and his teeth bared in a rictus of impotent wrath.

The cell door crashed open, an Immortal halfway across the threshold with sword drawn.

"Empress!"

Melanna, who had not otherwise moved the merest fraction of an inch, waved him to stillness. Her eyes never left the prisoner's. "Goodbye, Cardivan. I don't expect we will speak again."

Rising, she departed the cell, and never once looked back.

*

Melanna couldn't face the throne room. Not with bodies still in the streets, and wounded facing an uncertain future in the lunassera's hands. Come evening, she'd again don the finery of Empire to lavish leadership and gratitude on strangers. But for the moment, she welcomed the relative peace of her outer chambers ... even if some of those gathered therein were little more than strangers themselves.

"The city is secure." Elim Jorcari stood at crisp attention by the door, wary of intruding on an Empress' privacy, despite invitation. Or perhaps he was nervous to be alone in a company of women. Brave men cultivated strange terrors. "What warriors we have stand ready vigil, *savim*."

Melanna took a sip of honeyed tea. Sweetness washed away the last of the dungeon's sourness. "Your lodge-mates?"

"Among others. I sent word to Kinholt and Vescarin in your name. Their chieftains provided warriors and apologies in equal measure. Others will follow. Between those, the lodges, the retired and the survivors of Cardivan's treachery, we have enough to hold the walls until Prince Aeldran returns."

Apara, restored to gowned splendour and hair woven with jewelled chains almost certainly *not* hers – and her eyes for the first time smoky with courtly makeup – offered an amused snort from her station by the window. A frown touched Sera's lips, the rest of her expression concealed beneath her silvered mask. The room's fifth occupant – and other than Melanna, the only one seated – offered no reaction at all. Roslava Orova had said almost nothing since Melanna had dismissed the guards, and bore Sera's suspicious glances with sullen dignity and a bloodless face that offered reminder she was yet far from hale.

A warrior of the old tradition, a thief, a priestess and a Tressian knight. Strange counsel for an Empress to seek, but somehow fit for the times.

Melanna set the cup aside. "It's a dangerous thing to speak for the Empress without her leave, jasaldar."

Not content with navigating the previous day's strife without so much as a scratch, Jorcari conspired to appear clear-eyed and alert despite having taken only three hours' sleep. "You bade me secure the city, my Empress. If I have overstepped, my life is yours to take."

It was just about possible to hear apology in his words, but Melanna found none in his tone. "That would be poor reward for all you've done. But make no habit of such things. I must be able to trust my champion."

Impossibly, he stood straighter. "*Savim*, I cannot—"

"Refuse? Absolutely correct. The Empress' word is law, is it not?" She smiled to soften an arch tone. "Not all traditions are without value. I hope recent events will serve as a lesson for the royal guard, not a reason for dissolution. I can think of no better tutor. Chakdra will command my Immortals, but will answer to you in all things. Until you're satisfied the lesson has taken, this palace belongs to the lunassera, and the royal guard are merely guests."

Tavar Rasha would have died anew to hear those words, but he'd have understood. Melanna only hoped Kaila warmed to Jorcari as much as she had Shar Rasha, whose Last Ride she'd officiate beneath the moon that very night. When the grim gates of Ravencourt Temple creaked open, six Immortals – volunteers all – would bear their captain into the mists. Melanna could barely afford to lose them, but there were few enough honours she could offer the dead. One last battle in the Raven's own land would have to suffice.

Jorcari offered a low bow. "I would be honoured . . . *essavim*."

Stiffness receded from Melanna's shoulders, though in truth she'd entertained few doubts about his acceptance. Warrior's pride was ever a dependable motivator. Besides, she'd already fought a similar, fiercer battle that morning, and won despite all odds. Speaking of which . . .

"What of my icularis?" she asked.

Apara's left eyelid flickered, but her voice was confident enough. "Those I've been able to contact – and convince of my authority – are torn between guilt and fury. If traitors remain within their ranks, I don't imagine we'll hear from them ever again this side of the mists." She shrugged. "I've sent riders south bearing variants of the letter to Prince Aeldran. Which copies arrive, and when, will prove instructive."

Melanna struggled to hide her surprise. She'd never have considered that particular opportunity. "Haldrane would have approved."

That much she was certain of, even if her own feelings towards the dead spymaster were less clear. His loyalty had never been in question, but his objectivity? He'd run out of road long before he'd stopped walking, and paid with his life.

"I doubt it," Apara replied. "He'd little good to say about me."

"And now he's dead, through his own error," said Sera. "This tells us something about the value of his opinions."

Jorcari grunted his amusement.

Melanna nodded to herself. Yes, she'd chosen well. Sera to safeguard her life and that of her daughter, Apara to be her eyes and ears, and Jorcari to rebuild that which Cardivan – and her own laxness – had broken.

Aeldran was a jarring absence, but would return. Aware that eyes other than his might read her letter, Melanna had spoken guardedly, assuring him all was well, and that his presence was requested as soon as he was able. But she'd striven to emphasise that it was not merely her consort whom she missed, but also her husband. She'd kept too many at a distance these past years – her daughter's father should not be among them.

That left one other matter undone before crowns and courts called the Empress to face a people who had fought and died for her.

"And what of you, Lady Orova?" Melanna fought to keep level tone. Despite all that had happened, it took effort not to think of the Tressian as an oathbreaker and an enemy. She had, in fact, been the most monstrous of foes, though Melanna herself had not beheld her thus. But even an Empress could not always choose her allies, nor those to whom she was indebted. "These others, I reward with service. But what can I offer the woman who saved my daughter's life?"

"You can set me free," she replied in accented Rhalesh, "so I can return home."

Jorcari scowled at words as rigid as their appearance.

Melanna took some small relief in the fact that the past clung as heavily to Orova as to herself. "You're not my prisoner, but my guest . . . one who is not yet fully recovered." Rising, she spread her hands. "You and I share an unhappy history. Maybe it's our fate to be enemies. But I swear on my daughter's life that when the lunassera declare you fit, I will grant you a horse and escort – whatever you demand. I've already set your Eastshires free. One knight, however formidable, is of little concern."

Orova scowled. "If I agree, I will make one demand of you now."

"Which is?"

"By now, my wife likely fears I'm dead or captured. Let her know otherwise, and I shall abide. With the Eastshires free, who knows? If the message is delivered correctly – and it is truly understood that I'm a guest, not a prisoner – perhaps we need not be enemies at all."

Peace. Her father had entertained it, then employed its promise as a ruse. Melanna herself had scorned it as impossible. But the world was changing. Old ways were breaking down. With Cardivan's belligerence unmade, could the enmity between Republic and Empire truly belong to the past? As much as her head warned otherwise, Melanna's heart stirred at the notion.

"Can you write a letter?" she asked. "Something your wife will know comes only from you, and without duress?"

"I can."

Melanna turned her attention to Apara, who scowled, but offered a slow, pensive nod. "Then she'll have it before the day is out."

Forty-Seven

Noon brought brooding skies – a promise that while the snows had receded, winter's grasp was far from broken. Beyond Tarvallion's makeshift wall, tents and campfires lay thick upon the Silverway's banks. Viktor was grateful for the Ice Wind, whose gusts swept away the worst of the host's bellicose song and overripe stench.

Thrydaxes. Tattooed Thrakkian mercenaries whose lacquered armour and black garb owed no allegiance save to coin. Whose plaited beards and boisterous manner were thought uncouth in the Republic, but whose valour was ever dependable. Viktor gripped the rampart and stifled a scowl. Shameful it had come to this – that Tressia could no longer fight its own wars. But circumstance, like the men who endured it, prospered where it would.

"These are our allies?" Sidara murmured at his shoulder.

Her tone wasn't *quite* disgusted – she'd been raised better than that – but certainly held reluctance. Certainly, the rough Thrakkian wool-claith and mismatched chain and lamellar lent a brigandish aspect, one well earned by deeds past – the folk of the south had ever been reivers and corsairs.

"You'll find no better, so long as there's coin," he replied.

"I've never seen anything like it." Sidara's awe carried through into her expression. "There are so many."

"The tragedy of peace is that it is never given, only seized."

"Josiri says otherwise."

He snorted. "Josiri sometimes beholds not the world, but his wish of what the world could be. I envy his vision, however flawed."

"Will they be enough?"

"Let us hope so."

Coin had lured near eight thousand thrydaxe horsemen north. Axes, bows and spears ready to fight for a foreign land. In number alone, they almost doubled the thin army Viktor had dredged up from the benighted Republic. In experience, they far surpassed it.

Of the seven regiments Izack had deemed fit to march, fewer than one in ten soldiers had survived the sight and smell of a real battlefield. The two thousands of Drazina were little better – scarcely an echo of the chapterhouses of old. Viktor regretted the absence of the veteran 14th – Arlanne Keldrov's old command – but Izack had argued that the Southshires needed one steady regiment on hand in case of trouble at the Thrakkian border.

As for the rest? Essamere, Fellnore, Lancras and obliterated Prydonis marshalled barely three hundred between them. Most were billeted in a city whose streets remained too empty. Others were still on the road. Add to that the sixty or so kraikons and near two hundred simarka directed by Sidara's will? It made for a host greater than any Viktor had accompanied to the field, much less led. Enough to overcome the Silsarian veterans who held the Eastshires, that much was certain. But if the Empress fanned the flames of overdue justice to outright war, the future grew far less certain.

Aware his countenance offered little comfort to a young woman weighed down by her own fears, Viktor offered a smile. "We shall prevail."

"Easy for you to say, Uncle." Use of the familial term betrayed unease. "You don't lose."

"So folk say."

"So *you* say."

"You sound like your father." Viktor's smile broadened unbidden. "I suppose it must seem the highest arrogance."

"I'd never question a man who can't lose."

"And now you sound like your mother." He laid a hand on her shoulder, and felt twice the giant – even in full armour, Sidara seemed like a child beside him. "Yes, I allow folk to speak of me thus, but only because it gives them confidence. May I tell you something I've told no other?"

Her eyes shone with curiosity. "If you wish, Uncle."

He hesitated. Speaking from the soul had never been comfortable. "I am at my best when others believe in me, and my worst when they do not. Perhaps we all are. That, more than anything, is the power of duty, and of love. It drives us to be more. To be better. So let those who follow me believe I cannot lose. That faith is a weapon as sure as any steel. And we will need all the weapons we can marshal in coming days. Including your light."

"And if light alone isn't enough?"

He stooped, bringing his eyes level with hers. "Make it so. The daughter of Malachi and Lilyana Reveque could do no less."

Doubt faded from her expression. "I won't let you down, Uncle."

He nodded. Josiri had indeed been wrong to keep Sidara from battle. Had he been so driven at her age? Viktor had been little older when Katya Trelan's death had altered the course of his life. Simpler days, before he'd mastered his shadow. Memory offered the vaguest recollection, and what Viktor glimpsed he scarcely reconciled with the man he'd become. Perhaps it would be so for Sidara.

"I know."

He rose at footsteps on the stairs, loath to betray emotion to any other. Sidara needed to see beneath his certainty in order to find her own. Others needed to see the man who couldn't lose.

Not that Viktor doubted the newcomers' commitment. Zephan Tanor, master of Essamere, in hunter's green. Sevaka Orova, her eyes clouded with a loss Viktor understood too well. And of course, the indestructible, indefatigable Izack. Yes, there were others Viktor would have wished at his side – Elzar and Calenne foremost among them – but there were few companions better for the road ahead.

Viktor met each gaze in turn, and found naught to trouble him. Apprehension perhaps, but that was to be expected. "Are we prepared?"

Izack stared across the river. He offered the Thrakkian encampment a brief nod of approval and rapped gauntleted knuckles on stone. "It'll take an hour yet before the last regiment arrives. A little longer to provision them for the onward march, but we await your order."

Tanor cleared his throat. "We've had plenty of refugees clear the border this past day. Folk telling tales that the garrisons at Kendrog, Halga and Mishvor are gone. Maybe Haldravord too."

Izack glared. "Of course they're empty. Shadowthorns know we're coming by now."

Tanor scowled. "Not necessarily. For all they know, this is a show of strength to make Thirava behave." He exchanged a glance with Sevaka. She offered no reply save a taut nod. "Do you know how few eastwealders have made it across the border in recent months? A dozen, no more. We've had near a hundred this past day, and they're all telling the same story."

"Civilians love telling stories." Izack folded his arms. "I don't doubt they tell them to the shadowthorns' purpose."

Viktor held up a hand. "You believe this a trap?"

"Thirava'll not give up his throne without a fight. Let's be clear, I'm not accusing anyone of deception, but a man at flight sees the world strangely. I've a bad feeling about the coming days."

Zephan chuckled. "Strip the cheese from your suppers. A heavy gut makes every dream portentous."

Viktor cleared his throat. "If the shadowthorns seek to ensnare us, we shall trust to valour and duty to see us through. To a Droshna's darkness . . . and to our Lady of Light."

Looking very much as if she wished herself elsewhere, Sidara pinched her lips and offered a curt nod. She'd learn bravado. Better the lesson begin now, before the air filled with the thunder of drums and the whistle of arrows.

"I leave Tarvallion in your charge, Governor Orova," said Viktor. "You've militia enough to hold the city?"

"Assuming Selnweald stays quiet." She barely glanced at him, her grey eyes far away. "We've long memories in Tarvallion. All of us."

Was there something amiss in her tone? Some shrouded hostility?

It didn't matter. Personal grievances would wait.

Viktor set his back to the rampart. "Then I leave the city in your keeping. For the rest of you? Return to your commands. We march at dusk. Death and honour await."

Sevaka spoke little as she made her way back to Brackenpike Manor. Nor did she pay great heed to streets thronged with marching soldiers, save what little was required to go untrampled. For their parts, neither

Zephan nor Izack seemed to notice – or were at least too polite to pass comment – but as they arrived at the front gates and the parting of the ways, she at last found her voice.

"What if he's wrong?"

Izack shrugged. "If it's a trap, we'll best it. Our recruits may be raw, but the Thrakkians know their business … So does the Reveque girl." He tugged at his army uniform. "I may be forced to play dress up, but I've still got my pride."

"It's not the trap that worries me." Sevaka paused, searching for words to frame nebulous concern. "It's Viktor."

Zephan frowned. "What do you mean?"

"I don't *know*. At times, it's like nothing has changed. At others …?" Should she tell them about Rosa's claims of stolen memory? "He was always given to bleakness, but there's an edge to him now. An urgency. Don't you feel it?"

"Sounds like treason to me," said Izack, deadpan. "Tie her up, would you, Tanor? But mind her teeth. She's a biter."

Sevaka shot him a sour look. "If you think I'm imagining it, have the decency to say so."

"Perhaps you need to lay off the bedtime cheese as well." Izack shrugged. "You supported this, back in the city."

"I know." Sevaka shook her head, weary with frustration. "Maybe it's not the 'what', but the urgency. Maybe it isn't even Viktor at all, but me. I told Rosa that if something befell her, I'd avenge her. Part of me still wants to, but the rest screams that it would be a mistake."

Zephan laid a hand on her arm. "We'll find Rosa, if—"

"If she's there to be found?" Sevaka broke off, aware she'd snapped. "I know."

Izack nodded. "And if she's not? I'll take great bloody pleasure in delivering you Thirava, a selection of knives and the blindest of blind eyes." He cocked his head. "Or maybe it'll be hammers? Maybe both. Variety's a pleasure all its own."

She shuddered. "I'll pass."

"Suit yourself." He offered another shrug. "Look, maybe Viktor *has* lost what little sunny side he used to have, but he's never steered us wrong. We've abandoned the Eastshires too long."

He was right – about the Eastshires, if nothing else – so why did it *feel* wrong? Sevaka clung to the cold, silent certainty in the pit of her stomach that Rosa still lived. She told herself it was a holdover from the strange bond they shared with the dead, and not a flight of heartbroken fancy.

"Take care of yourselves," she said at last. "Both of you."

Izack slapped Zephan's shoulder with enough force to set him staggering and received an exaggerated eye roll from the younger man for his trouble. "Don't you worry about this whippersnapper – I'll keep an eye on him. Essamere has the honour of serving as my bodyguard until I say otherwise. Lord Marshal I may be, but my place is in the thick of the fight."

"Slowing us down," said Zephan.

Izack narrowed an unfriendly eye. "More treason, is it?" He shook his head sadly. "Come on, Tanor. We've laggards to rouse and shadowthorns to thump."

Sevaka clasped Izack's hand and kissed Zephan on the cheek. Then she passed through the gate and up the uneven steps of Brackenpike's tangled gardens. As she reached the top she glanced back. Both had gone. Swallowed up by the east.

When she turned again, she found herself staring into a mirror.

Or almost so. The other woman was older, though the difference was less pronounced than at their last meeting, years before – as if time had left her untouched. Then there was the auburn hair with its badger's streak, the heaviness of eye sockets darkened by makeup of a sort seldom employed west of the Ravonn.

Hand to her mouth, Sevaka staggered, overwhelmed by memories of a cold night and colder steel deep in her belly. "Apara?"

Apara's throat bobbed. Pale lips pinched tight. A hand darted beneath robes more shadowthorn than Crowmarket, and emerged clutching an envelope. "From Rosa."

"Rosa?" Sevaka blinked, the Ice Wind carrying away old fears. "I don't understand . . ."

"Read it." For a moment, she looked as though she meant to say nothing more, but pressed on anyway, her low-tongue flecked with a Hadari accent. "She's alive. She didn't want you to worry."

Sevaka brushed trembling fingers across the delicate, copperplate letters of her own name. Unmistakeably Rosa's hand – no one else was so fastidious. Her heart turned cartwheels. The rest of her stared numbly. "Where is she?"

Another hesitation. Sevaka recognised the tiny twitch of the cheek that so often marred her own attempts at impassive expression. Strange to share habits with a woman she barely knew.

"Tregard," Apara replied. "I ... One of the Empress' agents rescued her from Thirava's cells. And then Rosa saved the Empress' daughter from assassins."

The bold, implausible claim could only ever have been true. Of course it was what Rosa would have done. The Rosa that Sevaka had fallen in love with long ago, before the Raven had driven them apart and then brought them back together.

"A shield first, and a sword second," Sevaka murmured.

"If you want more, read the letter."

Apara turned to leave. Sevaka, screwing scraps of courage tight, grabbed her wrist. Her gut ached as fingers closed about the rigid metal of concealed talons. She swallowed hard. That was in the past. How many times had she dwelled on this moment? Hoped for it?

"And you?" Still shaking, she met Apara's gaze. "What of my sister?"

"She ... " Her throat bobbed, and she looked away. "She has to go."

"I understand. I do. I don't know what to say either." Sevaka shook her head. "No, that's not true. What happened before ... What you did to me ... It wasn't your fault. It was our mother's. If we remain strangers, she's won."

"It's not that simple."

"Nothing ever is." She twitched the envelope. "Even without this, I'd have forgiven you. Go if you must, but promise you'll return. Just once, if that's all you can bear. But please, say you will."

Apara gave a long, slow nod. "All right."

Sevaka relaxed her grip and watched the other descend to the street. She barely dared breathe for fear of awakening herself from what had to be a dream. Rosa was alive! And Apara ... ? Perhaps Izack was right. Perhaps the fears were only in her mind. Unable to wait any longer, she ripped open the envelope and began to read.

*

Hood pulled low, Apara navigated Tarvallion's busy streets, habits honed in Dregmeet's crowds guiding her through the bustle with scarcely a jogged shoulder. With every step, she fought the urge to return to the manor's overgrown gardens. So many times, she'd almost left the letter with a servant and fled to the anonymity of the streets. She'd tormented herself with fantasies of swords drawn and guards summoned. Her mother's harsh, disappointed glower stretched across her sister's face. Instead, there had been forgiveness. Hope. For all that the steps leading away from Brackenpike were reluctant, they were lighter than those that had carried her there.

Lingering at a street corner long enough for a pair of constables to pass by – old instincts died hard – Apara slipped into the ruined streets bordering Tremora Gardens and its forlorn, overgrown towers. Retracing her steps through the firebreak bonfires, ever-careful not to stray into the coiled briars of Selnweald's sweet-scented overgrowth, she at last came to the old Lunastran chapel and the crumbled likeness of a sleeping cat upon its lintel.

The mists came readily enough at her call, seeping into the archway behind a pulpit.

"Apara Rann."

She froze, throat so tight that a panicked breath stuttered to nothing. A voice out of the past. One she'd laboured to forget. She silently pleaded the mist gate to hasten.

"Lord Droshna," she croaked. "It's been a long time."

Slowly, reluctantly, she turned about. The chapel's far end was cloaked in the shadow that had once made her a slave, the boundary between magic and master blurred at the edges. The Viktor Droshna she recalled – the Viktor *Akadra* – had been a man. The one who bore down upon her filled the space between the sagging rafters and the rubble-strewn floor. An eternal's altered perception, or a difference in him?

Him. It had to be. The pressure of his being reminded her too much of the Raven . . . even of Ashana.

"I believe I instructed you to do better with your life when last we met," Droshna replied. "Have you done so?"

"I'm free of the Crowmarket," she stammered.

He drew closer, shadows writhing. "And yet you still wear thieves' garb. And there's something else ... the Raven no longer holds you close, does he? Where once you were shrouded in feathers, there's only moonlight."

Apara shuddered as the first tendrils of shadow buried beneath her skin. But beneath the revulsion, something else stirred. A memory of contentment. A piece of her recalled what it was like to be smothered by Droshna, to act only as he wished. A primal longing that echoed through her bones. She wanted to be sick. To flee into the mists.

To her horror, Apara found she could do neither. Sensation was already cold and distant, her limbs numb. Even the sound of the streets had faded to nothing.

"Ashana ... saved me from the Raven," she gasped. "I'm free of him, too."

He cocked his head. "The Empress' patron. Curious that I should find you in Tarvallion now, of all times. While our armies muster to unmake old wrongs. Tell me, little crow, what brings you here?"

The shadow writhed beneath Apara's skin, urging obedience. The small, treacherous piece of her soul joined it. Her mouth filled with words not her own: confession of her friendship with the Empress that would give Droshna every reason to kill her. Frantic, she choked them back.

"I wanted to see ... my sister."

The shadow howled its disdain through her thoughts.

Droshna shook his head. "Don't lie to me. I can afford neither mercy nor patience, not with so much at stake." The shadow pulsed, sheathing Apara's thoughts with ice. "Tell me everything."

A whimper stammered free. Apara felt herself slipping into shadow. Something servile arose in its place. Her recent nightmares awoke, and she trapped within. Helpless. Powerless.

No.

The last time Droshna had shackled her thus, she'd come back to herself covered in blood, her mother's corpse at her feet. But she'd been younger then. Ephemeral. A woman without the strength to do what she knew was right.

Droshna wasn't the same. Nor was she.

A flick of her wrist and the talons snapped free of their housing.

She lunged at Droshna's heart with every ounce of eternal strength at her command.

The air crackled with ice. Her talons shattered. The shadow beneath Apara's skin boiled into her lungs, her veins. Droshna's hand closed about her throat and tipped back her head. His eyes bored into hers.

"Tell me everything," he rumbled.

The world rushed black, and the treacherous, broken piece of herself that Apara had hoped dead so long cried out in delight.

Buoyed by Apara's visit and Rosa's letter, Sevaka's good mood survived the curt summons to Tarvallion's jail. It endured the perfunctory, cold-eyed Drazina who'd replaced Corporal Setherin's avuncular presence. It tolerated Izack's and Zephan's awkward greetings, and Viktor's brooding silence. And then Viktor flung open the cell door, revealing a listless Apara, her wrists and ankles shackled and her outer robes divested, hanging from a chain like a side of meat in a butcher's window.

Joy boiled away.

Heart afire, Sevaka rounded on Viktor. "What have you done to her?"

His expression didn't even flicker. "She will recover."

"She shouldn't have to!"

Sevaka twisted away before the urge to strike him became unbearable. She drew closer to Apara. Close enough to catch the involuntary spasm of muscle that spoke to a life not fled. To hear the small, plaintive murmurings of a child lost to nightmare. Apara's eyes remained fixed on a point only she could see. She offered no reaction when Sevaka pressed a hand to her cheek. That there wasn't a mark on her only made it worse.

"Can you hear me? Apara?"

Apara's eyes twitched but found no focus. A thin moan eased from her lips.

Sevaka spun about, her fury instead now directed at Izack and Zephan. "Are you part of this?"

"No." Zephan's jaw clenched tight. "Before Lunastra, I am not."

"Izack?"

"She's a spy." He spoke softly, the conciliatory tone so rare that it might have given Sevaka pause, were she not lost to wrath. "By rights, she should be dead already."

"She brought me a letter! From Rosa!" She threw it at Izack. "Read it! The Empress is freeing the Eastshires. She wants peace! That's why the garrisons are empty. It's over!"

He caught the letter, but made no attempt to read. "Does it say the rest?"

Sevaka drew up short. "What do you mean, the rest?"

"Your sister is the head of the Empress's icularis," rumbled Viktor. "She's been her confidante for some years now."

Sevaka blinked. "How do you know?"

"She has no secrets from me."

Sevaka looked again on Apara. Rosa's claims of what Viktor had done to her a year before took on fresh significance. Had he left Rosa thus after Darkmere? "What does that matter now? The Eastshires are free and without a drop of blood shed. Let her go!"

Viktor and Izack exchanged a glance. Zephan's glare remained frosty.

"There's something else," said Viktor. "The bulk of the Empress' army is deployed far to the south, suppressing internal divisions. What remained in Tregard was all but wiped out by recent treachery. The city is defenceless. It offers opportunity."

Rage receded, leaving something shuddering and cold in its wake. "What do you mean?"

"If the Eastshires are empty of shadowthorns, we can be at the city's walls in less than three days. The Kingdom of Rhaled *is* the Empire. With one stroke, we'll avenge the slaughter of generations and deal such a blow that the shadowthorns might never again threaten the Republic."

"Rosa is in Tregard."

"And can you think of a better means of ensuring her freedom?" Viktor stepped closer, voice and eyes burning. The chamber's shadows lengthened. "We cannot let opportunity pass us by."

"Vengeance? The Republic used to be about justice. So did you, Viktor!" snapped Sevaka, her eyes again on Apara. "If you're wrong, you'll be throwing lives away for nothing. Worse, for something we already have!"

"And when has peace with the shadowthorns ever lasted?" growled Viktor. "When have their claims of friendship ever borne fruit?"

And just like that, he was a stranger. Perhaps he'd always been and she'd never realised. A man for whom wars would never end, because there'd always be one more reason to strike the tinderbox. And maybe the shadowthorns deserved it. All Sevaka's life, the Republic had watched its eastern border, wary of invasion. Was Viktor right? Or did she consider that possibility only because she feared what she might have to do if he was not?

"At least set Apara free," said Sevaka. "Surrender her to my custody."

"If she escapes, she'll carry word to Tregard. I can't risk that."

"Escape? Look at her, Viktor!"

"I told you, she'll recover soon enough."

"That you speak with such confidence makes me wonder how often you've done this, and to whom."

Viktor stiffened. "The spy stays, under the watch of my Drazina. Do not test me on this, Sevaka. We'll discuss this again when the war is settled."

"It'll be settled without me." Zephan's voice shook. For the first time, Sevaka realised his wrath was directed not at her, nor even Apara, but at Viktor. "And it will happen without Essamere."

Izack grimaced. "Zephan—"

"No, Izack." Zephan stood before Viktor, eye to eye, a face habitually calm crowded with anger. "You sold me this endeavour on the promise of taking back our land. Freeing our people. That's done. Tregard passed from our hands before my great-grandfather was born. It is a wound long closed. Essamere is a shield, not a sword. That will not change under my watch."

"Then perhaps that watch should belong to another?" rumbled Viktor.

He started forward. Icy air stung Sevaka's lungs.

Izack moved between them, his face riven by rare unhappiness, and rarer uncertainty. "Enough! This doesn't do anyone any bloody good, does it?"

Lip curling, Viktor turned away. "Get out of my sight, Tanor."

"Gladly." His eyes dwelling briefly on Izack's, Zephan offered Sevaka a stiff bow. "Can I offer you escort back to Brackenpike, Governor Orova?"

Sevaka's throat bobbed, sick at the prospect of leaving Apara thus. But what could she do? Nothing yet, but she'd damn well find *something*. "I'd be honoured, Master Tanor." She turned her gaze on Viktor's back. "Rosa was right about you, Viktor. I should have listened."

Offering silent farewell to Apara, she followed Zephan up the jail's long stair and into fresh air. Only when the place was far behind did she tug on Zephan's arm, bringing him to a halt.

"What happens now?" she asked.

He didn't meet her gaze, his eyes instead on the fingers of his left hand as they clenched and unclenched. "I must speak with the others of my order. If they don't agree with me, Viktor will have his wish." He let his hand fall and stared back toward the jail. "I expected better of Izack."

"Of them both." Sevaka hesitated. They'd spoken so easily about treason barely an hour before. There was little humour in the prospect now. "Whichever way it goes, find me when you're done. I have a request."

Maladas, 11th Day of Dawntithe

Says I, we'll strike Endala's pact, before we run aground.
Though damned I be, and all my line,
'Tis better cursed, than drowned.

Volro's Lament, The King of Fathoms

Forty-Eight

"This is hopeless," said Constans. "Might as well go grubbing around in a rockfall for a specific pebble."

Altiris stifled a yawn and leaned back against a lamp post. Twanging knees and sore heels spoke to a day and night of fruitless trudging from beggar's nest, to hovel, to hospice, to workhouse. "And I thought you were good."

Constans made play of rearranging his cloak against the cold and stared up at the ailing moon, pale in a greying sky. "A fearless seeker of ne'er-do-wells and vagabonds, am I, dear Devn." Florid theatrical tone yielded to his normal speaking voice. "But we've been at this all night, and not a sign. At least I *think* so. You still haven't told me who we're looking for."

"I told you. A woman who speaks little and hides her face. Probably trying to leave the city, or at least lose herself in it."

"And *I* told *you* that matches half the beggars in Tressia. Don't you know anything more?"

"Only that she's more slender and graceful than those beggars. And that she's in danger."

For the dozenth time since dusk, Altiris considered making full confession. For the dozenth time, he decided against. Constans' loyalty to his adopted father notwithstanding, it was increasingly clear that the Lord Protector was engaged in business that was unwholesome, if not downright wicked. Ignorance was a shield.

By rights, he shouldn't have gone to Constans at all, but Hawkin had missed a handhold on the downward climb, and joined a broken ankle to a broken wrist for the privilege. The city was a big place, and Altiris had few folk he trusted enough to involve – especially if the tower's erstwhile captive truly had been Calenne Trelan. Involving Lord Trelan without certainty was surely inadvisable. If only Sidara had still been in the city. Her pride of simarka would have found Calenne within hours. Almost three days since she'd left Tressia. She might already be ...

He shook away the ghoulish thought – a useless gesture, for it always returned readily enough – and stared anew at the dark spires and brooding windows of the Waycross Theatre. Despite the facade, it was little more than a shelter for those on the run from the constabulary. Another dead end, probably, but what choice did he have but to continue the search? There'd be little chance of making fresh entrance to the clocktower. Calenne was the proof Zarn wanted – that Lord Trelan *needed*, even if he didn't know it.

"Leave me to it," Altiris offered. "I can manage."

Constans snorted. "When has *that* ever been true?" He swept a hand towards the theatre, the actor's diction returning. "No faithless friend am I to abandon thee in needful hour."

Altiris shook his head, certain that the boy was no longer even offering quotation, merely expositing what he considered to be fitting words. Yet he was grateful for Constans' presence. Burdens were better shared than shouldered alone.

"Besides," Constans went on. "A knight *should* aid a damsel in distress, should he not?"

He stared at Altiris, eyes agleam but wary still. What a strange place the Republic had become where a son of storied line expected mockery for doing what was right. Or perhaps it had always been so? Either way, the friendship of those who held honourable course was the most valuable of treasures ... even if Constans kept his own honour carefully concealed from most. That he offered even a glimpse of it now was touching in a way that Altiris couldn't wholly explain.

"He should." Pushing away from the lamp post, Altiris clapped the boy on the shoulder. "But let me do the talking this time? All those thees and thous attract attention."

"Methinks thou art roused to envy most unseemly." Constans shrugged. "Have it your way."

*

The door creaked open. A handful of men in long, tattered coats filed through the tiered seats and clambered onto the stage. It had been a beautiful place before decades of grime had obscured the patterned walls. Calenne's heart, already at low ebb, sank further. Wolfish eyes gleaming in the lantern light told her all she needed to know. She drew the hood of her stolen cloak tighter, hiding immobile features already in shadow.

The leader, a man in threadbare jacket and worse beard, folded his arms. The others peeled off, two to either side.

[[You're Kiril?]]

She spoke softly, having learned through trial and error that it best concealed the singsong hollowness of her voice. Hours of false leads and hurried conversations from the shadows had at last offered up hope.

"I am indeed." He offered a sly smile. "Malia at the Hooked Hound says you want out of the city. That right?"

[[Yes. Can you help me?]]

"Maybe." He shrugged. False disinterest, for his eyes didn't waver. "Where are you bound?"

[[Eskavord.]]

"Eskavord?" The others readily joined Kiril's laughter. "Eskavord's gone, love. Nothing there but cyraeths and ash, not for years."

[[Still, that's where I want to go.]]

"Won't be cheap. Drazina have gone from the streets, but the gates remain guarded. Three crowns."

So much? [[I can pay one.]]

And that had been gathered painstakingly enough, slipping coins from drunkards' pockets – far easier than when she'd played a similar game with Josiri, when still a girl.

Kiril narrowed his eyes. "You can do better, well-spoken lass like you. That dress alone's worth a hundred times what I'm asking."

[[I'll trade you: the dress for new clothes, and passage south.]]

He stepped closer, head tilting side to side as he sought a glimpse beneath her hood. "Who are you, lass? What're you running from?"

Calenne backed away. [[That's not your concern.]]

"It is if someone's paying to get you back." Kiril snorted and spread his hands. "What? You reckon you're the only bride who's bedded down with regrets?"

A shape blurred to the left. A hand closed about Calenne's wrist. She spun around, balled fist crunching into the fellow's face. He dropped back with a howl, fingers clasped to a bloodied nose. It might have felt good, had not her hood slipped free, laying bare a porcelain face that would never pass for human.

"Demon!"

The shout came from Calenne's right, the dull whistle of a sweeping cudgel sounding a heartbeat before the blow set her staggering.

Kiril drew back, eyes wide. "Kill it!"

Others closed, raining down blows on Calenne's head and arms. As with the strike of Tzila's sword, they awoke no pain, but a buzzing, grinding vibration almost as bad. As she grabbed at a cudgel, a dulled sword chimed against her skull. A second cudgel cracked against her leg. The knee buckled, pitching her to the floor.

She lashed out with a foot and set an attacker staggering. A sword hissed down. Without thinking, Calenne raised a hand to ward off its strike. The scrape of steel on clay tore the glove free and left a jagged crack on the polished alabaster skin. Golden light tinged with smoky vapour seeped from the wound, its brilliance casting malicious shadows across the attackers' faces.

Another cudgel-blow landed across the back of Calenne's head. The world faded beneath buzzing vibrations of light and shadow.

The door slammed open. A familiar voice rang out. "Leave her alone!"

Five men. One clutching a bloodied nose. Three in the prosecution of a beatdown. A huddled shape in torn gown and tattered cloak, daylight streaming from cracks across her forearms and skull. More than enough to banish Altiris' weariness and uncertainty. "I said leave her alone!"

The leader – for weren't the leaders of such men always the ones who hung back? – spun to face him. "Ain't your business, boy!"

"That's what your watchkeepers said. They're sleeping off our disagreement."

"Brave words," sneered the leader. "This your demon, is it?"

Another crack crazed across Calenne's brow. Caged daylight set shadows flickering. Altiris' knuckles whitened on a sword as yet undrawn. "I won't ask again."

A dagger glinted in the leader's hand. One of his thugs pulled back from beating the defenceless Calenne. "Strong words too, for a man alone."

Altiris jumped onto the stage. "I'm not alone."

Shadows pulsed in the stage's wings. The rightmost thug grunted as Constans buried a fist in his stomach. Before he righted, the boy locked his hands and brought them down on the man's neck.

"Can't miss an entrance like that, can I?"

The second able-bodied thug cried out as Calenne yanked away his leg. Constans sprang towards the third. Altiris closed on the leader.

The dagger dropped, the fellow backing away with hands raised in surrender. "Let's talk about this."

"Let's not."

Altiris' punch jarred every bone between fingertips and shoulder, but felt glorious. The leader vanished over a chair's scuffed upholstery and didn't rise. Shaking his fist to soothe stinging knuckles, Altiris looked across the stage in time to see Constans boot the bloody-nosed one between the legs, and again in the head as he doubled over.

Without missing a beat, the boy spun around and offered his habitual showman's bow, one hand tucked to his stomach, the other at his spine. "Ta da!"

Calenne reached her feet and backed away, the light seeping from her wounds by turns blinding and unseen as she turned this way and that, trying to keep them both in sight.

Constans stared at her, brow furrowed and corner of his mouth curled. "This is who we were looking for? You might have said. She's hard to miss."

[[Who are you?]] snapped Calenne.

Dipping, she retrieved a fallen cudgel and brandished it first at Constans, then at Altiris.

He held out his hands, silently urging her to calm. "We're friends. This is Constans. My name's Altiris Cz... Altiris Trelan." Constans favoured him with a look that differed only in degrees to the one recently offered to Calenne. Altiris returned it with a nod. "Thank you for not killing anyone, by the way."

The boy flashed a grin and a flourishing salute. "You see? I *do* listen sometimes, whatever my sister says."

The thug at his feet groaned, his hand reaching for a discarded sword. Constans stomped on his fingers, the crackle of snapping bone lost beneath the fellow's howl. A kick to the head, and the thug went still. Constans offered Altiris a shrug.

Still very much a work in progress.

Altiris turned his attention to Calenne. "If you're who I think you are, I suppose that makes you my aunt."

She gave a hollow snort. [[That makes me sound ancient.]]

The cudgel dipped. Altiris chanced another step. "Are you hurt?"

Porcelain fingers *glinked* against forehead. [[I'm not sure I *can* be hurt. But I think I might be harmed.]]

"I don't understand. They shouldn't have been able to do that. Not if you're like Ana—"

Dark eyes swirled. Her body went taut. [[I'm nothing like Anastacia Psanneque.]] Calenne broke off, perhaps recognising the ridiculousness of the words. [[What happens now? Will you take me to Josiri?]]

Altiris took a deep breath. She seemed rational enough, but if she chose not to cooperate . . . ?

"No. At least, not yet. But there's someone who'd very much like to meet you. It's safe."

She glanced between him and Constans, who for his part had returned to regarding her with suspicion. Perhaps it would have been better to tell him, after all.

[[How do I know I can trust you?]]

"Because I give you my word as a Trelan and a Phoenix," Altiris replied.

Calenne's fingers slid from her forehead. [[Those who claim that plumage end badly.]] She sighed. [[Very well. Take me where you will.]]

Kurkas, as was increasingly his wont, was already up and around when Stonecrest's doorbell chimed. Silently bemoaning aching bones, he opened the door to the rising dawn and offered a nod to the tousle-haired boy waiting on the porch, folded letter in hand. Not a city herald. Not even a herald at all. In fact, he looked all too much like the guttersnipes and keelies Kurkas himself had run with at that age.

"Letter."

Kurkas snatched it from the boy's outstretched hand, surprised to see his own name scrawled on the front. He didn't believe the contents on the first read, so read it again, slower. They didn't improve on the second, nor the third. Trouble risen with the dawn.

No life for an honest soldier.

When he looked up again, the boy was still there.

"And what do you want?"

"Was promised a penny."

"Course you were." Might even have been true. Nonetheless, Kurkas dug in his pocket for a coin and tossed it into waiting hands. "Go on, get."

Closing the door, he found Anastacia tottering down the stairs, swaddled in a thick housecoat. Dark rings under her eyes spoke to overindulgence in hours not so very long past. Only her hair looked at all presentable, and that by dint of not being hers.

"Must you make that unseemly racket?" Brittle voice allied well with dishevelment that went beyond tiredness.

"I'm sorry." Kurkas pitched his voice just a hair too loud for someone wallowing in a hangover. "Late night, was it? Finding wine a bit less friendly when you've only a mortal's constitution to rely on?"

It should have been a straightforward enough revelation – especially as Anastacia had taken every opportunity to self-tutor since becoming flesh and blood. But so far, that lesson hadn't taken. Or at least not enough to vanquish desire for pleasures too long denied. Far as Kurkas could tell, she'd made determined assault on every form of temperance going. He found the prospect exhausting.

She clung to the banister. "Don't be tedious, Vladama."

"Lord Trelan about?"

"He's gone for a walk to clear his head."

Kurkas grunted. Burdens of work, or reluctance to linger in bed with a hungover Anastacia snoring like a drain? Either way, it saved him the prospect of running around behind his lordship's back. "Put some clothes on. We're wanted elsewhere."

"I'm not going anywhere . . . " She swayed and pressed knuckles to her lips. "Except back to bed."

Kurkas stifled a flash of annoyance. He considered getting her to read the letter, but found he'd no patience for it. Anastacia, Lady of Aristocratic Disdain, he knew how to deal with, and even liked.

Anastacia, Queen of Hangovers, was a very different prospect, and one he was much less inclined to humour. Besides, it'd be some hours before she was anything other than a liability. Especially if there was trouble waiting.

If? There was always bloody trouble waiting.

"Suit yourself. Wouldn't want you to put yourself out or anything."

Ignoring her belligerent stare, he stepped out into the morning and slammed the door behind.

Zarn pinched the bridge of his nose. "I still don't believe it. Not that I doubted your word, Altiris. But you must admit that to see *her* in the flesh . . . ? No offence, my dear."

He stared across what he'd wryly referred to as The Merrow's Lair. A broad cellar beneath Woldensend's west wing that by its contents had in times past served as both dungeon and armoury, before finding employment as a wine cellar. Why he'd insisted on conversing there, Altiris wasn't sure – especially as he'd by all evidence dismissed the servants.

From her position beside a stack of hogsheads, Calenne offered a hollow, bitter laugh. Her wounds seemed less than they had at the Waycross Theatre, the light dimmer. He'd seen Anastacia heal in similar fashion, the living clay remoulding itself over time. For all Calenne's claim that they were different, she and the Anastacia of recent memory were very much the same.

Zarn shook his head. "Remarkable. Simply remarkable. A soul stolen intact from the Raven and freed to walk the world. One might even call it a miracle."

Altiris glanced at Constans, a glowering, stationary presence by the stairs. He'd questioned the wisdom of bringing the boy to Woldensend, but had in the end decided it worth the risk – not that he'd any means to keep Constans away, in any case.

The boy had listened strait-laced as Zarn had laid out the case against his adoptive father, offering little response save the occasional reluctant nod. Constans reserved his glower not for Zarn, whom he seemed to have taken to well enough, but Hawkin – and she returned it readily. She sat on a bench beneath a rack of rusted weapons, right arm and ankle bound tight and a crutch close to hand. Constans' smile on thus seeing the woman who'd betrayed his family and once held him at dagger-point had been brief, but wicked.

And Zarn had certainly made a damning case, the dim lantern light of the cellar adding to the feel of conspiracy. Forbidden books. The secrets that swirled about Tzila. Confirmation from an informant in the Drazina that Kasvin was indeed dead, and that Lord Droshna had been the last to see her alive ... and Calenne's testimony above all.

Calenne had spoken reluctantly at first, haltingly confirming Altiris' suspicions of her being a prisoner in all but name. Then Zarn had repeated his accusation that Josiri's decisions were not wholly his own. His words coaxed forth a flood, Calenne's reluctance gone: the Lord Protector's erratic nature, his encouragement of the dockside uprising – even that he'd murdered his own father, years before. No one had paid more rapt attention than Constans, who far from defending his adopted father seemed determined to plumb the depths of his deeds.

"You wanted proof against Viktor," said Constans. "You have it. What happens now?"

Zarn turned to stare through the open drapes into the grey dawn. "I need to speak with a few acquaintances. Droshna may have dissolved the Council, but influence remains."

[[And Josiri? I want to see him.]]

"In time, I promise," Zarn replied smoothly. "I'll request a meeting as soon as we're done here. It's my hope he'll be receptive."

[[What if he isn't?]]

"He's starting to see some of the truth for himself. I'm relying on you to convince him the rest of the way." Zarn beckoned to Altiris. "How were the streets? Quiet?"

"Not a single Drazina in sight. The checkpoints are unmanned."

Zarn nodded. "Josiri is a good man, given room and time to think. It's why Malachi wanted him to be First Councillor. We were to make it law, the day he died."

"I didn't know."

"No one does. No one else survived. It's my hope yet to tell him. But before that comes, we must set him free." His voice faded, his manner becoming distant. "Just a little longer. Then I can ..."

The words petered to nothing, his eyes fixed on the floor. Then he could … what? Share his secret with Lord Trelan? Rest? Die? Having glimpsed beneath Zarn's mask, Altiris couldn't be certain. Was Kasvin calling him from the mists? Could he ever be free of her, even in death? Calenne's presence challenged mortality in so many ways, and Altiris cared for none of them.

Hawkin stirred. "Then we can all go back to our lives. Maybe even make amends for mistakes made." Cold expression thawed, a muscle twitching in her cheek as she stared at Constans. "I know you and me have unfinished business, my bonny. A proper little blade you've become. It suits you."

His hand drifted to a scabbarded dagger's hilt, then checked as Altiris drew closer. A scowl, a sharp nod, and the hand receded. Hawkin lapsed into silence.

Altiris gripped Constans' shoulder and lowered his mouth to the lad's ear. "Good man."

Zarn shook his head, back in the living world once more. "Lady Trelan, I must ask that you remain here." He gestured towards the iron-barred door of the old liquor cellar, hived off from the main chamber by thick stone walls. "Indeed, I'm afraid I must insist. Josiri has reason enough to distrust me already, without me promising his long-dead sister and offering only an empty house."

[[Am I to trade one cage for another?]] she said icily.

"What if one of us stayed with you?" said Constans. "It'll only be for what, a few hours?"

"If that," said Zarn. "I expect matters to move very swiftly."

"Then I volunteer." Constans offered Calenne a low bow. "After all, she's practically my adoptive mother."

[[Thanks. That somehow makes me feel even older than being an aunt.]]

"You're dead," said Hawkin sourly. "That makes you older than everyone."

"It seems the least I can do," Constans insisted. "My father – my *real* father – would approve, I'm sure."

Altiris, who couldn't recall the last occasion on which Constans had willingly mentioned Malachi Reveque thus, grunted his surprise.

"You've duties. What if you're missed? The last thing we need is vengeful Drazina scouring the streets – especially if Tzila gets involved. It had better be me. No one who's not in this room will miss me."

"And not even all of *them*," said Hawkin.

Constans scowled, but nodded. "Even a fool may speak truth when fortune fills his sails."

[[Is that a yes?]]

Altiris hung his head, despairing of Constans' fondness for what he thought poetry. "It's a yes." He gestured towards the makeshift cell. "Shall we?"

After brief hesitation, Calenne hitched up her ruined skirts and passed through the iron door.

Altiris followed. Zarn eased the door shut, slipped the bolts and snapped the padlock into place. The key vanished into the pocket of his tailored jacket. "Try not to upset her."

Altiris glanced at Calenne, who'd perched on an upturned barrel, eyes downcast and thoughts a mystery. "Don't be long."

Zarn offered a wry smile and withdrew, leaving Altiris to stare at Constans through the bars. "Thank you for today, Constans. Your sister would be proud."

"I don't need my sister's approval." Constans stared down as his feet, brow creasing and his voice lowered almost to a whisper. "And for what it's worth, I really am sorry."

"About what?"

"I knew if I stuck with you long enough, I'd find Hawkin. You keep bad company."

Too late, the pieces clicked into place. "Constans! No!"

Altiris lunged through the bars. Constans pulled away, the tails of his coat slipping through his fingers.

Zarn turned. "Raven's Eyes! What—?"

His challenge ended in a sodden, gasping huff, Constans' dagger rammed up under his ribcage. Eyes wide, he grabbed at the lad's shoulder, lips fumbling for words but without breath to drive them. Constans twisted the dagger free and let him fall.

Altiris heaved at the bars. The door rattled, but didn't move. "Hawkin! Get out of here!"

Hawkin lurched upright. Crutch braced against broken tile, she staggered towards the stairs.

In one smooth motion, Constans reversed the bloody dagger and let fly. Hawkin cried out and collapsed in a heap by the doorway, the blade buried to the hilt in the back of what *had* been her good leg. Still, she crawled on.

Altiris threw a frantic look at Calenne. "Help me!"

Porcelain hands clamped about iron. [[Together.]]

Still the door didn't move. Anastacia would have ripped it clean away, back in the day. Calenne wasn't as similar to her ersatz sister-in-law as she appeared.

Blood pooling beneath him, Zarn rolled onto his side, a breathy gurgle in his throat that might have been Kasvin's name, or might have been nothing at all. His eyes lost their lustre and he lay still.

Constans bore down on Hawkin.

"Constans!" shouted Altiris. "You don't have to do this."

"Yes I do." Constans' eyes stayed on Hawkin as she dragged herself onto the lowermost step. "I trusted her. My parents trusted her, and she betrayed us all. The blade rights deeds gone wrong, dear Devn."

He drew a second dagger from concealment from beneath his cloak.

[[And what do you deserve?]] asked Calenne. [[What do you want?]]

Constans froze, eyes darting between Hawkin and the point of the dagger in his hand. "I want to prove myself worthy of the gift Viktor gave me. To be strong. Not weak as Josiri is weak. As Malachi was weak."

"Your magic," Altiris murmured, the truth obvious in hindsight. "It's not yours at all, but a piece of Droshna's shadow."

Constans rounded, teeth bared and eyes furious. "It's mine! He gave it to me!"

Hawkin reached the third step, a bloody trail behind.

Calenne gave a hollow sigh. [[Viktor's gifts come with a price. Don't you see that? Look at me! Do you think he did this for me, or for him?]]

"At least I'm grateful."

Spinning on his heel, Constans bore down on Hawkin.

"I thought we were friends!" shouted Altiris.

"We are. That's why you're still alive."

Winding fingers through her hair, Constans knelt across Hawkin's back. "You remember holding a dagger to my throat, Hawkin? I begged you to let me go. I wept. Viktor said I should put it behind me, so I shall. Will you beg? Will you weep?"

Hawkin gasped as he yanked back her head. "Called it right before, my bonny. Proper blade you've become. More vranakin than vranakin." She raised her voice, the blade now at her throat. "Guess you were right, Altiris. There's no outrunning the past."

She died without a scream. Just the rasp of steel on sinew, and the red flood of a ripper's grin.

Constans rose, limbs trembling and his dark coat sheeted black. Then, with a hooded glance at the cage, he fled the Merrow's Lair.

Forty-Nine

Armoured against the coming day by a walk about Stonecrest's grounds, Josiri was halfway between an abandoned breakfast and the vast pile of paperwork waiting in his study – one swollen by recent necessity of taking copious notes during any meeting – when the doorbell chimed. Kurkas' absence making it apparent he wasn't in ready earshot, Josiri trudged to answer.

Halfway there, it struck him how empty the house felt. Not just with Altiris and Sidara gone to divergent – if equally reckless – fates. He'd barely glimpsed a hearthguard all morning. Coming to a halt as the doorbell chimed anew, he told himself it was nothing, and hauled back the door.

"I'm sorry, Josiri. I didn't know where else to come."

Sevaka was a dark, unsteady shape against dawn's light, her hair in disarray and the sour stench of travel thick on the air. Behind and below her stood a horse, its reins lashed about a bollard at the foot of the entrance stairs. And slumped in her arms, eyes distant and face pale ...

"Apara?" He forced back a rush of concern. "Here. Let me help you."

Soon, they had Apara stretched out on a drawing room sofa. Through it all, she barely acknowledged Josiri's existence. Indeed, she seemed unaware of everything.

Tugging on the servant's pull-call, Josiri glanced from one sister to the other. "What is this, Sevaka? What happened to her?"

Sevaka crossed to the dresser and poured a generous measure of brandy. She spluttered as much onto her sleeves and the polished countertop as she swallowed, but it returned colour to her cheeks – even if it couldn't touch the dark circles beneath her eyes.

"It's Viktor," she stuttered. "He—"

Sevaka twisted away as a maid entered the room. She halted, eyes wide and mouth agape at the ragged, lifeless bundle on the sofa.

Josiri took a long step between them, hands ushering the maid to calm. "It's all right, Ellyren." She nodded, lips pursed. "I need a physician fetching from Saint Selna's, Ana woken, the horse on the drive stabling . . . oh, and find Kurkas. Get as much help as you need, do you understand?"

Ellyren gave hurried curtsey and withdrew.

"What's happened to Viktor?" said Josiri.

"It's not what's happened," Sevaka snapped. "It's what he's done."

No obvious injuries, but again that mattered little where an eternal was concerned. Josiri knelt beside the sofa and took Apara's hand. Cold, for all that mattered. But eternal flesh *was* cold.

"He knows," she murmured, no more cognisant of his presence than before. "He knows. He knows."

"She brought proof that Rosa's alive," said Sevaka. "The next time I saw her, Viktor had her hanging like a piece of meat. He'd picked her mind apart, just like he did Rosa after Darkmere."

Josiri's thoughts, already treading dark paths, delved further from the light. "What do you mean?"

"Before Rosa left, she told me why they'd become estranged. She said he'd taken her memories, or at least sealed them so far away she couldn't reach them."

"He'd never do such a thing!" The rejection was instinct, and rang false even as Josiri uttered the words. There was little Viktor wouldn't do out of need. There'd been ample proof in recent days. "Not without reason," he added softly.

"We're talking of Rosa," snapped Sevaka. "What reason could he have? She told me it was like her thoughts were bounded by black fog. That the more she reached for them—"

"The more distant they became."

Cold nausea arose in Josiri's gut and crept outward, sucking the breath from his lungs and turning thoughts to molasses. He fumbled at a table to steady himself, almost dashing a vase to the floor.

"Yes ... that's right," said Sevaka. "How did you know?"

A part of him didn't want to say, because saying made it real. Ever since Anastacia had forced him to realise his memory was failing, he'd hoped – prayed – she was wrong. That there was some other explanation. But not this. "Because it's been happening to me, too."

Impossibly, Sevaka's face fell further.

"He knows," breathed Apara, the words frantic, pained. "He knows."

Josiri swallowed hard and closed his eyes. It didn't help. "Why does she keep saying that?"

"There's been an uprising in Tregard. The Empress won, but the city's vulnerable." Sevaka gazed mournfully at Apara. "Viktor tore the knowledge from Apara's mind. He means to take the city."

"He doesn't have the soldiers." Easier to dwell on that than the rest. "Not to seize Tregard *and* reclaim the Eastshires."

"The Empress has already freed the Eastshires."

So easy to see how events had unfolded. With her throne secure, Melanna Saranal had proven herself capable of more than empty promises. And Viktor ...? Josiri swallowed a rush of bile. Viktor saw only an enemy to be humbled, repaid for the dead of years past. Yet even before the prospect of renewed, pointless war, the personal betrayal was a hot knife in Josiri's heart. How many pieces of him had Viktor scattered to the winds to ensure his cooperation? His blindness? How many of his actions in recent days – even recent years – had truly been his own?

Brotherhood. Friendship. Had any of it been true? Or had he only ever been a means to an end?

Had Altiris been right?

It took him a moment to recognise the low, guttural moan as his own. In striving to control it, he succeeded only in setting free the wrath rising behind. A wild sweep of his hand sent the vase crashing against the wall.

"A little early for a party, isn't it?" Anastacia stood in the doorway, immaculately gowned and mocking smile in place despite her evident hangover. She backed away as Josiri rounded on her. "What is this?"

Josiri grimaced, unable to find the words – to even know where to start seeking them. He gestured to Apara. "Can you help her?"

"I've told you before, I don't have a healer's touch."

"Please," said Sevaka, her eyes bright with tears.

Gathering her skirts, Anastacia knelt beside the sofa, one hand about Apara's and another pressed flat against her brow. Fitful daylight skittered across her fingertips, gone as soon as seen.

Striving for semblance of composure, Josiri turned his attention to Sevaka. "How did you get here?"

"Zephan Tanor refused any part of this. After Viktor marched, his knights helped me free her from the Drazina. We're all fugitives now." Her lip twitched. "There were deaths."

Breathing deep, Josiri sought something – some anchor – to stop himself being swept away. His gaze settled on Anastacia. Her attention fully on Apara, she offered no word, nor even a sign she'd seen. His world steadied nonetheless.

He laid a hand on Sevaka's arm. "You were right to come."

She nodded distantly. "How did you know her, Josiri? It took me a moment to recognise her, but you knew Apara at once. Why is that?"

There was no accusation in Sevaka's tone, but guilt spurred forth all the same. Viktor wasn't the only one with secrets, but now wasn't the time to confess to his meetings with Melanna Saranal.

Anastacia came to his rescue. "Her mind is broken." Solemn tone lay at odds with a face seldom other than impish. "But it's healing. Were she ephemeral, she'd already be dead."

The door opened. Sergeant Brass, eyebrow twitching in suspicion, gathered himself to something resembling attention. "You wanted me, lord?"

"I wanted Captain Kurkas." The old title returned as habit.

"Not here, sir. Half the guard's gone too."

"Vladama had an errand." Anastacia shrugged. "I don't know what."

Josiri scowled. Secrets everywhere, and no answers worth the name. He smoothed a hand across his brow to ease troubled thoughts. As he let it fall, he jostled his jacket's breast pocket and the eyeglasses within. Shalamoh's eyeglasses. Shalamoh – a man deep in Viktor's counsel.

You're no use to anyone if you're not seeing things clearly.

Shalamoh's parting words now sounded less like advice, and more like the cleverness of a man who delighted in concealed knowledge.

Something gleamed amid murk-drowned thoughts. Not a solution, but a way forward. The mere *possibility* of understanding.

It would do.

The makeshift cell offered little room for pacing. Altiris managed barely three strides between bars and the gentle curve of the cellar's brick wall. But it was better than sitting there *waiting* for fate to unfold.

[[Will you stop that?]] said Calenne, sitting cross-legged on the floor. [[It's annoying.]]

Altiris halted and threw up his hands in frustration. "It helps me stay calm."

[[It's still annoying.]]

He gazed across the weapon racks and barrels half-hidden in the shadows of the Merrow's Lair. Hawkin and Zarn stared back with dead eyes. His fault, for all that both had earned death. Too busy drawing contingencies against Zarn being untrustworthy, he'd not thought to worry about Constans. Recklessness at work again, this time not the bravado of the blade, or the desire for status, but the wayward pride of thinking he'd seen something in Constans that the boy's own sister had missed.

He slammed a fist against the bars.

Calenne stared at Zarn, his body – and the precious key – out of reach. [[It wasn't your fault.]]

"Then whose was it?"

[[You're not responsible for the boy's actions.]]

How could she be so sanguine? Constans would return with Tzila, and Calenne would be a prisoner again. Altiris' own fate was all the murkier. Evading it relied on a troublesome series of ifs. *If* the dregrat had delivered the letter. *If* Kurkas believed him. *If* he acted in time. If. If. If. Slim hopes to hang on ... or to avoid a hanging.

"You're very calm," he said at last. "Want to let me in on the secret?"

Calenne cocked her head, the dark swirl of her eyes dancing with amusement. [[I'm waiting for my moment. A friend once told me that's all you can do. Wait for your moment, and seize it with both hands.]]

For the first time, Altiris perceived not a doll in tattered finery, but the Phoenix of Davenwood who'd destroyed an Emperor's dreams. "This friend ... Lord Droshna?"

[[Lord Akadra, he was then. He was so strange. Proud, but humble. Cruel when he needed to be, but capable of such kindness.]] She shook her head angrily. [[And now I wonder if I beheld only what I wanted to see – maybe even what *he* wanted me to see.]]

Altiris tensed as footsteps sounded on the stairs. Moment of truth, one way or another. Hopefully Calenne was right, and it was a moment worth seizing.

A drawn sword preceded a battered uniform upon whose tabard the outline of a golden phoenix could be faintly seen. Kurkas gazed around the cellar, expression blank and yet still managing to be judgemental.

"What a pretty picture," he drawled. "Want to paint in the colours for me?"

Altiris grinned, his breathing easier. "Zarn's jacket, there's a key. We might not have a lot of time."

"There's a key, he says, as if that's the only thing on my mind." Kurkas stuck his head around the stairway door. "Down here!"

He stepped towards the cage and went utterly still as Calenne rose to her feet and made play of dusting down her dress.

[[Captain Kurkas, is it? You got old.]]

He took a half-step back, eye narrowing in suspicion. His face was otherwise immobile – a shield, Altiris knew only too well, for racing thoughts. "Yeah, I daresay I did. Lady Trelan? Or is it Lady Akadra?"

[[Trelan,]] she replied firmly. [[Definitely Trelan.]]

"Yeah. Thought the voice was familiar." He shifted his glare to Altiris. "Your letter might have said something about this. Is it for real?"

Altiris hesitated. Kurkas' reaction was precisely why he'd said nothing of Calenne, asking only that he and Ana come to Woldensend to hear something important, but to come prepared for unpleasantness. "Lord Droshna stole her from the Raven and put her in a body like Ana's."

"Did he now?" Kurkas' voice was calm. Too calm. A shield for unseen emotion. "The great and sublime Lady Plant Pot is nursing a sore head. Living life a little too full, if you take my meaning."

Footsteps heralded Jaridav's entrance to the cellar. A friendly nod at Altiris, a puzzled stare at Calenne, and then her attention darted to settle on Kurkas.

"Stalder keeping watch?" asked Kurkas.

She grinned. "Mostly he's complaining about the cold."

Kurkas nodded at Zarn's body. "Apparently that corpse is guarding the key. See to it, would you?"

Jaridav offered a suspicious glance at Calenne, a friendlier one at Altiris, and set about her search.

"Gotta admit, you sound like her, more or less," said Kurkas. "But better folk than me or the lad here have been fooled before. Care to set my mind at ease?"

She shook her head. [[If all Viktor told me of the other Calenne was true, there's nothing I can say that will convince you these memories are mine, and not his.]]

Altiris nodded. Calenne Akadra – the mad doppelganger a mourning Lord Droshna had woven from the Dark – had known only what he had of Calenne *Trelan's* life. "Lord Trelan needs to hear what she has to say."

"You reckon?" said Kurkas, eye still on Calenne. "Got the key yet?"

"Sir." Jaridav sprang to her feet, slipped the key into the padlock ... but stopped short of turning it. "You sure about this?"

"No." He shrugged. "Do it anyway."

Altiris swung open the door and embraced Kurkas. "Thank you for coming."

"Any time." Stepping back, he shook his head. "But this? Her? This is no end of trouble."

[[You've no idea how much. Viktor—]]

A scream echoed down the stairs, the sound of a falling body close behind.

"Stalder!" Kurkas started towards the stairs.

"No! Stay together! It's Tzila. Maybe Constans too. They're here for Calenne." Altiris crossed to the nearest weapon rack. He tossed a longsword to Calenne and drew another for himself. "Tzila's like her."

"Is she now?" said Kurkas.

"Only ... I don't think she's quite right."

They formed a line opposite the doorway, Kurkas and Altiris in the centre, Jaridav to the left, and Calenne on the right.

Long shadows tugged at Tzila's cloak and bases, her swords already drawn. Jaridav crooked her fingers in the sign of the sun and tapped them to her brow. Altiris shuddered as the blank-eyed sallet helm turned towards him, the gaze worse for knowing what lay beneath.

"Might as well head out." Slovenliness gone from his manner, Kurkas fixed Tzila with an unblinking stare. "You're outnumbered, lass, and we're none of us playfighting this time."

[[Calenne comes with me.]]

Kurkas closed his eye. His shoulders slumped. When he next spoke, it was with the voice of an old, disappointed man. "Oh, Viktor. You stupid bloody bastard."

A crack showed between leaf and jamb. Josiri put his shoulder to the timbers and it sprang open. A muffled cry retreated behind. The bright streets of Highvale gave way to an entrance hall's gloom, Shalamoh little more than a shadow as he scrambled away.

Josiri caught him on the drawing room threshold. Hands about Shalamoh's shirt collar, he bore the thin, grey man past the low table with its lonely, flickering firestone lantern, and slammed him up against the shelves. A book, jarred loose, struck Josiri's shoulder a glancing blow and fell open on the floor.

"Have you gone mad?" Shalamoh's toes skidded as they sought purchase on the floor.

"Maybe," growled Josiri.

Anastacia swept into the room. Viara Boronav was a pace behind, her face troubled.

"We're drawing a crowd, lord."

"Keep them back," snapped Josiri, his eyes on Shalamoh's. "No one else comes in. Not even if they're with the constabulary."

"I . . . I don't have authority to do that."

"Do you have a sword?"

"Yes."

"Then you've all the authority and purpose anyone in this damn city ever cares about."

An audible swallow and she was gone. Anastacia stooped to reclaim the fallen book. "*The Ninth Book of Astarria*. Provocative. I thought my sister Azyra had destroyed all of these."

"There seems to be some misunderstanding," gasped Shalamoh. "Surely we can discuss it equably?"

"What was Viktor doing at Darkmere?"

Shalamoh blinked. "I really cannot stress how little I'm at liberty to speak on the matter. Discretion, remember?"

Josiri slammed him again against the shelves. "And if I insist?"

"Only a fool welcomes pain." The knowing glint was back in his eye, the panic of Josiri's sudden arrival fading. "But I suspect my tolerance for receiving is far higher than yours for doling it out."

"This really is a fascinating book." Anastacia riffled through the pages. "Very valuable. Irreplaceable, in fact."

She brought her free hand down on the firestone lantern. Glass shattered under the blow, blood welling up from a dozen small cuts. The crystal darkened, its brilliant firelight gathering instead about her fingers. Without looking, she brought her hand up to caress the book's lower corner. Smoke coiled away as paper blackened, the bitter stink of it filling the room.

Shalamoh's eyes went wide. "No, I beg you! There's no other copy. Please!"

Anastacia withdrew her hand. A careless breath extinguished a tongue of flame clinging to the pages. A click of her fingers banished the rest. "Talk."

"You almost told me last time I was here," said Josiri. "Men like you love to show your cleverness, so show me now."

"You think you know me?" Shalamoh offered him a baleful stare. "Hah!"

"Then prove me wrong." He eased Shalamoh to the ground and let him loose. "Or do I send Ana to find a tinderbox?"

The other rubbed at his throat, eyes resentful. "He wanted to reach the spirits of the dead."

Anastacia made a small, disgusted noise. "*Ephemerals*. I give up. I really do."

"He came to me, and I told him of something I'd read about in *The Undawning Deep* – a relic Malatriant used to breach the Otherworld's mists for her own ... eccentric purposes. That fool Orova ruined everything and we recovered only a fragment, but it was enough to make an attempt."

Josiri touched his eyes closed. On the journey over, he'd almost – *almost* – convinced himself he'd overreacted. "An attempt at what?"

"Cheating the Raven's grasp, of course. With the foundry gone, Lord Droshna was convinced the Republic would only survive if it found new warriors. Soldiers that never tire and never question – who'd no fear of death, for they could always be reborn into new bodies of bronze, or of clay." Shalamoh shook his head. "Only it didn't work, not entirely. The fragment wasn't enough. He snatched but a single soul. The Raven fought him, leaving nothing but shreds of who she'd been. She was quite mad, poor thing, even after he'd papered over the cracks with his own shadow."

"He doesn't learn, does he?" murmured Anastacia. "He doesn't *listen*."

Josiri nodded, sickness gnawing at his stomach. "Who was she?"

"Some old comrade he admired. I didn't ask. Discretion, remember? But you've met her."

"Tzila."

Shalamoh sniffed. "So there is some small intellect behind those eyes?"

Tzila hadn't arrived on the scene until months after Darkmere. And then there was her brutal duelling performance the day of Elzar's funeral. "But it ended there?"

"That's when Lord Droshna ceased consulting me." He shrugged. "But he roused my interest. I heard whispers that Governor Orova had died, but returned from the mists hale and whole. I thought if I could learn more, Lord Droshna might welcome me back into his confidence. That together we might unlock death's secrets and forge the army he desired."

"Why?" Anastacia wiped her bloody hand clean on Shalamoh's shirt. "Why are you helping him?"

"Because he is of the Dark."

Josiri glared at him. "That's not an answer."

"Oh, but it is," said Shalamoh, voice thick with urgency. "The Dark shapes us. We shape it. We shape *him*. He wants to be a hero. A champion. But the more we perceive him as something else, the more he becomes that instead. I decided it was better to help him be a hero. The Republic's saviour."

Was it possible? The Dark may have been malleable – it was the firmament of all existence – but Viktor? Josiri had seldom met anyone more single-minded. No, this was sophistry. A philosophical game by which Shalamoh justified his actions. "By enslaving the dead?"

"Better them than us, don't you think?"

"Should've known when we crossed swords back at Stonecrest," said Kurkas. "Pointing out my arm. My eye. The ones you took. Trying to tell me, weren't you, Halvor?"

Altiris glanced from one to the other. *Revekah* Halvor? Lord Trelan's mentor? The woman who'd given herself to the pyre, spitting defiance even as Malatriant possessed her?

She cocked her head. [[My name is Tzila.]]

Altiris marked the southwealder accent. The hint of Thrakkian. Was it possible?

"No it ain't." Kurkas' words crackled with anger, his body shaking. "No it ain't! I hear it in your voice. It's in how you move, now I'm looking for it. Raven take me for not seeing it. And Droshna for doing this to you!"

Calenne's fingers *glinked* against her porcelain cheek. [[It's true, isn't it? You used to visit me when I was very little, bringing messages from mother. If I cried, you'd take my hand and stroke my cheek, just as you did in the clocktower.]]

Tzila stepped forward, at last coming free of the shadows and into the cellar's uncertain light. [[You'll come with me. The others may leave.]]

Her curved blades whirled a circle about her wrists and came up at guard.

"She's going nowhere with you," said Kurkas.

Tzila pivoted flawlessly towards him.

Kurkas edged back, never breaking contact with her blank stare. "You remember our final chat, in Branghall's gardens? Fine wine and fine words." For all that he spoke softly, the words were brittle. "Said I'd look for you on that last bastion, when all other walls have fallen, yeah?"

[[You said ...]] She froze. [[You said we'd hold it together.]]

"Yeah, that's right." Kurkas nodded, a tear shining on his cheek and his throat taut. Altiris' heart ached in sympathy. "So how about we put down our swords, and let Calenne go back to her brother, like she wants? That *is* what you want?"

[[More than anything.]] Calenne's sword drooped. [[Revekah, please. You were never anyone's servant. Just let us go.]]

"Come on, Halvor," said Kurkas. "Show me some of that pig-headed stubbornness! I don't pretend to know half of what's gone on here, but you tried to kill Droshna, back in the day! You really going to do his deeds now?"

[[Kurkas . . . I don't . . .]] Tzila's voice shook. [[What's happened to me?]]

Altiris caught the blur of shadow too late. The gathering of light and dark as Constans lunged free of the wall behind Kurkas.

"No!" shouted Altiris.

Even as Altiris dived to intercept, Constans' dagger plunged between Kurkas' shoulders. Once. Twice.

An age too late, Altiris tackled Constans before the third fell, shoulder pinning him against brick. The boy cried out as his ribs flexed. Eyes red-rimmed and murderous, Constans aimed a wild slash at Altiris' face. As Altiris ducked away from the wicked blade, the boy dived across a barrel and vanished into shadow once more.

Tzila started forward across Kurkas' body, the spell of camaraderie broken with his fall. The curved swords whirled to the attack. Jaridav screamed and reeled away in a spray of blood. Turning, Altiris fumbled a desperate parry and paid the price in balance lost. As he fell, Tzila bore down, swords whirling to the kill.

Suddenly Calenne was between them. Tzila's left-hand blade screeched against Calenne's longsword; her right bit deep into a porcelain forearm in a golden blaze. Daylight flared as Tzila rammed her helm into Calenne's face. The longsword dropped. Tzila's booted foot set Calenne staggering.

Tzila closed the distance, swords whirling.

Altiris scrambled away. A memory clicked. "For the Phoenix!"

As in the clocktower, Tzila froze at the old battle cry that had so defined Revekah Halvor.

Calenne – the light from her wounds scattering the cellar's shadows – shoved Tzila from behind, sending her stumbling through the cell doorway.

Heart pounding, Altiris scrambled upright, snapped the padlock into place and backed away as Tzila hurled herself at the bars. Again and again, the door rattled in its hinges, but it held.

Altiris spun around, scouring the shadows for a sign of Constans. The howling, furious Tzila aside, there was only himself, Calenne and four motionless bodies.

Or not quite. Though Jaridav lay every bit as still as Zarn and Hawkin, breath bubbled and rasped across Kurkas' lips, the lid of his good eye fluttering as Altiris knelt beside him and squeezed his hand tight.

Behind, iron bars clanged with Tzila's renewed attempts at freedom. In hindsight it was obvious why Constans had gone for Kurkas first – he'd almost gotten through to Tzila. Revekah Halvor was gone again, subsumed by the creature Lord Droshna had created.

"Don't you dare die, Vladama," he breathed, the words ragged. "Don't you dare."

"...sah." Kurkas' eye fluttered closed.

Fifty

Calenne waited in the drawing room's silence, the light from the window vying with the fading luminescence of healing wounds. Alone again. Was this ever to be her fate? It had been thus at Branghall, where she'd watched the business of the town from the ruined observatory. Not that she'd much to observe. The windows opened onto a garden far tidier than the one she'd been inconstant mistress of at Branghall, but there was no one in sight. Indeed, but for the muffled voices in the adjoining room – sometimes quiet, sometimes raging, she might have been entirely alone, dreaming in the mists of brighter days to come.

She found bitter, inescapable irony in her situation. Almost all her life, she'd belonged in but one place and yearned to be free of it. Now she ached for the familiarity of Branghall and belonged nowhere at all. A jest only the wicked or the divine might find amusing.

[[I suppose you think this is funny?]] she murmured.

But if the Raven heard, he offered no sign.

Calenne turned her attention to the window once more. No guards. That at least was different. She could run. Leave Stonecrest behind and seek some other place. Some solitude. But hadn't flight been her existence's other constant? She had to stop running sometime, otherwise it wasn't really a life at all.

She stared down at the smooth, unfeeling porcelain of spread hands. Life. Whatever she had, it wasn't that.

The door creaked. With guilty start, Calenne gathered herself, hands looped at her waist, shoulders rounded. The very image of respectability, were one inclined to overlook the torn and filthy dress – the unfinished, alien aspect of her being.

Josiri set the door to, lips torn between thoughtful frown and a deeper, angrier scowl. He looked so much older than intervening years should have demanded, lined and greying, the weight of burdens unseen and unknown. But still the brother who'd raised her from girlhood to womanhood. With whom she'd laughed and quarrelled over everything and nothing.

Sorrow and joy mingling where her heart should have lain, Calenne started towards him. He stumbled back, revulsion soon hidden, but unmistakeable. Forgotten heart overborne, Calenne stumbled to a halt, for the first time glad that tears were denied her.

"I'm told you claim to be my sister." He didn't meet her gaze. "But I've had this trick played on me before. And by Viktor, no less."

[[And you fear I'm another?]]

"I hope not." His throat bobbed. "Altiris thinks you're not, and I've doubted him too much of late. But I'm learning hope counts for little in Viktor's shadow, save where it serves him."

Strange to hear such heartbroken regret in Josiri's voice. His rock, Viktor had named him. [[He's not the man I remember.]]

"I imagine few of us are . . . if you truly remember anything at all."

Calenne's temper, never at its most level around Josiri, began to slip. [[It's not kind to speak of me as if I'm not real. I didn't have to come here.]]

He started forward, then checked his step just as she'd earlier checked hers. "I want to believe. You've no idea how much."

[[Then tell me what it would take.]]

Josiri shook his head. "I don't know. I'm sorry." He turned to leave and halted, fingers on the door handle. For all that he said nothing, stuttered breaths told their own tale.

[[I know there's nothing I can say that you can trust – that you might fear I once told Viktor and he since conjured into some imposter.]] Calenne heard her voice tremble, and pressed on for fear it might fail entirely. [[If you send me away, I will go. You'll never see me again. But don't let us part as we did before. That, I couldn't bear.]]

"Do you remember, after Mother died?" He spoke without turning.

"You slept so poorly. I'd wake to find you curled up in the chapel, one of her old cloaks swaddled around you, tears streaming down your face."

[[And you'd hold me until first light, never once with a word of complaint. A champion to protect me against the coming of the Black Knight.]] She chanced a step closer. [[Only it wasn't the chapel, but the library. And it wasn't Mother's cloak, but yours. The one you wore when you tried to bring me safe out of Eskavord. The *sword* was Mother's. You'd set it in my lap, and promised I'd never be helpless. That Trelans were never helpless. Because Trelans were stubborn.]]

"We are that." He turned, his eyes bright with tears. "You understand this proves nothing?"

Calenne nodded, her hopes ashen. [[Yes.]]

"You know I'd be a fool to trust you? Especially now?"

[[Yes.]]

Josiri drew down a deep breath and straightened. For the first time since he'd entered the room, he was a stranger to her, older and sturdier. The rock Viktor had claimed him to be.

Closing the distance between them, he took her hands. "I'd sooner die a thousand times a fool than risk you believing I don't love you, Enna."

Fire blazed anew beneath the ash. An unbidden cry – half sob, half heartfelt joy – spilling free, Calenne flung her arms about her brother and held him in embrace fit to last out all the turnings of the world. Perhaps she yet had a place where she belonged.

[[I hate that name,]] she breathed.

"I know."

Sevaka returned to Stonecrest as dusk fell, steadier for a solid five hours of sleep behind her, and steadier still for deeds performed since waking. Receiving direction from Sergeant Brass, she found Josiri on the stone bench beneath the latticework gazebo, staring across the gardens. She knew the brittleness in his eyes well enough from brief glimpses of her own in the mirror.

"The palace is ours."

He nodded. "Hollov give any trouble?"

"She tried, but having Essamere at my back did wonders for my confidence. She led her ruffians off as meekly as a lamb." Zephan had come readily enough at Josiri's call, and Viktor had left few enough Drazina in the city to make trouble. "They're holed up in the Meldagate barracks for now. Jezek's picking over Viktor's quarters. Lots of muttered prayers punctuated by very unpriestly oaths. He'd like to consult with Ana over some of the things he's found."

"A churchman seeking her advice?" Josiri laughed mirthlessly. "She'd love that on any other day."

Sevaka nodded, not wanting to tread on private grief. "What about you? Any success?"

"Hardly any. If Constans is still in the city, he's staying clear of the constabulary. Tzila was gone by the time Captain Raldan got to Woldensend ..." He rubbed at his brow. "Or maybe I should call her Revekah. I don't know any longer."

"You believe all that?"

"Kurkas does. That's good enough for me." He grimaced. "I've seen too much to doubt something just because it's impossible. There's no coming back from this. There can't be. Thank Lumestra the city's quiet."

There was a calm about Josiri now, a man badly bowed but far from beaten. Sevaka was glad of that. She'd been drowning ever since leaving Tarvallion. It perhaps helped that Josiri was an old hand at insurrection.

"And your sister? If that's who she is?"

"It's Calenne." Firm words lacked firm tone.

"You're certain?"

He shrugged. "I'm trying to learn from my mistakes."

"And if this is another?"

"Calenne or not, she deserves our protection until she proves unworthy. But it's *her*. I won't let her down again."

Sevaka nodded, humbled. Where Viktor's certainty had appalled, Josiri's offered up only quiet dignity. "What do we do now?" she murmured.

"What we always do: everything we can. Even if we don't want to." He shook his head. "I've sent heralds on swift horses. I doubt he'll listen, but it had to be tried ... if only to salve my conscience."

"Maybe he'll turn back."

"Which will still leave us with the problem of what to do with him. Viktor's gone too far, and we've no choice but to go further." He rose. "Thank you for all you've done. We'll discuss the next stage on my return."

"Where are you going?"

"It's better you don't know."

Sevaka frowned. "You sound like Viktor."

"And isn't that something? The more I try to be my own man, the more alike we become."

Wreathed in bitter laughter, he walked away.

When no one answered Altiris' diffident knock, he eased open the door and slipped into the gloom. He'd expected sparseness of furnishings and possession, and in this wasn't disappointed. But what *was* there were far finer than he'd ever have imagined. A row of unblemished books sat atop a hatchwork-veneered dresser. The wardrobe was the same, the swirling golds and silvers set in the dark timber more delicate than anything else in the house. Even in the thin glow of a hooded lantern, the mirror gleamed.

And one last detail, a statuette of Lumestra and Lunastra entwined in embrace, spoke to a spirituality unsuspected, and certainly never given voice. Vladama Kurkas, born to the vranakin and reared in the gutter, held hidden treasures close. Altiris felt like an intruder, uninvited and unwanted.

Not that Kurkas was in any position to offer invitation. He wasn't in a position to offer much of anything. Shallow, fitful breaths barely stirred the sheets nor parted his lips.

"How is he?" Altiris whispered.

Anastacia sat still as a statue at the bedside, head bowed and Kurkas' hand in hers. "Too much blood lost and too many years behind, the physicians say. Sidara could help him. *I* could help him, had I ever bothered to learn how."

Altiris swallowed a rush of sorrow. "If I ever see Constans again, I'll break his neck."

"You might as well snap mine alongside," murmured Anastacia. "I should have been there."

"It wouldn't have changed anything." The old Anastacia – the plant pot in body as well as name – might well have done so, but not the mortal creature she'd become. "This isn't your fault."

"Isn't it? The whole time I was bound to the clay, I prayed to my mother, even though I knew she couldn't hear me. I begged to be restored to flesh. To live among those I love, not as some distant, deathless observer, but as one of you. And perhaps she *did* hear me, after all. Perhaps she's not as dead as I believed, for my dearest wish was granted. But ever since, I've wallowed in selfishness and sensation. Revelling in what was once forbidden and thinking of nothing but my own delight. Now this irritating, irreverent, bewildering . . . " She wiped her eyes with the back of her hand, stared at it and scowled. "Don't tell me I couldn't have made a difference. I should have found a way."

Altiris moved to stand behind Anastacia and laid a hesitant hand on her shoulder. So hard to imagine the unshakeable Lady Plant Pot begging for anything, much less of a deceased mother she so often claimed to hate. It made the confession poignant, and impossible to answer.

Warm fingers found his and held them tight. "I was better as a creature of stone."

Ghosts hung heavy as ever to the walls of Silvane House, the brooding facade lent portent by slivers of moonlight as much as Josiri's grim mood. Apara waited beyond the gate, her eyes clear but restless, and her face weary. She clung to the rambler's staff as if it were her only support.

"She's here. I've told her only that it's urgent."

Josiri sighed. Easier had the answer been otherwise. Or difficult in a different way. "And you?"

"I don't know." Her face creased. "I think . . . I think pieces of me are still missing."

Josiri understood all too well. Knowing the cause of his broken memory had done nothing to restore that which he'd lost – which Viktor had *taken*. Even now, he tried not to think on it. The shame. The violation. He couldn't afford anger, not tonight. "Are you coming in?"

"I need to be alone with the moon for a time. Call for me when you're done."

Josiri found the mansion door open in welcome, the treasures and trinkets within bereft of dust. The drawing room blazed with light and life where all else was cold and dark.

Melanna Saranal waited beside the fire. "Every time I see you, Josiri, you look worse."

"Today I learned that my closest friend has betrayed me. A second has one foot in the mists, with the other soon to follow. Much of what I believed or have known is under siege. However I look, I feel far worse."

"It's the way of rule," said Melanna. "Our triumphs are louder, but failures echo further. I've had reminder myself of late, and I'm determined to do better. Apara will have told you of the Eastshires?"

"After a fashion."

Melanna stared at him strangely. "I ask no thanks, but I would have expected a little joy."

She knew why he'd asked to speak with her. Not the whole of it, maybe not even some of it, but only a fool would have answered urgent summons and not conjured suspicions. Josiri, confronted again by the enormity of what he had to do, felt the words he'd intended to speak slip from his grasp.

"Better them than us," he said instead. "That's what someone told me today. As if an evil blow can be forgiven so long as it falls somewhere beyond sight."

Melanna drew closer, her face crowded with concern. Fingertips brushed his arm, the lacquered nails shining in the firelight. "Josiri . . . What is it?"

There was no longer any choice. No escape from what he'd determined to do – what he *had* to do in order to live with himself. If he, like Apara, was to take back a piece of his soul.

"In his pursuit of victory, the Lord Protector has gone mad."

Josiri spoke slowly, gaze averted. Easier to stare into the fire than Melanna's eyes.

"Victory?" said Melanna. "He has no need. The Gwyraya Hadar offers you peace."

"Viktor doesn't *want* peace." He forced the words out, faster and faster, for fear he'd lose the courage to speak. "He knows Tregard is undefended. He means to have an army of some seventeen thousand soldiers and mercenaries at your walls in two days. He seeks nothing less than Rhaled's destruction."

Melanna withdrew her hand, clenching her fingers to still their tremor. "Why are you telling me this, Josiri? What do you expect me to do?"

"As of this afternoon, I speak for a reconvened Privy Council. Viktor Droshna acts without our authority and without our protection. I urge you to safeguard your people."

Even if those steps meant Viktor's death. Or Izack's. Or Sidara's. Or any one of the thousands of men and women who marched beneath the Lord Protector's banner.

She drew in a sharp breath, colour returning to her cheeks. "You still haven't told me *why*."

"Because I find I cannot sit idle while an evil blow falls elsewhere. Because you once made yourself a traitor to your people to save mine, and that debt cannot go unanswered." He sighed. "Perhaps even because we might have been friends, had paths run but a little different."

Exhausted, he turned away. A hand at his shoulder held him back.

"We *are* friends, Josiri. I think perhaps we always were. And as ever, you shame me with your generosity. In Ashana's light, I swear I will not forget."

Fifty-One

Melanna stared into her bedchamber's fire and felt little of its warmth.

Two thousand warriors. That was all Cardivan's treason had left her. Two thousand spears, salvaged from garrisons and Veteran's Lodges, supplemented by old soldiers quartered in the city. Oh, there were others. Boys and girls old enough to lift a sword. But to hold Tregard's wall against Tressian soldiers? To keep to their courage when the air screamed with stone and fire, and blood's sour tang tainted every breath?

Melanna bit back a flash of anger at Apara, without whom Droshna would not have known Tregard's weakness until it had passed. It wasn't her fault, though what words of consolation Apara had tolerated had little eased her torment. Melanna could scarcely conceive having another pick apart her thoughts. The most complete of degradations, and all the worse for being a long-held nightmare made real. Better that Apara had returned to Tressia with her sister and Josiri. She was safer from Droshna there than in Tregard.

Two thousands to meet Droshna's seventeen. The city walls worked in her favour, of course. But only until they were breached, and Melanna had respect enough for Tressian siege-craft to know that was a matter of days at most. And they'd be hard days indeed.

Had Aeldran already returned, it might have been different. He'd ridden south with three thousand spears, and headed home with many of those freed from watching the border at Mergadir. Perhaps five in all. Combined with those already in Tregard, it was enough to match Droshna's Thrakkian rabble and unblooded conscripts – certainly enough to make any siege a grim prospect for the attacker. But Aeldran remained at least two days distant. If Josiri's estimate was correct, Droshna would round Fellhallow's southern extent and cross the western border no later than the coming noon.

How quickly joy turned to dust. Two days to rejoice in a throne secured, and now imperilled worse than before. Two days since Tregard had risen to save its Empress, and now that same Empress was powerless to save them in return. She'd overcome the troubles of the past with a drawn sword and the defiance of her forefathers. Neither would serve here, save to salve aching pride.

Should she then surrender? Offer generous terms and yield holdings? Melanna shook her head in angry dismissal. To capitulate was to invite disaster as certain as the one offered by siege. No Empire could prosper beneath a rule so chastened.

Then what?

Leaving the bedchamber's warmth behind, Melanna exited onto the balcony and gazed up at the moon. The sight offered scant comfort, its light as distant as Ashana's aid. Would the Goddess come if she called? If she did, what then? In offering aid, Ashana broke her bargain with Jack, leaving Melanna his to claim. Did a Bride of Fellhallow offer more salvation than a dead Empress?

But something more held Melanna back from offering prayer. On the one hand, a nation saved and an adopted daughter lost to Jack. On the other, that same daughter dead, and thousands with her. How could Melanna ask Ashana to make that choice and yet claim to love her as a daughter should?

The coming war was not of Ashana's making, but Melanna's own. The road she'd walked lay thick with dead. Her hands dripped with Tressian blood – the currency by which she'd purchased her crown. That debt now screamed to be paid. Whatever Droshna's madness, she'd earned his hatred. Youth might excuse it and ambition justify it, but not to the dead or to those who sought vengeance in their name. The deeds of the past echoed forth to smother her future.

"I deserve this."

Melanna spoke without meaning to, the words lost to the cool breeze almost before she heard them. But their truth lingered. All she'd done since taking the throne didn't matter. The small justices meted out and divisions healed – her striving to be a kinder, fairer ruler than her father. The blood she'd spilled would cling to those deeds – to her – for as long as she wore the crown. The crown Ashana had promised she'd pass to a daughter.

But Ashana had ever claimed prophecy was merely a word to justify deeds, or their lack.

If Kaila was to inherit the throne, her mother's deeds needed to count now, more than ever. Two days prior, the people of Tregard had risked all for their Empress. If Melanna didn't prove herself worthy of that sacrifice then they'd died for nothing.

The Empress was not the Empire. The people were. And the Empress' debts had to be paid.

There, on the balcony, her skin raised to gooseflesh by the chill Wintertide night, Melanna finally understood what she had to do. From a field of impossible choices, only one offered semblance of hope and shred of honour.

The scent of smoke lingered amid the old wood's fire-blackened remains. But there was something else too – a floral musk that tarried on the tongue and roused the senses even as it drove out the cold.

The remnant of the old oak loomed against the stars, ruling over its charred court in death as it had in life. Or perhaps not. Moonlight offered glimpse of unseasonal green buds, renewal stirring in Melanna's childhood companion as elsewhere in the wood. A promise that not all harms were for ever.

Heart hammering, she turned to flee the terror that had walked with her across the gardens. The bright lights of the palace called to her, begged her to take counsel, to find another way.

Brick by brick, Melanna rebuilt her composure. Fear faded. She'd come to bargain, not to beg. Weakness invited exploitation.

"Lord Jack?"

No answer. Clinging tight to the last of her courage, Melanna pressed on.

"My mother owed you a debt, and I will not pay it. But I will offer you a bargain in its place."

A gust of wind howled about the oak, bearing fragments of ashen bark into the night. Melanna gritted her teeth, mindful that even a single misspoken word might offer more than intended.

"My realm is beset by an army I cannot defeat. They will cast down all I have ever striven for, and render it dust. My daughter will never know the throne that is her birthright, and my people will suffer." At the last, words almost failed her. "My bargain is this: deliver Rhaled from its enemies, and once my daughter's rule is unassailable – not one day sooner – I will be your queen."

With the words spoken, Melanna saw her future dwindle almost to nothing. Ten years until Kaila was old enough to assume the throne in her stead. Ten years, and no time at all, but a greater span than any other offered that bleak night. A bargain with the divine bound all parties. If Jack agreed the terms, Kaila *would* take the throne, and Melanna would have ten years to prepare her for its burden. Prophecy would be fulfilled, and all debts repaid.

She closed her eyes. "Do you agree the bargain, Lord Jack?"

His answer came in a rustle of branches, and on windblown laughter neither malicious, nor entirely kind.

Tzadas, 12th Day of Dawntithe

When the wheel of history turns, it is better to be the axle than to cling to its treads.

from Eldor Shalamoh's "Historica"

Fifty-Two

Thick clouds choked the sky, robbing the world of Lumestra's light. Viktor didn't care for himself. Sunlight, like the firestone lanterns that were its echo, had grown wearying in recent years, fraying his shadow – and therefore himself – with even the gentlest caress. But sunlight had ever been a herald of portentous victory. Its lack was ... disappointing.

Still, the shadowthorn army on the valley ridge's shrinking snows was barely worthy of the name. Two thousand spears, no more, and precious little cavalry, all clinging to the scrap of high ground where the road veered northeast to skirt Fellhallow's dark boughs.

They'd arrived with the dawn, too late to contest the broad arches of Argatha Bridge. A motley array of banners and shields from three generations of Empire, the blazons hailing back to two dead Emperors and an Empress soon to follow. For Melanna Saranal was there, her banner, fluttering in the Dusk Wind so that the silver owl spread its wings across a field of emerald silks.

In the space between, three companies of King's Blue wayfarers contested the steep valley slopes with shadowthorn outriders. Arrows and quarrels hissed back and forth beneath grim skies.

"No volley," muttered Izack. "Unusual."

Viktor grunted. Shadowthorn tradition was to offer three volleys in salute: one for Ashana, one for the Empress and one for her heir. "They offered no salute before they broke Ahrad's walls."

Ahrad, once the enduring fortress on the border between Republic and Empire. Its ruins lay in Tressian hands again for the first time in six long years, overrun the previous day by the vengeful blades of the 7th, 10th and 11th whose forebears had perished when Kai Saran's Avitra Briganda had burst across the Ravonn. Supported by kraikons, they'd taken all save the central keep and Viktor had left that besieged with no hope of relief.

"Maybe they've heard there's not supposed to be a battle today?"

Izack stared directly ahead, his unwillingness to meet Viktor's gaze no less telling than his tone. He'd never have spoken thus within earshot of the soldiery. The wayfarers were far ahead and the battle line a quarter mile behind. No other could have heard save Sidara, who shifted uncomfortably in her saddle.

"Josiri has no authority over this campaign," growled Viktor. The missive had been polite enough, if insistent, and as with much of what sprang from Josiri's thoughts cared for the moment, and not the future. "Nothing has changed."

"Nothing has changed?" Izack swept a hand downhill, past the sprawling, serried ranks of King's Blue and Thrakkian pennants glittering with ice – past the towering, sparking kraikons, the pride of attentive simarka and sheer ravine of Argatha Gorge – to the Ravonni lowlands. On a clear day, Ahrad's ruins would have been visible on the horizon. "What we set out to do, we've done. Unless your pride's hurting that the Hadari gave you a gift, not a fight?"

"It's not done until our lands are secure," said Viktor, his shadow uncoiling as temper flared. "Essamere used to understand that."

Izack stiffened in his saddle, furious – as he should have been – at the reminder of his sword-siblings' desertion. Worse than desertion. Outright defiance. Josiri's herald hadn't been the only one to reach the army. Another had borne from Tarvallion's reeve, laying out in stark terms Zephan Tanor's liberation of Apara Rann. Happily, that second herald had found Viktor alone, gifting him chance to marshal waning patience. *The irony of order is that it foments indiscipline.* An old sermon, and never truer. Even on the threshold of historic times unity crumbled, the men and women Viktor had trusted so long pulling in different directions, more afraid of the price than eager for the prize.

"I don't understand why they offer battle at all," said Sidara.

"Buggers don't have a choice," said Izack. "They lost the bridge, so the ridge is their best bet. Nothing but open ground between here and Tregard. A stand here will hurt us, might even slow us. I wish they'd bloody surrender, but good sense is a flighty wench."

Viktor gritted his teeth and brought his temper to heel, his shadow alongside. "Have the shields locked, and send them forward behind Sidara's constructs. The thrydaxes will manage the flanks, but this victory *must* belong to Tressians. We take back what was ours." He paused. Perhaps there was a middle ground to be sought. "Offer mercy to those who yield, and steel to those who do not. I trust this meets with your approval, Izack?"

For a long moment, the other offered no reply, his gaze on the duelling outriders and wayfarers on the gorse-strewn hillside.

"If these are your orders, Lord Protector," he replied at last, "then I'll see them done. But you'll need to find yourself a new Grand Marshal after."

Kicking his heels to his steed's flanks, Izack spurred through the snow towards the waiting lines. Sidara watched him go, her unease a pressure on Viktor's thoughts.

"It's not his fault," he murmured. "Nor Josiri's. Nor Sevaka's. They're weary. They want peace, and who am I to begrudge that? I yearn for it as much as they, and wish I could believe it so easily won. Every ephemeral has limits, and I fear they've reached theirs."

"But not you, Uncle?" said Sidara.

"I want nothing more than to leave all this behind, and seek a quiet life far from drums and buccinas." He shook his head. Now was not the time to dwell on Calenne, and the promises of a future not yet earned. "I must endure. You'll understand as you grow into your birthright. You and I are tempered by forces the others cannot comprehend. We are more than mortal, and our burdens will always be greater because of it. So long as we have the means to act, we must do so . . . even if others do not understand."

She nodded. "I won't fail you."

So easy to see where her thoughts lingered. Silverway Dock, and all that had gone awry. He'd been much the same before Davenwood, dwelling on mistakes made and imperfections past. Such doubts ate at the soul like nothing else. Kind words could not ease their chafing, but anger drove them out. Wrath was the font of valour and purpose when the killing began. It had held Viktor together at Davenwood; it would hold Sidara together today.

He held her gaze. "The warriors you face today are kin to those who murdered your father, who set fires blazing across the Eastshires and left the ruins thick with unburied dead. Mercy will wait until the battle is done. Concern yourself with justice, and do your father proud." He paused, letting silence lend weight to the next words spoken – words that had shaped Sidara long before she'd first donned a uniform. "We fight to protect those we love. Never forget that."

Sidara swallowed, cheeks colouring as she took the words as criticism. Then she rallied, her irises gleaming gold, and clasped a hand to her breastplate in salute.

"At your command, my Lord Protector."

Melanna had been alone before, but never like this. No matter the over-lapping battle lines stretching along the crest to left and right. No matter the banners raised in defiance. No matter Elim Jorcari's solemn, silent presence at her left shoulder and Chakdra's golden scales to her right. All was distant, the fading embers of a dream. She was alone against the stain of Tressian shields spreading across the lower slopes. Three staggered lines, running west to east. Each wider and deeper than her own. The debts of reckless youth come due.

Friends might have anchored her, but all her friends were far else-where, and better for them that they were so. Apara was in Tressia. Aeldran's vanguard was still a day and a half away. Sera remained in Tregard, charged with safeguarding Kaila and evacuating the city – tasks in which Roslava Orova had pledged assistance, offering no explanation save a line of verse concerning a broken sword and a shield.

No Ashana. Nor her Huntsman riding out from parted mists, his spear shining bright as it had at Ahrad. Melanna had dreamt of him in the small hours, the equerries of the Court of Eventide riding at his back, but she knew the dream was but a dream. Even Jack had offered no reply save laughter, no matter how she'd pleaded with the shadows of the old wood.

She was alone.

On the roadway far below, the Tressian lines gathered pace beneath numeralled banners of King's Blue and silver thread. The shrill cry of pipes awoke tremor beneath Melanna's feet as thrydaxes galloped forward.

Havildars bellowed orders and the outriders retreated uphill, the skirmish ended by the onset of Thrakkian horse archers. Kraikons strode on, great swords tight in metal fists. Simarka loped ahead, streamers of golden light crackling behind. The enemy, vast before, now seemed a tidal wave fit to sweep the hillside clear and leave no trace.

Had ever Melanna doubted that this was a doomed fight, born of pride, she did so no longer.

A lament swelled on the Dusk Wind. Close, mournful harmonies of farewell offered by those who knew that their hour had come. Old men of the Veteran's Lodges, young women scarcely come to the warrior's trade, lunassera scattered throughout the line so the Goddess' blessing might befuddle the constructs, and everything between.

Kithaga narai. The archaic words, spun from ancient tongue, and yet so familiar from a hundred memorials – a promise of remembrance to kith and kin – spanned the myriad leagues of regret and drew Melanna back to the hillside. For the first time since taking her place in the line, she felt the closeness of comrades, tasted the bitter perfume of moorland gorse; the bite of the wind, and the rumble of a belly she'd lacked heart to fill.

Jorcari hoisted his sword aloft. "Saranal Amyradris!"

"*Saranal Amyradris!*" The cry echoed along the line, the lament abandoned to defiance.

Shame stirred. Was this how an Empress faced death?

No.

Brushing aside Chakdra's restraining hand, Melanna pushed her way through to the front rank and turned about. Back to the advancing foe, she let her golden shield fall and tugged free her helm. Her helm, and the crown bolted in place atop. The crown that she'd spent her life pursuing, and which had brought nothing but sorrow. She tossed it to Chakdra, who lingered in the front rank, his brow furrowed as one witnessing unfolding insanity, but uncertain of its form.

"I am not your Empress! Not today!" shouted Melanna, her voice trembling and the words wild on her lips. "We come to this place already dead, and the dead have no monarch save the Raven. Blood! Valour! These coins purchase hope for our kin. I gladly pay the toll, for the dead have nothing to fear! If this is to be our Last Ride, let us go to it in glory! Kithaga narai!"

"*Kithaga narai!*" Perhaps a hundred returned the cry.

"Kithaga narai!"

"*Kithaga narai!*" Swollen by new voices, Chakdra and Jorcari's among them, the words hammered back louder than before.

"Kithaga narai!"

"*Kithaga narai!*"

The third and final cry drowned out the rumble of hooves. Melanna reclaimed her shield and her place in the front rank and stared across the valley. At an army that could not be beaten, but would be taught a lesson to echo through the ages.

This was how an Empress faced death.

The first arrows fell like rain far to Melanna's right, the Thrakkian thrydaxes of the west flank having found firmer ground than those to the east. In the centre, the Tressian line rippled as hump-backed pavissionaires presented crossbows. Kraikons lumbered to the charge. The constructs worried her. Before, there'd always been the hope of killing the proctors who gave them orders, but there were none in sight. Hammers would have to serve.

Jorcari locked his shield to hers. For a heartbeat, Melanna didn't see him at all, but her father come from Evermoon to witness her last battle. But the moment passed, and he was the grim-faced Blackwind veteran once more.

"Ignore the giants," he murmured. "The line is all that matters. At thirty paces, sound the charge. Tear the leading ranks to ruin and it might give the others pause."

Melanna nodded, knowing sound advice when she heard it. She'd spoken true – there was no survival worth having that day. Better to end in glory, as her father had.

Arrows whistled overhead, the volley opening gaps in the Tressian advance. The survivors bore down, thick as flies on the carrion field the hillside would soon become.

A hundred paces. Close enough to make out individuals in the Tressian lines.

Eighty paces. The ground shook as kraikons lumbered to the charge, simarka streaming before them.

Fifty. Melanna swept her sword – the Goddess' flameless sword – to grey skies. Drums boomed, the rhythm quickening as clansmen made clash of spear-staff on shield.

The owl banner rippled and snapped as the wind veered north. The bitter scent of moorland yielded to sweet, unseasonal pollen – musky, and thick with forgotten years.

The sky shook to a hollow, yawning groan.

A rustling, crackling sound swallowed the mournful sigh. The fanfare of the swarm, or of leaves caught in a gale. Something Viktor hadn't heard in six long years, and had hoped never to hear again.

"Sound the withdrawal!"

Buccinas brayed the descending triplets of retreat, but the newly woken Ice Wind bore them back across the river. Viktor, a score of paces to their front, heard barely a whisper. The soldiers of Izack's advance could have heard nothing.

Thick with foreboding and mounting wrath, Viktor rounded on the knot of officers pressed into service as adjutants. "Find the commanders! Order the retreat!"

Confused eyes met his. Too young. Too untested to read shifting fortune. Too innocent of the world's horrors.

"Go!" he roared.

The day darkened, his shadow slipping free. Adjutants spurred away on startled steeds, cloaks streaming as they galloped headlong after Izack's assault.

Sidara, her posture already rigid as glass, stiffened further. The halo of light about head and shoulders flickered. "What is it?" Her voice, normally so light and musical, was brittle, unswerving. Older, somehow. She twisted in the saddle, the golden fire in her eyes setting Viktor's shadow writhing. "What's happening?"

New shapes appeared on the ridgeline. Thousands upon thousands. A horde of tangled briar-creatures, like poppets twisted from branch and bramble by an enthusiastic child; not quite man-shaped in their gangling limbs and lopsided aspect, but fashioned as imitation. Strawjacks. Whispering Ones. Livasdri. The ice-crusted nightmare of Hallowsiders who, praying for untroubled sleep and plentiful harvest, left tribute of vittles and kin at the forest's edge. They came not as lines ordered for battle, but as leaves upon the storm, their mad rush billowing and ebbing according to individual pace.

They spilled past the flanks of the shadowthorn lines and rushed downhill.

As the first dizzying motes of pollen tantalised Viktor's senses, he glimpsed thornmaidens amid the horde. They capered and pirouetted about their misshapen brothers, bright petals curling and falling from their hair as the seasonless magics of Fellhallow yielded to the Wintertide of the wider world. And behind them all, vast lurching four-legged shapes with high, briared shoulders and low snouts, crowned with tangled horns and stubbled, mossy hides. Thornbeasts – something else Viktor had once thought only fable.

At the line's western extent, pavissionaires deployed as a skirmish screen stumbled away from the oncoming mass, only to be overtaken by thorns. On their flank, the Thrakkian advance stuttered, riders slumping in their saddles as thornmaidens' intoxicating pollen did its wicked work. The sweep of a kraikon's sword snatched a half-dozen strawjacks to splinters, then the giant fell, borne backwards by a score of others. Brilliant daylight scattered beneath sullen clouds.

Sidara grabbed at her saddle's horn for balance. "Uncle?"

The foremost of the three assault lines vanished beneath the tide of strawjacks.

Paralysed not by windblown poison, but the disbelief of waking nightmare, Viktor scarcely registered the awed, horrified murmurs from the reserve at his back, or the screams echoing on the Ice Wind. It couldn't be! After Govanna, the gods had foresworn involvement in ephemeral war. Or so Josiri had said. But Josiri had been wrong before. Ephemeral or divine, he was ever too ready to believe heartfelt tale.

Shields buckled beneath a thornbeast's impact, bodies scattering behind. The second assault line halted, rippling back as its soldiers beheld the unfolding horror to their fore. The hillside gleamed bronze as simarka crashed into the mass of strawjacks, the kraikons scattered across the battlefield converging on the point where Izack's banner had vanished. Scrape of metal and thorn vied with screams, daylight flaring as forest-demons pried metal apart and freed captive light.

Breathing as one in the throes of exertion, Sidara turned stricken gaze on Viktor. "There are too many. I can't—" She gritted her teeth. Her halo glowed bright enough to itch at Viktor's skin. On the hillside, light danced about bronze shoulders and sculpted manes. "Viktor!"

Jarred from nightmare as much by Sidara's tone as his shadow's discomfort at her halo, Viktor glanced behind at forces yet held in reserve. Curse Essamere and their faithlessness. And Sartorov for seceding. What remained was scarcely their match. Drazina knights, mounted and foot, drilled and loyal but woefully inexperienced. Commander Tallar's lightly armed wayfarer auxiliaries. Conscripts of the 2nd, 8th and 16th, whom he'd only ever intended to offer sight and smell of the enemy, for they were the greenest in the army. Numbers fit to cow a humbled Rhaled, but to face the divine?

But what else was there, save retreat and thus abandonment of those who'd followed their Lord Protector to the field? Besides, he had his shadow, and a Lady of Light rode at his side. Jack was not the only divinity come to Argatha Bridge. Heirs of Malatriant and Lumestra were present also.

Let the Lord of Fellhallow intrude. Let him face the man who could not lose, and be humbled for it.

"Commander Tallar?" Viktor spread his shadow wide and let the words ripple within, cheating the unnatural wind. "Sound the advance!"

Buccinas flared, the murmurs lost beneath the shouts of officers and sergeants. Breath steaming in the cold, Viktor unslung his claymore. The weight of it hastened rising confidence. Not for him the general's place behind the lines, while others fought in his name. Nor at the head of a council's table, burdened with petty governance. For three decades, his home had been the battlefield. It called him now.

As Drazina formed up around, Viktor spurred closer to Sidara, his voice too low to carry. "Stay close to me. I promised Josiri I'd bring you home safe. I would not be a liar in this."

Cheeks taut, she unslung her shield from her shoulders, and drew her sword. "I'm not afraid."

Of course she was. To be otherwise was to be a fool. But fear was the wellspring of courage. For all the concerns Viktor bore for the soldiers at his back, he carried none for the daughter of Lilyana and Malachi Reveque.

He swept the claymore high, the exhilaration of coming battle abuzz in his veins and his shadow howling its delight. "Death and honour!"

"*Death and honour!*"

Fifty-Three

Melanna wept, never knowing if elation or loss urged tears forth, salvation's joy dashed against unyielding despair.

Song and battle cry had long departed the Hadari ranks. Shields were grounded. Spears at rest. Death they had pledged and death there was, though none was borne or dealt by Rhaled's children. Forgotten by the very battle they'd come to fight, they watched, awestruck, as the assault line buckled, Thrakkian axe and Tressian halberd counting little against Fellhallow unleashed. Lunassera fell to their knees, offering unspoken prayer to their distant goddess. Unblooded warriors gaped while veterans adopted the distant stare of men lost in old battles.

"Goddess guard me," breathed Chakdra. "What miracle is this?"

"Jack fought the Tressians at Govanna," rumbled Jorcari. "Perhaps he holds a grudge?"

How Melanna wished to believe that. How she wished she could silence the small, horrified voice that screamed at her for a fool. The bargain had been struck. The price would follow. All she'd wished for. All she'd feared.

The Thrakkians on the western flank were already in full retreat, streaming downhill, a tideline of black-garbed dead at their back and strawjacks lumbering behind. A lone thornmaiden, the flowers of her briared hair falling as withered petals, had strayed from the pursuit. Clutching a corpse to her breast, she turned a courtly waltz atop the dead, each strut and whirl set to the rhythm of screams.

To the east and in the centre, the Tressians fought on, the second and third lines embattled as Fellhallow's host overwhelmed the first. The howls of the dying vied with the crunch and snap of briar. Roots dragging the wounded down through the churned snow until their mouths filled with mud and their struggles were lost from sight.

"It's not a grudge," said Melanna, the words spoken without conscious intent. "Fellhallow now stands as the guarantor of Rhaled's throne, and the throne of Empire."

She broke off, her throat thick. A lunassera shot her a poisonous glance. Chakdra regarded her without comprehension. How far had her words carried? What whispers would they birth in coming days?

"What are your orders, my Empress?" said Jorcari. "Your warriors stand ready. Do we go forward?"

She shook her head, sickened by a hillside already thick with dead. More corpses to haunt her dreams. That they were Tressians seemed no longer to matter. More bodies to prop up her throne. Their deaths bought Rhaled's survival, and the lives of those who'd followed their Empress to Argatha Bridge. But the thought of expending even a single Rhalesh life to speed Jack's victory filled her throat with bile.

"No," she said, the words heavy as her heart. "Our part here is ended."

As she turned to leave, light and shadow swept the hillside.

Viktor's claymore struck the strawjack's ivy-clad torso in a spray of dying leaves. Ice-crusted branches woven in imitation of musculature shattered to fragments, laying bare a ribcage of mouldered bone. Livid green eyes blazed one last time in the jagged mask of the creature's face, and then its wreckage was lost behind the Drazina's thundering hooves.

Cheers rang out as men and women found faltering courage in the knowledge that the forest-demons could be slain. The third line surged uphill to rescue the second. Viktor forged on, Sidara radiant at his side, her longsword smeared with ichor and daylight mantled about her shoulders. With them came the riders of the reserve, Drazina with lances lowered and wayfarers with sabres slashing.

The second line was all but hidden beneath a writhing, clawing mass of branches. The first could not be seen. But there was no time for doubt, nor to conjure Izack's fate. Viktor gave himself to tremor of hooves and his shadow's wild joy.

He swept on into the billowing pollen-clouds, the air unbreathable.

Senses swimming, Viktor set loose his shadow. Frost crackled along the claymore's blade. Strawjacks turned turgid, writhing fronds slowing as chill bit deep. Steel hacked down through a misshapen shoulder, scattering bone and briar. Halberds came forward to settle the rest, sergeants' cries restoring order to a line embattled.

A knot of Drazina galloped past to Viktor's left and paid for valour with death, snatched from their steeds by strawjacks' gangling arms. The last died in a thornmaiden's embrace, idiot grin fixed in place even after briars tore out his throat. Viktor's claymore took the thornmaiden's head before the corpse stopped twitching, her last utterance a spill of excited laughter.

"Rally!" Viktor stood tall in his stirrups, sword aloft. "Reform the line!"

Survivors of the third line joined the second, bolstered again by the infantry of the reserve. As a new shield wall arose amid the bloody wreckage, Viktor cast about for Sidara.

A blaze of daylight revealed her to the east, a shrinking band of Drazina about her. Uphill, where Viktor at last glimpsed Izack's banner, a lone kraikon shuddered and toppled sideways beneath a thornbeast's charge, light hissing from rents in its armour. Sidara cried out and slid from her saddle, the horse bolting from beneath her.

Crackling triumph, strawjacks crowded in.

"Yah!"

Leaving the reforming line to Tallar's care, Viktor spurred across the hillside. Others rode with him. Drazina. Conscripts rescued from the rout. The claymore bit deep and pulled free through shards of frost-speckled brambles. An axe sheared away a strawjack's head, and thudded into the mud as whipping fronds dragged its master from his saddle.

Viktor slipped from his saddle before his horse stopped, claymore hacking a strawjack's legs away. A Drazina's sweeping blade split the creature's head. Awash in pollen, Viktor shouldered the thrashing wreckage clear and knelt beside Sidara.

"I told you to remain close."

Shield discarded, she pushed herself upright on trembling arms.

"Your promise is not mine," she breathed. "I'm fine."

Viktor didn't waste breath gainsaying the lie. Sidara's gaunt face spoke to the reflected toll of her destroyed charges. She put a piece of her light – her *self* – within the constructs to grant them purpose. What became of that sliver of soul when the host fell dark? Viktor didn't know – he'd never asked – and the weight of that ignorance lay heavier than ever.

He stood, hand hooked beneath her shoulder to help her rise, and beheld disaster.

The momentum of his charge had fizzled almost to nothing. Tallar's line, in the process of reforming at last sight, shuffled downhill as a fresh strawjack onslaught broke across its shields. The rear ranks were an open wound, King's Blue uniforms bleeding away south to the safety of the bridge. The west flank was a charnel of bodies and swaying thorns, the east full of galloping horses and panicked cries. And everywhere, the broken, mangled hulks of simarka and kraikons, as mournful in their way as the flesh and blood masters they'd failed.

An army fit to end the threat of Rhaled for generations, lost to slaughter and rout in less than an hour. Defeat came for the man who could not lose, and mocked his ambition.

Sidara swayed, her face more haggard than ever. "It's done, Viktor."

Furious, he rounded on her, uncaring that a score of wavering Drazina witnessed his fury. "No! Not while we've strength to fight!" He cast a hand northwards to Izack's banner, where crackling forest-demons made butchery of the first line's survivors. "Would you have me abandon Izack?"

"No!" She spat the word and followed it tiredly. "There's nothing more we can do."

"There's always something more!" he roared. "Find your strength! We cannot let this pass!"

Heart seething, Viktor closed his eyes and stretched his shadow across the hillside as he'd once done at Govanna. A twitch. A tug. The dead rose. Tressians. Thrakkians. One corpse after another, crawling from the carnage to oppose the foe. Black spots danced behind his eyes, the pressure worsening with every cadaver that clawed its way upright. He fell to his knees, and gripped the dead tight. They couldn't fight. He didn't need them to. They needed only to give the strawjacks pause, and give hope to those who fought on.

Thus had he won the field at Govanna. Thus would he win again.

Viktor's will clamped about them like a fist, the dead stood tall. Snarling satisfaction, he opened his eyes.

The strawjacks came on, ignoring the dead, lurching ever onwards to foes with blood yet to spill. The outermost edge of Viktor's band vanished beneath seething fronds. To the west, Tallar's banners fell as the shield wall dissolved into a mass of fleeing, doomed souls.

"No!"

Brow streaming with cold sweat, he gripped the dead tighter, striving by will alone to instil spark of life and thus deliver salvation. But for all his striving, the dead defied him as they ever had. He sank to one knee, and then the other. His shadow writhed and raged. The darkness behind his eyes flowed forth and smothered sight.

The last thing he heard was Sidara's scream.

The thornbeast shouldered a pavissionaire aside and stomped down on Izack's chest, driving him into the mud. His breastplate, already scored and crumpled from the impact of the creature's gnarled, cervine horns, buckled. Air shuddered from tortured lungs. Ribs snapped. Izack scrabbled for a sword flung beyond reach when the demon had knocked him flying.

The thornbeast reared up. Izack abandoned his attempt for the sword and slid his dagger from its sheath as the creature stomped down. Driven as much by the demon's strength as Izack's own, the honed steel parted the tangled branches between its toes. Again the thornbeast reared. Its hooting, crackling cry rippled with pain. Strawjacks crunched beneath thrashing feet.

Ignoring the red hot stab of broken ribs, Izack rolled clear of the beast's flailing horns and snatched up his sword.

"Come on then, you ugly bastard!"

The thornbeast lumbered to the charge, scattering sightless, stumbling corpses before it.

A woman's scream split the air. Not fear, nor panic, but loss and rage. Rage above all. Izack just about registered the voice as Sidara's when a sucking, howling wind lit the sky to flame.

A hot wind brushed Izack's exposed skin, not searing but warming, caressing. A summer's day beneath bleak clouds. Golden rays woke the thornbeast's briaried flesh to flame, and flame to stinging soot. Light faded. The false wind died and the true regained mastery, bearing the crackling, alien screams of strawjacks away south.

His throat thick with ash, Izack cuffed at streaming eyes and stared north along a scorched, arrow-straight path perhaps two-hundred paces wide. At a forest of wizened and blackened strawjacks, reduced to charred statues, golden embers sparkling and fires burning upon the scrub. Beyond them, beyond Tressians caught within the forest but miraculously untouched by the flames, the hillside fell deathly still. Shadowthorns frozen in the act of withdrawal or fallen to their knees, mouths agape. Forest-demons stood motionless to either side of the blackened pathway, alien emotion unreadable as the wind tugged at frond and briar.

But it was the view a half mile to the south, where scorched ground yielded to melting snows and muddy green, that stole what little breath Izack's ravaged lungs sifted from the bitter, ashen air. A vast, spread-winged bird-shape reached towards the clouds, its pinions ablaze with golden, leaping flame. Sidara was a dark figure at its heart, arms upraised.

"Raven's Eyes," breathed Izack.

The light flickered as Sidara fell to her knees, the firebird dissipated by the wind. The battlefield breathed deep.

Tearing his gaze from Sidara, Izack beheld the hillside anew. Hundreds of strawjacks snatched to oblivion by the golden flames, but many times more remained upon the crest. Of his own, Izack marked precious few. A dozen here. A score there. Bands of men and women clinging to tattered banners atop the dead. Thousands strained and squalled to make passage of the bridge below, but the hillside – the battle – had been lost long ago. Sidara's miracle offered no victory. It only staved off disaster.

Too like Govanna, for his liking. Mortals caught between the divine.

"Fall back to the bridge!" Ash clogged Izack's cry. He hawked to clear it. "Fall back!"

Soldiers streamed down the hill through scattered fires, faces as awestruck and soot-blackened as he knew his own to be, bearing their wounded and leaving the dead behind. Izack went with them, thoughts as numb as his limbs and eyes always on a motionless foe, wary for the pursuit that would tear them all to ruin.

That pursuit still hadn't come by the time Izack reached the blackened tidemark where a filthy Sidara knelt beside a motionless Lord Droshna.

"A phoenix shall blaze," she muttered, the words singsong. "A phoenix shall ... "

"B-bloody did." Izack cursed himself for his stutter. But how could one not be wary of someone capable of ... all this? "You did good, lass."

She stared blankly, golden eyes fading blue, looking but not seeing. The young woman he remembered, but something else also. Something he'd never understand. Something to be respected. Maybe even feared. He glanced back uphill. No maybe about it.

Deciding – hoping – that Sidara would keep, Izack turned his attention on Lord Droshna. "He still among the living?"

A Drazina nodded. "Yes, sir."

"Idle bastard, as usual." Glibness turned bitter. "Get him out of here."

As soldiers hurried to obey, Izack turned his attention on Sidara once more. "Don't make me carry you. Folk'll talk."

She blinked, eyes snapping to focus for the first time, and allowed him to help her rise.

They joined the stumbling retreat, Izack half-carrying her and guiding her steps. Still the pursuit held off. Were Jack's children afraid? Did such creatures feel fear? Or did they simply judge their duty done?

The answer came as Izack reached the crowded neck of the bridge, its form the yawning, groaning cry that had heralded Fellhallow's first coming. Warned by horrified gasps, Izack stared back towards the slope, and a living forest again on the move.

"Blessed Lumestra," breathed a Drazina.

What little of the soldiery had kept their order stumbled back across the bridge, eyes wide.

Heart ebbing further, Izack stared south across the bridge, at moorland thick with rout. Thousands had died on the hillside. Thousands more would perish to Fellhallow's vengeance. But the bridge could be held. The gorge's sides were steep; the Silverway strong. The bridge was all. And even an hour might make all the difference.

Funny how life offered choices that were no choice at all.

Ha-bloody-ha.

"Stand your damn ground!" bellowed Izack. "I said STAND!"

A few heeded, the muster field's obedience deep in their bones. Conscripts. Drazina. Even a few Thrakkians. They weren't Essamere – Lumestra, what he'd have given for that! – but they knew him, knew his voice. A score. One hundred. Two. Weary. Bloodied. Uniforms torn but backbones straight. The rest ran on, duty abandoned in hope of survival. So easy to become one of them. To cast down arms and flee. Easy, but impossible.

A soldier's life wasn't his own to spend. Others were his to save.

Izack shoved Sidara to the far bank, towards the Drazina bearing Lord Droshna from the field. "Get out of here, lass. Tell Droshna I wish ..." What? That he'd listened to Josiri? That he'd argued harder against taking the field that day? That he'd joined his voice to Zephan's and Sevaka's back at Tarvallion? All of those things were true, but had come too late to count. No point in saying them now. "Tell him I wish our road had led elsewhere."

"I can fight." She started angrily back, a stumble making lie of the words. "I'm staying!"

"You can barely walk." He flung out an arm to stop her, wincing as broken ribs shifted with even that small effort. "Lass, if you could do again what you did back there, I'd have you in a heartbeat. But you can't, can you?"

She glared at him. "I—"

"Can you?"

"I have a sword."

"A sword isn't enough." Setting lips level with her ear, he lowered his voice. "Droshna's going to need you, especially after today. Don't go throwing your life away out of pride."

"I might say the same to you."

Izack snorted. "Me? I already told him he'd need a new Lord Marshal before the day's end. Should've kept my big mouth shut, shouldn't I? Go. Don't make me have you dragged away."

She scowled, a wan flicker of gold leaving her eyes as soon as it arrived. "You wouldn't dare."

Izack conveniently forced a smile. "Try me."

Sidara narrowed her eyes. Then without a word, she strode away.

"Good lass." Spinning on his heel, Izack grabbed a sergeant by the shoulder and hauled her to the centre of the bridge. "Make the line! Shields tight!"

Little by little, the shield wall formed across the central arch. Stragglers took their places, weapons levelled. As the first strawjacks reached the far bank, a thrydaxe's black pennant was found and raised high for Lumestra to see. Izack grunted approval and took to the front rank. Wasn't a battle without a banner, even if it wasn't your own. Time to be Essamere – to be a shield for those that couldn't fight for themselves – one last time. A fellow could do worse. Maybe even atone for the mistakes that had led him to Argatha Bridge in the first place.

"All right, you dozy lot!" he roared. "Let's make this one for the histories! Until Death!"

Argatha Bridge's defenders held for long hours after the last of their routed fellows had vanished from sight. Melanna – alone upon the ridgeline save for a steed – watched the black pennant fall three times into the crackling mass of strawjacks, only for it to rise anew.

She couldn't say why she felt compelled to bear witness. Some perversion of spirit, goading her to drink the bitter day to its dregs? Or perhaps it was regard for those who fought on against all odds? The kinship of the sword transcended all other loyalty. So hard to know, with her heart awash in relief and dread.

As brooding dusk drew in, the pennant fell for a fourth and final time, and did not rise. A triumphant, yawning groan echoed up from the riverside, and was met by another from Fellhallow's eaves.

Turning her back on the charred and bloody field, Melanna hauled herself into the saddle. As she did so, she glimpsed a masked, gangling figure on the forest's edge, ragged cloak gathered close, and green eyes blazing against the gathering dusk. He was gone as soon as seen, but the chill in Melanna's bones lingered.

Lumendas, 14th Day of Dawntithe

We worry too much over eternity when it is the
moments that count. A hundred chances pass us by
each day, unremarked and unseen.

from the sermons of Konor Belenzo

Fifty-Four

Melanna heard the cheers long before she reached Tregard's walls. Word of salvation had far outpaced the army, reversing hurried evacuation and filling the streets with adulation. Triumphal Gate had welcomed many a victorious army, though few so gladly. Songs rang out, confetti of dried petals and silvered paper streamed from rooftops. Flasks of tarakeet and Lasmanora whiskey were pressed into soldiers' hands.

Jorcari and the others lost themselves to the embrace of loved ones they'd thought never to see again. Melanna watched from beneath Emperor Alfric's banner, apart from it all, at once an Empress' privilege and burden.

By the time she reached the marketplace, the celebrating populace had grown so thick that words were needed to clear passage. Jorcari at her side, she spurred ahead of the column.

"We have been tested, but we have triumphed!" She filled her voice with every scrap of confidence she could muster. "We have found enemies where we should have found friends, and allies in the unlikeliest places. A new dawn rises for Rhaled and for the Empire! Praise..."

She faltered as a new sight reached her eyes. An effigy at the marketplace's heart. Old timbers covered in torn canopies, treated with woodstain, it towered over the crowds, arms spread wide and the smooth arc of its mask tilted heavenward. Artless though it was, there was no mistaking it as anyone other than Jack o' Fellhallow. Melanna swallowed, a chill returning to her bones.

"Praise Ashana," she finished, and hoped no one heard the tremor in her voice.

The crowd cheered, and at last parted. Melanna rode on alone.

Two figures waited at the top of the stairs, a half-circle of servants gathered three paces behind. Sera, white robes immaculate. Orova, her pallor healthier than at their last meeting, but walking with the aid of a stick and plainly ill at ease in a black and silver dress. A third, caring nothing for decorum, bounded down the steps two at a time, arms spread in greeting.

"Madda!"

Melanna left her fears in the saddle and threw her arms about her daughter, holding her tight enough to cheat even the Raven's claim. She closed her eyes, banishing the cheer of the crowd as she had her fears, heeding instead the miracle of life dearer than her own. The warmth against her skin. Hurried breaths caught between excitement and fears of abandonment not yet forgotten, never committing fully to either.

"Did you miss me, Madda?" asked Kaila.

"In every moment," Melanna replied.

Yes, Jack would claim his due, but it was worth it. Bargain had bought Kaila's future, and thousands more besides. And there were yet many long years in which to see her grow. Not as a fugitive or a hostage, but into an Empress who'd eclipse her mother in happiness and wisdom.

Kaila squirmed and pulled away, eyes narrowing in suspicion. "Why are you crying?"

Melanna brushed her cheek. "Tears of joy, *essavim*. Nothing to burden yourself with."

Kaila nodded happily, and allowed Melanna to lead her up the steps. Sera offered a low bow, Orova a nod; neither with any great friendliness.

"Am I to congratulate you on your victory?" said Orova sourly.

"I wish none of it had been necessary." Melanna scratched surreptitiously at her left wrist, which itched something fierce. Her whole body was a mass of bruises and chafed skin – reminders of long hours in the saddle. "I don't expect you to believe me."

"Is Viktor among the dead?"

"Would it trouble you if he were?"

An eyelid flickered. "Your messenger claimed you sheltered those who fled. Is *that* true?"

"I ordered them freed once battle was done. They were no harm to anyone." As the rout had gathered pace, Tressians had sought safety in the Hadari lines, less afraid of shadowthorns than demons. She'd ordered the ranks opened to them, and the strawjacks had lumbered off in search of other victims. Few of those taken had been the cold-eyed veterans of Davenwood and Ahrad. Girls and boys, mostly. Strong enough to hold a sword and stand the line. A mirror of the Imperial practice of tithing, and horrific in the reflection. Sparing them had come easily. "My war was never with your people, but factions within my own. I understand that now."

Orova's lip curled. "If you seek forgiveness, do so elsewhere."

Irritation flared, but quarrelling with a guest was unseemly, especially today. "Has Apara returned?"

"Not so I know."

Which meant she was still in Tressia, or yet further afield. That, at least, gave identity to another scrap of loss. In some indefinable way, Tregard wasn't *home* with Apara elsewhere. Just as Aeldran's absence diminished the city in a manner Melanna had never truly noticed. But Aeldran was returning. Apara might for ever remain out of reach, beyond what solace Melanna could offer. A friend deserved better. Friendship *demanded* better.

"You asked of Lord Droshna," she said, before her thoughts turned dark. "He was borne from the field, though I do not know his fate. I hold him responsible for recent deaths, as should you. Should he cross my path again, I will do so forcefully."

Orova scowled, though Melanna had the sense she was not the sole target of disfavour.

She crouched, eye to eye with Kaila, mercifully still and silent throughout the exchange. "*Essavim*, perhaps you and Lady Orova would do me the kindness of inspecting the banquet preparations? One cannot have a celebration without a feast. The cooks might even have some honeycomb to spare."

Eyes shining, Kaila smoothed her hair across her shoulders and raised a hand for Orova to take. "Come, Shar Rosa. Honeycomb is the *best* breakfast."

Orova's scowl deepened. But it cleared swiftly enough, the reluctant smile telling a tale as plainly as Kaila's use of the *shar* honorific. Offering Melanna a final appraising glance, she took the girl's hand and withdrew.

"She seldom left Orova's side this past day," said Sera. "The woman has seen every inch of the palace twice over, and heard every tale Kaila knows to tell. She's been worn ragged. I began my watch fearing your daughter might need protecting from your guest. The reverse was truer."

Melanna's eyes remained on the retreating pair. "She's better at making friends than her mother. I hope the knack never leaves her. Friends are important." She shifted her gaze to Sera. "And should always speak their mind."

The lunassera straightened, steeling herself. "There is always a price for Jack o' Fellhallow's aid. Your father learned this too late. I thought you knew better."

"Ashana left us to stand alone." Melanna hung her head, the smile worn for Kaila receding as consequence again clamoured for attention. "And my people celebrate salvation in a city that would otherwise have burned around them."

"But the bargain—"

"Is mine alone, and the debt alongside. When it comes due, I will pay it unflinching, but for today I will strive for happiness. Will you permit me that, Sera?"

She hesitated, lips pursing beneath the silver half-mask. "Of course, Ashanal."

Viktor stared east across the rushing waters of the River Ravonn and beheld nothing but failure amid the melting snows.

The army that had followed him to Argatha Bridge? Gone. More to rout than to the Raven, or so his officers assured him, but regathering it would take days, if it was possible at all. What constructs remained were pitiful, battered creatures, badly in need of repair and barely fit to guard the siege lines at Ahrad. Most had been destroyed, their wreckage abandoned by an army in flight. Those few Thrakkians who'd held their order had already ridden for home, claiming their contract was for the Eastshires' recapture, not to die to demons across the border.

Stantin Izack, most loyal of the souls who'd marched east under his orders? Gone. A colossal weight upon Viktor's shoulders, the burden multiplied first by the uncivil tone of their last parting, again by the fact that Izack's caution had been proven proper, and one last time by the faithfulness shown to the very end.

Hopes of an Empress humbled and Tregard taken? Gone. Opportunity had been lost. Moreover, if Fellhallow and the Empire stood as one, there would be no other. Indeed, the days ahead might hold a great deal of strife. Reports from wayfarers and the smattering of borderers still under Viktor's command suggested that the ancient forest had returned to slumber. But what stock could really be set in such claims?

His reputation as a man who achieved the impossible? Gone. Viktor told himself that renown shouldn't have mattered when set against other losses. When set against the dead.

But it did, and burned all the darker.

Harms to the self were nothing. Even if his limbs still trembled with the aftermath of his shadow's exertion and his thoughts buzzed with its restlessness. The crisp scent of the rushing river fell distant, dreamlike. The hubbub from the siege encampment a quarter mile to the north was little better. Only the sunlight felt real, its unsettling caress more mockery than balm.

He'd been a fool to puppeteer the dead. He'd known what it might cost, known even then that it wouldn't work. Why else had he pursued the possibility of porcelain soldiers so long? Desperation had chosen his actions, and he fortunate not to be among the dead. That he was not was source of both shame and hope. Shame for surviving where others had not, and the hope that he might one day deliver justice already overdue.

What else was there? He stared north, to the palisades and tents of the siege lines. Ahrad would again be theirs within a week, assuming Jack o' Fellhallow's mischief was done. That might have counted for something, except Josiri would claim the ruins could have been theirs without a fight. It might even have been true.

Viktor scowled away the thought. Times were dire enough without surrendering to doubt. Josiri brought enough of his own to any conversation.

A twig snapped, the scuff of boot close behind.

"I left orders I was not to be disturbed," he said without turning. The growl in his voice should have set the intruder to flight.

"I need to speak with you, Uncle." Sidara's voice shook, apprehension and resolve battling for dominance. Resolve won. "I *must* speak with you."

Little question as to what had brought her there. She'd been as much a stranger to the woebegone encampment as he, but since waking Viktor had pieced together enough accounts of the battle to understand her role. Had he suspected she'd concealed such power, things might have been very different . . .

He willed dourness away. It obeyed only in part, but a part was enough to regain mastery of self and temper. Turning carefully, the better to subdue the dizziness of sunlight, he sought a reassuring smile. He found none.

"If it's wisdom you seek, mine lies at low ebb."

Sidara picked her way across the stones and joined him at the riverside. She scarcely looked upon him, her eyes downcast to the water. Her entire self was frayed. Not just the uniform – though that was unusual enough – but her manner also. Even the radiant light Viktor perceived through his shadow. Abandoning the search for a smile, he settled for a softened tone.

"What troubles you?"

Her throat bobbed. "I failed everyone, just as I failed my parents."

"You saved us."

A half-truth, for salvation had come as much from Izack and those who'd held Argatha Bridge. But Izack lay beyond Viktor's ability to offer comfort. The events of Midwintertide had proven how far the dead lay beyond his grasp.

Sidara hung her head. "And what of the slain? The wounded who burned on the hillside? The constructs in my charge?" She paused, her voice shaking. She'd always regarded the simarka as pets, more than tools of war. A foolish notion, though Viktor understood the sentiment that drove it. "Did I save them? After you collapsed, the light called for me to set it free. Why couldn't it have done so sooner?"

"If I've learned anything about magic, it's that it possesses fearsome will. It must be dominated if you've any hope of remaining sane."

"I thought I'd done so. It's been so quiet these past years."

"Perhaps because you hadn't need. You say it called for you. Perhaps you called for it?"

Sidara pinched her lips tight, her eyes fixed on the Ravonn's seething waters. "Then it *is* my fault. I could have acted sooner."

After brief hesitation – the personal more challenging than ever while swathed in his own grim mood – Viktor laid heavy hand on her shoulder. "I didn't mean it thus. Battle is a catalyst that rouses strength from weakness and valour from a timorous heart. All that I am, it taught me. The lessons are not always kind." He spoke slowly, choosing his words with uttermost care. "But we can still learn from them, if we possess the strength to do so."

Colour returned to Sidara's cheeks. "I couldn't control it. Freed, it did precisely as it wished and carried me alongside. I was everywhere, a piece of me in every tongue of flame. I felt the forest-demons wither and burn in my grasp. The dying slipped into Otherworld at my caress." She spoke faster and faster, maudlin tone yielding to reflected exhilaration. "So perfect. So beautiful."

Breathless, she shuddered and shrank inwards.

"I felt myself slipping away, and Lumestra help me, I *wanted* to. I longed to run for ever across the hillside, and live within the light. I've never felt such desire, and dared not trust it. So I sought reprieve in a phrase Altiris clung to in the dark times on Selann. They bound me back to him, and through him to the world." She splayed her hands between them, light glimmering from fingertip. "I've felt empty ever since."

Stifling discomfort awoken by her light, Viktor closed his hands about hers. Had he misread her mood as he had her words? She'd sent the mortally wounded on their way. A necessary kindness, though doubtless burdensome in aftermath. And if that were so, was she seeking absolution, or permission? Viktor more than any knew the lure of glimpsing a secret one unwittingly concealed from oneself . . . the temptation of learning more.

"What would you have me say?" he murmured.

"Tell me how to control the magic," she pleaded. "How *you* control it."

He winced. "You'd do better to ask Anastacia."

"Ana isn't here." She gazed up. "I wear this uniform to save lives. I want folk to look to me for safety."

"And you brought it when I could not."

"I killed our own!"

"You brought them mercy."

"I should have brought them life!" Breath rattling in her throat, she broke off. "For that, I have to learn what is possible, and what is not. Even if I risk losing myself to the light."

Her words struck a chord, the resonance of a kindred spirit. Sidara teetered on the brink of the same despair he'd felt many times. Kinship demanded he do all he could.

"I cannot teach you to control the light," he said. "It and I are too different. But I have it within me to share a portion of my shadow. *That* I could teach you to control, and through those lessons offer insight elsewhere."

Sidara drew her hands free, her brow furrowing. "I don't know ... I don't ... Your shadow?"

Reticence was to be expected. His shadow was of the Dark, and the Dark's reputation was less than savoury. "It's a weapon, as your light is a weapon. One to be bent to purpose, and sorely needed." Seeing that his words found little purchase, he sought another tack. "It has been the making of your brother."

"Constans?" She gaped. "Constans has magic?"

Was that anger? Surprise? Jealousy? Perhaps a little of all. Having no blood siblings of his own, Viktor poorly understood the paradoxes of love and envy that bound them. "A piece only. The mastering of it taught him discipline." He offered a thin smile. "You must admit, it was a lesson sorely needed. I was glad to offer it."

"Why didn't he tell me?"

"I asked him to keep it hidden."

"Another lesson in discipline?"

"In part. But you know the power of superstition. It distorts perception, and your brother is already perceived unfavourably enough."

"That's true ... " Sidara shook her head. "I can't, Viktor. I'm sorry."

"You came to me for help. This is all I can offer."

"And I'm grateful, but the light writhes in your shadow's presence. Carrying a piece of it within me – I fear the two would tear me apart in quarrel."

So she was sometimes as discomfited in his company as he was hers? But sought his company and counsel regardless? Malachi would have been proud of her. "I've faith that you'd master them."

She offered a wan smile. "I don't. So it seems I must find another way."

Viktor was struck by temptation to make the decision for her, or else smother her objections in shadow and seek forgiveness after. There was so much at stake. Not just Sidara's sanity, but an Eastshires whose liberation would mean nothing if it could not be defended against Fellhallow's malice. Sidara's light *was* a weapon, and one that had proved itself more apt to the task than shadow. With the Republic in the balance, how could he even hesitate? Especially with that particular, peculiar note in her voice. One that betrayed curiosity ... perhaps even yearning.

But hesitate Viktor did, weighed down by the lesson of Izack's death. He'd erred too much and others had paid the price. Trust was a mirror: unoffered, it could never be returned. Sidara's choices had to remain her own.

"As you wish."

The palace throne room, so austere and seemly in the cold light of day, was entirely other when furnished for banquet. The scent of woodsmoke and roasted meat wafted between tables already stained with grease and scraps. Goblets chimed a hundred toasts. Drunken cries from men and women gave voice to a hundred more. A time for warriors to indulge – a celebration mirrored in every street.

Melanna had witnessed it first as a girl, sneaking glimpses through door-cracks and spyholes, marvelling at the transformation of stone-faced warriors to wild rogues. Later she'd done so as a princessa at her father's side, unwanted and ill-regarded by so many. As Empress, she'd held aloof, indulging sparingly and comporting herself as a ruler should.

Not that night.

As soon as Kaila was banished to their private quarters, she left High Table – and the empty seat that should have been Aeldran's; the place that had been set for Orova as manners demanded, but remained unfilled as expectation allowed – and gave herself to the merriment. Jorcari an ever-present shadow, she moved from table to table, joining warriors and chieftains in mirth and toast. Most welcomed her with wary eyes, fearing a joke at their expense. They relaxed readily, her soft smiles and softer words aided by wine and mead partaken. As it had been for her father, so it was for Melanna. Welcome it was, for it banished the day's lingering fears.

And perhaps she'd indulged wine more than intended. For as midnight approached and tables were dragged away to clear a dancer's ring about the central fire, Melanna found herself among the blur of faces and wine-soured air, breathless as the reel quickened pace. She welcomed the ache and the giddiness. And if there were those who saw the woman first, and Empress but regretfully, she welcomed that too.

The great door boomed beneath a fist's strike. A blare of trumpets silenced fiddle and pipe. The double leaves swung inwards. Golden gleamed in the gloom, betraying warriors not in the soft silks of banquet, but the battlefield's scales. They strode into the firelight, befuddled souls clearing a space before them. Low murmur rose to a growl.

"I've ridden hard for this?" Aeldran's voice boomed through the sudden silence. "I thought to find Tregard besieged or ablaze, and instead I find my Empress cavorting with our warriors!"

Melanna's dance partner – a minor prince of Illacar whose smile had been rather more pleasing than his club-footed steps – shrank away. Freed, Melanna faced Aeldran square on across the thinning crowd. "And this troubles you, *essavir*?"

Frown gave way to a smile. "Only if I'm unwelcome."

She extended her left hand, twitching as the banished itch returned full force. "Your place is here. Will you not claim it?"

The growl became a cheer. Aeldran strode forward, the warriors at his back claiming seats and goblets forsaken. Others readily made room, at last marking what Melanna had seen from the start – that not one carried a blade.

Aeldran took Melanna's hand and made to kneel. Raising him up, she kissed him full on the lips and grinned at his surprise. The fondness of the absent heart or of wine taken? She knew not, and cared little. Only that his return had restored a piece of her also.

The music began anew, the revels of the dancers offering the strange privacy of the crowd.

Aeldran's fingers brushed the curve of her cheek, tracing a fading scar earned during the battle for Tregard. "You are well, *essavim*? I have news from Incalia Tiranal, should you wish to hear it."

Cardivan's niece? "Is it good?"

"I think so, yes."

"Then it will wait."

As servants fetched vittles for the newcomers, Melanna led her consort away through the dancers, and left the throne room behind.

The newcomer arrived as dusk fell, passing through Commander Tallar's picket lines and reaching Viktor's tent without voice raised or challenge given. That alone would have been cause for concern. Viktor tolerated circumvention of military protocol poorly at the best of times, and with his mood growing steadily darker as reports tallied the full cost of the disaster at Argatha Bridge, gave no quarter in remonstration.

Or rather, such had been his intent. Horrific news all but erased his distaste for the bearer's conduct. Sending a herald for Sidara, Viktor lost himself in contemplation of a world shifting into a new and decidedly unwelcome configuration. He barely noticed her arrival, aspect neater than at their previous meeting, but expression guarded.

"You sent for me, Uncle?"

He beckoned her inside the tent and gestured for her to sit opposite the table that served as his desk. "I've had word from Tressia. It appears I have been deposed."

Even now, it took every scrap of self-control to pretend reason when every instinct called him to rage. Every scrap, and still not enough.

Sidara flinched as the shadows deepened around her. "I don't understand."

The corner's gloom shifted as Constans at last deigned to reveal himself. Sidara started in alarm, then returned his flowery bow with a scowl.

"Is that all? I expected at least a little panic." Constans shot Viktor a knowing look. "Oh, I see how it is. Someone's been giving away my secrets."

Viktor ignored him. "Josiri's new council is remaking the city in its image – which explains the orders we received yesterday morn. The Drazina I charged with keeping order have been detained or killed by the traitors of Essamere. Tzila is missing. I expect to be summoned to account for my actions before dawn rises, if an assassin's blade doesn't find me first ... We know all too well the company Governor Orova keeps," he finished bitterly.

Sidara sprang to her feet, her face taut. "What about Ana? Josiri . . . ?" She swallowed, an edge creeping into her voice. "Altiris?"

"Ana and Josiri are well enough, I imagine," said Constans. "Josiri is after all the architect of these woes."

"No!" Viktor shook his head and fought again for calm. "I cannot accept that. He is used, perhaps. A figurehead for others. We've quarrelled much of late, and I've given him little reason to trust me. His part in this arises from misunderstanding, nothing more."

Constans offered a disbelieving sigh. "Open your eyes, Father! He's at the very heart of it. He—"

"Enough!" Viktor bellowed.

He upended the table, spilling candles and papers across the floor. Ice crackled across timber uprights and the surviving candelabra. His shadow's cold stole the air from his lungs.

Constans stumbled away, face pale.

Sidara sprang to her feet, her composure badly shaken. "Altiris! What has become of him?"

Viktor returned Constans' enquiring glance with a heavy-hearted nod. The news would only fester with delay.

"I'm sorry, dear sister," said Constans, his brow furrowed in sympathy. "He died when Essamere stormed the palace. His last words were that I should flee the city before it was too late. He stayed true to Tressia – to the Lord Protector – to the last. It was humbling to see."

Her face fell. "What . . . ? No." Sidara stumbled, hand grasping blindly for the chair's support. She missed her footing, but Constans darted forward and steadied her, one hand at her shoulder and another at her elbow. "You're lying. You always lie to me . . ."

Pulling away, she collapsed in the chair, head in her hands and straggled golden hair streaming past her fingers.

Viktor's wrath shrank in abeyance at sorrow so close to his own. Constans had offered no word of Calenne, save that she'd been taken to Josiri's keeping. It was Viktor's most fervent hope that she'd find no harm there, but guarantees were fast becoming a thing of wild imagining. What a fool he'd been to hold silent of her return.

Kneeling, he struggled for words to salve Sidara's pain, and his own fears. None came.

"He was example to us all," murmured Constans. "I'd just come around to liking him, too."

Something in his tone struck Viktor as amiss. But then neither solemnity nor loss came readily to the lad. To hear both at once was sure to carry strangely.

Sidara's head snapped up. Red-rimmed, golden eyes held no tears. Only a fury that turned Viktor's blood to ice. "This can't go unanswered."

"It won't," rumbled Viktor. "I'd intended to oversee Ahrad's capture and refortification, but what use is it looking to the Republic's armour if its heart is rotten?"

She blinked. "You mean to march on the city?"

"With what? The army is gone and I've spent five years making Tressia impregnable. Even if I strip Ahrad's siege lines of every soldier, I'd not have a tenth of what I needed. But I must see for myself what has been done. Perhaps this is all a tragic misunderstanding, and the situation recoverable without bloodshed."

"And if not?" asked Constans.

"It will not be the first time I've stepped alone into the enemy's maw."

"I'm coming with you." Golden eyes brooked no argument. "I'll see Altiris' killers brought to account."

Her tone left nothing of the nature of that accounting to Viktor's imagination. "No. I'll not place us all in the noose. The siege remains in Commander Tallar's care. Leave the surviving kraikons and simarka to ensure it remains so, but take what Drazina remain and head to Castle Prangav, in the Heartweald. Both of you." Viktor glanced up at Constans and received a reluctant nod in reply. "Wait there until I send word."

"And if no word comes?" asked Constans.

"Then I am likely dead, or a prisoner, and the Republic will need you free."

"I won't let you do this," Sidara bit out.

Viktor let friendliness fall away. "You will, because it is not your uncle who asks, but the Lord Protector to whom you swore an oath who *commands*."

She stood, rigid and unflinching. "Yes, my lord."

Viktor nodded, proud. Josiri had wanted to keep her from war? He'd been a fool. Or perhaps that too had been part of so far-reaching scheme only now revealed? "I won't lie. There may yet be the darkest of days ahead. They might ask of us that which we do not wish to give. But I promise you that this will pass, and we shall see justice done."

Sidara made to leave but halted at the tent flaps, the tears in her heart at last present in her eyes. "Your offer ... Would you share your shadow with me?"

He regarded her, pleased and wary at the change of heart. "What of your concern it would make poor companion for your light?"

The corner of her mouth twisted. Her gaze left his to contemplate unseen eternities. "The world is different now. I have to be different too. More than ever, I need to be in control."

Viktor waved at Constans. "Leave us."

The boy scowled, but obeyed, leaving them alone in flickering candlelight.

"You're certain of this?" Viktor scried Sidara's face for a trace of doubt, but her expression was a mask. "There may be pain, if it works at all."

"Then better now, when I'm numb to so much."

He nodded. "Take my hands."

After brief hesitation, she obeyed, her thin fingers smooth against his calloused palms. Breathing deep, he closed his eyes and let his shadow flow between them.

Sidara whimpered, but snarled the weakness away. Viktor's shadow hissed reluctance, but he drove it on, deeper – down through the radiant glory of her soul, aiming ever for her heart.

Drowning in sunlight, his shadow howled displeasure. So different to when he'd done the same for Constans, for whom it had been more like the tether with which he'd once bound Apara Rann. Painless. Immediate. Irreversible.

This was more akin to exorcism of Rosa upon Govanna Field, where he'd cast out the Raven's blight and restored her to sanity. But even that was poor comparison. The Raven's mists had parted readily, but not Sidara's light. It fought, searing his shadow, the skin of his palms rising to blisters in sympathy. She'd been right, there could be no parity between the two. There could be only master and servant.

Again Sidara cried out. Her hands shifted against Viktor's and tried to pull away. Fearing the shock of separation might doom the attempt for ever, he held her close and sent his shadow again to the fray.

The light retreated before his onslaught. On the brink of collapse, he wove a cage about it, as he had many times for his own shadow. Raging brilliance faded with freedom. One last flaring, and it was done.

Viktor opened his eyes as Sidara sank against him and lowered her gently to her knees.

"Can you hear me?" Worry set in when no answer came. The fear that he'd done more than he'd intended, and thus inflicted harm. "Sidara?"

Her hand tightened on his arm. Eyes fluttered open, golden irises fading to piercing blue, to inky, smoky black. "I can ... feel it," she gasped. "Moving around my soul. Talking to me."

"And what does it say?"

"That I should listen to you, Uncle."

Viktor's shoulders sank in relief. Perhaps this would work, after all. "Good. Because you've much to learn, and little time in which to do so."

The balcony was about as different from the throne room as it was possible to be. There, Melanna's skin had sweltered in the close, fire-laden air. Here, the cold night rippled it to gooseflesh beneath her robes. Aeldran, now clad as simply as she, held the worst at bay through embrace, her disarrayed hair against his shoulder and his arms looped about her waist. Together they beheld the distant lights and laughter of the city proper, unremarked and unobserved.

A strange place to find contentment, but little better company in which to find it. Had the time apart brought them closer, or was it simply the knowledge of foreshortened years urging her to take what comfort she might in what remained? Did it even matter, so long as the heart was settled?

"Your thoughts are distant, *essavim*." Aeldran kissed the back of her head and drew away. "Has it anything to do with the boarded-up windows in your chambers?"

Melanna cursed softly, letting darkness hide her scowl. She'd hoped he hadn't noticed, not with the drapes drawn and distraction aplenty closer to hand. But now wasn't the time to broach the details of her bargain with Jack, nor the unsettling compulsion awakened in her by sight of the old wood. It would only be trouble, and trouble would wait ... if Aeldran had to be told at all.

"Tell me about Incalia Tiranal," she said instead. Advancing to the balcony's edge, she scratched idly at her itching wrist, seeking to still the sensation or at least spirit it elsewhere.

A soft grunt warned that the change of topic had not gone unnoticed. "Dotha Silsaria sends a pledge of unyielding friendship."

She shook her head. "The House of Tirane has never been short of promises. It's the deeds that bring woe."

"Perhaps she foresaw your scepticism. Her cousin, Prince Thirava, came by swift horse to Calandil, and was promptly jailed. Apparently he met with an accident shortly thereafter."

Melanna stared out towards Ravencourt Temple with its black spires and the flickering, ethereal plumes of blue-white ghostfires holding the dead at bay. Thirava. The last piece in a cruel puzzle. Incalia had taken swift steps to secure her throne. Other intent would reveal itself in time. Whether Incalia's or that of Cardivan's allies in the Gwyraya Hadar.

"Then I suppose the matter will keep," she said at last, though her thoughts were less on distant Silsaria, and more on ... what? In truth, she couldn't say. Too much wine.

"I imagine there's no great hurry." Even facing away, Melanna heard Aeldran's smile. "You *are* well? You seem different."

The urge to tell all bubbled to the surface, even though it would dispel the illusion of peace. Melanna turned her back on the city. "Good different, or bad different?"

He leaned down to kiss her cheek. "Time will tell." Straightening, he withdrew to the balcony door. "I thought to look in on our daughter, if you can spare me?"

"Of course. If there's a Tressian walking the corridors, stay your hand."

Aeldran frowned. "A Tressian?"

"Lady Orova."

"*That* Lady Orova?"

"She saved Kaila." Knowing it an imperfect explanation, Melanna cast around for another. Tiredness led her astray. "She sleeps poorly."

"I see." It was plain Aeldran did not, but he took mercy on her bewilderment. "It seems a great deal has changed, but Kaila's knack for twisting souls about her little finger has not."

Offering a small smile, he slipped from the balcony. Melanna again stared out across the city. At the lives and loves spared from the sword by her bargain with Jack. How could it not be worth it? And she'd ten years to make matters right with those she loved. Ten years before Kaila could claim the throne Jack had sworn to preserve.

The itch returned to her inner wrist. Fleeting. Damnable. Impossible to ignore. Without looking, Melanna bit back irritation and scratched harder than before.

Something brushed against her fingertips, feather light and gossamer thin. She gave it a frustrated tug and snatched it away, only for a stab of pain to send her sinking against the balcony. She opened her fingers. A flap of skin fluttered to the balcony floor. Cold settling in the pit of her stomach, Melanna raised her left hand.

There was no blood. No red raw and chafed flesh. Merely a tear in the skin an inch wide and two long, running from base of her palm and across her wrist As she curled her fingers, woven briars flexed where flesh should have lain, their thorns ripping at unblemished skin.

Jack's mark. A reminder of all she'd promised and of what she'd one day become.

Throat thick with bile, Melanna fell to her knees and wept.

Astridas, 15th Day of Dawntithe

Trust glitters brightest in the darkness.

Ithnajîm proverb

Fifty-Five

Strange, thought Viktor, how history repeated itself. The roadway before King's Gate, normally so full at that hour, was deserted save for a double line of soldiers, Essamere green to the fore and King's Blue behind. He glimpsed others on the rampart. More than was usual for simple sentry duty. And to complete the mirror of days long gone, a friend waited on the road, expression unwelcoming. Not Rosa, as it had been after the Battle of Davenwood, but Josiri with a councillor's soft cloth as his raiment, and a sword buckled at his waist.

Constans' warnings buzzing about his thoughts, Viktor dismounted. Battle-worn black cloak brushing the roadway, he led his horse the rest of the way.

Josiri strode to meet him. Viktor slowed, using the extra time to read his brother's manner. Stiff. Unfriendly. Was he truly a pawn in all this? Doubts had formed in long hours on the road. So much of what he'd done could be misinterpreted – Calenne, in particular – especially after he'd found nothing but failure in the east. But whether Josiri or his co-conspirators acknowledged it, their actions laid a road to a civil war the Republic could scarcely afford.

With Josiri a dozen paces away, Viktor halted. "Brother."

Distaste wrinkled Josiri's brow. "Don't call me that."

So that was how matters lay? "This is not the welcome I expected."

"You were ordered to bring your army home."

"If such missives were sent, they passed me on the road." That much was true, for Viktor had met no heralds on his westward ride.

Josiri's expression hardened. "So where is the army?"

"As I brought the Empress to battle, Fellhallow roused against us," Viktor replied bitterly. Two days was not nearly enough to lessen that burden. "We were overrun, lost to slaughter and rout."

Josiri paled. "What of Sidara? Izack?"

"Sidara lives, and acquitted herself proudly." Viktor shook his head. "Izack bought our lives with his own. One among thousands."

Josiri's shoulders slumped, his eyes downcast to the roadway and his lips pinched tight. "Damn you, Viktor. Why couldn't you have listened? Or am I to believe those first heralds never found you either?"

"I am Lord Protector of this Republic. None may command me. Not even you ... brother."

Josiri straightened. For the first time, he bore authority as a mantle. A look that might have suited him – that Viktor might have applauded – under other circumstances. "No longer. The Tressian Republic again takes guidance from a council. From many voices, rather than one."

Viktor bit back an angry retort. "And yours is pre-eminent?"

"For the moment."

So Constans *had* been correct. Josiri wasn't merely part of this, but its instigator? Viktor sought kinship in his brother's expression, and found nary a flicker. The betrayal hurt more than the deed. Heeding his shifting mood, Viktor's shadow uncoiled. Breath frosted on the air.

"And if I decide otherwise?" Viktor growled.

Josiri took a half-step back, then rallied, meeting Viktor's glare head on, the petulance of self-righteousness rising to the fore. "Submit to the Council's judgement. You'll have opportunity to make your case."

His shadow hissed. Soldiers paled as the grey morning fell deeper into gloom. One or two stepped back, eyes wide. Josiri held his ground.

"And what would you have me explain?" asked Viktor.

"You stand accused of treason and witchcraft."

"Charges of convenience."

"Not today. And there are others. Complicity in the deaths at Silverway Docks. Murder. Violations of self and soul. Come quietly, Viktor. I argued long and hard with the others to offer this choice."

"Then you stand as my defender, brother?" Perhaps Constans had been wrong, after all.

"As your accuser. For Calenne. For Revekah. For myself."

The betrayal cut deeper for recent hopes. Not trusting himself to speak, Viktor stared past Josiri to the assembled soldiery. Barely thirty, even counting those upon the walls. Well within his shadow's gift to overcome, so long as others weren't hidden close by. Certainly not enough to contain him if he sought to depart. It was almost insulting. Viktor strove to remind himself that he'd come to talk, not brawl. Even in the face of provocation.

"And should I refuse to yield?"

"Then you make truth of my fears." Josiri stepped closer, his expression carved from stone. He raised a hand. A dozen crossbows presented above the battlements. "And I'll have no choice at all."

For all he strove otherwise, Viktor's temper began to slip. "You think that'll stop me?"

"I think an innocent man would protest, not threaten." He stepped closer, until the two were barely a dozen strides apart. "And yes, I do. Silver, Viktor."

Overcome by bitter laughter, Viktor gestured at the Essamere ranks. "You stand here with traitors at your back and accuse me of the same? You meet me with threats? I thought you knew better than that."

"Then we're both of us fools, because I thought better of you. See where it's got us."

Typical Josiri. Holier-than-thou arrogance. Seeking equivalence of strife where none existed. "Have your rabble stand down, and I'll accompany you. This 'council' of yours may level its charges."

"The Council isn't yet ready to question you. You'll go to confinement until they are."

In the end, it was the flaunting of petty authority that did it. It wasn't enough to question, to accuse. Josiri and his as-yet unnamed conspirators sought humiliation alongside. Before Argatha Bridge, Viktor might have indulged them. Not now. He'd been patient enough.

The roadway drowned in darkness, the cries of blinded soldiers reaching Viktor's ears before he was aware he'd set it free. Crossbows fell from masterless hands and fell to the roadway from the ramparts. A silver bolt, loosed by the impact, spat away into the murk. Knights sank to their knees.

Only Josiri stood firm, trapped in the eye of the storm while Viktor's shadow raged about the roadway. Pale, he advanced, sword untouched, as the shadow howled.

"Viktor!"

Closing, Viktor hauled Josiri off his feet and raised him high. "I never thought it'd be you who betrayed me!"

They might have been alone in the darkness, save for the cries of those caught in his shadow. King's Gate, the city itself – even the fields bordering the road – all felt distant, removed from the world.

"I'm trying to keep my promise," gasped Josiri. "To stop you if the Dark overtook you."

Viktor cast him to the roadway. "This isn't about the Dark! This is about loyalty!"

"Is it?" Slowly, painfully, Josiri rose on one elbow. "Look around, Viktor. Tell me this isn't about the Dark. Someone recently told me that you're not responsible for what you've become. That your shadow makes you a reflection of our fears. I don't believe him. I've never known you to be anything other than in complete control. Prove me right. For Calenne's sake, if not your own."

"You'd threaten your own sister?" Did he even recognise Calenne for what she was, or did paranoia rule him, as Viktor had feared?

"Never. But what do you suppose she'd say to see you now?"

A good question, and one to which Viktor found no ready answer. Josiri's promise to curtail his actions if the Dark took him, once a comfort, now caged them both. That there was tyranny afoot within the city – within *his* city – he no longer doubted, but if Josiri spoke true, there was yet hope it could be excised. But not like this. A man who came to the walls in anger could only ever be perceived as a monster.

Inch by inch, Viktor drew back his shadow. Grey morning reclaimed roadway and rampart; the scattered, gasping soldiers who'd thought to prove themselves his superior and had learned the terrible depth of their error.

Viktor unslung his claymore and cast it to the roadway. He held out his hands to be shackled.

The drawing room's log fire tantalised in a way Calenne couldn't describe. Sensation was part of it, or rather the memory of the same. Not as powerful as when she'd beheld flames from the clocktower's window, but unmistakeably *there*.

Was it pain? She no longer had any point of reference. Pain was long in her past. It was certainly discomfiting, but then wasn't discomfort as much a part of the mind as the body? Still, she embraced it, and marvelled at the act's perversity. Was she so broken a soul that only the unwholesome found purchase? Was that why she'd drawn the curtains? Certainly, peace came easier in the darkness. Or perhaps it was because she didn't want anyone to see her kneeling in the hearth's soot, staring into fire.

Enough of Stonecrest's inhabitants regarded her strangely as it was. Not Josiri, of course, with whom she'd spoken as often as his newest, painful duties allowed, and taken rare delight in beholding the man he'd become. Not Altiris, who'd accompanied her on walks about the grounds, not as a guard, but as a solicitous friend, though his thoughts were plainly with his distant lover when they were not with the comatose Kurkas. Not Anastacia, who had been so sympathetic – even *kind* – that Calenne had for the first time glimpsed the creature her brother loved, rather than the one she'd always loathed. But the others? In too many eyes, she was tainted, declaimed as a demon by expression, if not words. Justice, of a sort, for she'd ever levied that charge against Anastacia. It wasn't even the clay that provoked their fear, but association with a fallen hero.

The Raven lowered himself into a chair. Calenne spared him barely a glance, and went back to watching the flames.

"I see you've exchanged one cage for another."

[[Shut up.]]

"Very dignified." Planting a walking cane between his feet, he leaned forward and propped his chin on the handle. "It's not good to seek truth in flame."

[[I didn't ask.]] Calenne sighed and tore her attention from the hearth. The ruin of the Raven's face looked better, the starscape less ragged where it met torn flesh. And it was *his* face alone, the goateed society gentleman no longer flickering in and out with the Hadari widow. A sign that he, at least, was on the mend? [[And I'm not a prisoner. I can leave whenever I'd like.]]

"You don't belong here."

[[And where do I belong?]]

The Raven tilted his head, expression speaking volumes.

[[Otherworld? I've just found my brother again. I'm not going back.]] A fatuous statement, for the Raven collected all in the end. It would be the height of foolishness to consider this anything more than a reprieve. [[Not yet.]]

"Hmm." He twisted in the chair and stared into the flames. "May I offer some advice?"

[[Do I seriously have a choice?]]

"No." A thin smile chased across his lips. "The ephemeral world is no place for the dead. Stay, and you put everyone around you at risk."

Calenne regarded him warily. [[Is that a threat?]] It didn't sound like one. Indeed, the Raven sounded almost solicitous, his ready charm a far cry from the anger of previous meetings.

He waved a spread palm across his face. "You might notice I'm feeling much more like myself. It has brought a certain ... clarity, shall we say. In all the turnings of the Celestial Clock, there has always been a Raven. Always the *same* Raven, while so many of my siblings take new faces and new forms. I've beheld the rise and fall of entire worlds. Dark has yielded to the dawn, then returned with the dusk. I'd be a dull sort if I didn't learn to recognise patterns in all that." He shrugged, a weary smile tugging at the corner of his mouth. "You'll return to my keeping soon enough. When the time comes, don't fight it."

Not a threat, and not quite an apology. [[I—]]

The door creaked open, a shard of daylight cutting through the gloom.

"Why are you sitting in the dark?" Josiri frowned, his hand still on the door. "Is someone with you?"

Calenne glanced at the Raven's empty chair. [[Apparently not. Altiris is watching over Captain Kurkas. I think he feels responsible.]]

Josiri nodded, the corner of his mouth twitching.

Gathering ashen skirts, Calenne rose to offer embrace. For all that physical sensation was denied her, she found solace in his closeness. As much memory as the warmth of the flame, but no less reassuring. Especially today. Letting go, she stepped away. [[Is it done?]]

He snorted, his expression weary and troubled. "Done? It's barely begun. But at least Viktor came quietly enough in the end. He's in the clocktower, shackled with silver and closely guarded. It seemed the best place to hold him."

There was a certain symmetry in that. Calenne wasn't sure how it made her feel. [[Is he hurt?]]

"Only in his pride."

[[And you?]]

He set the door to and sank into a chair, hand to his brow. "This all feels like some terrible dream. At one moment, I can't believe it's possible. At the next I curse myself for not seeing its inevitability. So many warnings, and I missed them all." He scowled. "And now? Now, I'm as damned as he..."

Those last words seemed to speak to a different burden, though Calenne couldn't divine what. [[During my time in the clocktower, Viktor spoke highly of you. Often with frustration, but never without fondness. Whatever he's done, he loves you.]]

"Does he?" Josiri leaned forward, drained. "He's never listened to me, not in anything that matters. And now I know that when my arguments tired him, he simply... changed my mind for me and crumbled adjoining memories to dust. I don't think I'll ever know how many decisions were truly mine. Maybe none of them since the day he brought you back to Branghall. Maybe I've been his plaything ever since."

Calenne sat opposite. [[I won't believe that. For you, the change has been gradual, across years. To me it's plain that Viktor's not the same man, however much he pretends otherwise. I don't know that he's even a wicked man, though he's certainly adrift. As you and I were adrift when we first met him.]]

Josiri shook his head. "We were proud. Selfish. He's killed, and worse than killed. He's treated those he called friends like puppets. There's no comparison."

[[And what if that's only because you and I lacked the ability?]] asked Calenne. [[You yearned so much to finish our mother's work and see the Southshires freed. Could you have resisted the temptation to make things right, no matter the cost?]]

He scowled and hid his face in his hands. "You're supposed to find peace in the mists, little sister, not wisdom. It's impolite."

Calenne would have smiled, had she been able. [[What's to happen now?]]

"That's for the Council." Josiri sighed. "No one much cares that Viktor murdered his father or Kasvin, both of which could be said to be justified. The last year or so of his protectorship borders on tyranny, but tyranny is unremarkable enough in our fine Republic, so long as it's legal. Too many would find no fault in him pressing his invasion of the Empire against orders . . . But the rest? It doesn't look good. We'd be fools to believe that Rosa, Apara and I were the only ones whose memory and will he violated."

He stared into the fire, fingers working restlessly and his brow knotted. A full minute passed before he spoke again, the words crackling with emotion.

"We have the vranastone Viktor used to bring you back. It's locked away in Duskvigil Church, alongside a series of texts that Ana went pale to behold. She's been working with Shalamoh, offering him snippets about her life on Astarria in exchange for cooperation. Meaningless scraps, she says, but you should see his eyes light up." Josiri snorted in weary amusement. "Even with Tzila missing, there's damning proof enough."

[[That's not her name. Call her Revekah.]]

He grimaced. "But she's *not* Revekah. Only the part of Revekah Halvor Viktor stole from the Raven. The rest of her is the Dark, so Shalamoh said. Mad, as all born of the Dark are mad."

Calenne shuddered at the reminder of what so easily could have been her fate.

"Shalamoh said she was meant to lead an army of the dead," said Josiri. "And Viktor's actions since have proven he'd have done more with it than secure our borders. Malatriant's heir raising an undead army fixed on conquest? Jezek's already talking about sending Viktor to the pyre."

Cold gathered at the core of Calenne's being. For all that she abhorred Viktor's recent actions, the prospect of his death provoked dread. [[Of course he is!]] she spat. [[He's a churchman. Makrov was the same.]]

"Jezek isn't his predecessor. He's gone out of his way to help set things right, marshalling every church under his authority – and a few others besides – to distribute rations to the needy, and offer shelter to those who have none. A bright spark in dark days. But he's afraid. They're all afraid." Josiri glanced at her, his eyes empty. "I'm afraid too, when I'm not angry. Which isn't often."

Irritation flared. [[Let me speak to them.]]

"That's not a good idea."

[[So you don't trust me?]]

"It's not you I don't trust. You're part of Viktor's guilt. I argued long and hard to save you from the consequences. Without Sevaka and Ana backing me up, I don't know that I'd have prevailed." He scowled. "They call me their First Councillor, but they're watching me closely. I'm tainted, you see. Too close to Viktor. If you involve yourself, I don't know how it will end."

Calenne read the lie in his eyes. He knew, all right. She calmed herself. Arguing with Josiri came naturally – a peculiar thing to have missed, though she had – but it wouldn't keep Viktor from the flames.

[[Do you *want* to save him?]]

His face flushed. "What I want doesn't matter," he snapped.

[[That's the old Josiri talking. The one who hid in Branghall while the Southshires burned.]]

He glared at her. "Fine. Do *you* want to save him, knowing what you do?"

[[I once thought Viktor my future. The Black Knight become my saviour. Now? I don't know how I feel. I don't know how I feel about almost anything. The world's so distant without sensation.]] Calenne heard self-pity crowd her singsong voice. She forced it back. On this topic, at least, her feelings were clear. [[I'd save the man who saved *me*. I believe he's still in there, though he's lost his way. Do you want to save him? Can you forgive him?]]

He hesitated. "I don't know."

[[You need to be sure. You need to know what he deserves. For your sake, if not Viktor's.]]

And for hers. For if Josiri couldn't save Viktor from his mistakes, Calenne had little chance of doing so. She who'd surely stand beside him on the pyre. The prospect of death renewed should have awoken *something*. Fear, at the least. Maybe the Raven was right. She didn't belong to the ephemeral world any longer, save for when she chose to.

Josiri nodded and forced a smile. "Two morsels of wisdom in one day? I'm honoured."

[[I offered little enough when I was alive,]] she replied primly, relieved to have broken through his malaise, if only for a moment. [[I'm trying to correct the shortfall.]]

"And you do." Rising, he kissed her brow. "Thank you. I'll return when I can."

Then he was gone, and Calenne again alone with the tantalising flames.

Fifty-Six

The walk to King's Gate had taken every inch of courage. Every step a mile, every breath labouring beneath the weight of events to come. Only anger had kept Josiri moving, one foot in front of the other. He'd clung to it, used its strength in place of his own. The walk to the palace was worse, because even anger needed fuel to burn, and his was all but spent. There was only a terrible, enervating weariness of body and soul, one that well surpassed fatigue.

Drained, he wanted nothing more than to sleep, to open his eyes only when the matter was settled. Not that he could. Haunted by the dead of Argatha Bridge, he'd managed barely a wink for two nights, though he'd striven to hide that fact from anyone but Anastacia. He knew it'd only get worse when an official tally of the slain came in. Deaths that would for ever linger on his conscience, for all that he'd not truly been their architect.

Worse was the ineluctable truth lying foursquare in his path. Even at King's Gate, he'd had the luxury of pretence. He could live in a world where this was all tragic misunderstanding. Once in the clocktower, that world would be gone.

If it had ever existed.

And so Josiri trudged on through the deepening dusk, barely acknowledging wary glances from Brass and Kelver. There were only the cobbles beneath his feet, and the mocking visage of the future gazing back.

Once inside the palace, they passed through Viktor's quarters without challenge. Four Knights Essamere stood guard at the clocktower door.

Silver sigils glinted on lintel and threshold, swirling patterns that dizzied the eye. Anastacia's work. The heavy bolts had been fixed by a steelsmith to supplement the heavy lock. No chances taken.

The knights' captain exchanged a glance with his companions, and met Josiri on the stairs. "Can I help you, Lord Trelan?"

Josiri unbuckled his sword and held it out. "I want to speak to him."

A careful note crept into his tone. "The Council say Lord Droshna's to have no visitors until his fate's decided."

Prudent. Even welcome, save for the fact that it was the first Josiri had heard of it. Evidence of events moving further beyond his control? "I'm the First Councillor." The title lent further degree of nauseating unreality to events. "You may consider that decree overruled."

The captain offered a slow nod. Unconvinced, but unwilling to make a challenge of it. Josiri almost wished he would. Anything for an excuse to turn aside and return to Stonecrest.

"As you say, my lord." The captain took Josiri's sword. Another knight set about the process of unlocking and unbolting. "We'll be right here, should anything go amiss."

Josiri nodded, heeding the double meaning. "Thank you."

Leaving Brass and Kelver behind, he approached the gloomy threshold.

And hesitated.

The sense of standing on a precipice returned, stronger than ever. Still not too late. He could walk away, leave the matter for another day, another person.

But Calenne had been right. He had to know, if only for himself.

He stepped inside.

The door swung shut behind, the bright lanterns of the corridor banished. A sole lamp suspended from the rafters took up their labours, so dull as to leave as much in shadow. Silver sigils gleamed about the barred windows, and in great concentric circles spiralling out from the centre of the floor. Anastacia had been busy indeed. The furnishings of Calenne's confinement had long since been removed. Only an iron bedstead remained, and a plain chair beside – both of them at the centre of the silver wards.

Viktor sat on the latter, eyes closed and head bowed. Silvered shackles bound his wrists, and were in turn secured by chain to a heavy eyebolt in the floor. He wore no armour, only simple black garb that blurred where it touched shadow.

"Brother. Have you come to set me free? Or perhaps you're here to kill me?"

Josiri stifled a chill and stepped closer. Viktor was the prisoner, so why did *he* feel trapped? "I'm trying to save your life. Jezek and the others, they think you should go to the pyre. And here am I, fool that I am—" He lowered his voice and strove for calm. "I came to talk. Lumestra knows I didn't want to. Calenne suggested I should."

His lip twitched. "How is she?"

"Better for being free of this place."

Viktor sighed and opened his eyes. "I only ever wanted to keep her safe."

"From me? She is, at any rate, better off than that *thing* you've made of Revekah, so I suppose I should thank you for that."

For a long moment, Viktor said nothing. Then he nodded slowly. "I wish that had gone otherwise. But the Republic needed defenders, and I needed someone who knew a soldier's trade. Someone I trusted."

"Someone to be the first of an army? Shalamoh told me. Only I know it's a lie. If you'd been certain of it working, you'd have brought back Calenne right from the start. But you weren't, and Revekah was expendable, wasn't she? Now she's trapped, one foot in both worlds, drowning in the madness of the Dark."

"And without that, I'd never have learned enough to rescue Calenne," said Viktor. "The Revekah I knew would gladly have taken the risk."

"Maybe she would," Josiri bit out. "Had you asked."

They stared at one another in silence, eyes locked in the gloom.

"What did you want to discuss?" said Viktor at last. "Can it be that you no longer possess the courage of your convictions?"

Josiri hesitated. "I honestly don't know."

"You should fix that. A usurper needs confidence to keep what he's stolen." Bitterness welled beneath the words. "You should be prepared for what you've set in motion."

Josiri's blood ran cold. "Is that a threat?"

"It's simply what will be. Your allies will turn on you, as you turned on me."

"You *really* consider yourself the victim in all this?"

"I'm the one manacled to the floor."

Josiri grimaced. "You made it necessary."

"By restoring a fractured realm to peace and prosperity? I don't expect you to understand what it costs. From our very first meeting you've always left the difficult decisions to me."

"That's not true," snapped Josiri.

"Isn't it? You spent years watching the Council oppress the Southshires, but did nothing until I forced the issue." Viktor cocked his head. "Again and again, you've let me bear the brunt of what must be done, then quibbled about my methods. You know nothing of sacrifice."

"Nothing of sacrifice?" Josiri strode closer, his voice rising to a shout. "How do you suppose the Hadari knew you meant to march on Tregard?"

Viktor's eyes hardened. His voice, unfriendly from the first, shaded darker still. Nothing compared to the guilt Josiri felt for his part in the deaths at Argatha Bridge. "Rann. I should have torn her apart when I had the chance."

"You did more than enough to her."

"Did I? And here I thought it was only me you'd betrayed." Viktor sprang to his feet. Too late, Josiri realised he'd stepped within the chain's extent. As he made to back away, Viktor's hands clamped about his throat, choking off any attempt at raising the alarm. "I should break your neck!"

Dark eyes burned into Josiri's. He met them unblinking. "Do it," he rasped. "You think those deaths don't haunt me? The only reason I've hope of ever sleeping again is because I know that if I'd said nothing, more would have died."

He gasped for breath that wouldn't come. The room mottled and turned darker still.

Snarling, Viktor shoved him away. "You were my friend! My brother!"

His shoulders heaved, the chain taut between shackles and eyebolt.

Josiri doubled over, one hand outflung for balance, the other rubbing at his throat. "Was I?" he gasped. "You twisted me inside out! Made sure I did what you wanted, when you wanted it, and drowned the memory in shadow so I wouldn't remember. Are those a brother's deeds? You say I betrayed you? You betrayed me first."

The chain went slack. The fury in Viktor's expression turned wary. "Explain."

He needed no notes for this. Betrayal had seared the memories into his soul.

"I've found my signature on so many decrees. Some I remember refusing. Others I've no recollection of at all, though it's there, right alongside Izack's." He faltered. How many of Izack's choices had been his own in recent months? Izack, whose death would for ever stain both their consciences ... assuming Viktor had one. "Ana worried my memory was failing. I stared into the future and beheld dotage before my time. And then I learned what you did to Rosa after Darkmere. I got to wondering how many thoughts and deeds in recent years have truly been ours."

Viktor's face crumbled. "I never broke your trust, Josiri. At least ... I didn't mean to." He sank heavily on the chair. "I was tempted, so many times. Just a nudge, here or there. Overcome that cursed stubbornness of yours so you'd for once do the right thing without argument. I don't know, maybe ... Maybe I did."

Caught off guard by the confession, Josiri watched him closely, wondering how much, if anything, he should believe. Hope flared, a part of him yearning that there might, even now, be a way back. "How can you not know?"

"Sometimes my shadow acts on my desires and leaves me none the wiser," growled Viktor. "You know this. You've seen it. Raven's Eyes, but I've despaired of changing your mind often enough. I don't think there's any way to know, not for certain."

Josiri nodded, recalling fleeting memories of Calenne Akadra. The woman Viktor had woven from the Dark without knowing. "And Rosa?"

Viktor grunted. "The Raven turned her against me at Darkmere. It was that or kill her. I'd no choice."

Hope stuttered and faded. "You say that a lot, Viktor."

"I don't follow."

"I've done a lot of thinking in your absence." Josiri thrust his hands into his pockets. "There's a pattern, stretching back through the years I've known you. A problem arises – one no other can solve. And while everyone is in disarray, in strides Viktor Akadra, head high and voice firm."

Josiri jabbed a finger at Viktor, but eyes always wary of the chain's extent. "He's a man who doesn't lose. Who can't be swayed by circumstance or counsel. He does precisely as he wishes, and snatches victory from the jaws of defeat. But there's always a price. Oh, never to you, though you play the victim in aftermath. You do remorse so terribly well. But I'm not buying it any longer."

Viktor sat back, face immobile. "I've only ever done what's necessary."

"You do as you please, with not a thought to the consequences!"

"Untrue."

Josiri held up a bunched hand and extended his thumb. "Seven years ago, Malachi would have brought Ebigail and your father to trial, had you not taken it upon yourself to kill them. Who knows how much easier a time he'd have had with the Council had their crimes been laid bare?" Forefinger joined the thumb. "The following year, during the Avitra Briganda, you lied to me about Calenne Akadra."

"I didn't know what she was!"

"No. You thought she was my sister, and still you hid her from me. When the Dark overtook her and she started killing—"

"I dealt with the matter."

"You *destroyed* her."

"I had—"

"No choice?" Josiri shook his head. "I beheld a terrified woman, struggling with the notion that her life was a lie. Perhaps we could have helped her, but you did what you always do when those you love prove inconvenient – you forge on, Raven take the consequences and the hindmost."

"You dare suggest you knew that creature better than I?" rumbled Viktor.

"I might not, had we discussed the matter, but you always refused." The index finger joined the others. "Malachi wanted me to replace him as First Councillor. Konor Zarn knew. Did you?"

"I ... suspected."

Renewed anger drove back surprise. "But instead, you pressured me into supporting your ascension to Lord Protector. Was even that my choice, or another of your *necessities*?"

Viktor gave no response, and thus offered deafening reply.

Josiri breathed deep on a failed search for calm. "And Constans?

Lumestra knows he was never that likeable, but what you've done to him ... ?"

Thunder gathered about Viktor's brow. "I gave him *discipline*, which is more than you ever managed."

"You *infected* him with your shadow. That same shadow you claim sometimes acts beyond your control! What possessed you to do such a thing?"

"It was the making of him!"

"He tried to murder Kurkas! But for Altiris, he'd have succeeded."

Viktor frowned, subsided. "Altiris? I thought ... " He shook his head, his voice thick with concern. "I didn't know about Vladama, I swear. Will he live?"

"I don't know." Josiri rubbed his brow. "He awoke for a time this morning, but ... I don't know."

Viktor slumped in his chair and stared at the floor. "You paint a damning portrait, brother."

Did the familial honorific suggest contrition? Did it matter? Josiri could no longer say for sure. The last of his anger bled away, leaving a hole at the core of his being. "It's warranted. Personal betrayals aside, you've turned this city into what the Southshires once was. Checkpoints. Distrust. Steel to solve the problem of unrest. But that's how you solve every challenge, isn't it, Viktor? Only it looks a damn sight less heroic when you're doing it to your own people."

"I've wept for the dead." Even now he sounded affronted.

"And what are tears worth to my mother? To Calenne Akadra? Revekah? To the dead of Silverway Dock? To those who died at Argatha Bridge? And everyone in between?" Josiri cast a frustrated hand towards him. "Bad enough that you leave a trail of bodies behind, but you never acknowledge that you've done so. You never *learn*. Everything you touch falls into ruin, but it's always someone else's fault. Some *necessity* provoked by another's hand. And I have to wonder, is this pride or is this malice? Are you even Viktor Akadra any longer? Or the Dark wearing his shape? Or perhaps I just hope that, because it makes me less of a fool for ever trusting you."

He turned away, overcome by weariness.

*

Viktor stared thoughtfully at Josiri's back. Impressive, in its way, that he'd gleaned so much truth in so short a time. Indeed, the gaps in his knowledge were gaps in Viktor's also, who even now couldn't judge the rightness of Josiri's claims about coercion and stolen memories. It awoke the possibility that his shadow – now cowering deep within his soul, away from the preponderance of silver – had cast its influence more widely than he'd known.

Rosa, yes. Apara Rann, certainly – and both with good reason. Josiri? Others? Malatriant had warned of the possibility at Eskavord, years ago – that his shadow would bend others to his will, even without his guidance. He'd dismissed it then, and dared not do so now. It would explain Sevaka's inconstant support. Had Elzar truly chosen to aid him against the Raven, or had his shadow forced this issue?

Impossible. He was in control of his shadow. Had been so for a long time.

But he'd thought that before. And all the while lived a lie. Was he doing so again? Worse, was he entertaining that possibility to forsake responsibility for choices made?

There was no way to know.

Had he become everything he'd sworn never to be? Malatriant's heir in purpose as well as power? The mere possibility set something cold gnawing at his core. How easily one became a tyrant.

And Constans? The boy had lied about Altiris' death for no other reason than a cruel jest at Sidara's expense. He'd trusted the boy too much. That was plain to see. And if wickedness yet remained in his shadow, what fate had he condemned Constans to? Even Sidara, with whom he'd lately shared another piece of himself?

Ironic, that he'd returned home hoping that reason might prevail. And so it had, but in a manner wholly other to the one he'd expected. If he could no longer swear which actions belonged to his shadow and which belonged to him, then he'd lost his way, and Josiri was right to hold to his promise.

Viktor swallowed to clear a throat suddenly dry. "I don't know what you want from me, brother. You value my apologies even less than my tears, but I offer both, and in whatever quantities are required." He hung his head. "I only ever wanted to protect this Republic. Whatever amends I can make, I will . . . if I am permitted."

He'd never intended to remain Lord Protector for ever. He'd done all he'd set out to achieve. Perhaps it was time to retire. Return to the simple life that had brought him such peace. And this time, if he was fortunate, with Calenne at his side.

Josiri's shoulders dipped. He nodded without turning, his relief palpable even in gloom. "I'll talk to the Council, but I can make no promises."

Viktor stifled a growl. Josiri had accused him of not learning from the past and now revealed himself to be every bit as bad. First Councillor, and he was still trying to forge consensus, rather than impose it. But to say as much was to shatter the brittle accord just struck.

"Is Calenne safe?" he said instead.

"Yes. And always will be, so long as I live."

Viktor nodded. That pledge, at least, he could trust. "I'd like to speak with her."

Josiri halted at the door. "I'll see what can be done."

Sevaka reached the council chamber in the early hours to find that she was the last to arrive. Or so she thought. As she took her seat at the table – not her mother's old seat, as a point of principle – she realised that neither Josiri nor Anastacia were in attendance.

A second sweep of the room confirmed they were the only absentees. Zephan Tanor, the brooding scowl of recent days still clinging to his chiselled features. Captain Raldan, still very much resembling a man who thought himself an intruder. The grey-haired Jeska Soren, speaking for the trader's guild after Konor Zarn's death. And at the table's head – in the chair that would otherwise have been Josiri's – Avriel Jezek.

"Governor Orova." The archimandrite's haggard, sleep-lorn expression made him look a good decade older than his middle-years. "I apologise for the lateness of the hour, but some things cannot wait. I trust we're not distracting you from something important?"

"Not at all."

Sevaka had been with Apara when the herald had found her. They'd shared the day together, though they'd spoken little. For all that her sister seemed mostly in command of her wits, she flinched in terror at the smallest of noises. That night, as for the two preceding it, Silvane House blazed with lantern light fit to banish every scrap of shadow.

"Good." Jezek nodded. "Then we can begin."

Sevaka frowned. "Without the First Councillor? Without Lady Psanneque?"

"I fear so." Grimacing, he steepled his fingers. "There's no delicate way to put this, so I'll be blunt. Josiri visited Lord Droshna today, in direct contravention of this council's orders."

"They've a lot to discuss," Sevaka replied. "Josiri has suffered from Viktor's actions more than anyone."

"That's the crux of our concern," said Jeska Soren, speaking with the precision for which she was known. "Our worry is that Lord Droshna retains unhealthy influence over him. Such things cannot be discounted when dealing with witchery."

Sevaka glanced from one to the next, and found only expressions set in unflinching accord. "This is ridiculous. Josiri was the first to denounce Viktor."

"Did you know he also gave the shadowthorns warning of our army's approach?" asked Zephan. "He told Lord Droshna as much today, according to the shieldbearers keeping watch."

She had, of course. Not in advance, but after Josiri and Apara had returned. Instinct warned her against admitting as much. "That's hardly proof that Viktor holds sway over him. Quite the reverse."

"But it does speak to erratic judgement and divided loyalties," said Jezek. "If we're to put this lamentable mess behind us, we must do so quickly and boldly. Steps must be taken that we cannot expect Josiri to approve. For his good and for ours, we need to be rid of Viktor Droshna, and every trace of his heresy ... including that abomination Josiri claims is his sister."

What? "Calenne is an innocent in all this. She's a victim."

"Calenne Trelan may be," said Soren. "But she's been dead for years. Who knows what influence Lord Droshna wields over Josiri through that demon?"

Again Sevaka cast about the table, seeking support. It would have been easier if any of them looked like they were enjoying the matter. Some pettiness to leverage in Calenne's defence. But if any of her peers took glee in the moment, it was well concealed. All looked as weary as she felt. Weary, and scared. "She's no demon. You can't punish her for Viktor's mistakes."

Jezek's face fell. "I was afraid you'd be resistant. Perhaps there's some truth in Master Shalamoh's claims, after all."

Sevaka's blood turned to ice. "What claims?"

"That you're as much an abomination as she."

He continued speaking, joined in debate by Raldan and Soren. Lost in private torment, Sevaka didn't hear a word. It was even true, wasn't it? They'd both returned from the mists. That the Raven had given her up willingly didn't matter, even if she'd means of proving it.

The strike of Zephan's fist on the table dragged her back to horrific reality.

"Enough!" Centuries of Essamere resonated in his voice. "Witch hunts and wild accusations belong to the past. Leave them there."

Sevaka pinched her lips tight and nodded, glad that her trembling hands were out of sight beneath the table.

"You're correct, of course," said Jezek. "I'm sorry, governor. I fear I'm not fashioned for such horrible times."

Zephan offered Jezek a less than friendly glance. "Be that as it may, we do this cleanly, or we don't do it at all."

Soren leaned forward. "Then we have your support, and the support of Essamere?"

"You do."

"Then I call the matter to a vote." She scowled. "And may Lumestra help us all."

Jeradas, 16th Day of Dawntithe

Malatriant's chief evil lay not in the deeds she bade others perform, but in those deeds others performed in her name without ever once being asked.

Fear is the death of decency.

from Eldor Shalamoh's "Historica"

Fifty-Seven

The Hayadra Grove always looked splendid in dawn's first light, and that winter morning was no exception. The alabaster trees shone, their crowns no less majestic for the dearth of leaves. The Shaddra, marred and blackened though she was, seemed twice the presence at that hour, her broad branches spread in welcome across the temple ruins. Even the air seemed crisper, lighter – separate from the sour, earthy stench of surrounding streets. Beautiful in all ways; inspiration for poet and preacher alike, and yet Altiris' heart remained at low ebb.

Too many losses. Too many betrayals. And no justice for anyone. Kurkas with one foot in the mists. Anastacia withdrawn and furious with guilt. Izack – whom Altiris had liked, for all that he'd found him intimidating – dead on the border.

But there were moments of gladness amid the sorrow. Lord Trelan's reunion with Calenne had been a joy to behold, as if each held a piece of the other that had been missing too long. Effusive thanks had dispelled Altiris' fears that his master – his *father* – harboured any ill will. Indeed, even caught up in all that occurred, Lord Trelan had insisted on having the adoption notarised without delay – though both agreed that formal declaration would wait for a happier time, if one ever arrived.

The Eastshires were free. Tressia itself was already so different. With the Drazina gone and checkpoints empty, the mood of the streets seemed lighter. The Hayadra Grove was more crowded with celebrants and idlers than in days past, a few of whom offered curious glances at the pair of Phoenixes in their midst, but no hostility. Kasvin had been right, at least in part, and Altiris found himself hoping it brought her soul a measure of peace.

And more important than all of that, Sidara was *alive*.

Even so, no one seemed to know where she was, and for all Lord Trelan's assurances of her forgiveness, Altiris dared not believe them until he heard it for himself. But at least there was a dream of the future to cling to. Constans was another matter.

"You're miles away." Receiving no response, Viara nudged his shoulder. "Farthing for your thoughts?"

Altiris scowled. "They're not worth it."

She glanced at the base of the Shaddra's trunk and shrugged. "He's not here."

"I know." Just like Constans hadn't been there yesterday, or the day before that, at dawn or at dusk. A slim hope that he'd be creature of habit enough to return to the grove, despite everything. But it had to be tried. At least at dawn Altiris could be certain of the lad's absence. No shadows in which to hide. Dusk was another matter. "We should head back."

"We could take the long way? It's a beautiful morning. We should enjoy it."

Translation: *he* should enjoy it.

Altiris supposed Viara was right. A week before, he'd been a fugitive. Now he was reinstated, all sins forgiven and a Trelan, no less. The last part still seemed unreal. Better to take pleasure in what moments he could.

Turning his back on the Shaddra, Altiris struck out for Sinner's Mile.

Halfway there, he slowed to a halt. The crowd's mood shifted as its numbers swelled. A covered wagon appeared at the crest of Sinner's Mile. Instinct roused, anticipation all too familiar from his time on Selann. Trapped in compounds and hovels, the slaves had never known *what* was brewing, only that it *was*.

Viara glanced about. "What is it?"

"I don't know." The first uniforms showed beneath the crowded terraces of Sinner's Mile. Not Drazina, thankfully. Constables. Regular army. A smattering of Essamere. Tabards Altiris had come to trust. So why did he feel so ill at ease? "Nothing good."

Stonecrest would wait.

*

Stonecrest's door sprang open as soon as Josiri turned the key, the knocker forcing her way into the entrance hall when it was barely more than ajar.

"You have to leave, now." Sevaka doubled over, fighting for breath. "Take Calenne and get out of the city."

Josiri frowned, expectations realigning. "I don't understand."

"The Council are afraid Calenne's a demon. They're going to burn her."

Josiri reeled, throat dry. The Council? But he was First Councillor . . . "You're mistaken."

"I got away as soon as I could." She straightened, grey eyes brimming with urgency. "Essamere are on their way to take her. They'll be here any moment."

Your allies will turn on you, as you turned on me.

Josiri swallowed, Viktor's warning starker in the daylight than the clocktower's gloom.

"He was right," he murmured. "He's always right."

[[Josiri?]] Calenne emerged from the drawing room, the expressionless mask of her face tilted in enquiry. [[I heard the commotion. What's wrong?]]

Stricken, he faced her. No time for explanations, much less to wake Anastacia. "We have to get you out of here. Can you ride?"

[[I think so. I mean, I haven't tried since—]]

The door crashed open. Brass crossed the threshold and slammed it shut behind, his not-inconsiderable weight braced against the timber. "Beg your pardon, sir." His normally lugubrious tone held urgency. "Just saw a dozen Essamere knights breach the gate without so much as a warning or a by-your-leave. They took Beckon and Jarrock at sword point."

Two hearthguards down already. With Altiris and Viara out in the city, Jaridav and Stalder dead at Tzila's hands, that left what? Three, Brass included? Not enough to contest Essamere, even if he could gather them in time.

"The kitchens," snapped Josiri. "The servants' door to the stables. Move!"

He shoved Calenne on her way and made to follow.

The kitchen door crashed open. Hunter's green and drawn steel crowded the doorway. In the same heartbeat, the front door bucked and sent Brass flying. Zephan Tanor entered, his sword scabbarded. Six helmed and cloaked knights came behind. The first planted a foot on Brass' chest. The others, joined by those from the kitchen, fanned out in encirclement, weapons levelled.

"Don't make this more difficult." Zephan stepped into the circle and removed his helm. The silver grandmaster's circlet gleamed in the lantern light. "There's no need for bloodshed."

Furious, Josiri bore down, careless of the naked swords. "No need? You break into my home to drag my sister to the pyre, and you say there's no need?"

His expression set like stone. "That's not your sister, Josiri, but a demon. Only you can't see it."

Calenne hung her head. Her hollow, bitter laughter echoed across the hallway.

"Is the grandmaster of Essamere now an authority in matters divine?" growled Josiri. "She is Calenne Trelan. My sister. The Saviour of Davenwood, returned to us by a miracle."

"It's a demon, birthed by witchcraft. It must burn."

"No!"

Josiri lunged, his fingers closing on Zephan's scabbarded sword. Before he had it even halfway drawn, the grandmaster's gauntleted fist struck him reeling. Stars exploded behind Josiri's splotchy eyes. His mouth crowded with the taste of blood. Calenne's hands found his shoulders, steadying him as the dizziness passed.

"There's no need for this!" shouted Sevaka.

"This is what you voted for," Zephan rejoined.

"Jezek would have put me on the pyre alongside if I hadn't!"

The circle closed in.

"Are we debating demons and I wasn't invited?" said Anastacia. "I think I'm offended."

Josiri looked up to see her standing halfway along the stairs, immaculately gowned and her arms folded over the banister.

She peered down with rank disfavour. "I've been named a demon more times than I can count, often by men in archimandrite's robes. Those who profess faith see demons everywhere but their own tawdry souls." She smiled throughout, but there was ice in her tone. "Goodness knows Calenne and I have never exactly been close, but tell me, what has she *done*?"

"She is a familiar for Lord Droshna's influence," Zephan replied stiffly.

"Nonsense. Viktor never needed that. It's what makes him so dangerous."

"The archimandrite says otherwise."

"Why *of course* he does." Standing upright, she began a graceful descent. "Calenne's no more a demon than I am. Perhaps you should take me too ... if you think you can."

Josiri gaped, horrified. "Ana—"

"Quiet, dear. We're learning so much." Daylight blazed into being about Anastacia's bunched fist. It flickered, scattering almost at once. She held Zephan's gaze, defiant, as though it had only been a warning. But the slight sag of her shoulders didn't escape Josiri, nor did the fact that the knuckles of her other hand were white where it gripped the banister. As in her duel with Tzila, what magic she'd possessed as a serathi spirit refused to heed a mortal woman's call. "How far do you want to take this, Master Tanor?"

Zephan met her gaze head on. "It's already gone too far. But I know my duty."

Josiri wiped a trickle of blood from his lip. "She's *not* a demon. Why won't you listen?"

"You know how this city works," Zephan bit out. "If I leave in failure, it won't be the end of the matter. Your stubbornness will damn you. Others will come, and they'll not be gentle. How many more would you have die to save a demon's life?"

Arms thrust at his sides and voice breaking, Josiri advanced once more. "If you want my sister, you'll have to take me also."

"And me," said Anastacia, the words as solemn as they were unexpected. "And I will *not* go quietly."

"Lady Orova," Zephan said tersely. "Do you stand with the Council, or with them?"

Sevaka hung her head. "What you're doing is no different to what Viktor did to my sister. Can't you see that? How quickly this city makes us into those we abhor." Sighing, she raised her eyes to meet his.

"I'm with them. As you should be. A shield, not a sword. Isn't that the Essamere way?"

"I'm trying to be a shield. Can't you see that?"

[[Is no one to ask my opinion?]]

Intent chimed loud beneath Calenne's question. She stood motionless at the heart of the sword-ring, eyes downcast and hands looped at her waist.

[[When the time comes, don't fight it,]] she murmured. [[He knew.]]

"Who knew?" asked Josiri. "Viktor?"

[[The Raven. He told me that if I insisted on staying here, I'd put others at risk.]] She met Josiri's gaze, smoky eyes blazing with emotion in a cold, expressionless face. [[I can't allow that.]]

The Raven? Josiri glanced about, for a moment believing he might catch a glimpse of the Keeper of the Dead. "No!"

[[I won't let you die for me. Not when I'm already dead.]]

Eyes filling with tears, he stepped closer. "Don't do this. We'll find a way."

[[Ever since I returned, I've had visions of fire. I thought they belonged to the past, but perhaps they were prophecy.]] She laid a hand on his arm. [[You need to let me go. Viktor never could, and it's led him into wickedness. Don't make the same mistake.]]

Heart aching, Josiri flung his arms about her. The doll's body seemed colder and smaller than ever. "I won't let them take you." The words scraped at a ragged, ashen throat.

Calenne returned the embrace with fearsome strength. [[These last few days have been a gift – a chance to see who you've become. I love you. I'm proud of you. Never forget that.]] She glanced up at the stairs. [[Look after him ... demon.]] The last was spoken with wry inflection.

Anastacia nodded. "To my last breath."

"Take her!" said Tanor.

Knights pressed forward. Hands dragged them apart.

"Calenne!"

Josiri's struggles earned him a cuff about the head. When his vision cleared, Calenne stood on Stonecrest's threshold, silver shackles about her wrists and two knights to either side. Others shepherded Brass, Sevaka and Anastacia towards the drawing room.

"Don't let them leave. I'll send word when it's done." Zephan donned his helm. "I'm sorry, Lord Trelan. This has to happen. It's—"

"Necessary?" What Josiri had intended as bleak laughter stuttered to a raw, rattling moan. "Sevaka's right. You've more in common with Viktor than you think. At least take me with you. She shouldn't face this alone."

"And risk you fomenting the crowds to mischief?"

Josiri stared towards the door. Calenne was mere paces away, but beyond reach of anything save words. Speech came haltingly, overwhelmed by the racing emotions that sucked away his breath, and set the world shuddering. Exhausted from sleepless nights and the horror of the present, Josiri felt words disintegrate even as he sought them, crushed by the invisible fist closing about his heart. But if ever there was a time for stubbornness, it was now.

"I love you, little sister," he gasped. "I'll look for you come Third Dawn."

For a moment, she stood framed in the morning sunlight, no longer the creature of cold clay and falsehood who'd re-entered his life, but Calenne as Josiri remembered her, with unruly black hair and sparkling sapphire eyes.

Then the door slammed, and she was gone.

"... and only by casting out the Dark in our midst can we move forward into light."

Archimandrite Jezek had a long way to go before being remembered fondly as a public speaker, Altiris decided. The reedy, uncertain voice and tediousness of the sermon were only part of it. The man looked as though he wanted to be anywhere but where he was, which was atop a small scaffold hurriedly erected at the crest of Sinner's Mile, well beyond the hayadra trees, but close enough to draw association from the holy site.

But for all that, Jezek had the crowd's rapt attention. Or maybe he didn't. Maybe, like Altiris, their eyes were drawn to the ghoulish presence of the wagon within the ring of King's Blue shields. No longer covered, the wagon's bounty of kindling and timber lay revealed beneath the morning sun. Even from fifty yards back, its purpose stood plain. To erase all doubt, a lone serene stood beside a lit brazier, unlit torch in hand.

"It's the Lord Protector," he muttered. "They're really going to burn him."

He'd not witnessed a burning since leaving Selann. Indeed, there hadn't been one in the city for many years – decades, if those attempted by Ebigail Kiradin were discounted. And yet Altiris felt no stirring of sympathy. After Silverway Dock, Calenne and the revelations of what he'd done to Lord Trelan, Lord Droshna deserved his fate.

Viara shuddered. "I don't believe it."

He nodded at the wagon, and the lone, upright stake at its heart. "You think they've gathered all that for nothing?"

Toward the crest, the crowd shrank back, voices raised to the heckle and jeer. A column of Essamere knights marched into sight, their grandmaster at their fore. And at their heart, head held high and unflinching before the crowd's disdain . . . ?

"No . . . " breathed Altiris. "This isn't right."

"A demon stands in our midst," shouted Jezek, the words cutting above the tramp of boots and the crowd's tumult. "To spare its victims, we send it to the fire."

Calenne, a demon? Altiris didn't believe it for a moment. She was a Trelan. A Phoenix. As he was a Phoenix. And where was Lord Trelan? Did he even know what was happening?

"Out of my way!" Leaving Viara behind, Altiris threaded his way through the crowd, picking up speed with every step. "In the First Councillor's name, clear the way!"

"Altiris!" Viara grabbed at him. He pulled free and kept moving. "Lieutenant!"

He was halfway to the ring of shields when Calenne reached the wagon. Jezek at last fell silent. A choir of serenes struck up a dirge, beautiful voices raised in mournful song.

"Let her go!" bellowed Altiris.

A constabulary sergeant blocked his path. "You've no authority here, Phoenix."

Altiris swung. The sergeant dropped, his helmet bouncing across the cobbles. Ignoring the crowd's sudden outrage, Altiris lowered his shoulder to a join between two shields. A bone-jarring impact, and he was through, the dirge faltering as serenes scattered. He ran for the wagon.

Fresh shields barred his path. Not the King's Blue of the conscript army, but Essamere green.

"Give it up!" bellowed Grandmaster Tanor. "We don't want to hurt you."

Shields rushed in, not as a line, but a noose. Wherever Altiris turned, another barred his path. In moments, they had him pinned in a circle of steel – unable to move, let alone draw his sword. He punched and kicked. Shields shuddered, but held.

Throat thick with despair, he looked up at the wagon, where Calenne was now bound to the stake, the skirts of her dress pooled across kindling. "I'm sorry!"

The expressionless face gazed down, dark eyes swirling.

[[This isn't your fault. This isn't your moment.]] She tilted her head in what might have been amusement, though Altiris couldn't see how. [[And what else can one expect from northwealders, anyway?]]

So saying, Calenne twisted as much as her bindings would allow and glared at Jezek. Startled, the archimandrite lost his grip on his sceptre of office, which tumbled into the crowd.

[[Well?]] she snapped. [[Get it over with!]]

The lone serene thrust her torch into the brazier. The fire lit at once, the thick, bitter aroma of oils and alchemist's powder dancing on the breeze. Step by solemn step, she advanced on the wagon.

Viktor didn't recognise the fire's significance at first. Just another flicker of light, glimpsed out of the corner of his eye. Only as it grew did it claim his attention – the hungry, leaping tongues at the top of Sinner's Mile clearly visible from the clocktower's newly barred window. Shoulders pricking, he rose from the chair and drew as close to the window as the chain permitted. Close enough to see the speck of darkness at the flames' distant heart.

A burning. The fate Josiri had warned would be his, now delivered upon another.

"No!"

He turned his attention to the door, to the knights waiting beyond. "Set me free! I beg you! I can't let her die! Not again!"

No response came.

Overcome by fury, Viktor hauled at the chain. He kicked and hammered at the eyebolt. He braced his feet against the floor and heaved until the shackles dug into his flesh and blood slicked his wrists. He heard himself howling, keening, and fought all the harder, letting the pain feed his frenzy.

Again and again, he strained, until muscles ached and mangled wrists screamed. The madness of methodicality, all the time pleading silently to any deity who'd listen that the chain might shatter. That his shadow might tear free of silver. That he might yet save Calenne from her tormentors.

His world shrank almost to nothing, bounded only by the fire on the hill, and the hollow, hammering wrath that strove against the chain.

And somewhere along the line, the tiniest of pressures in his thoughts – one so small Viktor had never before paid it any heed – winked out, and left only darkness.

Its vanishing did what pain and weariness could not, sent his madness howling away and left cold, trembling clarity. Shaking head to foot, he collapsed into the chair, tearful gaze fixed on the crest of Sinner's Mile and its dying flames.

Calenne was gone. The one person he'd sworn never to fail, dragged to the flames. Despite Josiri's claims of fairness. Despite his promise of protection. And for what? To punish him? The cruelty of petty men and women, unable to grasp what truly mattered, consumed by jealousy of those who could. The eastern border was threatened anew by an alliance between the shadowthorns and the forest demons of Fellhallow, and how did they respond? By snarling and howling like rabid dogs, snapping at any who might save them. Preying upon one another because they knew no other way.

And now Calenne was dead. Calenne, who'd feared him for a monster, but loved him for the man. Calenne, to whom he'd long ago given the best part of himself, and had perished anew with it in her keeping.

The man had tried to play game of whispers and bargains that ruled Tressia – ruled the world entire. But the other players hadn't heeded the man, not even those who claimed kinship. They'd lied to him. Betrayed him. And before the end – perhaps even that very day – they'd render him as ash on the wind.

Josiri had accused him of never learning from the past. In that, at least, he'd been right. He'd been a fool to expect better from his peers. The Republic had only ever grown weeds and treachery.

Viktor started as something heavy fell against the door. A wet scream followed close behind. A scrape of steel on steel, and the dull rush of a dying breath.

He scrambled to his feet as the door opened. A knight's corpse toppled across the threshold. Others lay unmoving on the stairs. With a whisper of steel, Tzila returned her sabres to their scabbards and offered a low bow.

Viktor pinched his eyes shut at the grim humour of the rescue's timing. Too late to save Calenne, but perhaps not too late for everything. "Free me."

So swollen was his throat, he barely recognised his own words, but Tzila nodded and set about searching the bodies. The key swiftly found, she twisted his shackles open and hurled them away. Freed of the silver, Viktor's shadow came howling back, the flaring of pain as it overcame Anastacia's runework sharp, but brief. With it came fresh sense of purpose. Josiri and the others . . . They'd sought to break him. They'd failed. They'd always fail.

[[We should go,]] said Tzila. [[Someone might have heard.]]

Viktor stared at the featureless sallet helm. She'd never spoken before. He even caught a hint of Revekah Halvor's southwealder accent. A sign that her creation was not as flawed as he'd feared? A slim hope when set against all else, but a hope it remained . . . and perhaps a promise that matters could yet be set right, if he had the strength.

"We'll leave the city. At least for now." Viktor glanced again towards the spent pyre, resolve burning in his broken heart. The man had failed. If it took the monster to save Tressia from itself, so be it. "But first, I need to find something."

Calenne awoke into mist, at once lighter and heavier. But even that recollection was distant, dreamlike. An after-image of fire and a jeering crowd. Fragmented just enough to tantalise and frustrate.

She stared down at outspread hands. No longer cold clay, but not quite flesh. Pallid, translucent, their small motions trailing vapour into mist.

It all felt so familiar, though she couldn't say why. Nor why it troubled her so. A part of her felt at ease, even while the rest screamed.

The mists receded. A cobbled street faded into view. Jettied eaves and narrow cottages. Like Eskavord, before the flames consumed it. As the flames had twice consumed her. Pale figures drifted beneath a green-grey sky, their bodies rippling to mist below the waist, all of them unaware or uncaring of her presence. All save one. He was dark where the others were pale, a feathered domino mask worn above a trimmed goatee, and a slender cane perfect accompaniment to tailcoat and high-crowned hat.

"Welcome home, Miss Trelan," said the Raven.

Fifty-Eight

Altiris returned to Stonecrest heartsick and weary, the failures of the morning exacerbated by time held in custody at the Sinner's Mile watch house and the long walk back. The morning sunshine was but a memory, lost behind black skies and torrential rain driven nearly horizontal by a ferocious Dawn Wind. Streets emptied of people were already full of broken branches and shattered tiles. If Calenne's burning had been intended to please Lumestra, it had surely failed.

Run-off pattered on the tiles as he peeled off the rain-sodden cloak, the warmth from the hallway hearth prickling welcome across his skin.

Anastacia rushed to greet him, subdued tone as rare as her embrace. "Altiris?"

"I tried to save her," he stuttered. "You have to believe me."

"Viara told me everything." Green eyes met his, the compassion welling behind rarer even than the embrace. "It's not your fault."

Altiris almost believed her. The benefit, he supposed, of seeking solace from a serathi, however transformed. It was no consolation at all that Calenne wouldn't have felt the flames. "Lord Trelan, is he—"

"Josiri's sleeping. I asked Adbert's wife to mix something to keep him that way." No one but Anastacia used Brass' loathed first name. No one else dared. "After everything that's happened, he needs time away from the world."

Scowling, she turned away and stared into the hearth.

"It never gets any easier," she said. "Ephemerals are so stupid. So ready to lash out at what they don't understand . . . Present company excepted. And I'm no better."

Altiris stepped closer, wincing as water trickled down his neck. "That's not true."

She glanced back to offer full benefit of an eye roll. "Save the flattery for Sidara. I know what I am. All the time we were together at Branghall, I treated Calenne like a child, and in the end she went to her death so nobly. I don't know that I could do that. Calenne. Revekah. Izack. Malachi. That shrew Lilyana. Maybe even Vladama, if his fever returns. Everyone around me dies, Altiris, and my first thought is always for myself. I'm supposed to be better than that."

"Has there been any word of Sidara?"

"She's not at Ahrad. Sevaka sent a herald. None of the Drazina are. But an army can't hide for ever. Someone will send word." She offered a small smile. "She's alive."

"Assuming Lord Droshna's word can be trusted."

"Now, more than ever, Viktor's promises are nothing to me. But I'd know if it were otherwise. So would you. The piece of herself she left with you would tell you."

The echo of the magic with which she'd once saved his life. That had shielded him from Kasvin's domination. "I hope you're right."

"In this, if in little else." Anastacia brightened. "Perhaps I should pay Viktor a visit. I'm of a mood to ask him a few questions, and care little about how I get the answers."

"Lord Droshna's escaped. They think it happened while Calenne . . . " Altiris swallowed, the event still too near for words to frame. "Four dead knights, and no alarm given."

"Tzila?"

"I don't know who else could. Grandmaster Tanor thinks he's left the city. He's sent heralds to every corner of the Republic bearing warrants of arrest."

She snorted. "As if Zephan Tanor's judgement is worth anything. I'm surprised he didn't have you locked up."

He grimaced. "To be honest, I never felt much like a prisoner – not after the fires were out. He sat with me while I was in the watch house. He didn't say much, not that made any sense, anyway. He'd the look of a man caught between impossible choices, who feared he'd made the wrong one."

Anastacia arched an eyebrow. "And what does that look like, exactly?"

"Lord Trelan, for the most part."

A scowl became a sigh. "You need to lose that habit. He's your father now. Call him Josiri."

Easy for her to say. Not so easy for him to do. "Yes, *Mother.*"

Narrowed eyes threatened a terrible fate. "The things we do for love . . . " Her voice faded, the mock-arch expression become one steeped in thought. "Viktor hasn't left the city. Not yet. I know where he's going. Come on!"

Plucking a greatcoat from the porch's coat rack, she made for the outer door.

Altiris grabbed her arm. "Shouldn't we wake Lord Trelan?"

She shot a forlorn glance at the stairs, doubt creasing her brow. Doubt, and something Altiris couldn't quite identify. Close to fear, but not quite. However lightly she'd spoken of Lord Trelan's condition, she was hurting to see him thus. "You couldn't even if you wanted to."

Swallowing his misgivings, Altiris reached for his cloak.

However bad the wind in Tressia's built-up streets, it was worse in the exposed lychfields of Duskvigil Church. Save for the scattered tombs and headstones, the ancient structure stood alone on a rock-strewn promontory, surrounded on three sides by a sheer, dizzying plunge into waves driven to white-crested frenzy by the howling wind. An outpost of wild, elder days, barely part of the city at all. A place for pilgrims, penitents – and, according to Anastacia, for relics the archimandrite deemed too corrupting to keep around righteous folk.

Staggered by a gust, Altiris grabbed at a tomb. Soil crumbled beneath his foot, sending a scatter of small pebbles bouncing away down the rutted path. A handful vanished over the ragged, grassy tufts of the cliff edge.

Coat and skirts streaming behind, Anastacia strode on towards the crooked spire. Taking a deep breath, Altiris followed, forearm raised to keep stinging rain from his eyes.

He stumbled across the first bodies a moment later. A man and a woman in constabulary tabards, just beyond the low wall that marked the boundary between lychfield and the church's inner ward. Sentries, their vigilance in vain. The woman lay against a headstone in a pool of rain-diluted blood, her sword alongside. The man bore no obvious wounds, only a wide-eyed, terrified rictus, and a patina of frost glistening across uniform and blued, mottled flesh.

Glancing away, Altiris stumbled after Anastacia, who stood at the base of the winding, serpentine stairway that led up to the church proper. The lower steps were thick with bodies. Altiris' gut twitched as he realised what he'd at first taken for a broken statue was in fact another corpse, frozen solid and shattered across a plinth.

"Lord Droshna did *this*?" Foolish words, but he could summon no others.

Anastacia nodded, her jaw set though the rest of her shook with the cold. "We're too late."

Altiris stared up at the church and its towering, golden statue of Lumestra, her arms spread in welcome towards the eastern horizon. "All this for a lump of rock. He's mad."

She shook her head viciously, voice barely audible over the wind. "That lump of rock is a piece of a vranastone. It's how he brought Calenne back from the mists. It's capable of so much more. I've spent three days in this place, keeping Shalamoh blind to the rest." She sighed. "Of course Viktor would try again. He's never once learned from his mistakes."

Altiris swept a disbelieving arm at the bodies. "But this is murder!"

"And when has Viktor ever let death unseat his dreams?" Anastacia gazed up at Lumestra. "Our darkest moments reveal us for who we are. He was always apt to this. We just looked the other way."

The wind dropped. A scream echoed down from the church.

Altiris started towards the steps. "He's still here."

Anastacia seized his arm. "No. Go back for help. Find Grandmaster Tanor. The Essamere chapterhouse isn't far."

Altiris stared again at the bodies, the cold gathering in his bones nothing to do with the wind. What could the two of them do that the church's defenders had not? Facing Lord Droshna across drawn steel was bad enough. To contest his shadow? Anastacia was right. "We can't lose him."

"We won't. I'll keep watch. If he leaves, I'll follow and send word."

At last, he realised that she shook not with cold, but anger. "You go. I'll stay."

"You'll be faster." She cracked a mirthless smile. "Obey your mother. Hurry back."

"All right. But please, Ana ... take no chances."

She nodded, her eyes still on the rain-lashed statue. "I've none left to take."

Viktor braced his feet against the floor and heaved. With a screech of grinding stone, the tomb's lid slid clear and cracked against marble flagstones. The musty smell of ancient dust rose to contest the bitter tang of blood. And there, amid yellowed bones and tattered vestments: the tomes stolen from the clocktower, and the vranastone's jagged fragment. Dancing specks of pale green light flickered to contest the feeble glow of shattered lanterns. His shadow seethed, malcontent on consecrated ground.

"No good can come of this!" cried Shalamoh.

Turning, Viktor stared past the altar and along the corpse-choked pews of the nave. Constables. Conscripts. Essamere knights. The old fool in golden robes who'd thought to bar the threshold with nothing save a broken-down old sunstave. The serenes who'd offered misguided prayers to contain the vranastone's supposed evil. All as dead as Saint Selna, in the care of whose desiccated bones they'd hurried to conceal his prize. But secrets lasted only as long as defiance. They'd not remained defiant long.

He recalled few of the deaths. He'd set his shadow free, and that had been that.

They'd been warned. They'd made their choice. Foolishness was not courage.

"Calm yourself, Master Shalamoh," rumbled Viktor.

Shalamoh thrust a trembling finger in his direction. Even with his eyeglasses cracked and his grey clothes spattered with others' blood, he conspired to dignity.

"This is an abomination!"

"How can you say that? You who set my feet on the path?"

"I was wrong. The world is better off without magic, and without gods."

Viktor snorted. He'd once thought the same. An excuse for timidity. A cage the weak fashioned for the strong. "You lack vision."

He turned his attention to the casket once more. If the bones of a saint held magic, they revealed nothing of their bounty as he ripped the vranastone free. His senses crowded with Otherworld's presence. The scent of forbidden days and forgotten lives. The whispers of the dead, pining for freedom.

"No!"

Shalamoh lunged, reaching for the vranastone. Viktor's shadow embraced him, hauling him high above the pews. Eyeglasses shattered on the flagstones. Cries of terror choked off as darkness smothered his sight and oily tendrils crawled across his lips. The air crackled with ice.

No remorse, not even for Shalamoh whose aid had once been invaluable. Gratitude too was sometimes foolishness.

Viktor's shadow pulsed. Shalamoh's cries weakened, his struggles alongside.

The church's interior blazed bright as the sun.

The flash of pain and the shadow's scream came as one. Viktor threw up his hands in reflex, though he was already blind, the vranastone falling back into Saint Selna's uncertain care. He sank against the tomb. Heard the thud as Shalamoh struck timber pews. The shriek of his flailing shadow, and the howl of the wind about the church's time-worn stones.

Anastacia's voice rang out above them all.

"I should have done this the first moment you entered our lives!" The words rippled and shook, something more behind them than mere ephemeral purpose. A chime of distant bells. Sweet voices raised in chorus. Echoes of faded worship long past, drawn into the present at the command of Lumestra's exiled daughter. They hurt as the burst of daylight had hurt. "But you were such a charmer. So earnest. So righteous. How we've paid."

Splotches cleared from Viktor's sight. Through slitted fingers, he glimpsed her – a dark, bedraggled shape advancing along the corpse-strewn nave with fists clenched. As she passed, lanterns exploded to brilliance, their broken glass falling as glittering rain. The eyes of serathi caryatids blazed with daylight. Viktor gritted his teeth, and sought mastery of his panicked shadow. He bellowed as his clothes began to smoulder.

"Do not trust the Dark, whatever form it takes, however noble its aspect!" shouted Anastacia. "My mother cast me to this world to contain it. I failed. Always too worried with what I wanted and what I stood to lose. No more. Even if it takes the last of me. Even if I have to drain every scrap of wonder from these stones, I will see that you hurt no one else!"

Caught between his shadow's pain and his own, Viktor collapsed across the open tomb. Saint Selna's bones crumbled, their dust borne away upon rising thermals. *The Undawning Deep. Testament of Ways. Vitsimar.* Books that had taken years to uncover burst into hungry flame. The fire spread to Viktor's gloved hands, racing through his clothes and searing his flesh. Gasping through the pain, he reached again for his shadow. Transfixed by Anastacia's light, it offered no response.

"No!" he spluttered, his own voice as distant as the tolling bells. "You cannot stop me!"

"Oh, but I can." There was no satisfaction in Anastacia's voice, but nor was there pity. "Why do you suppose I let Jezek house your wretched trove here? The divine doesn't linger in Forbidden Places alone. The stones sing with my mother's love for this church."

She meant to kill him, and between light and flame, he was powerless to stop her. His nostrils thick with the bitter scent of burning, Viktor sought another way. Skin crackling, he twisted to face her. Even so close, she was nothing but a dark ember haloed in daylight.

"I'm trying to save what I love," he stuttered.

With a creaking, mournful groan, a statue plunged from above the altar and shattered on the floor. A caryatid cracked clean down the middle, the light in its eyes fading as it crumbled to dust.

"So am I."

Anastacia reached out to him. Fire raced along his sleeves to his shoulders. The air filled with the stink of burning flesh.

She stumbled. The brilliance of her halo faded, revealing a face frozen in dismay.

"No . . ." she breathed.

A bead of bright blood showed at the corner of Anastacia's lips. She brushed at it with the back of her hand, eyes disbelieving, and crumpled sideways, the last of the light falling away alongside. Freed of its prison, Viktor's shadow flooded back. He drew it closer than ever, set it running beneath his skin where it smothered the fire and pain of burning flesh, though not its memory. Between Viktor and the altar, revealed by Anastacia's collapse, Tzila twirled a bloodied sabre once about her wrist and returned it to its scabbard.

"Where were you?" Viktor gasped, his words rippling with the shadow that stifled his pain.

[[I saw movement on the cliff.]]

"Help me stand."

Tzila hauled him upright. A section of roof, weakened by the caryatid's destruction, gave a yawning groan. An avalanche of stone, timber and tile collapsed into the nave. Spluttering, Viktor doubled over in the cloud of stinging dust. He stared with mounting horror at flaking, igneous hands charred black by flame, livid flesh and golden light showing through the cracks. His fingers shook, though his shadow's embrace held the pain at bay. He clenched them tight.

It didn't matter. It would heal. He'd go on.

And what of Anastacia? Another traitor, though it came as no surprise.

He glanced at where she'd fallen and saw only a bloody smear in the dust. Anastacia was gone.

So was the vranastone.

A desperate haul on the reins, and the borrowed destrier slowed to a halt at the boundary wall. Altiris, never less than ungainly while on horseback, dropped to the path, stumbling for balance as the wind redoubled its fury. He was moving before he found it, running pellmell to where he'd last seen Anastacia. Ahead, fitful flames danced atop the church's sunken roof. Behind, knights dismounted with grace born of practice.

He'd been gone half an hour, no more. But what if he were too late?

"Spread out!" shouted Grandmaster Tanor, his voice fighting a losing battle with wind and rain. "Find Lord Droshna, but don't try to take him alone!"

Altiris reached the foot of the steps, dismay quickening to panic. "She's not here!"

Had Droshna left, and Anastacia with him? Her strange behaviour at their parting screamed for attention an age too late.

Tanor's gauntleted hand closed about Altiris' shoulder. "If Anastacia's here, we'll find her."

Altiris nodded, but the grandmaster was already moving, sword naked in his hand and cloak hissing and snapping in the wind.

Halfway up the winding steps, a shout rang out across the promontory. "There!"

Knights broke into a run, converging on a dark shape running headlong down the path, silken cloak and bases streaming like smoke behind. Tzila.

"I want her taken alive!" shouted Tanor, though the Dawn Wind carried his words out to sea. Vaulting the wall's low parapet, he joined the pursuit.

Altiris' eyes were drawn back to the church. Two knights made arcing advance from the south, as indirect a course as the cliff edge would allow. Another approached across the broken, grave-strewn ground to the north. Tzila was leaving. Droshna was likely long gone. What had become of Anastacia? Worry returned, thicker and fiercer than ever.

Taking the stairs two at a time, he ran for the church's main gate.

Fears of a vengeful Droshna scattered as he passed from the porch to the dust-strewn charnel of the nave. So many bodies. Had any still lived when he'd ridden for help? Could he have saved them, or would he simply have perished alongside? Altiris at once recognised the latter as the truth, though it did little to quell his guilt.

As he picked his way towards the altar, one of the bodies moved.

Heart leaping, Altiris spun, sword levelled. Shalamoh, his grey garb white with dust, spluttered and raised a shaking hand to ward him off.

"Droshna ... He came for the vranastone." He broke off, coughing. "But she took it. She was ... magnificent."

"Ana?" Altiris stepped closer, nearly losing his footing on the rubble. "Where is she?"

But Shalamoh had gone again, whether to unconsciousness or to the Raven, Altiris couldn't immediately tell. Then his eyes settled on the bloody trail leading to the chancel's northern door, and nor did he care.

*

The crumbling soil threatened at any moment to pitch Viktor onto the jagged rocks far below. The wind screamed impotence above, its fury cheated by the cliff's overhang, bearing the fading cries of pursuit and the worst of the rain out to sea. Every step jarred at burnt and blackened flesh, but he pressed on, following the bloody tell-tales of Anastacia's passage. The pursuit bothered him not at all. Tzila would lead it away. But Anastacia? Every moment she was gone from sight was a moment in which she might escape.

It was therefore with grim delight that he glimpsed her as he rounded the next corner. She sat on the path barely six paces away. Pale as the doll she'd once been, and motionless, eyes closed, her back against rock and the vranastone in her lap. The white chalk of the cliff face ran pink with diluted blood. Barely a span beyond, the path plunged down a treacherous incline.

Viktor staggered closer. A spill of stone skittered away from his foot and plunged into the sea. Anastacia started to wakefulness. Vranastone tucked close to her chest, she stumbled to her feet and propped a shoulder against the rock, eyes defiant despite her tremors.

"Give me the stone!" he bellowed, his voice still strange with the shadow's overlay. "There's still time. You can live."

Not that her life mattered any longer, now she'd betrayed him.

She shook her head. "I'm done putting myself before others."

Was she really so deluded? "If the living cannot defend the Republic, the dead must."

"Is that all Calenne was to you? Someone handy with a sword?"

"She was everything to me!" he shouted, his voice raw. "And now the mists have her for ever. I'll never see her again! What I do next, I do in her memory and her name!"

As he spoke, he reached out with his shadow, let it slip beneath her thoughts. Nudging, persuading. Seeking the leverage that would make her see the necessity of all he'd done.

Anastacia laughed, even that small motion setting her tottering. "You're wasting your time. Whatever my body has become, my soul is serathi. You're just a shadow of a shadow. I'll give you nothing."

Viktor drew his sword, untouched since his assault on the church. "Then I'll take it from your corpse."

"Oh, Viktor," she shook her head in disappointment. "You really won't."

Pushing away from the cliff, Anastacia took the vranastone's fragment in both hands, green light flickering across her pallid face.

Seized by horrific premonition, Viktor started forward. He was still a pace distant when her arms convulsed. The vranastone chimed once off the path, again off an outcrop twenty feet below. A wave crowned white as it broke the surface, and then it was gone, Viktor's hopes drowning alongside.

The channel lay full fathoms deep. Chance might wash the vranastone up on the shore, but a search of years would never uncover it. Even his shadow found no trace.

"No!" Lunging, he closed a flaking, charred hand about Anastacia's throat and slammed her against the cliff. "What have you done?"

"It was never meant for this world," she gasped. "The sea will keep it safe from you. It'll keep the dead – and the living – safe from you."

Viktor almost killed her in that moment. It would have taken almost no effort to snap Anastacia's neck or cast her to the sea. The only thing that held him back was the certainty that for all her bravado, she was almost gone. A quick death – after all she'd stolen from him – was a gift undeserved. Robbed of the ability to grant life to the deserving, he could at least withhold mercy.

Stepping back, he dropped Anastacia to the path, and stalked back through the rain.

Altiris had barely taken a dozen steps down the coast path when a shadow loomed.

"Ana?"

He knew the answer even as he spoke. The shape was too tall, too bulky to mistake for Anastacia's petite form. Hope had made him ask the question. Horror set him scrambling back as the rain parted and Viktor Droshna stood revealed.

Or what had once been Viktor Droshna.

All trace of the self-effacing man who'd joked at Midwintertide was gone, as too were the hero Altiris had sought to impress and the tyrant who'd loosed soldiers on Silverway Dock. His arms were charred to the elbow. Beyond that it was impossible to tell what was seared flesh and what was cloth. A cloak of living shadow writhed about his shoulders, its presence frosting the air even at a distance.

Altiris' sword fell from his nerveless hand. He lost his footing as he scrambled away, and went the rest of the way on heels and palms as Droshna stalked closer. He yelped at the sudden shock of the cliff face at his back. Shadow flooded about him. Its cold lending bite to every breath, the emptiness of Droshna's eyes tearing at fleeting sanity.

Altiris Trelan, who'd faced death so many times on Selann, in Dregmeet and in other places besides, knew with utter, heart-stopping certainty that the Raven hovered close.

Droshna walked on without a backward glance, shadows rippling and writhing behind.

Breath still stuttering with fear, Altiris somehow found his feet and pressed on through the rain. Droshna hadn't had the vranastone, so perhaps Anastacia hadn't come this way after all. Pinkish stains in the chalk told another story and he ran on, as much to put distance between him and the Dark-wreathed apparition as out of hope of finding Anastacia.

He found Anastacia at the path's end, a limp bundle of flesh and cloth lying in the mud.

"Ana!"

He fell to his knees beside her and gathered her up in his arms. Cold to the touch. Almost as cold as the receding shadow. Bloodshot, sightless eyes blinked and found focus.

"Viktor . . ."

"I saw him," he babbled. He'd been right to feel the Raven's presence. But the Keeper of the Dead hadn't come for him. "He walked right past me, as if I wasn't worth the effort. I was too scared to follow."

A bloodless lip twitched in approximation of a smile. Her fingers brushed his cheek. "Good boy. He's always been a man on the edge. Not any more . . . but I've put the vranastone beyond his use. That will have to . . ." Her voice, already little more than a whisper, faded to nothing.

The panic of Droshna's passing became something more urgent. "You should have waited."

"Tell Josiri I'm sorry." Her eyes fell closed. "Tell him there'll always be a piece of me . . ."

Altiris took her hand. Squeezed it tight as if that alone could keep her from the mists. "Don't go, Ana. Please."

No answer came. Neither word, nor faltering breath.

Anastacia's hand slipped from his, her body become shimmering golden dust before it fell. Its radiance drove out the cold, bathing grey cliffside in gentle sunlight.

Then a gust of wind bore it out to sea, and Altiris was alone.

Maladas, 17th Day of Dawntithe

What is tyranny, save unchallenged hubris?

from the sermons of Konor Belenzo

Fifty-Nine

Viktor's spirits, already wandering dark places, sank further as he rode into the ruins of Castle Prangav. Like so many of the Republic's bastions, Prangav's heyday lay long in the past, its walls toppled during a ducal squabble, and its stones picked over by commoners seeking building materials. A fitting redoubt for a cause in disarray.

The wounds inflicted by Anastacia's treachery were the least of Viktor's worries. With his shadow knitted to his flesh, the pain from his burns was at distant ebb, and easily suppressed – save for when he peeled away his gloves and beheld the full horror beneath. But to pass among the campfires and tents of his surviving Drazina – men and women who'd stood by him first in defeat and now in exile? All looking to him for leadership and hope where he'd little of the one, and nothing at all of the other.

Tzila kept pace through the mud, her thoughts unreadable. Viktor envied her. For all his shadow's talents, its embrace couldn't numb him to mistakes made, and the bitter harvest yet to come.

"Watch the road," he murmured. "If we've drawn curious eyes, put them out."

[[Yes, lord. May I ask you something first?]]

Still strange to hear her speak. Could it be that the Raven was losing his grip? And was that to the good, or the bad? "Whatever you wish."

[[I keep seeing things that aren't there. A phoenix banner, bright beneath the sun. Faces I should know, but don't recognise. Why?]]

Another new development, and worrying by its timing. Though prior discussions had perforce been one-sided, Tzila had never shown any awareness of her past. Should he tell her of the woman she'd been? He'd always sworn he would, if memories returned. The goal had been to welcome Revekah Halvor back to the living world; Tzila had been the necessary compromise. But now, with matters growing ever more dire? He was more reliant on her than ever.

"Pay them no mind," he replied. "It's weariness. It will pass."

The sallet helm bobbed a nod. [[Yes, lord.]]

A tug on the reins and she rode away. Tireless. Unflinching. A reminder of the army that might have been, but for Anastacia's interference.

"Viktor!"

Sidara met him at the overgrown steps of what had once been the keep, wisps of shadow trailing behind as she ran to greet him. Did that speak to control, or its lack? Constans hung back, arms folded, his expression a study in disinterest while his sister's held only concern. Dismounting, Viktor surrendered to her embrace, their shadows bleeding together. He winced as cloth rubbed charred and blistered skin.

Blue eyes peered up at him. "What is it?"

If only she knew the complications tied to that question. Weary from the long ride, Viktor lacked the heart to tell her. "Nothing that cannot wait."

Sidara nodded, contrite but unconvinced. "Of course." She pursed her lips. "And the city? What did you find?"

He closed his eyes, drained by the act of recollection. "It is all as Constans warned. Josiri has betrayed us. The Republic is returning to old ways. Corruption and suspicion. Weakness celebrated as strength. Faithlessness as virtue."

"Josiri really is a traitor?" Sidara's disbelief echoed about their shared shadow.

"Yes." Even now, it took effort not to weep. "He has abandoned everything for which he once stood. I was fortunate to escape with my life."

The truth went deeper, of course. The explanation didn't touch on the pursuit through Tressia's streets. Of stolen horses ridden hard through the rain.

"And Ana?" She grew more urgent. "What of her?"

Opening his eyes, Viktor laid a hand on her shoulder. "I'm sorry." His heart aching at Sidara's crestfallen expression, he chose his next words with uttermost care lest their bond of shadow undermine him. The lie was necessary. The truth – and any confrontation – would wait until she saw for herself how far the Republic had fallen. Then, she'd understand how Anastacia had forced his hand. "The Republic of laws I forged is gone. Now, superstition rules callow hearts. That superstition killed Anastacia."

Her eyes rushed black, a glint of gold brief and barely seen. She stood to attention, expression hard and voice raw with loss. "What are your orders?"

Viktor took in the courtyard. The keep approach, empty on his arrival, was crowded with Drazina. Distant enough for privacy, but expectant, waiting. Even Constans yearned for *something* to cling to, for all he strove to conceal it. Viktor nodded to himself. Whatever losses he'd borne, responsibility remained. To those who followed him. To a stolen Republic. He couldn't give up and remain the man he held himself to be.

Turning about, he stood as tall as injuries allowed and raised his voice to a shout. "All is as we feared! But we will fight on. This isn't over!"

Quiet nods answered his declaration. Not the outpouring of defiance for which Viktor had hoped, but he supposed it was all he deserved. A foundation to build on, and he was thankful for it. But what next? His mind, numb with weariness, held no answer. No vranastone. A few hundred Drazina against a fortified city. An impossible campaign, some would have said. But not for Viktor Droshna, the man who couldn't lose.

"I need to rest," he told Sidara. "But we cannot stay here. Have everyone ready to march. Wake me when it's done."

She nodded, a tremor in her cheeks the only sign of the loss echoing beneath. "Where are we bound?"

Viktor grunted softly. In this, at least, only unvarnished truth would serve. "I don't know. Perhaps to Indrigsval. Armund af Garna will give us shelter. Maybe even an army, if he sees profit in it." And if tidings of Argatha Bridge had not already rusted Thrakkian mettle. "But I'll need you more than ever in coming days . . ." He caught Constans looking at him. " . . . *both* of you."

"Yes, Uncle," Sidara replied. "I won't let you down."

She saluted and strode away into the encampment proper.

"Why do you favour her over me?" asked Constans, his voice thick with hurt.

"Because she needs to hear it more," Viktor replied, careful that his words wouldn't carry. "She lacks your certainty."

"That's not all she lacks. There was a fight yesterday. A petty quarrel over guard duty, of all things." He sniffed. "Steel was drawn. Sidara used her shadow to break it up. *Almost* killed everyone involved."

Did he disdain his sister's lack of control, or her lack of resolve? It'd do no good to ask, and Viktor found he'd little patience for playing Constans' games. "Tell me again how Altiris died."

Constans dipped his head, a wry smile playing across his lips. "So I lied to her. What does it matter if we both got what we wanted? She's properly part of our family now. A Droshna." The smile became a grin. "And you lied about Anastacia. A knave knoweth falsehood's chime, rung softly though it be."

Viktor hoisted Constans off his feet by a fistful of shirt. "Anastacia *is* dead. She made the mistake of standing against me. Remember that."

Constans nodded, his face pale. Already regretting the flash of temper, Viktor let him drop and went to find his tent.

Calenne wandered beneath a green-black sky. What colourless landmarks Otherworld offered dissolved and reshaped around her with every step. Cobbled streets gave way to flagstoned promenades or wooded dells without rhyme or reason, the old mingling and melding with the new or falling away into the green-white mists almost before they'd formed. Nor was there aught to indicate the passage of time, save the swirl of ghostly etravia spirits drifting endlessly about, forging onwards to unknown destinations. She might have walked for hours, days or barely at all; traversed untold miles, or a few hundred steps.

Recollection was less memory than dream ... or nightmare. Sight and sound lacked definition. Reality, unquestioned in life and palpable even in the muted existence of clay – felt more like a lie woven for oneself. Even Calenne's body – if a vaporous, translucent approximation could be called such – felt indistinct, diffuse. Her flesh, skin and bone no more real than her gown, and all of it bleeding steadily into mist.

Sighing frustration, she halted. Small tendrils of her being drifted onwards, borne by currents she couldn't feel. "Where am I even trying to go?"

Nearby etravia offered no reply. They never spoke, nor registered her presence. If she blocked their path, they simply drifted through her. Did she appear any different to them? Was her own perception at fault? Had she even spoken, or merely thought she had? Was even now another adrift soul speaking to her, trying to elicit response? A crowd of strangers, all alone, unable to see or hear another's efforts to reach them? Trapped until Third Dawn.

Calenne shuddered. Pure reflex, for she'd no skin to prickle, nor awareness of cold or heat. The motion sent more of her bleeding into the mists, her hands growing diffuse, her fingers streaming away like smoke in the wind.

With a flash of horror, Calenne reeled herself in, though without being at all aware of how she did so. Fading flesh regained wan colour and fingers their shape. She flexed them, and wondered how long she might keep herself whole. Or even if she wanted to. What point to such a dreadful, washed-out existence? She almost longed for the clay.

Almost.

At least here she was free, for whatever that freedom was worth. And at least her sacrifice had spared Josiri, Altiris . . . even Anastacia.

She glanced up, eyes drawn to a darkness she'd missed before. A black, spiralling stain reaching beyond skeletal branches and tiled rooftops, into a lurid sky. Unpleasant, perhaps, but difference – any difference – was good.

Calenne set off, the trees and buildings sinking back into mist as they always had. The stain remained. She strode on through fields and moorland, along winding streets and across the stones of a ruined wall, urgency growing with every step.

Until at last, in a formal garden, overgrown with black weeds, she reached the darkness' source.

A pyre of furniture and fallen timber stood in the garden's centre, ramshackle and uneven. So similar to the one that Calenne had lately occupied, and yet different. Lurid green flames graced its kindling, sending a rush of thick, black smoke spiralling above. And at the heart, a woman's ghostly echo, wreathed in smoke, her face blackened and contorted in voiceless agony.

Calenne advanced through inattentive etravia, close enough now for recognition.

"Revekah," she murmured. "What have they done to you?"

"They?" sniffed the Raven. "This isn't my doing. This is your beloved Viktor's work. The form of it, though? That's all her. We see what her soul feels."

He stood beside the pyre – though Calenne was certain he hadn't before – hatted, coated and masked.

"He tried to bring her back to the living world," she said. "You're the one holding her here."

He shrugged. "This is where she belongs. I'm well within my rights."

Calenne stared at Revekah. She'd never known the other woman well, but to see her like this? Worse, that this would have been her own fate, had Viktor sought her first. She'd not felt the pyre's heat, but read in Revekah's torment every searing caress the clay had spared her.

"Does Viktor know?"

The Raven tapped his cane on the flagstones and tutted. "The question is, does he care?"

"Let her go. She doesn't deserve this."

"Life is seldom about what we deserve. Why should death be different?" He stalked closer, scant friendliness falling away. "I am the wronged party, not her."

"She's the one suffering!" snapped Calenne.

"I wouldn't let it bother you. You'll be beyond such cares soon enough." He seized Calenne's hand and raised it between them, gloved fingers splayed against hers ... only hers were scarcely recognisable as such – pale traceries of downy mist, more memory than form. "Viktor gave you a reprieve, but you're long overdue to move on."

Horrified, Calenne drew herself back together. The Raven tilted his head, the corner of his goatee twitching. "Interesting."

Snatching her hand away, Calenne sought leverage in half-forgotten stories. "What if I offer a trade? The gods love to bargain, don't they?"

The Raven stepped away, his back to the pyre's emerald flames. "*Love* is a word much overused."

"So it's pride?" said Calenne, voice thick with disgust. "For all your fine words, all your friendliness, you're torturing her out of pride?"

The mists darkened to match the Raven's sudden scowl. For all that he retained mortal guise, Calenne had the impression of a vast, bird-headed shape stretched against the skies.

"Don't think to understand my motives!" he shouted. "Otherworld is *my* realm. It follows *my* rules. I will not be lectured by some scrap of upstart soul!"

Instinct demanded Calenne back away. Cower. Apologise. She over-ruled it all. Instinct belongs to the living, and she'd not been that for some time. And Trelans were stubborn. In the face of needless cruelty, doubly so. For the first time, she understood how her mother's fire had burned so hot.

"You're as bad as Viktor!"

The ground shook. Closing the distance between them, the Raven seized Calenne by the throat. Tendrils of her being rippled away as he tightened his grip.

"Maybe I am," he snapped, the domino mask's beak inches from her nose. "And if not, maybe I should be. But one thing is for certain, Miss Trelan: I need not answer to you."

A shove, and Calenne fell, unravelling into the mists, ice beneath the sun. She tried to cry out, but found no voice. Sight and sound followed the words into the abyss, and memory, last of all.

"Viktor?"

He opened his eyes, drawn from a dreamless, black sleep. Sidara stood at the tent flaps, face crowded with uncertainty. Sunlight streaming through the gap set Viktor's shadow seething. Groggy, he propped himself onto an elbow. Still fully clothed, he barely remembered crawling onto the bed.

"How long have I slept?"

"It's past noon. The camp's taken down, all save this. We can march whenever you're ready."

He swung upright and stood, scowling at the pain crackling along his arms. Fishing a replacement from the haversack at the bed's foot, he peeled off his soiled, bloodied shirt.

"Uncle . . . " Sidara started forward, her eyes wide. "Your arms . . . "

Viktor nodded. Thanks to his shadow's embrace, they looked far worse than they felt, crusted black skin above livid, blistered flesh still burning. "Others . . . Others suffered more. I can hold a sword. Nothing else matters."

She stepped closer, the golden light about her fingers topped by a writhing plume of shadow. "Let me help you."

Viktor's own shadow hissed its distaste. He held out a hand to ward her off. "I regret your light is no balm to me. I wish it were otherwise."

Sidara nodded and stepped away. "How did it happen?" Her face fell. "They sent you to the pyre, didn't they?"

How soon the conversation strayed onto delicate ground, but lies would only make matters worse. Wincing only a little as he pulled on the clean shirt, Viktor sought a response that would serve.

"I confess, I have misled you. My return to Tressia was not solely to test the truth of your brother's reports . . . I wanted to see Calenne, and bring her safe out of the city."

She frowned. "Josiri's sister? You're mistaken, Uncle. She's been dead for years."

"I found a way to bring her back. Elzar's light and my shadow, channelled through a relic recovered from Darkmere." Elzar. One more reason to fight on. One more sacrifice to be respected. "That vranastone existed in our world and the Raven's – a tether binding the living to the dead. We cheated the Raven's grasp and restored Calenne to a body of clay."

Swallowing, she pursed her lips, eyes bright with grief. "Like Ana's?"

He nodded, a piece of him aching in empathy with Sidara's loss, even if he didn't share it. "In practice, it's nothing more than creating constructs. The power of the soul harnessed in place of Lumestra's magic. But I knew others would call it witchcraft." Old mistakes crowding close, he sat heavily on the bed. "That they'd name Calenne an imposter, or worse. So I kept her secret. Just yesterday, those who call themselves Tressia's Council – Josiri among them – sent her to the pyre."

She screwed her eyes shut. "Josiri killed his own sister?"

"He stood by as she burned," Viktor replied. "That's almost worse. He's not the man we remember. His political machinations are only part of this. The shadowthorns were ready for us at Argatha Bridge because he gave warning we were coming. If only I'd seen what he'd become. Perhaps Anastacia and Calenne would still be alive."

Aghast, Sidara brushed her left forearm with her fingertips, mirroring the path of his wounds. "You earned these trying to save her ..."

He grunted. "They came later, when I tried to reclaim the vranastone. Its keepers ... fought harder than I could have imagined. In the end, they triumphed. The vranastone is lost to me."

"And with it, hope of retrieving Calenne? I'm so sorry, Uncle."

Viktor closed his eyes, sealing the guilt and rage of preceding days in the darkness. "No. She was lost to me even then. Otherworld's mists are vast, and the Raven a jealous warden. He'll keep her from me for ever." He brushed away a tear. "But we could have used the vranastone to set things right. Together, you and I could have remade Elzar's miracle. Calenne was only ever meant to be the first to return. I thought to raise an army out of Otherworld, their service exchanged for a new lease of life. With an army like that ...? When the shadowthorns come again with Fellhallow at their back, those supine fools on the Council will roll over and beg. Everything we've fought for will be lost."

"You'll find a way, Uncle. You always do."

He nodded, though found little agreement. His talk of finding aid from Armund af Garna, thane of Indrigsval, was talk alone. Armund had refused direct support not a month before, brokering terms with the now-dead thrydaxes instead of committing his own forces. Another friend proven unworthy in a moment of need. But what else was there? Perhaps the thane could be persuaded to make amends. "I hope you're right."

She laid a hesitant hand on his. He barely felt it. The shadow's embrace left him numb to more than pain. "I am with you to the end, Uncle."

"You know that it may not be my fight to finish? It may yet fall to you to see our people protected."

She grimaced, but nodded. "Yes."

Of course Sidara understood. Constans never would. The boy had cleverness, but little sense of duty. Strange how years altered perspective. Years ago, when Malatriant had striven to make him her inheritor, Viktor had not grasped her drive to do so. Still didn't, in truth, but he at last had a glimmering. Immortality was more than flesh. It was legacy. When the time came, Sidara would be a worthy heir.

"A hard road lies ahead, but I could hope for no better companion."

Sidara backed away, embarrassed ... but pleased as well, he thought. "Death and honour."

"Death and honour."

Reaching for the tent flaps, she paused. "You said Calenne was to be the first, but Tzila ... I never noticed before, but now I can feel the shadow clinging to her. She's the same, isn't she?"

Even now, he heard no judgement. Just a woman wrestling with a puzzle. Whatever else she'd learnt from Anastacia, Sidara retained an open mind ... or was it his shadow, easing her to his way of thinking? Did it matter, so long as it was done?

"Tzila is ... different. It takes Lumestra's light to make a body whole. Elzar made it so for Calenne. I saved Tzila alone, and rescued only pieces. That's why she is how she is – part of her remains in the Raven's jealous keeping. I hold together what remains as best I can."

"Then Tzila exists in both worlds?" Sidara spoke slowly, carefully, shaping emergent thought with words more than expressing one. "And if she does ... "

Was it really that simple? Unbidden laughter spilled free of Viktor's lips. "Why did I not see it?"

He traced the thought to its end and found no flaw. Tzila's fractured soul, already steeped in shadow, trapped in both worlds but belonging wholly to neither – as the vranastone had belonged to neither – could serve as the bridge. One foot in the mists and one in the light. Through her, he could reach from the living realm into Otherworld's heart.

A once-bleak future burgeoned with possibility. All he needed were souls eager to escape the Raven's grasp. Angry enough to fight. Defiant enough to face the armies of the traitor Council without hesitation.

He had the answer at once. Perfect symmetry. Proof that for all his missteps, his course had always – *always* – been correct. With Sidara's help, he'd yet save the Republic from itself.

"We march south."

Sixty

Nothing had changed in Eskavord since Viktor's last visit, but then nothing ever did any longer. The provincial town lingered only in memory, erased by the fires that had purged Malatriant from the shores of the mortal world. In its place, a field of fire-blackened stones barely visible through Otherworld's intrusive, unyielding mists. A Forbidden Place, haunted by the scent of bitter memories and whispers on the edge of hearing. Every Ascension for five years he'd trod the ash, seeking absolution from those he'd failed, clinging to the hope of reunification.

Branghall, the Trelan ancestral home, dominated the western horizon, a black, angry presence of uncertain shape. The remnant of the church – spire and roof gone, chancel open to the black, cloud-choked skies – held sway over what had once been the marketplace. Echoes of other structures remained. A gable wall. A beam. A pillar. A spill of rubble about a knee-high wall. Grave markers of lives lost in a battle they'd never known they'd faced, souls snuffed out and bodies dancing to Malatriant's command. All of it drowning in ash.

A jerk of the reins brought Viktor's horse to a standstill – by chance, or unconscious design, at the very spot where Malatriant had tricked him into embracing her magic.

If my legacy is to be a shining realm of privileged squabbles, with you as its champion and Calenne at your side, then so be it. I wish you the joy of making it so.

Had she known even then how matters would unfold? That even had he conquered the Dark and pressed it to righteous purpose, others would fall over themselves to cast down what he'd built? To think he'd once walked from Eskavord thinking his battles done. But battles were like art. They might change form or become abandoned, but they were never truly finished. There was always more to do.

It was the one consolation of losing Calenne that he was now freed to the pursuit.

"Uncle?" Sidara cantered to his side, eyes dark as the mists drew her shadow to the surface. Brittle tone belied composed expression. "You're making our soldiers nervous. You've done nothing but stare into space for a quarter hour."

Blinking away old memories, he gazed back across the column of Drazina, some on horseback, most on foot. Too many pale faces and restless eyes. Timorousness that went beyond defeat-eddied morale. Northwealders all, they'd grown up far from the Forbidden Places that dotted the Southshires. For them, the dead belonged to Otherworld, and the living to the light. They didn't yet understand how little such absolutes held sway.

Constans clattered to a halt between Viktor and Sidara, his horse a little ahead of hers and his posture crafted to shield his sister from view.

"They're cowards. Send them away." His voice held no trace of his sister's wariness.

Viktor scowled. Jealousy was one thing. Disrespect another. Foolishness something else. "The Republic is theirs to defend as much as ours."

"Look at them." Constans cast out an arm, his voice pitched loud enough to carry, but low enough for denial. "They'll seize any excuse to flee."

"Enough!" Viktor leaned over his saddle, shadow curling about his shoulders. "If you cannot show respect, then I release you from service and duty. You may leave whenever you wish."

Constans flinched as if struck, suddenly crestfallen. "My place is with you."

"It's wherever I decide."

"He didn't mean it," said Sidara. "We're all on edge."

Constans chased away a grimace with a twist of his lips, his displeasure obvious. But he nodded. "I'm sorry, Father. I spoke out of turn."

"Follow your sister's example," said Viktor. "She's lost more than any of us, but comports herself with dignity."

A twitch of Constans' cheek told him the admonition had hurt, as it was meant to. A test was nothing without bite. "Yes, Father."

Viktor nodded his satisfaction and turned his attention to the Drazina. For all their brashness, Constans' words held a kernel of truth. Beaten, harried and faced with matters beyond ephemeral ken, it was all too possible the Drazina would desert him.

"I understand your fears," he rumbled. "But there is no malice in this place. Those voices you hear belong to men and women abandoned by the Council as we were abandoned by the Council. They yearn for a second chance, as *we* yearn for a second chance. Harden your hearts, and it will be ours."

A few nodded and stood straighter, purpose returning. But only a few. Most retained harried aspect. Too much uncertainty. Viktor didn't blame them for that, damnably inconvenient though it was.

He had to excise that uncertainty.

Closing his eyes, Viktor set his shadow free across the Drazina, smothering their fear as it smothered the pain from his burns. A handful yielded with reluctance, felt in the flaring of spirit as the shadow drew tight about troubled thoughts, and heard in sharp intake of breath. But resistance never lasted. By the time Viktor opened his eyes, those gazing back were bereft of doubt, fear gone and purpose in its place. His purpose.

"For the Republic!" he bellowed.

For the Republic! Fists crashed against breastplates. Constans and Sidara offered salute alongside, though they alone had needed no urging.

Muffled hoofbeats on the stone bridge heralded Tzila's return from the eastern mists. Viktor spurred to greet her. "Well?"

[[I found a handful of scavengers on the southern boundary. They fled at first sight of me. Eskavord is ours.]]

Viktor nodded. "Then we can begin."

Eskavord's lychfield brought back old memories, few of them welcome, but what better place to treat with the dead? Though none of those Viktor sought had been buried in the church's shadow – or had indeed been buried at all – the ash-drowned gardens and skeletal, long-dead yews retained a strong connection to the mists.

Sidara was a nervous presence beneath one such tree, her hands clasped tight together. Her attention split between Viktor and the solemn, silent Tzila kneeling between them. With the Drazina standing watch on Eskavord's boundary, quarrying clay from the western fields or ridden east to the abandoned, ash-strewn fortress of Cragwatch in search of weapons, Constans was left the only other observer – a subdued, suspicious presence in the gaping maw of what had once been the church's vestry door.

Had he been too harsh with the boy before? Probably. Viktor was all too aware that kindness was so seldom in his gift. If only Constans was more like his sister in temperament. If only Sidara had given herself fully to his cause long ago. So much pain could have been avoided.

He glanced at the row of androgynous clay figures lying atop the ash. A mere six to begin with: grey, hastily fashioned and unfired. Artistry held second place to urgency. Their crudity made them even more alike to Ocranza statues than the body he'd made for Calenne. And perhaps that was fitting. In stories, Ocranza had ever been guardians of the living, forerunners even to Belenzo's kraikons. It was a suitable lineage, born of the oldest traditions. All they'd lacked was life. Not so *his* Ocranza.

"Are you ready?" he asked.

Sidara nodded, doubts locked away behind her eyes. Yes, so much stronger than her brother. "Viktor ... If this works, is there any hope for Altiris?"

The pain in her voice chimed with Viktor's own at losing Calenne. So simple to ease it. To tell her that he'd spared the lad, despite provocation to do otherwise. But truth would lead to more questions, and questions to distraction. He needed Sidara focused – maybe even in pain, if it goaded her to do what the Republic required.

He could make things right afterwards. Josiri had led Altiris astray. Once that influence was removed, anything was possible. And if the corruption went deeper? Well, there was always the shadow. If it could quell the Drazina's fear, it could surely rid Altiris of misguided sentiment. Nothing so crude as what Apara Rann had forced him to. Just a nudge. A caress.

He nodded. "If it is at all possible to bring you together, I will do so. You have my promise."

She offered uncertain smile, not yet ready to believe. Or perhaps she'd a better ear for equivocal truths than he'd suspected? "Then we should begin."

"Open yourself to the shadow," said Viktor. "I'll guide you."

Closing his eyes, he beheld the lychfield through his shadow's eyes. Constans became a wisp of darkness in vision's periphery, Tzila an inky, swirling stain upon the ash.

Sidara's pale presence darkened as she set her own shadow free. As they joined, Viktor felt her light seething in the cage he'd made for it. His shadow hissed at its touch. He ignored it. Shadow could reach into Otherworld, it could grant flexion to immobile limbs, but only light set free the soul. Only light could fire the clay into useful form.

Taking a deep breath, he reached out through Tzila. His shadow's perception of Eskavord shifted, overlaid with an echo filled with twisted buildings and lurid green skies. Flickers of soul, sensed but never seen through ephemeral eyes, gathered to vaporous etravia spirits milling through the streets, directionless and without purpose.

Sidara's sharp intake of breath warned Viktor that she saw them too. "Have no fear," he said. "They won't hurt you. They're barely aware."

Her shadow-form rippled a nod. Viktor reached out to the nearest etravia, drew it tight in gossamer strands of shadow as he'd once done with Tzila's soul. Flickers of memory roused at the touch. A man, slain by Malatriant during her conquest of Eskavord. He reached for another. This one had been a young woman – a serene – barely old enough to know anything of life. A third was a wolf's-head, his soul trapped on the gallows.

All of them as much a part of the living realm as the Raven's domain. Everything he'd sought. Everything the Republic needed.

"Do you feel them?"

Sidara offered a taut nod. "Yes. They're ... beautiful."

"Set free your light. Bring them home."

Radiance cracked through Sidara's shadow, daylight from thunder-clouds. Even braced though he was, Viktor shied away, its touch – even the suggestion of contact – sending a searing shiver through his shadow.

And yet he could almost . . . *feel* it. The bridge between his magic and Sidara's allowing him to endure a force that should have boiled him away to nothing. Through his shadow's slitted eyes, he glimpsed a vast apparition at Sidara's back. A woman like but unlike, washed of all colour save dawnlight, and her hands on Sidara's shoulders.

Tzila went rigid. Daylight enveloped the captive souls.

They screamed.

Sidara staggered, her shadow-self convulsing in pain. "They don't want to!"

Viktor felt it now. The reluctance. The fear. Not Sidara's. Not his. Not even the Raven's. But something deeper and more pervasive. The defiance of timber before the flame, or steel beneath the blacksmith's hammer. "It will pass! Keep going!"

"I can't!"

"You must!"

Sidara gritted her teeth and sank to one knee. The light flickered, shadow rushing into the gaps. Traceries of light and dark raced across the outer skin as the clay fired from within. Constans shied away, a hand thrown up to ward off the heat. Viktor felt it prick his skin, but between shadow's embrace and the elation of success, he paid it no heed.

The clay bodies exploded in a hollow, searing rush.

The shockwave threw Viktor gasping to his knees. Pottery shards tugged at his skin and pattered off his armour. Constans shrieked and flung himself behind the doorway's remnant as clay fragments pinged off stone. Sidara fell to hands and knees in the ash, chest heaving. Tzila remained unmoving, untouched as light and shadow danced about her.

"I told you . . ." breathed Sidara. "I told you they didn't want to."

Frustration welling, Viktor stumbled upright and stared at the ruin of the three broken figures. No! Not when he was so close! "You're mistaken. We try again. I know it's hard, but—"

Sidara staggered to her feet, her shadow-self stuttering. "No, Viktor. This is wrong. Can't you feel it?"

"And what of the Republic?" he asked, beseeching in word and tone. "What of those who look for us to protect them from those who'd see the shadowthorns conquer all? To defend them against the demons of

Fellhallow? Would you have the living hold the line when the dead might serve in their place? The dead have nothing to lose!"

Shadow bled from Sidara's eyes, replaced by gold. "The light tells me otherwise."

"It's wrong."

"Are you so sure? How can we know? We'll find another way. But I can't do this." Swallowing, she met his gaze. "I *won't* do it."

Even now, Viktor caught glimpses of the apparition at Sidara's back. He'd thought her a manifestation of magic, as the phoenix she'd conjured into being at Argatha Bridge. But what if she were something more? Something holding Sidara back. What if she wasn't, and he heard Sidara's voice alone?

In that suffocating moment of failure, Viktor realised it didn't matter. "You will."

Bringing together his hands, Viktor locked his shadow tight about Sidara. The piece of himself he'd lent her roused at his call, smothering her cries, smothering the light. It fought back, searing and screaming as he forced it back into her soul. Viktor shook before it, the pain worse than any war wound, worse even than the fires Anastacia had sent through his flesh.

But with failure the only alternative, he did what he'd always done best: he endured.

The apparition dissipated to nothing as the light faded. Gold faded from Sidara's eyes, overcome by the shadow burrowing beneath her skin and across her soul. Viktor caged the light as deep as he dared, close enough to call upon, but distant enough that it wouldn't rule her judgement.

Her struggles ceased, the fuel of defiance snuffed out. Viktor felt a piece of Sidara's soul calling to him, welcoming him as Apara's had done at Tarvallion. He gladly acceded, smoothing away objection and reluctance as he had his Drazinas' fear until only purpose remained.

When Viktor at last drew back his shadow, he beheld Sidara and saw only reflection. Her eyes were wholly black, their sockets dark with spidery veins – the shadow he'd lent no longer mantled, but threaded through her soul. This was Sidara as she should have been, spared doubt and uncertainty. Viktor had set her free from the light's treacherous whispers and others' compromises.

Sidara breathed deep of the mists, her abyssal eyes wide in wonder, as though perceiving the world for the first time. Her stillness rippled through their shared bond, reluctance gone and her legacy of light now at the command of the shadow from which it had once sprung.

For all the joy the sight occasioned, Viktor felt a part of him die inside. A small, ailing fragment too weary to endure. He didn't mourn it. He knew he'd not miss it.

"We try again."

Sidara nodded. "Yes, Uncle."

Awareness came gradually. A sound. A flash of memory. A flicker of movement. All of it distant. All of it shrouded in greenish-white. The process slow and frustrating; agonising, and yet somehow soothing.

The more she focused on those fleeting sensations, the stronger they became.

A name teetered on the edge of thought. Her name?

She seized it tight; held it closely, jealously. To hold something, she needed hands, so she wove them from the mists, never once questioning what hands were, or how she knew of them. A body followed, for the thought of hands alone was absurd, if not macabre.

As the last strand of the body wove to completion, taking the name into herself seemed the thing to do, so she did precisely that. Thus Calenne Trelan's soul took root, and stood shivering in Otherworld's mists.

"Queen's Ashes," she muttered, turning her spectral hands over and over as though they held the answer. "What just happened to me?"

The mists screamed with swirling etravia, drawn into the skies like hurricane-strewn clouds. The flames of Revekah's pyre – no longer green, but uttermost black – leapt into vortex, embers scattering across the colourless gardens. The Raven stood before the pyre, one hand jammed on his hat as his coat tails fluttered and snapped in the winds.

He turned as Calenne forged towards him through the winds, his brow creasing in surprise. "You're supposed to be gone for good."

She stifled a jolt of horror. The Raven had truly meant to be rid of her? What did that even mean? Why hadn't it worked? "What's happening?"

"He's stealing from me! Again! And he's using her to do it!"

He could only mean Viktor. And if Viktor was again seeking the souls of the dead ...? Calenne shuddered. After all she'd experienced since Viktor had brought her out of Otherworld, the prospect offered no solace, only foreboding. Yes, he'd striven to free her from the Raven – against her wishes – but even that had been selfish more than selfless. "So stop him."

"I can't!"

"I thought you were the Keeper of the Dead!"

The Raven glared in impotent frustration. Calenne felt herself unravelling again, even before the angry wave of his hand.

The souls fought as they had before, but with Sidara now freed of her doubts, resistance was for nought. Shadow tight about his prizes, Viktor wedded them to the clay. He loosed the shackles about Sidara's light, permitting just enough to spill free so that the lifeless might live. Still the light fought him, twisting this way and that in his grasp, Sidara looking raptly on as he fought to contain rebelliousness.

Clay seared to rigidity. Limbs roused to motion. One by one, the reborn clambered to their feet, their androgynous shells smoothed by the heart of their creation, their eyes burning dark within expressionless faces.

"It's done!" Overcome with relief, Viktor turned to Sidara. "It worked!"

She offered modest incline of the head. Calm. Respectful. No trace of her earlier conflict. "Was there ever any doubt?"

Elated, Viktor set his gaze on his creations once more. "My name is Viktor Droshna, Lord Protector of the Tressian Republic. I rescued you from the mists so that together we might save our people. I regret the rudeness of your awakening, but time is short, and my need great."

They regarded him in silence, no word of objection or agreement voiced.

He looked closer at clay that should have been smooth, and was not. Shadow oozed beneath a crust of grey stone, islets on a dark and viscous river. Not just at the joints, but everywhere – even around the eyes, where the cracks imitated the spiderwork veins about Sidara's own.

Cold wormed its way into Viktor's heart. Tzila had been thus when first reborn, her clay skin solidifying over the course of days. Calenne had been whole from the first. Tzila had been silent. Calenne, while incapable of reason, had keened like a lost soul.

Suspicion became certainty as Viktor performed deeper examination. He studied each Ocranza in turn, seeking a glimmer of Sidara's light. He found only shadow, gumming together fragments of sundered souls. Disbelief became despair, became fury. In restraining the light, he'd foolishly unmade his own intent. With triumph in his grasp, he'd erred and could lay the failure at no other door. His dream of soldiers reborn to a righteous war was dust. He'd sought to restore the dead, and through them the Republic. But his newborn Ocranza would never earn new life, for they'd no identity, no yearning, no purpose.

Could he overcome the issue? Perhaps in time he might learn how to seek the proper balance of light and Dark, but time was the one resource he could little afford. Even now, the shadowthorns were drawing up their plans to invade a weakened Republic, and there was no one fit to stand in their path save he.

Breath hot in his throat, Viktor urged himself to stillness.

He'd purpose enough for ten thousand souls, and perfection was seldom a soldier's lot.

"You will follow me into battle." He made no question of the words. How could they not? What life they possessed sprang from him. They were of the Dark, as he was of the Dark – as Calenne Akadra had once been of the Dark. As Sidara was now of the Dark. They were one. And they were only the beginning. "The Republic will be saved from itself."

As the Ocranza knelt in homage, Viktor turned to Sidara. "We need more clay. Hands to shape it. Weapons with which to fight."

She offered a smile, her reflected pride at what they'd done rippling through the Dark. "The expedition should have returned from Cragwatch by now. If not, I'll go myself."

Offering salute, Sidara picked her way through the ashen lychfield to what had once been the street. Left alone with Tzila and her unmoving siblings, Viktor examined his prospects, and allowed that they were better than he'd first believed. A soldier he remained, and soldiers understood the unattainability of perfection. There were souls enough in Eskavord to remake the Republic's fortunes. That was all that mattered. The dead were dead. He owed them nothing.

A whisper of movement drew his attention to the church's ruined doorway. Constans – about whom Viktor had completely forgotten – gaped at the kneeling Ocranza.

He recovered himself as Viktor approached. "What did you do to my sister?"

His expression gave nothing away, as was so often the case.

"You wanted her to be family," rumbled Viktor. "Now she's closer than ever. So will you be, in time."

Constans' cheek twitched, the flare of jealousy banished almost as soon as seen. "Yes, Father."

Tzadas, 18th Day of Dawntithe

Faith is better placed in friends than distant gods.

from the diaries of Malachi Reveque

Sixty-One

The day was to be a good day, for it brought freedom.

Not that Cardivan Tirane had suffered any great physical burden since his imprisonment. Melanna Saranal, Empress in nothing but name, had held true to her promise. Save for the barred windows and the bricked-up doors – the one leading into the palace proper being the one exception, and guarded day and night – the quarters she'd provided would have been generous to a guest, let alone a hated rival.

Yet confinement remained confinement. And for all her virtues – and Cardivan reluctantly admitted that his captor possessed one or two – Melanna lacked the deviousness of mind to fully appreciate his reach. Coin and reputation travelled far. Cardivan had taught her that lesson once before. Today, another began.

A polite knock sounded. Cardivan allowed himself a small smile and departed the gilded bedchamber. The outer door was already closing, a glint of gold and white silk in the corridor serving as reminder that his was a guard drawn not only from the Immortals, but also the incorruptible lunassera of Mooncourt Temple.

Gazindar laid the tray upon the table and offered a low and respectful bow. In a palace of upstarts, the servant at least knew his place. "Good day, *savir*."

"And to you." Cardivan examined the tray's contents. Fennel tea. Bread. A generous portion of jakiri, the succulent aroma of spiced meat tantalising even at a distance. "I commend your efforts. This must have taken time to prepare."

Gazindar shook his head. "It's simply a matter of approaching the proper people."

Cardivan stifled a sigh. But for all its artless staging the message was clear: preparations were complete. He plucked a sliver of jakiri from its plate. The meat dissolved on his tongue, leaving tantalising aftertaste of garlic and bergamot.

"That might prove expensive," he said.

"No more than you might expect," Gazindar replied.

Cardivan grunted, though coin was hardly his first concern. His surviving agents in the city had paid Gazindar a prince's ransom in exchange for treachery. Another such sum had lured rescuers to Tregard. Not that it mattered. Only freedom mattered. "And I can expect my evening meal at the usual time?"

Gazindar twitched a brief smile. No actor, indeed. "A little delayed, *savir*. There may be some small commotion towards the approach of dusk."

Cardivan nodded. "My thanks."

Gazindar bowed and departed, leaving Cardivan to contemplate a repast for which he'd no longer any appetite. Momentous times made food seem so *trivial*.

Crossing to the barred window, he stared out across the city. The view was everything Melanna had promised, taking in a span of Emperor's Walk and the marketplace beyond. It would be the work of long months to rebuild what he'd lost. He'd a treacherous niece to cast down and a son to avenge, an army to rebuild, alliances to shore up. But white beard belied vital heart. He had those years and more. And it all began with an open door at dusk, a rush of blades and fast horses. Many would die for his freedom, but their families would be compensated. Generosity lay at the heart of loyalty.

As Cardivan took a sip of tea, he caught a wisp of a new scent. The sweet fragrance of rot, laced with unfamiliar perfume. Nose wrinkling, he set the cup aside. The fragrance grew stronger, cloying. It fuzzed the senses, lent distance to frescoed walls and the glint of sunlight in the streets beyond barred glass.

Cardivan squeezed his eyes shut and pinched the bridge of his nose. The world snapped back into focus, but the scent remained.

A crackling, rustling scrape sounded from the bedchamber.

Cardivan spun about to see vines writhing across the threshold. An impossible wind tumbled desiccated leaves across the polished floor. Briars coiled through gentle mist to wend about table leg and chair. A hunched, gangling shape gathered at the inner doorway, framed by tattered robes the colour of decay. Green flame leapt in the eyeholes of a wooden mask, featureless but for a single, jagged scar.

Cardivan scrambled away, his horrified cry rasping to nothing in a mouth suddenly dry.

{{Greetings, my king,}} buzzed Jack.

Sevaka arrived at Silvane House to find its door open. It always was, though she could never decide whether some magic made it thus, or because Apara always saw her approach and left it ajar. Even at that hour, with the morning sun lending warmth to winter days, firestone lanterns blazed in every room, holding at bay shadows, and the memories they provoked.

She found Apara overlooking the overgrown gardens. Clad again in Hadari silks, she contrived to look more dignified than Sevaka managed even on her best days. Until you looked in her eyes. No matter how bright the sun, no matter how many lanterns Apara lit, some shadows couldn't be banished.

But her embrace was warm enough. For all that Apara was a stranger, Sevaka's heart again filled with gratitude that she might not for ever be so.

"How are you?"

Her gaze on the gardens, Apara offered a wan smile. "Would you believe, I don't know?" Her voice was little more than a whisper. "For six years, I had a home. A place in the world where no one could touch me. Now? I don't know that I fit anywhere. You?"

"I've been with Josiri."

Apara grimaced. "How is he?"

Sevaka sighed, haunted anew by a feeling of uselessness. "How do you think? He's lost more these past few days than I have in a lifetime. First Calenne, and now Anastacia." Flesh or clay, Anastacia had been more vibrant, more *alive* than anyone Sevaka had ever met. Acknowledging she was gone left a hole in her heart a mile wide. "I couldn't tell you how he can even get out of bed, but he does. Even insisted attending Council this morning. I don't know what was worse, watching him try to string words together, or how the others treated him. Even when he managed to get a sentence out, someone would say something soothing and press on as if he'd said nothing at all. They're trying to be kind, but you can see he makes them uncomfortable."

"They should be uncomfortable," said Apara. "They executed his sister."

Sevaka fought back a rush of guilt. That she'd been part of that decision, however coerced, would stay with her for ever. "They could have set him on that pyre alongside, had they wanted. Warning the Empress was treason."

"It was the right thing to do."

For the first time, Apara's words carried weight. Even a hint of their mother's fire. The day grew warmer for it.

"I know. But when did that ever matter?" Sevaka took a deep breath, not wanting to sour the moment further, but knowing she must. "We've had a herald from Ardva. Governor Keldrov reports that Viktor has occupied Eskavord's ruins."

"Good," said Apara, her eyes still on the garden. "Then he's a long way off."

"She also claims he's raising a new army within the mists. Warriors fashioned from clay and seething with shadow. Already a thousand strong, and growing with every moment."

"And the Council doesn't believe her?"

"The Council believes, all right. But they refuse to act." She flung up her hands in frustration. "They're clinging to the hope that this will pass by, though they have to know it won't. And it's the Southshires. Some prejudices die hard. Why send the folk of the north to perish defending southwealders? Oh, they might approve action once Viktor crosses the Tevar Flood, but by then it'll be too late."

Sevaka stared out across the gardens, though caught no sign of whatever offered Apara solace.

"I don't know what we're going to do. Zephan wants to act, but has fewer than a hundred knights left. The Council won't authorise mobilising what soldiers we have left, and even if they would it'll be days yet before the regiments scattered at Argatha Bridge are fit to march, let alone fight." Despair bled away, frustration building to defiance. "I mean to do all I can, even if it amounts to nothing."

"I can't be part of it," murmured Apara, her voice cracking. "I can't face him again."

Sevaka concealed disappointment behind a nod. "I'm not asking you to. But someone should warn the Empress. Because after Viktor's done with us, she'll be next."

"And you care?"

Sevaka hesitated, uncertain how to express something she couldn't explain even to herself. "I shouldn't, but I do." She smiled without humour. "Perhaps it's because I know our mother would *hate* it."

At last, Apara tore her gaze from the garden. "She would, wouldn't she? Tell me everything."

After a morning spent conciliating Imperial business and the prospect of noon approaching sooner than it should, Melanna gladly retreated to her balcony's solitude. Just her and the city, laid out below.

But solitude ushered unhappy thoughts to the surface. Elbow-length gloves couldn't conceal Jack's mark from memory, nor banish the persistent itch. In the balcony's quietude, she could almost *feel* the briars shifting beneath her skin, edging ever outwards through tendon and sinew. Part of her, and yet not.

"Even an Empress cannot outrun her past," she murmured.

"Nor can any of us."

There was little scope for concealment on the balcony, but Apara had somehow contrived to find enough to remain unnoticed without treading in shadow. Or perhaps she'd made no effort to do so, and Melanna's own preoccupations had done the work?

"I shan't be offended if you call for your guards." Wan smile belied Apara's words. "Am I welcome?"

Overwhelmed by emotion that owed much to both gladness and sorrow, but committed to neither, Melanna embraced her.

Tension eased from Apara's shoulders. The one-sided embrace became mutual, and Melanna's burdens melted into memory. They'd return, of course they would, but if coming years were to count for anything, she had to seize moments of joy.

"Always." She drew back, the better for Apara to see the truth in her eyes. "Tregard is your home for as long as you wish."

Apara shook her head, on guard once more. "What I did—"

"You were a victim. You aren't responsible."

Apara gave a slow, unhappy nod. She didn't believe. Perhaps she never would. Her tone, already wintery, grew bleaker still. "It's about him that I've come."

Melanna's mood darkened, the moment of happiness as fleeting as she'd feared. "Tell me."

Passing inside, she rang for tea and pulled up a chair before the hearth. Apara sat opposite and with only brief hesitation launched into an account of all that had happened since Argatha Bridge. Of Droshna's madness. Of resurrected women sent to the fire. Of a serathi gone to dust in defiance of Droshna's growing malice. Of an army gathering in the Southshires. Tea was delivered and went cold, untouched and unlamented. Appetite withered.

Calenne Trelan, Melanna recalled as a courageous clash of steel at Davenwood and little more. Anastacia, she'd never met. But Josiri? Who'd given her so much and asked for nothing in return? Who'd by his friendship saved her family at the cost of his own? But more than that, Melanna's thoughts dwelled on Droshna. His shadow, not unfittingly, loomed over all.

"I did this." She barely managed even those words, so thick was guilt about her lungs. Glory in victory. Fortitude in defeat. Honour always. She'd striven to live by that credo. She'd failed. "He'd removed himself from the world. The Avitra Briganda brought him back. *I* brought him back. Whenever he kills, my hand is on the sword alongside his."

Apara scowled. "If I'm not responsible for what Viktor Droshna has done, nor are you."

Melanna forced a smile. "Maybe."

A new Age of Dark. The dead bound in service to conquer the living, and the living shackled to a single, tyrannous will. The Avitra Briganda had begun to prevent such a fate. Corrupted by pride and ambition, it had instead ushered it into being.

She'd ushered it into being.

Melanna closed her eyes, acknowledging the irony that stillness came easier in darkness. *Too* easily. Thought eased away. The sweet scent of dew and the soothing rustle of windblown leaves rose to take its place. Melanna started, eyes snapping open. She spread a hand across her chest to ease a pounding heart. She'd already forgotten what had set it racing.

She refocused on Apara. Droshna. They'd been talking about Droshna. "What does your sister mean to do?"

"To gather what forces she can, and put an end to this."

"Can she?"

"With the Council's backing? Perhaps."

"You'll want to tell Lady Orova, of course. You'll find her playing nursemaid to my daughter." It wasn't entirely true, for no Hadari nursemaid would have thought to tutor so young a child in sword-craft, which was precisely what Lady Orova had taken it upon herself to do, albeit – at Jorcari's insistence – with the very bluntest of blunt sticks. "I'm sure Kaila would be delighted to see you, Shar Apara."

"No."

Surprised by the brusqueness of response, Melanna opened her eyes.

"I'm not to tell Rosa," Apara clarified. "I promised Sevaka."

"I don't follow."

"Sevaka wants her safe. She's worried Rosa's history with Droshna will make her reckless."

"Lady Orova is a warrior," Melanna replied. "It's not for you to shield her."

"I'm simply honouring my sister's request." Apara twitched a brief frown. "Her first such request . . . and likely her last."

Melanna found the deceit abhorrent but let the matter lie. "Will you stand with her?"

Apara looked away, her posture suddenly shrunken, as if she wanted to pull herself inside the chair and go unnoticed. "I can't. If he sees me again – if his shadow touches me – I don't know what I'll become. Even the thought . . ."

"I don't pretend to understand what Droshna's taken from you," said Melanna, "but if you don't find a way to take it back, you'll be for ever lost in his shadow, even if you never cross his path again."

"And what do you know of it?" snapped Apara, head in her hands. "Do you know what it's like to hear yourself speak, to see yourself move, and know that it's not you at all? Shouting, screaming, hammering on the glass between what you *are* and what *is*, and have no one hear you?"

The itch in Melanna's wrist flared to wakefulness. She set her other palm atop it, and strove to ignore the creeping, crawling sensation beneath the glove's fabric.

"I don't," she lied. "I hope never to do so."

"Then you know nothing at all!" She broke off, eyes red-rimmed. "I'm sorry."

Leaving the chair, Melanna crouched at Apara's side, gloved hands about hers. "I spoke out of turn. You're my dearest friend, and have my support in whatever course you choose. But remember this. You and I have seen sights granted to no other. We've walked the mists at the behest of the Goddess of the Moon. We've lingered beneath the stars of the Celestial Clock, and beheld the bickering of gods. There are powers in this world greater than the Dark, even if only for a moment. You will be free of him, Apara. I promise."

Apara nodded, a tremulous smile fighting to be seen. "Thank you, *essavim*."

"What do you mean, he's missing?" asked Melanna.

"I cannot explain it, Empress," said Chakdra, his discomfort visible even at the distance afforded by throne and dais. "I made inspection of King Cardivan's chambers myself. He's nowhere to be found."

Melanna laid her hand on the Goddess' sword, again hanging from the throne's armrest. It was half the comfort with the cool metal shielded by her glove, but half a comfort was better than none. How quickly the world crumbled.

Aeldran stirred from his station at Melanna's shoulder, his voice gruff with precursor to fury. "Have his guards held for questioning. Double the patrols."

Chakdra nodded. "Already done, my prince. I've sent word to Mooncourt, requesting others of the lunassera aid the search." He scowled as he spoke. Bad enough that the lunassera had already stolen so many of the Immortals' duties. That he'd sent for them at all spoke to his shame. "The prisoner will be found."

"See that he is," said Melanna. "Keep me informed."

Chakdra bowed and departed the throne room, two Immortals falling into step as he reached the door.

Aeldran moved to follow. "If you need me, *essavim*, I'll be with our daughter."

She nodded, grateful. "Thank you." Struck by sudden thought, she rose and halted him with a touch of her hand. "You'll find Apara in my chambers. Tell her what's happening."

"Of course."

Then Aeldran too was gone, leaving Melanna alone with Jorcari and the lunassera posted watch at the door. "I want to see for myself."

Jorcari grunted. "You should stay here, *savim*." He offered a lopsided shrug. "But I know you won't, so at least stay close."

Leaving the throne room behind, they passed through corridors until they at last came to the east wing. The two lunassera stationed at the entrance to Cardivan's chambers bowed and withdrew without a word.

What lay within was too ... ordinary. Not a furnishing out of place. No blood. The window bars remained sturdy, the gloom of dusk gathering beyond. A half-plate of jakiri sat on the table, the dregs of cold tea beside and cutlery set in the manner of unfinished business. Calm. Collected. No signs of a struggle. Cardivan's rescuers had come and gone without trace. All too easy to imagine his smug, supercilious smile.

Melanna shook her head. Of course the rescuers hadn't vanished without trace. Cardivan had suborned his guards as he'd done so many others, which meant he'd somehow found purchase on lunassera, as well as Immortals. Curse the man and his silver tongue.

"There's nothing to learn here, *savim*," murmured Jorcari. "What matters now is that you and your family are kept safe."

Safe. As if there could ever be such a thing. "I should have killed him when I had the chance."

"You'll have that chance again, my Empress."

For all that Jorcari's words – his *promise* – helped, Melanna couldn't bring herself to leave. Skirting the table and its untouched meal, she entered Cardivan's bedchamber. Here too, she found nothing out of place. And yet for all that there was *something* on the air. Not a sensation she could name, but unmistakeable for all that.

As she turned to leave, a dark sliver beneath the windowsill caught her eye. Crouching, she reached out to take it. A coil of black briar. She stared at it without seeing. The strange sensation surged, bringing with it a whisper and rustle of leaves.

Breath came slow, heavy – contrast to a quickening pulse. She felt a repeated, insistent tug at her wrist. Another, heavier, at her shoulder. A voice, distant, muffled.

"Empress? Empress?"

Melanna shook her head. Her thoughts cleared. She looked up to see Jorcari standing over her, his hand on her shoulder. The briar lay entangled about the fingers of her left hand. Her right scratched idly at her left wrist through the silken glove. Grimacing, she brought it to stillness and stood up.

Jorcari leaned closer. "What is it?"

Wincing, she let the briar fall. "Nothing," she lied. "Nothing at all. You're right. There's nothing to be learned here. I need you to go out into the city. Make sure there's no trouble at Triumphal Gate."

"My place is with you, Empress."

"Cardivan's gone." That was true enough, at least. "And I'll be safe enough with the lunassera."

Jorcari scowled but, offering a bow, he obeyed.

Only when she was certain he'd gone did Melanna peel back the edge of her glove. She let it fall back at once. Throat crowded with nausea, she clung to the windowsill, unable to think, and barely able to breathe.

Melanna felt the change as soon as she crossed into the old wood. The scents of the garden, subdued in winter, grew sharper, glorious in a manner she'd never known. Bruised grass and broken leaves. The rich, mellow warmth of pulsing sap. She *felt* life rising beneath the cracked, ashen boughs, reclaiming what the fire had stolen. Overwhelming. Intoxicating. She might even have found it beautiful, but for Jack's betrayal.

He'd lied to her. Bad enough he'd set Cardivan free, but to advance his claim upon her at the same time . . . ? Over and over, she re-examined their pact, and found no loophole to exploit. *Deliver Rhaled from its enemies, and once my daughter's rule is unassailable – not one day sooner – I will be your queen.* A bargain with the divine bound all parties. Unassailable truth revealed as lie.

And yet for all Melanna clung to hatred and resentment, they slipped ever further from her grasp. With every step, urge assailed her to shed clothing and skin and run naked beneath the ashen boughs. To sleep in the embrace of the soil, stem and root. To partake experiences for which she'd no name, but knew without doubt could be hers. Nauseating, invigorating desires that belonged to someone else – some*thing* else.

Again and again, Melanna cloaked herself in fury at what Jack had done. But each time, a little less of her remained. A little less cared at the foolishness of coming there alone. By the time she reached the oak, she trembled with the effort of recollection. Not just of the anger that had borne her there, but even her own name.

{{You shouldn't be here, not yet.}} Jack's gangling shadow drifted behind the oak, granted barest shape by what little moonlight cheated the clouds. For the first time, he wasn't alone. A dozen others stood silhouetted beyond, briars curling and twitching in the breeze. She knew the shapes well enough. Strawjacks. {{My gift is barely complete.}}

"I don't want your gifts. I want you to keep your promise!" She swayed, the rejoinder sapping reserves under strain.

{{My gift *is* my promise.}} Puzzlement rippled beneath the words. Puzzlement . . . and hurt? {{Won't you come and see?}}

Despite her better judgement, Melanna edged closer. Rot joined the profusion of scents, no less enticing than the others, for all its foulness.

The first of Jack's companions shambled closer, its likeness revealed beneath the moon. Not a strawjack, or rather not quite – not yet. Cardivan Tirane's thorn-wreathed corpse was still recognisable as such, if barely. Briars burrowed through gaping wounds, crawled beneath his eyes and over his tongue. Exposed bone glinted as flesh sloughed steadily, remorselessly away, rebound with fronds and pallid green tendrils.

Melanna gazed at the dead eyes and felt no remorse, no sympathy – only a shudder of fascination she'd couldn't be certain belonged to her at all.

As she watched, more of the macabre assemblage lurched into sight, not the mere dozen Melanna had first glimpsed, but a full score.

Some, she knew. Thirava Tirane, though he was barely recognisable as such, and by his presence revealing there was much more to his supposed accident than his cousin Incalia had reported. Queen Agrana of Novona, and King Bodra of Kerna – Cardivan's allies in the Gwyraya Hadar. One of Melanna's own servants. Three Immortals in Rhalesh green, and another in Icansae scarlet. Others, arrayed in all the colours of the Empire, rendered to sweet, rotting flesh and the cycle of root and stem.

"What is this?" murmured Melanna.

Jack hunched closer, strangely hesitant. {{My promise fulfilled. Kaila's throne secure.}} He spoke faster, the buzzing, crackling voice quickening in breathy excitement. {{My daughters have been most assiduous in seeking them out. And now they are yours, a wedding gift fit for a queen on the night her debt comes due.}}

He reached out a tangled, rag-clothed hand.

Melanna watched numbly as her own rose to take it. Thoughts drifted away on clouds of sweet, succulent decay.

"No!" She snatched back her hand. "This isn't what you promised!"

Jack jerked away, rising to his full, twisted height before sinking again to a hunch. {{It is *more* than I promised.}} Even now, he didn't sound angry, but hurt. A child blind to transgression. {{I'd no need to be so thorough, but I wanted you to be content. I didn't want you afraid for your daughter. A daughter is always a treasure.}}

Melanna sagged. *Once my daughter's rule is unassailable, I will be your queen.* Her words. Her bargain. She'd sought to postpone this day until Kaila was of age. Jack, blithely or not, viewed it otherwise.

"She needs her mother."

{{She has a father.}}

Aeldran would die to defend Kaila. And die he would, if Droshna again turned his eye to the east. "And if he isn't enough?" she snapped.

{{Our bargain was that she'd live to rule, never for how long.}}

Heartsick, Melanna spun away. "You knew that wasn't what I meant."

{{The bargain isn't what is meant, but what is agreed.}} For the first time, anger buzzed beneath the words. It yielded to wounded disappointment. {{But I give you my promise, freely and without bond, that for as long as Fellhallow's roots wend about this thin, brittle world, your daughter's enemies will be mine. She will live long in happiness, and pass into mist only when the seed of her life is spent.}}

"And what is your promise worth?" she replied bitterly.

{{Everything.}} He issued a great, rumbling sigh. {{Though if it is your wish to break the bargain, I will not stop you. But you know how I am bound.}}

For a moment, temptation arose to accept, even knowing the cost to Tregard – to the Empire. For a moment only. Jack hadn't deceived her. She'd deceived herself. How could she even consider having others pay her debts?

Her debts . . .

Jack was not her only creditor. Droshna was a stain upon her ledger. She couldn't pass from the life she'd known without at least an attempt at reckoning.

With supreme effort, Melanna drew herself together. "I've business left undone and farewells to offer. I cannot be your queen until they are settled."

{{Then you break the bargain.}}

"No!" Turning, she clasped her hands. "You've shown yourself to be kinder than your legend, and I ask only for a little more time. If I'm anything more to you than a prize, you must grant me this."

Jack snarled and twisted away. {{You seek to cheat me. As all cheat me.}}

Swallowing, Melanna cast around for something he might believe. "I swear . . . I swear on my daughter's life, that I do not. I just need a little time."

He swung about, green fire dancing in the eyes of his mask. {{You have until midnight.}}

Sixty-Two

Kaila slept as she ever had, snoring like a flooded gutter. Melanna watched from the bedside chair, searing into memory every curve and crease of her daughter's face, locking the likeness away in the hope she might retain even a fraction of remembrance.

Resolve to wake Kaila had faltered the moment Melanna had set foot in the room. How could she explain what was to come when she could barely hold back her own tears? Every inch of skin itched, at once too loose and too tight. Worse, Melanna too often felt her thoughts straying, lost in leaf and loam, in the yearning for something she didn't understand. She couldn't risk Kaila seeing that. Better that their last memories of each other be unmarred.

Rising, she kissed Kaila's brow. "Sleep well, *essavim*. You have been my life, and will always have my love."

Heart brimming, she left the room. Tears held at bay for Kaila's sake welled free. As she crossed the landing, a shadow pulled free of the wall and limped to block her path.

"I was told you were prowling around," said Aeldran. "She's safe."

Melanna nodded. "I know. Cardivan will trouble us no longer."

"So I heard." He drew closer, suspicion in his eyes. "Just as I heard you'd withdrawn the guards from this part of the palace. And now I find our chambers in darkness. What is all this, *essavim*?"

She flinched away and hugged herself tight about the shoulders. "Cardivan is dead. I ordered the guards withdrawn and the lights doused because I wanted to see our daughter, and not be seen in exchange." She hesitated. "I have to go away. Tonight. I will not return."

She felt his gaze upon her as he sought jest in her words. "I don't understand."

"To save Tregard, I made a deal with Jack. I'm to be his queen."

He rocked as if struck, a clenched fist going to his lips before falling away alongside a muttered, breathy curse. "How could you do this? To Kaila? To me? To your people?"

"I thought I'd found a compromise, but Jack deceived me." No, that wasn't right, was it? Now more than ever, Aeldran deserved the truth. For the first time, she met his gaze, no longer needing to conceal the aftermath of tears. "I deceived *myself*, and now the debt is due."

Aeldran touched his eyes closed. When he opened them again, they were hard as stone. "No!" His finger stabbed at the air between them. "I won't permit this!"

"It's not yours to deny," hissed Melanna. "If I break the bargain, Jack will return everything to how it was. He doesn't have a choice. He will lay Tregard to waste, and my debt – my mother's debt – will pass to Kaila."

He reached for her, thought better of it, and spread his hands between them. "There must be a way. Speak to the lunassera! To Ashana! It doesn't have to end like this."

She heard the quiet desperation in his tone, the anger building behind. A warrior Aeldran remained – he'd seek solution through the sword and it would be his doom. But in that moment words escaped her, drifting away on the scent of pollen and dead leaves.

"I'll have the wood burned again," growled Aeldran. "And this time, I'll see it's—"

He broke off as Melanna dropped her silken glove at his feet, though it wasn't the glove itself that reduced him to silence, but what it no longer concealed.

Beneath her elbow, no scrap of skin remained. What had been flesh was now twisted bramble and vine, strands of willow flexing in sinew's stead. Hidden by the gown's sleeve, the skin of her upper arm hung loose, the limb beneath already ridged and twisted. When she'd first seen it thus in Cardivan's chambers, nausea had all but overwhelmed her. Now she felt only curiosity for what might follow, and loathed herself for it.

{{This is done, *essavir*,}} she murmured. {{There is nothing more to say. Our daughter will rule. That is enough. Prophecy *will* be fulfilled, and all debts repaid.}}

Aeldran's throat bobbed, anger draining from his expression. He took her hands in his, the marred as readily as the hale. His eyes gleamed. "You won't let me accompany you, will you?"

{{No.}} Melanna swallowed, willing the crackling buzz from her voice. "Your sword has saved me in the past. Your strength has been mine more often than I've told you. Neither will serve here. It's my debt, and a journey only I can take."

"Then ..." Aeldran screwed his eyes shut. "Then what would you have me do?"

"Be the father Kaila needs," said Melanna. "Have her learn early all the lessons you and I learned too late. And have her remember me well, if you can bear it."

She embraced him, surrendering one last time to closeness too often spurned, losing herself in the warmth, the feel, the smell of him. How fortunate she'd been to have Aeldran at her side, just as Kaila was fortunate to have him as a father. Another memory to hold close within the briar, were she able.

And then the moment was spent, as all moments are. She left him without backward glance, passing through the darkened halls until she came again to the birchwood balcony, and the silver glory of Tregard below.

"Is it done?" asked Apara.

"It is. You're almost my last farewell, and I don't know what to say."

"I do. My words before, about being trapped behind glass ... I didn't know." She hung her head. "I'm sorrier than I can say. You're sure there's nothing—"

Melanna laid her gloved hand against Apara's chest. Another friendship she couldn't say how she'd earned. One of so many. "Certain. Deliver my message, and I'll be content. Ashana walk with you, Apara. And thank you for everything."

This time, reknitting her etravia came faster, easier, urged on by instincts Calenne barely recognised as her own. She rose into an Otherworld becalmed, the vortex's winds dropped almost to nothing. What other etravia wandered Revekah's dead pyre-gardens did so untroubled. Not so the Raven, who sat just beyond the flames, elbows on crooked knees and hat between his feet. Head bowed and hackles high, he resembled his namesake more than ever.

"Is it ended?" asked Calenne.

"You're back, are you?" He no longer sounded angry, only resigned. "It's only a pause. Even the mighty Viktor Droshna has his limits."

Calenne drifted closer, careful not to meet the agonised gaze of Revekah's burning soul. "I still can't believe that he's doing it at all."

"A man who kills a serathi might aspire to much that is forbidden."

"Anastacia?" Calenne felt colder than ever. "He killed Anastacia?"

"To all intents and purposes."

Nausea crowded in. They'd never been close, she and Anastacia, but still ... "Why?"

"She sought to stop him. That's enough, these days."

"Is she here?"

"Not everyone takes the same path, at the same speed."

Why couldn't he just say no? Beset with a sense of loss she knew she'd not earned, Calenne stared up at the vortex. This wasn't the work of the man who'd saved her from wolf's-heads beneath Davenwood's eaves. Nor the one who'd inspired her to become the woman – the leader – of which she'd been so proud. Then there'd been that time he'd nursed her through the winter. Or that day at Valna where, outnumbered, he'd sent Thrakkian raiders howling back to the border. *That* Viktor hadn't just loved her, he'd shown kindness to strangers, even though he'd received little of his own.

Wait. What?

Frozen, Calenne re-examined her memories. She and Viktor had barely spent the most chaste of nights together, never mind a whole winter. And Valna? She could just about place it on a map, but not summon to memory its uneven palisade, squat chimneys and the spire of an overgrown temple rising behind ...

Other recollections rushed to the fore. Glimpses of a life not lived – or at least, not by her. And yet, they *were* her memories, indivisible from her being.

Panicked, she looked up to see the Raven staring at her with sour amusement. "Can I help you?"

She hesitated. "I'm remembering things, but they're not my memories. Only . . . I think they are, but they can't be."

"That's very clear."

He was enjoying this. Watching her in anticipation of the penny dropping. "You know, don't you?"

The Raven pursed his lips in that damnable, better-than-you smile. Then he scooped his hat back onto his head and shrugged. "Once upon a time, there was a selfish, embittered young creature. You'd not like her very much. But someone did. When she died, that someone fashioned a version of her from the Dark and together they lived a happy lie."

Calenne sagged. Felt pieces of herself spiral away into the mist. Viktor had been wrong. She wasn't who she thought she was. Not the original, but the copy. "I'm not Calenne Trelan at all, am I? I'm Calenne Akadra."

The Raven wagged a finger. "Might I finish?"

She nodded mutely. It seemed easier that way.

"Thank you. Anyway, in time, this ersatz – and not entirely sane – young lady also perished. She came to Otherworld, as all eventually do. Twice now, you've constituted yourself against my wishes, thrashing around for any scrap of being that might give you form. You're not Calenne Akadra, but she is part of you. You made her so."

Calenne's thoughts raced. Had she done such a thing? How would she even know? "That's impossible."

He hooked an eyebrow. "Look around, Miss Trelan. Consider to whom you're speaking, and where. Impossible is our Tzadas, and every other day of the week besides. It's routine. Even ordinary, if you'll allow yourself the imagination. Don't think I'm any happier than you. The Dark is beyond my grasp, which means there's a part of you I can't affect. It's very vexing, let me tell you. When I banish someone, I like them to *stay* banished."

"You're saying I destroyed her!" It mattered more than it should.

"Not exactly. Calenne Akadra was only ever half alive, and you had as much claim to the half that lived as anyone else. She was never able to help herself. Perhaps she chose to help you. Ephemerals do put such store by self-sacrifice. It might be she thought it made her more human."

Calenne stared down at herself. Her sense of identity, besieged ever since Viktor had drawn her back into the ephemeral world, shuddered anew. She *felt* like herself, but what use was that? Calenne Akadra had been her mirror. And the memories were so *real*. Memories made by a stranger, and yet not. The life that could have been. The life she'd wanted and been denied.

The vortex quickened, the winds returning.

"Oh good," said the Raven, glumly. "He's starting again."

Calenne gazed into the swirling skies. No longer sure of much of anything, she knew one thing with ironclad, immovable certainty. The Viktor she'd loved – who'd loved *her* in a life she'd never led – would hate the lost and twisted soul he'd become.

Akadra, Trelan or amalgam of both, she'd responsibility yet.

Josiri's study was a haven of calm, the subdued bustle of the household sealed behind the door's stout timbers, the rain banished behind leaded glass. Only the crackle of the hearth and the slow tick of the clock intruded on his thoughts. Or at least, upon the place where he knew his thoughts should be. The void within him was a jealous lodger, and permitted no rival.

He'd forgotten so much in recent months, the memories drowned beneath Viktor's shadow. If only he could forget anew. But no, he wasn't that fortunate. And in truth, he didn't *want* to forget – merely to be free of the loss and the pain. Forgetting meant losing the last of Anastacia, and that prospect hurt more than the memories.

He knew he should rise from the chair. Take a walk. Eat something. Break the cycle of hours spent staring at the desk and the upside-down book, pages spread and spine broken. Left out in defiance of his wish that this room, at least, remain tidy. A first printing of Kespid's *A Walk to Ingcross*. Rare. Valuable. Anastacia hadn't cared. She'd seen only a book to be read. One of kind, changed for ever by the whirlwind of her existence. He lacked the heart to move it. As long as it was still there, there remained the possibility she might return to move it herself.

Even false hope remained hope. Viktor had left him nothing else. Not even a body to bury.

A knock sounded at the door.

He ignored it.

The door opened anyway. Altiris entered. Composed as a highblood should be. As Josiri should have been. "You have guests."

Josiri swallowed to clear a dry throat. "Offer my apologies and send them away."

"They're worried about you. *I'm* worried about you."

"I'm fine. Leave me be."

"You need to hear them out."

"Why, when no one listens to what I have to say in return? Not my friends. Not the Council I founded. Maybe they're right. I let Viktor do this. I killed Ana as surely as he did."

He broke off to fight resurgent tears. No matter how many he shed, more remained.

"This wasn't your fault. In that moment, Ana saw a chance and she took it, even knowing what it might cost. She was trying to protect us. Tell me you'd have done it differently in her place."

Altiris' eyes lingered on Anastacia's discarded book. "Come down. Listen to what they have to say. And then, if it's your wish, I'll lock all the doors. You need see no one ever again." He paused, steeling himself. "Please . . . Josiri."

Up close, dignified facade no longer concealed loss behind. Anastacia's murder had left a void in so many hearts. She'd have loved that almost as much as she'd have loathed it. And Sidara . . . For all anyone knew, she was already dead. The prospect gnawed at Josiri too, in those rare moments when his grief ebbed. It surely weighed heavier on Altiris.

Was there anything more selfish than claiming monopoly on loss?

Falteringly, he rose. "I'll listen. I promise nothing more."

Leaving the study, Josiri followed Altiris down the stairs, steadying rubbery legs with a hand ever on the banister. How long since he'd last eaten? He couldn't remember.

The drawing room held not the handful of guests Josiri had expected, but a small crowd. Altiris joined Sevaka and Zephan by the hearth. The rest of the Phoenixes – Viara, Brass, Beckon, Jarrock and Kelver – stood a little to one side. None met Josiri's gaze.

That the drawing room was fuller than it had been since Midwintertide only served as reminder of how much had changed. Elzar, Izack and Anastacia lost to the mists. Kurkas still lingering on the threshold.

Sidara fallen to a fate unknown. Constans and Viktor seduced by their own worst instincts.

Josiri sought refuge in poor humour. "Is no one watching the grounds?"

Zephan grunted. Another one unable to meet his gaze. "I've ten knights standing sentry, and as many again on patrol. Anyone who causes trouble at Stonecrest tonight will have the fright of their fore-shortened lives."

Josiri bit back anger. For all that Viktor had doomed Calenne, Zephan had dragged her to the flames. "You think this makes up for anything?"

"No. Nor am I asking it to. I'm here to discuss the future, not the past." Zephan shook his head. "But if I were, I'd beg your forgiveness. I've no excuse save fear, and that's no excuse at all."

A graceful apology, had Josiri the heart to accept it. "Why are you here?"

"You know what Viktor's doing," said Sevaka. "You know where it'll lead. He has to be stopped."

As if it were that simple. "This morning, I spent two hours trying to convince the Council of that very fact. They ignored me. Are you here to tell me they've changed their minds?"

Sevaka shook her head. "No."

"Then there's nothing to be done." Overcome by fresh weariness, Josiri turned to leave. "If you'll excuse me, it's late and I'm tired."

A new voice checked him at the door. One no less weary than his own. A gruff, city-dweller's accent he'd lost all hope of hearing. "And when did Josiri Trelan ever give a single bloody damn what the Council thinks?"

Kurkas, hidden until that moment by the heavy shadows at the room's far end, hobbled to his feet. He moved stiffly, more a man of advancing years than ever. Even so, the sight stirred Josiri to sluggish relief. Maybe even gladness.

"Vladama? You're awake?"

Kurkas' brow furrowed, an echo of pain and loss creasing his worn features. "Answer the bloody question."

"Viktor has an army!" snapped Josiri.

"And when did *that* bloody matter?" Kurkas rejoined, his voice no longer that of a friend, but of a disgusted drill sergeant.

Josiri flinched, but held his ground. "When one was needed, and was nowhere to be found."

Kurkas snorted. "Seems to me we've been here before, you and me. *One is a man alone. Two are a beginning.* You told me that, back before you dragged this city kicking and screaming out of the Crowmarket's clutches." He swept his hand about the drawing room. "There's nine of us here. Ten, counting yourself. And more to come. Ain't that right, Master Tanor?"

Zephan nodded. "Every shield I have left."

Did they really not see the hopelessness of it all? "Have you read Keldrov's letter?" said Josiri. "Viktor has at least a thousand, and his numbers grow by the hour. Ten or a hundred, it won't matter. He's beyond us. He always was! The only thing ever holding him back was his need to be seen as a hero. He's free of that now."

Kurkas shrugged. "You think I don't know what Lord Droshna is?" He spoke faster, anger beneath the words. "He was my friend a damn sight longer than he was yours, and you better believe I'll put him in the ground for what he's done."

"You'll never have the chance," said Josiri. "He'll kill you."

"Probably he will. But I owe it to the plant pot and Halvor to at least *try.*"

Revekah. He'd forgotten about her. Another victim.

"You don't leave a wolf on the prowl," Brass put in. "Only makes trouble later."

Brass was part of this? *Brass,* who'd never met a duty he couldn't shirk? Josiri looked about the room, for the first time gleaning the gathering's true intent. "You're not asking for my approval. You've already decided to go."

Phoenixes nodded. Sevaka offered a mirthless smile. "That's about the size of it."

Altiris stepped forward. "I saw what Lord Droshna's become. There's no road back for him." His tone grew subdued, his expression haunted. "And I need to know what's happened to Sidara."

"We wanted to offer you the chance to come with us," said Zephan.

"What can I do that Essamere cannot? I've no authority," Josiri added bitterly. "The Council's made that clear."

"Do you have a sword?" asked Viara.

"Of course I have a sword," he replied, irritation edging out weariness.

"Then you've all the authority and purpose anyone in this damn city ever cares about."

He snorted. "Is everyone to throw my words back at me tonight?"

"For as long and as often as it takes," said Kurkas. "There comes a point in every soldier's life, sah, where you don't fight because you think you can *win*, but because if you don't *try* you've already lost."

"You're the only one Viktor might heed," said Sevaka. "Maybe this doesn't have to be a fight."

Talk to Viktor? After all he'd done? What would he even say? Could he even bring himself to speak? "You believe that?"

She grimaced. "No."

"Then we're back to me being a man with a sword." Josiri sighed, uncertain why he still argued. Weariness and fear were so closely mingled about his heart as to defy untangling. "What difference does one sword make?"

"Perhaps it's not about the sword, but the man who carries it, and why."

The stale scent of Otherworld's mists followed Apara into the room. Zephan moved to intercept her, only to be checked by Sevaka's hand and a shake of her head.

Kurkas snorted. "So much for the watchfulness of Essamere. What do you want, lass?"

Apara went utterly still – a woman re-examining recent choices and wishing she'd chosen otherwise. "To walk back out that door and pretend I never heard the name Viktor Droshna." She shared a glance with Sevaka. A nod exchanged left both women standing taller than before. "But I can't. Because if I do, whatever follows won't be a life. I'll carry his shadow wherever I walk. So will you."

There was always that. What more could Viktor do that he hadn't already? He'd only be finishing what he'd begun on the clifftops at Duskvigil Church. Josiri held the revelation close. Weariness retreated before its warmth.

"I also carry a message from the Empress. She's aware of what gathers in the south ... " Apara tailed off, a shadow touching her eyes, then pressed on. "She regrets that she can promise no aid, and wishes it were otherwise. But she'd have you understand, Josiri, that the Empire is changing in ways she never thought possible, and that this is your doing as much as hers. She says that you, more than anyone, taught her that the sword is not the only measure of honour, and that she will treasure your friendship to the last."

Josiri had the sense that the morbid undertone was not meant for him, though instinct counselled against enquiring further in public. Still, Melanna was right. The sword was not the only measure of honour. The sword allowed one to fight for what was truly valuable: the faithfulness of friends yet living, and justice for those already lost . . . whether to death, or to madness. Viktor had taught him that lesson years before.

He took in the gathering. Soldiers. Highbloods. The daughters of a woman who'd persecuted his family. The grandmaster of a knightly order that had betrayed his mother. An ex-vranakin, now pledged to the service of the Hadari Empire. Northwealders all, Altiris aside. They should have been his enemies, but they were his friends.

For the first time since entering the drawing room, Josiri asked himself what Ana would have done. He at once realised the question's irrelevance. She'd made her choice at Duskvigil Church. How could he do less?

Weariness faded. Fear melted away. Even sorrow, his constant companion in recent days, receded. Not gone. Josiri knew they'd never wholly leave him, but they retreated far enough that he could at last think like a man of whom he could be proud.

"I once promised Viktor I'd stop him," he said. "Whatever it takes. Whatever it costs. So it looks like I'm coming with you."

Sera accompanied Melanna on the long walk to Mooncourt Temple. The lunassera had come without being called, and sought no explanation for why her Empress was hooded and cloaked beyond recognition. Melanna had the impression Sera knew anyway – had perhaps foreseen this outcome from the day she'd returned from Argatha Bridge. But Sera offered neither judgement nor rebuke as they passed the colonnades of Emperor's Walk – merely quiet companionship – and bowed low as Melanna headed deeper in the temple alone.

The air beneath the sanctum mound was sharper, sweeter, than at her last visit. When Melanna closed her eyes, she felt the roots of the birch trees burrowing through the soil, as if a piece of her did so alongside. She drove the sensation from her mind, faltering lips giving shape to familiar prayer.

"Blessed Ashana. Guide your ephemeral daughter."

A chill crept across her shoulders. She drew tight the hooded cloak, worn to shield her from onlookers' view as she'd hurried along Emperor's Walk. It no longer fitted as it should.

"Blessed Ashana. Guide your ephemeral daughter."

"She will not come. You know this."

Melanna caught her breath at the deep, fibrous voice. So familiar, for all that it had gone unheard so long. Not since he'd led her through the mists to the Celestial Clock, and the meeting place of the gods. The mists took you anywhere, if you knew the route. "So you always say."

Opening her eyes, she saw a shadow moving against the gloom. An antlered helm, green eyes blazing beneath. A cloak of captive stars atop armour.

"Even my presence courts disaster," rumbled the Huntsman. "Go, before it's too late."

Melanna gripped her hood. "It's already too late."

Shame made her hesitate. Shame, and alien exhilaration that couldn't understand why she sought to hide. Overcoming both, she drew back the hood.

The fire in the Huntsman's eyes dimmed. His tone grew tender. "She will come. Even if I have to drag her."

Was that humour in his tone? Melanna had always believed she knew Ashana well enough, but the Huntsman – and their bond – remained a mystery. She'd no chance to ask. He was already gone, and she alone with thoughts that came increasingly hard.

A beetle emerged from between crystal-set roots and scurried across the floor. Melanna traced its passage with a crooked forefinger that no longer bent quite as it once had. Unbidden, the beetle reversed course, rushing up over her hand and burrowing between the woven stems of her wrist and out of sight. The only horror she felt was that she felt none at all.

"Melanna."

A soft glow from the sanctum's deeper chambers heralded Ashana's arrival. And it *was* Ashana, not the mortal guise she'd worn at their last meeting. Beautiful. Ageless. Stricken.

Melanna fought the urge to flinch away. {{Mother.}}

Ashana rushed closer. Moonlight tingled where she touched cheek and brow.

"What have you done?" She sounded angry, and sad, and everything between.

{{What I had to.}} There was no banishing the crackle from her voice now. {{I gave Jack what he wanted to save my people.}}

"Do you understand what this means?" Ashana's eyes touched closed. "Jack is the essence of rebirth, and his nature distorts even his own desires. Those who come to him as queen are never as he first beheld them."

{{I know.}} The prospect sickened and thrilled in equal measure. {{It's as though . . . There's another "me" inside my head. She's getting stronger, and I'm drifting away on clouds of pollen. By midnight, I'll be gone, and she'll take my place.}}

"Oh, Melanna . . . " Ashana shook her head, the moonlight dimming. "I can't undo this. It would end divine truce. This world will fall into war and Third Dawn will come."

{{I'm not asking you to. This is payment for deeds past, and I will bear it.}}

"Then why have you come?"

{{Because I wanted to see you while I'm still myself. Because kindness must be repaid, and sacrifice honoured.}} Melanna's thoughts drifted, unravelling in the soothing scent of root and moss. She drew them back. Just a little longer. {{The fate we feared has come to pass. Viktor Droshna is lost to the Dark. Those who were once my enemies mean to stop him, but cannot do so alone. They need help. Light must drive out the shadow.}}

Ashana narrowed her eyes. "You'd have me aid those who sought your death? Who persecute their own kind for the sin of worshipping the moon over the sun?"

{{I owe Josiri Trelan a debt, and I . . . }} Melanna swayed, her thoughts wandering. {{ . . . I can no longer repay it.}}

"No," said Ashana, her voice cold. "I will show them no kindness."

{{Then you let the Dark reclaim its hold on the world!}}

"That isn't certain, even now."

Melanna read the lie in the Goddess' eyes. The desperate hope.

{{We did this, you and I! Your fear. My ambition. We garbed ourselves in righteousness, waded in blood, and created the very future we sought to deny! And so I ask: does the Goddess who raised me as her own, who taught me the value of honour and of life, pay her debts?}}

{{Lady Orova.}}

Rosa awoke, old fears of treachery rising to the surface. But there were no blades in her darkened bedchamber. Nothing at all save a shaft of moonlight through drapes dancing in the breeze. It shaped a cloaked, hooded figure beside a balcony door left ajar.

"Who's there?"

She sat up and reached for an absent sword. Guest though she was, certain privileges lay beyond the pale.

{{Melanna.}} A dour chuckle rippled through the gloom, the rustle of leaves in the wind. {{I appreciate I may not sound like myself. I'm breaking a promise to be here, so perhaps I'm not even myself at all. Perhaps I only think that I am.}}

Rosa heard it now, the familiar voice beneath the buzzing consonants. Little cause for ease, given all else. The Empress had no need to creep about her own palace, much less gain ingress via the balcony – itself no small feat. Wrapping the bedclothes about herself, she rose.

"What do you want?"

Steel shone in the dark. Rosa cast about for something, anything, that might serve as weapon. The sword remained at middle guard. Between that and her hooded robes, the Empress resembled a sepulchral guardian, struck from stone to stand watch over a tomb.

{{This sword used to stand for something. For some, it was hope. For others, honour. What hope I have is spent. The rest I give to you, so that what remains of my honour may mean something. It can never make up for what my pride has done to your people. But I'd have this sword stand for hope again, one last time.}}

"I don't understand."

{{Viktor Droshna recruits an army from the dead of Eskavord. Your wife and your friends mean to stop him. I'd help them if I could, but I cannot. And so I offer my sword. May it shine for you as it once did for me. That in bringing hope to others, it might again find its fire.}}

Melanna scabbarded the sword and held it out.

Rosa stared blankly, racing emotion dispersing sleep's vestige. Grim satisfaction that her accusations about Viktor had found validation. Sorrow that her oldest friend had fallen so. Fear for Sevaka ...

Determination most of all.

She took the sword. Lighter than she'd expected. "Eskavord is three days' ride, and on bad roads. Even if I leave at once ... What if I can't get there?"

{{Have faith.}}

Rosa snorted. Divinities had never offered her comfort, only pain. "In whom?"

{{In the end ...? In the end, I don't know that it matters. We have to trust to ourselves, and trust the deed that follows. Glory in victory. Fortitude in defeat. Honour always. Whatever the price.}}

"I don't understand."

Melanna drew back her hood. Amber eyes glinted beneath a brow of knotted stems. A mane of briars and black roses spilled across her shoulders. Where the cloak parted, it revealed neither flesh nor raiment, only woven frond and willow-stem in the likeness of woman's form.

Blood rushing cold, Rosa stumbled back. "What happened to you?"

Thorn-touched cheeks twitched. {{I am Empress no more. A greater realm calls me to be its queen and I must go, else all shall be lost.}}

Rosa blinked. Though she comprehended little of what she beheld, she readily grasped the cause. Not so long ago, a similar fate had almost been hers. A pact with the divine that asked nothing in barter but one's humanity. A Queen of Thorns, where Rosa had so nearly been Queen of the Dead. And for the first time, she wondered what other common ground they might have known. At Govanna Field, her humanity slipping away, Rosa had thought only of retribution. Melanna Saranal, the treacherous Empress of the East, had chosen a harder path.

"I'm sorry." The words were useless, but she felt bound to offer them.

Parting the drapes, Melanna reached for the balcony door. {{Farewell, Lady Orova.}}

Rosa started forward, urged by sensation she couldn't name. "For the past. For the harm levied against my countryfolk. For betrayal . . . " She swallowed, the words hard for all their necessity. "You have my forgiveness . . . For whatever it's worth."

Melanna halted, frozen in moonlight. Lips the texture of cracked leaves formed a smile. Then she passed beneath the drapes and into the night.

Rosa, no more than a pace behind, found the balcony empty of all save a discarded cloak, and black petals dancing on the wind.

In the distance, a clock chimed midnight.

Lunandas, 19th Day of Dawntithe

In the end, it may not be hope of victory that drives you to fight, but the knowledge that doing nothing is worse than defeat.

from the Saga of Hadar Saran

Sixty-Three

The marchers didn't belong in the mists. A hundred or so in all, they moved with purpose and at speed, unhindered by those of their number who wore blindfolds, or were carried. Shields and tabards were not the mournful whitish-green of the etravia parting about them, but retained an echo of ephemeral colour. Hunter's green and King's Blue. As Calenne drew closer, leaving the becalmed vortex and the horror of Revekah's pyre behind, she recognised a face at the column's head.

"Josiri?" She hurried through the etravia, disbelieving the evidence of her senses, but desperate to attract his attention. "Josiri! Can you hear me?"

He marched on, his gait awkward in armour she'd never seen him wear, companions gathered close. Calenne recognised other faces now. Sevaka. Altiris. Kurkas. The knight who'd brought her to the pyre. All following a black-garbed figure striding beneath an unfurled banner of sword and eagle, a firestone lantern burning atop its pole. Calenne knew her as well, though the meeting had been brief. Apara Rann. She looked as though she wished she were somewhere else.

Why were they here? Where were they going?

Calenne quickened, her vaporous form drifting over wall and debris until she was foursquare before the column's line of march.

"Josiri!"

Still the marchers strode on, strode *through* her. Ephemeral flesh contesting a space held only by anchorless soul. Overcome with nausea, Calenne dragged herself from their path and back to the roadside. As she did, an unfamiliar marcher moaned, staring this way and that before breaking ranks and bolting for a crumbling doorway. The knight's file-mates caught her, blindfolded her, and dragged her back to the column.

"Otherworld is no place for the living," said the Raven from his perch on a nearby wall.

"Why are they here?" asked Calenne. "What is this?"

He shrugged, eyes on a column already halfway swallowed by the mists. "I'd say they want to be somewhere in something of a hurry. Time and distance don't work the same as in the living realm, not if you know the paths, and dear Apara always had a knack." He tapped his cane on the ground. "As to the 'where', I think you might hazard a guess."

Obvious, in hindsight. "They're going after Viktor."

"So one assumes." The Raven glanced over his shoulder to the smoke of Revekah's pyre, just visible across a building of a style Calenne didn't recognise. "I can't say I rate their chances."

"Then help them."

"I told you, I can't," he snapped. "I made a bargain not to interfere in the ephemeral world. If I break that pledge, there'll be worse to fret about than Viktor's trifling sins."

This time, Calenne heard something else beneath the anger. She pressed on, voice thick with contempt. "To think, I used to be afraid of you. All those tales about the Keeper of the Dead. I slept with lanterns lit when I was little, afraid you'd snatch me into the shadows." That was before Zanya and her mother's death, of course. The Black Knight Viktor Akadra had haunted her dreams thereafter. "I wish I'd known then that mighty Raven was nothing more than a frightened old man in a crumpled coat!"

He sprang down from the wall, gait hunched and angular, the after-image of an abyssal corvine shape again flickering in the mist behind. The air shook with shrieking voices. "Then perhaps you should be scared of him again!"

He thrust his spread hands towards her in a shove. For all that it never made contact, it *hurt*. Already fraying, Calenne sought something, anything, to keep her being anchored and whole. She found nothing. Strand by strand, she came unravelled.

Her last sight was of the column's trailing end vanishing into the mists.

*

Josiri spread his hand against the tree and doubled over, spluttering as damp air filled his lungs. For all that the mists were no less prevalent in the living realm than in Otherworld, they felt somehow more whole-some. Or perhaps it was simply that the world no longer shifted and blurred. Part of him wished it did. All the better to hide the horror that Eskavord had become.

Seven years since he'd been here last. Seven years of avoiding his ancestral home. His dukedom. Beyond sparse trees, the fire-blackened ruin of Eskavord's north wall was just about visible – the mist granting shape even under black, oppressive skies. Its palisade had long since gone to ash, but the stones beneath still stood proud. The space between remained as grey as at Josiri's last glimpse, the carpet of ash undisturbed by winds that never found real purchase in the Southshires' newest Forbidden Place.

He righted himself and stared southwest to where Branghall's ruins waited beyond the veil of mist. So many years and so many leagues trav-elled, and yet so little had changed. Perhaps nothing had changed since he'd parted from Viktor at the foot of Drannon Tor, he bound for Tressia, and Viktor to an exile's life. Strange to regard such days as happier times.

The bobbing lanterns of what only the generous might call an army formed up beneath the gold and green banner and the circle of light from its lantern. Ninety knights, a half-dozen hearthguard. Two politicians and a thief turned assassin, turned spymaster. Most were pale from the passage of Otherworld. Josiri had been fortunate, having walked its paths in Ashana's company; Altiris and Kurkas for less auspicious reasons. For all others save Apara, it had been a new and unpleasant experience, marked by haunted expressions and shaking limbs. Even Essamere's valour had limits.

Infantry all, for no one had wanted to trust a horse within the mists. He hoped it'd be enough.

It wasn't that the Council weren't convinced Viktor was a threat. Quite the opposite – they were frozen in fear of what he might do if provoked. Better to let the storm blow out and calm return. Only … Josiri knew Viktor too well to believe that was a possibility. Horror was brewing in the Southshires – the only question that remained was whether it would be Tressia or the Hadari Empire that would suffer first.

The usurpers, or the ancient enemy? Ironic then that Josiri, who as little as seven years before would have happily watched both drown in shadow, found himself charged with their deliverance.

"Night already?" Sevaka, like Josiri himself, cut an unfamiliar figure in borrowed armour. She wore an Essamere tabard unearned, save through Zephan's insistence. "We've not been marching that long."

"Time runs different in the mists, but it's not night." Apara's pensive eyes stared southward. "It's the Dark. This is how it was after Davenwood. He had me bring him here, last time . . . "

She twisted away, the thought unfinished.

Josiri caught Sevaka's worried glance and drew closer to Apara. "You should go," he murmured. "You've done enough. Leave the rest to us."

"Could you?" Apara replied.

He glanced down at his tabard, at the golden phoenix embroidered on King's Blue. The phoenix he hated, and wore only to remind himself of what he owed Viktor, good and bad. One way or another, the day would clear all debts. "I have to finish this."

Steel crept into grey eyes. "So do I."

Leaving the sisters to contemplate an uncertain future, Josiri rejoined his knot of hearthguard – or what remained of it – all of them burdened with lanterns and wrapped bundles slung across their backs. Viara and Beckon stood in hushed conversation off to one side. Jarrock and Kelver stared at the growing Essamere shield wall. Brass made gloomy appraisal of Eskavord's distant wall. Altiris nodded pensively at his approach. Only Kurkas, hunch-shouldered though he was from a long march he'd not been fit for in the first place, seemed at ease. But then, he wore only leather where the others wore full armour – a sign of flagging reserves.

"Looks like this is it, sah."

"You've a site picked out for what we discussed?"

"Over there," Altiris pointed to a low hummock on the treeline, far to the east, and halfway to Eskavord's walls. "Brass says it's a good spot."

Brass grunted. "Brass said it *might* be a good spot."

"You really think he'll meet with you, lord?" asked Viara.

"I know I have to *try*."

"I should be with you," said Altiris. "There's nothing I can do over there."

Josiri laid a hand on Altiris' shoulder and met him eye to eye. The lad had come a long way in a few short weeks, more than worthy of the Trelan name, but he'd plenty of lessons ahead. "I've Essamere to keep me safe, and Phoenixes should stand together. If I've learned nothing else, I've learned that." Lowering his voice, he addressed the other fear lingering in Altiris' eyes. "We'll find her. I'm not losing any more family today, do you hear me?"

Altiris nodded. "Yes ... Father."

Satisfied that warning had hit home alongside reassurance, Josiri drew back, careful to meet each Phoenix's gaze in turn. "We've seen some times, haven't we?"

Words dried on his tongue. Anastacia would have known what to say. Something irreverent, insulting, but with affection beneath. The hole in his heart grew a size larger.

"I feel I should say something, but I can't find the words. Just know that I'm proud." Moved by uncertain emotion, Josiri held out his hand. "Thank you for everything, Vladama."

Kurkas gripped his hand tight and nodded, a little of his Raven-may-care insouciance returning. "Go on, get. Don't want me to start crying, do you?"

He didn't look like a man about to weep, but then he probably didn't have the energy to spare. Not that there was any point telling Kurkas to sit this out. Josiri stared north through the mists, summoning to mind the muddy field outside Zanya where his mother's dreams had died. He and Kurkas had fought on opposite sides in that battle. Eskavord's razing might have felt like it only yesterday, but Zanya seemed impossibly far in the past.

A cry of alarm drew his attention west, to a scattering of dark figures emerging from Davenwood's deeper reaches.

Altiris started forward, hand on his sword. "Trouble?"

Josiri shook his head, the newcomers close enough for him to recognise King's Blue shields bearing the numeral of the 14th. Keldrov's old regiment. "I don't think so. Get in position."

Leaving no chance for reply, he headed back through the sparse trees, skirting the Essamere line to greet the newcomers and beckoning Zephan and Sevaka to his side. He spotted a familiar face soon after, garbed in armour and cloth not worn for years.

"Arlanne? This is a day for old uniforms."

"Lord Trelan. Master Tanor. Governor Orova." Governor Keldrov offered a weary salute, well matched to a face that had aged a decade in a few short weeks. "Tell me the Council's sent more than this?"

Sevaka snorted.

"The Council sent nothing at all," said Zephan, another soul who'd aged badly in the newborn year. "This was all we could gather."

Josiri had taken the new arrivals to be the 14th's vanguard. Fresh appraisal of battered and bloodied faces – and paucity of numbers – corrected that impression. He saw barely thirty, and nary an officer among them. "What happened?"

"We went in when the skies turned black. Lord Droshna was waiting." Keldrov's eyes lost their focus. "A few Drazina, and rank upon rank of clay soldiers, the Dark seething beneath their skin. He calls them Ocranza – like the guardian statues – and it's not unfitting. They're not as bad to fight as if they were kraikons, but they're bad enough."

"Blessed Lunastra," murmured Zephan. "Can they be killed?"

"Yes. We found that out the hard way. That skin of theirs looks tough, but it's nothing to steel. I don't know that they feel pain, but they're like foundry constructs. Break the shell and the magic escapes. Then some of our own they ... they just ... " She shook her head, voice fading as a faraway look came into her troubled eyes. "They turned on their comrades. Tore them apart from the inside just as the lines closed. It was a slaughter."

Josiri scowled, the description too similar to the influence Viktor had wielded over Apara, himself ... Lumestra knew how many. That he no longer felt the shadow save in absent memories didn't mean it wouldn't return, if Viktor chose. He touched a hand to the pendant of Saint Selna hanging at his neck. Guardian of Lost she might have been, but the silver mattered more. Each of them wore a similar token, blessed that morning by the serenes of the Highmount Church – something to cheat the influence of Viktor's shadow, or so Josiri hoped.

But Keldrov's report offered good news alongside. Proof that Viktor's Ocranza were no hardier than Calenne's clay form, and leagues apart from Anastacia's porcelain body. A handful like Anastacia would have slaughtered every soldier he'd brought from the north. But then

Anastacia had been unique, not just for her serathi spirit, but for the craftsmanship of her doll's creation. No stolen soul and patchwork body could ever be her equal. An imperfect army for a misguided cause.

"What are his numbers?" asked Sevaka.

"We gave good account of ourselves before ..." Keldrov scowled. "Maybe five hundred of these Ocranza, and fifty Drazina – at least, that I saw."

Worse than they'd hoped for. Better than they'd feared. "Are your soldiers fit to fight?" asked Josiri.

Earnestness returned to haggard features. "We can do no other."

"Form up behind my lot," said Zephan. "We'll bear the brunt, and look to you for support."

"Agreed." Keldrov raised a hand. "14th!"

King's Blue peeled off towards the thin shield wall. Keldrov lingered, her troubled gaze directed towards Eskavord. "Don't let this be for nothing. We've ..." She tailed off. "Josiri, I need ... I have to ... I ..."

Hand on her brow, she fell silent, pained expression a clue to burdened soul. Josiri, who'd earlier struggled for words, more than understood. Keldrov had been Viktor's staunchest supporter in recent years.

"You're not responsible for what he's done, Arlanne," Josiri said softly.

She nodded, her furrowed brow suggesting she wanted to say more. Instead, she walked away as one on the point of collapse. Sevaka watched her go, brow furrowed and eyes troubled, her manner that of one trying to pin down a stray thought. A feeling Josiri had known all too well of late.

"You still want to talk to him?" Zephan's steady rumble dragged Josiri's attention back to the matter in hand. "The 14th was at full strength. Izack kept it so in case our Thrakkian neighbours made trouble. A thousand swords, gone. He'll break you in half and not even blink."

"How confident are you in the alternatives?" asked Josiri.

He offered no reply.

Josiri stared bleakly at Eskavord's empty north gateway. "Then let's get this over with."

"Viktor! Will you speak with me, brother?"

Viktor was waiting on a restless horse at the north gateway when

Josiri's voice rang out. He watched as the other closed to within fifty paces of the gate, twice as far again from the Essamere banner and its swarm of lanterns beneath the ragged trees. Josiri the traitor, come to barter and hector as he always did. His strength lay in wearing others down.

But still . . .

Hope remained that perhaps Josiri had recognised the wrongness of his stance. Nothing could forgive Calenne's death, but the rest? For all he pretended otherwise, Josiri was a spiritual man and others would easily have twisted that to their own ends. Had he come to his senses, now Anastacia was gone? That possibility tempted Viktor to rare hope. Family should be together, and Josiri *was* family. He proclaimed as much, even now.

"Viktor! Will you speak with me?"

Viktor stared down the rubble of the ruined street to the Ocranza standing silently in the mist, awaiting the nudge of will that would loose them to battle.

He felt Drazina and others nearby, or more precisely the specks of shadow with which he'd quieted their troubles. Some fought his influence, though never enough to be wholly free. No matter. They were a temporary solution, while Sidara raised enough Ocranza for his needs. Keldrov had inflicted heavy losses before he'd brought her to heel, the southern approach littered with bodies of flesh and clay. But with Otherworld open to him, such losses were easily replenished.

Yes. It was worth the risk. After all, what risk could there truly be? With old limitations cast aside, one man alone was of no threat. If nothing else, talking bought time for Sidara to draw forth new soldiers. She'd no need of his presence, not with Constans and Tzila at her side.

The matter settled, he rode for the gate.

"He's actually going for it," murmured Kurkas. "And alone, too."

Lying prone a short distance behind, Altiris fought the urge to rise up and see for himself, but one set of eyes – well, eye – above the hummock and its thin bushes was already a risk. Not much of one, as their lanterns were darkened so as not to give them away, but even that would have been too much. Bad enough to know that they were much closer to Josiri and Lord Droshna than to the Essamere lines.

The only clue Altiris had to his fellow Phoenixes' positions lay in the small sounds. Viara lay somewhere to his right, her breathing uneven as she sought to control fear. Brass a little further to the left, sounding like a beast at slumber. The others lay further back, awaiting the signal, muttered prayers and the scuff of knee and elbow betraying nervousness.

Altiris' veins coursed hot and cold, anticipation vying with apprehension. Hope of being reunited with Sidara contested the hollow dread that it was already impossible. One road led to joy, the other to impenetrable darkness. And so he counted away the pulse of his heart, trying not to think about how every breath drew in wisps of ash from the ground beneath him, and waited.

The hoofbeats slowed. Viktor became a dark, armoured shape, framed by a cloak of writhing shadow and his unshaven face void of expression. He looked . . . empty. Josiri could think of no other word to describe it. Even imprisoned in the clocktower, there'd yet been a trace of his friend. Now? Though Viktor's features were the same, they belonged to a stranger. Or maybe it was easier to think of him thus. Conscience bore a stranger's death easier than a friend's.

"Viktor."

"Josiri." Viktor made no move to dismount. "You wanted to speak. I'm here."

His tone was measured, calm. But then Viktor had never wanted for reason, even at his most unreasonable. Josiri set his free hand on the pommel of his sword and drew his lantern close, guilt at Viktor's shying from the light eased away by memory of recent deeds.

"I wanted to give you chance to explain." He circled round to the south, his back towards Eskavord. "One last chance."

Viktor mirrored the movement, his horse's hooves rousing sprays of ash. A rumbling, snorting laugh echoed through the mists. "And here was I, thinking you'd found your senses. You know the Republic cannot stand without me."

"Then perhaps it shouldn't stand at all." Josiri halted, his back westward to Branghall's hidden ruins. "Everything you've done—"

Viktor glared and leaned low over his horse's neck. "Everything *I've* done? You betrayed me to the shadowthorns! When the demons of

Fellhallow wreak slaughter on the Eastshires, will that be my fault as well? When our cities burn and the populace are taken for slaves? Will you cling to vacillating principle and blame me for the loss? I'm trying to save us. Can't you see that?"

Cold stung the back of Josiri's throat. He felt *something* whisper across his soul. It spoke with a voice like his own, and yet different. Urging, nudging. Viktor's shadow, not quite held at bay by Saint Selna's pendant, but revealed by it. Or perhaps he only recognised it because he'd been looking? Because he knew Viktor would seek to twist him as he had before?

Did it even matter, when so much of what Viktor said was true? There was no guarantee Melanna wouldn't seek reprisals. Such had been the way of Republic and Empire for generations. Blow and counterblow. Revenge and retaliation. The past was no longer relevant. The future was everything.

Weariness hung heavier than ever. Arguments marshalled in hope of changing Viktor's mind bled away into the mist. A part of Josiri knew his malaise to be the work of Viktor's shadow, but only a small part. The rest yearned to *believe*.

"It *is* a last chance," said Viktor, "but that opportunity belongs not to me, but to you. I'm prepared to forgive you, brother. The Republic still needs you. I still need you. Help me save our people."

Leaning low in the saddle, he held out his hand.

"That's it," hissed Kurkas. "Get in position."

Phoenixes scrambled to their feet, the scrape of boot on ash joined by the whisper of arrows drawn from quivers. Altiris hung back, letting others find vantage upon the hummock. As with Jarrock and Beckon, he'd never learnt an archer's trade. Not like Viara, who'd indulged target shooting as only a highblood could, or Kelver, who refused to admit where he'd honed his craft. As for Brass, the retired poacher? The terror of the Akadra estates was in a league of his own.

Taking care to keep low, Altiris followed them onto the summit and knelt at Kurkas' side.

As promised, Lord Droshna's back was to the hummock, haloed in the drifting mist by light from Josiri's lantern. Altiris scarcely believed the cold calculation of Josiri's plan. Hard enough to lure a man out under terms of truce while all the while manoeuvring him into an archer's sights, but when that man was your brother? Altiris hated Lord Droshna almost as much as he feared him – had done since the night of Anastacia's murder – but knew with unflinching certainty that his own loathing was nothing to his adoptive father's.

Or perhaps it wasn't hate at all, but love? Whatever else had occurred, Lord Droshna was no longer the man he'd been. Death was mercy as much as justice, and love roused death as readily as hate. What if roles were exchanged, and it wasn't Lord Droshna framed in lantern light, but Josiri ... or Sidara? What if their deaths would save thousands? Would love or hate accomplish the deed better?

Altiris didn't know, and prayed to Lumestra that he'd never find out.

The creak of bowstrings married with effort's exhalation. Silvered arrowheads glinted with reflected lantern light. The light and safety of the Essamere shield wall felt worlds away.

"Wait for it," murmured Kurkas, his cautioning hand barely a shadow in the darkness. "Wait for the signal ... "

Josiri stared at Viktor's hand, not gauntleted, as he'd first thought, but armoured in ridged, writhing shadow. Beneath, he glimpsed charred skin, still molten with daylight. In the same moment, he felt a little of that daylight's warmth. Its brightness. Not from Viktor, but from within. Only for a moment, but long enough to remember what had brought him back to unhappy Eskavord. The betrayal greater than all others. Weariness yielded to anger, and in turn drove the shadow from his soul.

He stepped away. "Why did you kill Ana?"

Viktor drew back his hand and sat high in the saddle once more. "She left me no choice."

Josiri shook his head. "You see? There's that sentiment again. Never you to blame, always someone else."

"She meant to kill me!" He held out his hands, the shadow hissing away to reveal the full horror of his wounds. "I'm still burning, and you call her the victim?"

"And how many had you already murdered when Anastacia found you?" said Josiri. "I've been to Duskvigil Church, Viktor. I've seen your handiwork. Shalamoh warned me there was nothing left of you worth saving. Lumestra help me, but he was right!"

"Josiri—"

"You shouldn't have killed her, Viktor. I might have listened otherwise." Anger faded, leaving emptiness behind. "I'm not here as your friend, your brother, or on behalf of the Republic. I'm not here to talk you round, nor offer redemption. I made you a promise six years ago. I made another yesterday, on the cliff where Ana died. You've made me so many promises over the years, and kept none. This is me keeping mine. I'm here as your executioner, Viktor."

He raised the lantern.

Arrows whistled through the mist.

One clattered off Viktor's left pauldron and spiralled away. Another missed entirely, whipping past Josiri's shoulder into the darkness. Staggered by the first arrow, Viktor twisted in his saddle, searching for the source.

Then came the third. Brass' arrow, for certainty. A poacher cared not if the game was spooked, so long as he knew where it would run.

Viktor roared and slumped across his horse's neck. A pale shaft protruded between armoured plates halfway between hip and left armpit. The steed sprang away towards Eskavord, Viktor barely half in the saddle, great clouds of ash rising behind.

"No!" yelled Josiri.

But Viktor was already gone from sight.

Disgusted, Josiri trudged back towards the Essamere lines. They'd never had much of a chance, but that didn't ease his disquiet at the failure. Poor odds were better than none at all, and theirs were about to get a good deal worse.

Apara met him halfway, her face pinched and her voice wary. "I saw him fall. Is he dead?"

Josiri shook his head as the first footfalls sounded. The tremor of soldiers on the march. He stared back towards a gateway suddenly thick with activity.

"No. So now we do it the hard way."

Sixty-Four

The Ocranza came forth in a line wider and deeper than the lantern-lit Essamere ranks. Neither the lockstep of a single mind, nor the shambling of witless thralls. Warriors with bodies of cracked stone floating on a sea of Dark, wearing no raiment but the embrace of shadow. Weapons were the harvest of old battlefields, swords alongside axes and war hammers, as many of foreign make as Tressian – testament to the Southshires' troubled past. A few shields had the stylised sword and hill of long-abandoned Cragwatch. Most bore neither blazon nor crest, their rotting planks smeared with grave-loam. No banners. No pride. Just a dark tide come to drown a defiant shore.

But no Viktor. Not yet. Standing beneath the limp Essamere banner, a wall of locked shields reaching left and right and what remained of his friends beside him, Josiri clung to the hope that even now his oldest friend was bleeding his last into Eskavord's ash.

"Blessed Lunastra," said Zephan. "*This* is the future Lord Droshna would offer the Republic?"

Murmurs elsewhere in the Essamere ranks echoed their grandmaster's disgust.

"Not the one he intended," Josiri replied. "But Viktor's intent never mattered much."

Zephan grunted. "I suppose it's too much to hope that they need lanterns to see?"

No lanterns dotted the Ocranza line, whereas every third knight in Essamere's rear ranks held one high, their shields grounded at their feet.

"Viktor's sensitive to the light," said Josiri. "Maybe they are too."

"I thought he'd have more," said Sevaka.

There were still hundreds, more than the combined forces of Essamere and the 14th's survivors, but not desperately so. "We can thank Arlanne for that." He glanced behind, past the lanterns and grim faces of the second rank to where the knot of King's Blue, Keldrov at their fore, waited among the trees with swords drawn. "But this can't be everything."

Apara, little more than a shadow with lanterns blazing about her, nodded. "No Drazina."

"Maybe they've abandoned him?" asked Zephan.

Josiri shuddered, the memory of the shadow's caress returning. He'd expected it, had armoured himself with blessed silver to thwart its influence, and still had almost been overcome. "He won't let them. They'll fight for him whether they want to or not." Did that include Sidara? Her light offered advantages others didn't possess. She'd have resisted, and even before his madness Viktor had shown little tolerance for defiance. "Either way, we hold to the plan. Master Tanor holds the east, I the west. We break the first wave, go in hard, and take the fight to Viktor."

Easier said than done, but wasn't that ever the way?

Bleak thoughts threatening to overwhelm him, Josiri pushed his way clear of the shield wall.

For a long moment, he beheld the advancing line, thicker and deeper than his own. The wall of expressionless faces. Then he turned to face those who'd followed him to Eskavord's ashen field. So many faces so much younger than his own. All of them looking as Josiri had felt at Zanya, at Davenwood, in the Hayadra Grove with vranakin howling around him and the city falling into mist ... as he felt right now. At Zanya, his mother's confidence had fanned fear to flame. Viktor and Calenne had achieved the same at Davenwood. In the Hayadra Grove, Anastacia's divine glory had promised victory where words could not.

But words were all Josiri had.

"I don't want to make a big deal about this, but the future turns on what comes next." He offered a wry smile, and took heart from the ripple of amusement. "Lord Droshna's no longer our protector, our champion, our hero ... our friend. He's a rabid wolf, lost to the Dark. If we don't stop him here, today, his madness will consume everything."

He swept his gaze along the line, meeting every pair of eyes that would meet his.

"Yes, we're outnumbered! But so was the last army to fight for the Southshires, and we sent the Hadari running for the border!" Sentiment that had come hard earlier now flowing free, Josiri thrust his sword towards the Ocranza line, the reflected confidence of Essamere feeding his own. "We know they can be sent back to the mists! We know it's a mercy! So let's remind Lord Droshna what it is to be Essamere! What it is to fight for the Southshires! For the Republic!"

"Until Death!" shouted Zephan.

"Until Death!" Hilts hammered against shields, the drumbeat marking the syllables.

"Until Death!"

Impossibly, the chant grew louder. *"Until Death!"*

Altiris lay prone on the hummock's crest beside Kurkas, praying fervently that none of the Ocranza glanced his way. Most had already marched past, blocking the retreat to the Essamere shield wall, barely visible beyond.

"All right, sah," murmured Kurkas. "You're in charge ... What do you want to do?"

Altiris glanced into the darkness that concealed the other Phoenixes. Between injuries and sheer bulk, neither Kurkas nor Brass was good for the sprint. The others might have made it, but Phoenixes stood together.

But that didn't mean they were out of the fight. The Ocranza had passed, their shields towards Essamere, and their backs exposed. Brass, Kelver and Viara each had a full quiver. It'd call down trouble, sure as sunrise, but it was better than doing nothing.

"Brass, Kelver, Boronav," Altiris hissed. "Get up here."

Neither battle cry nor challenge heralded the Ocranza charge, neither clarion, nor drum. There was only the thunder of feet, and shadow thickening in the mists.

"Steady!" Zephan's shout echoed from the east. "Steady!"

Josiri leaned into his shield, sword levelled across its rim, the press of bodies claustrophobic and comforting. Hungry strides devoured the ashen ground between. Lantern light gave shape to unfinished faces and smoky eyes. Clay platelets floating on seas of shadowy flesh.

Some Ocranza clasped swords in textbook guard, others whirled them high, or dragged blades behind to furrow the ash. For every shield braced and levelled, another hung by its straps. What had begun as a line grew ragged. This was no army, but a mob, untrained and untested. And no mob could beat the glory of Essamere – not without far greater numbers than Viktor brought to bear.

Hope, distant for days, rekindled.

"Death and honour!" shouted Josiri.

"Death and honour!"

The leading edge of the charge crashed home.

Josiri's shield shook beneath an axe blow. He thrust, steel hissing over the upper rim. Brief resistance. A crunch of clay. His shield sagged under a body's weight, and the Ocranza scraped clear. Its body fell at his feet, no longer a warrior of stone and shadow, but a shell of empty clay, cracked and soulless.

Then shadow blurred before Josiri's shield, and he'd attention for nothing but survival.

He fell into old patterns. The thrust of the sword, the twist to free the blade. Trusting to one's shield, and to the shield of one's neighbours. Lessons drilled for long ago Zanya, and little atrophied by passing years. He fought on through the screams, through the grunt of effort and dull thump of blade finding flesh. He blotted out the rising stench of blood and sweat.

Brittle the Ocranza might have been, but they were strong. Tireless. Every blow set Josiri's shield shuddering. Every block or parry jarred the bones at wrist and elbow, threatening to rip the sword clean from his hand. Every attack was a brutal flurry that ceased only when clay flesh was pierced, and the shadow hissed free.

But most unnerving of all was that the Ocranza made no sound. No cry of exultation to accompany triumph, nor pain to mark their passing.

The knight to Josiri's right fell writhing, armour rent and an axe buried in her ribs. Ocranza hurled themselves at the breach. Another knight strode into the gap to remake the wall, shield braced and lantern discarded. He went down, blood beneath his helm and an Ocranza kneeling on his chest. The attacker's sword stabbed down again and again, silencing the gurling cries.

Arrows hissed through the mist and thumped home into the press of backlit bodies. An Ocranza collapsed, shadow hissing away across the skies. Another staggered, easy meat for Grandmaster Tanor's thrust. Altiris watched it all uneasy, desperate to act.

Brass grunted and reached for another arrow.

"This could be going worse," said Beckon.

"Don't say that out loud," replied Kurkas. "You never know who might be listening."

"Reckon the gods care?"

"Who's talking about the gods? Plenty of nasties around here without them involved."

Bowstrings hummed. Altiris, his nerves increasingly jarred, didn't see arrows strike home. The others knew their business, and the darkness felt closer and more oppressive with every ash-laden breath. As if he were being watched, and didn't know it. Just because he saw nothing didn't mean there was nothing there. He could almost *feel* something, creeping closer.

"Quiver's empty," murmured Brass. "What now?"

Altiris dragged his attention back to the lights of Essamere.

What now indeed? Though the Ocranza were greatly thinned, they still outnumbered Essamere to overbearing degree. But still . . . the battle was turning, and for the better. And even if it weren't, there wasn't much they could achieve without arrows.

The sensation of being watched returned, stronger than ever.

"Group up," Altiris murmured. "We're heading back to the others."

"No!" cried a familiar voice. "Wait!"

Darkness pulsed at Altiris' shoulder. He twisted aside, blind grab closing about a throat. Pivoting at the waist, he heaved the interloper across his shoulder and dropped him in the ash. Before the other could move, he had the point of his sword against his throat and a foot on his chest.

"Jarrock?" breathed Altiris, eyes never leaving his captive. "I think we might risk a little light. Brass? Boronav? Let me know if anything comes our way."

Light from a coaxed lantern spilled across the hummock. Just enough to give shape to the assembled Phoenixes and the spluttering bundle at Altiris' feet.

"Stay your hand, dear Devn," said Constans, his hands outspread. "A friend am I."

"A friend?" Kurkas limped closer. "I ought to cut your bloody heart out!"

The shield wall buckled inwards. Ocranza flooded into the gap. A war hammer crashed against Josiri's shield. The impact drove him back, arm numbed and footing treacherous.

"Close the line!" he bellowed. "Close up!"

His gut soured, knowing it was already too late. A gap two shields wide became three, became four. The Ocranza surged into the breach. Josiri heard screams behind, and knew knights in the second rank were dying.

And then Apara was in the gap, sword darting without thought to her own defence. An Ocranza collapsed, shadow hissing from a wound in its misshapen chest. She shouldered another aside and thrust down.

She shrieked as an axe thudded into her back. Flinched as a sword cut deep into her arm. Staggered beneath a war hammer's merciless strike. But still Apara stood – still she fought – her garb torn, but her eternal flesh bloodless and unyielding. Only when the tide of Ocranza ebbed did she sink to her knees.

"*Until Death!*"

Hunter's green shields pressed forward, sealing the gap. The assault ebbed, attackers' numbers run thin in their attempt to breach the wall.

Gauntleted hands dragged Apara clear. As the wall rebuilt, Josiri gratefully yielded his place to an unwearied knight and pushed his way to her.

She knelt in the ash, limbs shaking but the wounds of the war hammer's strike already healing. Bone crackled as her right hand twisted a lolling left back into place. Black blood trickled across her fingers and dissipated to silvered vapour.

Marking Josiri's approach, she shook her head. "I'll be all right."

Dropping his useless shield, he helped her stand. "More than 'all right'. You just saved us all."

Constans squirmed and went still as Altiris' sword point grazed his throat.

"What do you want?" said Altiris in a bitter whisper.

"To help." Tone and expression pleaded.

Kurkas squatted and made meticulous search of lad's clothing. He tossed two daggers onto the ash. "You believe that rot?"

Altiris shook his head. Constans *sounded* genuine, but he'd done so before, all in service of a lie. "Not a word."

Kurkas tugged a third dagger from Constans' boot and tucked it into his own belt. "You want to do it, or shall I?"

No clue in Kurkas' voice to tell whether he meant it. Could be he didn't know himself. Constans' betrayal remained too fresh for Altiris to untangle his own feelings, let alone another's. And Kurkas had almost died.

"He's all yours," he said, his eyes on Constans.

Kurkas drew his sword.

"No!" yelped Constans, his eyes wide. "I know where Sidara is! She needs your help."

The claim sent a jolt clean through Altiris' spine and deep into his heart, just as Constans had surely meant it to. He exchanged a glance with Kurkas. "You believe him?"

"My aching back aside, he's Droshna's creature. Be fools to listen."

"It's—" Constans lowered his voice as Altiris gave a warning jab of his sword. "It's true, I swear. Viktor shared his shadow with her as he did me, but it's different. She looks the same, but it's like there's a piece of him behind her eyes."

Altiris grimaced, awash with churning, helpless horror. But grisly memories of the Merrow's lair held him back from believing. "Sidara suddenly matters to you? Enough to betray your father?"

"She's my sister!"

"Like that's mattered for years," said Kurkas.

Altiris stepped away. "Make it quick, captain."

"Yes, sah!"

"Viktor chose her over me," said Constans, breathless. "I wanted us all to be a family, but as soon as he had her, I didn't matter any longer. Even in the Dark, she outshines me."

The boy swallowed, eyes bright with humiliation. A pitiful, selfish confession from a broken, jealous soul. It made so much sense of Constans' contradictory behaviour. He so wanted to be loved, to be valued. Of course he'd found that under Droshna's guardianship . . . or he'd thought he had. Even now, it wasn't clear whether Constans wanted to help Sidara, or merely depose her from his rightful place in his father's affections. Not that it mattered much.

"Now that, I believe." Kurkas sheathed his sword. "What do you want to do?"

As if there was any choice. "Viara? Do you have a spare bowstring?" Catching it cleanly, Altiris dragged Constans to his feet and bound his wrists tight. Every other moment, he shot pensive glance towards the battle. "I'm going after Sidara. I have to. Vladama, you'll take the others to Lord Trelan."

Kurkas brought his heels together. "Certainly bloody won't, sah."

"Vladama . . ." Altiris abandoned an attempt to meet his gaze. It wasn't the darkness so much as the fact that Kurkas wouldn't meet his in return. The drill sergeant's recourse.

Jarrock grunted. "Lord Trelan said we should stay together."

"And you know what he'd say if he were here," put in Viara.

Altiris searched for help in Kelver and Beckon's faces, and found none. "Sergeant Brass? Talk some sense into them, would you?"

"Like anyone ever listens to me."

Kurkas grinned. "Looks like the matter's settled, don't it?"

With a last glance towards the lights of Essamere, Altiris admitted defeat. He prodded Constans towards Eskavord. "You want to make things right, now's your chance."

A final welter of blood – a ragged bellow – and Sidara drew the arrow free. She hissed as the bloody silvered head brushed a fingertip. Her shadow's discomfort resonating with Viktor's own, she cast the arrow angrily to the lychfield's ash. Viktor slumped against the church wall, gasping as his shadow's screams finally ceased.

Tzila looked silently on from amid a crowd of motionless Ocranza. Others laboured beside a cart, fashioning clay into bodies that would soon be needed. Drazina set to guard Sidara's work stared outward into the ruins. Constans was nowhere to be seen, as was so often the case when there was work to be done.

Sidara leaned close, visage twisted in concern. "Better, Uncle?"

Viktor nodded. "Thank you."

Pain remained, but pain was nothing to silver's touch. Sensation flooded back, his resurgent shadow joining anew to the subservient slivers he'd sent elsewhere. He was disgusted at how poorly his Ocranza fared. Reflex had hurled them forth, unsupported and untrained, while silver had him blind. He'd treated them like soldiers, when they were not. Not yet. He'd still much to learn, but he'd do so. He had to, were the Republic to be saved.

He didn't need to tell Sidara, of course. She already knew. She'd already seen, written in their shared shadow.

Standing tall, Viktor beheld the waiting Ocranza, the gathered Dark no obstacle to his sight for it was a part of him. A mere two hundred, but they'd serve now he was fit to lead them.

Sidara waved a hand towards the forms waiting to be roused. "Will you need more?"

She swayed, exhaustion of recent hours in lined features and lidded eyes. Viktor longed to grant her rest – she'd laboured so long and so diligently this past day – but he couldn't afford reprieve. Not yet. He set his shadow billowing between them, buttressing her flagging spirit with his own.

"As many as you can, and soon."

Her eyes snapped fully open, dark and lustrous. Lips formed a proud smile even as her cheeks grew a shade more wan. "Yes, Uncle."

Satisfied, Viktor again turned his attention to the Ocranza.

"Come with me."

The words were habit, for they read his intent in shadow more than sound. Viktor felt the anger seething beneath their shadow, the fury that he'd read as flaw in Tzila, when in truth it was a gift. Anger birthed strength. And strength was sorely needed.

But he'd other servants, too. Seeded when the 14th had made doomed assault on Eskavord.

Reaching forth with his shadow, he set them loose.

*

Sevaka was fighting from the second rank when the screams sounded. Not along the shield wall, but *behind*.

Even as she turned, the chime and grunt of desperate fighting broke out. Knights who'd thought themselves safe in the rear ranks found themselves assailed. Not by Ocranza, but by new enemies come howling out of the darkness.

The survivors of the 14th.

"Behind!" Sevaka shouted, her voice already hoarse. "Behind!"

Lanterns blinked out, shattered in their wielders' hands or falling with their slain bodies. Darkness rushed in, sucking life and hope from the mists. Screams found new timbre. The darkness filled with the thunder of running feet. The shield wall, weakened from behind, shuffled back.

Ocranza surged through the gaps, quickening the slaughter. A clash of lines became a contest of individuals – a contest where numbers counted more than skill. It grew steadily more uneven as lanterns died beneath the smothering Dark.

"Essamere!" Sevaka snatched the banner from its bearer's hand and hoisted it high in the failing light. "Rally to me! Essamere!"

She cast around, searching for sign of Josiri or Apara.

The western end of the Essamere line was already dark.

"Essamere!"

A few heeded her now, shields gathering to the banner's lantern. Too few.

Zephan stumbled through the mists, helm gone, armour bloodied and sword dragging behind. He dropped to one knee and sprawled, eyes skyward.

"Zephan!"

As Sevaka started towards him, another figure slunk into the circle of light, her eyes drowning in darkness, tell-tale black spiderwebs creeping outward across her skin.

Bloodied sword still in her grip, Keldrov staggered and clapped her hands to the sides of her head. "Tried to tell you ... warn you ... He wouldn't let me." She screamed and fell to her knees. "All one in the Dark ... All one ... Help me!"

Sevaka stared, soul-sick and numb, remembering how Keldrov had spoken of soldiers of the 14th turning on their own. She'd thought the phrasing odd at the time, but had dismissed it as exhaustion. Viktor had them now – had held them for the moment his thralls would do the most damage.

"I'm sorry."

Sevaka rammed her sword forward – the only help she had to offer. Pained features softening to gratitude, Keldrov slipped sideways into ash and did not rise.

"Zephan?"

The banner now more support than burden, Sevaka knelt beside the dying grandmaster. His eyes darted, sightless. Bloodied lips muttered half-formed words, breathy, faltering. As shields formed a protective ring about them, she let her sword fall and held his hand tight. Even in the face of disaster, some lives mattered more. Another friend slipping away, and she powerless to prevent it.

Above her, shields shuddered beneath fresh blows, the silent Ocranza joined by the corrupted soldiers of the 14th.

"Lunastra," murmured Zephan, left hand tight about his moon pendant. "Blessed . . ."

The prayer faltered on his dying breath, and he was gone.

Leaden, Sevaka rose to her feet. She saw no lanterns beyond the score or so knights ringed about her, only the dead and the dying. Here and there, the fight continued, knots of Essamere with battered shields and bloodied tabards. And in the distance, away towards Eskavord's mist-wreathed gate, a new line of Ocranza marched into view, a tall, shadow-cloaked figure striding at their head.

Viktor.

There'd never been much of a chance, she'd known that from the first. They'd all known. Defiance counted for something. Even to the last. If Viktor wanted her dead, he could do the deed himself.

Arm shaking, she raised the banner high. "Essamere . . . !"

Sevaka faltered, belatedly wondering why she could see Viktor at all if there were no lanterns to light the darkness. The mist was shining, no longer the greenish-white of invasive Otherworld, but pearlescent silver as a brilliant half-moon reclaimed the skies.

She didn't know why she started to laugh, only that she did. Zephan hadn't offered prayer. With his dying breath, he'd beheld a miracle.

A hunter's horn rang out, sonorous and vibrant.

When it faded, there were riders among the mists. Riders clad in darkened scale and cloaks of fallen leaves, their faces hidden by sombre helms fashioned in the likeness of birds. All of them more smoke than substance, a dream roused on winter flame and drawn thither by a favourable wind. All save the two who rode at their head.

One rode a white stag, green fire blazing beneath his antlered helm, and his cloak swirling with the light of captive stars. Ashana's demon, who'd cast down the gates of Ahrad with his starlight spear and set loose the horror of the Avitra Briganda.

Sevaka should have feared him, and perhaps would have done so, but for the woman at his side. A woman who sat astride a steed of shadow and moonlight, who wore an Empress' golden scales and silken robes, but no Empress was she. White hair shone bright beneath the moon.

Sevaka gaped, forlorn laughter lost to wonder. "Rosa?"

Sixty-Five

The hunter's horn rang out. The ground shook.

From Eskavord's gate, Ocranza mustering behind him, Viktor watched with mounting fury as their scattered siblings of the first assault became the riders' prey. Spears dipped and punched home, leaving trails of streaming shadow. Brittle clay shattered under spectral hooves. Essamere – broken and dismayed after the 14th's intervention – gaped wide-eyed at salvation.

Hunter's instinct was all, the riders splitting and reforming like a flock of birds. Where saddles emptied, the steeds dissipated into swirling autumn leaves. No words of exultation rang through the mists, no battle cries, no orders – only the thunder of hooves and the winding of that accursed horn, its antlered bearer dark behind a starlit spear. The Court of Eventide, set loose from myth to besiege the future. And riding at their head, a woman Viktor had once counted among his closest friends . . .

But then Rosa had been the first to betray him, hadn't she?

Even awash in outrage, Viktor knew he should have been afraid. He knew the equerries from myth, and their Huntsman from reports of Ahrad's fall, six years before. He'd faced others of the divine at the close of that war, and knew too well what perils such contests held for ephemeral men.

But instead, what few doubts he yet entertained vanished for ever at the sight.

That Ashana sent her lackeys to Essamere's aid was final proof of Josiri's treachery. But it also offered hope. Even at the height of the Avitra

Briganda, Ashana had withheld the Court of Eventide from aiding the shadowthorns. That she loosed it now betrayed her fear. It proved that Viktor held within his hand the secret to casting down the faithless Empire sheltering beneath her skirts. In her desperation, Ashana offered Viktor certainty. She offered the Republic no mere survival, but a promise of pre-eminency.

All he need do was triumph. No mortal man could have done so, but he was Viktor Droshna, scion of the Dark and redeemer of Malatriant's tainted legacy. There was little beyond him, if he set his shoulder to the wheel and his mind to purpose.

He hefted his claymore aloft. "Forward!"

The bobbing will-o'-the-wisp of the lantern turned sharply and headed south through the ruins. Crouched low behind the remnant of cottage walls, Kurkas beckoned back into the dark.

"Quickly," he hissed.

Boronav's hooded lantern roused to a dull glow. The rest of the Phoenixes gathered to the crossroads corner, Altiris in the lead, the bound Constans sandwiched between Brass and Kelver. All of them on edge, though Kurkas couldn't blame them for that. The nostalgia-laden smell of the mist, the prickle of ash at the back of the throat, the screams of battle echoing from the north. Plenty to set a soul shivering, even without the darkness.

"More Drazina?" Altiris asked, his tone brittle. Again, no surprise. He'd more at stake than any of them.

Kurkas crooked a smile. "You know how it is. Turn over a rock . . ."

The attempt at humour fell flat. Truth was, he wasn't feeling much for funny stuff himself. Every time he thought on what Lord Droshna had done, he wanted to scream.

For all that oath sworn to the Republic said otherwise, a soldier's first loyalty was to his friends. To have your oldest betray so many others? That was hurt enough to match his barely healed wounds. Every step sent fire racing along his spine. More, Kurkas knew the clamminess at his back wasn't sweat alone. The bandages hadn't been meant to stand up to this. He'd not told Altiris. The lad would never have let him be part of if he'd known the truth. But you stood with your friends, or what were you? And now there was a damsel in need of rescue – not that Sidara had ever struck Kurkas as one susceptible to distress. You didn't turn your back on that.

He snorted. Vladama Kurkas, the romantic. Who'd have thought?

"How far now?" he asked Constans.

The boy nodded west. "She's in the old lychfield ... or she was."

Kurkas closed his eye, mapping years-old memories of Eskavord atop imperfect glimpses of its ruins. Reduced to Dark-haunted rubble, one building looked much like another. But they'd not crossed the Grelyt River, so they'd not passed the church. Couldn't be far.

"Queen's Ashes ... " muttered Jarrock.

Kurkas snapped his eye open onto disaster.

Eskavord, drowning in the Dark until that moment, now shone. Moonlit mist gave shape to ashen wastes and crumbled buildings ... to the foursome of a second Drazina patrol advancing down the eastern street.

Shouts and drawn swords betraying mutual recognition, they barrelled forward.

Altiris swore softly and strode into the street proper, midway between a cottage's collapsed wall and a sharp drop into an ash-clogged drainage ditch.

"Phoenixes! To me!"

Kurkas nodded his approval. They had the numbers, and it was as good a spot as any ... Or it would have been, but for shouts erupting from the direction of the first patrol. Others sounded away towards the northern wall.

No life for an honest soldier.

Jarrock and Kelver joined Altiris' thin line.

"It's about to get cosy." Kurkas rolled his shoulder in fruitless attempt to banish its stiffness.

"We're Phoenixes," Altiris said stiffly. "We can handle this."

"No!" said Boronav. "You and Kurkas keep going. We'll draw these others off. Give you your chance."

Brass scowled. "She's got a point."

Altiris rounded on him, furious. "What happened to Phoenixes standing together?"

Kurkas gripped Altiris' shoulder. "They're right, lad. We'll not reach Sidara with this lot on our heels."

Altiris screwed his eyes tight, but nodded. "Nothing reckless, Viara."

She smiled. "From a Phoenix? Perish the thought."

With a last glance at the approaching Drazina, Altiris struck out west, shoving Constans before him. Exchanging a nod with Brass, Kurkas followed. His last glimpse before following Altiris into the cover of the ruins was of a thin line in the glowing mist, swords drawn and shields steady.

"Come on, you dozy bastards!" Viara shouted towards the oncoming Drazina. "Scared, are you?"

"She didn't have that mouth on her when she joined up," said Kurkas. "You're a bad influence, lad."

Expression taut, Altiris slipped deeper into the ruins.

The moonlight mare knew its business better than any destrier Rosa had ever known. She lined up charge after charge to utter perfection, the strike of the unfamiliar sword and the crackle of shattered clay mere formality. Perhaps that was for the best, as Rosa had neither bridle nor spurs with which to offer command.

Rosa was grateful for the judder of hooves and the ache in her scarred shoulder – the weight of one sword in her hand, and rattle of another, still scabbarded, at her back. They offered proof that this was not a dream. And so much *was* dreamlike. Had been since the Huntsman appeared beneath her balcony. She barely recalled walking to meet him, much less mounting the moonlight steed. What had come after was hazier still. Mists and a garden of white trees. Lithe, silver women binding her in armour and tending with a touch wounds that should have taken days to heal. Then the sound of the hunting horn had drawn her back to ashen fields and friends beset. A knight's duty bright beneath the shining moon.

The mare veered left and picked up speed. Rosa hacked down. Felt brief resistance of clay beneath the steel. Then the mare was moving once more, galloping alone to relieve an embattled ring of green shields, heedless of the danger offered by spears levelled in her path.

An Ocranza crunched to broken shards beneath insubstantial hooves.

A scraped parry. A plunging thrust and another collapsed, shadow bleeding from empty eyes. Rosa's backswing scattered a third. The mare reared, a spear in its chest and its flailing hoof caving in a clay skull.

Rosa grabbed at a handful of mane. Her fingers closed on brittle leaves. Others swirled about her as she fell, the scent of old summers and fading seasons thick in her throat. She struck the ground winded, a cloud of ash rising about her. A crunch of broken clay, and an Ocranza collapsed alongside, shadow peeling into the mist. Then a gauntleted hand found hers.

It took Rosa a moment to recognise a face that didn't belong above a knight's torn cloak and battered armour. But only a moment. With a cry of joy, she flung her arms about Sevaka.

"What are you doing here?"

Sevaka pulled away and grinned, and the night grew brighter for it. "I might ask you the same. You're hopeless. Even when I try to keep you from a fight, you still find a way."

"An Empress' gift. Her penance."

The Ocranza driven off and respite earned, the shield ring reformed, a tattered banner above. Rosa glanced around at familiar faces. No more than a dozen. Knights she'd trained. Fought alongside. And one who was no knight at all. "Apara?" Seized of urgency, she gripped the thief's arm. "Josiri? Have you seen him?"

Apara shook her head. "Not since the wall collapsed."

"What about Zephan?"

Sevaka shook her head, cast of brow telling the rest of the tale. Rosa gazed across the ashen fields to the shadow-wreathed line at Eskavord's gate. One shadow darker than any. A murmured, half-remembered prayer spilled unbidden from her lips.

What had Viktor become? Could she have stopped it if she'd spoken out earlier? If she'd warned Josiri instead of running off to play wolf's-head in the Eastshires?

Sevaka frowned. "I thought the Empress could offer no aid."

"She could *promise* no aid," said Apara. "She hoped, but she didn't know. Is that her sword?"

Rosa unslung the scabbarded blade from her back. "It is. She wanted it to stand for hope again."

Apara frowned. "Then it should be drawn."

"Not by me." She paused, seeking words to frame unclear sentiment. "If I wield that sword, I'll never set it down. I haven't the strength to do so. The Empress gave it to me, but I think she meant it for Josiri. Find him, Apara."

Apara grimaced, her eyes towards Eskavord and the shadow at its gates. Then she gave a terse nod and fled the ring, scabbard clutched to her chest.

Rosa stared across the battlefield. What had begun as a unified charge had descended into a hundred scattered contests. All save for where the Huntsman's spear shone through the mists, two score equerries at his back, riding headlong towards Viktor's line of Ocranza.

"Shouldn't you be with them?" asked Sevaka.

Rosa glanced mournfully at the dying swirl of leaves that had once been her steed. "Ephemeral or divine, it seems there's not a steed I can't fall off. It might be I'm not a very good knight. But if this is where it ends, I'll face it with you." Tugging free her helm, she kissed Sevaka. Held her close so that not even the Raven could part them, were that his wish. "No more running away."

Across the mists, near and far, Ocranza driven back by the Huntsman's charge gathered anew. And in their path, the weary, the scattered and the dazed. Sword-siblings and shieldbearers of Essamere, without leadership, without hope.

No. Never that. Not while she lived.

She swept her sword high. "Essamere!"

The Drazina folded without a sound, wits struck clean away by Kurkas' fist. Her companion fared better only in that Altiris caught his falling body, rather than letting it fall. Kurkas, with only a single arm to work with and his back throbbing, had neither the sympathy nor the energy to waste. Resolve softened when the woman rolled onto her back, eyes skyward. Black eyes, with dark spiderweb cracks beneath the brows.

"Mine's the same," murmured Altiris. "What is it?"

"He's in their heads," Kurkas replied. "All the way in."

Last time he'd been in Eskavord, the entire population had danced to

Malatriant's tune. What one had felt, they'd all felt. No sign of that with this pair. And the eyes ... Hard to be sure with so much time between, but they didn't look *as* bad. For whatever that was worth.

"He said he'd taken away their fear," said Constans, hands still bound and his eyes watchful.

"Yeah, it starts that way," said Kurkas. "But I've seen how it ends."

He shared a glance with Altiris, marked the lad's hollow gaze. How far gone was Sidara? Was there anything left to save? If there wasn't ...? Kurkas made a silent promise that it wouldn't be Altiris' burden to bear.

By unspoken assent, they crept towards the southwest corner, where blackened and tumbled stone gave way to the lychfield's forest of ash-swallowed graves. Tzila knelt at the bleak garden's heart, hands on her knees and head bowed. Sidara stood behind – or at least something that looked *mostly* like Sidara, for she was as dark-eyed as the unconscious Drazina and deathly pale. Where light so often mantled her shoulders, there was only shadow, writhing, caressing.

Kurkas caught Altiris' sharp intake of breath and grabbed his shoulder. "Steady, lad. Nothing stupid."

The shadow pulsed. Clay bodies lain along the lychfield's western edge twitched to life, darkness oozing beneath the platelets of their skin. Without a word of command from Sidara or Tzila, they formed into a column and marched into the northern streets. A handful of Drazina set about shovelling clay from the back of a wagon.

"It's not Droshna's army at all," murmured Altiris. "It's Sidara's."

He sounded sick. Kurkas couldn't blame him. "Did you not see the others? Do you not see her eyes? She's his hands in this. That's all."

"And what if there's nothing of her left?"

The bitter, heartbroken words hung on the air, inviting the answer neither of them wanted to hear.

"She's still Sidara, at least a little," said Constans. "I tried talking to her, but she's never listened to me. She'll listen to you. Why do you think I came looking for you?"

Kurkas shook his head. "As easy as that, eh?"

"Probably not." Determination crept into Altiris' face. "But I have to try."

Kurkas stared again across the lychfield. Not good odds. Tzila alone could handle them both. And that was before you considered the half a dozen Drazina in ready sight . . . and Sidara.

He slipped Constans' dagger from his belt. "Hold out your hands."

Altiris stepped between Constans and Kurkas. "You can't be serious."

"It's that stage of the game," Kurkas replied. "You walk away from the table, or you give it everything, hope your instincts are true, and pray you're not playing the high proctor, Lumestra rest his cheating soul."

"After what he did?" hissed Altiris.

Kurkas tried to ignore the dull, red throb and his clammy shirt. "It's somewhat present in my mind."

Altiris scowled, but nodded.

"Hands, boy." Kurkas jabbed the dagger in the air between them. "You don't want to know what this second chance'll cost if you let me down."

Constans offered a shaky version of his florid bow. Strands of bowstring slithered from his wrists. "A repentant soul, am I."

Altiris glared. "How . . . ?"

"I undid it *ages* ago, but I didn't want you to be nervous." The arrogance slipped from his voice. "I won't let you down, Devn."

"Give him the dagger," muttered Altiris, "before I throttle him."

Kurkas hesitated, then slapped the dagger into Constans' outstretched palm. "Can you handle the Drazina?"

"Pfff."

Taking the answer as a yes, Kurkas stared back across the lychfield. "Make your girl see sense, lad. Leave the rest to us."

Altiris threw him a suspicious look. "What about Tzila?"

"We've old business to settle."

Constans cleared his throat. "Altiris . . ."

"What?"

"Sidara might be a bit surprised to see you. *More* surprised, I mean."

"And why's that?"

Constans winced. "I told her you were dead . . . " He brightened. "But I said you'd died heroically."

Altiris scowled.

"Of course you did," said Kurkas.

He drew his sword and stepped clear of concealment. The throbbing weight in his back grew hotter, heavier, but he somehow kept it from his voice.

"Oi, Halvor! You owe me a rematch!"

Shouts rang out as the Drazina at the wagon scrambled for weapons and came forward. Sidara's gaze snapped up, shadow swirling about her shoulders. At once, she hunched over, hands at her ears and eyes screwed shut. Tzila reached her feet, the motion graceful as ever.

A whisper of motion at Kurkas' left and a Drazina fell, Constans' dagger in his throat. The boy was on him in moments, and then had both a dagger and a sword.

"Sidara!" Altiris went past to Kurkas' right.

Then Tzila was before him, sabres drawn and approaching with the manner of a spider glad that a fly had invited itself in for lunch.

"Still time to pick the right side, Halvor," said Kurkas.

[[I don't know that name.]]

Her lunge became a feint, became a slash that slit the leather on Kurkas' thigh and drew blood beneath. He stumbled back, cursing the stiffness of old bones. A scream sounded to his left as Constans claimed another victim.

[[You're too slow, old man.]]

Rich, coming from her. Halvor had at least a decade over him, and that was before you factored in that she was dead and he wasn't. Well, not yet. "Who're you calling old?"

She stalked closer, left-hand sabre whirling and the right at high guard. [[You couldn't beat me before. You can't now.]]

The words had an unpleasant ring. Truth always did. Kurkas forced a shrug, and felt something warm ooze along his spine. "Yeah, well. Some things you just gotta do. You used to understand that."

Gripping his sword tight, he charged.

Sixty-Six

This time, pulling herself back together *hurt*, a riot of spasm and contortion that left Calenne blind and shuddering, still more mist than form. Lying curled on her side in Otherworld's mists, arms clutched to her chest and knees practically touching her chin, she couldn't decide whether the pain made her more real, or less. She knew only that she was furious. At Viktor. At the Raven. At herself for being so useless. Was there anything worse than watching fate unfold, unable to act?

The tremors subsided. Vaporous fingers gained firmity. Sight returned, and with it the horrific image of Revekah's spirit pyre and the vortex of mist . . . only now, the tableau was changed.

The garden was gone, replaced by a lychfield, its headstones crooked teeth in an ashen jaw. Through drifting etravia, Calenne glimpsed darker shapes, too real to be part of Otherworld's shifting realm.

Steel flashed, blood spattering ash. A Drazina collapsed. Constans twisted away into a pall of shadow as another struck out in revenge, the sword striking sparks from a gravestone. His hand dripping blood and his left leg buckling, Kurkas parried one flashing sabre and lurched away from another. Tzila bore down, her steps no longer a dancer's, but a hunter come to finish her prey.

And in the centre, at the foot of a pyre Calenne knew at once they couldn't see, stood a young woman with matted, filthy blonde hair, her hands clamped over her ears and her eyes screwed tight. The Raven stood behind her, lips level with her hands, his words lost to distance.

But it was about Tzila that the shadow was darkest, a thousand gossamer tendrils lashing and writhing about her shoulders, a match for the flames consuming Revekah's soul self. Unless, of course, they weren't really flames at all. Not any longer.

Calenne frowned, struck by the nagging sense that she'd seen something important, but not understanding *what*.

Altiris came into sight, sword in his hand, for all that he looked unready to use it. "Sidara!"

"Leave me alone!"

Shadow pulsed at Sidara's shriek, hurling the Raven back. Hat and cane gone, he landed awkwardly against the pyre's steps. Mist rolled back in, hiding the lychfield and its inhabitants behind the dying garden.

"What was that?" asked Calenne.

"Back again? Lucky me." Scowling, the Raven reclaimed his hat and lurched to his feet. "I'm not permitted to act directly, but I thought I might try talking sense into her. You saw how that went."

She stared into the mists, desperate for a glimpse of the mortal realm. "Try again."

"I don't think so."

The tone struck Calenne more than the words. Weary, affronted . . . even childish – as if no party in unfolding events were more injured than he. She opened her mouth in retort and closed it again just as quickly. She'd tried arguing with the Raven before, and achieved nothing. Just like the arguments she'd shared with Josiri had never done any good. Pride seldom yielded to passion. Only reason. Even when everything was *unreasonable*.

Calenne stared again at the bonfire, the dark flames leaping into the vortex above. And just like that, she understood. Perhaps the Raven understood too, but pride wouldn't allow him to act upon it. Pride, or some peculiar arrangement of worlds – the duties of the Keeper of the Dead. But the Keeper of the Dead was a god before anything else, and where gods were concerned, Calenne knew one truth above all others, hammered home by fairy tale and fable.

She took a deep breath – or whatever passed for breath, in her strange circumstance – and met the Raven's petulant gaze. "I offer you a bargain."

He tilted his head, eyes watchful beneath the mask. "Now?"

A tone meant to quell found no purchase on Calenne. Fear belonged to the living, not one who'd died a handful of times over. "Why not?"

He snorted. "Very well. I'm listening. What do you want?"

"Let's start with what I can give you."

"Oh, this should be good. A scrap of soul thinks to set the terms of trade? How—"

Calenne cut off his sneer with a wave of her hand – a gesture she'd seen her mother use, long years ago. It felt natural. "I'll strike the blow you cannot. You're not free to act. I am. I'll give you revenge against Viktor. That's my offer."

The Raven shook his head in derision. "And how do you propose to make good on your bargain? You've some small, *irritating* resilience here, but out there . . . ?" He turned his back.

"Then let's talk about what you're to give me in return," said Calenne.

With the spectral riders barely thirty yards distant, Viktor loosed his shadow.

It came reluctantly at first, weakened by his generosity of sharing it with Sidara, the Ocranza, the survivors of the 14th, others. But hissing disfavour at the mist's reflected moonlight, it obeyed, gathering pace as it slithered across the ash. He sent it forth not to blind, as he had in times past, nor to raise the slain as puppets, but to kill.

It overtook the leading equerries, ghostly flesh and armour shattering as its cold burrowed deep. A galloping wedge of spears became a field of glistening chunks and swirling leaves, the riders of Eventide torn from moonlight's embrace and back into legend. The wedge became a ragged line of emptied saddles and broken spears.

Yet still they came on, the Huntsman at the fore, armour thick with rime, his stag's antlers lowered. His equerries were ephemeral souls, but he was something older, deeper. Infused with moonlight, and the Dark that was its sire. The demon who'd cast down Ahrad's walls, and lain waste its armies. He'd been stronger then, vibrant with the full moon's light and brimming with a goddess' holy wrath. But even now, with the half-moons of Eventide and Evermoon in balance, no mere shadow could unmake him, not alone. The Dark shied from his starlight spear, its weariness become Viktor's own.

"Brace!" roared Viktor.

Shields crashed together to his fore, driven by Viktor's willpower as much as his word. The Huntsman's horn sounded anew, and the starlight spear lowered to the charge. Viktor dragged his shadow back from the expanse of ash and fading leaves, and bound it about him as armour.

The night sky shuddered as the riders crashed home. Shields split. Bodies sailed through the air. Souls scattered, their clay shells sundered by spear and hoof. The front rank buckled, lost beneath shadow and autumn leaves. Viktor staggered as pieces of the Dark – of him – ripped free of ephemeral mooring, the souls they'd caged lost again to the Raven's embrace.

The starlight spear blazed bright. Viktor raised his claymore to high guard in challenge, and swung.

At the last moment, the spear twitched, the Huntsman's reactions swifter than sight. The claymore's arc, intended to strike the spearhead aside in preparation for a disembowelling thrust, met only empty air. Not so the Huntsman's spear. Shadow-armour parting before its brilliance, the blazing head punched through plate and hauberk, and deep into flesh.

Viktor's world turned to fire.

Spear deep in his shoulder, he skidded backwards through the ash, his own bellow of pain as distant and unfamiliar as the strike of the stag's hooves. Green eyes blazed. Unremitting. Uncaring.

And then they were gone, lost in a blur of white and captive stars, and Viktor was face down in the ash.

As Altiris drew level with the wagon, Sidara at last faced him. So close, there was no mistaking the Dark's influence, marked by dark eyes and spreading spiderweb cracks across cheek and brow. But there was something else. An edginess. A distraction. As if she didn't really see him at all.

"I don't want to fight you." Even the *idea* shivered Altiris to his stomach. Not least because if it came to a fight, he'd no chance of winning. "Can't you see what Viktor's done to you?"

She stared at him, hands slipping from her ears.

A Drazina's scream sounded off to Altiris' left. He ignored it and edged closer, fighting to meet Sidara's evasive gaze. "Sidara—"

Her cold, bitter laugh jerked him to a halt. "So it's apparitions now, is it?"

He edged closer. "It's me. It's Altiris."

"Altiris is dead! They killed him!" Shadow spilled free across her shoulders. Her expression contorted in misery. "Is this the best trick the Raven can manage?"

What did the Raven have to do with anything? He risked another step.

What was there to say? What *could* he say that madness or imposter would not? He'd never had much of a plan. Only a hope that Sidara's love for him – and if not love, then at least their friendship, however tested – might snap her out of what Viktor had done. That it might at least give her pause. Denied his very identity by delusion and deceit, even that naive hope sputtered to nothing.

He'd wondered before if he could kill her, if called to. Would it come to that?

Her shadow pulsed to embrace him. Altiris cried out as ice crackled across his limbs, the pain as sharp as it was immediate. He heard his sword drop, but didn't feel it slip from numbed fingers.

"Altiris is dead." Sidara stalked closer, her rictus fluctuating between wrath and sorrow. Even her voice was not her own. Something darker lurked beneath. "Whatever you are, you'll join him."

Altiris fell to hands and knees, leaden tongue fumbling for words that would stop her from killing him. Shivered breaths stung the back of his throat and burned his lungs. That she meant to, he'd no doubt.

But in that moment, he felt something stir deep within. A shard of radiant light. Sidara's light, the piece left behind when she'd saved his life years before; that had held Kasvin's seductive will at bay in Sothvane. The shadow recoiled before it, the cold alongside. Sidara yelped and staggered away, shadow unwinding.

Every inch an agonising, frozen mile, Altiris rose to his knees. Worthless, leaden fingers sought his sword.

Eyes murderous, Sidara bore down anew. The light blinked out, smothered. A candle guttering at midnight. Shadow rushed in, colder than ever. Altiris' pulse slowed, the drab colours of Eskavord's ruins growing more muted still.

"Don't do it, Sidara." Through dimming eyes, Altiris saw Constans approach, his hood back and empty hands held up in surrender. "It's him. Not a trick. Not a deceit. It really is Altiris."

She rounded on him, shadow writhing. "You told me he'd died!"

"I always lie to you, remember?" He scowled away a grimace. "I wanted you to be more like me. But no one should be like me, least of all you. One's enough. One's too many."

Sidara drew herself up. "You always lie to me. That's true." Her laughter rippled through the shadow. "You're lying to me now."

Her shadow heaved, flinging Constans away. He caromed off a tomb and went still, blood gushing from a wound on his scalp and seeping away into the ash.

Freed in the moment she'd lashed out at Constans, Altiris regained his feet. Juddering fingers at last found his sword.

"Sidara, please." The words were like grit in his throat. "Come back to me."

She looked down at her brother's motionless body, shadow seething about her shoulders.

"This is what Viktor needs me to be." For all Sidara's words offered reply, Altiris had the sense she'd forgotten about him. She stared down at herself – hands spread and darkness curling about her fingers – and again at Constans. "What the Republic needs me to be."

She sagged. For a moment Altiris thought he glimpsed daylight beneath the shadow's pall, like thunder crackling behind clouds. But then it was gone, if it was ever there. With it went her last doubts, her back straighter than before and her eyes clear. The Lady of Light lost to shadow. The wellspring of Viktor's army, and the means by which he'd drown the Republic in Dark. Lost in contemplation of the brother she'd likely killed. Distant. Distracted.

Vulnerable.

Shivering and heartsick, his knuckles aching about his sword's grips, Altiris staggered towards her.

Viktor's right arm collapsed as he made to stand, his shoulder screaming. Vision blurred, the ruins of Eskavord's gateway indistinguishable from the night sky. Breath rasped hot over his tongue. Ahead, the battle raged on. Behind, the mournful call of the Huntsman's stag, and the staccato double-thump as it gathered to the charge.

Again, Viktor tried to stand. Again his arm buckled, and he fell.

But something else arose. The old fire. The determination that had seen him through countless battlefields of the spirit or the sword. The reminder that all things turned on a single moment, for good or for ill. That triumph and defeat turned on such moments. Made a man a hero, or a failure.

He'd come too far to fail now.

He'd been wrong to fear Ashana's lickspittle, who was but an echo of moonlight. The Dark was older, and he its master.

Viktor stuffed the wound with shadow. Made the Dark's cold strength his own and banished even the idea of pain. This time, the arm buckled, but held.

Fingers closing about his claymore and drawing strength from its weight, Viktor rose into the Huntsman's path. As the starlit spear dipped, Viktor sent forth his shadow. Light rose to meet it, the magic of the Huntsman's creation roused in opposition to the Dark from which it had been fashioned. It had preserved him while his equerries had surrendered to ice, and would do so again. But Viktor had never meant to win the contest, only to distract.

The spearpoint twitched. Not much, but it was all the opening Viktor sought.

Viktor sprang forward into the Huntsman's path, claymore upright and scraping the spear-shaft's inner edge. Blinding starlight scraped past his head. Blood hissed to scalding vapour as the tip sliced his brow. Pain boiled to fire, and fire to strength.

The claymore shuddered in his charred hands as he drove it up under the Huntsman's ribs, the momentum of charge and counter-charge driving the point up through his armour. Roar of effort melding with his foe's pained bellow, Viktor drove the Huntsman backwards off the stag.

They struck the ashen ground with a bone-jarring impact. An antler snapped. The claymore's steel sank deep into the Huntsman's divine flesh, pinning him to the soil. Driven to his knees and heaving for breath, Viktor clung to the grips for support.

"This is the might of Ashana's demon?" he said, voice thick with disgust. "Can she do no better?"

Beneath him, the Huntsman stirred, green eyes fading beneath his helm. "Probably. But we all serve our purpose. This was never her battle to fight." Ragged gasps turned to a deep, vibrant chuckle. "... and I was only ever a distraction."

A chill gathering in his heart, Viktor staggered upright, eyes outward across a battlefield thick with swirling leaves, the last of the equerries overmatched by the Ocranza. But beyond, a line of green shields, broader and thicker than it had been since he'd returned to the battlefield. The broken and dismayed returned to purpose he'd striven to strip away. Beneath the banner, Rosa held her sword high. The familiar cry rang out.

"Until Death!"

The Huntsman's chuckle blossomed to throaty laughter. Overcome by wrath, Viktor twisted his claymore and wrenched it free. A wind sprang up, stirring the leaves of the Huntsman's passing. But his mocking laughter lingered.

The pain of his wounds pulsing beneath shadow, Viktor gazed beyond the Ocranzas' reforming line to the Essamere advance. Fury sought to set his shadow upon them as he had the Huntsman's charge. Reason warned that to do so was folly. That what remained of his ephemeral body stood on the brink of collapse. Only the Dark held it together.

Still, the advantage remained his. He'd won more battles with his shadow held in check than with it loosed. His Ocranza outnumbered Essamere. That advantage would only grow as Sidara dredged more soldiers from the clay. Essamere would be swept away, Rosa alongside. One last victory, and a Republic to remake.

As he started towards the Ocranza lines, his shadow shuddered with a piece of it rooted elsewhere. Not in pain, but confusion. Courage shaken and slipping away.

Sidara.

Viktor swore, belatedly realising that the Essamere line was empty of too many faces that should have been there. Too much to hope they'd perished in battle. A distraction, the Huntsman had named himself. By chance or design, Essamere had become the same. If he lost Sidara? If he failed her as he had so many others?

Turning on his heel, Viktor left Essamere to contest the Ocranza and strode back through the gate. Ruined streets passed in a blur, each stride undercut by pain even his shadow couldn't fully contain.

He forged on as the sounds of battle renewed split the air, leaving behind the ashen cobblestones of the marketplace where Malatriant had for ever altered his life's course. Past the winding road and the wall behind which Branghall's broken-arched ruins reached up at the moon. To the stone bridge and the gorge below, where the swift-flowing Grelyt River fled Eskavord's desolation for haler fields.

It was there Viktor at last found his path blocked. At the bridge's crest stood a helmless man in battered armour and torn phoenix tabard, an Essamere shield at his feet and sword point-down on the cobbles. His expression was as weary as Viktor's own.

"Hello, brother," said Josiri. "Time to make an end of this."

Sixty-Seven

Viktor halted before the bridge, eyes on the Grelyt's rushing waters and claymore against his uninjured shoulder. The other shoulder screamed beneath the shadow's embrace, a fit match for the aftermath of Anastacia's light still seething in his charred hands. Try though he might, he could manage no hatred for Josiri, not for betrayal in the city, nor ambush hidden beneath promise of parley. His heart held only weariness, and a sense of inevitability birthed by cosmic humours.

Of course it had to end there, on that bridge. On the spot where Katya Trelan had once given herself to the Raven for want of the courage to live, her son now did the same.

Such a waste.

Viktor reached out through his shadow, and recanted as his wounds screamed for attention. Even an hour before, he could have ended Josiri's threat with barely a thought. Now, to assail him with shadow carried too great a risk. His whole being felt diffuse, as much a part of the Dark as the Dark was of him.

He needed no shadow to beat Josiri. He'd laid low emperors in his time, and fought an Empress to a standstill. All through steel and discipline, and the will to triumph. He was a hero, a champion. Josiri was only a man. An ordinary man. Viktor had killed more ordinary men than he could readily count.

But Sidara's disquiet was a growing blight in his thoughts, and he feared delay as greatly as defeat. He risked a little shadow, reaching out to the umbral presence of Ocranza in nearby streets. To Drazina further east, their minds awash with thoughts of survival as they fought a running battle with Phoenixes. A caress of shadow – a nudge – and it was done, and Viktor free to grant Josiri the Raven's mercy.

"Are we really to do this, brother?" he asked.

Josiri hesitated before replying, his aspect no less weary than Viktor's own. "What choice have you left me?"

Viktor snorted. How small he seemed. Not just in stature, but in vision. He cursed himself for not seeing it before.

"I thought it was I who blamed my failings on others."

Josiri's only reply was to sweep his sword to the formal salute. For all the steel in his voice, his limbs shook. Impossible not to admire the man for marching knowingly into death. Viktor resolved that the Republic's histories would hold no record of this moment. Let future generations believe Josiri loyal to the last. He could do that much for the man who'd been his closest friend.

He returned the salute and strode onto the bridge.

Viktor raised his sword to a two-handed high guard, letting his left arm bear the burden of the injured right. At once, Josiri shrank back, slipping into a defensive stance, shield to the fore. His limbs no longer shook, and the point of his longsword held steady.

The claymore looped about, the blade rising to threaten Josiri's left side. Steel chimed, the longsword's parry as textbook as the stance. Slower than it should have been, but Viktor allowed that neither of them were at their best in that hour.

With a cry borne of the day's frustrations, Viktor launched a flurry of short, efficient strikes at Josiri's head. A dull scrape sounded as the shield cheated the first. Others found empty air as Josiri retreated. Viktor thrust before the other regathered himself. Josiri's cloak tore beneath steel.

Pressing his advantage, Viktor cleared the bridge's crest, a roll of the wrists making feint of a downward arc in favour of a vicious slash at Josiri's left. Taken off guard by the superior reach granted by Viktor's height and the claymore's length, Josiri again let his shield weather the blow. It bucked, the rim clattering against armour.

Again Viktor pressed in. Steel flashed between them as Josiri went on the offensive for the first time. Viktor's hurried parry struck the slash away, but there was another, another, another, each attack flowing seamlessly into the next. A practised, blurring rhythm that sent Viktor scrambling back across the bridge's crest.

Harrowed eyes tight, Josiri advanced, ash billowing about his feet.

A thrust cheated a slow parry as they recrossed the bridge's crest. Steel shrieked as Viktor's breastplate turned the blow his sword could not. Unbidden, regret arose that they'd never duelled in comradeship, not even between the red pennants on Stonecrest's lawn. Unthinkable that after everything Josiri might prove the better swordsman.

Frustration gorged on pride and flared to fury. Roaring, Viktor swung a downward two-handed haymaker, fit to cleave a man in two. Josiri stepped aside. Too late, Viktor realised he'd meant to tempt such recklessness.

Even as the claymore sparked against cobbles, the longsword blurred silver beneath moonlight.

Viktor hurled himself away. The rising lunge meant to take his throat instead scored his left cheek. Warmth sheeted Viktor's face and neck, the tang of blood sharp above the bitter, ashen air.

Snarling, he let loose a portion of his shadow. Let resurgent pain lend much-needed purpose. One sweep of the claymore battered Josiri's shield wide. Another sliced deep into Josiri's exposed forearm, severing the shield's straps and drowning the vambrace in blood.

As Josiri cried out, Viktor gathered him up in shadow and hurled him against the bridge's northern wall. A sweep of the claymore ripped the longsword from Josiri's hand and sent it skittering down the bridge's western slope.

"Why did you make me do this?" Viktor bellowed, loss and fury a poisonous mix in his ravaged heart. "We were brothers!"

Trapped in the shadow's embrace, Josiri offered no reply.

Even in that moment, a piece of him yearned to stay his hand. To show mercy. But only a piece. In a single, smooth moment he raised the claymore and hacked down.

"No!"

The cry and the blur of movement came as one.

Flesh parted beneath the claymore's blade. Collarbone and ribs snapped, the sensations travelling up Viktor's arm to awaken shudder-ing empathies. And yet, there was no blood. The blow sent to bestow mercy Josiri no longer deserved fell not upon him, but a pale woman in shadowthorn robes, her grey eyes cold and unflinching.

Apara Rann cried out as Viktor ripped the claymore free. Again, as he seized her by the throat. Whirling, he slammed her against the bridge's wall, scattering loose stone from the parapet and into the rushing Grelyt below.

Another loose end. Another act of mercy gone awry. How long would he suffer the mistakes of his past?

"Have you not learned your place, thief?" he demanded.

Her right hand clawed at his. Her left hung limp at her side. "Right now?" she hissed. "It's between you and Josiri."

"Foolish to be so, without even a sword."

Somehow, she smiled. "Oh, I had one. I gave it away."

Red rage crowding his vision, Viktor sent what he could afford of his shadow flowing into her, seeking to break her anew. But the riven, pathetic woman of Tarvallion's cells was a stranger to them both. He weaker, and she stronger in ways that defied ready words. His shadow, already stretched to breaking point, recoiled.

Apara's smile turned vicious. "I'm not your slave any more."

With a roar, Viktor hurled her across the parapet. A splash of white in the darkness, and she was lost to the rushing waters. Chest heaving with exertion and anger, Viktor straightened.

As he did so, the night paled.

Josiri staggered into sight, bloody, tattered and weary beyond words, the sword in his hand blazing with alabaster flame.

"We're not done, Viktor."

Tzila spun on her heel, right-hand sabre slashing at Kurkas' head, the left at his midriff. He ducked the former, flung a hurried block at the latter, and stumbled away. Lungs labouring fit to burst and his heartbeat a stampede, he propped a shoulder against a statue. The empty-eyed serathi stared back.

He hoped the others were doing better than he was.

"For the Phoenix, Halvor," he gasped. "Don't you remember? Sunshine, shadowthorns . . . all that good stuff?"

Words that had twice frozen Tzila barely gave her pause. A sabre arced down. Kurkas flung himself aside. Steel chimed off stone. He staggered about, eyes scrying the black sallet helm for crumb of comfort. Some sign his words were getting through. Lumestra knew his sword wasn't.

[[That's not my name.]]

"But it is!" he said. "It *is*! Droshna's just made you forget, that's all. Come on, Halvor! You really gonna bend a knee to a northwealder and not even *question*?"

He hobbled into a colonnade of tombs. Last resting place of Eskavord's wealthy before rebellion and war had scattered its families. High-roofed sepulchres, guarded by dead yews and yet more graven serathi, their features thick with dust and ash.

A moment. Just needed a moment to get his breath back.

Who was he kidding? He'd not been Halvor's match in life, with all his parts and pieces, let alone now, with his leg throbbing and his life bleeding away into his shirt. Main thing was to keep her away from Altiris. Give the lad time to talk sense into Sidara.

He glanced back through the mist. No sign of Tzila on the path between the tombs.

"Come on, Halvor. Snap out of it!"

Still no sign. Had she wandered off? Was she even now sticking a blade in Altiris' back? Getting stabbed in the back wasn't an experience Kurkas could recommend.

He edged back the way he'd come. At last, Tzila stepped into sight, sabres again at her sides, the points inches from the desiccated vines and yew roots choking the path.

But there was movement behind as well, betrayed by the scrape of stone upon stone and the crackle of long-dead fibres.

Risking a glance, Kurkas saw Ocranza moving amid the tombs, cutting off his retreat.

He sighed, and shook his head. Like that, was it? Fair enough. Couldn't say he'd not had a good run. Better to go out on a high.

Putting the last of his strength behind his sword, he threw himself at Tzila.

For the first time, she retreated, sabres flashing to a parry. Kurkas' thrust became a feint, became a neck-high slash, the moves flowing from aching shoulder to creaking wrist. No thought now to the deeds.

No worries of Altiris, or Lord Trelan, or other comrades lost to the mists. Only survival instincts earned in Dregmeet's cruel streets, honed in the army and practised to perfection on the battlefield. The sick fury at how Lord Droshna had contorted so fine a woman into an obedient puppet.

Tzila twisted from a lunge. Silk torn from her cloak fluttered atop a tomb. [[You can't win. Too old and tired.]]

"You think I don't know that?" Kurkas replied, breath hot in his throat. The realisation she no longer bothered even to parry hurt more than his throbbing back.

[[Then why fight?]]

He slashed again, the sword heavier in his hand than ever. "If you were *really* her, you'd know."

Another lunge went wide, cheated by a slow pirouette. A sabre's guard crashed into his cheek, rattling teeth and running the world red. Lungs heaving, Kurkas fell to one knee and spat blood into the ash.

From the moment Viktor's claymore first met the Goddess' sword, Josiri knew he couldn't win. For all that the flame kept Viktor's shadow at bay, it couldn't do the same for his steel. Only strength might do that, and Josiri's rapidly faded, seeping from the gash in his left arm. He clung two-handed to the grips as a drowning man to driftwood, the moonlight flame his only warmth in a world growing steadily colder.

Again and again, Viktor hammered at him. No longer recognisable as himself. Barely recognisable as a man. A grim apparition, cloaked in shadow. A hole in the world.

Somehow Josiri met Viktor's steel with his own, old lessons roused in desperation for a fight far beyond him. But for every blow countered, another cheated the flame. Armour blunted some. Too many slipped through, slicking steel and rushing garments red.

The world beyond the alabaster flame grew dreary and fuzzed, but within the flame Josiri found purpose. The will to carry on, even when every inch of him screamed, or else had fallen silent.

The claymore arced down. Josiri sent the white flame to meet it, the blow driving him to one knee. Fire raced along the locked swords, Viktor darker than ever behind it.

"The dutiful son!" bellowed Viktor. "Determined to repeat his mother's mistakes!"

The blades slipped with a banshee screech. Hilts met.

"This isn't about my mother," gasped Josiri. "This is about my promise to *you*."

Muscles screaming, he heaved the swords aside. Old stone crumbled beneath the claymore's strike, more of the bridge's abused northern wall plunging into the seething Grelyt.

As Viktor stumbled away, Josiri rose on rubbery legs.

"You won't win!" snarled Viktor.

"I will," gasped Josiri. The sword dipped to the road, too heavy for what little of him remained. "And if I don't, another will. It's the rule of the Southshires, Viktor. Don't you see that? A Phoenix will come. The chains will be broken. The darkness never lasts!"

With a roar that owed more to madness than to man, Viktor barrelled forward, claymore hacking down. Somehow, Josiri brought the Goddess' sword up to meet it.

Fire faded with a dull *crack*. Ashana's sword, her last gift – the last hope, offered by an enemy who had become the finest friend – split asunder, the upper part pinwheeling away.

The blow's force sent Josiri sprawling to the roadway, jagged hilt in hand, numbed limbs cold as the fire's warmth departed, leaving him with the dying embers of a life pushed beyond its limit.

Viktor loomed above, eclipsing even the moon.

The night grew darker. Josiri heard the mists calling, their song sweet and solemn, their welcome soothing to bones aching for rest. And there in the darkness, he glimpsed a familiar, impossible sight. A pale, vaporous figure moving purposefully through the mists, arms crossed and hands clasped to her chest.

"Calenne?" he breathed.

After so long trapped within the mists or in a body of clay, Calenne's senses rebelled at the ephemeral world's glory. Even beneath moonlight, the colours were brighter, the sounds crisper. And the smells . . . The foulness of sweat. The coppery miasma of Josiri's blood. Sickness crowded her thoughts. She forced it back. Nausea was of the body, and she nothing but spirit. A cyraeth set loose from Otherworld at the Raven's hand to settle old business.

"Leave my brother be, Viktor," she said. "You know he's right."

Viktor turned, the shadow swirling about him. "Calenne?" The claymore fell as bruised and bloodied features cracked to disbelieving joy. "What is this? How ... ?"

So dreadful he looked, no longer even the Black Knight of her unquiet dreams but a suffocating, malevolent spirit become mockery of a man ... And yet, she felt the allure. The piece of her that had been Calenne Akadra belonged to him, was *part* of him. It yearned for unity, and its yearning became hers also.

Calenne tamped it down, held tight to the squirming bundle wrapped in her arms. The Raven's collateral. A bargain to deliver a god's vengeance, and perhaps a measure of peace to those touched by Viktor's madness.

"You're lost, Viktor. Can't you see that? You're everything you swore never to be."

His expression darkened with hurt. "So you turn on me as well?"

"On what you've become." Drawing level with Josiri's body, she sought traces of life and found almost nothing. She choked back the memory of tears, and cursed herself for arriving too late. "Not what you were."

She spread her hands and a pale, ghostly raven took wing. It spiralled through mists, climbing ever higher, and flew away east.

The light shifted as Ocranza closed in behind. Tzila stepped closer. Slow. Deliberate. Kurkas flinched as the sabre's icy point slipped under his chin.

He met the sallet helm's empty gaze one last time. "One last bastion? D'you remember? You and me against the world. Whatever happened to that?"

Kurkas started as a spectral raven came screeching out of the western mists, ghostly feathers streaming behind. It shot past his shoulder and, without slowing, dived straight at Tzila, passing through breastplate and tabard with a ripple of green-white light. Sabres slipping from her hands, she doubled over, clutching at a tomb for support.

Bemused, but never one to let opportunity pass him by, Kurkas stumbled to his feet. An Ocranza's shield-barge threw him to the ground, vision swimming as his head hit stone.

Expressionless shadow-set faces blotted out the moon.

The war hammer smote Sevaka's shield and set her staggering. The Ocranza trudged on, its backswing hurling aside a knight and forcing the gap wider. Others barrelled in its wake, and were met in turn by a rush of green from Sevaka's right, Rosa at its head.

"Essamere!"

The hammer-wielder toppled back, its arm shattered by the strike of Rosa's sword. Sevaka rammed her own notched blade forward and cast another back into the mists.

But through the rush of battle, one clarion rang true: the Ocranza were too many, and Essamere too few.

Helping a bruised knight to her feet, Sevaka stared toward Eskavord. At the foes yet between them and the gate. Ocranza. Stray survivors of the 14th in King's Blue. Drazina in midnight black. Perhaps a hundred. Perhaps more. And her strength was spent. Essamere was spent. Too many dead, and of those who remained, few could hold both sword and shield.

But still they came, gathering one last time to the hawk and the sword.

"It's death to go down there," said Rosa.

"I've been dead before." Sevaka forced a smile. "And you're going, aren't you?"

"Only because you'll be there."

A hundred thoughts vied for expression as their eyes met. A thousand words to go for ever unsaid because, in the end, their life together had been too brief. But there were worse ways to meet an end, and no better company in which to do so.

"Until Death, Lady Orova."

Rosa nodded, lips tight and eyes shining. "Until Death, Lady Orova."

Sevaka lifted her sword anew, no longer her heaviest burden. With Essamere at her back and her love beside her, she went smiling to her doom.

Steel flashed over Kurkas' head, the crunch of clay close behind. An Ocranza staggered back, shadow oozing from a broken skull and into the night. Another collapsed, a sabre buried to the hilt in its chest. A third managed two parries before its shadow bled free.

Tzila reached down, hand spread.

[[One last bastion, Vladama?]] Though she looked the same in aspect and posture, the voice was different. Still hollow, but rounded, softer ... though with bite behind. A woman ill-accustomed to suffering fools gladly, even when they were friends.

Elation surging through the pain, Kurkas took Tzila's – *Revekah's* – hand. "Being awfully familiar, ain't you, Halvor?"

[[Shut up.]]

Bones creaking and an idiot grin on his face, Kurkas reached his feet. "Knew you'd come back to me," he lied.

[[I don't remember any of it,]] she replied softly. [[Not in detail. Just glimpses through the Dark. And rage ... So much rage, and none of it mine.]]

"Then you don't remember me handing your arse to you in that duel?"

She tilted her head. [[No you didn't.]]

Impossibly, he felt his grin broaden. "No I didn't. Glad to have you back, you old baggage."

Revekah flinched and shrank back. [[Anastacia ... What have I done?]]

Swaying with exhaustion, Kurkas grabbed her shoulder. "Wasn't you." The words seemed worthless, pitiful. Never much one for finer feelings, he'd no idea how to ease a pain he knew he'd never fully understand. "She knew that. Bloody knew everything, did the plant pot."

Breath crackling and popping in his chest, Kurkas peered at the Ocranza drawing nearer through the mists. Eschewing his sword, he reclaimed a mace from amid broken clay and set his back to Revekah's. Too many to beat, but not too many to fight ... not with a friend at his side.

One last bastion indeed.

As to last words? Well, what else could they be?

"For the Phoenix, Captain Halvor?"

The sabres came up. [[For the Phoenix.]]

Sidara shrieked and doubled over, golden light again flaring beneath shadow. Trembling, uncertain – the sword in his hand feeling more useless than ever – Altiris edged closer.

"I know you're still in there, Sidara. I can see you fighting what he's done to you."

She straightened, dark eyes murderous. The light died, smothered by ascendant shadow. Frost crackled along Altiris' sword and stung his cheeks. "The Republic needs Viktor, and he needs me. I won't fail him!"

Gone were the accusations of apparitionhood, Altiris realised. Did Sidara see him for who he was? Or did she simply no longer care? How much did Droshna's shadow influence her sight? Influence *her*? Or was he grasping at straws, desperate for anything offering hope that the Sidara he loved still existed?

Gritting his teeth against the cold, Altiris pressed on. "The Republic needs many things, but Droshna isn't one of them. He lost his fight against the Dark long ago. He'll drag us all down with him before he's done!"

"Maybe he should!" Sidara's eyes blazed gold, shadow rimming them as smoke rings flame. "Maybe that's what the Republic deserves."

"How can you say that?"

"They killed Ana! Viktor told me."

The words made sense of so much. "Sidara ... *Viktor* murdered Ana."

Shadow rushed back, drowning gold in darkness. It swirled about them both, concealing all else from sight, whipping ash and mist to a storm. The cold dug deeper.

"You're lying!" shouted Sidara.

"I've *never* been able to lie to you, even when I've wanted to! Ana ... She tried to stop all this, and Viktor killed her for it. I held her as she died. I watched the wind blow her soul out to sea. But she never stopped fighting him. Nor will I, even if it kills me too."

Altiris cast aside his useless sword. A sword he knew he'd never be able to use. It vanished into spiralling shadow, lost to sight.

"But I won't fight you. I can't. If that's weakness, I don't care." Willing shaking limbs to motion, he closed the last distance and took her hands. Warmth and chill rippled across chafed, frostbitten skin as Light and Dark fought for mastery of her soul. "As long as I've known you, you've wanted to help folk. To protect them from things they can't fight. Well, they need you now! *I* need you!"

Golden light crackled through the shadow-storm. Fitful. Sputtering. Sidara doubled over, shadow burning across shuddering shoulders.

"Help me!" she screamed.

Altiris clung tight. "However I can. With whatever I have to give. I will *always* catch you. But you don't need my help. You've never needed it. You're Sidara Reveque. The Lady of Light. And if history and scripture agree on anything, it's that light burns away shadow."

Sidara's eyes tightened as she pulled away. The tremor subsided from her shoulders. Fists clenched and tears running down her face, she screamed – no longer in loss or confusion, but in wrath fit to set the world ablaze.

Light overtook the lychfield and the ruined church, the night suddenly bright as day.

Sixty-Eight

Sunlit fire raged across the eastern skies. Borne aloft on Sidara's full-throated scream, it leapt higher and higher. Dancing flames burned away the mists and coalesced to a spread-winged form against the night sky, a storm of burning dust herald to its fury. The Phoenix of Argatha Bridge come to Eskavord.

And Viktor's shadow *howled*.

He felt it flee Sidara, its agony his as fire consumed it from within. His connections to the Ocranza – to the Drazina and survivors of the 14th – blinked out one by one. Burned to nothing as the Dark writhed.

The blaze of light brought the Essamere charge to a stumbling standstill. Rosa turned away too late, her vision seared by purpled splotches and the after-image of a vast and wondrous firebird. Cries of amazement echoed around her as the phoenix-shape faded into the diffuse glow of an early dawn.

But Rosa had eyes only for the Eskavord gate, and a fading of another sort.

The Ocranza host that had promised death moments before stood unmoving, shadow streaming from cracks in clay skin. One by one, they collapsed in upon themselves, weapons falling from frozen hands and limbs shattering on the ground. The living souls among them – Drazina and the survivors of the 14th – freed of that same shadow, fell to their knees and wept.

"Blessed Lumestra," murmured Sevaka.

*

The Ocranza shuddered before Kurkas' mace even struck, toppling backwards to shatter amid the ruins of those already bested. All around, the tale was the same – murderous, tireless assailants become motionless statues, become scattered potsherds amid the ash.

"I don't bloody believe it!" Weariness fled and pain forgotten, he cast down the mace. "Would you look at that, Halvor?"

Receiving no answer, he turned to find her sitting on a tomb's edge, sallet helm removed and her porcelain face towards the east, and the promise of a rising sun. Shadow fled like smoke from her empty eyes.

"No." Kurkas' knee cracked on stone as he scrambled to reach her. He barely felt it. "Not you too! Not after all this!"

[[I don't belong here.]] Revekah cocked her head, the motion stiff, reluctant. [[But thanks for not giving up on me.]]

He nodded, his throat sore. "You did good, Halvor." Clasping bloody fingers to a fist, he offered one last salute. "Keep a spot for me on that bastion. You and me, we ain't done."

She offered no reply, just stared off into the distance. One more statue amid the ash.

Tears pricking his cheek, Kurkas sank down beside her, and watched the sun come up.

Viktor desperately gathered back what little of his shadow yet obeyed, taking into himself the gifts spread so generously. The sheer, suffocating *rush* of it all stole his breath away, roused anger to grim heights as his dream of the Republic's salvation crumbled.

"What is this?" he bellowed. Josiri was beyond answer, his broken body in puddled gore upon the bridge's crest. He rounded on Calenne. "What have you done?"

"What you once did for me. I gave someone a chance to find their truth. It wasn't hard. You make enemies like no other man I've known. And you've spread yourself too thin."

Blood roaring in his veins, Viktor grabbed at her.

She drifted back, vaporous form slipping through his fingers and eyes welling with pity. "The Ocranza. Sidara. All those poor, broken souls you've twisted to your cause. A tapestry of shadow, unravelled by a single loose thread. One you left dangling when you should have given her peace."

"You?"

"Tzila. Revekah. Half of her in the Raven's keeping, and half in yours. The conduit by which you dredged your soldiers from Otherworld. You, Revekah and Sidara, all woven together, and together to the dead. Returning Revekah to the living world – making her whole – unravelled those threads. Your soldiers have peace, and Sidara is free."

Through the black raging clouds of his thoughts, Viktor grasped her meaning. "You bargained with the Raven?"

"He believes so. He hates you so much he gladly set Revekah free, if only for a little while. In truth, I offered him only what I'd already promised myself. That you'd pay for what you've done. In my name. In Josiri's. And in that of the honourable, decent man I once loved, and whose face you wear." She drew closer, almost translucent in the rising sunlight. "Viktor Akadra died long ago. Viktor Droshna dies today."

Viktor spread his arms, chest heaving with bitter laughter. With anger came strength. The strength of a Dark no longer divided filled every fibre of his being. Even as his ephemeral body ebbed, the rest of him – the only part that any longer mattered – grew stronger still.

"And who will kill him? You? A formless cyraeth fading in sunlight? Josiri?" He cast a contemptuous hand towards the body on the bridge. "He already tried. The Raven's too craven to challenge me again, or else why send you as his herald?"

Viktor knew he was raving, but what else was there now? Surrounded by ingrates and betrayers, his dreams unmade. But the Dark was eternal, and he was of the Dark. It could all begin again, all—

Feeling warmth at his back, he turned to see Sidara on the road, the church's broken spire at her back. Filthy and haggard, but with sunlight ablaze about her shoulders.

Altiris staggered at her side, sword in hand. Further back, more uniforms. Phoenixes. Drazina, freed from his shadow's urging. And away to the west, beyond the bridge, a glimpse of hunter's green.

"It's over, Uncle," said Sidara. "Can't you see that? Look at what you've become. What you sought to make of me. Of us all."

Viktor's shadow shied from the light and he alongside, for what remained of him was held deep within it. One last betrayal. One final trust broken. After all he'd given her – after all his hopes – Sidara too stood against him. But Sidara was the key. Swords and steel were nothing to the Dark. Only the light mattered – the light, and its dousing.

Gathering his shadow close, he leapt, claymore a wicked arc against the sky.

Light blazed between them. Its backwash hurled Altiris away. It seared Viktor's shadow to smoke and fed the fires Anastacia had buried in his ruined hands. But still the sword descended, fit to cleave Sidara head to toe.

Hands aflame, she caught the blade a hand's breadth from her brow. The impact drove her to her knees, blood streaming from her palms.

Viktor snarled and strove to tear free. The claymore remained unflinching, trapped in a cage of light. With no other recourse, he sent his shadow at her, drowning its fear with his own rage. Radiance rose to meet it, his bellow conjoining Sidara's cry of pain.

Mist faded into rising light. Yet the more Josiri strove to reknit woolly thoughts, the faster they slipped away. Eyes sought focus, and found nothing. What sound existed lay on the edge of hearing, separate from the half-world in which he lay. There was only pain. The weight of leaden limbs. Cobbles digging into his back.

And failure. Failure above all.

A grey shape marred blurred vision. A familiar voice rose out of murk.

"Hoist your sorry carcass, Josiri. You going to let the bastard win after all this?"

Eyes cleared and alighted on the impossible. Receding blond hair and tanned features twisted halfway between jest and frown. A stare that offered scant nonsense, and tolerated none in return.

"Izack?"

Other figures joined the first, they no less impossible than he. A part of Josiri knew they weren't real, but spectres conjured from the delirium of his wounds. The rest struggled to believe.

"At least he remembers your name," Malachi Reveque told Izack, a wry smile tugging at the corner of his mouth. "That's more than I expected."

"You promised to protect my daughter." Lilyana pulled from her husband's side and drifted closer, golden hair spilling beneath a satin veil that did nothing to hide a worried frown. "She needs you."

Sidara? Josiri frowned, the flare of sunlight beyond the mist finding new meaning.

"But it hurts," he murmured.

"You're wasting your time," sneered Ebigail Kiradin, her arms folded and her back to the others. "He's spineless, just like his mother. No use to anyone."

Elzar exchanged a glance with Izack and shook his head. "You're not helping, Ebigail."

"Of course not," she snapped. "Why ever might you think I'd want to?"

She turned away and froze, her gaze locked with a tall, dark-haired woman, who stood at a distance, her arms folded, and her lips twisted.

"Then remain silent." Katya Trelan, gone so long from Josiri's life that it took him a moment to recognise his own mother, offered him an appraising nod. "Words never mattered as much as deeds, anyway."

They faded into the mists summoned from a dying mind, replaced by a slight, impish-featured woman with snow-white curls, eyes glinting with daylight and sable wings furled behind. Beautiful beyond words. Almost painful to look upon. She, at least, seemed almost real, if diminished. An echo of who she'd been. The piece of herself she'd once anchored in his soul, forgotten until this moment.

"Ana ... " Josiri croaked. Loss returned, and pain with it. "Is this a dream? Or is it a memory?"

"We are our memories, Josiri. A walking record of triumphs and failures. What we've gained, and what we stand to lose."

She'd said that, the day of her fall from the palace balcony. Before all this had begun. So afraid of being left behind.

"I've lost everything," he replied. "I've nothing left."

"You know that's not true." Anastacia crooked a smile. "You'll always have me, wherever you go."

Anastacia retreated before a newcomer's approach, one somehow realer for all that she lacked the others' substance. Cold, slender and the very palest of greys, the last of the delusion retreated before her, dark streets rising again out of mist.

Calenne shared a nod with the after-image of Anastacia and reached down a translucent, vaporous hand. Ghostly lips forming a smile Josiri had so seldom seen in all the long years of their life together. Behind her, two silhouettes snapped into focus against the night sky, one wreathed in shadow, the other shining with sunlight.

"Stand up, big brother. Trelans are stubborn. Let the world see it, one last time."

Josiri's hand found hers, and with it one last inch of purpose.

Even lost in the agony of Sidara's light, Viktor felt the Goddess' broken sword slide between his ribs – no longer ablaze, but steel served where magic could not. The shadow felt nothing. What remained of the man roared in pain. It lashed out a backhanded blow, hurling Josiri away.

In that moment of distraction his shadow, masterless for barely a heartbeat, boiled away from Sidara's vengeful light, peeling apart piece by piece and howling to nothing.

Bereft of protection, Viktor's body burned anew. Robbed of the Dark's deception, the truth blazed brighter still, searing away the madness that had ruled him since Calenne's second death – the lies in which he'd cloaked himself for months, years.

The truth burned hotter than any flame. It cut deeper than the Light. A hundred missteps, born of impatience. A noble goal worn away by a thousand lies and corrupted to its core.

And arrogance. Arrogance above all. For believing he'd held the whole of the answer, rather than a piece. For not heeding the warnings of those he loved, and violating their trust. And in the end, for believing he could control the Dark, and thus allowed it to make its desires his own. How else had he come to the Southshires, an army of Dark-shackled thralls at his command, lost in dreams of a realm remade in his image?

Malatriant had named him her heir, and so he was, not just in power, but in deed.

In the hour of her defeat, the Tyrant Queen had bade him forge her legacy into a shining realm, were that his wish. She'd always known it couldn't be done. That the Dark would shape him as it had shaped her. Every step along that road, forward or back, had led here.

Another man might have recognised the danger. But not Viktor

Droshna, the man who'd forsaken family name to boast of his shadow. The man who'd recognised the flaw in everyone but himself.

That hadn't been the Dark's doing. For that, he'd no one and nothing to blame but himself.

The man who'd believed he couldn't lose, and so had lost everything.

Silhouettes danced beyond the light, a commotion of voices, growing louder.

Caught between Dark and the Light, Viktor Akadra wept, his tears hissing to steam.

"I can't do this."

Viktor barely heard Sidara's words, but he felt her falter, the light fading with ebbing resolve. Even now – even after all he'd done – she couldn't bring herself to be his slayer.

Letting the claymore fall, he took her pale, perfect hands in the blackened ruin of his own.

"End it."

Golden eyes brimmed with hurt. "But you're free! It's over!"

So tempting to believe that. So seductive to think he might somehow atone for all he'd done through righteous deed. But he'd thought that way before, and those thoughts had dragged him deeper into the Dark.

"It'll never be over, not while I live." The words came harder now, the last of the shadow curling to nothing in Sidara's radiance, and strength failing alongside. "Make me a lesson to last out the ages. A warning to all of the perils of the Dark."

Sidara nodded, her eyes full of tears. How gratifying to yet be thought worthy of sorrow.

"Thank Josiri," croaked Viktor, "for keeping his promise."

The fire raged deeper. The pain unbearable, inevitable.

And in that last moment before his body burst to ash, Viktor Akadra – who'd striven ever to be a good man, for all that fate had chosen otherwise – at last glimpsed what it was to live a life beyond shadow, and free of the Dark.

With one last cry – more like the laughter of a gambler who'd cheated a crooked game than the howl of a damned soul – it was over. His back propped against the bridge's wall, Josiri's dimming eyes saw the wind darken with soot and the glory of Sidara's light fade into the rising dawn. He heard the cheers of men and women who'd borne witness to a miracle, and felt nothing but an abiding peace.

"Josiri!" Sidara stumbled to her knees beside him, her wan face streaked with dirt and the horror in her eyes reflecting what he already knew of his wounds. "Don't go! Let me help you!"

Light gathered about Sidara's trembling, bloody hands. Soothing. Calm. But she shuddered as she reached for him, her strength expended in a battle Josiri knew he'd never truly understand. But even in fading sight he recognised well enough a soul teetering on the brink.

Breath bubbling in his throat, he closed his few working fingers over hers. "I'm too far gone. Save your strength. You'll need it."

"No. I can't . . . "

She didn't understand. Hadn't seen enough of life to recognise what was bound to follow. But she'd learn. She'd have to.

Altiris appeared at Sidara's shoulder, his expression no less stricken. "Josiri? Let her—"

"My choice," Josiri murmured. "Sometimes . . . that's all we have."

He stared past them both, to the cobbles blackened by Viktor's passing. And beyond, barely a pale outline against the thinning mist, a pale and watchful figure.

"He said to thank you, at the end," murmured Sidara. "He said you kept your promise."

Josiri sighed, the acknowledgement strange source of pride, even now.

With his last strength, he gazed up at Altiris, who'd laid a comforting hand on Sidara's shoulder. "The Trelan name's . . . yours now." He managed a smile as Sidara's hand found Altiris', and held it tight. "And any who'd share it with you. Wear it well . . . and remember . . . not all stubbornness is a sin."

He'd meant to say something else, about family or about blood – or about legacy, which he supposed was the same thing – but the words wouldn't come. Suddenly tired, Josiri let his eyes fall closed to gather his thoughts.

When he opened them again, Altiris and Sidara were gone, as were the sunlight and the cheers, the worry and the pain. There were only the mists, thicker than before, and Calenne, her hand extended in greeting. Eskavord's streets, no longer ruined, loomed overhead as they had when he'd been a boy. And in the west, Branghall's towers stretched into a green-black sky thick with circling ravens.

"Come along, Josiri," said Calenne. "Let me take you home."

Jeradas, 23rd Day of Dawntithe

A phoenix shall blaze from the darkness.
A beacon to the shackled; a pyre to the keepers of
  their chains.

from the sermons of Konor Belenzo

Sixty-Nine

Tregard's glittering colours were in abeyance, bright canopies and silks exchanged for the drab greys of mourning. They'd remain so for days to come, commemorating not only those slain in Cardivan's uprising, but also for an Empress whose fate would remain for ever a mystery. And yet, for all that, Apara felt only joy as she passed beneath Triumphal Gate, the relief of a weary traveller at last come home.

Buffeted by winter floodwaters and battered on the rocks, she'd dragged herself onto the Grelyt's western bank as the Phoenix had risen over Eskavord and come again to the bridge, sodden and cold, long after Josiri's spirit had fled to the Raven's keeping. The dark stain marking Viktor Droshna's last moments she'd regarded without flicker of emotion, lest even triumph offer his spirit one last satisfaction. Not so her reunification with Sevaka, which had occasioned the most profound of joys. One she'd promised to repeat.

But Tressia wasn't Apara's home, not any longer. And so she'd ridden north and east with one last burden, eschewing the mists for the freedom of open skies.

She threaded the tangled streets towards the palace, taking delight in the small pleasures of lives lived free. Children quarrelling in the streets. The commotion of barter. The simple affection of folk and family. Even the new statue of crooked Jack, holding court above the marketplace as it had done since the Battle of Argatha Bridge, did little to douse her spirits. Only when Jorcari ushered her into the throne room did her resolve falter.

Aeldran glanced up from his position beside the empty throne, a wave of his hand silencing a robed worthy mid-flow. "Leave us."

Courtiers shuffled away, leaving Apara alone with the regent, his Immortals, his lunassera and the golden, graven visages of the gods. The chamber's emptiness suddenly oppressive, Apara approached the dais, and offered a bow.

"Am I welcome, my prince?"

Heartbeats eked past without reply. In the silence, Apara conjured emotions on a face she couldn't see. Resentment. Distrust. Anger. All of them just. All of them unfair.

Fingertips beneath her chin bade her rise, and Apara saw at once how badly she'd misjudged Aeldran's mood. Trembling lips betrayed a man struggling with unaccustomed emotion and determined not to grant it licence.

"Always," he rumbled. "Is the House of Saran's debt paid?"

"To the last coin. Viktor Droshna's shadow has passed from this world. But not without cost."

Immortals started forward as she unslung the scabbard from her back. Jorcari checked them with crisp word of command.

After the briefest hesitation, Aeldran took the scabbard and drew forth what remained of the Goddess' sword. Perhaps a foot of steel remained beyond the hilt, ending in a jagged spike. He turned it over in his hands, fingers gracing the blade with a lover's caress, perhaps hoping to feel the resonance of Melanna's spirit within the steel.

"It will be reforged," he said. "Goddess willing, it might even be the stronger for it. Sometimes it is so, do you not agree, *savim*?"

Apara heard a question behind the question, and wondered how much Aeldran knew of her recent trials. In any case, the answer was the same for both her and the sword. Some things *were* stronger after being broken. "Time will tell."

Nodding, Aeldran resheathed the sword and gave it over to an Immortal's care. "And is it your intention to reassume the duties bestowed by the late Empress?"

"If it pleases."

His lips cracked in a careful smile. "On behalf of the Princessa Kaila Saranal, I accept your service, Apara Rann. And for myself—"

He broke off as a breathless Immortal rushed into the chamber. "Forgive the interruption, my prince, but your daughter cannot be found."

Aeldran's face closed like a steel trap. "Jorcari?"

The champion was already on the move, barking orders as he headed for the door. Aeldran followed at a limping run, the guarded joy of moments before erased by worry.

Yet through it all, Apara felt no concern, though its absence refused all enquiry. As commotion overtook the neighbouring rooms, she departed the throne room and passed into the inner gardens, instinct driving her ever on to the old wood. After the briefest hesitation on its threshold, she passed within, the undergrowth spreading wide before her in welcome.

And there, in the centre of the path, she found Kaila Saranal, sitting in the dirt and babbling earnestly at a wool-stuffed dark-haired doll in golden armour.

Apara eased closer, her eyes on briars and boughs that now bore little trace of the Midwintertide fire. A tingle along her spine warned against complacency.

"You shouldn't be out here, my princessa."

Kaila looked up, eyes narrowed. "Why not, Shar Apara?"

"It's not safe."

Suspicion became a frown. "Yes it is. The Lady in the Green said so."

The tingle became a shudder. "Is she here now?"

"She sings to me at night when I can't sleep. She won't hurt me."

Apara nodded absently, her eyes on a patch of undergrowth perhaps a dozen strides deeper into the wood, where a dead tree cast long shadows into the morning. Amber eyes stared back, devoid of recognition, for all that she recognised them in return. Or not so much the eyes, but the briared face that was no longer human.

Apara swallowed, her heart brimming. "No, *essavim*, she won't. But you should come inside. Your father is worried."

Kaila nodded. "That's what the Lady said. But she also said that sometimes it's good for a father to worry over his daughter."

The amber eyes blinked out. A rustle of branches rippled away, deeper into the wood. Kaila offered no resistance as Apara hoisted her up and bore her out of the wood.

Halfway to the boundary, Kaila stirred. "Father says that Madda has gone away. He said I'll never see her again."

That her voice held more confusion than sadness did nothing to prevent Apara's own sorrow rising. "That's true, *essavim*," she said softly. "But I suspect you're never far from her thoughts."

With a last glance back at the empty wood, Apara bore the Empress-to-be to face a father's relieved chastisement.

A scrape of the shovel – a last effort from weary muscles – and it was done. A small patch of bare earth beneath fire-blackened walls and grey skies. The eastward-facing headstone bore two names, though only one body lay beneath. The grave was deep enough to hold the bones of Josiri Trelan safe until Third Dawn summoned them again into light. Altiris had hoped the sight would ease his heartache, but in that moment the loss hung heavier than ever.

Thrusting the shovel into the sod, he wiped his brow on his shirtsleeve and stared up at the ruins of Branghall, shrouded in mist, as they'd been ever since fires had driven Malatriant to the Raven's care seven years before. The soft fragrance of churned soil mingled with the scent of yesterdays. The three days spent recuperating in Ardva felt as though they'd never happened.

"I feel like I should say something," he murmured, "but I can't find the words."

Sidara, the ruins of her Drazina uniform replaced with a simple gown, slipped her hands about his waist and drew him close. Blue eyes glimmered gold above a sad smile. She'd held respectful distance throughout his labours, close enough for comfort, but understanding his need for solitude.

"Then say nothing," she said. "Just *be*. They'd understand."

Altiris nodded, though it wasn't so simple.

Pulling away, he stared towards the estate's gate, where the surviving members of the Stonecrest hearthguard – *his* hearthguard – kept watch in order to ensure a moment of privacy. Blue-white ghostfires burned beneath the crumbling gateway, the purity of fleenroot and silver holding unquiet spirits at bay. Eskavord retained its share of those. Indeed, the numbers had grown in recent days.

Of the knights who'd fought that final battle against Lord Droshna, fewer than half yet lived. Of the Drazina who'd followed their master to Eskavord, even fewer. Of the 14th, massacred in battle and its survivors broken to the

Dark, no more than a dozen remained, and they were haunted by terrible dreams. As for the Phoenixes? Kelver had died in the darkness, saving Viara's life from an Ocranza's axe. Jarrock, from his wounds two days prior. Brass had lost a finger – his *favourite* finger, whatever that meant – but Viara and Beckon had come through almost unscathed.

Unscathed, but keeping poor watch. At least, so the three figures climbing the shallow slope suggested. Then again, Altiris wouldn't have wanted to be the one to bar their way. Some battles couldn't be won.

He found he didn't mind. Solitude carried a body only so far, and every moment in the mists bore the burden of years.

"You didn't think we'd leave you to do it *all* alone, did you, Lord Trelan?"

Altiris winced. Even swathed in bandages and bruised where he was not, Kurkas conspired to infuriating manner. "Don't call me that, Vladama."

Kurkas mustered the distant parade-ground stare Altiris suspected he'd be seeing a great deal more often, but his good eye twinkled. "Right you are, my lord."

Rosa – yet another personal name Altiris was learning to use, however uncomfortable it made him – gave Kurkas a wicked nudge with her elbow. "Behave."

Kurkas adopted an expression of wounded innocence and received a scowl in return.

Sevaka offered Altiris a sympathetic smile. "You didn't have to do any of it alone."

"Josiri gave me everything, and for so little in return. This was the least I could do." Turning, Altiris stared at the modest grave. "The Council wanted him for the Hayadra Grove's catacombs, did you know that? A grand ceremony beneath the Shaddra, with fanfare and speeches. In life, they never knew quite what to do with him. In death, they acclaim Josiri Trelan a hero. But he never belonged to them. He belongs to the Southshires. He should rest here. He earned it."

He fell silent, the words that had escaped him in solitude coaxed free in company.

"But why here?" said Rosa. "Why not the cathedral at Kreska?"

"A tomb next to Konor Belenzo?" Kurkas grunted. "Oh, that would've been a thing to see."

"Because this was his home, and because . . . " Altiris tailed off, fearing his hopes would sound foolish. After all, they were founded on so little. A dying promise, half-heard in the rain on the clifftop at Duskvigil Church. "It doesn't matter."

One by one, they knelt before Josiri's grave – a hallowed farewell, for all it lacked the ceremony of incense and golden death masks. Kurkas knelt the longest – he more than any other had two farewells to offer. When it came to Rosa's turn, she laid her sword atop the bare earth. The hilt at the headstone and the blade pointing east. Her shield, with its Essamere crest, she retained.

"Has there been any word of Constans?" asked Sevaka.

Sidara's brow creased with hurt. "I saw him in Ardva yesterday, watching me from the shadows. When I called out, he fled into the night. You should have seen his face. You can see the guilt eating at him."

Kurkas grunted. "Bloody well should feel guilty."

Altiris' own feelings about Constans were harder to parse. The awkward boy who loved showmanship and poetry, and was so desperate to be liked. The cold-hearted killer, twisted by Hawkin's betrayal, who'd driven his own sister into the Dark out of envy. Even now, Altiris couldn't swear to which was real, and which was the mask. Possibly Constans didn't know himself. Sidara certainly didn't. But her brother he remained.

"Just be glad he's alive," said Sevaka. "The rest will attend to itself."

"Speaking of which, what happens now . . . " Kurkas let the words hang just long enough to offer hope that he'd not end them with the dread title. " . . . my lord?"

Altiris closed his eyes, trepidation returning. The archimandrite's letter had contained more than polite expectation concerning Josiri's interment. "Tomorrow, we ride north. Lord Trelan and the Lady Reveque are called to take their seats on the Council." He paused, overcome by dread. "They're going to eat me alive."

Sidara kissed him on the cheek. "You'll do fine." Reassuring tone turned apprehensive. "It's not you they'll want to set on a pedestal."

False smile concealed the truth of intervening days. Rumours had reached Ardva ahead of their weary convoy. Whispers of Phoenixes and sunlit miracles amid the mists. Crowds had greeted them, drawn

to behold the Lady of Light who had banished the Dark. The first petitioners had arrived at noon the following day, begging for Lumestra's
blessing. Sidara had hidden herself in the convent's hospice soon after,
lost in the business of healing Eskavord's wounded, Ardva's only two
beaten-up simarka standing jealous guard at the door. But hour by hour,
the crowds had swollen, a portent of what surely awaited in Tressia itself.

"Might be it's for the best," said Kurkas. "Hard to ignore the Phoenix
of Prophecy, especially when she's got a scowl like yours. Might be you
can change things for the better."

Sidara favoured him with that very scowl. "That's what Viktor thought."

Altiris stifled a sympathetic grimace. The Phoenix of Prophecy. So
many had claimed that title. Now it, in turn, had claimed Sidara. She'd
spent three sleepless nights in his arms, staring into a future drowning
in a legacy of light, terrified what it portended: to be for ever alone in a
crowd, acknowledged, but never truly *seen* beneath its radiance.

"Viktor was different," said Sevaka.

"Because of the Dark?" Sidara shook her head violently. "The Dark
was the means, not the motive. It compounded his mistakes, but they
remain *his* mistakes. What if the light does the same for me? It's come
close already, so many times."

She stared off into the mists. Altiris wondered what she saw. The
carnage at Silverway Dock? At Argatha Bridge? Something else? She'd
spoken so little about what she'd done in the clutches of Lord Droshna's
shadow, and he knew better than to force the topic.

"Viktor was different because he always stood alone, even when he
claimed otherwise," Sevaka replied. "Once he'd settled on an answer, he
never stopped to consider if it was the *right* answer. For him, strength
was always the sword, and never the shield. In that, he was more like my
mother than either would ever admit. Josiri knew better. Your parents
knew better. *You* know better."

"And if I forget?"

Rosa laid a hand on her shoulder. "Then we'll remind you. You're
never alone unless you want to be. I wish Viktor had recognised that.
He saved me from myself so many times. I wish I could have saved
him just the once, but he never would have let me." She scowled, lost
in memory, then rallied to something approaching cheer. "Trust me,

you'll find friends in the strangest of places, if you only allow yourself to look."

Sidara seemed to find comfort in the words, a little of the tension
bleeding from her shoulders. Altiris wondered if she was thinking, as he was, of the impoverished faces at Seacaller's Church at
Midwintertide. Of the others like them who'd never had anyone to
speak for them on the Council, but did now. At least, if he found
courage enough to do so.

In that moment, Altiris promised himself he would, however hard the
road ahead. There was no better way to honour the Trelan name, and
not all stubbornness was sin. What would Kasvin have made of that? He
found himself hoping that she too had found a measure of peace.

"Will we see you in Tressia?" he asked.

"In time. There's work to be done in the Eastshires, and it's as good a
place as any to rebuild Essamere – if indeed I'm the right person to do
so." Rosa shared a glance with Sevaka. "But first I've—"

"We've . . . " corrected Sevaka.

"*We've* respects to pay further east," Rosa offered a wry smile. "It
might be better if you kept that part to yourselves. Today, there's peace.
Tomorrow . . . ?"

"Tomorrow there will also be peace," said Sidara firmly. "Or we've
learned nothing."

And with that, hands were shaken and embraces exchanged. One by
one, they began the walk to Branghall's gate. Altiris hung back, instincts
prickling. Halfway down the slope, he glanced back towards the ruins.
For a moment, he glimpsed a shimmering figure at the graveside, an
after-image of daylight, wings spread beneath grey skies, hand aloft
in farewell.

Sidara pressed a hand to her lips, eyes shining with wonder.

"Ana always said there was a piece of her still bound here," murmured
Altiris. "She tried to tell me again at the end. I never really understood
what she meant, but I hoped."

"That's why you didn't want him buried at Kreska?" said Sidara.

He nodded. "I thought it worth the chance. I hope they find one
another again in the mists."

The mists shifted, the golden figure lost to sight as if she'd never been.

"They will," said Sidara. "Rosa's right. We're none of us alone unless we want to be."

His last sorrow borne away by miracle, Altiris kissed her, and lost himself in the warmth and wonder of a life yet to come. Hand in hand, they left Branghall's ghosts behind, and passed into a future bereft of shadow.

Calenne watched Altiris and Sidara from atop the blackened remnant of Branghall's gatehouse, far enough from the ghostfires' poisonous light to suffer only the mildest discomfort. Little by little, they were lost to sight, voices muted by the mists. The Raven sat beside her, heels kicking above the empty gate and hat propped on the stones between them.

"You didn't want to talk to them?"

She shook her head. "I thought I did, but life'll be complicated enough without an undead aunt lurking in the wings."

He snorted. "If you ask me, that only makes the idea more appealing." He cocked his head, goatee twitching in thought. "So what *will* you do next?"

"It's up to me?"

"Let's say it is."

Feeling steadily more unreal – no easy feat in current circumstances – Calenne stared at him. In all their conversations, the Raven had been annoyed, arrogant, affronted . . . but never friendly. This felt almost like an apology.

"This is a trap, isn't it? Some reprisal for annoying you."

A gravelly laugh rippled through the mists. "Not in the least. You upheld your bargain. As far as you and I are concerned, all is settled." He cast a hand beyond the ghostfire-light, encompassing the drifting etravia. "I'm not sure you belong among these listless souls. Otherworld is for a very *particular* kind of dead. One way or another, you're something else. But by all means, continue lurking. It'll be refreshing to have someone to talk to while we wait for darling Lumestra to pull herself back together and usher in Third Dawn."

"Even if you've no power over me?"

He shrugged. "Perhaps that's part of the appeal. When every day's the same, any change is for the better."

Calenne dropped down from the gatehouse and stared back at Branghall. Her home for more years than she remembered, and all that time she'd wanted nothing more than to be free of it.

"In the clocktower," she said slowly, feeling out the thought as she went, "you told me there were a dozen worlds beyond this one."

The Raven jammed his hat on his head and smiled down. "Oh, there are. Realms of grey stone and iron skies, where steel serpents rumble through the darkness. Shining worlds where magic is lifeblood, and others where it's derided as myth. Lands forged by giants. Ruled by serathi. Where silver knights fight an eternal battle against sullen shadows and bitter flames. Everything in between. You could journey a lifetime and never tread them all."

A frisson of excitement quickened at the possibility. "I think I'd like to try. Can I?"

The mists thickened. Branghall grew dark and thence became nothing at all.

"That's not for me to say," said the Raven, though Calenne could no longer see him. "The mists run where the mists run, but the first step is up to you."

A dozen worlds. In life, she'd never even made it as far as Thrakkia. Was it possible to stray further still in death?

There was only one way to find out.

Taking the memory of a breath, Calenne Trelan closed her eyes and set out.

Acknowledgements

Whew. We're here. At the end of Book 3. Did you ever think we'd get here? I'll be honest – I'm still getting used to the idea.

I'm writing this roughly two and a half years after I started writing *Legacy of Ash*, but I've known how Viktor and Josiri's story would end for upwards of twenty. Of course, plenty's changed along the way. New characters and conflicts have found their way into the tale. The world of Aradane is far richer than I could ever have imagined it becoming, but ... twenty years, man.

I think it'll be at least another twenty before it really sinks in.

So what happens next? At time of writing, I don't actually know. A trilogy ends, and with it an era, but the Empire and Republic go on, marching remorselessly into the Light of Third Dawn. Fresh legacies, burdens and conflicts await. Maybe we'll get to explore them together – I'd certainly like to – we'll have wait and see.

But that's the future. Let's stop and enjoy the moment. I mean, if you're actually reading this bit, I'm guessing you enjoyed a few other moments up to this point, right? And while we're doing that, there are a few folk I'd like to thank.

As ever, deepest and most heartfelt thanks go to my wife Lisa for her patience, support, beta reading, and general tolerance of the fact that my brain's never, ever what you might call *off*, and I'm extraordinarily grateful for all the times I've turned a car journey or vacation into an impromptu plotting session. She's not yet developed a twitch when she hears the words *"I think I've worked out what happens next in this bit ..."* or *"So, I've had another idea ..."* No mean feat.

Beyond that, a tip of the hat to my agent John Jarrold – a man who's learning that there is no level of detail I won't fret about when the mood takes me, but is never less than a rock. Another to my editor at Orbit, James Long, for ensuring that not only this book, but the whole trilogy, makes at least a lick of sense.

Thanks also to Joanna Kramer and her team; Suzannah Runnacles and Andy Hawes for saving me from the worst of my abstract grammar and typing failures; Viv Mullett for a very shiny (and increasingly densely populated) map; the team at M Rules for making the book's innards so nice; and the dynamic duo of Larry Rostant and Charlotte Stroomer for yet another knockout cover. As ever, my endless gratitude to Nazia Khatun and Angela Man for making sure I show up, answer questions and otherwise do a passable impression of a human being when it's time to promote the books.

And last but not least, I'd like to thank you, dear reader. You just finished a book I never thought would see print, and if you're reading this, you probably liked it. So you're awesome. Don't forget it.

Now, put the book down, and go show the world how awesome you are. You've earned it.

extras

orbit

meet the author

MATTHEW WARD is a writer, cat-servant and owner of more musical instruments than he can actually play (and considerably more than he can play *well*). He's afflicted with an obsession for old places – castles, historic cities and the London Underground chief among them – and should probably cultivate more interests to help expand out his author biography.

After a decade serving as a principal architect for Games Workshop's *Warhammer* and *Warhammer 40,000* properties, Matthew embarked on an adventure to tell stories set in worlds of his own design. He lives near Nottingham with his extremely patient wife – as well as a pride of attention-seeking cats – and writes to entertain anyone who feels there's not enough magic in the world.

Follow him on Twitter @TheTowerofStars

Find out more about Matthew Ward and other Orbit authors by registering for the free monthly newsletter at orbitbooks.net.

if you enjoyed
LEGACY OF LIGHT

look out for

THE SHADOW OF THE GODS

Book One of the Bloodsworn Trilogy

by

John Gwynne

THE GREATEST SAGAS ARE WRITTEN IN BLOOD.

A century has passed since the gods fought and drove themselves to extinction. Now only their bones remain, promising great power to those brave enough to seek them out.

As whispers of war echo across the land of Vigrið, fate follows in the footsteps of three warriors: a huntress on a dangerous quest, a noblewoman pursuing battle fame, and a thrall seeking vengeance among the mercenaries known as the Bloodsworn.

All three will shape the fate of the world as it once more falls under the shadow of the gods.

extras

Set in a brand-new, Norse-inspired world and packed with myth, magic, and vengeance, The Shadow of the Gods *begins an epic new fantasy saga from bestselling author John Gwynne.*

Chapter One

Orka

The year 297 of Friðaröld, The Age of Peace

"Death is a part of life," Orka whispered into her son's ear.

Even though Breca's arm was drawn back, the ash-spear gripped tight in his small, white-knuckled fist and the spearhead aimed at the reindeer in front of them, she could see the hesitation in his eyes, in the set of his jaw.

He is too gentle for this world of pain, Orka thought. She opened her mouth to scold him, but a hand touched her arm, a huge hand where Breca's was small, rough-skinned where Breca's was smooth.

"Wait," Thorkel breathed through his braided beard, a cold-misting of breath. He stood to her left, solid and huge as a boulder.

Muscles bunched in Orka's jaw, hard words already in her throat. *Hard words are needed for this hard world.*

But she held her tongue.

Spring sunlight dappled the ground through soft-swaying branches, reflecting brightly from patches of rimed snow, winter's

last hoar-frost kiss on this high mountain woodland. A dozen reindeer stood grazing in a glade, a thick-antlered bull watching over
the herd of cows and calves as they chewed and scratched moss and
lichen from trunks and boulders.

A shift in Breca's eyes, an indrawn breath that he held, followed
by a burst of explosive movement; his hips twisting, his arm moving. The spear left his fist: a hiss as sharp iron sliced through air.
A flush of pride in Orka's chest. It was well thrown. As soon as the
spear had left Breca's grip she knew it would hit its mark.

In the same heartbeat that Breca loosed his spear, the reindeer he
had chosen looked up from the trunk it had been scraping lichen
from. Its ears twitched and it leaped forwards, the herd around it
breaking into motion, bounding and swerving around trees. Breca's
spear slammed into the trunk, the shaft quivering. A moment later
there was a crashing from the east, the sound of branches cracking, and a form burst from the undergrowth, huge, slate-furred
and long-clawed, exploding into the glade. The reindeer fled in all
directions as the beast loped among them, oblivious to all around
it. Blood pulsed from a swarm of wounds across its body, long teeth
slick, its red tongue lolling, and then it was gone, disappearing into
the forest gloom.

"What . . . was that?" Breca hissed, looking up at his mother and
father, wide eyes shifting from Orka to Thorkel.

"A fell-wolf," Thorkel grunted as he broke into motion, the
stealth of the hunt forgotten. He pushed through undergrowth
into the glade, a thick-shafted spear in one fist, branches snapping,
Orka and Breca following. Thorkel dropped to one knee, tugged a
glove off with his teeth and touched his fingertips to droplets of the
wolf's blood, brushing them across the tip of his tongue. He spat,
rose and followed the trail of wolf-blood to the edge of the glade,
then stood there peering into the murk.

Breca walked up to his spear, the blade half-sunk into a pine
tree, and tried to pull it free. His body strained, but the spear didn't
move. He looked up at Orka, grey-green eyes in a pale, muddied
face, a straight nose and strong jaw framed with crow-black hair, so

much like his father, and the opposite of her. Apart from his eyes. He had Orka's eyes.

"I missed," he said, his shoulders slumping.

Orka gripped the shaft in her gloved hand and tugged the spear free.

"Yes," she said as she handed Breca his spear, half-an-arm shorter than hers and Thorkel's.

"It was not your fault," Thorkel said from the glade's edge. He was still staring into the gloom, a thick braid of black, grey-streaked hair poking from beneath his woollen nålbinding cap, his nose twitching. "The fell-wolf startled them."

"Why didn't it kill any of those reindeer?" Breca asked as he took his short spear back from Orka.

Thorkel lifted his hand, showing bloodied fingertips. "It was wounded, not thinking about its supper."

"What did that to a fell-wolf?" Breca asked.

A silence.

Orka strode to the opposite end of the glade, her spear ready as she regarded the dark hole in the undergrowth from where the wolf had emerged. She paused, cocked her head. A faint sound, drifting through the woodland like mist.

Screams.

Breca joined her. He gripped his spear with both hands and pointed into the darkness.

"Thorkel," Orka grunted, twisting to look over her shoulder at her husband. He was still staring after the wounded wolf. With a last, lingering look and shake of his fur-draped shoulders he turned and strode towards her.

More screams, faint and distant.

Orka shared a look with Thorkel.

"Asgrim's steading lies that way," she said.

"Harek," Breca said, referring to Asgrim's son. Breca had played with him on the beach at Fellur, on the occasions when Orka and Thorkel had visited the village to trade for provisions.

Another scream, faint and ethereal through the trees.

"Best we take a look," Thorkel muttered.

"Heya," Orka grunted her agreement.

Their breath misted about them in clouds as they worked their way through the pinewoods, the ground thick and soft with needles. It was spring, signs of new life in the world below, but winter still clung to these wooded hills like a hunched old warrior refusing to let go of his past. They walked in file, Orka leading, her eyes constantly shifting between the wolf-carved path they were following and the deep shadows around them. Old, ice-crusted snow crunched underfoot as trees opened up and they stepped on to a ridge, steep cliffs falling away sharply to the west, ragged strips of cloud drifting across the open sky below them. Orka glanced down and saw reed-thin columns of hearth fire smoke rising from Fellur, far below. The fishing village sat nestled on the eastern edge of a deep, blue-black fjord, the calm waters shimmering in the pale sun. Gulls swirled and called.

"Orka," Thorkel said and she stopped, turned.

Thorkel was unstoppering a leather water bottle and handing it to Breca, who despite the chill was flushed and sweating.

"His legs aren't as long as yours," Thorkel smiled through his beard, the scar from cheek to jaw giving his mouth a twist.

Orka looked back up the trail they were following and listened. She had heard no more screams for a while now, so she nodded to Thorkel and reached for her own water bottle.

They sat on a boulder for a few moments, looking out over the land of green and blue, like gods upon the crest of the world. To the south the fjord beyond Fellur spilled into the sea, a ragged coastline curling west and then south, ribbed and scarred with deep fjords and inlets. Iron-grey clouds bunched over the sea, glowing with the threat of snow. Far to the north a green-sloped, snow-topped mountain range coiled across the land, filling the horizon from east to west. Here and there a towering cliff face gleamed, the old-bone roots of the mountain from this distance just a flash of grey.

"Tell me of the serpent Snaka again," Breca said as they all stared at the mountains.

Orka said nothing, eyes fixed on the undulating peaks.

"If I were to tell that saga-tale, little one, your nose and fingers would freeze, and when you stood to walk away your toes would snap like ice," Thorkel said.

Breca looked at him with his grey-green eyes.

"Ach, you know I cannot say no to that look," Thorkel huffed, breath misting. "All right, then, the short telling." He tugged off the nålbinding cap on his head and scratched his scalp. "All that you can see before you is Vigrið, the Battle-Plain. The land of shattered realms. Each steppe of land between the sea and those mountains, and a hundred leagues beyond them: that is where the gods fought, and died, and Snaka was the father of them all; some say the greatest of them."

"Certainly the biggest," Breca said, voice and eyes round and earnest.

"Am I telling this tale, or you?" Thorkel said, a dark eyebrow rising.

"You, Father," Breca said, dipping his head.

Thorkel grunted. "Snaka was of course the biggest. He was the oldest, the father of the gods; Eldest, they called him, and he had grown monstrous huge, which you would, too, if you had eaten your fill each day since the world was born. But his children were not to be sniffed at, either. Eagle, Bear, Wolf, Dragon, a host of others. Kin fought kin, and Snaka was slain by his children, and he fell. In his death the world was shattered, whole realms crushed, heaved into the air, the seas rushing in. Those mountains are all that is left of him, his bones now covered with the earth that he ruptured."

Breca whistled through his teeth and shook his head. "It must have been a sight to see."

"Heya, lad, it must have been. When gods go to war, it is no small thing. The world was broken in their ruin."

"Heya," Orka agreed. "And in Snaka's fall the vaesen pit was opened, and all those creatures of tooth and claw and power that dwelled in the world below were released into our land of sky and sea." From their vantage point the world looked pure and unspoiled, a beautiful, untamed tapestry spread across the landscape in gold and green and blue.

But Orka knew the truth was a blood-soaked saga.

She looked to her right and saw on the ground the droplets of blood from the injured wolf. In her mind she saw those droplets spreading, growing into pools, more blood spraying, ghostly bodies falling, hacked and broken, voices screaming . . .

This is a world of blood. Of tooth and claw and sharp iron. Of short lives and painful deaths.

A hand on her shoulder, Thorkel reaching over Breca's head to touch her. A sharp-drawn breath. She blinked and blew out a long, ragged sigh, pushing the images away.

"It was a good throw," Thorkel said, tapping Breca's spear with his water bottle, though his eyes were still on Orka.

"I missed, though," Breca muttered.

"I missed the first throw on my first hunt, too," Thorkel said. "And I was eleven summers, where you are only ten. And your throw was better than mine. The wolf robbed you. Eh, Orka?" He ruffled Breca's hair with a big hand.

"It was well cast," Orka said, eyeing the clouds to the west, closer now. A west wind was blowing them, and she could taste snow on that wind, a sharp cold that crackled like frost in her chest. Stoppering her water bottle, she stood and walked away.

"Tell me more of Snaka," Breca called after her.

Orka paused. "Are you so quick to forget your friend Harek?" she said with a frown.

Breca dropped his eyes, downcast, then stood and followed her.

Orka led them on, back into the pinewoods where sound was eerily muted, the world shrinking around them, shadows shifting, and they climbed higher into the hills. As they rose the world turned grey around them, clouds veiling the sun, and a cold wind hissed through the branches.

Orka used her spear for a staff as the ground steepened and she climbed slick stone that ascended like steps alongside a white-foaming stream. Ice-cold water splashed and seeped into her leg-bindings and boots. A strand of her blonde hair fell loose of her braid and she pushed it behind one ear. She slowed her pace, remembering Breca's short legs, even though there was a tingling in her blood that set her muscles thrumming. Danger had always had that effect on her.

"Be ready," Thorkel said behind her, and then Orka smelled it, too.

The iron tang of blood, the stench of voided bowels.

Death's reek.

The ground levelled on to a plateaued ridge, trees felled and cleared. A large, grass-roofed cabin appeared, alongside a handful of outbuildings, all nestled into a cliff face. A stockade wall ringed the cabin and outbuildings, taller than Orka.

Asgrim's steading.

On the eastern side of the steading a track curled down the hills, eventually leading towards the village of Fellur and the fjord.

Orka took a few steps forwards, then stopped, spear levelled as Breca and Thorkel climbed on to the plateau.

The stockade's wide gates were thrown open, a body upon the ground between them, limbs twisted, unnaturally still. One gate creaked on the wind. Orka heard Breca's breath hiss through his lips.

Orka knew it was Asgrim, broad shouldered and with iron-grey hair. One hairy arm poked from the torn sleeve of his tunic.

A snowflake drifted down, a tingled kiss upon Orka's cheek.

"Breca, stay behind me," she said, padding forwards. Crows rose squawking from Asgrim's corpse, complaining as they flapped away, settling among the treetops, one sitting upon a gatepost, watching them.

Snow began to fall, the wind swirling it around the plateau.

Orka looked down on Asgrim. He was clothed in wool and breeches, a good fur cloak, a dull ring of silver around one arm. His hair was grey, body lean, sinewed muscles showing through his torn tunic. One of his boots had fallen off. A shattered spear lay close to him, and a blooded hand-axe on the ground. There was a hole in his chest, his woollen tunic dark with crusted blood.

Orka kneeled, picked up the axe and placed it in Asgrim's palm, wrapping the stiffening fingers around it.

"Travel the soul road with a blade in your fist," she whispered.

Breca's breath came in a ragged gasp behind her. It was the first person he had seen dead. Plenty of animals; he had helped in slaughtering many a meal for their supper, the gutting and skinning, the soaking of sinew for stitching and binding, the tanning of leather for the boots they wore, their belts and scabbards for their seaxes. But to see another man dead, his life torn from him, that was something else.

At least, for the first time.

And this was a man that Breca had known. He had seen life's spark in him.

Orka gave her son a moment as he stood and stared wide-eyed at the corpse, a flutter in his chest, his breath quick.

The ground around Asgrim was churned, grass flattened. A scuffed boot print. A few paces away there was a pool of blood soaked into the grass. Tracks in the ground led away; it looked like someone had been dragged.

Asgrim put someone down, then.

"Was he the one screaming?" Breca asked, still staring at Asgrim's corpse.

"No," Orka said, looking at the wound in Asgrim's chest. A stab to the heart: death would have come quickly. And a good thing, too, as his body had already been picked at by scavengers. His eyes and lips were red wounds where the crows had been at him. Orka put a hand to Asgrim's face and lifted what was left of his lip to look inside his mouth. Gums and empty, blood-ragged sockets. She scowled.

"Where are his teeth?" Breca hissed.

"Tennúr have been at him," Orka grunted. "They love a man's teeth more than a squirrel loves nuts." She looked around, searching the treeline and ridged cliff for any sign of the small, two-legged creatures. On their own, they could be a nuisance; in a pack, they could be deadly, with their sharp-boned fingers and razor teeth.

Thorkel stepped around Orka and padded into the enclosure, spear-point sweeping in a wide arc as he searched.

He stopped, stared up at the creaking gate.

Orka stepped over Asgrim into the steading and stopped beside Thorkel.

A body was nailed to the gate, arms wide, head lolling.

Idrun, wife to Asgrim.

She had not died so quickly as her husband.

Her belly had been opened, intestines spilling to a pile on the ground, twisted like vines around an old oak. Heat still rose from them, steaming as snow settled upon glistening coils. Her face was misshapen in a rictus of pain.

It was she who did the screaming.

"What did this?" Thorkel muttered.

"Vaesen?" Orka said.

Thorkel pointed to thick-carved runes on the gate, all sharp angles and straight lines. "A warding rune."

Orka shook her head. Runes would hold back all but the most powerful of vaesen. She glanced back at Asgrim and the wound in his chest. Rarely did vaesen use weapons, nature already equipping them with the tools of death and slaughter. There were dark patches on the grass: congealed blood.

Blood on Asgrim's axe. Others were wounded, but if they fell, they were carried from here.

"Did men do this?" Thorkel muttered.

Orka shrugged, a puff of misted breath as she thought on it.

"All is lies," she murmured. "They call this the age of peace, because the ancient war is over and the gods are dead, but if this is peace . . ." She looked to the skies, clouds low and heavy, snow falling in sheets now, and back at the blood-soaked corpses. "This is the age of storm and murder . . ."

"Where's Harek?" Breca asked.

orbit

Follow us:

/orbitbooksUS

/orbitbooks

/orbitbooks

Join our mailing list
to receive alerts on our
latest releases and deals.

orbitbooks.net

Enter our monthly
giveaway for the chance
to win some epic prizes.

orbitloot.com